W9-BIE-437

GREAT TV & FILM DETECTIVES

GREAT TV & FILM DETECTIVES

A COLLECTION OF CRIME MASTERPIECES FEATURING
YOUR FAVORITE SCREEN SLEUTHS

The Reader's Digest Association, Inc.
Pleasantville, New York/Montreal/London/Hong Kong/Sydney

A READER'S DIGEST BOOK

This edition published by The Reader's Digest Association, Inc.,
by arrangement with Orion Publishing Group

Library of Congress Cataloging in Publication Data:
Great TV and film detectives: a collection of crime masterpieces featuring your favorite screen sleuths.
p.cm
Selected by Maxim Jakubowski
ISBN 0-7621-0578-X
1. Detective and mystery stories, English. 2. Detective and mystery stories, American. I. Jakubowski, Maxim

PR1309.D4G735 2005

823'.087208-- dc22 2005046597

For more Reader's Digest products and information, visit our Web site:
rd.com (in the United States)
readersdigest.ca (in Canada)
rdasia.com (in Hong Kong)
readersdigest.com.au (in Australia)
readersdigest.co.uk (in the United Kingdom)

Printed in Spain

3 5 7 9 10 8 6 4 2

Contents

Introduction

Maxim Jakubowski

Dramas involving crimes and the detectives who try to solve them have been flashing across large silver screens right from the earliest days of movie film production. When television came along, the number of detectives portrayed on small home TV screens increased exponentially. Many people actually conjure their image of real-life policemen and private detectives based on fictional characteristics of the sleuths they see on the screen on a regular, if not daily, basis.

The crime genre with all its mystery and suspense, thrills, and chills—and often its wonderful characterization—lends itself to action-packed scenes so well that it would be unthinkable for film and TV producers not to continue to tap into its creative riches forever.

The relationship between crimes recorded on the page and acted on the screen is an intimate one, since at one time or another during their career, many actors and actresses assume the role of a highly recognized fictional sleuth. Some of these characters are so popular that they are brought to life again and again in succeeding generations, each time under the guise of a new and younger actor's face. (Think of the many incarnations of Sherlock Holmes, Hercule Poirot, Philip Marlowe, and Miss Marple, just to mention a few of the more famous ones. British actor Clive Owen, who won a recent Best Supporting Actor award, is still affectionately remembered as the face of the lovable rogue Nick Sharman, who appears in this collection.

Even though many people may automatically conjure up the face of a familiar actor or actress in connection with detective personages, perhaps it's more fair to remember that many intrepid, and sometimes quirky and all-too-fallible, sleuths first appeared in short stories and novels. And the history of crime and detective fiction is such a rich and rewarding mine of plots, intrigues and unforgettable heroes, some of whom are featured in this book. Many of the other major names are missing because we simply ran out of space and also because some famous characters only appear in novels and not in short form. But I am confident you will enjoy this trawl through the delights of film and TV detectives and might even become curious enough to do some investigating of your own, discovering authors, books or movies and TV series you had hitherto overlooked.

As Alfred Hitchcock once put it: "These great detectives are unique, they are intensely individual. They range from the deceptively stolid tenacity of French Inspectors to the Gallic and mercurial intuitiveness of Hercule Poirot. Some are eccentric, some ordinary; some naive, some sophisticated. Here are professionals and amateurs, rich dilettantes and hard-working police officials."

I couldn't have put it better, but then Hitch was an expert at presenting criminal inquiries on both screen formats; indeed, it's what he's best remembered for. I would just add that he wrote those words shortly before another Golden Age of crime writing began to flourish, many of whose great new exponents are also included in this anthology: Ian Rankin, Jeffery Deaver, John Harvey, Lawrence Block, Sara Paretsky, and more.

What wonderful films he could have directed had he had access to such incredible new suspense writing!

So, enjoy this panorama of past and present detectives, and marvel at their deductive skills and their subtle intelligence and persistence.

I Can Find My Way Out

Ngaio Marsh

Dame Ngaio Marsh is regarded as one of the "Great Ladies" of English mystery's golden age. Between the years 1932–1982, Marsh wrote thirty-two classic English detective novels, gaining her international acclaim. In the novel *A Man Lay Dead* (1934), Marsh first introduced Detective Chief Inspector Roderick Alleyn, a solid and erudite character. Educated at Eton, Alleyn trained as a diplomat before joining Scotland Yard and is considered one of the most famous policemen in detective fiction. Alleyn is ably assisted by the inquisitive journalist Nigel Bathgate and later by the redoubtable Shakespeare-quoting Inspector Fox. Alleyn's wife, Troy, an artist, is an excellent foil to her husband and does much to enhance and broaden the story lines. Inspector Alleyn was most recently seen on network television in the BBC series *The Inspector Alleyn Mysteries,* with Simon Williams appearing first in the pilot feature episode in 1990. This proved successful and was followed in 1993 by five feature-length episodes starring the distinguished British stage and screen actor Patrick Malahide as Alleyn, with William Simons as Inspector Fox.

At half-past six on the night in question, Anthony Gill, unable to eat, keep still, think, speak, or act coherently, walked from his rooms to the Jupiter Theater. He knew that there would be nobody backstage, that there was nothing for him to do in the theater, that he ought to stay quietly in his rooms and presently dress, dine, and arrive at, say, a quarter to eight. But it was as if something shoved him into his clothes, thrust him into the street and compelled him to hurry through the West End to the Jupiter. His mind was overlaid with a thin film of inertia. Odd lines from the play occurred to him, but without any particular significance. He found himself busily reiterating a completely irrelevant sentence: "She has a way of laughing that would make a man's heart turn over."

Piccadilly, Shaftesbury Avenue. "Here I go," he thought, turning into Hawke Street, "towards my play. It's one hour and twenty-nine minutes away. A step a second. It's rushing towards me. Tony's first play. Poor young Tony Gill. Never mind. Try again."

The Jupiter. Neon lights: I CAN FIND MY WAY OUT—*by Anthony Gill.* And in the entrance the bills and photographs. Coralie Bourne with H. J. Bannington, Barry George and Canning Cumberland.

Canning Cumberland. The film across his mind split and there was the Thing itself and he would have to think about it. How bad would Canning Cumberland be if he came down drunk? Brilliantly bad, they said. He would bring out all the tricks. Clever actor stuff, scoring off everybody, making a fool of the dramatic balance. "In Mr. Canning Cumberland's hands indifferent dialogue and unconvincing situations seemed almost real." What can you do with a drunken actor?

He stood in the entrance feeling his heart pound and his inside deflate and sicken.

Because, of course, it was a bad play. He was at this moment and for the first time really convinced of it. It was terrible. Only one virtue in it and that was not his doing. It had been suggested to him by Coralie Bourne: "I don't think the play you have sent me will do as it is but it has occurred to me—" It was a brilliant idea. He had rewritten the play round it and almost immediately and quite innocently he had begun to think of it as his own although he had said shyly to Coralie Bourne: "You should appear as joint author." She had quickly, over emphatically, refused. "It was nothing at all," she said. "If you're to become a dramatist you will learn to get ideas from everywhere. A single situation is nothing. Think of Shakespeare," she added lightly. "Entire plots! Don't be silly." She had said later, and still with the same hurried, nervous air: "Don't go talking to everyone about it. They will think there is more, instead of less, than meets the eye in my small suggestion. Please promise." He promised, thinking he'd made an error in taste when he suggested that Coralie Bourne, so famous an actress, should appear as joint author with an unknown youth. And how right she was, he thought, because, of course, it's going to be a ghastly flop. She'll be sorry she consented to play in it.

Standing in front of the theater he contemplated nightmare possibilities. What did audiences do when a first play flopped? Did they clap a little, enough to let the curtain rise and quickly fall again on a discomforted group of players? How scanty must the applause be for them to let him off his own appearance? And they were to go on to the Chelsea Arts Ball. A hideous prospect. Thinking he would give anything in the world if he could stop his play, he turned into the foyer. There were lights in the offices and he paused, irresolute, before a board of photographs. Among them, much smaller than the leading players, was Dendra Gay with the eyes looking straight into his. She had a way of laughing that would make a man's heart turn over. "Well," he thought, "so I'm in love with her." He turned away from the photograph. A man came out of the office. "Mr. Gill? Telegrams for you."

Anthony took them and as he went out he heard the man call after him: "Very good luck for tonight, sir."

There were queues of people waiting in the side street for the early doors.

At six-thirty Coralie Bourne dialed Canning Cumberland's number and waited. She heard his voice. "It's me," she said.

"O, God! darling, I've been thinking about you." He spoke rapidly, too loudly. "Coral, I've been thinking about Ben. You oughtn't to have given that situation to the boy."

"We've been over it a dozen times, Cann. Why not give it to Tony? Ben will never know." She waited and then said nervously, "Ben's gone, Cann. We'll never see him again."

"I've got a 'Thing' about it. After all, he's your husband."

"No, Cann, no."

"Suppose he turns up. It'd be like him to turn up."

"He won't turn up."

She heard him laugh. "I'm sick of all this," she thought suddenly. "I've had it once too often. I can't stand any more. . . . Cann," she said into the telephone. But he had hung up.

At twenty to seven, Barry George looked at himself in his bathroom mirror. "I've got a better appearance," he thought, "than Cann Cumberland. My head's a good shape, my eyes are bigger, and my jaw line's cleaner. I never let a show down. I don't drink. I'm a better actor." He turned his head a little, slewing his eyes to watch the effect. "In the big scene," he thought, "I'm the star. He's the feed. That's the way it's been produced and that's what the author wants. I ought to get the notices."

Past notices came up in his memory. He saw the print, the size of the paragraphs; a long paragraph about Canning Cumberland, a line tacked on the end of it. "Is it unkind to add that Mr. Barry George trotted in the wake of Mr. Cumberland's virtuosity with an air of breathless dependability?" And again: "It is a little hard on Mr. Barry George that he should be obliged to act as foil to this brilliant performance." Worst of all: "Mr. Barry George succeeded in looking tolerably unlike a stooge, an achievement that evidently exhausted his resources."

"Monstrous!" he said loudly to his own image, watching the fine glow of indignation in the eyes. Alcohol, he told himself, did two things to Cann Cumberland. He raised his finger. Nice, expressive hand. An actor's hand. Alcohol destroyed Cumberland's artistic integrity. It also invested him with devilish cunning. Drunk, he would burst the seams of a play, destroy its balance, ruin its form, and himself emerge blazing with a showmanship that the audience mistook for genius. "While I," he said aloud, "merely pay my author the compliment of faithful interpretation. Psha!"

He returned to his bedroom, completed his dressing and pulled his hat to the right angle. Once more he thrust his face close to the mirror and looked searchingly at its image. "By God!" he told himself, "he's done it once too often, old boy. Tonight we'll even the score, won't we? By God, we will."

Partly satisfied, and partly ashamed, for the scene, after all, had smacked a little of ham, he took his stick in one hand and a case holding his costume for the Arts Ball in the other, and went down to the theater.

At ten minutes to seven, H. J. Bannington passed through the gallery line on his way to the stage door alley, raising his hat and saying: "Thanks so much," to the gratified ladies who let him through. He heard them murmur his name. He walked briskly along the alley, greeted the stage doorkeeper, passed under a dingy lamp, through an entry and so to the stage. Only working lights were up. The walls of an interior set rose dimly into shadow. Bob Reynolds, the stage manager, came out through the prompt entrance. "Hello, old boy," he said, "I've changed the dressing rooms. You're third on the right: they've moved your things in. Suit you?"

"Better, at least, than a black hole the size of a bathroom but without its appointments," H. J. said acidly. "I suppose the great Mr. Cumberland still has the star room?"

"Well, yes, old boy."

"And who pray, is next to him? In the room with the other gas fire?"

"We've put Barry George there, old boy. You know what he's like."

"Only too well, old boy, and the public, I fear, is beginning to find out." H. J. turned into the dressing-room passage. The stage manager returned to the set, where he encountered his assistant. "What's biting *him?*" asked the assistant. "He wanted a dressing room with a fire." "Only natural," said the A. S. M. nastily. "He started life reading gas meters."

On the right and left of the passage, nearest the stage end, were two doors, each with its star in tarnished paint. The door on the left was open. H. J. looked in and was greeted with the smell of grease paint, powder, wet white, and flowers. A gas fire droned comfortably. Coralie Bourne's dresser was spreading out towels. "Good evening, Katie, my jewel," said H. J. "La Belle not down yet?" "We're on our way," she said.

H. J. hummed stylishly: "*Bella filia del amore,*" and returned to the passage. The star room on the right was closed but he could hear Cumberland's dresser moving about inside. He went on to the next door, paused, read the card, "Mr. Barry George," warbled a high derisive note, turned in at the third door and switched on the light.

Definitely not a second lead's room. No fire. A wash basin, however, and opposite mirrors. A stack of telegrams had been placed on the dressing table. Still singing he reached for them, disclosing a number of bills that had been tactfully laid underneath and a letter, addressed in a flamboyant script.

His voice might have been mechanically produced and arbitrarily switched off, so abruptly did his song end in the middle of a roulade. He let the telegrams fall on the table, took up the letter and tore it open. His face, wretchedly pale, was reflected and endlessly rereflected in the mirrors.

At nine o'clock the telephone rang. Roderick Alleyn answered it. "This is Sloane 84405. No, you're on the wrong number. *No.*" He hung up and returned to his wife and guest. "That's the fifth time in two hours."

"Do let's ask for a new number."

"We might get next door to something worse."

The telephone rang again. "This is not 84406," Alleyn warned it. "No, I cannot take three large trunks to Victoria Station. No, I am not the Instant All Night Delivery. No."

"They're 84406," Mrs. Alleyn explained to Lord Michael Lamprey. "I suppose it's just faulty dialing, but you can't imagine how angry everyone gets. Why do you want to be a policeman?"

"It's a dull hard job, you know. . . ." Alleyn began.

"Oh," Lord Mike said, stretching his legs and looking critically at his shoes, "I don't for a moment imagine I'll leap immediately into false whiskers and plainclothes. No, no. But I'm revoltingly healthy, sir. Strong as a horse. And I don't think I'm as stupid as you might feel inclined to imagine—"

The telephone rang.

"I say, do let me answer it," Mike suggested and did so.

"Hullo?" he said winningly. He listened, smiling at his hostess. "I'm afraid—" he began. "Here, wait a bit . . . Yes, but . . ." His expression became blank and complacent. "May I," he said presently, "repeat your order, sir? Can't be too sure, can we? Call at 11 Harrow Gardens, Sloane Square, for one suitcase to be delivered immediately at the Jupiter Theater to Mr. Anthony Gill. Very good, sir. . . . Thank you, sir. . . . Collect. Quite."

He replaced the receiver and beamed at the Alleyns.

"What the devil have you been up to?" Alleyn said.

"He just simply wouldn't listen to reason. I tried to tell him."

"But it may be urgent," Mrs. Alleyn ejaculated.

"It couldn't be more urgent, really. It's a suitcase for Tony Gill at the Jupiter."

"Well, then—"

"I was at Eton with the chap," said Mike reminiscently. "He's four years older than I am so of course he was madly important while I was less than the dust. This'll learn him."

"I think you'd better put that order through at once," said Alleyn firmly.

"I rather thought of executing it myself, do you know, sir. It'd be a frightfully neat way of gatecrashing the show, wouldn't it? I did try to get a ticket but the house was sold out."

"If you're going to deliver this case you'd better get a bend on."

"It's clearly an occasion for dressing up though, isn't it? I say," said Mike modestly, "would you think it most frightful cheek if I—well I'd promise to come back and return everything. I mean—"

"Are you suggesting that my clothes look more like a van man's than yours?" "I thought you'd have things—"

"For Heaven's sake, Rory," said Mrs. Alleyn, "dress him up and let him go. The great thing is to get that wretched man's suitcase to him."

"I know," said Mike earnestly. "It's most frightfully sweet of you. That's how I feel about it."

Alleyn took him away and shoved him into an old and begrimed raincoat, a cloth cap and a muffler. "You wouldn't deceive a village idiot in a total eclipse," he said, "but out you go."

He watched Mike drive away and returned to his wife.

"What'll happen?" she asked.

"Knowing Mike, I should say he will end up in the front stalls and go on to supper with the leading lady. She, by the way, is Coralie Bourne. Very lovely and twenty years his senior so he'll probably fall in love with her." Alleyn reached for his tobacco jar and paused. "I wonder what's happened to her husband," he said.

"Who was he?"

"An extraordinary chap. Benjamin Vlasnoff. Violent temper. Looked like a bandit.

Wrote two very good plays and got run in three times for common assault. She tried to divorce him but it didn't go through. I think he afterwards lit off to Russia." Alleyn yawned. "I believe she had a hell of a time with him," he said.

"All Night Delivery," said Mike in a hoarse voice, touching his cap. "Suitcase. One." "Here you are," said the woman who had answered the door. "Carry it carefully, now, it's not locked and the catch springs out."

"Thanks," said Mike. "Much obliged. Chilly, ain't it?"

He took the suitcase out to the car.

It was a fresh spring night. Sloane Square was threaded with mist and all the lamps had halos round them. It was the kind of night when individual sounds separate themselves from the conglomerate voice of London; hollow sirens spoke imperatively down on the river and a bugle rang out over in Chelsea Barracks; a night, Mike thought, for adventure.

He opened the rear door of the car and heaved the case in. The catch flew open, the lid dropped back and the contents fell out. "Damn!" said Mike, and switched on the inside light.

Lying on the floor of the car was a false beard.

It was flaming red and bushy and was mounted on a chin piece. With it was incorporated a stiffened mustache. There were wire hooks to attach the whole thing behind the ears. Mike laid it carefully on the seat. Next he picked up a wide black hat, then a vast overcoat with a fur collar, finally a pair of black gloves.

Mike whistled meditatively and thrust his hands into the pockets of Alleyn's raincoat. His right-hand fingers closed on a card. He pulled it out. "Chief Detective-Inspector Alleyn," he read, "C. J. D. New Scotland Yard."

"Honestly," thought Mike exultantly, "this is a gift."

Ten minutes later a car pulled into the curb at the nearest parking place to the Jupiter Theater. From it emerged a figure carrying a suitcase. It strode rapidly along Hawke Street and turned into the stage door alley. As it passed under the dirty lamp it paused, and thus murkily lit, resembled an illustration from some Edwardian spy story. The face was completely shadowed; a black cavern from which there projected a square of scarlet beard which was the only note of color.

The doorkeeper, who was taking the air with a member of stage staff, moved forward, peering at the stranger.

"Was you wanting something?"

"I'm taking this case in for Mr. Gill."

"He's in front. You can leave it with me."

"I'm so sorry," said the voice behind the beard, "but I promised I'd leave it backstage myself."

"So you will be leaving it. Sorry, sir, but no one's admitted be'ind without a card."

"A card? Very well. Here is a card."

He held it out in his black-gloved hand. The stage doorkeeper, unwillingly removing his gaze from the beard, took the card and examined it under the light. "Coo!" he said. "What's up, governor?"

"No matter. Say nothing of this."

The figure waved its hand and passed through the door. "'Ere!" said the doorkeeper excitedly to the stagehand, "take a slant at this. That's a plain clothes flattie, that was."

"Plain clothes!" said the stagehand. "Them!"

"'E's disguised," said the doorkeeper. "That's what it is. 'E's disguised 'isself."

"'E's bloody well lorst 'isself be'ind them whiskers if you arst me."

Out on the stage someone was saying in a pitched and beautifully articulate voice: *"I've always loathed the view from these windows. However if that's the sort of thing you admire. Turn off the lights, damn you. Look at it."*

"Watch it, now, watch it," whispered a voice so close to Mike that he jumped. "O.K.," said a second voice somewhere above his head. The lights on the set turned blue. "Kill that working light." "Working light gone."

Curtains in the set were wrenched aside and a window flung open. An actor appeared, leaning out quite close to Mike, seeming to look into his face and saying very distinctly: "God: it's frightful!" Mike backed away towards a passage, lit only from an open door. A great volume of sound broke out beyond the stage. "House lights," said the sharp voice. Mike turned into the passage. As he did so, someone came through the door. He found himself face to face with Coralie Bourne, beautifully dressed and heavily painted.

For a moment she stood quite still; then she made a curious gesture with her right hand, gave a small breathy sound and fell forward at his feet.

❦ ❦ ❦ ❦

Anthony was tearing his program into long strips and dropping them on the floor of the O. P. Box. On his right hand, above and below, was the audience; sometimes laughing, sometimes still, sometimes as one corporate being, raising its hands and striking them together. As now; when down on the stage, Canning Cumberland, using a strange voice, and inspired by some inward devil, flung back the window and said: "God: it's frightful!"

"Wrong! Wrong!" Anthony cried inwardly, hating Cumberland, hating Barry George because he let one speech of three words override him, hating the audience because they liked it. The curtain descended with a long sigh on the second act and a sound like heavy rain filled the theater, swelled prodigiously and continued after the house lights welled up.

"They seem," said a voice behind him, "to be liking your play."

It was Gosset, who owned the Jupiter and had backed the show. Anthony turned on him stammering: "He's destroying it. It should be the other man's scene. He's stealing."

"My boy," said Gosset, "he's an actor."

"He's drunk. It's intolerable."

He felt Gosset's hand on his shoulder.

"People are watching us. You're on show. This is a big thing for you; a first play, and going enormously. Come and have a drink, old boy. I want to introduce you—"

Anthony got up and Gosset, with his arm across his shoulders, flashing smiles, patting him, led him to the back of the box.

"I'm sorry," Anthony said, "I can't. Please let me off. I'm going backstage."

"Much better not, old son." The hand tightened on his shoulder. "Listen old son—" But Anthony had freed himself and slipped through the pass door from the box to the stage.

At the foot of the breakneck stairs Dendra Gay stood waiting. "I thought you'd come," she said. Anthony said: "He's drunk. He's murdering the play."

"It's only one scene, Tony. He finishes early in the next act. It's going colossally."

"But don't you understand—"

"I do. You *know* I do. But you're a success, Tony darling! You can hear it and smell it and feel it in your bones."

"Dendra," he said uncertainly.

Someone came up and shook his hand and went on shaking it. Flats were being laced together with a slap of rope on canvas. A chandelier ascended into darkness. "Lights," said the stage manager, and the set was flooded with them. A distant voice began chanting. "Last act, please. Last act."

"Miss Bourne all right?" the stage manager suddenly demanded.

"She'll be all right. She's not on for ten minutes," said a woman's voice.

"What's the matter with Miss Bourne?" Anthony asked. "Tony, I must go and so must you. Tony, it's going to be grand. *Please* think so. *Please*."

"Dendra," Tony began, but she had gone.

Beyond the curtain, horns and flutes announced the last act.

"Clear please."

The stagehands came off.

"House lights."

"House lights gone."

"Stand by."

And while Anthony still hesitated in the O.P. corner, the curtain rose. Canning Cumberland and H. J. Bannington opened the last act.

As Mike knelt by Coralie Bourne he heard someone enter the passage behind him. He turned and saw, silhouetted against the lighted stage, the actor who had looked at him through a window in the set. The silhouette seemed to repeat the gesture Coralie Bourne had used, and to flatten itself against the wall.

A woman in an apron came out of the open door.

"I say—here!" Mike said.

Three things happened almost simultaneously. The woman cried out and knelt beside him. The man disappeared through a door on the right.

The woman, holding Coralie Bourne in her arms, said violently: "Why have you come back?" Then the passage lights came on. Mike said: "Look here, I'm most frightfully sorry," and took off the broad black hat. The dresser gaped at him; Coralie Bourne made a crescendo sound in her throat and opened her eyes. "Katie?" she said.

"It's all right, my lamb. It's not him, dear. You're all right." The dresser jerked her head at Mike: "Get out of it," she said.

"Yes, of course, I'm most frightfully—" He backed out of the passage, colliding with a youth who said: "Five minutes, please." The dresser called out: "Tell them she's not well. Tell them to hold the curtain."

"No," said Coralie Bourne strongly. "I'm all right, Katie. Don't say anything. Katie, what was it?"

They disappeared into the room on the left.

Mike stood in the shadow of a stack of scenic flats by the entry into the passage. There was great activity on the stage. He caught a glimpse of Anthony Gill on the far side talking to a girl. The callboy was speaking to the stage manager who now shouted into space: "Miss Bourne all right?" The dresser came into the passage and called: "She'll be all right. She's not on for ten minutes." The youth began chanting: "Last act, please." The stage manager gave a series of orders. A man with an eyeglass and a florid beard came from farther down the passage and stood outside the set, bracing his figure and giving little tweaks to his clothes. There was a sound of horns and flutes. Canning Cumberland emerged from the room on the right and on his way to the stage, passed close to Mike, leaving a strong smell of alcohol behind him. The curtain rose.

Behind his shelter, Mike stealthily removed his beard and stuffed it into the pocket of his overcoat.

A group of stagehands stood nearby. One of them said in a hoarse whisper: "'E's squiffy." "Garn, 'e's going good." "So 'e may be going good. And for why? *Becos* 'e's squiffy."

Ten minutes passed. Mike thought: "This affair has definitely not gone according to plan." He listened. Some kind of tension seemed to be building up on the stage. Canning Cumberland's voice rose on a loud but blurred note. A door in the set opened. "Don't bother to come," Cumberland said. "Good-bye. I can find my way out." The door slammed. Cumberland was standing near Mike. Then, very close, there was a loud explosion. The scenic flats vibrated, Mike's flesh leapt on his bones and Cumberland went into his dressing rooms. Mike heard the key turn in the door. The smell of alcohol mingled with the smell of gunpowder. A stagehand moved to a trestle table and laid a pistol on it. The actor with the eyeglass made an exit. He spoke for a moment to the stage manager, passed Mike, and disappeared in the passage.

Smells. There were all sorts of smells. Subconsciously, still listening to the play, he began to sort them out. Glue. Canvas. Grease paint. The callboy tapped on doors. "Mr. George, please." "Miss Bourne, please." They came out, Coralie Bourne with her dresser. Mike heard her turn a door handle and say something. An indistinguishable voice answered her. Then she and her dresser passed him. The others spoke to her and she nodded and then seemed to withdraw into herself, waiting with her head bent, ready to make her entrance. Presently she drew back, walked swiftly to the door in the set, flung it open and swept on, followed a minute later by Barry George.

Smells. Dust, stale paint, cloth. Gas. Increasingly, the smell of gas.

The group of stagehands moved away behind the set to the side of the stage. Mike edged out of cover. He could see the prompt corner. The stage manager stood there with folded arms, watching the action. Behind him were grouped the players who were not on. Two dressers stood apart, watching. The light from the set caught their faces. Coralie Bourne's voice sent phrases flying like birds into the auditorium.

Mike began peering at the floor. Had he kicked some gas fitting adrift? The callboy passed him, stared at him over his shoulder and went down the passage, tapping. "Five minutes to the curtain, please. Five minutes." The actor with the elderly makeup followed the callboy out. "God, what a stink of gas," he whispered. "Chronic, ain't it?" said the callboy. They stared at Mike and then crossed to the waiting group. The man said something to the stage manager who tipped his head up, sniffing. He made an impatient gesture and turned back to the prompt box, reaching over the prompter's head. A bell rang somewhere up in the flies and Mike saw a stagehand climb to the curtain platform.

The little group near the prompt corner was agitated. They looked back towards the passage entrance. The callboy nodded and came running back. He knocked on the first door on the right. "*Mr. Cumberland! Mr. Cumberland!* You're on for the call." He rattled the door handle. *"Mr. Cumberland!* You're on."

Mike ran into the passage. The callboy coughed wretchingly and jerked his hand at the door. "Gas!" he said. "Gas!"

"Break it in."

"I'll get Mr. Reynolds."

He was gone. It was a narrow passage. From halfway across the opposite room Mike took a run, head down, shoulder forward, at the door. It gave a little and a sickening increase in the smell caught him in the lungs. A vast storm of noise had broken out and as he took another run he thought: "It's hailing outside."

"Just a minute if *you* please, sir."

It was a stagehand. He'd got a hammer and screwdriver. He wedged the point of the screwdriver between the lock and the doorpost, drove it home and wrenched. The screws squeaked, the wood splintered and gas poured into the passage. "No winders," coughed the stagehand.

Mike wound Alleyn's scarf over his mouth and nose. Half-forgotten instructions from antigas drill occurred to him. The room looked queer but he could see the man slumped down in the chair quite clearly. He stooped low and ran in.

He was knocking against things as he backed out, lugging the deadweight. His arms tingled. A high insistent voice hummed in his brain. He floated a short distance and came to earth on a concrete floor among several pairs of legs. A long way off, someone said loudly: "I can only thank you for being so kind to what I know, too well, is a very imperfect play." Then the sound of hail began again. There was a heavenly stream of clear air flowing into his mouth and nostrils. "I could eat it," he thought and sat up.

The telephone rang. "Suppose," Mrs. Alleyn suggested, "that this time you ignore it."

"It might be the Yard," Alleyn said, and answered it.

"Is that Chief Detective-Inspector Alleyn's flat? I'm speaking from the Jupiter Theater. I've rung up to say that the Chief Inspector is here and that he's had a slight mishap. He's all right, but I think it might be as well for someone to drive him home. No need to worry."

"What sort of mishap?" Alleyn asked.

"Er—well—er, he's been a bit gassed."

"*Gassed!* All right. Thanks, I'll come."

"What a bore for you, darling," said Mrs. Alleyn. "What sort of case is it? Suicide?"

"Masquerading within the meaning of the act, by the sound of it. Mike's in trouble."

"What trouble, for Heaven's sake?"

"Got himself gassed. He's all right. Good night, darling. Don't wait up."

When he reached the theater, the front of the house was in darkness. He made his way down the side alley to the stage door where he was held up.

"Yard," he said, and produced his official card.

"'Ere," said the stage doorkeeper. "'Ow many more of you?"

"The man inside was working for me," said Alleyn and walked in. The doorkeeper followed, protesting.

To the right of the entrance was a large scenic dock from which the double doors had been rolled back. Here Mike was sitting in an armchair, very white about the lips. Three men and two women, all with painted faces, stood near him and behind them a group of stagehands with Reynolds, the stage manager, and, apart from these, three men in evening dress. The men looked woodenly shocked. The women had been weeping.

"I'm most frightfully sorry, sir," Mike said. "I've tried to explain. This," he added generally, "is Inspector Alleyn."

"I can't understand all this," said the oldest of the men in evening dress irritably. He turned on the doorkeeper. "You said—"

"I seen 'is card—"

"I know," said Mike, "but you see—"

"This is Lord Michael Lamprey," Alleyn said. "A recruit to the Police Department. What's happened here?"

"Doctor Rankin, would you . . . ?"

The second of the men in evening dress came forward. "All right, Gosset. It's a bad business, Inspector. I've just been saying the police would have to be informed. If you'll come with me—"

Alleyn followed him through a door onto the stage proper. It was dimly lit. A trestle table had been set up in the center and on it, covered with a sheet, was an unmistakable shape. The smell of gas, strong everywhere, hung heavily about the table.

"Who is it?"

"Canning Cumberland. He'd locked the door of his dressing room. There's a gas fire. Your young friend dragged him out, very pluckily, but it was no go. I was in front. Gosset, the manager, had asked me to supper. It's a perfectly clear case of suicide as you'll see."

"I'd better look at the room. Anybody been in?"

"God, no. It was a job to clear it. They turned the gas off at the main. There's no window. They had to open the double doors at the back of the stage and a small outside door at the end of the passage. It may be possible to get in now."

He led the way to the dressing room passage. "Pretty thick, still," he said. "It's the first room on the right. They burst the lock. You'd better keep down near the floor."

The powerful lights over the mirror were on and the room still had its look of occupation. The gas fire was against the left-hand wall. Alleyn squatted down by it. The tap was still turned on, its face lying parallel with the floor. The top of the heater, the tap itself, and the carpet near it, were covered with a creamish powder. On the end of the dressing table shelf nearest to the stove was a box of this powder. Farther along the shelf, grease paints were set out in a row beneath the mirror. Then came a wash basin and in front of this an overturned chair. Alleyn could see the track of heels, across the pile of the carper, to the door immediately opposite. Beside the wash basin was a quart bottle of whiskey, three parts empty, and a tumbler. Alleyn had had about enough and returned to the passage.

"Perfectly clear," the hovering doctor said again. "Isn't it?"

"I'll see the other rooms, I think."

The one next to Cumberland's was like his in reverse, but smaller. The heater was back to back with Cumberland's. The dressing shelf was set out with much the same assortment of grease paints. The tap of this heater, too, was turned on. It was of precisely the same make as the other and Alleyn, less embarrassed here by fumes, was able to make a longer examination. It was a common enough type of gas fire. The lead-in was from a pipe through a flexible metallic tube with a rubber connection. There were two taps, one in the pipe and one at the junction of the tube with the heater itself. Alleyn disconnected the tube and examined the connection. It was perfectly sound, a close fit and stained red at the end. Alleyn noticed a wiry thread of some reddish stuff resembling packing that still clung to it. The nozzle and tap were brass, the tap pulling over when it was turned on, to lie in a parallel plane with the floor. No powder had been scattered about here.

He glanced round the room, returned to the door and read the card: "Mr. Barry George."

The doctor followed him into the rooms opposite these, on the left-hand side of the passage. They were a repetition in design of the two he had already seen but were hung with women's clothes and had a more elaborate assortment of grease paint and cosmetics.

There was a mass of flowers in the star room. Alleyn read the cards. One in particular caught his eye: "From Anthony Gill to say a most inadequate 'thank you' for the great idea." A vase of red roses stood before the mirror: "To your greatest triumph. Coralie darling. C.C." In Miss Gay's room there were only two bouquets, one from the management and one "from Anthony, with love."

Again in each room he pulled off the lead-in to the heater and looked at the connection.

"All right, aren't they?" said the doctor.

"Quite all right. Tight fit. Good solid gray rubber."

"Well, then—"

Next on the left was an unused room, and opposite it, "Mr. H. J. Bannington." Neither of these rooms had gas fires. Mr. Bannington's dressing table was littered with the usual array of greasepaint, the materials for his beard, a number of telegrams and letters, and several bills.

"About the body," the doctor began.

"We'll get a mortuary van from the Yard."

"But—surely in a case of suicide—"

"I don't think this is suicide."

"But, good God! D'you mean there's been an accident?"

"No accident," said Alleyn.

At midnight, the dressing room lights in the Jupiter Theater were brilliant, and men were busy there with the tools of their trade. A constable stood at the stage door and a van waited in the yard. The front of the house was dimly lit and there, among the shrouded stalls, sat Coralie Bourne, Basil Gosset, H. J. Bannington, Dendra Gay, Anthony Gill, Reynolds, Katie the dresser, and the callboy. A constable sat behind them and another stood by the doors into the foyer. They stared across the backs of seats at the fire curtain. Spirals of smoke rose from their cigarettes and about their feet were discarded programs. "Basil Gosset presents I CAN FIND MY WAY OUT by Anthony Gill."

In the manager's office Alleyn said: "You're sure of your facts, Mike?"

"Yes, sir. Honestly. I was right up against the entrance into the passage. They didn't see me because I was in the shadow. It was very dark off-stage."

"You'll have to swear to it."

"I know."

"Good. All right, Thompson. Miss Gay and Mr. Gosset may go home. Ask Miss Bourne to come in."

When Sergeant Thompson had gone Mike said: "I haven't had a chance to say I know I've made a perfect fool of myself. Using your card and everything."

"Irresponsible gaiety doesn't go down very well in the service, Mike. You behaved like a clown."

"I *am* a fool," said Mike wretchedly.

The red beard was lying in front of Alleyn on Gosset's desk. He picked it up and held it out. "Put it on," he said.

"She might do another faint."

"I think not. Now the hat: yes-yes, I see. Come in."

Sergeant Thompson showed Coralie Bourne in and then sat at the end of the desk with his notebook.

Tears had traced their course through the powder on her face, carrying black cosmetic with them and leaving the greasepaint shining like snail tracks. She stood near the doorway looking dully at Michael. "Is he back in England?" she said. "Did he tell you to do this?" She made an impatient movement. "Do take it off," she said. "It's a very bad beard. If Cann had only looked—" Her lips trembled. "Who told you to do it?"

"Nobody," Mike stammered, pocketing the beard. "I mean— As a matter of fact, Tony Gill—"

"*Tony?* But *he* didn't know. Tony wouldn't do it. Unless—"

"Unless?" Alleyn said.

She said frowning: "Tony didn't want Cann to play the part that way. He was furious."

"He says it was his dress for the Chelsea Arts Ball," Mike mumbled. "I brought it here. I just thought I'd put it on—it was idiotic, I know—for fun. I'd no idea you and Mr. Cumberland would mind."

"Ask Mr. Gill to come in," Alleyn said.

Anthony was white and seemed bewildered and helpless. "I've told Mike," he said. "It was my dress for the ball. They sent it round from the costume-hiring place this afternoon but I forgot it. Dendra reminded me and rang up the delivery people—or Mike, as it turns out—in the interval."

"Why," Alleyn asked, "did you choose that particular disguise?"

"I didn't. I didn't know what to wear and I was too rattled to think. They said they were hiring things for themselves and would get something for me. They said we'd all be characters out of a Russian melodrama."

"Who said this?"

"Well—well, it was Barry George, actually."

"Barry," Coralie Bourne said. *"It was Barry."*

"I don't understand," Anthony said. "Why should a fancy dress upset everybody?"

"It happened," Alleyn said, "to be a replica of the dress usually worn by Miss Bourne's husband who also had a red beard. That was it, wasn't it, Miss Bourne? I remember seeing him."

"Oh, yes," she said, "you would. He was known to the police." Suddenly she broke down completely. She was in an armchair near the desk but out of the range of its shaded lamp. She twisted and writhed, beating her hand against the padded arm of the chair. Sergeant Thompson sat with his head bent and his hand over his notes. Mike, after an agonized glance at Alleyn, turned his back. Anthony Gill leaned over her: "Don't," he said violently. "Don't! For God's sake, stop."

She twisted away from him and gripping the edge of the desk, began to speak to Alleyn; little by little gaining mastery of herself. "I want to tell you. I want you to understand. Listen." Her husband had been fantastically cruel, she said. "It was a kind of slavery." But when she sued for divorce he brought evidence of adultery with Cumberland. They had thought he knew nothing. "There was an abominable scene. He told us he was going away. He said he'd keep track of us and if I tried again for divorce, he'd come home. He was very friendly with Barry in those days." He had left behind him the first draft of a play he had meant to write for her and Cumberland. It had a wonderful scene for them. "And now you will never have it," he had said, "because there is no other playwright who could make this play for you but I." He was, she said, a melodramatic man but he was never ridiculous. He returned to the Ukraine where he was born and they had heard no more of him. In a little while she would have been able to presume death. But years of waiting did not agree with Canning Cumberland. He drank consistently and at his worst used to imagine her husband was about to return. "He was really terrified of Ben," she said. "He seemed like a creature in a nightmare."

Anthony Gill said: "This play—was it . . . ?"

"Yes. There was an extraordinary similarity between your play and his. I saw at once that Ben's central scene would enormously strengthen your piece. Cann didn't want me to give it to you. Barry knew. He said: 'Why not?' He wanted Cann's part and was furious when he didn't get it. So you see, when he suggested you should dress and make-up like Ben—" She turned to Alleyn. "You see?"

"What did Cumberland do when he saw you?" Alleyn asked Mike.

"He made a queer movement with his hands as if—well, as if he expected me to go for him. Then he just bolted into his room."

"He thought Ben had come back," she said.

"Were you alone at any time after you fainted?" Alleyn asked.

"I? No. No, I wasn't. Katie took me into my dressing room and stayed with me until I went on for the last scene."

"One other question. Can you, by any chance, remember if the heater in your room behaved at all oddly?"

She looked wearily at him. "Yes, it did give a sort of plop, I think. It made me jump. I was nervy."

"You went straight from your room to the stage?"

"Yes. With Katie. I wanted to go to Cann. I tried the door when we came out. It was locked. He said: 'Don't come in.' I said: 'It's all right. It wasn't Ben,' and went on to the stage."

"I heard Miss Bourne," Mike said.

"He must have made up his mind by then. He was terribly drunk when he played his last scene." She pushed her hair back from her forehead. "May I go?" she asked Alleyn.

"I've sent for a taxi. Mr. Gill, will you see if it's there? In the meantime, Miss Bourne, would you like to wait in the foyer?"

"May I take Katie home with me?"

"Certainly. Thompson will find her. Is there anyone else we can get?"

"No, thank you. Just old Katie."

Alleyn opened the door for her and watched her walk into the foyer. "Check up with the dresser, Thompson," he murmured, "and get Mr. H. J. Bannington."

He saw Coralie Bourne sit on the lower step of the dress circle stairway and lean her head against the wall. Nearby, on a gilt easel, a huge photograph of Canning Cumberland smiled handsomely at her.

H. J. Bannington looked pretty ghastly. He had rubbed his hand across his face and smeared his makeup. Florid red paint from his lips had stained the crepe hair that had been gummed on and shaped into a beard. His monocle was still in his left eye and gave him an extraordinarily rakish look. "See here," he complained, "I've about had this party. When do we go home?"

Alleyn uttered placatory phrases and got him to sit down. He checked over H. J.'s movements after Cumberland left the stage and found that his account tallied with Mike's. He asked if H. J. had visited any of the other dressing rooms and was told acidly that H. J. knew his place in the company. "I remained in my unheated and squalid kennel, thank you very much."

"Do you know if Mr. Barry George followed your example?"

"Couldn't say, old boy. He didn't come near me."

"Have you any theories at all about this unhappy business, Mr. Bannington?"

"Do you mean, why did Cann do it? Well, speak no ill of the dead, but I'd have thought it was pretty obvious he was morbid-drunk. Tight as an owl when we finished the second act. Ask the great Mr. Barry George. Cann took the big scene away from Barry with both hands and left him looking pathetic. All wrong artistically, but that's how Cann was in his cups." H. J.'s wicked little eyes narrowed. "The great Mr. George," he said, "must be feeling very unpleasant by now. You might say he'd got a suicide on his mind, mightn't you? Or don't you know about that?"

"It was not suicide."

The glass dropped from H. J.'s eye. "God!" he said. "God, I told Bob Reynolds! I told him the whole plant wanted overhauling."

"The gas plant, you mean?"

"Certainly. I was in the gas business years ago. Might say I'm in it still with a difference, ha-ha!"

"Ha-ha!" Alleyn agreed politely. He leaned forward. "Look here," he said: "We can't dig up a gas man at this time of night and may very likely need an expert opinion. You can help us."

"Well, old boy, I was rather pining for a spot of shuteye. But, of course—"

"I shan't keep you very long."

"God, I hope not!" said H. J. earnestly.

Barry George had been made up pale for the last act. Colorless lips and shadows under his cheek bones and eyes had skillfully underlined his character as a repatriated but broken prisoner-of-war. Now, in the glare of the office lamp, he looked like a grossly exaggerated figure of mourning. He began at once to tell Alleyn how grieved and horrified he was. Everybody, he said, had their faults, and poor old Cann was no exception but wasn't it terrible to think what could happen to a man who let himself go downhill? He, Barry George, was abnormally sensitive and he didn't think he'd ever really get over the awful shock this had been to him. What, he wondered, could be at the bottom of it? Why had poor old Cann decided to end it all?

"Miss Bourne's theory," Alleyn began. Mr. George laughed. "Coralie?" he said. "So she's got a theory! Oh, well. Never mind."

"Her theory is this. Cumberland saw a man whom he mistook for her husband and, having a morbid dread of his return, drank the greater part of a bottle of whiskey and gassed himself. The clothes and beard that deceived him had, I understand, been ordered by you for Mr. Anthony Gill."

This statement produced startling results. Barry George broke into a spate of expostulation and apology. There had been no thought in his mind of resurrecting poor old Ben, who was no doubt dead but had been, mind you, in many ways one of the best. They were all to go to the Ball as exaggerated characters from melodrama. Not for the world— He gesticulated and protested. A line of sweat broke out along the margin of his hair. "I don't know what you're getting at," he shouted. "What are you suggesting?"

"I'm suggesting, among other things, that Cumberland was murdered."

"You're mad! He'd locked himself in. They had to break down the door. There's no window. You're crazy!"

"Don't," Alleyn said wearily, "let us have any nonsense about sealed rooms. Now, Mr. George, you knew Benjamin Vlasnoff pretty well. Are you going to tell us that when you suggested Mr. Gill should wear a coat with a fur collar, a black sombrero, black gloves and a red beard, it never occurred to you that his appearance might be a shock to Miss Bourne and to Cumberland?"

"I wasn't the only one," he blustered. "H. J. knew. And if it had scared him off, *she* wouldn't have been so sorry. She'd had about enough of him. Anyway if this is murder, the costume's got nothing to do with it."

"That," Alleyn said, getting up, "is what we hope to find out."

In Barry George's room, Detective Sergeant Bailey, a fingerprint expert, stood by the gas heater. Sergeant Gibson, a police photographer, and a uniformed constable were near the door. In the center of the room stood Barry George, looking from one man to another and picking at his lips.

"I don't know why he wants me to watch all this," he said. "I'm exhausted. I'm emotionally used up. What's he doing? Where is he?"

Alleyn was next door in Cumberland's dressing room, with H. J., Mike and Sergeant Thompson. It was pretty clear now of fumes and the gas fire was burning comfortably. Sergeant Thompson sprawled in the armchair near the heater, his head sunk and his eyes shut.

"This is the theory, Mr. Bannington," Alleyn said. "You and Cumberland have made your formal exits; Miss Bourne and Mr. George and Miss Gay are all on the stage. Lord Michael is standing just outside the entrance to the passage. The dressers and stage staff are watching the play from the side. Cumberland has locked himself in this room. There he is, dead drunk and sound asleep. The gas fire is burning, full pressure. Earlier in the evening he powdered himself and a thick layer of the powder lies undisturbed on the tap. Now."

He tapped on the wall.

The fire blew out with a sharp explosion. This was followed by the hiss of escaping gas. Alleyn turned the taps off. "You see," he said, "I've left an excellent print on the powdered surface. Now, come next door."

Next door, Barry George appealed to him stammering: "But I didn't *know*. I don't know anything about it. I don't know."

"Just show Mr. Bannington, will you, Bailey?"

Bailey knelt down. The lead-in was disconnected from the tap on the heater. He turned on the tap in the pipe and blew down the tube.

"An air lock, you see. It works perfectly."

H. J. was staring at Barry George. "But I don't know about gas, H. J. H. J., tell them—"

"One moment." Alleyn removed the towels that had been spread over the dressing shelf, revealing a sheet of clean paper on which lay the rubber push-on connection.

"Will you take this lens, Bannington, and look at it. You'll see that it's stained a florid red. It's a very slight stain but it's unmistakably greasepaint. And just above the stain you'll see a wiry hair. Rather like some sort of packing material, but it's not that. It's crepe hair, isn't it?"

The lens wavered above the paper.

"Let me hold it for you," Alleyn said. He put his hand over H. J.'s shoulder and, with a swift movement, plucked a tuft from his false moustache and dropped it on the paper. "Identical, you see. Ginger. It seems to be stuck to the connection with spirit gum."

The lens fell. H. J. twisted round, faced Alleyn for a second, and then struck him full in the face. He was a small man but it took three of them to hold him.

"In a way, sir, it's handy when they have a smack at you," said Detective Sergeant Thompson half an hour later. "You can pull them in nice and straightforward without any 'will you come to the station and make a statement' business."

"Quite," said Alleyn, nursing his jaw.

Mike said: "He must have gone to the room after Barry George and Miss Bourne were called."

"That's it. He had to be quick. The callboy would be round in a minute and he had to be back in his own room."

"But look here—what about motive?"

"That, my good Mike, is precisely why, at half-past one in the morning, we're still in this miserable theater. You're getting a view of the duller aspect of homicide. Want to go home?"

"No. Give me another job."

"Very well. About ten feet from the prompt entrance, there's a sort of garbage can. Go through it."

At seventeen minutes to two, when the dressing rooms and passage had been combed clean and Alleyn had called a spell, Mike came to him with filthy hands. *"Eureka,"* he said, "I hope."

They all went into Bannington's room. Alleyn spread out on the dressing table the fragments of paper that Mike had given him.

"They'd been pushed down to the bottom of the can," Mike said.

Alleyn moved the fragments about. Thompson whistled through his teeth. Bailey and Gibson mumbled together.

"There you are," Alleyn said at last.

They collected round him. The letter that H. J. Bannington had opened at this same table six hours and forty-five minutes earlier, was pieced together like a jigsaw puzzle.

"Dear H. J.

Having seen the monthly statement of my account, I called at my bank this morning and was shown a check that is undoubtedly a forgery. Your histrionic versatility, my dear H. J., is only equaled by your audacity as a calligraphist. But fame has its disadvantages. The teller recognized you. I propose to take action."

"Unsigned," said Bailey.

"Look at the card on the red roses in Miss Bourne's room, signed C. C. It's a very distinctive hand." Alleyn turned to Mike. "Do you still want to be a policeman?"

"Yes."

"Lord help you. Come and talk to me at the office tomorrow."

"Thank you, sir."

They went out, leaving a constable on duty. It was a cold morning. Mike looked up at the facade of the Jupiter. He could just make out the shape of the neon sign: I CAN FIND MY WAY OUT by Anthony Gill.

The Secret Garden

G. K. Chesterton

G. K. Chesterton's Father Brown stories first appeared in the *Saturday Evening Post* in July 1910. These timeless classics describe an unassuming little priest who solves crimes by imagining himself inside the mind and soul of the criminal and understanding his motives. This "transcendental Sherlock Holmes" with a cherub face, glasses and unworldly simplicity has entertained countless generations of readers with his uncanny understanding of the villainous mind. When developing the character of Father Brown, Chesterton wanted to construct a comedy in which a priest should appear to know nothing and in fact know more about crime than the criminals.

Aristide Valentin, Chief of the Paris Police, was late for his dinner, and some of his guests began to arrive before him. These were, however, reassured by his confidential servant, Ivan, the old man with a scar, and a face almost as gray as his moustaches, who always sat at a table in the entrance hall—a hall hung with weapons. Valentin's house was perhaps as peculiar and celebrated as its master. It was an old house, with high walls and tall poplars almost overhanging the Seine; but the oddity—and perhaps the police value—of its architecture was this: that there was no ultimate exit at all except through this front door, which was guarded by Ivan and the armory. The garden was large and elaborate, and there were many exits from the house into the garden. But there was no exit from the garden into the world outside; all round it ran a tall, smooth, unscalable wall with special spikes at the top; no bad garden, perhaps, for a man to reflect in whom some hundred criminals had sworn to kill.

As Ivan explained to the guests, their host had telephoned that he was detained for ten minutes. He was, in truth, making some last arrangements about executions and such ugly things; and though these duties were rootedly repulsive to him, he always performed them with precision. Ruthless in the pursuit of criminals, he was very mild about their punishment. Since he had been supreme over French—and largely over European—political methods, his great influence had been honorably used for the mitigation of sentences and the purification of prisons. He was one of the great humanitarian French freethinkers; and the only thing wrong with them is that they make mercy even colder than justice.

When Valentin arrived he was already dressed in black clothes and the red rosette—an elegant figure, his dark beard already streaked with gray. He went straight through his house to his study, which opened on the grounds behind. The garden door of it was open, and after he had carefully locked his box in its official place, he stood for a few seconds at the open door looking out upon the garden. A sharp moon was fighting with the flying rags and tatters of a storm, and Valentin regarded it with a wistfulness unusual in such scientific natures as his. Perhaps such scientific natures have some psychic prevision of the most tremendous problem of their lives. From any such occult mood, at least, he quickly recovered, for he knew he was late, and that his guests had already begun to arrive. A glance at his drawing-room when he entered it was enough to make certain that his principal guest was not there, at any rate. He saw all the other pillars of the little party; he saw Lord Galloway, the English Ambassador—a choleric old man with a russet face like an apple, wearing the blue ribbon of the Garter. He saw Lady Galloway, slim and threadlike, with silver hair and a face sensitive and superior. He saw her daughter, Lady Margaret Graham, a pale and pretty girl with an elfish face and copper-colored hair. He saw the Duchess of Mont St. Michel, black-eyed and opulent, and with her were her two daughters, black-eyed and opulent also. He saw Dr. Simon, a typical French scientist, with glasses, a pointed brown beard, and a forehead barred with those parallel wrinkles which are the penalty of superciliousness, since they come through constantly elevating the eyebrows. He saw Father Brown, of Cobhole, in Essex, whom he had recently met in England. He saw—perhaps with more interest than any of these—a tall man in uniform, who had bowed to the Galloways without receiving any very hearty acknowledgement, and who now advanced alone to pay his respects to his host. This was Commandant O'Brien, of the French Foreign Legion. He was a slim yet somewhat swaggering figure, clean-shaven, dark-haired, and blue-eyed, and, as seemed natural in an officer of that famous regiment of victorious failures and successful suicides, he had an air at once dashing and melancholy. He was by birth an Irish gentleman, and in boyhood had known the Galloways—especially Margaret Graham. He had left his country after some crash of debts, and now expressed his complete freedom from British etiquette by swinging about in uniform, saber and spurs. When he bowed to the Ambassador's family, Lord and Lady Galloway bent stiffly, and Lady Margaret looked away.

But for whatever old causes such people might be interested in each other, their distinguished host was not specially interested in them. No one of them at least was in his eyes the guest of the evening. Valentin was expecting, for special reasons, a man of worldwide fame, whose friendship he had secured during some of his great detective tours and triumphs in the United States. He was expecting Julius K. Brayne, that multimillionaire whose colossal and even crushing endowments of small religions have occasioned so much easy sport and easier solemnity for the American and English papers. Nobody could quite make out whether Mr. Brayne was an atheist or a Mormon or a Christian Scientist; but he was ready to pour money into any intellectual vessel, so long as it was an untried vessel. One of his hobbies was to wait for the American Shakespeare—a hobby more patient than angling. He admired Walt Whitman, but thought that Luke P. Tanner, of Paris, Pa., was more "progressive" than Whitman any day. He liked anything that he thought "progressive." He thought Valentin "progressive," thereby doing him a grave injustice.

The solid appearance of Julius K. Brayne in the room was as decisive as a dinner bell. He had this great quality, which very few of us can claim, that his presence was as big as his absence. He was a huge fellow, as fat as he was tall, clad in complete evening black, without so much relief as a watch chain or a ring. His hair was white and well brushed back like a German's; his face was red, fierce and cherubic, with one dark tuft under the lower lip that threw up that otherwise infantile visage with an effect theatrical and even Mephistophelean. Not long, however, did that *salon* merely stare at the celebrated American; his lateness had already become a domestic problem, and he was sent with all speed into the dining-room with Lady Galloway on his arm.

Except on one point the Galloways were genial and casual enough. So long as Lady Margaret did not take the arm of that adventurer O'Brien, her father was quite satisfied; and she had not done so, she had decorously gone in with Dr. Simon. Nevertheless, old Lord Galloway was restless and almost rude. He was diplomatic enough during dinner, but when, over the cigars, three of the younger men—Simon the doctor, Brown the priest, and the detrimental O'Brien, the exile in a foreign uniform—all melted away to mix with the ladies or smoke in the conservatory, then the English diplomatist grew very undiplomatic indeed. He was stung every sixty seconds with the thought that the scamp O'Brien might be signaling to Margaret somehow; he did not attempt to imagine how. He was left over the coffee with Brayne, the honorary Yankee who believed in all religions, and Valentin, the grizzled Frenchman who believed in none. They could argue with each other, but neither could appeal to him. After a time this "progressive" logomachy had reached a crisis of tedium; Lord Galloway got up also and sought the drawing-room. He lost his way in long passages for some six or eight minutes: till he heard the high-pitched, didactic voice of the doctor, and then the dull voice of the priest, followed by general laughter. They also, he thought with a curse, were probably arguing about "science and religion." But the instant he opened the *salon* door he saw only one thing—he saw what was not there. He saw that Commandant O'Brien was absent, and that Lady Margaret was absent too.

Rising impatiently from the drawing-room, as he had from the dining-room, he stamped along the passage once more. His notion of protecting his daughter from the Irish-Algerian ne'er-do-well had become something central and even mad in his mind. As he went towards the back of the house, where was Valentin's study, he was surprised to meet his daughter, who swept past with a white, scornful face, which was a second enigma. If she had been with O'Brien, where was O'Brien? If she had not been with O'Brien where had she been? With a sort of senile and passionate suspicion he groped his way to the dark back parts of the mansion, and eventually found a servants' entrance that opened onto the garden. The moon with her scimitar had now ripped up and rolled away all the storm wrack. The argent light lit up all four corners of the garden. A tall figure in blue was striding across the lawn towards the study door; a glint of moonlit silver on his facings picked him out as Commandant O'Brien.

He vanished through the French windows into the house, leaving Lord Galloway in an indescribable temper, at once virulent and vague. The blue-and-silver garden, like a scene in a theater, seemed to taunt him with all that tyrannic tenderness against which his worldly authority was at war. The length and grace of the Irishman's stride enraged him as if he were a rival instead of a father; the moonlight maddened him. He was trapped as if by magic into a garden of troubadours, a Watteau fairyland; and, willing to shake off such amorous imbecilities by speech, he stepped briskly after his enemy. As he did so he tripped over some tree or stone in the grass; looked down at it first with irritation and then a second time with curiosity. The next instant the moon and the tall poplars looked at an unusual sight—an elderly English diplomatist running hard and crying or bellowing as he ran.

His hoarse shouts brought a pale face to the study door, the beaming glasses and worried brow of Dr. Simon, who heard the nobleman's first clear words. Lord Galloway was crying: "A corpse in the grass—a blood-stained corpse." O'Brien at least had gone utterly out of his mind.

"We must tell Valentin at once," said the doctor, when the other had brokenly described all that he had dared to examine. "It is fortunate that he is here;" and even as he spoke the great detective entered the study, attracted by the cry. It was almost amusing to note his typical transformation; he had come with the common concern of a host and a gentleman, fearing that some guest or servant was ill. When he was told the gory fact, he turned with all his gravity instantly bright and businesslike; for this, however abrupt and awful, was his business.

"Strange, gentlemen," he said as they hurried out into the garden, "that I should have hunted mysteries all over the earth, and now one comes and settles in my own back yard. But where is the place?" They crossed the lawn less easily, as a slight mist had begun to rise from the river; but under the guidance of the shaken Galloway they found the body sunken in deep grass—the body of a very tall and broad-shouldered man. He lay face downwards, so they could only see that his big shoulders were clad in black cloth, and that his big head was bald, except for a wisp or two of brown hair that clung to his skull like wet seaweed. A scarlet serpent of blood crawled from under his fallen face.

"At least," said Simon, with a deep and singular intonation, "he is none of our party."

"Examine him, Doctor," cried Valentin rather sharply. "He may not be dead."

The doctor bent down. "He is not quite cold, but I am afraid he is dead enough," he answered. "Just help me lift him up."

They lifted him carefully an inch from the ground, and all doubts as to his being really dead were settled at once and frightfully. The head fell away. It had been entirely sundered from the body; whoever had cut his throat had managed to sever the neck as well. Even Valentin was slightly shocked. "He must have been as strong as a gorilla," he muttered.

Not without a shiver, though he was used to anatomical abortions, Dr. Simon lifted the head. It was slightly slashed about the neck and jaw, but the face was substantially unhurt. It was a ponderous, yellow face, at once sunken and swollen, with a hawk-like nose and heavy lids—the face of a wicked Roman emperor, with, perhaps, a distant touch of a Chinese emperor. All present seemed to look at it with the coldest eye of ignorance. Nothing else could be noted about the man except that, as they had lifted his body, they had seen underneath it the white gleam of a shirt front defaced with a red gleam of blood. As Dr. Simon said, the man had never been of their party. But he might very well have been trying to join it, for he had come dressed for such an occasion.

Valentin went down on his hands and knees and examined with his closest professional attention the grass and ground for some twenty yards round the body, in which he was assisted less skillfully by the doctor, and quite vaguely by the English lord. Nothing rewarded their grovelings except a few twigs, snapped or chopped into very small lengths, which Valentin lifted for an instant's examination and then tossed away.

"Twigs," he said gravely. "Twigs, and a total stranger with his head cut off; that is all there is on this lawn."

There was an almost creepy stillness, and then the unnerved Galloway called out sharply:

"Who's that? Who's that over there by the garden wall?"

A small figure with a foolishly large head drew waveringly near them in the moonlit haze; looked for an instant like a goblin, but turned out to be the harmless little priest whom they had left in the drawing-room.

"I say," he said meekly, "there are no gates to this garden, do you know?"

Valentin's black brows had come together somewhat crossly, as they did on principle at the sight of the cassock. But he was far too just a man to deny the relevance of the remark. "You are right," he said. "Before we find out how he came to be killed, we may have to find out how he came to be here. Now listen to me, gentlemen. If it can be done without prejudice to my position and duty, we shall all agree that certain distinguished names might well be kept out of this. There are ladies, gentlemen, and there is a foreign ambassador. If we must mark it down as a crime, then it must be followed up as a crime. But till then I can use my own discretion. I am the head of the police; I am so public that I can afford to be private. Please Heaven, I will clear every one of my own guests before I call in my men to look for anybody else. Gentlemen, upon your honor, you will none of you leave the house till tomorrow at noon; there are bedrooms for all. Simon, I think you know where to find my man, Ivan, in the front hall; he is a confidential man. Tell him to leave another servant on guard and come to me at once. Lord Galloway, you are certainly the best person to tell the ladies what has happened, and prevent a panic. They also must stay. Father Brown and I will remain with the body."

When this spirit of the captain spoke in Valentin he was obeyed like a bugle. Dr. Simon went through to the armory and routed out Ivan, the public detective's private detective. Galloway went to the drawing-room and told the terrible news tactfully enough, so that by the time the company assembled there the ladies were already startled and already soothed. Meanwhile the good priest and the good atheist stood at the head and foot of the dead man motionless in the moonlight, like symbolic statues of their two philosophies of death.

Ivan, the confidential man with the scar and the moustaches, came out of the house like a cannon ball, and came racing across the lawn to Valentin like a dog to his master. His livid face was quite lively with the glow of this domestic detective story, and it was with almost unpleasant eagerness that he asked his master's permission to examine the remains.

"Yes; look, if you like, Ivan," said Valentin, "but don't be long. We must go in and thrash this out in the house."

Ivan lifted the head, and then almost let it drop.

"Why," he gasped, "it's—no, it isn't; it can't be. Do you know this man, sir?"

"No," said Valentin indifferently; "we had better go inside."

Between them they carried the corpse to a sofa in the study, and then all made their way to the drawing-room.

The detective sat down at a desk quietly, and even with hesitation; but his eye was the iron eye of a judge at assize. He made a few rapid notes upon paper in front of him, and then said shortly: "Is everybody here?"

"Not Mr. Brayne," said the Duchess of Mont St.-Michel, looking round.

"No," said Lord Galloway in a hoarse, harsh voice. "And not Mr. Neil O'Brien, I fancy. I saw that gentleman walking in the garden when the corpse was still warm."

"Ivan," said the detective, "go and fetch Commandant O'Brien and Mr. Brayne. Mr. Brayne, I know, is finishing a cigar in the dining-room; Commandant O'Brien, I think, is walking up and down the conservatory. I am not sure."

The faithful attendant flashed from the room, and before anyone could stir or speak Valentin went on with the same soldierly swiftness of exposition.

"Everyone here knows that a dead man has been found in the garden, his head cut clean from his body. Dr. Simon, you have examined it. Do you think that to cut a man's throat like that would need great force? Or, perhaps, only a very sharp knife?"

"I should say that it could not be done with a knife at all," said the pale doctor.

"Have you any thought," resumed Valentin, "of a tool with which it could be done?"

"Speaking within modern probabilities, I really haven't," said the doctor, arching his painful brows. "It's not easy to hack a neck through even clumsily, and this was a very clean cut. It could be done with a battle-axe or an old headsman's axe, or an old two-handled sword."

"But, good heavens!" cried the Duchess, almost in hysterics, "there aren't any two-handled swords and battle-axes round here."

Valentin was still busy with the paper in front of him. "Tell me," he said, still writing rapidly, "could it have been done with a long French cavalry saber?"

A low knocking came at the door, which, for some unreasonable reason, curdled everyone's blood like the knocking in Macbeth. Amid that frozen silence Dr. Simon managed to say: "A saber—yes, I suppose it could."

"Thank you," said Valentin. "Come in, Ivan."

The confidential Ivan opened the door and ushered in Commandant Neil O'Brien, whom he had found at last pacing the garden again.

The Irish officer stood up disordered and defiant on the threshold. "What do you want with me?" he cried.

"Please sit down," said Valentin in pleasant, level tones. "Why, you aren't wearing your sword? Where is it?"

"I left it on the library table," said O'Brien, his brogue deepening in his disturbed mood. "It was a nuisance, it was getting—"

"Ivan," said Valentin, "please go and get the Commandant's sword from the library." Then, as the servant vanished, "Lord Galloway says he saw you leaving the garden just before he found the corpse. What were you doing in the garden?"

The Commandant flung himself recklessly into a chair. "Oh," he cried in pure Irish, "admirin' the moon. Communing with Nature, me boy."

A heavy silence sank and endured, and at the end of it came again the trivial and terrible knocking. Ivan reappeared, carrying an empty steel scabbard, "This is all I can find," he said.

"Put it on the table," said Valentin, without looking up.

There was an inhuman silence in the room, like that sea of inhuman silence round the dock of the condemned murderer. The Duchess's weak exclamations had long ago died away. Lord Galloway's swollen hatred was satisfied and even sobered. The voice that came was quite unexpected.

"I think I can tell you," cried Lady Margaret, in that clear, quivering voice with which a courageous woman speaks publicly. "I can tell you what Mr. O'Brien was doing in the garden, since he is bound to silence. He was asking me to marry him. I refused; I said in my family circumstances I could give him nothing but my respect. He was a little angry at that; he did not seem to think much of my respect. I wonder," she added, with rather a wan smile, "if he will care at all for it now. For I offer it him now. I will swear anywhere that he never did a thing like this."

Lord Galloway had edged up to his daughter and was intimidating her in what he imagined to be an undertone. "Hold your tongue, Maggie," he said in a thunderous whisper. "Why should you shield the fellow? Where's his sword? Where's his confounded cavalry—"

He stopped because of the singular stare with which his daughter was regarding him, a look that was indeed a lurid magnet for the whole group.

"You old fool!" she said in a low voice without pretence of piety. "What do you suppose you are trying to prove? I tell you this man was innocent while with me. But if he wasn't innocent, he was still with me. If he murdered a man in the garden, who was it who must have seen—who must at least have known? Do you hate Neil so much as to put your own daughter—"

Lady Galloway screamed. Everyone else sat tingling at the touch of those satanic tragedies that have been between lovers before now. They saw the proud, white face of the Scotch aristocrat and her lover, the Irish adventurer, like old portraits in a dark house. The long silence was full of formless historical memories of murdered husbands and poisonous paramours.

In the center of this morbid silence an innocent voice said: "Was it a very long cigar?"

The change of thought was so sharp that they had to look round to see who had spoken.

"I mean," said little Father Brown, from the corner of the room, "I mean that cigar Mr. Brayne is finishing. It seems nearly as long as a walking stick."

Despite the irrelevance there was assent as well as irritation in Valentin's face as he lifted his head.

"Quite right," he remarked sharply. "Ivan, go and see about Mr. Brayne again, and bring him here at once."

The instant the factotum had closed the door, Valentin addressed the girl with an entirely new earnestness.

"Lady Margaret," he said, "we all feel, I am sure, both gratitude and admiration for your act in rising above your lower dignity and explaining the Commandant's conduct. But there is a hiatus still. Lord Galloway, I understand, met you passing from the study to the drawing-room, and it was only some minutes afterwards that he found the garden and the Commandant still walking there."

"You have to remember," replied Margaret, with a faint irony in her voice, "that I had just refused him, so we should scarcely have come back arm in arm. He is a gentleman, anyhow; and he loitered behind—and so got charged with murder."

"In those few moments," said Valentin gravely, "he might really—"

The knock came again, and Ivan put in his scarred face.

"Beg pardon, sir," he said, "but Mr. Brayne has left the house."

"Left!" cried Valentin, and rose for the first time to his feet.

"Gone. Scooted. Evaporated," replied Ivan, in humorous French. "His hat and coat are gone, too, and I'll tell you something to cap it all. I ran outside the house to find any traces of him, and I found one, a big trace, too."

"What do you mean?" asked Valentin.

"I'll show you," said his servant, and reappeared with a flashing naked cavalry saber, streaked with blood about the point and edge. Everyone in the room eyed it as if it were a thunderbolt; but the experienced Ivan went on quite quietly:

"I found this," he said, "flung among the bushes fifty yards up the road to Paris. In other words, I found it just where your respectable Mr. Brayne threw it when he ran away."

There was again a silence, but of a new sort. Valentin took the saber, examined it, reflected with unaffected concentration of thought, and then turned a respectful face to O'Brien. "Commandant," he said, "we trust you will always produce this weapon if it is wanted for police examination. Meanwhile," he added, slapping the steel back in the ringing scabbard, "let me return you your sword."

At the military symbolism of the action the audience could hardly refrain from applause.

For Neil O'Brien, indeed, that gesture was the turning point of existence. By the time he was wandering in the mysterious garden again in the colors of the morning the tragic futility of his ordinary mien had fallen from him; he was a man with many reasons for happiness. Lord Galloway was a gentleman, and had offered him an apology. Lady Margaret was something better than a lady, a woman at least, and had perhaps given him something better than an apology, as they drifted among the old flower beds before breakfast. The whole company was more light-hearted and humane, for though the riddle of the death remained, the load of suspicion was lifted off them all, and sent flying off to Paris with the strange millionaire—a man they hardly knew. The devil was cast out of the house—he had cast himself out.

Still, the riddle remained; and when O'Brien threw himself on a garden seat beside Dr. Simon, that keenly scientific person at once resumed it. He did not get much talk out of O'Brien, whose thoughts were on pleasanter things.

"I can't say it interests me much," said the Irishman frankly, "especially as it seems pretty plain now. Apparently Brayne hated this stranger for some reason; lured him into the garden, and killed him with my sword. Then he fled to the city, tossing the sword away as he went. By the way, Ivan tells me the dead man had a Yankee dollar in his pocket. So he was a countryman of Brayne's, and that seems to clinch it. I don't see any difficulties about the business."

"There are five colossal difficulties," said the doctor quietly; "like high walls within walls. Don't mistake me. I don't doubt that Brayne did it: his flight, I fancy, proves that. But as to how he did it. First difficulty: Why should a man kill another man with a great hulking saber, when he can almost kill him with a pocket knife and put it back in his pocket? Second difficulty: Why was there no noise or outcry? Does a man commonly see another come up waving a scimitar and offer no remarks? Third difficulty: A servant watched the front door all the evening; and a rat cannot get into Valentin's garden anywhere. How did the dead man get into the garden? Fourth difficulty: Given the same conditions, how did Brayne get out of the garden?"

"And the fifth?" said Neil, with eyes fixed on the English priest who was coming slowly up the path.

"Is a trifle, I suppose," said the doctor, "but I think an odd one. When I first saw how the head had been slashed, I supposed the assassin had struck more than once. But on examination I found many cuts across the truncated section; in other words, they were struck *after* the head was off. Did Brayne hate his foe so fiendishly that he stood sabring his body in the moonlight?"

"Horrible!" said O'Brien, and shuddered.

The little priest, Brown, had arrived while they were talking, and had waited, with characteristic shyness, till they had finished. Then he said awkwardly:

"I say, I'm sorry to interrupt. But I was sent to tell you the news!"

"News?" repeated Simon, and stared at him rather painfully through his glasses.

"Yes, I'm sorry," said Father Brown mildly. "There's been another murder, you know."

Both men on the seat sprang up, leaving it rocking.

"And, what's stranger still," continued the priest, with his dull eye on the rhododendrons, "it's the same disgusting sort; it's another beheading. They found the second head actually bleeding into the river, a few yards along Brayne's road to Paris; so they suppose that he—"

"Great Heaven!" cried O'Brien. "Is Brayne a monomaniac?"

"There are American vendettas," said the priest impassively. Then he added: "They want you to come to the library and see it."

Commandant O'Brien followed the others towards the inquest, feeling decidedly sick. As a soldier, he loathed all this secretive carnage; where were these extravagant amputations going to stop? First one head was hacked off, and then another; in this case (he told himself bitterly) it was not true that two heads were better than one. As he crossed the study he almost staggered at a shocking coincidence. Upon Valentin's table lay the colored picture of yet a third bleeding head; and it was the head of Valentin himself. A second glance showed him it was only a Nationalist paper, called *The Guillotine,* which every week showed one of its political opponents with rolling eyes and writhing features just after execution; for Valentin was an anti-clerical of some note. But O'Brien was an Irishman, with a kind of chastity even in his sins; and his gorge rose against that great brutality of the intellect which belongs only to France. He felt Paris as a whole, from the grotesques on the Gothic churches to the gross caricatures in the newspapers. He remembered the gigantic jests of the Revolution. He saw the whole city as one ugly energy, from the sanguinary sketch lying on Valentin's table up to where, above a mountain and forest of gargoyles, the great devil grins on Notre Dame.

The library was long, low, and dark; what light entered it shot from under low blinds and had still some of the ruddy tinge of morning. Valentin and his servant Ivan were waiting for them at the upper end of a long, slightly sloping desk, on which lay the mortal remains, looking enormous in the twilight. The big black figure and yellow face of the man found in the garden confronted them essentially unchanged. The second head, which had been fished from among the river reeds that morning, lay streaming and dripping beside it; Valentin's men were still seeking to recover the rest of this second corpse, which was supposed to be afloat. Father Brown, who did not seem to share O'Brien's sensibilities in the least, went up to the second head and examined it with his blinking care. It was little more than a mop of wet white hair, fringed with silver fire in the red and level morning light; the face, which seemed of an ugly, empurpled and perhaps criminal type, had been much battered against trees or stones as it tossed in the water.

"Good morning, Commandant O'Brien," said Valentin, with quiet cordiality. "You have heard of Brayne's last experiment in butchery, I suppose."

Father Brown was still bending over the head with white hair, and he said, without looking up:

"I suppose it is quite certain that Brayne cut off this head, too."

"Well, it seems common sense," said Valentin, with his hands in his pockets. "Killed in the same way as the other. Found within a few yards of the other. And sliced by the same weapon which we know he carried away."

"Yes, yes; I know," replied Father Brown submissively. "Yet, you know, I doubt whether Brayne could have cut off this head."

"Why not?" inquired Dr. Simon, with a rational stare.

"Well, Doctor," said the priest, looking up blinking, "can a man cut off his own head? I don't know."

O'Brien felt an insane universe crashing about his ears; but the doctor sprang forward with impetuous practicality and pushed back the wet white hair.

"Oh, there's no doubt it's Brayne," said the priest quietly. "He had exactly that chip in the left ear."

The detective, who had been regarding the priest with steady and glittering eyes, opened his clenched mouth and said sharply: "You seem to know a lot about him, Father Brown."

"I do," said the little man simply. "I've been about with him for some weeks. He was thinking of joining our church."

The star of the fanatic sprang into Valentin's eyes; he strode towards the priest with clenched hands. "And perhaps," he cried, with a blasting sneer, "perhaps he was also thinking of leaving all his money to your church."

"Perhaps he was," said Brown stolidly; "it is possible."

"In that case," cried Valentin, with a dreadful smile, "you may indeed know a great deal about him. About his life and about his—"

Commandant O'Brien laid a hand on Valentin's arm. "Drop that slanderous rubbish, Valentin," he said, "or there may be more swords yet."

But Valentin (under the steady, humble gaze of the priest) had already recovered himself. "Well," he said shortly, "people's private opinions can wait. You gentlemen are still bound by your promise to stay; you must enforce it on yourselves—and on each other. Ivan here will tell you anything more you want to know; I must get to business and write to the authorities. We can't keep this quiet any longer. I shall be writing in my study if there is any more news."

"Is there any more news, Ivan?" asked Dr. Simon, as the chief of police strode out of the room.

"Only one more thing, I think, sir," said Ivan, wrinkling up his gray old face, "but that's important, too, in its way. There's that old buffer you found on the lawn," and he pointed without pretence of reverence at the big black body with the yellow head. "We've found out who he is, anyhow."

"Indeed!" cried the astonished doctor. "And who is he?"

"His name was Arnold Becker," said the under-detective, "though he went by many aliases. He was a wandering sort of scamp, and is known to have been in America; so that was where Brayne got his knife into him. We didn't have much to do with him ourselves, for he worked mostly in Germany. We've communicated, of course, with the German police. But, oddly enough, there was a twin brother of his, named Louise Becker, whom we had a great deal to do with. In fact, we found it necessary to guillotine him only yesterday. Well, it's a rum thing, gentlemen, but when I saw that fellow flat on the lawn I had the greatest jump of my life. If I hadn't seen Louis Becker guillotined with my own eyes, I'd have sworn it was Louis Becker lying there in the grass. Then, of course, I remembered his twin brother in Germany, and following up the clue—"

The explanatory Ivan stopped, for the excellent reason that nobody was listening to him. The Commandant and the doctor were both staring at Father Brown, who had sprung stiffly to his feet, and was holding his temples tight like a man in sudden and violent pain.

"Stop, stop, stop!" he cried; "Stop talking a minute, for I see half. Will God give me strength? Will my brain make the one jump and see all? Heaven help me! I used to be fairly good at thinking. I could paraphrase any page in Aquinas once. Will my head split—or will it see? I see half—I only see half."

He buried his head in his hands, and stood in a sort of rigid torture of thought or prayer, while the other three could only go on staring at this last prodigy of their wild twelve hours.

When Father Brown's hands fell they showed a face quite fresh and serious, like a child's. He heaved a huge sigh, and said: "Let us get this said and done with as quickly as possible. Look here, this will be the quickest way to convince you all of the truth." He turned to the doctor. "Dr. Simon," he said, "you have a strong headpiece, and I heard you this morning asking the five hardest questions about this business. Well, if you will ask them again, I will answer them."

Simon's pince-nez dropped from his nose in his doubt and wonder, but he answered at once. "Well, the first question, you know, is why a man should kill another with a clumsy saber at all when a man can kill with a bodkin?"

"A man cannot behead with a bodkin," said Brown calmly, "and for this murder beheading was absolutely necessary."

"Why?" asked O'Brien, with interest.

"And the next question?" asked Father Brown.

"Well, why didn't the man cry out or anything?" asked the doctor. "Sabers in gardens are certainly unusual."

"Twigs," said the priest gloomily, and turned to the window which looked on the scene of death. "No one saw the point of the twigs. Why should they lie on that lawn (look at it) so far from any tree? They were not snapped off; they were chopped off. The murderer occupied his enemy with some tricks with the saber, showing how he could cut a branch in mid-air, or whatnot. Then, while his enemy bent down to see the result, a silent slash, and the head fell."

"Well," said the doctor slowly, "that seems plausible enough. But my next two questions will stump anyone."

The priest still stood looking critically out of the window and waited.

"You know how all the garden was sealed up like an air-tight chamber," went on the doctor. "Well, how did the strange man get into the garden?"

Without turning round, the little priest answered: "There never was any strange man in the garden."

There was a silence, and then a sudden cackle of almost childish laughter relieved the strain. The absurdity of Brown's remark moved Ivan to open taunts.

"Oh!" he cried. "Then we didn't lug a great fat corpse on to a sofa last night? He hadn't got into the garden, I suppose?"

"Got into the garden?" repeated Brown reflectively. "No, not entirely."

"Hang it all," cried Simon, "a man gets into a garden, or he doesn't."

"Not necessarily," said the priest with a faint smile. "What is the next question, Doctor?"

"I fancy you're ill," exclaimed Dr. Simon sharply, "but I'll ask the next question if you like. How did Brayne get out of the garden?"

"He didn't get out of the garden," said the priest, still looking out of the window.

"Didn't get out of the garden?" exploded Simon.

"Not completely," said Father Brown.

Simon shook his fists in a frenzy of French logic. "A man gets out of a garden, or he doesn't," he cried.

"Not always," said Father Brown.

Dr. Simon sprang to his feet impatiently. "I have no time to spare on such senseless talk," he cried angrily. "If you can't understand a man being on one side of a wall or the other, I won't trouble you further."

"Doctor," said the cleric very gently, "we have always got on very pleasantly together. If only for the sake of old friendship, stop and tell me your fifth question."

The impatient Simon sank into a chair by the door and said briefly: "The head and shoulders were cut about in a queer way. It seemed to be done after death."

"Yes," said the motionless priest, "it was done so as to make you assume exactly the one simple falsehood that you did assume. It was done to make you take for granted that the head belonged to the body."

The borderland of the brain, where all monsters are made, moved horribly in the Gaelic O'Brien. He felt the chaotic presence of all the horse-men and fish-women that man's unnatural fancy has begotten. A voice older than his first fathers seemed saying in his ear: "Keep out of the monstrous garden where grows the tree with double fruit. Avoid the evil garden where died the man with two heads." Yet, while these shameful symbolic shapes passed across the ancient mirror of his Irish soul, his Frenchified intellect was quite alert, and was watching the odd priest as closely and incredulously as all the rest.

Father Brown had turned round at last, and stood against the window with his face in dense shadow; but even in that shadow they could see it was pale as ashes. Nevertheless, he spoke quite sensibly, as if there were no Gaelic souls on earth.

"Gentlemen," he said, "you did not find the strange body of Becker in the garden. You did not find any strange body in the garden. In face of Dr. Simon's rationalism, I still affirm that Becker was only partly present. Look here!" (pointing to the black bulk of the mysterious corpse) "You never saw that man in your lives. Did you ever see this man?"

He rapidly rolled away the bald, yellow head of the unknown and put in its place the white-maned head beside it. And there, complete, unified, unmistakable, lay Julius K. Brayne.

"The murderer," went on Brown quietly, "hacked off his enemy's head and flung the sword far over the wall. But he was too clever to fling the sword only. He flung the head over the wall also. Then he had only to clap on another head to the corpse, and (as he insisted on a private inquest) you all imagined a totally new man."

"Clap on another head!" said O'Brien staring. "What other head? Heads don't grow on garden bushes, do they?"

"No," said Father Brown huskily. And looking at his boots; "there is only one place where they grow. They grow in the basket of the guillotine, beside which the chief of police, Aristide Valentin, was standing not an hour before the murder. Oh, my friends, hear me a minute more before you tear me in pieces. Valentin is an honest man, if being mad for an arguable cause is honesty. But did you never see in that cold, gray eye of his that he is mad? He would do anything, anything, to break what he calls the superstition of the Cross. He has fought for it and starved for it, and now he has murdered for it. Brayne's crazy millions had hitherto been scattered among so many sects that they did little to alter the balance of things. But Valentin heard a whisper that Brayne, like so many scatter-brained skeptics, was drifting to us; and that was quite a different thing. Brayne would pour supplies into the impoverished and pugnacious Church of France; he would support six Nationalist newspapers like *The Guillotine.* The battle was already balanced on a point, and the fanatic took flame at the risk. He resolved to destroy the millionaire, and he did it as one would expect the greatest of detectives to commit his only crime. He abstracted the severed head of Becker on some criminological excuse, and took it home in his official box. He had that last argument with Brayne, that Lord Galloway did not hear the end of; that failing, he let him out into the sealed garden, talked about swordsmanship, used twigs and a saber for illustration, and—"

Ivan the Scar sprang up. "You lunatic," he yelled. "You'll go to my master now, if I take you by—" "Why, I was going there," said Brown heavily. "I must ask him to confess, and all that."

Driving the unhappy Brown before them like a hostage or sacrifice, they rushed together into the sudden stillness of Valentin's study.

The great detective sat at his desk apparently too occupied to hear their turbulent entrance. They paused a moment, and then something in the look of that upright and elegant back made the doctor run forward suddenly. A touch and a glance showed him that there was a small box of pills at Valentin's elbow, and that Valentin was dead in his chair; and on the blind face of the suicide was more than the pride of Cato.

The Case of the Widow

Margery Allingham

Rivaling Agatha Christie in the British detective genre, Margery Allingham's heroic character Albert Campion is regarded as one of the more interesting of British detectives. An English gentleman and scion of a noble house, Campion is described as well-educated, adventurous yet inconspicuous and, along with the rough-and-tumble manservant Lugg, helps Scotland Yard with their trickiest of cases. Allingham's deft portrayal of characters and situations, and the humor and charm with which they are told, have provided Campion with a devout and ever growing readership since 1920. Campion was played by British actor Peter Davison in two series of BBC adaptations of Allingham's stories, shown in the United States by PBS in the 1980s. Lugg was played by Brian Glover, and Inspector Oates by Andrew Burt.

The second prettiest girl in Mayfair was thanking Superintendent Stanislaus Oates for the recovery of her diamond bracelet and the ring with the square-cut emerald in it, and Mr. Campion, who had accompanied her to the ceremony, was admiring her technique.

She was doing it very charmingly; so charmingly, in fact, that the superintendent's depressing little office had taken on an air of garden-party gaiety which it certainly did not possess in the ordinary way, while the superintendent himself had undergone an even more sensational change.

His long dyspeptic face was transformed by a blush of smug satisfaction and he quite forgot the short lecture he had prepared for his visitor on The Carelessness Which Tempts the Criminal, or its blunter version, Stupidity Which Earns Its Own Reward.

It was altogether a most gratifying scene, and Mr. Campion, seated in the visitor's chair, his long thin legs crossed and his pale eyes amused behind his horn-rimmed spectacles, enjoyed it to the full.

Miss Leonie Peterhouse-Vaughn raised her remarkable eyes to the superintendent's slightly sheepish face and spoke with deep earnestness.

"I honestly think you're wonderful," she said.

Realising that too much butter can have a disastrous effect on any dish, and not being at all certain of his old friend's digestive capabilities, Mr. Campion coughed.

"He has his failures too," he ventured. "He's not omnipotent, you know. Just an ordinary man."

"Really?" said Miss Peterhouse-Vaughn with gratifying surprise.

"Oh yes; well, we're only human, miss." The superintendent granted Mr. Campion a reproachful look. "Sometimes we have our little disappointments. Of course on those occasions we call in Mr. Campion here," he added with a flash of malice.

Leonie laughed prettily and Mr. Oate's ruffled fur subsided like a wave.

"Sometimes even he can't help us," he went on, encouraged, and, inspired, no doubt, by the theory that the greater the enemy, the greater the honor, launched into an explanation perhaps not altogether discreet. "Sometimes we come up against a man who slips through our fingers every time. There's a man in London today who's been responsible for more trouble than I can mention. We know him, we know where he lives, we could put our hands on him any moment of the day or night, but have we any proof against him? Could we hold him for ten minutes without getting into serious trouble for molesting a respectable citizen? Could we? Well, we couldn't."

Miss Peterhouse-Vaughn's expression of mystified interest was very flattering.

"This is incredibly exciting," she said. "Who is he? Or mustn't you tell?"

The superintendent shook his head.

"Entirely against regulations," he said regretfully, and then, on seeing her disappointment and feeling, no doubt, that his portentous declaration had fallen a little flat, he relented and made a compromise between his conscience and a latent vanity which Mr. Campion had never before suspected. "Well, I'll show you this," he conceded. "It's a very curious thing."

With Leonie's fascinated eyes upon him, he opened a drawer in his desk and took out a single sheet torn from a week-old London evening paper. A small advertisement in the Situations Vacant column was ringed with blue pencil. Miss Peterhouse-Vaughn took it eagerly and Mr. Campion got up lazily to read it over her shoulder.

Wanted: Entertainer suitable for children's party. Good money offered to right man. Apply in person any evening. Widow, 13 Blakenham Gardens, W.1.

Leonie read the lines three times and looked up.

"But it seems quite ordinary," she said.

The superintendent nodded. "That's what any member of the public would think," he agreed, gracefully keeping all hint of condescension out of his tone. "And it would have escaped our notice too except for one thing, and that's the name and address. You see, the man I was telling you about happens to live at 13 Blakenham Gardens."

"Is his name Widow? How queer!"

"No, miss, it's not." Oates looked uncomfortable, seeing the pitfall too late. "I ought not to be telling you this," he went on severely. "This gentleman—and we've nothing we can pin on him, remember—is known as 'The Widow' to the criminal classes. That's why this paragraph interested us. As it stands it's an ad for a crook, and the fellow has the impudence to use his own address! Doesn't even hide it under a box number."

Mr. Campion eyed his old friend. He seemed mildly interested.

"Did you send someone along to answer it?" he enquired.

"We did." The superintendent spoke heavily. "Poor young Billings was kept there singing comic songs for three quarters of an hour while W—I mean this fellow—watched him without a smile. Then he told him he'd go down better at a police concert."

Miss Peterhouse-Vaughn looked sympathetic.

"What a shame!" she said gravely, and Mr. Campion never admired her more.

"We sent another man," continued the superintendent, "but when he got there the servant told him the vacancy had been filled. We kept an eye on the place, too, but it wasn't easy. The whole crescent was a seething mass of would-be child entertainers."

"So you haven't an idea what he's up to?" Mr. Campion seemed amused.

"Not the faintest," Oates admitted. "We shall in the end, though; I'll lay my bottom dollar. He was the moving spirit in that cussed Featherstone case, you know, and we're pretty certain it was he who slipped through the police net in the Barking business."

Mr. Campion raised his eyebrows. "Blackmail and smuggling?" he said. "He seems to be a versatile soul, doesn't he?"

"He's up to anything," Oates declared. "Absolutely anything. I'd give a packet to get my hands on him. But what he wants with a kid's entertainer—if it is an entertainer he's after—I do not know."

"Perhaps he just wants to give a children's party?" suggested Miss Peterhouse-Vaughn and while the policeman was considering this possibility, evidently the one explanation which had not crossed his mind, she took her leave.

"I must thank you once again, Mr. Oates," she said. "I can't tell you how terribly, terribly clever I think you are, and how awfully grateful I am, and how frightfully careful I'll be in future not to give you any more dreadful trouble."

It was a charming little speech in spite of her catastrophic adjectives and the superintendent beamed.

"It's been a pleasure, miss," he said.

As Mr. Campion handed her into her mother's Daimler he regarded her coldly.

"A pretty performance," he remarked. "Tell me, what do you say when a spark of genuine gratitude warms your nasty little heart? My poor Oates!"

Miss Peterhouse-Vaughn grinned.

"I did do it rather well, didn't I" she said complacently. "He's rather a dear old goat."

Mr. Campion was shocked and said so.

"The superintendent is a distinguished officer. I always knew that, of course, but this afternoon I discovered a broad streak of chivalry in him. In his place I think I might have permitted myself a few comments on the type of young woman who leaves a diamond bracelet and an emerald ring in the soap dish at a public restaurant and then goes smiling to Scotland Yard to ask for it back. The wretched man had performed a miracle for you and you call him a dear old goat."

Leonie was young enough to look abashed without losing her charm.

"Oh, but I am grateful," she said. "I think he's wonderful. But not so absolutely brilliant as somebody else."

"That's very nice of you, my child," Mr. Campion prepared to unbend.

"Oh, not you darling." Leonie squeezed his arm. "I was talking about the other man—The Widow. He's got real nerve, don't you think? Using his own address and making the detective sing and all that . . . so amusing!"

Her companion looked down on her severely.

"Don't make a hero out of him," he said.

"Why not?"

"Because, my dear little hideous, he's a crook. It's only while he remains uncaught that he's faintly interesting. Sooner or later your elderly admirer, the superintendent, is going to clap him under lock and key and then he'll just be an ordinary convict, who is anything but romantic, believe me."

Miss Peterhouse-Vaughn shook her head.

"He won't get caught," she said. "Or if he does—forgive me, darling—it'll be by someone much cleverer than you or Mr. Oates."

Mr. Campion's professional pride rebelled.

"What'll you bet?"

"Anything you like," said Leonie. "Up to two pounds," she added prudently.

Campion laughed. "The girl's learning caution at last!" he said. "I may hold you to that."

The conversation changed to the charity matinee of the day before, wherein Miss Peterhouse-Vaughn had appeared as Wisdom, and continued its easy course, gravitating naturally to the most important pending event in the Peterhouse-Vaughn family, the christening of Master Brian Desmond Peterhouse-Vaughn, nephew to Leonie, son to her elder brother, Desmond Brian, and godson to Mr. Albert Campion.

It was his new responsibility as a godfather which led Mr. Campion to take part in yet another elegant little ceremony some few days after the christening and nearly three weeks after Leonie's sensational conquest of Superintendent Oate's susceptible heart.

Mr. Campion called to see Mr. Thistledown in Cheese Street, E. C., and they went reverently to the cellars together.

Mr. Thistledown was a small man, elderly and dignified. His white hair was inclined to flow a little and his figure was more suited, perhaps, to his vocation than to his name. As head of the small but distinguished firm of Thistledown, Friend and Son, Wine Importers since 1798, he very seldom permitted himself a personal interview with any client under the age of sixty-five, for at that year he openly believed the genus homo sapiens, considered solely as a connoisseur of vintage wine, alone attained full maturity.

Mr. Campion, however, was an exception. Mr. Thistledown thought of him as a lad still, but a promising one. He took his client's errand with all the gravity he felt it to deserve.

"Twelve dozen of port to be laid down for Master Brian Desmond Peterhouse-Vaughn," he said, rolling the words round his tongue as though, they, too, had their flavor. "Let me see, it is now the end of '36. It will have to be a '27 wine. Then by the time your godson is forty—he won't want to drink it before that age, surely—there should be a very fine fifty-year-old vintage awaiting him."

A long and somewhat heated discussion, or, rather, monologue, for Mr. Campion was sufficiently experienced to offer no opinion, followed. The relative merits of Croft, Taylor, Da Silva, Noval and Fonseca were considered at length, and in the end Mr. Campion followed his mentor through the sacred tunnels and personally affixed his seal upon a bin of Taylor, 1927.

Mr. Thistledown was in favor of a stipulation to provide that Master Peterhouse-Vaughn should not attain full control over his vinous inheritance until he attained the age of thirty, whereas Mr. Campion preferred the more conventional twenty-one. Finally a compromise of twenty-five was agreed upon and the two gentlemen retired to Mr. Thistledown's consulting room glowing with the conscious virtue of men who had conferred a benefit upon posterity.

The consulting room was comfortable. It was really no more than the arbor of bottles constructed in the vault of the largest cellar and was furnished with a table and chairs of solid ship's timbers. Mr. Thistledown paused by the table and hesitated before speaking. There was clearly something on his mind and Campion, who had always considered him slightly inhuman, a sort of living port crust, was interested.

When at last the old gentleman unburdened himself it was to make a short speech.

"It takes an elderly man to judge a port or a claret," he said, "but spirits are definitely in another category. Some men may live to be a hundred without ever realizing the subtle differences of the finest rums. To judge a spirit one must be born with a certain kind of palate. Mr. Campion, would you taste a brandy for me?"

His visitor was startled. Always a modest soul, he made no pretensions to connoisseurship and now he said so firmly.

"I don't know." Mr. Thistledown regarded him seriously.

"I have watched your taste for some years now and I am inclined to put you down as one of the few really knowledgeable younger men. Wait for me a moment."

He went out, and through the arbor's doorway Campion saw him conferring with the oldest and most cobwebby of the troglodyte persons who lurked about the vaults.

Considerably flattered in spite of himself, he sat back and awaited developments. Presently one of the younger myrmidons, a mere youth of fifty or so, appeared with a tray and a small selection of balloon glasses. He was followed by an elder with two bottles, and at the rear of the procession came Mr. Thistledown himself with something covered by a large silk handkerchief. Not until they were alone did he remove the veil. Then, whipping the handkerchief aside, he produced a partly full half bottle with a new cork and no label. He held it up to the light and Mr. Campion saw that the liquid within was of the true dark amber.

Still with the ritualistic air, Mr. Thistledown polished a glass and poured a tablespoon of the spirit, afterwards handing it to his client.

Feeling like a man with his honor at stake, Campion warmed the glass in his hand, sniffed at it intelligently, and finally allowed a little of the stuff to touch his tongue.

Mr. Thistledown watched him earnestly. Campion tasted again and inhaled once more. Finally he set down his glass and grinned.

"I may be wrong," he said, "but it tastes like the real McKay."

Mr. Thistledown frowned at the vulgarism. He seemed satisfied, however, and there was a curious mixture of pleasure and discomfort on his face.

"I put it down as a Champagne Fine, 1835," he said. "It has not, perhaps, quite the superb caress of the true Napoleon—but a brave, yes a brave, brandy! The third best I have ever tasted in my life. And that, let me tell you, Mr. Campion, is a very extraordinary thing."

He paused, looking like some old white cockatoo standing at the end of the table.

"I wonder if I might take you into my confidence?" he ventured at last. "Ah—a great many people do take you into their confidence, I believe? Forgive me for putting it that way."

Campion smiled. "I'm as secret as the grave," he said, "and if there's anything I can do I shall be delighted."

Mr. Thistledown sighed with relief and became almost human.

"This confounded bottle was sent to me some little time ago," he said. "With it was a letter from a man called Gervaise Papulous; I don't suppose you've ever heard of him, but he wrote a very fine monograph on brandies some years ago, which was greatly appreciated by connoisseurs. I had an idea he lived a hermit's life somewhere in Scotland, but that's neither here nor there. The fact remains that when I had this note from an address in Half Moon Street I recognized the name immediately. It was a very civil letter, asking me if I'd mind, as an expert, giving my opinion of the age and quality of the sample."

He paused and smiled faintly.

"I was a little flattered, perhaps," he said. "After all, the man is a well-known authority himself. Anyway, I made the usual tests, tasted it and compared it with the oldest and finest stuff we have in stock. We have a few bottles of 1848 and one or two of the 1835. I made the most careful comparisons and at last I decided that the sample was '35 brandy, but not the same blend as our own. I wrote him; I said I did not care to commit myself, but I gave him my opinion for what it was worth and I appended my reasons for forming it."

Mr. Thistledown's precise voice ceased and his color heightened.

"By return I received a letter thanking me for mine and asking me whether I would care to consider an arrangement whereby I could buy the identical spirit in any quantity I cared to name at a hundred and twenty shillings a dozen, excluding duty—or in other words, ten shillings per bottle."

Mr. Campion sat up. "Ten shillings?" he said.

"Ten shillings," repeated Mr. Thistledown. "The price of a wireless license," he added with contempt. "Well, as you can imagine, Mr. Campion, I thought there must be some mistake. Our own '35 is listed at sixty shillings a bottle and you cannot get a finer value anywhere in London. The stuff is rare. In a year or two it will be priceless. I considered this sample again and reaffirmed my own first opinion. Then I reread the letter and noticed the peculiar phrase—'an arrangement whereby you will be able to purchase.' I thought about it all day and finally I put on my hat and went down to see the man."

He glanced at his visitor almost timidly. Campion was reassuring.

"If it was genuine it was not a chance to be missed," he murmured.

"Exactly." Mr. Thistledown smiled. "Well, I saw him, a younger man than I had imagined but well informed, and I received quite a pleasant impression. I asked him frankly where he got the brandy and he came out with an extraordinary suggestion. He asked me first if I was satisfied with the sample, and I said I was or I should hardly have come to see him. Then he said the whole matter was a secret at the moment, but that he was asking certain well-informed persons to a private conference and something he called a scientific experiment. Finally he offered me an invitation. It is to take place next Monday evening in a little hotel on the Norfolk coast where Mr. Papulous says the ideal conditions for his experiment exist."

Mr. Campion's interest was thoroughly aroused.

"I should go," he said.

Mr. Thistledown spread out his hands.

"I had thought of it," he admitted. "As I came out of the flat at Half Moon Street I passed a man I knew on the stairs. I won't mention his name and I won't say his firm is exactly a rival of ours, but—well, you know how it is. Two or three old firms get the reputation for supplying certain rare vintages. Their names are equally good and naturally there is a certain competition between them. If this fellow has happened on a whole cellar full of this brandy I should like to have as good a chance of buying it as the next man, especially at the price. But in my opinion and in my experience that is too much to hope for, and that is why I have ventured to mention the matter to you."

A light dawned upon his client.

"You want me to attend the conference and make certain everything's above board?"

"I hardly dare to suggest it," he said, "but since you are such an excellent judge, and since your reputation as an investigator—if I may be forgiven the term—is so great, I admit the thought did go through my mind."

Campion picked up his glass and sniffed its fragrance.

"My dear man, I'd jump at it," he said. "Do I pass myself off as a member of the firm?"

Mr. Thistledown looked owlish.

"In the circumstances I think we might connive at that little inexactitude," he murmured. "Don't you?"

"I think we'll have to," said Mr. Campion.

When he saw the "little hotel on the Norfolk coast" at half-past six on the following Monday afternoon the thought came to him that it was extremely fortunate for the proprietor that it should be so suitable for Mr. Papulous's experiment, for it was certainly not designed to be of much interest to any ordinary winter visitor. It was a large country public house, not old enough to be picturesque, standing by itself at the end of a lane some little distance from a cold and sleepy village. In the summer, no doubt, it provided a headquarters for a great many picnic parties, but in winter it was deserted.

Inside it was warm and comfortable enough, however, and Campion found a curious little company seated round the fire in the lounge. His host rose to greet him and he was aware at once of a considerable personality.

He saw a tall man with a shy ingratiating manner, whose clothes were elegant and whose face was remarkable. His deep-set eyes were dark and intelligent and his wide mouth could smile disarmingly, but the feature which was most distinctive was the way in which his iron-gray hair drew into a clean-cut peak in the center of his high forehead, giving him an odd, Mephistophelean appearance.

"Mr. Fellowes?" he said, using the alias Campion and Mr. Thistledown had agreed upon. "I heard from your firm this morning. Of course I'm very sorry not to have Mr. Thistledown here. He says in his note that I am to regard you as his second self. You handle the French side, I understand?"

"Yes. It was only by chance that I was in England yesterday when Mr. Thistledown asked me to come."

"I see." Mr. Papulous seemed contented with the explanation. Campion looked a mild, inoffensive young man, even a little foolish.

He was introduced to the rest of the company round the fire and was interested to see that Mr. Thistledown had been right in his guess. Half a dozen of the best-known smaller and older wine firms were represented, in most cases by their senior partners.

Conversation, however, was not as general as might have been expected among men of such similar interests. On the contrary, there was a distinct atmosphere of restraint, and it occurred to Mr. Campion that they were all close rivals and each man had not expected to see the others.

Mr. Papulous alone seemed happily unconscious of any discomfort. He stood behind his chair at the head of the group and glanced round him with satisfaction.

"It's really very kind of you all to have come," he said in his deep musical voice. "Very kind indeed. I felt we must have experts, the finest experts in the world, to test this thing, because it's revolutionary—absolutely revolutionary."

A large old gentleman with a hint of superciliousness in his manner glanced up.

"When are we going to come to the horses, Mr. Papulous?"

His host turned to him with a deprecatory smile.

"Not until after dinner, I'm afraid, Mr. Jerome. I'm sorry to seem so secretive but the whole nature of the discovery is so extraordinary that I want you to see the demonstration with your own eyes."

Mr. Jerome whose name Campion recognized as belonging to the moving spirit of Bolitho Brothers, of St. Mary Axe, seemed only partly mollified. He laughed.

"Is it the salubrious air of this particular hotel that you need for your experiment, may I ask?" he enquired.

"Oh no, my dear sir. It's the stillness." Mr. Papulous appeared to be completely oblivious to any suggestion of a sneer. "It's the utter quiet. At night, round about ten o'clock, there is a lack of vibration here, so complete that you can almost feel it, if I may use such a contradiction in terms. Now, Mr. Fellowes, dinner's at seven-thirty. Perhaps you'd care to see your room?"

Campion was puzzled. As he changed for the meal, a gesture which seemed to be expected of him, he surveyed the situation with growing curiosity. Papulous was no ordinary customer. He managed to convey himself as open and simple as the day. Whatever he was up to he was certainly a good salesman.

The dinner was simple and well cooked and was served by Papulous's own man. There was no alcohol and the dishes were not highly seasoned, out of deference, their host explained, to the test that was to be put to their palates later on.

When it was over and the mahogany had been cleared of dessert, a glass of clear water was set before each guest and from the head of the table Mr. Papulous addressed his guests. He made a very distinguished figure, leaning forward across the polished wood, the candlelight flickering on his deeply lined face and high heart-shaped forehead.

"First of all let me recapitulate," he said. "You all know my name and you have all been kind enough to say that you have read my little book. I mention this because I want you to realize that by asking you down here to witness a most extraordinary demonstration I am taking my reputation in my hands. Having made that point, let me remind you that you have each of you, with the single exception of Mr. Fellowes, been kind enough to give me your considered views on a sample of brandy which I sent you. In every case, I need hardly mention, opinion was the same—a Champagne Fine of 1835."

A murmur of satisfaction not untinged with relief ran round the table and Mr. Papulous smiled.

"Well," he said, "frankly that would have been my own opinion had I not known—mark you I say 'known'—that the brandy I sent you was a raw cognac of nearly a hundred years later—to be exact, of 1932."

There was a moment of bewilderment, followed by an explosion from Mr. Jerome.

"I hope you're not trying to make fools of us, sir," he said severely. "I'm not going to sit here, and—"

"One moment, one moment." Papulous spoke soothingly. "You really must forgive me. I know you all too well by repute to dare to make such a statement without following it immediately by the explanation to which you are entitled. As you're all aware, the doctoring of brandy is an old game. Such dreadful additions as vanilla and burnt sugar have all been used in their time and will, no doubt, be used again, but such crude deceptions are instantly detected by the cultured palate. This is something different."

Mr. Jerome began to seethe.

"Are you trying to interest us in a fake, sir?" he demanded. "Because, if so, let me tell you I for one am not interested."

There was a chorus of hasty assent in which Mr. Campion virtuously joined.

Gervaise Papulous smiled faintly.

"But of course not," he said. "We are all experts. The true expert knows that no fake can be successful, even should we so far forget ourselves as to countenance its existence. I am bringing you a discovery—not a trick, not a clever fraud, but a genuine discovery which may revolutionize the whole market. As you know, time is the principal factor in the maturing of spirits. Until now time has been the one factor which could not be artificially replaced. An old brandy, therefore, is quite a different thing from a new one."

Mr. Campion blinked. A light was beginning to dawn upon him.

Mr. Papulous continued. There seemed to be no stopping him. At the risk of boring his audience he displayed a great knowledge of technical detail and went through the life history of an old liqueur brandy from the time it was an unripe grape skin on a vine outside Cognac.

When he had finished he paused dramatically, adding softly:

"What I hope to introduce to you tonight, gentlemen, is the latest discovery of science, a method of speeding up this long and wearisome process so that the whole business of maturing the spirit takes place in a few minutes instead of a hundred years. You have all examined the first fruits of this method already and have been interested enough to come down here. Shall we go on?"

The effect of his announcement was naturally considerable. Everybody began to talk at once save Mr. Campion, who sat silent and thoughtful. It occurred to him that his temporary colleagues were not only interested in making a great deal of money but very much alarmed at the prospect of losing a considerable quantity also.

"If it's true it'll upset the whole damned trade," murmured his next-door neighbor, a little thin man with wispy straw-colored hair.

Papulous rose. "In the next room the inventor, Mr. Philippe Jessant, is waiting to demonstrate," he said. "He began work on the idea during the period of prohibition in America and his researches were assisted there by one of the richest men in the world, but when the country was restored to sanity his patron lost interest in the work and he was left to perfect it unassisted. You will find him a simple, uneducated, unbusinesslike man, like many inventors. He came to me for help because he had read my little book and I am doing what I can for him by introducing him to you. Conditions are now ideal. The house is perfectly still. Will you come with me?"

The sceptical but excited little company filed into the large "commercial" room on the other side of the passage. The place had been stripped of furniture save for a half circle of chairs and a large deal table. On the table was a curious contraption, vaguely resembling two or three of those complicated coffee percolators which seemed to be designed solely for the wedding-present trade.

An excitable little man in a long brown overall was standing behind the table. If not an impressive figure, he was certainly an odd one, with his longish hair and gold-rimmed pince-nez.

"Quiet please. I must beg of you quiet," he commanded, holding up his hand as they appeared. "We must have no vibration, no vibration at all, if I am to succeed."

He had a harsh voice and a curious foreign accent, which Campion could not instantly trace, but his manner was authoritative and the experts tiptoed gently to their seats.

"Now," said Mr. Jessant, his small eyes flashing, "I leave all explanations to my friend here. For me, I am only interested in the demonstration. You understand?"

He glared at them and Papulous hastened to explain.

"Mr. Jessant does not mean the human voice, of course," he murmured. "It is vibration, sudden movement, of which he is afraid."

"Quiet," cut in the inventor impatiently. "When a spirit matures in the ordinary way, what does it have? Quiet, darkness, peace. These conditions are essential. Now we will begin, if you please."

It was a simple business. A clear-glass decanter of brandy was produced and duly smelt and sampled by each guest. Papulous himself handed round the glasses and poured the liquid. By unanimous consent it was voted a raw spirit. The years 1932 and 1934 were both mentioned.

Then the same decanter was emptied into the contraption on the table and its progress watched through a system of glass tubes and a filter into a large retort-shaped vessel at the foot of the apparatus.

Mr. Jessant looked up.

"Now," he said softly. "You will come, one at a time, please, and examine my invention. Walk softly."

The inspection was made and the man in the brown overall covered the retort with a hood composed of something that looked like black rubber. For a while he busied himself with thermometers and a little electric battery.

"It's going on now," he explained, suppressed excitement in his voice. "Every second roughly corresponds to a year—a long, dark, dismal year. Now—we shall see."

The hood was removed, fresh glasses brought, and the retort itself carefully detached from the rest of the apparatus.

Mr. Jerome was the first to examine the liquid it contained and his expression was ludicrous in its astonishment.

"It's incredible!" he said at last. "Incredible! I can't believe it. There are certain tests I should like to make, of course, but I could swear this is an 1835 brandy."

The others were of the same opinion and even Mr. Campion was impressed. The inventor was persuaded to do his experiment again. To do him justice he complied willingly.

"It is the only disadvantage," he said. "So little can be treated at one time. I tell my friend I should like to make my invention foolproof and sell the machines and the instructions to the public, but he tells me no."

"No indeed!" ejaculated Mr. Campion's neighbor. "Good heavens! It would knock the bottom out of half my trade."

When at last the gathering broke up in excitement it was after midnight. Mr. Papulous addressed his guests.

"It is late," he said. "Let us go to bed now and consider the whole matter in the morning when Mr. Jessant can explain the theory of his process. Meanwhile, I am sure you will agree with me that we all have something to think about."

A somewhat subdued company trooped off upstairs. There was little conversation. A man does not discuss a revolutionary discovery with his nearest rival.

Campion came down in the morning to find Mr. Jerome already up. He was pacing the lounge and turned on the young man almost angrily.

"I like to get up at six," he said without preamble, "but there were no servants in the place. A woman, her husband and a maid came along at seven. It seems Papulous made them sleep out. Afraid of vibration, I suppose. Well, it's an extraordinary discovery, isn't it? If I hadn't seen it with my own eyes I should never have believed it. I suppose one's got to be prepared for progress, but I can't say I like it. Never did."

He lowered his voice and came closer.

"We shall have to get together and suppress it, you know," he said. "Only thing to do. We can't have any single firm owning the secret. Anyway, that's my opinion."

Campion murmured that he did not care to express his own without first consulting Mr. Thistledown.

"Quite, quite. There'll be a good many conferences in the City this afternoon," said Mr. Jerome gloomily. "And that's another thing. D'you know there isn't a telephone in this confounded pub?"

Campion's eyes narrowed.

"Is that so?" he said softly. "That's very interesting."

Mr. Jerome shot him a suspicious glance.

"In my opinion . . ." he began heavily but got no further. The door was thrust open and the small wispy-haired man, who had been Campion's neighbor at dinner, came bursting into the room.

"I say," he said, "a frightful thing! The little inventor chap has been attacked in the night. His machine is smashed and the plans and formula are stolen. Poor old Papulous is nearly off his head."

Both Campion and Jerome started for the doorway and a moment later joined the startled group on the landing. Gervaise Papulous, an impressive figure in a long black dressing gown, was standing with his back to the inventor's door.

"This is terrible, terrible!" he was saying. "I beseech you all, go downstairs and wait until I see what is best to be done. My poor friend has only just regained consciousness."

Jerome pushed his way through the group.

"But this is outrageous," he began.

Papulous towered over him, his eyes dark and angry.

"It is just as you say, outrageous," he said, and Mr. Jerome quailed before the suppressed fury in his voice.

"Look here," he began, "you surely don't think . . . you're not insinuating . . ."

"I am only thinking of my poor friend," said Mr. Papulous.

Campion went quietly downstairs.

"What on earth does this mean?" demanded the small wispy-haired gentleman who had remained in the lounge.

Campion grinned. "I rather fancy we shall all find that out pretty clearly in about an hour," he said.

He was right. Mr. Gervaise Papulous put the whole matter to them in the bluntest possible way as they sat dejectedly looking at the remains of what had proved a very unsatisfactory breakfast.

Mr. Jessant, his head in bandages and his face pale with exhaustion, had told a heartbreaking story. He had awakened to find a pad of chloroform across his mouth and nose. It was dark and he could not see his assailant, who also struck him repeatedly. His efforts to give the alarm were futile and in the end the anaesthetic had overpowered him.

When at last he had come to himself his apparatus had been smashed and his precious black pocketbook, which held his own calculations and which he always kept under his pillow, had gone.

At this point he had broken down completely and had been led away by Papulous's man. Mr. Gervaise Papulous then took the floor. He looked pale and nervous and there was an underlying suggestion of righteous anger and indignation in his manner which was very impressive.

"I won't waste time by telling you how appalled I am by this monstrous attack," he began, his fine voice trembling. "I can only tell you the facts. We were alone in this house last night. Even my own man slept out in the village. I arranged this to ensure ideal conditions for the experiment. The landlady reports that the doors were locked this morning and the house had not been entered from the outside. Now you see what this means? Until last night only the inventor and I knew of the existence of a secret which is of such great importance to all of you here. Last night we told you, we took you into our confidence, and now . . ." He shrugged his shoulders. "Well, we have been robbed and my friend assaulted. Need I say more?"

An excited babble of protest arose and Mr. Jerome seemed in danger of apoplexy. Papulous remained calm and a little contemptuous.

"There is only one thing to do," he said, "but I hesitated before calling in the police, because, of course, only one of you can be guilty and the secret must still be in the house, whereas I know the publicity which cannot be avoided will be detrimental to you all. And not only to yourselves personally, but to the firms you represent."

He paused and frowned.

"The Press is so ignorant," he said. "I am so afraid you may all be represented as having come here to see some sort of faking process—new brandy into old. It doesn't sound convincing, does it?"

His announcement burst like a bomb in the quiet room. Mr. Jerome sat very still, his mouth partly open. Somebody began to speak but thought better of it. A long unhappy silence supervened.

Gervaise Papulous cleared his throat.

"I am sorry," he said. "I must either have my friend's notebook back and full compensation, or I must send for the police. What else can I do?"

Mr. Jerome pulled himself together.

"Wait," he said in a smothered voice. "Before you do anything rash we must have a conference. I've been thinking over this discovery of yours, Mr. Papulous, and in my opinion it raises very serious considerations for the whole trade."

There was a murmur of agreement in the room and he went on.

"The one thing none of us can afford is publicity. In the first place, even if the thing becomes generally known it certainly won't become generally believed. The public doesn't rely on its palate; it replies on our labels, and that puts us in a very awkward position. This final development precipitates everything. We must clear up this mystery in private and then decide what is best to be done."

There was a vigorous chorus of assent, but Mr. Papulous shook his head.

"I'm afraid I can't agree," he said coldly. "In the ordinary way Mr. Jessant and I would have been glad to meet you in any way, but this outrage alters everything. I insist on a public examination unless, of course," he added deliberately, "unless you care to take the whole matter out of our hands."

"What do you mean?" Mr. Jerome's voice was faint.

The tall man with the deeply lined face regarded him steadily.

"Unless you care to club together and buy us out," said Mr. Papulous. "Then you can settle the matter as you like. The sum Mr. Jessant had in mind was fifteen thousand pounds, a very reasonable sum for such a secret."

There was silence after he had spoken.

"Blackmail," said Mr. Campion under his breath and at the same moment his glance lighted on Mr. Papulous's most outstanding feature. His eyebrows rose and an expression of incredulity, followed by amazement, passed over his face. Then he kicked himself gently under the breakfast table. He rose.

"I must send a wire to my principal," he said. "You'll understand I'm in an impossible position and must get in touch with Mr. Thistledown at once."

Papulous regarded him.

"If you write your message my man will dispatch it from the village," he said politely and there was no mistaking the implied threat.

Campion understood he was not to be allowed to make any private communication with the outside world. He looked blank.

"Thank you," he said and took out a pencil and a loose-leaf notebook.

"Unexpected development," he wrote. "Come down immediately. Inform Charlie and George cannot lunch Tuesday. A. C. Fellowes."

Papulous took the message, read it and went out with it, leaving a horrified group behind him.

Mr. Thistledown received Mr. Campion's wire at eleven o'clock and read it carefully. The signature particularly interested him. Shutting himself in his private room, he rang up Scotland Yard and was fortunate in discovering Superintendent Oates at his desk. He dictated the wire carefully and added with a depreciatory cough:

"Mr. Campion told me to send on to you any message from him signed with his own initials. I don't know if you can make much of this. It seems very ordinary to me."

"Leave all that to us, sir." Oates sounded cheerful. "Where is he, by the way?"

Mr. Thistledown gave the address and hung up the receiver. At the other end of the wire the superintendent unlocked a drawer in his desk and took out a small red manuscript book. Each page was ruled with double columns and filled with Mr. Campion's own elegant handwriting. Oates ran a forefinger down the left-hand column on the third page.

"Carrie . . . Catherine . . . Charlie . . ."

His eye ran across the page.

"Someone you want," he read and looked on down the list.

The legend against the word "George" was brief. "Two" it said simply.

Oates turned to the back of the book. There were several messages under the useful word "lunch." "Come to lunch" meant "Send two men." "Lunch with me" was translated "Send men armed," and "Cannot lunch" was "Come yourself."

"Tuesday" was on another page. The superintendent did not trouble to look it up. He knew its meaning. It was "hurry."

He wrote the whole message out on a pad.

"Unexpected developments. Come down immediately. Someone you want (two). Come yourself. Hurry. Campion."

He sighed. "Energetic chap," he commented and pressed a bell for Sergeant Bloom.

As it happened, it was Mr. Gervaise Papulous himself who caught the first glimpse of the police car which pulled up outside the lonely little hotel. He was standing by the window in an upper room whose floor was so flimsily constructed that he could listen with ease to the discussion taking place in the lounge below. There the unfortunate experts were still arguing. The only point on which they all agreed was the absolute necessity of avoiding a scandal.

As the car stopped and the superintendent sprang out and made for the door Papulous caught a glimpse of his official-looking figure. He swung round savagely to the forlorn little figure who sat hunched up on the bed.

"You peached, damn you!" he whispered.

"Me?" The man who had been calling himself "Jessant" sat up in indignation. "Me Peach?" he repeated, his foreign accent fading into honest South London. "Don't be silly. And you pay up, my lad. I'm fed up with this. First I do me stuff, then you chloroform me, then you bandage me, then you keep me shut up 'ere, and now you accuse me of splitting. What you playing at?"

"You're lying, you little rat." Papulous's voice was dangerously soft and he strode swiftly across the room towards the man on the bed, who shrank back in sudden alarm.

"Here—that'll do, that'll do. What's going on here?"

It was Oates who spoke. Followed by Campion and the sergeant he strode across the room.

"Let the fellow go," he commanded. "Good heavens, man, you're choking him."

Doubling his fist, he brought it up under the other man's wrists with a blow which not only loosed their hold but sent their owner staggering back across the room.

The man on the bed let out a howl and stumbled towards the door into the waiting arms of Sergeant Bloom, but Oates did not notice him. His eyes were fixed upon the face of the tall man on the other side of the room.

"The Widow!" he ejaculated. "Well I'll be damned!"

The other smiled.

"More than probably, my dear Inspector. Or have they promoted you?" he said, "But at the moment I'm afraid you're trespassing."

The superintendent glanced enquiringly at the mild and elegant figure at his side.

"False pretences is the charge," murmured Mr. Campion affably. "There are certain rather unpleasant traces of blackmail in the matter, but false pretences will do. There are six witnesses and myself."

The man whose alias was The Widow stared at his accuser.

"Who are you?" he demanded, and then, as the answer dawned upon him, he swore softly. "Campion," he said. "Albert Campion . . . I ought to have recognized you from your description."

Campion grinned. "That's where I had the advantage of you," he said.

Mr. Campion and the superintendent drove back to London together, leaving a very relieved company of experts to travel home in their own ways. Oates was jubilant.

"Got him," he said. "Got him at last. And a clear case. A pretty little swindle too. Just like him. If you hadn't been there all those poor devils would have paid up something. They're the kind of people he goes for, folk whose business depends on their absolute integrity. They all represent small firms, you see, with old, conservative clients. When did you realize that he wasn't the real Gervaise Papulous?"

"As soon as I saw him I thought it unlikely." Campion grinned as he spoke. "Before I left town I rang up the publishers of the Papulous monograph. They had lost sight of him, they said, but from their publicity department I learned that Papulous was born in '72. So as soon as I saw our friend The Widow I realized that he was a good deal younger than the real man. However, like a fool I didn't get on to the swindle until this morning. It was when he was putting on that brilliant final act of his. I suddenly recognized him and of course the whole thing came to me in a flash."

"Recognized him?" Oates looked blank. "I never described him to you."

Mr. Campion looked modest. "D'you remember showing off to a very pretty girl I brought up to your office, and so far forgetting yourself as to produce an advertisement from an evening paper?" he enquired.

"I remember the ad," Oates said doggedly. "The fellow advertised for a kid's entertainer. But I don't remember him including a photograph of himself."

"He printed his name," Campion persisted. "It's a funny nickname. The significance didn't occur to me until I looked at him this morning, knowing that he was a crook. I realized that he was tricking us but I couldn't see how. Then his face gave him away."

"His face?"

"My dear fellow, you haven't spotted it yet. I'm glad of that. It didn't come to me for a bit. Consider that face. How do crooks get their names? How did Beaky Doyle get his name? Why was Cauliflower Edwards so called? Think of his forehead, man. Think of his hair."

"Peak," said the superintendent suddenly. "Of course, a widow's peak! Funny I didn't think of that before. It's obvious when it comes to you. But even so," he added more seriously, "I wonder you cared to risk sending for me on that alone. Plenty of people have a widow's peak. You'd have looked silly if he'd been on the level."

"Oh, but I had the advertisement as well," Campion objected. "Taken in conjunction the two things are obvious. That demonstration last night was masterly. Young brandy went in at one end of the apparatus and old brandy came out at the other, and we saw, or thought we saw, the spirit the whole time. There was only one type of man who could have done it—a children's party entertainer."

Oates shook his head.

"I'm only a poor demented policeman," he said derisively. "My mind doesn't work. I'll buy it."

Campion turned to him. "My good Oates, have you ever been to a children's party?"

"No."

"Well, you've been a child, I suppose?"

"I seem to remember something like it."

"Well, when you were a child what entertained you? Singing? Dancing? *The Wreck of the Hesperus?* No, my dear friend, there's only one kind of performer who goes down well with children and that is a member of the brotherhood of which Jessant is hardly an ornament. A magician, Oates. In other words, a conjurer. And a damned good trick he showed us all last night!"

He trod on the accelerator and the car rushed on again.

The superintendent sat silent for a long time. Then he glanced up.

"That was a pretty girl," he said. "Nice manners too."

"Leonie?" Campion nodded. "That reminds me. I must phone her when we get back to town."

"Oh?" The superintendent was interested. "Nothing I can do for you, I suppose?" he enquired archly.

Campion smiled. "Hardly," he said. "I want to tell her she owes me two pounds."

My Vacation in the Numbers Racket

Howard Engel

In his Canadian private eye, Benny Cooperman, Howard Engel presents us with what appears at first glance to be a mild-mannered, bookish and unlikely crime buster, based in the sleepy town of Grantham, Ontario. However, his exterior belies a shrewd and tough investigator whose tenacity is often at the root of his best detection work. P.I. Cooperman's mother regularly makes an appearance and, in this short story, demonstrates where Benny first got the sleuthing gene. With over fifteen novels and short-story collections, Engel has scripted many television and radio adaptations for the Canadian Broadcasting Company, including recent TV series of his novels *The Suicide Murders* and *The Ransom Game,* both featuring Saul Rubinek as the eponymous hero.

Dear Benny,

I was thinking of you all alone in that hotel room of yours with the frost making leaf-prints on your window, so I thought I'd see if I couldn't get this cassette machine working long enough to send you a letter. I think I've pushed the right button, but I don't think I've got the courage to try playing it back in case I wipe what I think I've recorded.

You'll be surprised to hear that your father and I are in Sarasota. You thought we were still in Miami, where I meant to send you a postcard, but things just happened too fast to send you a postcard. Right from the beginning this winter hasn't been like any other winter we've ever spent in Florida. I'll try to tell you what happened if I can still remember.

One thing I remember, and I'll start there, is the Red Cap. That's a place your father and I went with Shirl. Do you remember Shirl? She's that blonde that if it wasn't for me I think your father might have been nuts about back a few years. She used to work in his store, and then she started doing her hair up and moved to the millinery shop in the Leonard Hotel. That's where she used to hang out until she met Dave Steiner. He was the first man she ever met who had his shirts made to order. Dave might be a little shady in his business life but he was always generous where Shirl was concerned. We have been visiting them every winter for a few days since we started going to Miami. Which brings me back to the Red Cap, the lounge on the edge of Miami where Shirl and Dave used to take us. It's a kind of bar, but a real joint, if you know what I mean. Even for down there it's a joint. They call it the Red Cap, and it's a sort of Last Chance Saloon because it's open all night and it's so far away from everything. It's located right in the middle of these big, big . . . What-do-you-call-'ems? You know, storage tanks for gas? A huge field of them. And right across the road from the bar is the whole electric whatchamacallit for the whole city of Miami. A power station, not a sub-station or anything like that. And this joint just sits there in the middle of all that gas and electricity with its peeling sign winking on and off like it was something to be proud of.

They have a piano player there, some drunk that comes in all the time. They told me he used to be somebody but you could have fooled me. He leaned into the keyboard like he was protecting it with his body. I don't think I ever saw him look up, not even when the girl replaced his empty glass with a full one. He wasn't the only musician. When they finished their club dates, jazz musicians drop around on their way home. There was always some sort of jam session going on if you came in late enough.

The night I met Stone Eyes was the night it all started to happen. Dave and your father were out looking after some business together and were going to pick us up at the Red Cap. Shirl parked her convertible in back and we walked into that neon haze around the front door. So just before she starts telling jokes with the owner, Shirl tells me not to talk to anybody she doesn't introduce me to first. It's a safety precaution, I know that. But you know me; I'm always the little juvenile delinquent. And so I started talking to this tall guy sitting at the bar. He had eyes that looked like they were made of stone. I'd never in my life seen eyes like that. They looked like they were really made of stone. Anyway, I know you're going to say that we were all pretty stoned and sure, we were, because it was after four in the morning and Dave and Manny were busy like I told you.

So anyway, I looked around and everywhere there's something chipped or faded or falling apart: plastic liquor signs that light up, even neon in the windows writing the name of an American beer backwards. It's a really low place and the people in it . . . let's say that it's not where you expect to find ladies with pearls and twin sets, if you know what I mean. This is 159th Street after all: the last chance. You get all types here, millionaires and crooks. They say the mayor or former mayor used to come here all the time. One time Shirl told me that the guy she'd introduced me to owned half of Miami. Now, Benny, you know what I think of Miami. If it wasn't for the Canadian winter, they could give it to Castro. When you look at them all sitting there talking over their drinks you can't tell the crooks from the millionaires. And you know me. I couldn't care less which is which. Every crook Shirl ever introduced me to treated me like a lady. Anyway, I always talk to men in bars. You know, I tell them I'm from Canada and that I'm visiting friends in Miami and very soon we're talking. And so I was talking to this tall man in the gray suit with the eyes I was telling you about.

That night the orchestra was not great. In fact it was terrible. I was only listening with half an ear until it started playing "Windmills of My Mind." The guy with the eyes was humming into his drink. I leaned over and said to him, "That's from *Don Quixote,* isn't it?"

"What?" he asks.

"The music: 'Windmills of My Mind.' From the musical."

"Oh," he says, and I look into those stone eyes of his.

"That's Cervantes."

"Naw, that's Voltaire. *Candide,*" he says, "I'd know it anywhere. You're thinking of *The Man of La Mancha.* That goes different. It's a better book. Longer, but better. They both got a lotta giggles in 'em." And I can't get over it; in a place like that to be having an intellectual conversation with the man with the stone eyes. So, anyway, I don't agree with him about the music, naturally, but I ask him where he went to university. He looks surprised and smiles and says that he didn't even finish high school. Well, I don't tell him that I dropped out in junior fourth, but I compliment him on his reading.

"Ask me any question," he says.

"Is this a game or something?"

"Naw. Just quiz me about stuff. Try me on the Bible. I specialize on the Bible."

"Who was Malachi?"

"It means 'messenger' and he was the last of the Minor Prophets. He wrote a whole book. That was easy. Try me again."

"Who was Lazarus?"

"Trick question, huh?"

"What do you mean?"

"'Cause there were two of them. One in the parable of the Rich Man and the other one gets raised from the dead. Right?"

"How am I supposed to know? I just asked the first thing that came into my head." I asked him where he got his education and he started laughing.

"I did twenty years of reading in one stretch when I was in prison."

Well, I could have fallen right off my stool—like the time I broke my coccyx and Charlie Wilson from General Motors picked me up and called a doctor. I guess he could see my surprise. I think I let my mouth go slack.

"You got lots of time for reading in prison," he said. "I guess I've smoked more Bibles than most people have read."

I looked him over, but there was nothing of the jailbird about him except that his hair was cut shorter than you see nowadays. But that doesn't mean anything. His clothes were as good as your father's. So, I try to stop staring at him and ask him what he'd done to get sent to prison for twenty years.

"Name it," he said. My mouth was open again and I snapped it shut. "I guess I've done just about everything one time and another," he said. Then he told me that one of the things he'd done was kill his wife. So there I am sitting and laughing and talking about *Candide, Don Quixote,* and the Bible with a wife-killer. I go into a trance and when I hear what he's saying again he's talking about guns. ". . . too much respect for them to carry one. I hate wearing one under my coat in the heat. And you can get into a lot of trouble with guns. I'm all for gun control, you know. I heard about one old-timer with bad kidneys from Louisiana. His relatives riled him up so bad he took a few warning shots at them with a handgun. When it went off it severed the tube from his dialysis machine and he bled to death. I know another guy who thought he saw a prowler at the foot of his bed and shot his own pecker off. You'll have to forgive my language." I tried to show him that it was all right this time, but that I wasn't used to that kind of talk.

Just then the girl behind the bar with blue spots showing through her pancake make-up comes over with a drink for me. I tell her that I didn't order it and she tells me that he ordered it for me. I explain that I couldn't accept it, and she leans over the bar and tells me that in the three years this guy has been coming in here every night regular, this is the first time he'd ever bought anyone a drink. So, being me, I naturally accepted. He'd spent twenty years in prison for killing his wife and God knows what else he's done, and who ends up on the bar stool next to him? Me! Oh, I know, I'm terrible. But I can still picture those stone eyes of his and remember talking about Cervantes and Voltaire. Isn't that the limit? I mean, look: he could have gotten very ugly with me, you know. You accept a drink from some of these guys and they think they own you. One rye and water and you're bought and paid for.

So, anyway, your father and Dave came back around then. They saw me sitting at the bar and I waved to your father and said: "Manny, come over here, I want you to meet a friend of mine." Dave saw who I was talking to and went over to the table where Shirl was still talking to the owner. Manny and Stone Eyes shook hands but didn't exchange names. After that we left. I think I have a feeling that Stone Eyes knew Dave from someplace. I'm not sure. I know that Dave has never done time. Somebody else would have asked my educated ex-con all about his life in prison but not me. He would have expected that, and I always do the unexpected.

So anyway, after that we go back to Shirl and Dave's place, which is right there off 159th Street, and have a few more drinks and a few laughs. It's a nice place with patio and pool, and Shirl has fixed it up real cute with lamps she's made from kits you can buy for making colored plastic lampshades. That's about as artistic as she gets. I tried to get her interested in art once when she lived in Grantham, but she thought that the man taking the class was queer. Generally, if they don't have hair on their knuckles, she thinks they're queer. So we have a drink and a few laughs, like I say, because we were trying to cheer her up, take her out of herself after everything she'd gone through, what with the robbery and then the probation thing. Don't get me wrong, Benny, she didn't get probation for a robbery that *she'd* committed. I know they have some pretty strange friends, but apart from the numbers, they're very careful, Shirl and Dave. She isn't really any different from the girl who used to work in your dad's store in Grantham. You should meet Shirl again. She always liked you. Your father says that Shirl and Dave are very careful about the numbers, too. Shirl didn't tell anybody she was mixed up in it. The first few winters we came to Miami we didn't know anything about it. It was only after we heard about her being out on probation, we got to wondering about the big apartment, the pool, and everything. And she had to tell us when we asked her what it was she was on probation for. Then we remembered about the suitcase every Thursday and Saturday, how she was always taking it to a different motel to count out money and tally lists of numbers.

Well, your father, who as you very well know would never hurt a fly, was fascinated by this. He remembered how he'd carried the suitcase for Shirl on a couple of occasions and how sometimes he'd help her add up the accounts. To him it was no different from doing his books at the store. But I didn't want any part of it. I wondered whether it was the Mafia, but Shirl said it was an independent group. But she gave the Mafia its due. If you want anything done in Miami, including protection, you have to get it from the Mafia. The police, she said, are just a joke. Why, when we arrived in Miami this year, what with Shirl being depressed and everything, I have to give her Mafia connections their due. At the airport your father couldn't rent a car anywhere. We phoned Shirl and she said that she'd look after it. Inside of half an hour we had a rent-a-car, and not only that, but the guy turned back the speedometer about two hundred miles so that in the end we had the car for the whole two weeks and it only cost your father eighty dollars. If it wasn't for the saving and a few other things I'm going to tell you about, I'd be putting all this down in ballpoint in a letter instead of on a cassette. You know how I hate writing letters. Your father writes a beautiful letter, but you and your brother take after me. Remember how the camp counselor used to threaten you with no swimming if you didn't write home?

Now I don't want you to get me wrong. Your father and mother have not turned to a life of crime. God forbid. And you may not remember but Shirl is just about the most giving and wonderful person on earth. She's the best friend a girl could have and she's always thought the world of your father. But, to tell you the truth, she has run into a lot of unsavory characters. Even Dave. I once saw Dave shake her, right up against the wall of the patio of her apartment, and demand to have half of the money they got from Lou for not mentioning his name at the trial. Lou has always been good to Shirl. He's the guy who looks after the apartment and her other expenses. I think he was at one time sweet on Shirl. I wouldn't be surprised. Lou gave them fifty thousand for taking the rap for him.

When they got the fifty, Shirl and Dave went through it so fast you'd think that they knew it was going to be discontinued. They spent it like it was sea water. And they both used to live pretty high on the hog even in the old days. It took them less than four weeks to rip through that bankroll. They bought a second color TV with all sorts of Atari games. They got a Polaroid camera, you know, all that stuff. And Shirl got a new mink coat. In that climate! Two mink coats! The old one wasn't three years old and she didn't even have to trade it in.

I don't want you to get us wrong, Benny. The first time we went to Miami, as I was saying, we didn't dream about the numbers. I mean, when I think of all the clues there were: Dave and Shirl were always so careful about being followed, driving around the block to see if there was anybody parked by the apartment. That sort of thing. And, of course, not only did your father help out with the tallying, he even went around with Dave to all those black bars collecting bets and then delivering the money afterwards.

How can I defend us to you, Benny? We had no training for getting involved, that's all. Your father has kept books all his life, so naturally he became a little suspicious when he saw books with no names in them. In case you're shocked, let me tell you that we were too. Only we just woke up and found ourselves right in the middle of it.

Oh, they've had the numbers in Florida for years. This bunch was run by a gang from Detroit. The numbers were on short slips of paper, about two inches by four, in bunches held together by elastics. It's all on the up and up. There's no way you can cheat on it because the numbers are a combination of who won the first race at Jamaica or the last race at Santa Anita, or something like that. It's all in the open, and if you win, you know it, and if you don't, you're down two, three bucks. For a two-dollar win, you can get maybe two hundred more if it's a special combination win. It's like slot machines or the lotteries. Most of the time you lose, but if you win, Lou and his bunch can go down a couple of hundred thousand. Dave said once a few years ago Lou was borrowing cab fare one day and he owned the company a week later. Naturally, most of the time they don't lose, but they don't cheat at it. I mean you can't fix all those horse races, can you? For a racket, it's as honest as you can make it.

The robbery and Shirl and Dave taking the rap for Lou when the apartment was raided happened last summer. As she said, we missed the fireworks. We missed the court case, too. All the excitement. When we got back to Miami things were a lot different, more creepy. Dave gave me the willies. Manny liked Dave, but me, well, to be honest, I never much liked the look of him. He was like most of Shirl's men: big, dark fellows. Mediterranean types. They always looked like they were carrying guns under their jackets, but most of them weren't carrying anything more than maybe fifty pounds overweight.

Anyway, after the court case, Shirl and Dave got off. I don't know why they didn't deport Shirl. I don't understand how she stays there. It's this lawyer they've got. I can see why she wouldn't want to leave that place of hers; it's really a beautiful place. And she's got a toy poodle, Maggie, a wonderfully cute, dear little fellow. I adore Maggie, and you know about me and dogs as a rule: we can't stand one another. They know it and I know it. It's never been a problem. But I was telling you about the apartment. Wasn't I? The apartment? It's a palace, that's all. Five bedrooms, patio, pool, and a view over, well, I'm telling you that it wouldn't make it very hard for Manny and me to pack up and move down here and that's for sure. And if you want something, anything, Shirl or Dave or Lou knows somebody who can get it. Oh, it's just marvelous.

Where was I? Oh, the apartment. That's really one for the books. You have to see it. Anyway, the point I was making is that after the robbery, they, Shirl I should say, just let it go to rack and ruin. She lost heart, poor girl. Well, I guess, after all she went through, I mean. It must have been hell. A woman can get frightened of things a man doesn't have to worry about in a situation like that. Oh, the kid went through hell. And Dave? Not a scratch. He wasn't even there. I never trusted Dave. He looks like those movie torpedoes, and he acts like that's the way he wants to look. Tough, he-man. Not that Shirl ever went for the choirboy type. Like I said, she always went for the dark, brawny type with size eighteen necks. And most of them had a mean streak. Not like that boy from out Pelham Road she married out of Commercial. He had a real sweetness about him, but Shirl put him on the worry wagon with a vengeance. She preferred the flashy type: she couldn't help it. When they were loaded, Shirl's men always spent freely. They like Cadillacs in the drive and convertibles, if you please. One, two, make it three. Like Shirl and her minks. Same thing.

The numbers were always collected and counted in a new place every time. Shirl first got to use the apartment because it was used as one of the places. Then they didn't want to have anything in the apartment overnight. Wasn't it a big surprise that the Feds knew about the first time in months that there was stuff linking them to the numbers in the place. That can't have been just bad luck. It's like what it says in the mystery stories I read all night, somebody "shopped" them. Now, not only did they lose the money they were holding, but they are having to fight the tax people, you know, Internal Revenue, who want to count the numbers money as income, and undeclared income at that. I mean they had hundreds of thousands with them and none of it was theirs. There must have been a leak of some kind, because Lou and his cousin before him had been running numbers there without anything happening for years and years.

After the trial came the robbery. Shirl thinks there was something fishy about that too, and I don't blame her. When we came back this winter, Shirl was a different woman. She'd lost her—what's the word? Specialness? The thing that made men turn and look at her. You know I've known Shirl for years and we've been very close. We've gone through rough times together. So there was no fooling Manny and me when we got off that plane.

Shirl thinks the world of your father, Benny, and God bless him, he's not one for sitting around when there's work to be done. Anything before talk. That's your father. So, right away he starts cleaning up the place. She'd let it go downhill quite a bit, though who could blame her after what that kid has been through. I looked after Maggie, the poodle. Manny loves gardening. Me, I have a black thumb, can't make anything grow except that ivy I've been trying to kill off in the kitchen. Wouldn't you know it: if I wanted it to live, it would have died off years ago. But your father has a talent, as you know, and he started in on her place, trimming the hedge and cutting back the rubber plant, and cleaning the dead plants out of the place.

Manny bought some annuals. They have annuals all year round down there. He made a proper garden for the patio like we have at home. Oh, your father's wonderful at that sort of thing, while I sit back with a rye and water. Ha! That's my style. Especially when it comes to work. Shirl adores Manny. Always has, not that she'd try anything. Much more likely that he'd look too far into those baby-blue eyes of hers and fall in. I trust your father, but he's only human. Everybody loves Manny. Everybody. There's something sweet about him. You can smell it on his skin. Me? Well, they think I'm pretty special too, but oh, they all love your father.

Well, he cleaned out the pool, scrubbed it, vacuumed it, and replaced the burnt-out lights in the bottom. When at last the place started to look like something again,

Shirl started coming out of herself. You know how she can sound tough, but she didn't have to act that way with us. Not ever. We were always special for her and she never put on a show for us. One night she turned on the night lights in the pool and we all went for a swim. She still looked beautiful in that turquoise light, although she wouldn't wear a bikini any more. When we were all dried off and having a drink I had enough courage to ask her to talk about the robbery.

It was after four in the morning when she came home, parked her Cadillac in the drive, and let herself into the apartment. Dave wasn't with her. When she opened the door, they were inside waiting for her. They grabbed her from behind by the throat and mouth. She only saw stockinged faces and screamed into rubber gloves. They blindfolded her, put adhesive tape over her mouth, and tied her to a chair. She said they talked of raping her right at the start, but she made them understand that she had a heart condition, so they left her alone. Here's an interesting thing: they knew she was wearing a diamond pendant under her turtleneck sweater. Can you beat that? They knew which was her car. They took time collecting everything in the place that was fenceable. I learned that word from Ellery Queen. They made themselves Nescafé and went through every pillow, mattress, upholstered chair in the place with their knives. They even cut up the backs of her pictures. The poor kid! Shirl could hear the birds and the sounds of starting cars next door when they left. She knew that it was getting light on 159th Street. Before they left, they poured acid from the swimming pool shed into the pool. Then they left in her car. They found the Caddy a few days later. The cops, I mean, but they won't find the rest of her stuff. Even the cops told her not to hold her breath until that happened.

The rings! She had a seven-hundred-dollar Pucci and a diamond cut like—well, it was the only one of its kind. But the thing that got her was the swimming pool. Shirl couldn't talk about it too much. It was Dave who told us about the acid in the pool. He said that Shirl was broken up into little pieces when he got home after her call to him in New York. "She was a wreck for about a month, weren't you honey?" he said. "I nearly didn't have the heart to tell her about the pool, but she kept bugging me about why I had it drained. Didn't you, sweetheart? I tried lying to her, but that wasn't no good, so I had to tell her. And that got her started all over again. But she's all right now, huh? How's my little girl?" She was sick about that. If she had tried to go swimming, her skin would have been eaten right off by the acid. It makes you sick just thinking about it. It's funny, they didn't break up the place any in a malicious way, except for what I told you already, but they did that to the pool. I don't understand people doing a horrible thing like that.

The next day, I think it was, the three of us, Shirl, Manny, and I, went shopping. Dave was off on business of some kind. I wanted to get some postcards to let you get a taste of the balmy south to pin to your bulletin board. I knew you were looking after our plants and your brother says he likes to hear from us regularly. Not that either of you'd ever think to drop us a line. So we went into this arcade and were browsing around when suddenly Shirl looks at me, really scared, and says, "I've got to get out of here. I'll see you later." And off she goes into the crowd and out of the other end of the arcade. Well. You could have knocked me over with a lemonade. I looked at your father and he looked at me and for a minute we didn't know what to do. Like, it took us a minute to realize that Shirl had left so fast.

Anyway, I bought about half a dozen cards, got some stamps from the machine, and was sitting writing out one to your brother when Manny gives me a nudge. When I looked up, he nods at two men standing about ten feet away. They were watching us. One is a dumpy guy in a sports jacket and the other is wearing a pale blue nylon windbreaker with a zipper. There was no mistake about it. They were watching us. As soon as they saw that we saw them, the tall one in the windbreaker comes over and asks where Shirl is. How do you like that? I tell him it's none of his business.

"You don't understand," he says, "we're friends of hers. Is Dave with her?" He tried to look friendly and the chubby guy was nodding and tried to look agreeable.

"Well, you just missed her," I said, a little apprehensively. "She had some things to do."

"Well, that's too bad. At least we can give you a lift back to where you're staying."

"That won't be necessary," I said. "Thank you very much."

"We're driving right past 159th Street," the other one added.

"We're just shopping," Manny said, and added, "For the love of Mike!" to show that he was serious.

"I'm afraid I'm going to have to insist," said the first guy, trying to take my arm. He smelled of talcum powder like a baby. "Our car's parked right outside."

Well, I looked at Manny and your father looked at me, and there didn't seem to be anything we could do about it. They both wore smiles and seemed friendly enough. While the short one looked like a thug in the movies, I had to remind myself we weren't in the movies. Things like that don't happen to a couple having a holiday in Miami, for goodness' sake. So we went with them to the car which was double-parked at the front of the arcade. There was a man at the wheel and the motor was running.

If I was worried at all, I felt better as soon as I saw that the driver was old Stone Eyes from the Red Cap. The guy I was telling you about? He did a real double-take when he saw me. But he didn't smile or say anything. He just got out of the car and came around to open my door. Manny and I sat in the back with the one in the windbreaker and Stone Eyes and the heavyset one rode in front. For a while nobody said anything. Manny watched the streets run by the car windows and I kept my eyes on the backs of the necks in the front seat. What was I going to do? I'd never be able to remember where they were taking us. All the streets in Miami look alike to me. Or so I thought. After a while I could see these big gas drums, so I could roughly guess where we were. Stone Eyes ran into an empty parking lot and leaned back and said: "What do you say we all have a little drink?"

The waiter with the broom tried to say that the place was closed, but the men just walked right over him. The place looked different in the daylight. There were no shadowy places. Empty, it looked twice as big. Stone Eyes looked at Manny, but he said to me, "Look, why don't you sit at the bar for a sec. I'll join you after I have a word with my associates." He and the other two sat in the booth and started in on what sounded like the middle of a conversation. After about five minutes, he ambles over and sits next to us at the bar. I was sipping a rye and water and so was Manny. The waiter brought him a drink without even asking.

"My friends and I are a little curious about your plans here in Miami. I mean are you down here on a vacation, a visit, or what? They're a little concerned that may be you're not on a vacation at all, that maybe you're planning to settle down here and I don't mean in a retirement condominium. It's a friendly argument we're having. A little speculating, sure, but a few words from you can settle the whole thing. What do you say?" I could see the other two leaning this way from their booth, trying to hear as much as they could without getting up, but not making a big thing about not appearing to be listening at all. Manny looked pained, the way he gets when I use the garlic powder from the old house and we've run out of Gelusil. But as usual, it's your mother who opens her big mouth.

"We've been down here for about two weeks. Planning to stay three. You're not from the Department of Tourism or something. So, why the interest?" Of course I knew they weren't tourist inspectors, but I just come out with things. You know me. Stone Eyes thought about this for a minute while he took a slow sip from his drink.

"So, you're going back to Canada in a week, right?"

"That's right."

"And you're not in business down here, right?"

"Of course not."

"Good. Okay, that's all I got to know. Be right back." And over he goes to his pals again for another confab. Manny was looking at his fingernails. He gave me a weak grin. Stone Eyes came back to the bar. Your father just had time to say:

"It's going to be all right. You'll see." Stone Eyes looked at both of us, then reached for his drink. He didn't say anything until the glass was empty. He rubbed his mouth with a red bandanna he carried in his pocket.

"Okay, as soon as you're ready, I'll drive you home." He still didn't smile, I don't think I ever saw him do that. But this time his non-smile was as close to a smile as I ever saw him get. "One thing," he said as I was getting off my stool, "my associates would appreciate it if you didn't mix into Dave's and Shirl's business any more." I started to protest, but Manny had me by the upper arm before I could utter a syllable. "You know how things are in business," Stone Eyes continued, "people are superstitious about outsiders. You follow me? It's like our friend Candide. He got his nose busted a few times putting it into the wrong places. I don't mean this unfriendly. It's just that my friends don't understand people the way I do." We were now going out of the door of the Red Cap, and Stone Eyes held the door for your father and me. He took me to one side in the parking lot: "Look, what you do is this," he said, "you go back to Canada in a week, even sooner wouldn't hurt things none, and you don't say anything about what you've seen. That's all." He looked at me really hard with worry in those cold eyes, then he said, "Come on. I'll drop you at the house."

The ride back to Shirl's was much more relaxed. The short one was telling what his ten-year-old son told him about oil spills in the Gulf of Mexico. All three of them said something about the destruction caused by oil spills. Stone Eyes blamed it on lax shipping registry laws and referred to the Law of the Sea Conference that was going on someplace, and then the blue windbreaker got on to acid rain as we came to a stop in front of Shirl's. The other guy said that he was very impressed with the interest young people have in ecology. "Kids are really great the way they want to protect and preserve stuff." That was the end of it. We got out and said good-bye.

So, we let ourselves into the apartment. We didn't notice anything wrong, but when Shirl got back an hour later and when we told her what happened, she really went into orbit. I mean first of all she gets the shakes when she sees that Dave's stuff is gone from the closet. She checks the dressers and starts to cry. She asks us to describe the men we met and in less than no time we are packing ourselves into a limousine and on our way to the airport. Can you beat that? One minute I'm sitting in the sun with a tall, cool drink on the patio, the next I'm packing and Shirl's trying to smile and not fooling anybody. Shirl went with us to the airline terminal and gave us both a big hug as we got into the limo. The last we saw of her she was wiping tears from those huge blue eyes and slamming the door of her Caddy.

Now isn't that the darndest thing you ever heard? Of course I figured it all out on the flight to Sarasota. Shirl knew that Dave was in on the robbery because he knew about the acid in the swimming pool. How can you tell there's acid in a pool unless you told somebody to put it there? He pulled the robbery to put Lou off the scent. He must have been creaming the top off his numbers money. A lot of them try that. People get greedy, that's all. So Lou hired those thugs to shake things up to see if any change rolled out of our pockets that didn't belong to us. It all started looking like something in a paperback mystery novel. Isn't there a private eye down here who lives on a houseboat? John D. something. The whole two weeks sounds like a case he might have got involved in.

Anyway, your father and I are both well. You can pick us up at the airport on Tuesday, Flight 604 from Sarasota. And, Benny, don't forget to water my plants.

Love,

Mother

The Duke Alexander

Mickey Spillane

All Mickey Spillane wanted was enough money to build a house. In order to get the needed funds, he wrote a book. *I, the Jury* was published in 1947 and introduced the world to the most hard-hitting of private eyes, Mike Hammer. Spillane is the master of the "hard-boiled" detective story. Infusing his tales with sex and sadism, Spillane's books became a worldwide phenomenon. Even his name invoked images of the steamier side of law enforcement. In the character of Hammer, the most chauvinist avenger among classic private eyes, Spillane created a dark counterpart to the knightly Philip Marlowe. From the 1950s through the 1990s, Spillane's Mike Hammer has been the hero in over fifteen films, starring Darren McGavin, Kevin Dobson, and most notably Stacy Keach. Spillane himself portrayed his hard-nosed detective in his film *The Girl Hunters* (1963). For his extraordinary contribution to the mystery genre, in 1995 Spillane was recognized by the Mystery Writers of America and appointed a Grand Master.

I'm only minding my own business, see? I'm sitting there next to the window crouched down behind a magazine so the porter would get the idea and go away. All morning long he's been on my back, bringing me water, steering me to the diner and even shaving me. Yeah, he hauls me in the lounge outside the men's room and gives me a lather and blade job before I wake up even.

Sure, I slip him a buck and he says, "Thank you, Duke, sar." Then I got back to my seat with him standing so close I can reach out and touch him. Nobody else gets this treatment. Just me. The guy's got everybody turning around to look and I feel like a bug in the customer's potatoes.

If I go to move he's right there with, "Somethin' I can do, Duke, sar?" And no matter what I say he does it anyway. Can't even comb my hair. Duke, sar. That's all the guy knows. I told him my name was Mike and if he gotta call me anything, call me that. So what happens.

"Yes, sar, Mike Duke sar," he says. What a train. What a vacation.

Anyway, like I said, I'm only minding my own business when along comes this cupcake. He looked like a lampshade in a double-breasted suit that didn't fit and waddles up the aisle like a duck. Every time he passes a seat he looks at the guy sitting there, shakes his head then moves on. That is, until he gets to me. He gives one peek at me behind my magazine and his eyebrows shoot up to his hatband.

He shrieks, "Ah, you scoundrel . . . you brigand! So you think to elude me. You are contrariwise! He who is the retiree from the Sûreté. Now I have you caught flatfooted and never will you get away again until you pay me my moneys!"

What can a guy do in a situation like that? I yell, "Scram, ya bum, before I brain ya!" Yeah, I was pretty mad. Does he flinch? Nix . . . not a bit. He perches his hand on his hips and taps his foot impatiently.

After a couple of harrumphs, he says, "No . . . do not tell me. This time it is that you have the amnesia. You do not fool me, for I Alfred, know who you are. Now, do I get my moneys?"

"No," I tell him, good and loud.

He smacked his lips a few times. "You say no. How can you sit there and . . . all right, tell me why it is no."

"Because I don't owe ya none. Now scram."

"Oh, I . . . *sacre blue!* Overcome I am." He holds his head and shoulders. "This country she is mad. I demand payment!"

Real calm like, I tell him, "Chum, would you like a punch in the nose?"

I get a real hurt look for that remark. "Of course, certainly not. The thought is horrible to me. Why?"

"Because that's what you'll get if ya don't get outta here."

"Ah ha! Now it is that you will assault me. Very well, we shall see. I assure you that the gendarmerie will not treat the matter so lightly as I. You are practically chained to the wall of the Bastille right now!" The jerk snaps his fingers in my face. "Poof I go, but I shall return . . . then you will go, as they say in this country, to the hoosegow!"

Then he stamps off down the car with his chin out further than Mussolini's, slightly forcefully assisted through the door by a shove from my buddy, the porter. Natch, old toothy grin is my pal from then on. I wave him over confidentially. "Look," I whisper, "we got a section eight car tagged to this train?"

"Section eight, Duke, sar?" His face is blank, so I circle my finger around my temple and he gets the idea, then he makes like it was quite a joke. "No, sar, not so's I recollect. Very funny, Duke, Sar."

So I shrug my shoulders and go back to my mag. It's only ten minutes before we get to Washington, where I'd change to the Great Southern Special, then I'd be out of this rolling booby hatch.

That's what I thought.

I had a half-hour layover so I walked into the reservation desk to see if I can do any good about getting myself a bunk for the night instead of doing my sleeping at right angles to myself.

Do any good? Why, the guy at the desk gives me a pair of wide eyes. All of a sudden there I am with what amounts to the presidential suite on wheels. He's all spurts and splutters so I don't get half what he's talking about, but I sign my name, he gives me a very knowing smile like he's been let in on a state secret, and the merry-go-round starts to twirl again.

What a vacation! Two porters grab my bags and zip off, but instead of following them I duck into a normal looking place where a bored babe in gingham slides me a plate of bacon and eggs, no questions asked, and I get some of my strength back.

I shouldn't've taken so long to eat. Before I know it I hear my train being announced and I rip out of there on the double. You know what the squeeze is like in a train station. Sixty-five people trying to get through a four-foot doorway at the same time.

That's where they got the name bottleneck. Opening the gates is like pulling the cork. Everybody jams together, then pop . . . they get blown through. Sometimes they lose their clothes, sometimes, their baggage. Just as I was compressed into the breech I thought I lost my head.

A millimeter away I was staring at my own face! It took one look at me and said, "Eek, I am seeing double! You are not me, so who am I?" But before I could think of an answer to that one, someone pulled the trigger and I was shot through on the way to the train. Luckily, one of the porters got me, or I would have ended up with the engineer.

At half past twelve that night I popped straight up in my berth. I flipped the shade up so I could see my reflection in the glass and said, "That you, Mike?" The image nodded back vigorously, but I held my hand under my chin just to be sure it was my own skull that was doing the bobbing, then tried on a few grimaces for size. When I was sure that I wasn't a case of overdue battle fatigue, I threw my hands up and flopped back to sleep.

Okay, now do you blame me for trying to get out of there on the fly when we hit Memphis? But do you think it did any good? Huh! Before the train had jerked to a stop I was down at the wrong end, tossed my bags out on the platform and jumped for it.

I don't know what I expected, but it sure wasn't a million bucks worth of southern fried chicken on the hoof in a gray covert suit, a face to make you stop breathing and a figure to give you artificial respiration.

She had the prettiest little drawl, but the way she looked at me made me feel like I'd just crawled out from under a rock. She said, "I figured you'd have to come this way. Fortunately, Pam has a cold and couldn't meet you." I tried to talk but couldn't think of anything to say. Southern-fried motioned with her beautiful blond head. "The car is out back. Come along."

She didn't need a leash, I heeled perfectly. I'm far from being even a medium-size guy, but this dish came to where I'd hardly have to bend my head to kiss her. She had more dough on her back than I had in the bank, but already I had ideas about keeping her in buckskins. I thought to myself that maybe this wasn't going to be such a bad vacation after all. When we got to the extra deluxe super sports special that she obligingly called a car, I changed my mind.

She turned her head and couldn't keep the sneer out of her eyes. "I want you to understand something," she told me. "It is three days until the wedding. During that time I'll do everything in my power to make my silly sister see the light and chase you back to wherever you came from. If that doesn't work, maybe a little violence will help." Then I got the world's nastiest look. "You'll stay a lot healthier if you take the hint now," she reminded me.

About that time I got my voice back. It wasn't as strong as usual, but I could make a speech with it. "Now, look, sis," I grind out, "ordinarily I'm a fairly bright boy, but I've been swinging at curves ever since I left home, only hitting nothin' but flies. Just what in blazes goes on around here? I try to take a vacation and I get treated like a king, threatened like a criminal, then tossed back to the dogs like a college freshman at the senior prom. I even talk to myself face to face and that ain't logical. At first I thought it was me, but now I think the whole world is bats *but* me. Am I or ain't I Mike Hammer with a little office up in Manhattan? Is this or ain't it a vacation where I'm supposed to have a good time? And just who the hell are you?"

Think that made an effect? Nuts! She said, "You can stop being incognito with me, Alex. I can see you've spent a good deal of time being indoctrinated in sound American expressions, but for the time being you can put your office away and just be sure that my sister is one curve that isn't going to be tossed at you. Incidentally, I'm Pam's big sister. You know the grouchy one . . . Vinny. Now let's go before the brass band mother brought along finds out you've taken a powder. Daddy is waiting to have a prenuptial chat with you . . . alone."

So where did that leave me? If I took off on my own there was no telling what would happen. At least here I could put in a plug for myself if I needed it. I like to know what's going on. Besides, I was getting ideas about straightening out some of Vinny's curves. She sure could pitch 'em. I threw my bags in the back and got in the car.

We drove for about a half hour without saying a word, and then pulled up to a place that seemed to be a small mountain with the top cut off. Part of the Great Wall of China kept out busybodies, and the fancy sign that hung on the post by the driveway read HATHAWAY HEIGHTS. It should have been called incredible heights, because if you didn't see it you'd never believe it. Money was written all over the place, from the crew-cut lawns to the mansion that peeked at me through the magnolia trees.

A small army of servants marched out and surrounded the car. One picks up my bags like they were dirty socks and tiptoes in with them. When Vinny gets out they all bow like the Rockettes, but with me I get a lifting of the upper lip and a nod. At the end of the line is the chauffeur who mutters something very nasty as I go past. That did it. I turn on my heel and walk back.

The guy has got one of THOSE faces. For a chauffeur he's a grade A thug. Busted nose, thick lips and scar tissue over the eyes.

I said, "Punchy, did you just make silly sounds with your fat mouth?"

His hands folded into big hams.

"No, sir," he answers. Then as I go to walk away he mutters, "You'll get yours later!"

I'm a good guy, see? I can hold my temper just so long, and if I expected to hold it much longer I had to get out of there. I looked back at him over my shoulder and he must have thought I was scared, so he sneered at me.

Vinny grabbed my arm as I went up the steps. She was being very sweet all of a sudden. "Daddy's waiting to meet you, Alex. You're going to like daddy, and if you want him to like you real much you'll do just as he asks, won't you dear?"

She melted my temper with that "dear." I gave her a big, dreamy smile. "Why don't you do the asking, honey?"

Just like that she dropped my arm. "Louse!" she snapped.

What a contradiction she was! She got over it fast. The sweet smile came back and she steers me into the library. I've been in libraries before, and this one was just as big and just as quiet. And it had just as many books. Only the others never had a librarian who looked and scowled like a bear, ready to jump on you as you came in.

Before the bear could move Vinny said: "This is the Duke Alexander. I'm sure he's going to be reasonable."

Reasonable? He was even bigger than me, and like I already told you, I'm no midge. He said, "Am I supposed to bow or shake hands?"

I don't know what I was expected to do, but if he wasn't Vinny's old man I would have plastered him. As it was, I stuck out my hand. "I ain't pleased to meetcha," I said. The bear shows his teeth, wipes his hand on his pants like I do back on the job and mitts me.

Right away I could see this was a game with the old boy. Vinny smiles happily as his hand starts to crush mine into pulp and remarks, "Daddy used to be a steelworker, Alex. You wouldn't know it though, would you?"

I waited until Daddy was sweating a little bit, then stepped up the pressure some more. "Really?" I was being real bright. "I never would have known it. I was in the game awhile myself." Then I looked straight at Daddy. He was getting red in the face and he planted his feet and gave a last effort. "Yes, sir," I said when I heard his knuckles start to pop. "I sure ain't pleased to meetcha."

Daddy was real glad to let go of my hand. The old bear was a little on the cub side now, but his teeth still showed. He dropped in a chair behind the giant-size desk and rubbed his sore hand so I couldn't see it. Vinny had her lip between her teeth.

"Sit down," he barked.

So I sat. Daddy got right down to business. He pulled open a drawer and yanks out an oversize checkbook. "I imagine you know why I wanted to see you, Duke. Ever since I've had a bankroll, a royalty-minded wife and one foolish daughter, I've been keeping half the courts in Europe in cheese and crackers. Now how much do you want to go back where you came from?"

Well, it took me a long time, but I was beginning to catch on. If I had any sense, I would have spouted off a figure, grabbed at it and hit for Manhattan. But I don't have much sense. You can have fun on a vacation in more ways than one.

"Nuts, Daddy dear," I grinned, "I like it here."

Vinny slammed her palm against the arm of her chair. "Okay, Dad, he wants to play it dumb. He won't take a cash settlement because he thinks he can marry Pam and get all he wants. Let him go ahead. Let him try. Just let him try!"

"I'll be damned if I will!" He was a mad bear again. "Do you get out of here or do I throw you out?"

The ugly chauffeur must have been listening outside, because he came in on cat feet. "You callin' me, sir? Want I should throw the bum out?"

Mama saved the day for somebody. I knew it was Mama, because she was just what you'd expect to find in a joint like that. She burst into the room leading a pack of people that must have been the local society, because there was more diamonds and fancy duds there than at Tiffany's. Her face is smiling from ear to ear, and she spreads her arms wide open and shrieks, "Why, Duke. You naughty, naughty boy! Surprising us at home like this, just when I was beginning to believe you had missed your train!"

"Hi ya, Mama," I said. Then I squeezed her good. If they wanted an act, then they were going to get an act. It was about time I got into this game. Over her shoulder I began to wave at everybody and they waved back. Some duck grabs my hand and pumps it. Two babes crowding fifty tried to bow and almost split a dress. They got helped to their feet.

"But your voice, Duke . . . It has changed," Mama said seriously.

"Sure. I got some jerk from Brooklyn to gimme lessons in American and now I talk just like regular people. Good, ain't it?"

I sure made a funny with that one. Mama clutched her bosom. "Why, how quaint! Duke, you're marvelous." Vinny didn't think so, though. I saw her looking at me, her face as black as a thunderhead. As they say in books, I was getting a look that could kill.

Hot to get Vinny and Pop in bad with the battle axe, I dummy a story about how I got the wrong car at the station and was very luckily recognized by the charming elder daughter. Then I sprung the sticker. "But how's about Pam. Where's she?"

Mama petted my arm. "The poor dear has a horrible cold but I'm sure she's dying to see you at once. George! Why didn't you show the Duke upstairs when he arrived? The poor boy has traveled thousands of miles to see his intended and you keep him away. Shame!"

Everybody snickered but Pop and Vinny. They hadn't gotten a word in edgewise yet. Mama took my arm. "Come along . . . son. I know you can't wait to see your beloved."

"You can say that again, Mama." Her bosom rose and fell in a wind tunnel sigh.

She said to herself, "Goodness . . . just imagine, having a real duke in the family." I felt like adding . . . "at last" to her thoughts, because the way she said it, she had been trying for a long time.

Two maids were playing watchdog outside the door that kept Pam's germs to herself. They parted to let Mama do the honors, and with a flourish she threw the door open and pipes, "Pam, dear, there's someone to see you." With that she shoves me and I get propelled into milady's boudoir.

Pam was laying in bed holding a frilly handkerchief, up to her nose, blinking at me through watery eyes. She lets out, "Oh, Alexander, to think you have to find me like this!" then sets up a wailing that brings the house down.

I said, "Aw, take it easy kid. You only got a cold. How's every little thing?"

Behind me I heard the door open a little, so I spread it on thick. "Ain't I gonna get a little hello kiss, sugar?"

"You are not!" Vinny came at me with claws out, then remembers herself mighty sudden like. "But Alex, we don't want you catching Pam's cold . . . not with the wedding so close." She looked at her sister. "Don't you agree, Pam?"

My intended wrinkled up into a sneeze and Vinny pulled the covers up around her. She looked at us both very confidentially. "Now I'll tell you what we'll do. While you're recovering from the nasty cold, I'll have Alexander escort me around town and meet all your friends. Don't you think that will be best?"

"You . . . you sure you don't mind, Vinny?"

"Not at all, darling."

"But . . . Alex . . ."

"Don't worry about me, kid. I wanna get to know the lay of the land around here anyway. And don't worry about Vinny here. You can trust her, all right." I picked up Pam's limp hand from the bed and planted a smacker on her palm. "There's some healthy germs for you, honeybunch."

"Oh, Alex, you're so sweet," she said.

Vinny muttered something I didn't get.

Mama met us outside the door and Vinny told her the plans. I could see right off that Mama didn't like the idea, but I tut-tuted her objections and everything was okay again. Boy, this was the berries. With Mama, the Duke could do no wrong.

We took the tunnel entrance to the library where the old bear was camped in his den ready to pick my bones. When we came in he and the chauffeur, who were yappity-yapping at close range, jumped back trying to wipe the snug looks off their pans, and I knew that the no-good that was being bred had just been born.

Yep, maybe this wasn't gonna be such a bad vacation after all. Sometime during the day I had to get a wire off to my buddies who were expecting me at the fishing camp so they wouldn't tear up the countryside looking for me. Those guys were always pretty loyal to a mug who could never stay out of trouble.

The chauffeur took off at a nod from Popsie and left the three of us there alone. The bear kept an ear cocked for Mama's footsteps and growled, "Well?"

"Alex is going to be my escort for a while, Dad," Vinny told him. I could see the funny smile playing around her mouth. "A sister's duty, you know."

The bear stared at me. "I'm only going to ask you once more. How much will you take to clear out of here? Name it and it's yours. I'm willing to go any price to make sure my daughter marries a man instead of a floogie with a title."

"How about ten or twenty million." I wink at him.

His face got red up to his hair. "All right, Vinny, escort the gentleman about town. Be sure he sees the sights. All of them," he adds significantly.

I didn't even get time to change my shorts. Out we go, not to the sports special, but to a shining black limousine. Parked behind the wheel is Punchy, licking his chops. Vinny climbed in, with me after her and the wheels spun in the gravel.

Wherever we were going, we were in a hurry. "Nice country around here," I observed.

"Take a good look at it while you still can see it," she popped back.

Right then I thought it was time for a heart to heart talk. "Look, sister. Set me straight on the rules, will ya? I'm having a swell time and all that, but leave us name some places so I can figure ahead of time. I've been climbing a tree ever since I left Manhattan."

"Quit the act, Alex. I'm disgusted with you, your phony American accent and anything connected with you. This afternoon you had a chance to leave well enough alone, but you wouldn't have it. All right, take it anyway you want, but you're not going to marry Pam if I can help it. We don't want your kind near us. Mother's title happy and you're money mad. Poor Dad is the one who has to pay for it. Pam will forget you in a month or so, but if we have to go through much more of these international affairs, Daddy will wind up in the sanitarium."

"But you got me all wrong, baby. Ya see, there's been a switch. My tag is Mike Hammer. . . ."

"Yes, I know," Vinny interrupted. "You have an office in Manhattan, and you're on vacation."

"Yeah, that's it. All along the line people have been calling me Duke. Say, who is this guy anyway?"

Vinny turns and passes me over slowly. There was no doubt in her voice when she said, "Alex, although this is the first I've ever seen you in the flesh, so to speak, your picture has been staring at us from Pam's room, every newspaper and society news for this last year. All I've heard since Mother and Pam came back from Europe is Alex this and Alex that. You are a very clever actor, Alex. I imagine your kind must have to be. But it is no use. That scar on your cheek is no fake, is it? You got that in a duel, I heard. One you lost."

"As a matter of fact, cherub, I got it when some babe hit me with a flower pot. I was twelve years old."

"Anyway your eyes are not the same color. How do you account for that?"

"You mean the other guy got sad sack eyes too? Amazing!"

"The same height, about six one I should imagine. Yes, you even weigh the same, one-eighty."

"Two-oh-six," I put in.

"So you see, Alex, you don't have to try to assume another identity with me. You have too many definite characterizations. I know you for what you are."

"Aw, phooey," I said. I was getting sick of it all now. I was just going to tell Punchy to take me home when he started to slow down. We were way the devil out in the country, off on a side road somewhere. The birds and the bugs were trying to out chirp each other and if I hadn't been sore I might have enjoyed the scenery. Punchy got out, opened the back door.

"This way, sir," he snarls.

"What do you want?"

"I want to show you somethin'. Come on, hop out."

Vinny smirks, "Don't worry. It will be very interesting . . . jerk."

Now she was making me even madder. I climbed out and Punchy takes a little path up the field with me behind him. When we round the bend in the trees he throws his cap on the ground, gives me the old leer and snaps a roundhouse right over on me.

Poor Punchy, his timing was shot to hell. I kinda bent at the knees until it went over my head, then tapped him like the trainer used to tell me to, right where it counted. Punchy did a buck and wing, flapped his arms like a crow then sat down, he eyes like marbles. I put his hat back on and picked him up.

Vinny came running out to meet me. "Nick!" she yelled. "What happened to Nick?"

"He was gonna show me something but he tripped and his head hit a tree. What was he gonna show me up there anyway?"

"Nothing," she snapped. I sure was getting in bad. Vinny didn't know whether to believe me or not. I stowed Punchy in the backseat and got behind the wheel.

"You come in with me. By damn, I'm going to have me a vacation and you're going to like it." She slid in alongside me, but she didn't like it. It took me a half hour to get feeling good again. Hightailing it along the open road in the rig was something and ahead of me was the city. Yes, sir, I sure was enjoying myself.

That is, until I heard the siren come screaming up beside me. Two big state troopers give me the heave-ho sign, but since they had me dead to rights anyway, I was going to have a little fun out of it. I tramped on the gas and yelled, "Hang on!"

Boy oh boy, what a ride that was. Vinny was shouting at the top of her lungs for me to slow down and each time she hollered I jumped the needle up a notch. The police car was dropping away fast, and when I heard a couple of slugs smack the back of the heap it dropped away even faster. I'm allergic to bullets. And those guys weren't fooling. The turns saved us. We had a two-hundred-foot lead and bullets couldn't shoot around corners. Then when we hit the straightaway I gave it everything she had, and when I looked in the mirror you could hardly see the black sedan.

"You fool! You'll kill us all. Stop this instant!"

"Why chicken, I thought you had nerve. Golly, if I thought a little thing like that would scare a red-blooded American gal why I'd . . ."

"Who's afraid? Pam said you'd never driven a car in your life and I don't want to be run off a cliff by a crazy maniac at the wheel of something he's never handled!"

"Oh, there isn't a cliff for miles. Relax."

I didn't slow down a fraction until we hit the city limits, then I led a rat race up and down every street and alley I could find. We could hear sirens all over the place by that time. Every cop on wheels was cruising the town with an eye out for the limousine. I parked outside a theater, grabbed Vinny and yanked her out on the sidewalk.

"Now what, bright boy?"

"So we'll leave Punchy inside and he can tell the bulls how he was held up by a maniac, slugged and taken for a ride. Come on, we have a vacation to enjoy." I pulled her down the street on the gallop, and turned into the first place that carried a beer sign in the windows.

But we didn't get a beer. A miniature tornado jumps from a table and points a finger at me. "It is you! So you think you evade your debts. Now I have you on the spot and will wring my moneys from you. *Garçon! Garçon!* Call the gendarmes . . . at once. This man is a crook!"

"Not you again, pally," I yip. It was Alfred from the train.

"So," Vinny howls, "they even chase you in this country to get their money back. Now you're in for it . . . and brother, will I squeal on you! You won't get back to the old country for ten years! Waiter, call the cops!"

He didn't have to be told twice. The minute the little guy yelled he reached for the phone. Then when Vinny let loose, four guys detached themselves from another table and moved to cover the doorway. This kind of talk I could understand. I grabbed a pair of chairs and went for the roadblock.

If I could have reached it I would have been out of there in nothing flat, because the opposition didn't like the way I was moving those pieces of chromed steel and leather, but a hundred twenty pounds of southern fried chicken took me out high, and a butterball of one-fifty did the same on the low side, and the opposition moved for the pileup. A reinforcement in navy blew the whistle, and I went to the Black Maria.

"Aha yourself and shut up."

"So! You still insist you do not know me. Ho Ho. So I will prove it to you who you are. Tonight you have a nice bed in the clink and I will have my moneys. So! Ho ho!"

"And I," said Vinny, "will send you cigarettes. Nice moldy ones."

The cop at the end of the paddy wagon told everybody to shut up. Which was fine with me. I needed time to think. The wagon tore down the main drag, made a right turn and brakes screeched. The last mile began. I climbed out of the cage with the cop standing by, one hand on a billy, while the driver gave me the thumb to get inside. Vinny was absolutely overjoyed. She was loving every minute of it. So was Alfred. He marched in to present his case like a bantam rooster.

The cops on the inside were collecting us in a group with motions to be quiet when from outside came the most gosh-awful racket you ever heard. Somebody was yelling bloody murder, and a deeper, raspier voice was for the other guy to stop or be killed.

A whistle blew, two cars banged together and women shrieked. *Whoosh!* Just like that the doors bang open and I run in. No. It wasn't me, but it was me.

Hell, I didn't give it too much time. I got smart fast. Right behind me, in comes Punchy waving a club ready to bash out my brains. No, that other me's brains. It was all so confusing, but I was lucky. I saw it all before anyone else did and made a dive for the water cooler just as my other self buried himself in the arms of the cop that was supposed to be guarding me.

Somehow Punchy was disarmed, but he wasn't devoiced. He swore up and down that he'd rip me apart with his bare hands, he'd cut me into little pieces and make me eat them before I was dead.

Alfred started to voice first claims on my body and Vinny wanted to call the undertaker right away, but the cop stopped her. I don't know how the bulls managed it, but they got everybody into the room in front of the chief's desk before murder was committed. They left me out behind the cooler still in a fog. So I can take a joke. I had me a drink of water, patted the cooler affectionately, then found a side room to peek in on the proceedings.

The chief was next door to a stroke, Vinny was having a laughing spasm and Punchy was fit to be tied. But poor me. I stood there watching myself shake like a bowl of pudding. I cried out, "*Alors!* Woe is me! I am entirely innocent, I insist it. Here I am walking calmly down the street when I am attacked by this . . . this thing! I seek the protection of the noble police and what do I find? I am incarcerated! This cannot be America. I will refer the matter to my consulate! I will . . ."

"You will shut up," the chief told me. I mean the other me.

Punchy yelled, "He beaned me, that's what he did. Picked up a rock and beaned me, then stole the boss's car. He's a kidnapper!"

That was Vinny's cue. Yes sir, she agreed, she was kidnapped, right there in broad daylight. I was a villain, even worse. And, what was more, I was practically an extortionist to boot. At that moment who comes in but the state troopers. One look was all they needed. Yep, that was the guy who drove the car, Yup, yup. They had a good close look and couldn't forget a face like that, yup, yup.

I was up there screaming that it wasn't so. It was an international conspiracy so I couldn't take back good American dollars to the old country. It was a foul plot. No kidding, I like to split a gut watching it. The only trouble was that I felt sorry for myself even if it wasn't really me out there.

Then other people came in. The mama bear, the papa bear, and Pam, the baby bear. One peek at them and I let loose in a foreign language that switched back and forth to English in tones that implied that incredible heights was a suburb of Looneyville and that all was off in the wedding department. Mama fainted, Pam opens the dam and forth comes a flood of tears.

"So now the would-be duchess is cry!" I say. "Ha . . . never would you see the inside of a royal court. For your moneys I care not a pouf! So there!"

Papa plays it smart. He grabs me fast. (I mean the other me). He said, "Are you refusing to marry my daughter?"

"Of the certainty, that I am. Arrest me, torture me, I am unsways. I do not marry anyone."

Old Pop just grinned like a fool. So did Vinny. "I guess that tears it, Papa, we can go home now."

"But my moneys, what about my moneys?" Alfred hoots. "Am I to be deprived of my moneys? Am I to be deprived of my moneys what is owed me?"

I (the other me) gave him a haughty look. "It is a trifling sum. I will pay you someday."

"Now! I want it now!" Alfred did a dance.

Papa laughed. "It was worth it. How much does he owe you?"

"Three thousand American dollars. . . . Trifling sum, ha! It will take him all his life to earn that in the hoosegow. How do propose I should collect?" Papa showed him how in a swipe of his pen on a blank check.

Just then Mama came to and fainted all over again. Pam decided to stay out of it with a little faint of her own. Punchy fanned her with his hat, but he kept glowering at the Duke. By this time I was leaning against my doorjamb, out of breath from laughing. Honest, this was the best vacation I ever had in my life!

Vinny and the old bear had their heads together, then Papa stepped forward. Right away I saw he was a big man in these parts. His whisper was loud enough for me to hear. "Chief, do you think we can straighten this thing out of court. I'll be glad to pay any fines or damages and if you just jail this jerk, there really is liable to be some kind of international complications. What do you think?"

I knew that Pop was more concerned with the publicity angle than any across-the-ocean scandal, but the chief saw the wisdom in the words. The matter was straightened out then and there. While the Duke was putting his ruffled feathers back together, Vinny walked up to him. "You know, for a while there I was beginning to like you. Yet you almost have me fooled. I couldn't see how anybody could pick up a Brooklyn accent so fast. You almost, but not quite, sold me a bill of goods."

My heart did a flip. Then it flopped when the Duke looked at her as though she were crazy. "Silly girl," he sneered, and much to Punchy's disgust, stalked out.

I waited until they all stood outside on the sidewalk. Papa loaded the mama bear and Pam bear into one car, while Punchy held the door of the limousine open for Vinny. The Duke was nowhere around. I waited until Papa drove off, then came down the steps fast. "Hey, chicken, how about that beer we missed having?"

"You!" she gasped.

Punchy said something like, "Agrrr!" he came boiling around the car and sneered, then let loose with that roundhouse. I bent a little at the knees, again it breezed by, then I planted one on him in the other alley, and this time he did the buck and wing on the other foot.

"That guy will never learn," I said to Vinny.

She was standing there with her mouth wide open, staring at me with those big blue eyes. When I took her arm and took off down the street she was as limp as wet spaghetti.

I laughed because I got her point. She never saw the Duke dash in the station house ahead of Punchy. Sure, she thought Punchy happened to see me and came charging up to get his licks in while he could. Oh, great!

It took a while, but we reached the spot where I almost ordered the beer. We sat at the table a minute, then the waiter came up with a half empty bottle in his hand. "Can't you stay put, Mac?"

"Who, me?"

"Yeah, you."

Then I saw what he meant. The "other me." The door opened and the Duke came in. He was a sorry sight. Vinny shrieked and started at him, then at me, then back to him again. Right then her mind was in an awful state. Too bad. I patted her on the head and stood up. After all, I did owe the Duke something.

I went over and held out my hand. "Look, pal, how about letting you and me let bygones be bygones. I'll . . ."

"Eek! It is my doubles again. You have ruined everything. Ah ha! Ah ha! Now you come to me on bend knee for forgiving. No is the answer. Nothing I forgive, not one little thing! You have made me look a foolish, and for that I am objectionable!" His arms went wide and he shouts to the public, "This . . . this man, he has stole my train, my woman, my honor . . ." His eyes found the half-empty bottle on my table. "Now he's even drinking the beer I ordered yet!"

"No look, it was all a mis—"

"Do not now look me. It was the insult supreme and I am challenge you. To the death we fight." Up comes his hand and patty cakes me across the cheek. All is quiet. I see the bartender reaching for the phone.

Right then I looked over my shoulder at Vinny. "Now do you believe I'm just Mike Hammer with an office in Manhattan?"

Vinny nodded.

"Did you really mean that about sorta liking me?"

Vinny nodded again.

"Enough to get out of this place and go up where all the nuts are on the trees?"

This time she grinned her yes.

My face was still stinging from that slap though so I grabbed hold of the Duke's coat. "Okay, Buster, you asked for this, but remember something, from now on there ain't gonna be nobody what'll mistake me for you again!" It only took one solid punch to change the Duke's whole personality. His look too. The bartender was busy on the phone. I heard the siren wailing. I yanked Vinny to her feet and we beat out to a taxi.

"Union Station," I ordered.

"Where are we going?" Vinny asked. "Dad won't like this."

I grinned at her. "I don't know about that, chicken. He said he wanted a man in the family. Maybe now he'll get one. There's a train going north in five minutes and you better hope we make it. I don't think we can get your pop to talk us out of anything again."

The taxi was in time. I paid the driver as we unpiled, but I was slightly disturbed. Vinny hadn't said a word during the entire ride to speak of. As we ran for the train I gave her one last chance. "Want to back out, honey?" She shook her head.

"Then why so quiet?"

"I was just thinking . . ."

"Yeah?" the train jerked, started to pull out, and I shoved her aboard.

"When you socked the Duke back there so there wouldn't be any more mix-ups . . . Now he doesn't look like anybody . . . but you still look like the Duke!"

A white-sleeved arm shot out, pulled Vinny up, then grabbed me. I looked up into the grinning face of my pal, the same porter that came down with me.

"Glad to see you back, Duke, sar," he said.

I let out a long groan. "Oh no, not again!"

Vinny said, "See what I mean?"

I saw.

The Adventure of the Beryl Coronet

Sir Arthur Conan Doyle

Sir Arthur Conan Doyle's world-famous Baker Street sleuth, Sherlock Holmes, has appeared in a total of sixty stories and novels. His story "The Beryl Coronet" first appeared in an edition of *The Strand Magazine* of 1892, demonstrating the time-honored skills of one of the world's most famous fictional detectives and possibly one of the most recognizable fictional characters of all time. With his staggering intellect and brilliant powers of deduction, Holmes is the standard against which so many later fictional detectives must be measured, while the relationship with his trusty partner, Dr. Watson, has been the inspiration for many later pairings and partnerships. Sherlock Holmes has appeared in over two hundred and sixty film adaptations and many television series. The first and only American television series of Sherlock Holmes adventures, *The New Adventures of Sherlock Holmes,* was broadcast in 1954, starring Ronald Howard as Holmes and Howard Marion Crawford as Watson. On film, however, Basil Rathbone remains the archetypal Holmes. It is the British television series, produced by Granada Television with the late Jeremy Brett as Holmes, that has been one of the most popular to date. This series, consisting of thirty-six episodes and four films, began broadcasting in 1984.

"Holmes," said I as I stood one morning in our bow-window looking down the street, "here is a madman coming along. It seems rather sad that his relatives should allow him to come out alone."

My friend rose lazily from his armchair and stood with his hands in the pockets of his dressing-gown, looking over my shoulder. It was a bright, crisp February morning, and the snow of the day before still lay deep upon the ground, shimmering brightly in the wintry sun. Down the centre of Baker Street it had been ploughed into a brown, crumbly band by the traffic, but at either side and on the heaped-up edges of the foot-paths it still lay as white as when it fell. The gray pavement had been cleaned and scraped, but was still dangerously slippery, so that there were fewer passengers than usual. Indeed, from the direction of the Metropolitan Station no one was coming save the single gentleman whose eccentric conduct had drawn my attention.

He was a man of about fifty, tall, portly, and imposing, with a massive, strongly marked face and a commanding figure. He was dressed in a sombre yet rich style, in black frock-coat, shining hat, neat brown gaiters, and well-cut pearl-gray trousers. Yet his actions were in absurd contrast to the dignity of his dress and features, for he was running hard, with occasional little springs, such as a weary man gives who is little accustomed to set any tax upon his legs. As he ran he jerked his hands up and down, waggled his head, and writhed his face into the most extraordinary contortions.

"What on earth can be the matter with him?" I asked. "He is looking up at the numbers of the houses."

"I believe that he is coming here," said Holmes, rubbing his hands.

"Here?"

"Yes; I rather think he is coming to consult me professionally. I think that I recognize the symptoms. Ha! Did I not tell you?"As he spoke, the man, puffing and blowing, rushed at our door and pulled at our bell until the whole house resounded with the clanging.

A few moments later he was in our room, still puffing, still gesticulating, but with so fixed a look of grief and despair in his eyes that our smiles were turned in an instant to horror and pity. For a while he could not get his words out, but swayed his body and plucked at his hair like one who has been driven to the extreme limits of his reason. Then, suddenly springing to his feet, he beat his head against the wall with such force that we both rushed upon him and tore him away to the centre of the room. Sherlock Holmes pushed him down into the easy chair and, sitting beside him, patted his hand and chatted with him in the easy, soothing tones which he knew so well how to employ.

"You have come to me to tell your story, have you not?" said he. "You are fatigued with your haste. Pray wait until you have recovered yourself, and then I shall be most happy to look into any little problem which you may submit to me." The man sat for a minute or more with a heaving chest, fighting against his emotion. Then he passed his handkerchief over his brow, set his lips tight, and turned his face towards us.

"No doubt you think me mad?" said he.

"I see that you have had some great trouble," responded Holmes.

"God knows I have! A trouble which is enough to unseat my reason, so sudden and so terrible is it. Public disgrace I might have faced, although I am a man whose character has never yet borne a stain. Private affliction also is the lot of every man; but the two coming together, and in so frightful a form, have been enough to shake my very soul. Besides, it is not I alone. The very noblest in the land may suffer unless some way be found out of this horrible affair."

"Pray compose yourself, sir," said Holmes, "and let me have a clear account of who you are and what it is that has befallen you."

"My name," answered our visitor, "is probably familiar to your ears. I am Alexander Holder, of the banking firm of Holder & Stevenson, of Threadneedle Street." The name was indeed well known to us as belonging to the senior partner in the second largest private banking concern in the City of London. What could have happened, then, to bring one of the foremost citizens of London to this most pitiable pass? We waited, all curiosity, until with another effort he braced himself to tell his story.

"I feel that time is of value," said he. "That is why I hastened here when the police inspector suggested that I should secure your cooperation. I came to Baker Street by the Underground and hurried from there on foot, for the cabs go slowly through this snow. That is why I was so out of breath, for I am a man who takes very little exercise. I feel better now, and I will put the facts before you as shortly and yet as clearly as I can.

"It is, of course, well known to you that in a successful banking business as much depends upon our being able to find remunerative investments for our funds as upon our increasing our connection and the number of our depositors. One of our most lucrative means of laying out money is in the shape of loans, where the security is unimpeachable. We have done a good deal in this direction during the last few years, and there are many noble families to whom we have advanced large sums upon the security of their pictures, libraries, or plate.

"Yesterday morning I was seated in my office at the bank when a card was brought in to me by one of the clerks. I started when I saw the name, for it was that of none other than—well, perhaps even to you I had better say no more than that it was a name which is a household word all over the earth—one of the highest, noblest, most exalted names in England. I was overwhelmed by the honor and attempted, when he entered, to say so, but he plunged at once into business with the air of a man who wishes to hurry quickly through a disagreeable task.

"Mr. Holder," said he, "I have been informed that you are in the habit of advancing money."

"The firm does so when the security is good." I answered.

"It is absolutely essential to me," said he, "that I should have fifty thousand pounds at once. I could, of course, borrow so trifling a sum ten times over from my friends, but I much prefer to make it a matter of business and to carry out that business myself. In my position you can readily understand that it is unwise to place one's self under obligations."

"For how long, may I ask, do you want this sum?" I asked.

"Next Monday I have a large sum due to me, and I shall then most certainly repay what you advance, with whatever interest you think it right to charge. But it is very essential to me that the money should be paid at once."

"I should be happy to advance it without further parley from my own private purse," said I, "were it not that the strain would be rather more than it could bear. If, on the other hand, I am to do it in the name of the firm, then in justice to my partner I must insist that, even in your case, every businesslike precaution should be taken."

"I should much prefer to have it so," said he, raising up a square, black morocco case which he had laid beside his chair. "You have doubtless heard of the Beryl Coronet?"

"One of the most precious public possessions of the Empire," said I.

"Precisely." He opened the case, and there, imbedded in soft, flesh-colored velvet, lay the magnificent piece of jewelry which he had named. "There are thirty-nine enormous beryls," said he, "and the price of the gold chasing is incalculable. The lowest estimate would put the worth of the coronet at double the sum which I have asked. I am prepared to leave it with you as my security."

"I took the precious case into my hands and looked in some perplexity from it to my illustrious client."

"You doubt its value?" he asked.

"Not at all. I only doubt—"

"The propriety of my leaving it. You may set your mind at rest about that. I should not dream of doing so were it not absolutely certain that I should be able in four days to reclaim it. It is a pure matter of form. Is the security sufficient?"

"Ample."

"You understand, Mr. Holder, that I am giving you a strong proof of the confidence which I have in you, founded upon all that I have heard of you. I rely upon you not only to be discreet and to refrain from all gossip upon the matter but, above all, to preserve this coronet with every possible precaution because I need not say that a great public scandal would be caused if any harm were to befall it. Any injury to it would be almost as serious as its complete loss, for there are no beryls in the world to match these, and it would be impossible to replace them. I leave it with you, however, with every confidence, and I shall call for it in person on Monday morning."

"Seeing that my client was anxious to leave, I said no more but, calling for my cashier, I ordered him to pay over fifty one-thousand-pound notes. When I was alone once more, however, with the precious case lying upon the table in front of me, I could not but think with some misgivings of the immense responsibility which it entailed upon me. There could be no doubt that, as it was a national possession, a horrible scandal would ensue if any misfortune should occur to it. I already regretted having ever consented to take charge of it. However, it was too late to alter the matter now, so I locked it up in my private safe and turned once more to my work.

"When evening came I felt that it would be an imprudence to leave so precious a thing in the office behind me. Bankers' safes had been forced before now, and why should not mine be? If so, how terrible would be the position in which I should find myself! I determined, therefore, that for the next few days I would always carry the case backward and forward with me, so that it might never be really out of my reach. With this intention, I called a cab and drove out to my house at Streatham, carrying the jewel with me. I did not breathe freely until I had taken it upstairs and locked it in the bureau of my dressing-room.

"And now a word as to my household, Mr. Holmes, for I wish you to thoroughly understand the situation. My groom and my page sleep out of the house, and may be set aside altogether. I have three maid-servants who have been with me a number of years and whose absolute reliability is quite above suspicion. Another, Lucy Parr, the second waiting-maid, has only been in my service a few months. She came with an excellent character, however, and has always given me satisfaction. She is a very pretty girl and has attracted admirers who have occasionally hung about the place. That is the only drawback which we have found to her, but we believe her to be a thoroughly good girl in every way.

"So much for the servants. My family itself is so small that it will not take me long to describe it. I am a widower and have an only son, Arthur. He has been a disappointment to me, Mr. Holmes—a grievous disappointment. I have no doubt that I am myself to blame. People tell me that I have spoiled him. Very likely I have. When my dear wife died I felt that he was all I had to love. I could not bear to see the smile fade even for a moment from his face. I have never denied him a wish. Perhaps it would have been better for both of us had I been sterner, but I meant it for the best.

"It was naturally my intention that he should succeed me in my business, but he was not of a business turn. He was wild, wayward, and, to speak the truth, I could not trust him in the handling of large sums of money. When he was young he became a member of an aristocratic club, and there, having charming manners, he was soon the intimate of a number of men with long purses and expensive habits. He learned to play heavily at cards and to squander money on the turf, until he had again and again to come to me and implore me to give him an advance upon his allowance, that he might settle his debts of honor. He tried more than once to break away from the dangerous company which he was keeping, but each time the influence of his friend, Sir George Burnwell, was enough to draw him back again.

"And, indeed, I could not wonder that such a man as Sir George Burnwell should gain an influence over him, for he has frequently brought him to my house, and I have found myself that I could hardly resist the fascination of his manner. He is older than Arthur, a man of the world to his fingertips, one who had been everywhere, seen everything, a brilliant talker, and a man of great personal beauty. Yet when I think of him in cold blood, far away from the glamor of his presence, I am convinced from his cynical speech and the look which I have caught in his eyes that he is one who should be deeply distrusted. So I think, and so, too, thinks my little Mary, who has a woman's quick insight into character.

"And now there is only she to be described. She is my niece; but when my brother died five years ago and left her alone in the world I adopted her, and have looked upon her ever since as my daughter. She is a sunbeam in my house—sweet, loving, beautiful, a wonderful manager and housekeeper, yet as tender and quiet and gentle as a woman could be. She is my right hand. I do not know what I could do without her. In only one matter has she ever gone against my wishes. Twice my boy has asked her to marry him, for he loves her devotedly, but each time she has refused him. I think that if anyone could have drawn him into the right path it would have been she, and that his marriage might have changed his whole life; but now, alas! it is too late—forever too late!

"Now, Mr. Holmes, you know the people who live under my roof, and I shall continue with my miserable story.

"When we were taking coffee in the drawing-room that night after dinner, I told Arthur and Mary my experience, and of the precious treasure which we had under our roof, suppressing only the name of my client. Lucy Parr, who had brought in the coffee, had, I am sure, left the room; but I cannot swear that the door was closed.

Mary and Arthur were much interested and wished to see the famous coronet, but I thought it better not to disturb it."

" 'Where have you put it?' asked Arthur.

" 'In my own bureau.'

" 'Well, I hope to goodness the house won't be burgled during the night,' said he.

" 'It is locked up,' I answered.

" 'Oh, any old key will fit that bureau. When I was a youngster I have opened it myself with the key of the box-room cupboard.'

"He often had a wild way of talking, so that I thought little of what he said. He followed me to my room, however, that night with a very grave face.

" 'Look here, Dad,' said he with his eyes cast down. 'Can you let me have two hundred pounds?'

" 'No, I cannot!' I answered sharply. 'I have been far too generous with you in money matters.'

" 'You have been very kind,' said he, 'but I must have this money, or else I can never show my face inside the club again.'

" 'And a very good thing, too!' I cried.

" 'Yes, but you would not have me leave it a dishonored man,' said he. 'I could not bear the disgrace. I must raise the money in some way, and if you will not let me have it, then I must try other means.'

"I was very angry, for this was the third demand during the month. 'You shall not have a farthing from me,' I cried, on which he bowed and left the room without another word.

"When he was gone I unlocked my bureau, made sure that my treasure was safe, and locked it again. Then I started to go round the house to see that all was secure—a duty which I usually leave to Mary but which I thought it well to perform myself that night. As I came down the stairs I saw Mary herself at the side window of the hall, which she closed and fastened as I approached.

" 'Tell me, Dad,' said she, looking, I thought, a little disturbed, 'did you give Lucy, the maid, leave to go out tonight?'

" 'Certainly not.'

" 'She came in just now by the back door. I have no doubt that she has only been to the side gate to see someone, but I think that it is hardly safe and should be stopped.'

" 'You must speak to her in the morning, or I will if you prefer it. Are you sure that everything is fastened?'

" 'Quite sure, Dad.'

" 'Then, good night.' I kissed her and went up to my bedroom again, where I was soon asleep.

"I am endeavoring to tell you everything, Mr. Holmes, which may have any bearing upon the case, but I beg that you will question me upon any point which I do not make clear."

"On the contrary, your statement is singularly lucid."

"I come to a part of my story now in which I should wish to be particularly so. I am not a very heavy sleeper, and the anxiety in my mind tended, no doubt, to make me even less so than usual. About two in the morning. Then, I was awakened by some sound in the house. It had ceased ere I was wide awake, but it had left an impression behind it as though a window had gently closed somewhere. I lay listening with all my ears. Suddenly, to my horror, there was a distinct sound of footsteps moving softly in the next room. I slipped out of bed, all palpitating with fear, and peeped round the corner of my dressing-room door.

" 'Arthur!' I screamed, 'You villain! You thief! How dare you touch that coronet?'

"The gas was half up, as I had left it, and my unhappy boy, dressed only in his shirt and trousers, was standing beside the light, holding the coronet in his hands. He appeared to be wrenching at it, or bending it with all his strength. At my cry he dropped it from his grasp and turned as pale as death. I snatched it up and examined it. One of the gold corners, with three of the beryls in it, was missing.

" 'You blackguard!' I shouted, beside myself with rage. 'You have destroyed it! You have dishonored me forever! Where are the jewels which you have stolen?'

" 'Stolen!' he cried.

" 'Yes, thief!' I roared, shaking him by the shoulder.

" 'There are none missing. There cannot be any missing,' said he.

" 'There are three missing. And you know where they are. Must I call you a liar as well as a thief? Did I not see you trying to tear off another piece?'

" 'You have called me names enough,' said he, 'I will not stand it any longer. I shall not say another word about this business, since you have chosen to insult me. I will leave your house in the morning and make my own way in the world.'

" 'You shall leave it in the hands of the police!' I cried, half-mad with grief and rage. 'I shall have this matter probed to the bottom.'

" 'You shall learn nothing from me,' said he with a passion such as I should not have thought was in his nature. 'If you choose to call the police, let the police find what they can.'

"By this time the whole house was astir, for I had raised my voice in my anger. Mary was the first to rush into my room, and, at the sight of the coronet and of Arthur's face, she read the whole story and, with a scream, fell down senseless on the ground. I sent the house-maid for the police and put the investigation into their hands at once. When the inspector and a constable entered the house, Arthur, who had stood sullenly with his arms folded, asked me whether it was my intention to charge him with theft. I answered that it had ceased to be a private matter, but had become a public one, since the ruined coronet was national property. I was determined that the law should have its way in everything.

" 'At least,' said he, 'you will not have me arrested at once. It would be to your advantage as well as mine if I might leave the house for five minutes.'

" 'That you may get away, or perhaps that you may conceal what you have stolen,' said I. And then, realizing the dreadful position in which I was placed, I implored him to remember that not only my honor but that of one who was far greater than I was at stake; and that he threatened to raise a scandal which would convulse the nation. He might avert it all if he would but tell me what he had done with the three missing stones.

" 'You may as well face the matter,' said I. 'You have been caught in the act, and no confession could make your guilt more heinous. If you but make such reparation as is in your power, by telling us where the beryls are, all shall be forgiven and forgotten.'

" 'Keep your forgiveness for those who ask for it,' he answered, turning away from me with a sneer. I saw that he was too hardened for any words of mine to influence him. There was but one way for it. I called in the inspector and gave him into custody. A search was made at once not only of his person but of his room and of every portion of the house where he could possibly have concealed the gems; but no trace of them could be found, nor would the wretched boy open his mouth for all our persuasions and our threats. This morning he was removed to a cell, and I, after going through all the police formalities, have hurried round to you to implore you to use your skill in unravelling the matter. The police have openly confessed that they can at present make nothing of it. You may go to any expense which you think necessary. I have already offered a reward of one thousand pounds. My God, what shall I do! I have lost my honor, my gems, and my son in one night. Oh, what shall I do!"

He put a hand on either side of his head and rocked himself to and fro, droning to himself like a child whose grief has got beyond words.

Sherlock Holmes sat silent for some few minutes. With his brows knitted and his eyes fixed upon the fire.

"Do you receive much company?" he asked.

"None save my partner with his family and an occasional friend of Arthur's. Sir George Burnwell has been several times lately. No one else, I think."

"Do you go out much in society?"

"Arthur does. Mary and I stay at home. We neither of us care for it."

"That is unusual in a young girl."

"She is of a quiet nature. Besides, she is not so very young. She is four-and-twenty."

"This matter, from what you say, seems to have been a shock to her also."

"Terrible! She is even more affected than I."

"You have neither of you any doubt as to your son's guilt?"

"How can we have when I saw him with my own eyes with the coronet in his hands."

"I hardly consider that a conclusive proof. Was the remainder of the coronet at all injured?"

"Yes, it was twisted."

"Do you not think, then, that he might have been trying to straighten it?"

"God bless you! You are doing what you can for him and for me. But it is too heavy a task. What was he doing there at all? If his purpose were innocent, why did he not say so?"

"Precisely. And if it were guilty, why did he not invent a lie? His silence appears to me to cut both ways. There are several singular points about the case. What did the police think of the noise which awoke you from your sleep?"

"They considered that it might be caused by Arthur's closing his bedroom door."

"A likely story! As if a man bent on felony would slam his door so as to wake a household. What did they say, then, of the disappearance of these gems?"

"They are still sounding the planking and probing the furniture in the hope of finding them."

"Have they thought of looking outside the house?"

"Yes, they have shown extraordinary energy. The whole garden has already been minutely examined."

"Now, my dear sir," said Holmes. "Is it not obvious to you now that this matter really strikes very much deeper than either you or the police were at first inclined to think? It appeared to you to be a simple case; to me it seems exceedingly complex. Consider what is involved by your theory. You suppose that your son came down from his bed, went at great risk, to your dressing-room, opened your bureau, took out your coronet, broke off by main force a small portion of it, went off to some other place, concealed three gems out of the thirty-nine with such skill that nobody can find them, and then returned with the other thirty-six into the room in which he exposed himself to the greatest danger of being discovered. I ask you now, is such a theory tenable?"

"But what other is there?" cried the banker with a gesture of despair. "If his motives were innocent, why does he not explain them?"

"It is our task to find that out," replied Holmes. "So now, if you please, Mr. Holder, we will set off for Streatham together, and devote an hour to glancing a little more closely into details." My friend insisted upon my accompanying them in their expedition, which I was eager enough to do, for my curiosity and sympathy were deeply stirred by the story to which we had listened. I confess that the guilt of the banker's son appeared to me to be as obvious as it did to his unhappy father, but still I had such faith in Holmes's judgment that I felt that there must be some grounds for hope as long as he was dissatisfied with the accepted explanation. He hardly spoke a word the whole way out to the southern suburb, but sat with his chin upon his breast and his hat drawn over his eyes, sunk in the deepest thought. Our client appeared to have taken fresh heart at the little glimpse of hope which had been presented to him, and he even broke into a desultory chat with me over his business affairs. A short railway journey and a shorter walk brought us to Fairbank, the modest residence of the great financier.

Fairbank was a good-size square house of white stone, standing back a little from the road. A double carriage-sweep, with a snow-clad lawn, stretched down in front to two large iron gates which closed the entrance. On the right side was a small wooden thicket, which led into a narrow path between two neat hedges stretching from the road to the kitchen door, and forming the tradesmen's entrance. On the left ran a lane which led to the stables, and was not itself within the grounds at all, being a public, though little used, thoroughfare. Holmes left us standing at the door and walked slowly all round the house, across the front, down the tradesmen's path, and so round by the garden behind into the stable lane. So long was he that Mr. Holder and I went into the dining-room and waited by the fire until he should return. We were sitting there in silence when the door opened and a young lady came in. She was rather above the middle height, slim, with dark hair and eyes, which seemed the darker against the absolute pallor of her skin. I do not think that I have ever seen such deadly paleness in a woman's face. Her lips, too, were bloodless, but her eyes were flushed with crying. As she swept silently into the room, she impressed me with a greater sense of grief than the banker had done in the morning, and it was the more striking in her as she was evidently a woman of strong character, with immense capacity for self-restraint. Disregarding my presence, she went straight to her uncle and passed her hand over his head with a sweet womanly caress.

"You have given orders that Arthur should be liberated, have you not, Dad?" she asked.

"No, no, my girl, the matter must be probed to the bottom."

"But I am so sure that he is innocent. You know what woman's instincts are. I know that he has done no harm and that you will be sorry for having acted so harshly."

"Why is he silent, then, if he is innocent?"

"Who knows? Perhaps because he was so angry that you should suspect him."

"How could I help suspecting him, when I actually saw him with the coronet in his hand?"

"Oh, but he had only picked it up to look at it. Oh, do, do take my word for it that he is innocent. Let the matter drop and say no more. It is so dreadful to think of our dear Arthur in prison!"

"I shall never let it drop until the gems are found—never, Mary! Your affection for Arthur blinds you as to the awful consequences to me. Far from hushing the thing up, I have brought a gentleman down from London to inquire more deeply into it."

"This gentleman?" she asked, facing round to me.

"No, his friend. He wished us to leave him alone. He is round in the stable lane now."

"The stable lane?" She raised her dark eyebrows. "What can he hope to find there? Ah! this, I suppose, is he. I trust, sir, that you will succeed in proving, what I feel sure is the truth, that my cousin Arthur is innocent of this crime."

"I fully share your opinion, and I trust, with you, that we may prove it," returned Holmes, going back to the mat to knock the snow from his shoes. "I believe I have the honor of addressing Miss Mary Holder. Might I ask you a question or two?"

"Pray do, sir, if it may help to clear this horrible affair up."

"You heard nothing yourself last night?"

"Nothing, until my uncle here began to speak loudly. I heard that, and I came down."

"You shut up the windows and doors the night before. Did you fasten all the windows?"

"Yes."

"Were they all fastened this morning?"

"Yes."

"You have a maid who has a sweetheart? I think that you remarked to your uncle last night that she had been out to see him?"

"Yes, and she was the girl who waited in the drawing-room and who may have heard uncle's remarks about the coronet."

"I see. You infer that she may have gone out to tell her sweetheart, and that the two may have planned the robbery."

"But what is the good of all these vague theories," cried the banker impatiently, "when I have told you that I saw Arthur with the coronet in his hands?"

"Wait a little, Mr. Holder. We must come back to that. About this girl, Miss Holder. You saw her return by the kitchen door, I presume?"

"Yes. When I went to see if the door was fastened for the night I met her slipping in. I saw the man, too, in the gloom."

"Do you know him?"

"Oh, yes! He is the green-grocer who brings our vegetables round. His name is Francis Prosper."

"He stood," said Holmes, "to the left of the door—that is to say, farther up the path than is necessary to reach the door?"

"Yes, he did."

"And he is a man with a wooden leg?" Something like fear sprang up in the young lady's expressive black eyes. "Why, you are like a magician," said she. "How do you know that?" She smiled, but there was no answering smile in Holmes's thin, eager face.

"I should be very glad now to go upstairs," said he. "I shall probably wish to go over the outside of the house again. Perhaps I had better take a look at the lower windows before I go up." He walked swiftly round from one to the other, pausing only at the large one which looked from the hall onto the stable lane. This he opened and made a very careful examination of the sill with his powerful magnifying lens. "Now we shall go upstairs," said he at last. The banker's dressing-room was a plainly furnished little chamber, with a gray carpet, a large bureau, and a long mirror. Holmes went to the bureau first and looked hard at the lock.

"Which key was used to open it?" he asked.

"That which my son himself indicated—that of the cupboard of the lumber-room."

"Have you it here?"

"That is it on the dressing-table." Sherlock Holmes took it up and opened the bureau.

"It is a noiseless lock," said he. "It is no wonder that it did not wake you. This case, I presume, contains the coronet. We must have a look at it." He opened the case, and taking out the diadem he laid it upon the table. It was a magnificent specimen of the jeweler's art, and the thirty-six stones were the finest that I have ever seen. At one side of the coronet was a cracked edge, where a corner holding three gems had been torn away.

"Now, Mr. Holder," said Holmes, "here is the corner which corresponds to that which has been so unfortunately lost. Might I beg that you will break it off." The banker recoiled in horror.

"I should not dream of trying," said he.

"Then I will." Holmes suddenly bent his strength upon it, but without result. "I feel it give a little," said he, "but, though I am exceptionally strong in the fingers, it would take me all my time to break it. An ordinary man could not do it. Now, what do you think would happen if I did break it, Mr. Holder? There would be a noise like a pistol shot. Do you tell me that all this happened within a few yards of your bed and that you heard nothing of it?"

"I do not know what to think. It is all dark to me."

"But perhaps it may grow lighter as we go. What do you think, Miss Holder?"

"I confess that I still share my uncle's perplexity."

"Your son had no shoes or slippers on when you saw him?"

"He had nothing on save only his trousers and shirt."

"Thank you. We have certainly been favored with extraordinary luck during this inquiry, and it will be entirely our own fault if we do not succeed in clearing the matter up. With your permission, Mr. Holder, I shall now continue my investigations outside."

He went alone, at his own request, for he explained that any unnecessary footmarks might make his task more difficult. For an hour or more he was at work, returning at last with his feet heavy with snow and his features as inscrutable as ever.

"I think that I have seen now all that there is to see, Mr. Holder," said he. "I can serve you best by returning to my rooms."

"But the gems, Mr. Holmes. Where are they?"

"I cannot tell."

The banker wrung his hands. "I shall never see them again!" he cried. "And my son? You give me hopes?"

"My opinion is in no way altered."

"Then, for God's sake, what was this dark business which was acted in my house last night?"

"If you can call upon me at my Baker Street rooms tomorrow morning between nine and ten I shall be happy to do what I can to make it clearer. I understand that you give me *carte blanche* to act for you, provided only that I get back the gems, and that you place no limit on the sum I may draw."

"I would give my fortune to have them back."

"Very good. I shall look into the matter between this and then. Good-bye; it is just possible that I may have to come over here again before evening."

It was obvious to me that my companion's mind was now made up about the case, although what his conclusions were was more than I could even dimly imagine. Several times during our homeward journey I endeavored to sound him upon the point, but he always glided away to some other topic, until at last I gave it over in despair. It was not yet three when we found ourselves in our rooms once more. He hurried to his chamber and was down again in a few minutes dressed as a common loafer. With his collar turned up, his shiny, seedy coat, his red cravat, and his worn boots, he was a perfect sample of the class.

"I think that this should do," said he, glancing into the glass above the fireplace. "I only wish that you could come with me, Watson, but I fear that it won't do. I may be on the trail in this matter, or I may be following a will-o'-the-wisp, but I shall soon know which it is. I hope that I may be back in a few hours." He cut a slice of beef from the joint upon the sideboard, sandwiched it between two rounds of bread, and thrusting this rude meal into his pocket he started off upon his expedition. I had just finished my tea when he returned, evidently in excellent spirits, swinging an old elastic-sided boot in his hand. He chucked it down into a corner and helped himself to a cup of tea.

"I only looked in as I passed," said he. "I am going right on."

"Where to?"

"Oh, to the other side of the West End. It may be some time before I get back. Don't wait up for me in case I should be late."

"How are you getting on?"

"Oh, so so. Nothing to complain of. I have been out to Streatham since I saw you last, but I did not call at the house. It is a very sweet little problem, and I would not have missed it for a good deal. However, I must not sit gossiping here, but must get these disreputable clothes off and return to my highly respectable self."

I could see by his manner that he had stronger reasons for satisfaction than his words alone would imply. His eyes twinkled, and there was even a touch of color upon his sallow cheeks. He hastened upstairs, and a few minutes later I heard the slam of the hall door, which told me that he was off once more upon his congenial hunt.

I waited until midnight, but there was no sign of his return, so I retired to my room. It was no uncommon thing for him to be away for days and nights on end when he was hot upon a scent, so that his lateness caused me no surprise. I do not know at what hour he came in, but when I came down to breakfast in the morning there he was with a cup of coffee in one hand and the paper in the other, as fresh and trim as possible.

"You will excuse my beginning without you, Watson," said he, "but you remember that our client has rather an early appointment this morning."

"Why, it is after nine now," I answered. "I should not be surprised if that were he. I thought I heard a ring."

It was, indeed, our friend the financier. I was shocked by the change which had come over him, for his face which was naturally of a broad and massive mould, was now pinched and fallen in, while his hair seemed to me at least a shade whiter. He entered with a weariness and lethargy which was even more painful than his violence of the morning before, and he dropped heavily into the armchair which I pushed forward for him.

"I do not know what I have done to be so severely tried," said he. "Only two days ago I was a happy and prosperous man, without a care in the world. Now I am left to a lonely and dishonored age. One sorrow comes close upon the heels of another. My niece, Mary, has deserted me."

"Deserted you?"

"Yes. Her bed this morning had not been slept in, her room was empty, and a note for me lay upon the hall table. I had said to her last night, in sorrow and not in anger, that if she had married my boy all might have been well with him. Perhaps it was thoughtless of me to say so. It is to that remark that she refers in this note:

> MY DEAREST UNCLE:
> I feel that I have brought trouble upon you, and that if I had acted differently this terrible misfortune might never have occurred. I cannot, with this thought in my mind, ever again be happy under your roof, and I feel that I must leave you forever. Do not worry about my future, for that is provided for; and, above all, do not search for me, for it will be fruitless labor and an ill-service to me. In life or in death, I am ever
> Your loving
> MARY

"What could she mean by that note, Mr. Holmes? Do you think it points to suicide?"

"No, no, nothing of the kind. It is perhaps the best possible solution. I trust, Mr. Holder, that you are nearing the end of your troubles."

"Ha! You say so! You have heard something, Mr. Holmes; you have learned something! Where are the gems?"

"You would not think a thousand pounds apiece an excessive sum for them?"

"I would pay ten."

"That would be unnecessary. Three thousand will cover the matter. And there is a little reward, I fancy. Have you your check-book? Here is a pen. Better make it out for four thousand pounds."

With a dazed face the banker made out the required check. Holmes walked over to his desk, took out a little triangular piece of gold with three gems in it, and threw it down upon the table. With a shriek of joy our client clutched it up.

"You have it!" he gasped. "I am saved! I am saved!" The reaction of joy was as passionate as his grief had been, and he hugged his recovered gems to his bosom.

"There is one other thing you owe, Mr. Holder," said Sherlock Holmes rather sternly.

"Owe!" He caught up a pen. "Name the sum, and I will pay it."

"No, the debt is not to me. You owe a very humble apology to that noble lad, your son, who has carried himself in this matter as I should be proud to see my own son do, should I ever chance to have one."

"Then it was not Arthur who took them?"

"I told you yesterday, and I repeat today, that it was not."

"You are sure of it! Then let us hurry to him at once to let him know that the truth is known."

"He knows it already. When I had cleared it all up I had an interview with him, and finding that he would not tell me the story, I told it to him, on which he had to confess that I was right and to add the very few details which were not yet quite clear to me. Your news of this morning, however, may open his lips."

"For heaven's sake, tell me, then, what is this extraordinary mystery?"

"I will do so, and I will show you the steps by which I reached it. And let me say to you, first, that which it is hardest for me to say and for you to hear: there has been an understanding between Sir George Burnwell and your niece Mary. They have now fled together."

"My Mary? Impossible!"

"It is unfortunately more than possible; it is certain. Neither you nor your son knew the true character of this man when you admitted him into your family circle. He is one of the most dangerous men in England—a ruined gambler, an absolutely desperate villain, a man without heart or conscience. Your niece knew nothing of such men. When he breathed his vows to her, as he had done to a hundred before her, she flattered herself that she alone had touched his heart. The devil knows best what he said, but at least she became his tool and was in the habit of seeing him nearly every evening."

"I cannot, and I will not, believe it!" cried the banker with an ashen face.

"I will tell you, then, what occurred in your house last night. Your niece, when you had, as she thought, gone to your room, slipped down and talked to her lover through the window which leads into the stable lane. His footmarks had pressed right through the snow, so long had he stood there. She told him of the coronet. His wicked lust for gold kindled at the news, and he bent her to his will. I have no doubt that she loved you, but there are women in whom the love of a lover extinguishes all other loves, and I think that she must have been one. She had hardly listened to his instructions when she saw you coming downstairs, on which she closed the window rapidly and told you about one of the servants' escapades with her wooden-legged lover, which was all perfectly true.

"Your boy, Arthur, went to bed after his interview with you but he slept badly on account of his uneasiness about his club debts. In the middle of the night he heard a soft tread pass his door, so he rose and, looking out, was surprised to see his cousin walking very stealthily along the passage until she disappeared into your dressing-room. Petrified with astonishment, the lad slipped on some clothes and waited there in the dark to see what would come of this strange affair. Presently she emerged from the room again, and in the light of the passage-lamp your son saw that she carried the precious coronet in her hands. She passed down the stairs, and he, thrilling with horror, ran along and slipped behind the curtain near your door, whence he could see what passed in the hall beneath. He saw her stealthily open the window, hand out the coronet to someone in the gloom, and then closing it once more hurry back to her room, passing quite close to where he stood hid behind the curtain.

"As long as she was on the scene he could not take any action without a horrible exposure of the woman whom he loved. But the instant that she was gone he realized how crushing a misfortune this would be for you, and how all-important it was to set it right. He rushed down, just as he was, in his bare feet, opened the window, sprang out into the snow, and ran down the lane, where he could see a dark figure in the moonlight. Sir George Burnwell tried to get away, but Arthur caught him, and there was a struggle between them, your lad tugging at one side of the coronet, and his opponent at the other. In the scuffle, your son struck Sir George and cut him over the eye. Then something suddenly snapped, and your son, finding that he had the coronet in his hands, rushed back, closed the window, ascended to your room, and had just observed that the coronet had been twisted in the struggle and was endeavoring to straighten it when you appeared upon the scene."

"Is it possible?" gasped the banker.

"You then roused his anger by calling him names at a moment when he felt that he had deserved your warmest thanks. He could not explain the true state of affairs without betraying one who certainly deserved little enough consideration at his hands. He took the more chivalrous view, however, and preserved her secret."

"And that was why she shrieked and fainted when she saw the coronet," cried Mr. Holder. "Oh, my God! What a blind fool I have been! And his asking to be allowed to go out for five minutes! The dear fellow wanted to see if the missing piece was at the scene of the struggle. How cruelly I have misjudged him!"

"When I arrived at the house," continued Holmes, "I at once went very carefully round it to observe if there were any traces in the snow which might help me. I knew that none had fallen since the evening before, and also that there had been a strong frost to preserve impressions. I passed along the tradesmen's path, but found it all trampled down and indistinguishable. Just beyond it, however, at the far side of the kitchen door, a woman had stood and talked with a man, whose round impressions on one side showed that he had a wooden leg. I could even tell that they had been disturbed, for the woman had run back swiftly to the door, as was shown by the deep toe and light heel marks, while Wooden-leg had waited a little, and then had gone away. I thought at the time that this might be the maid and her sweetheart, of whom you had already spoken to me, and inquiry showed it was so. I passed round the garden without seeing anything more than random tracks, which I took to be the police; but when I got into the stable lane a very long and complex story was written in the snow in front of me.

"There was a double line of tracks of a booted man, and a second double line which I saw with delight belonged to a man with naked feet. I was at once convinced from what you had told me that the latter was your son. The first had walked both ways, but the other had run swiftly, and as his tread was marked in places over the depression of the boot, it was obvious that he had passed after the other. I followed them up and found they led to the hall window, where Boots had worn all the snow away while waiting. Then I walked to the other end, which was a hundred yards or more down the lane. I saw where Boots had faced round, where the snow was cut up as though there had been a struggle, and, finally, where a few drops of blood had fallen, to show me that I was not mistaken. Boots had then run down the lane, and another little smudge of blood showed that it was he who had been hurt. When he came to the highroad at the other end, I found that the pavement had been cleared, so there was an end to that clue.

"On entering the house, however, I examined, as you remember, the sill and framework of the hall window with my lens, and I could at once see that someone had passed out. I could distinguish the outline of an instep where the wet foot had been placed in coming in. I was then beginning to be able to form an opinion as to what had occurred. A man had waited outside the window; someone had brought the gems; the deed had been overseen by your son; he had pursued the thief; had struggled with him; they had each tugged at the coronet, their united strength causing injuries which neither alone could have effected. He had returned with the prize, but had left a fragment in the grasp of his opponent. So far I was clear. The question now was, who was the man and who was it brought him the coronet?

"It is an old maxim of mine that when you have excluded the impossible, whatever remains, however improbable, must be the truth. Now, I knew that it was not you who had brought it down, so there only remained your niece and the maids. But if it were the maids, why should your son allow himself to be accused in their place? There could be no possible reason. As he loved his cousin, however, there was an excellent explanation why he should retain her secret—the more so as the secret was a disgraceful one. When I remembered that you had seen her at that window, and how she had fainted on seeing the coronet again, my conjecture became a certainty.

"And who could it be who was her confederate? A lover evidently, for who else could outweigh the love and gratitude which she must feel to you? I knew that you went out little, and that your circle of friends was a very limited one. But among them was Sir George Burnwell. I had heard of him before as being a man of evil reputation among women. It must have been he who wore those boots and retained the missing gems. Even though he knew that Arthur had discovered him, he might still flatter himself that he was safe, for the lad could not say a word without compromising his own family.

"Well, your own good sense will suggest what measures I took next. I went in the shape of a loafer to Sir George's house, managed to pick up an acquaintance with his valet, learned that his master had cut his head the night before, and, finally, at the expense of six shillings, made all sure by buying a pair of his cast-off shoes. With these I journeyed down to Streatham and saw that they exactly fitted the tracks."

"I saw an ill-dressed vagabond in the lane yesterday evening," said Mr. Holder.

"Precisely. It was I. I found that I had my man, so I came home and changed my clothes. It was a delicate part which I had to play then, for I saw that a prosecution must be avoided to avert scandal, and I knew that so astute a villain would see that our hands were tied in the matter. I went and saw him. At first, of course, he denied everything. But when I gave him every particular that had occurred, he tried to bluster and took down a life-preserver from the wall. I knew my man, however, and I clapped a pistol to his head before he could strike. Then he became a little more reasonable. I told him that we would give him a price for the stones he held—one thousand pounds apiece. That brought out the first signs of grief that he had shown. 'Why, dash it all!' said he, 'I've let them go at six hundred for the three!' I soon managed to get the address of the receiver who had them, on promising him that there would be no prosecution. Off I set to him, and after much chaffering I got our stones at one thousand pounds apiece. Then I looked in upon your son, told him that all was right, and eventually got to my bed about two o'clock, after what I may call a really hard day's work."

"A day which has saved England from a great public scandal," said the banker, rising. "Sir, I cannot find words to thank you, but you shall not find me ungrateful for what you have done. Your skill has indeed exceeded all that I have heard of it. And now I must fly to my dear boy to apologize to him for the wrong which I have done him. As to what you tell me of poor Mary, it goes to my very heart. Not even your skill can inform me where she is now."

"I think that we may safely say," returned Holmes, "that she is wherever Sir George Burnwell is. It is equally certain, too, that whatever her sins are, they will soon receive a more than sufficient punishment."

The Red Silk Scarf

Maurice Leblanc

French author, journalist and police reporter Maurice Leblanc created Arsène Lupin, the French gentleman thief turned detective, in 1907. First featured in Leblanc's novel *Arsène Lupin, Gentleman Cambrioleur,* Lupin was described as a master of disguise whose criminal activities have more or less "unselfish" grounds. Lupin amuses himself by keeping one step ahead of the police and, in particular, Inspector Ganimard from the Sûreté. Lupin's adventures have been captured in more than sixty novels and short stories. In films, John Barrymore in 1932 (*Arsène Lupin*) and Melvyn Douglas in 1938 (*Arsène Lupin Returns*) both starred as the dashing rogue detective.

On leaving his house one morning at his usual early hour for going to the Law Courts, Chief Inspector Ganimard noticed the curious behavior of an individual who was walking along the Rue Pergolèse in front of him. Shabbily dressed and wearing a straw hat, though the day was the first of December, the man stooped at every thirty or forty yards to fasten his bootlace, or pick up his stick or for some other reason. And, each time, he took a little piece of orange peel from his pocket and laid it stealthily on the curb of the pavement. It was probably a mere display of eccentricity, a childish amusement to which no one else would have paid attention; but Ganimard was one of those shrewd observers who are indifferent to nothing that strikes their eyes and who are never satisfied until they know the secret cause of things. He therefore began to follow the man.

Now, at the moment when the fellow was turning to the right, into the Avenue de la Grande-Armée, the inspector caught him exchanging signals with a boy of twelve or thirteen, who was walking along the houses on the left-hand side. Twenty yards farther, the man stooped and turned up the bottom of his trousers legs. A bit of orange peel marked the place. At the same moment, the boy stopped and, with a piece of chalk, drew a white cross, surrounded by a circle, on the wall of the house next to him.

The two continued on their way. A minute later, a fresh halt. The strange individual picked up a pin and dropped a piece of orange peel; and the boy at once made a second cross on the wall and again drew a white circle round it.

"By Jove!" thought the chief inspector, with a grunt of satisfaction. "This is rather promising. . . . What on earth can those two merchants be plotting?"

The two "merchants" went down the Avenue Friedland and the Rue du Faubourg-Saint-Honoré, but nothing occurred that was worthy of special mention. The double performance was repeated at almost regular intervals and, so to speak, mechanically. Nevertheless, it was obvious, on the one hand, that the man with the orange peel did not do his part of the business until after he had picked out with a glance the house that was to be marked and, on the other hand, that the boy did not mark that particular house until after he had observed his companion's signal. It was certain, therefore, that there was an agreement between the two; and the proceedings presented no small interest in the chief inspector's eyes.

At the Place Beauveau the man hesitated. Then, apparently making up his mind, he twice turned up and twice turned down the bottom of his trousers legs. Hereupon, the boy sat down on the curb, opposite the sentry who was mounting guard outside the Ministry of the Interior, and marked the flagstone with two little crosses contained within two circles. The same ceremony was gone through a little farther on, when they reached the Elysée. Only, on the pavement where the president's sentry was marching up and down, there were three signs instead of two.

"Hang it all!" muttered Ganimard, pale with excitement and thinking, in spite of himself, of his inveterate enemy, Lupin, whose name came to his mind wherever a mysterious circumstance presented itself. "Hang it all, what does it mean?"

He was nearly collaring and questioning the two "merchants." But he was too clever to commit so gross a blunder. The man with the orange peel had now lit a cigarette; and the boy, also placing a cigarette end between his lips, had gone up to him, apparently with the object of asking for a light.

They exchanged a few words. Quick as thought, the boy handed his companion an object which looked—at least, so the inspector believed—like a revolver. They both bent over this object; and the man, standing with his face to the wall, put his hand six times in his pocket and made a movement as though he were loading a weapon.

As soon as this was done, they walked briskly to the Rue de Surène; and the inspector, who followed them as closely as he was able to do without attracting their attention, saw them enter the gateway of an old house of which all the shutters were closed, with the exception of those on the third or top floor.

He hurried in after them. At the end of the carriage entrance he saw a large courtyard, with a house painter's sign at the back and a staircase on the left.

He went up the stairs and, as soon as he reached the first floor, ran still faster, because he heard, right up at the top, a din as of a free fight.

When he came to the last landing he found the door open. He entered, listened for a second, caught the sound of a struggle, rushed to the room from which the sound appeared to proceed and remained standing on the threshold, very much out of breath and greatly surprised to see the man of the orange peel and the boy banging the floor with chairs.

At that moment a third person walked out of an adjoining room. It was a young man of twenty-eight or thirty, wearing a pair of short whiskers in addition to his moustache, spectacles, and a smoking jacket with an astrakhan collar and looking like a foreigner, a Russian.

"Good morning, Ganimard," he said. And turning to the two companions, "Thank you, my friends, and all my congratulations on the successful result. Here's the reward I promised you."

He gave them a hundred-franc note, pushed them outside and shut both doors.

"I am sorry, old chap," he said to Ganimard. "I wanted to talk to you . . . wanted to talk to you badly."

He offered him his hand and, seeing that the inspector remained flabbergasted and that his face was still distorted with anger, he exclaimed:

"Why, you don't seem to understand! . . . And yet it's clear enough . . . I wanted to see you particularly. . . . So what could I do?" And, pretending to reply to an objection, "No, no, old chap," he continued. "You're quite wrong. If I had written or telephoned, you would not have come . . . or else you would have come with a regiment. Now I wanted to see you all alone; and I thought the best thing was to send those two decent fellows to meet you, with orders to scatter bits of orange peel and draw crosses and circles, in short, to mark out your road to this place. . . . Why, you look quite bewildered! What is it? Perhaps you don't recognize me? Lupin . . . Arsène Lupin. . . . Ransack your memory . . . Doesn't the name remind you of anything?"

"You dirty scoundrel!" Ganimard snarled between his teeth.

Lupin seemed greatly distressed and, in an affectionate voice:

"Are you vexed? Yes, I can see it in your eyes. . . . The Dugrival business, I suppose. I ought to have waited for you to come and take me in charge? . . . There now, the thought never occurred to me! I promise you, next time . . . "

"You scum of the earth!" growled Ganimard.

"And I thinking I was giving you a treat! Upon my word, I did. I said to myself, "That dear old Ganimard! We haven't met for an age. He'll simply rush at me when he sees me!"

Ganimard, who had not yet stirred a limb, seemed to be waking from his stupor. He looked around him, looked at Lupin, visibly asked himself whether he would not do well to rush at him in reality and then, controlling himself, took hold of a chair and settled himself in it, as though he had suddenly made up his mind to listen to his enemy:

"Speak," he said. "And don't waste my time with any nonsense. I'm in a hurry."

"That's it," said Lupin, "let's talk. You can't imagine a quieter place than this. It's an old manor house, which once stood in the open country, and it belongs to the Duc de Rochelaure. The duke, who has never lived in it, lets this floor to me and the outhouses to a painter and decorator. I always keep up a few establishments of this kind: it's a sound, practical plan. Here, in spite of my looking like a Russian nobleman, I am M. Daubreuil, an ex-cabinet-minister. . . . You understand, I had to select a rather overstocked profession, so as not to attract attention."

"Do you think I care a hang about all this?" said Ganimard, interrupting him.

"Quite right, I'm wasting words and you're in a hurry. Forgive me. I shan't be long now . . . five minutes, that's all. . . . I'll start at once. . . . Have a cigar? No? Very well, no more will I."

He sat down also, drummed his fingers on the table, while thinking, and began in this fashion:

"On the 17th of October, 1599, on a warm and sunny autumn day . . . do you follow me? . . . But, now that I come to think of it, is it really necessary to go back to the reign of Henry IV, and tell you all about the building of the Pont-Neuf? No, I don't suppose you are very well up in French history; and I should only end by muddling you. Suffice it, then, for you to know that, last night, at one o'clock in the morning, a boatman passing under the last arch of the Pont-Neuf aforesaid, along the left back of the river, heard something drop into the front part of his barge. The thing had been flung from the bridge and its evident destination was the bottom of the Seine. The bargee's dog rushed forward, barking, and, when the man reached the end of his craft, he saw the animal worrying a piece of newspaper that had served to wrap up a number of objects. He took from the dog such of the contents as had not fallen into the water, went to his cabin and examined them carefully. The result struck him as interesting; and, as the man is connected with one of my friends, he sent to let me know. This morning I was waked up and placed in possession of the facts and of the objects which the man had collected. Here they are."

He pointed to them, spread out on a table. There were, first of all, the torn pieces of a newspaper. Next came a large cut-glass inkstand, with a long piece of string fastened to the lid. There was a bit of broken glass and a sort of flexible cardboard, reduced to shreds. Lastly, there was a piece of bright scarlet silk, ending in a tassel of the same material and color.

"You see our exhibits, friend of my youth," said Lupin. "No doubt, the problem would be more easily solved if we had the other objects which went overboard owing to the stupidity of the dog. But it seems to me, all the same, that we ought to be able to manage, with a little reflection and intelligence. And those are just your great qualities. How does the business strike you?"

Ganimard did not move a muscle. He was willing to stand Lupin's chaff, but his dignity commanded him not to speak a single word in answer nor even to give a nod or shake of the head that might have been taken to express approval or criticism.

"I see that we are entirely of one mind," continued Lupin, without appearing to remark the chief inspector's silence. "And I can sum up the matter briefly, as told us by these exhibits. Yesterday evening, between nine and twelve o'clock, a showily dressed young woman was wounded with a knife and then caught round the throat and choked to death by a well-dressed gentleman, wearing a single eyeglass and interested in racing, with whom the aforesaid showily dressed young lady had been eating three meringues and a coffee éclair."

Lupin lit a cigarette and, taking Ganimard by the sleeve:

"Aha, that's up against you, Chief Inspector! You thought that, in the domain of police deductions, such feats as those were prohibited to outsiders! Wrong, sir! Lupin juggles with inferences and deductions for all the world like a detective in a novel. My proofs are dazzling and absolutely simple."

And, pointing to the objects one by one, as he demonstrated his statement, he resumed:

"I said, after nine o'clock yesterday evening. This scrap of newspaper bears yesterday's date, with the words, "Evening edition." Also, you will see here, pasted to the paper, a bit of one of those yellow wrappers in which the subscribers' copies are sent out. These copies are always delivered by the nine o'clock post. Therefore, it was after nine o'clock. I said, a well-dressed man. Please observe that this tiny piece of glass had the round hole of a single eyeglass at one of the edges and that the single eyeglass is an essentially aristocratic article of wear. This well-dressed man walked into a pastry cook's shop. Here is the very thin cardboard, shaped like a box, and still showing a little of the cream of the meringues and éclairs which were packed in it in the usual way. Having got his parcel, the gentleman with the eyeglass joined a young person whose eccentricity in the matter of dress is pretty clearly indicated by this bright-red silk scarf. Having joined her, for some reason as yet unknown he first stabbed her with a knife and then strangled her with the help of this same scarf. Take your magnifying glass, Chief Inspector, and you will see, on the silk, stains of a darker red which are, here, the marks of a knife wiped on the scarf and, there, the marks of a hand, covered with blood, clutching the material. Having committed the murder, his next business is to leave no trace behind him. So he takes from his pocket, first, the newspaper to which he subscribes—a racing-paper, as you will see by glancing at the contents of this scrap; and you will have no difficulty in discovering the title—and, secondly, a cord, which, on inspection, turns out to be a length of whipcord. These two details prove—do they not?—that our man is interested in racing and that he himself rides. Next, he picks up the fragments of his eyeglass, the cord of which has been broken in the struggle. He takes a pair of scissors—observe the hacking of the scissors—and cuts off the stained part of the scarf, leaving the other end, no doubt, in his victim's clenched hands. He makes a ball of the confectioner's cardboard box. He also puts in certain things that would have betrayed him, such as the knife, which must have slipped into the Seine. He wraps everything in the newspaper, ties it with the cord and fastens this cut-glass inkstand to it, as a make-weight. Then he makes himself scarce. A little later, the parcel falls into the waterman's barge. And there you are. Oof, it's hot work! . . . What do you say to the story?"

He looked at Ganimard to see what impression his speech had produced on the inspector. Ganimard did not depart from his attitude of silence.

Lupin began to laugh:

"As a matter of fact, you're annoyed and surprised. But you're suspicious as well: 'Why should that confounded Lupin hand the business over to me,' say you, 'instead of keeping it for himself, hunting down the murderer and rifling his pockets, if there was a robbery?' The question is quite logical, of course. But—there is a 'But'—I have not time, you see, I am full up with work at the present moment: a burglary in London, another at Lausanne, an exchange of children at Marseilles, to say nothing of having to save a young girl who is at this moment shadowed by death. That's always the way: it never rains but it pours. So I said to myself, 'Suppose I handed the business over to my dear old Ganimard? Now that it is half-solved for him, he is quite capable of succeeding. And what a service I shall be doing him! How magnificently he will be able to distinguish himself!' No sooner said than done. At eight o'clock in the morning, I send the joker with the orange peel to meet you. You swallowed the bait; and you were here by nine, all on edge and eager for the fray."

Lupin rose from his chair. He went over to the inspector and, with his eyes in Ganimard's, said:

"That's all. You know now the whole story. Presently, you will know the victim: some ballet dancer, probably, some singer at a music hall. On the other hand, the chances are that the criminal lives near the Pont-Neuf, most likely on the left bank. Lastly, here are all the exhibits. I make you a present of them. Set to work. I shall only keep this end of the scarf. If ever you want to piece the scarf together, bring me the other end, the one which the police will find round the victim's neck. Bring it to me in four weeks from now to the day, that is to say, on the 29th of December, at ten o'clock in the morning. You can be sure of finding me here. And don't be afraid: this is all perfectly serious, friend of my youth; I swear it is. No humbug, honor bright. You can go straight ahead. Oh, by the way, when you arrest the fellow with the eyeglass, be a bit careful: he is left-handed! Good-bye, old dear, and good luck to you!"

Lupin spun round on his heel, went to the door, opened it and disappeared before Ganimard had even thought of taking a decision. The inspector rushed after him. But at once found that the handle of the door, by some trick of mechanism which he did not know, refused to turn. It took him ten minutes to unscrew the lock and ten minutes more to unscrew the lock of the hall door. By the time that he had scrambled down the three flights of stairs, Ganimard had given up all hope of catching Arsène Lupin.

Besides, he was not thinking of it. Lupin inspired him with a queer, complex feeling, made up of fear, hatred, involuntary admiration and also the vague instinct that he, Ganimard, in spite of all his efforts, in spite of the persistency of his endeavors, would never get the better of this particular adversary. He pursued him from a sense of duty and pride, but with the continual dread of being taken in by that formidable hoaxer and scouted and fooled in the face of a public that was always only too willing to laugh at the chief inspector's mishaps.

This business of the red scarf, in particular, struck him as most suspicious. It was interesting, certainly, in more ways than one, but so very improbable! And Lupin's explanation, apparently so logical, would never stand the test of a severe examination!

"No," said Ganimard, "this is all swank: a parcel of suppositions and guesswork based upon nothing at all. I'm not to be caught with chaff."

When he reached the headquarters of police, at 36 Quai des Orfèvres, he had quite made up his mind to treat the incident as though it had never happened.

He went up to the Criminal Investigation Department. Here, one of his fellow inspectors said:

"Seen the chief?"

"No."

"He was asking for you just now."

"Oh, was he?"

"Yes, you had better go after him."

"Where?"

"To the Rue de Berne. . . . There was a murder there last night."

"Oh! Who's the victim?"

"I don't know exactly . . . a music hall singer, I believe."

Ganimard simply muttered:—

"By Jove!"

Twenty minutes later he stepped out of the underground railway station and made for the Rue de Berne.

The victim, who was known in the theatrical world by her stage name of Jenny Saphir, occupied a small flat on the second floor of one of the houses. A policeman took the chief inspector upstairs and showed him the way, through two sitting rooms, to a bedroom, where he found the magistrates in charge of the inquiry, together with the divisional surgeon and M. Dudouis, the head of the detective service.

Ganimard started at the first glance which he gave into the room. He saw, lying on a sofa, the corpse of a young woman whose hands clutched a strip of red silk! One of the shoulders, which appeared above the low-cut bodice, bore the marks of two wounds surrounded with clotted blood. The distorted and almost blackened features still bore an expression of frenzied terror.

The divisional surgeon, who had just finished his examination, said:

"My first conclusions are very clear. The victim was twice stabbed with a dagger and afterward strangled. The immediate cause of death was asphyxia."

"By Jove!" thought Ganimard again. Remembering Lupin's words and the picture which he had drawn of the crime.

The examining magistrate objected:

"But the neck shows no discoloration."

"She may have been strangled with a napkin or a handkerchief," said the doctor.

"Most probably," said the chief detective, "with this silk scarf, which the victim was wearing and a piece of which remains, as though she had clung to it with her two hands to protect herself."

"But why does only that piece remain?" asked the magistrate. "What has become of the other?"

"The other may have been stained with blood and carried off by the murderer. You can plainly distinguish the hurried slashing of the scissors."

"By Jove!" said Ganimard, between his teeth, for the third time. "The brute of a Lupin saw everything without seeing a thing!"

"And what about the motive of the murder?" asked the magistrate. "The locks have been forced, the cupboards turned upside down. Have you anything to tell me, M. Dudouis?"

The chief of the detective service replied:

"I can at least suggest a supposition, derived from the statement made by the servant. The victim, who enjoyed a greater reputation on account of her looks than through her talent as a singer, went to Russia, two years ago, and brought back with her a magnificent sapphire, which she appears to have received from some person of importance at the court. Since then, she went by the name of Jenny Saphir and seems generally to have been very proud of the present, although, for prudence's sake, she never wore it. I daresay that we shall not be far out if we presume the theft of the sapphire to have been the cause of the crime."

"But did the maid know where the stone was?"

"No, nobody did. And the disorder of the room would tend to prove that the murderer did not know either."

"We will question the maid," said the examining magistrate.

M. Dudouis took the chief inspector aside and said:

"You're looking very old-fashioned, Ganimard. What's the matter? Do you suspect anything?"

"Nothing at all, Chief."

"That's a pity. We could do with a bit of showy work in the department. This is one of a number of crimes, all of the same class, of which we have failed to discover the perpetrator. This time we want the criminal . . . and quickly!"

"A difficult job, Chief."

"It's got to be done. Listen to me, Ganimard. According to what the maid says, Jenny Saphir led a very regular life. For a month past she was in the habit of frequently receiving visits, on her return from the music hall, that is to say, at about half past ten, from a man who would stay until midnight or so. 'He's a society man,' Jenny Saphir used to say, 'and he wants to marry me.' The society man took every precaution to avoid being seen, such as turning up his coat collar and lowering the brim of his hat when he passed the porter's box. And Jenny Saphir always made a point of sending away her maid, even before he came. This is the man who we have to find."

"Has he left no traces?"

"None at all. It is obvious that we have to deal with a very clever scoundrel, who prepared his crime beforehand and committed it with every possible chance of escaping unpunished. His arrest would be a great feather in our cap. I rely on you, Ganimard."

"Ah, you rely on me, Chief?" replied the inspector. "Well, we shall see . . . we shall see. . . . I don't say no. . . . Only . . . "

He seemed in a very nervous condition, and his agitation struck M. Dudouis.

"Only," continued Ganimard, "only I swear. . . . Do you hear, Chief? I swear . . ."

"What do you swear?"

"Nothing. . . . We shall see, Chief. . . . We shall see. . . ."

Ganimard did not finish his sentence until he was outside, alone. And he finished it aloud, stamping his foot, in the tone of the most violent anger:

"Only, I swear to Heaven that the arrest shall be effected by my own means, without my employing a single one of the clues with which that villain has supplied me. Ah, no! Ah, no!"

Railing against Lupin, furious at being mixed up in this business and resolved nevertheless, to get to the bottom of it, he wandered aimlessly about the streets. His brain was seething with irritation; and he tried to adjust his ideas a little and to discover, among the chaotic facts, some trifling detail, unperceived by all, unsuspected by Lupin himself, that might lead him to success.

He lunched hurriedly at a bar, resumed his stroll and suddenly stopped, petrified, astounded and confused. He was walking under the gateway of the very house in the Rue de Surène to which Lupin had enticed him a few hours earlier! A force stronger than his own will was drawing him there once more. The solution of the problem lay there. There and there alone were all the elements of the truth. Do and say what he would, Lupin's assertions were so precise, his calculations so accurate, that, worried to the innermost recesses of his being by so prodigious a display of perspicacity, he could not do other than take up the work at the point where his enemy had left it.

Abandoning all further resistance, he climbed the three flights of stairs. The door of the flat was open. No one had touched the exhibits. He put them in his pocket and walked away.

From that moment, he reasoned and acted, so to speak, mechanically, under the influence of the master whom he could not choose but obey.

Admitting that the unknown person who he was seeking lived in the neighborhood of the Pont-Neuf, it became necessary to discover, somewhere between that bridge and the Rue de Berne, the first-class confectioner's shop, open in the evenings, at which the cakes were bought. This did not take long to find. A pastry cook near the Gare Saint-Lazare showed him some little cardboard boxes, identical in material and shape with the one in Ganimard's possession. Moreover, one of the shop girls remembered having served, on the previous evening, a gentleman whose face was almost concealed in the collar of his fur coat, but whose eyeglass she had happened to notice.

"That's one clue checked," thought the inspector. "Our man wears an eyeglass."

He next collected the pieces of the racing paper and showed them to a news vender, who easily recognized the *Turf Illustré*. Ganimard at once went to the offices of the *Turf* and asked to see the list of subscribers. Going through the list, he jotted down the names and addresses of all those who lived anywhere near the Pont-Neuf and principally—because Lupin had said so—those on the left bank of the river.

He then went back to the Criminal Investigation Department, took half a dozen men and packed them off with the necessary instructions.

At seven o'clock in the evening, the last of these men returned and brought good news with him. A certain M. Prévailles, a subscriber to the *Turf*, occupied an entresol flat on the Quai des Augustins. On the previous evening, he left his place, wearing a fur coat, took his letters and his paper, the *Turf Illustré*, from the porter's wife, walked away and returned home at midnight. This M. Prévailles wore a single eyeglass. He was a regular race-goer and himself owned several hacks which he either rode himself or jobbed out.

The inquiry had taken so short a time and the results obtained were so exactly in accordance with Lupin's predictions that Ganimard felt quite overcome on hearing the detective's report. Once more he was measuring the prodigious extent of the resources at Lupin's disposal. Never in the course of his life—and Ganimard was already well advanced in years—had he come across such perspicacity, such a quick and far-seeing mind.

He went in search of M. Dudouis.

"Everything's ready, Chief. Have you a warrant?"

"Eh?"

"I said, everything is ready for the arrest, Chief."

"You know the name of Jenny Saphir's murderer?"

"Yes."

"But how? Explain yourself."

Ganimard had a sort of scruple of conscience, blushed a little and nevertheless replied:

"An accident, Chief. The murderer threw everything that was likely to compromise him into the Seine. Part of the parcel was picked up and handed to me."

"By whom?"

"A boatman who refused to give his name, for fear of getting into trouble. But I had all the clues I wanted. It was not so difficult as I expected."

And the inspector described how he had gone to work.

"And you call that an accident!" cried M. Dudouis. "And you say that it was not difficult! Why, it's one of your finest performances! Finish it yourself, Ganimard, and be prudent."

Ganimard was eager to get the business done. He went to the Quai des Augustins with his men and distributed them around the house. He questioned the portress, who said that her tenant took his meals out of doors, but made a point of looking in after dinner.

A little before nine o'clock, in fact, leaning out of her window, she warned Ganimard, who at once gave a low whistle. A gentleman in a tall hat and a fur coat was coming along the pavement beside the Seine. He crossed the road and walked up to the house.

Ganimard stepped forward:

"M. Prévailles, I believe?"

"Yes, but who are you?"

"I have a commission to . . ."

He had not time to finish his sentence. At the sight of the men appearing out of the shadow, Prévailles quickly retreated to the wall and faced his adversaries, with his back to the door of a shop on the ground floor, the shutters of which were closed.

"Stand back!" he cried. "I don't know you!"

His right hand brandished a heavy stick, while his left was slipped behind him and seemed to be trying to open the door.

Ganimard had an impression that the man might escape through this way and through some secret outlet:

"None of this nonsense," he said, moving closer to him. "You're caught. . . . You had better come quietly."

But, just as he was laying hold of Prévailles's stick, Ganimard remembered the warning, which Lupin gave him: Prévailles was left-handed; and it was his revolver for which he was feeling behind his back.

The inspector ducked his head. He had noticed the man's sudden movement. Two reports rang out. No one was hit.

A second later, Prévailles received a blow under the chin from the butt end of a revolver, which brought him down where he stood. He was entered at the Dépôt soon after nine o'clock.

Ganimard enjoyed a great reputation even at that time. But this capture, so quickly effected, by such very simple means, and at once made public by the police, won him a sudden celebrity. Prévailles was forthwith saddled with all the murders that had remained unpunished; and the newspapers vied with one another in extolling Ganimard's prowess.

The case was conducted briskly at the start. It was first of all ascertained that Prévailles, whose real name was Thomas Derocq, had already been in trouble. Moreover, the search instituted in his rooms, while not supplying any fresh proofs, at least let to the discovery of a ball of whipcord similar to the wounds on the victim.

But, on the eighth day, everything was changed. Until then Prévailles had refused to reply to the questions put to him; but now, assisted by his counsel, he pleaded a circumstantial alibi and maintained that he was at the Folies-Bergère on the night of the murder.

As a matter of fact, the pockets of his dinner jacket contained the counterfoil of a stall ticket and a program of the performance, both bearing the date of that evening.

"An alibi prepared in advance," objected the examining magistrate.

"Prove it," said Prévailles.

The prisoner was confronted with the witness for the prosecution. The young lady from the confectioner's "thought she knew" the gentleman with the eyeglass. The hall porter in the Rue de Berne "thought he knew" the gentleman who used to come to see Jenny Saphir. But nobody dared to make a more definite statement.

The examination, therefore, let to nothing of a precise character, provided no solid basis whereon to found a serious accusation.

The judge sent for Ganimard and told him of his difficulty.

"I can't possibly persist, at this rate. There is no evidence to support the charge."

"But surely you are convinced in your own mind, *monsieur le juge d'instruction!* Prévailles would never have resisted his arrest unless he was guilty."

"He says that he thought he was being assaulted. He also says that he never set eyes on Jenny Saphir; and, as a matter of fact, we can find no one to contradict his assertion. Then again, admitting that the sapphire has been stolen, we have not been able to find it at his flat."

"Nor anywhere else," suggested Ganimard.

"Quite true, but that is no evidence against him. I'll tell you what we shall want, M. Ganimard, and that very soon: the other end of this red scarf."

"The other end?"

"Yes, for it is obvious that, if the murderer took it away with him, the reason was that the stuff is stained with the marks of the blood on his fingers."

Ganimard made no reply. For several days he had felt that the whole business was tending to this conclusion. There was no other proof possible. Given the silk scarf—and in no other circumstances—Prévailles's guilt was certain. Now Ganimard's position required that Prévailles's guilt should be established. He was responsible for the arrest, it had cast a glamour around him, he had been praised to the skies at the most formidable adversary of criminals; and he would look absolutely ridiculous if Prévailles were released.

Unfortunately, the one and only indispensable proof was in Lupin's pocket. How was he to get hold of it?

Ganimard cast about, exhausted himself with fresh investigations, went over the inquiry from start to finish, spent sleepless nights in turning over the mystery of the Rue de Berne, studied the records of Prévailles's life, sent ten men hunting after the invisible sapphire. Everything was useless.

On the 28th of December, the examining magistrate stopped him in one of the passages of the Law Courts:

"Well, M. Ganimard, any news?"

"No, *monsieur le juge d'instruction.*"

"Then I shall dismiss the case."

"Wait one day longer."

"What's the use? We want the other end of the scarf; have you got it?"

"I shall have it tomorrow."

"Tomorrow!"

"Yes, but please lend me the piece in your possession."

"What if I do?"

"If you do, I promise to let you have the whole scarf complete."

Ganimard followed the examining magistrate to his room and came out with the piece of silk:

"Hang it all!" he growled. "Yes, I will go and fetch the proof and I shall have it too . . . always presuming that Master Lupin has the courage to keep the appointment."

In point of fact, he did not doubt for a moment that Master Lupin would have this courage, and that was just what exasperated him. Why had Lupin insisted on this meeting? What was his object, in the circumstances?

Anxious, furious and full of hatred, he resolved to take every precaution necessary not only to prevent his falling into a trap himself, but to make his enemy fall into one, now that the opportunity offered. And, on the next day, which was the 29th of December, the date fixed by Lupin, after spending the night in studying the old manor house in the Rue de Surène and convincing himself that there was no other outlet than the front door, he warned his men that he was going on a dangerous expedition and arrived with them on the field of battle.

He posted them in a café and gave them formal instructions; if he showed himself at one of the third-floor windows, or if he failed to return within an hour, the detectives were to enter the house and arrest any one who tried to leave it.

The chief inspector made sure that his revolver was in working order and that he could take it from his pocket easily. Then he went upstairs.

He was surprised to find things as he had left them, the doors open and the locks broken. After ascertaining that the windows of the principal room looked out on the street, he visited the three other rooms that made up the flat. There was no one there.

"Master Lupin was afraid," he muttered, not without a certain satisfaction.

"Don't be silly," said a voice behind him.

Turning round, he saw an old workman, wearing a house-painter's long smock, standing in the doorway.

"You needn't bother your head," said the man. "It's I, Lupin. I have been working in the painter's shop since early morning. This is when we knock off for breakfast. So I came upstairs."

He looked at Ganimard with a quizzing smile and cried:

"Pon my word, this is a gorgeous moment I owe you, old chap! I wouldn't sell it for ten years of your life; and yet you know how I love you! What do you think of it, artist? Wasn't it well thought out and well foreseen? Foreseen from alpha to omega? Did I understand the business? Did I penetrate the mystery of the scarf? I'm not saying that there were no holes in my argument, no links missing in the chain. . . . But what a masterpiece of intelligence! Ganimard, what a reconstruction of events! What an intuition of everything that had taken place and of everything that was going to take place, from the discovery of the crime to your arrival here in search of a proof! What really marvelous divination! Have you the scarf?"

"Yes, half of it. Have you the other?"

"Here it is. Let's compare."

They spread the two pieces of silk on the table. The cuts made by the scissors corresponded exactly. Moreover, the colors were identical.

"But I presume," said Lupin, "that this was not the only thing you came for. What you are interested in seeing is the marks of the blood. Come with me, Ganimard: it's rather dark in here."

They moved into the next room, which, though it overlooked the courtyard, was lighter; and Lupin held his piece of silk against the windowpane:

"Look," he said, making room for Ganimard.

The inspector gave a start of delight. The marks of the five fingers and the print of the palm were distinctly visible. The evidence was undeniable. The murderer had seized the stuff in his blood-stained hand, in the same hand that had stabbed Jenny Saphir, and tied the scarf round her neck.

"And it is the print of a left hand," observed Lupin. "Hence my warning, which had nothing miraculous about it, you see. For, though I admit, friend of my youth, that you may look upon me as a superior intelligence, I won't have you treat me as a wizard."

Ganimard had quickly pocketed the piece of silk. Lupin nodded his head in approval:

"Quite right, old boy, it's for you. I'm so glad you're glad! And you see, there was no trap about all this . . . only the wish to oblige . . . a service between friends, between pals . . . and also, I confess, a little curiosity. . . . Yes, I wanted to examine this other piece of silk, the one the police had. . . . Don't be afraid: I'll give it back to you. . . . Just a second . . . "

Lupin, with a careless movement, played with the tassel at the end of this half of the scarf, while Ganimard listened to him in spite of himself:

"How ingenious these little bits of women's work are! Did you notice one detail in the maid's evidence? Jenny Saphir was very handy with her needle and used to make all her own hats and frocks. It is obvious that she made this scarf herself. . . . Besides, I noticed that from the first. I am naturally curious, as I have already told you, and I made a thorough examination of the piece of silk which you have just put in your pocket. Inside the tassel, I found a little sacred medal, which the poor girl had stitched into it to bring her luck. Touching, isn't it, Ganimard? A little medal of Our Lady of Good Succor."

The inspector felt greatly puzzled and did not take his eyes off the other. And Lupin continued:

"Then I said to myself, 'How interesting it would be to explore the other half of the scarf, the one which the police will find round the victim's neck!' For this other half, which I hold in my hands at last, is finished off in the same way . . . so I shall be able to see if it has a hiding place too and what's inside it. . . . But look, my friend, isn't it cleverly made? And so simple! All you have to do is to take a skein of red cord and braid it round a wooden cup, leaving a little recess, a little empty space in the middle, very small, of course, but large enough to hold a medal of a saint . . . or anything . . . a precious stone, for instance . . . such as a sapphire . . . "

At that moment he finished pushing back the silk cord and, from the hollow of a cup he took between his thumb and forefinger a wonderful blue stone, perfect in respect of size and purity.

"Ha! What did I tell you, friend of my youth?"

He raised his head. The inspector had turned livid and was staring wild-eyed, as though fascinated by the stone that sparkled before him. He at last realized the whole plot:

"You dirty scoundrel!" he muttered, repeating the insults which he had used at the first interview. "You scum of the earth!"

The two men were standing one against the other.

"Give me back that," said the inspector.

Lupin held out the piece of silk.

"And the sapphire," said Ganimard, in a peremptory tone.

"Don't be silly."

"Give it back, or . . . "

"Or what, you idiot!" cried Lupin. "Look here, do you think I put you on to this soft thing for nothing?"

"Give it back!"

"You haven't noticed what I've been about, that's plain! What! For four weeks I've kept you on the move like a deer; and you want to . . . Come, Ganimard, old chap, pull yourself together! . . . Don't you see that you've been playing the good dog for four weeks on end? . . . Fetch it, Rover! . . . There's a nice blue pebble over there, which master can't get at. Hunt it, Ganimard, fetch it . . . bring it to master. . . . Ah, he's his master's own good little dog! . . . Sit up! Beg! . . . Does'ms want a bit of sugar, then? . . .

Ganimard, containing the anger that seethed within him, thought only of one thing, summoning his detectives. And, as the room in which he now was looked out on the courtyard, he tried gradually to work his way round to the communicating door. He would then run to the window and break one of the panes.

"All the same," continued Lupin, "what a pack of dunderheads you and the rest must be! You've had the silk all this time and not one of you ever thought of feeling it, not one of you ever asked himself the reason why the poor girl hung on to her scarf. Not one of you! You just acted at haphazard, without reflecting, without foreseeing anything. . . . "

The inspector had attained his object. Taking advantage of a second when Lupin had turned away from him, he suddenly wheeled round and grasped the door handle. But an oath escaped him: the handle did not budge.

Lupin bust into a fit of laughing:

"Not even that! You did not foresee that! You lay a trap for me and you won't admit that I may perhaps smell the thing out beforehand. . . . And you allow yourself to be brought into this room without asking whether I am not bringing you here for a particular reason and without remembering that the locks are fitted with a special mechanism. Come now, speaking frankly, what do you think of it yourself?"

"What do I think of it?" roared Ganimard, beside himself with rage.

He had drawn his revolver and was pointing it straight at Lupin's face.

"Hands up!" he cried. "That's what I think of it!"

Lupin placed himself in front of him and shrugged his shoulder:

"Sold again!" he said.

"Hands up, I say, once more!"

"And sold again, say I. Your deadly weapon won't go off."

"What?"

"Old Catherine, your housekeeper, is in my service. She damped the charges this morning while you were having your breakfast coffee."

Ganimard made a furious gesture, pocketed the revolver and rushed at Lupin.

"Well?" said Lupin, stopping him short with a well-aimed kick on the shin.

Their clothes were almost touching. They exchanged defiant glances, the glances of two adversaries who mean to come to blows. Nevertheless, there was no fight. The recollection of the earlier struggles made any present struggle useless. And Ganimard, who remembered all his past failures, his vain attacks, Lupin's crushing reprisals, did not lift a limb. There was nothing to be done. He felt it. Lupin had forces at his command against which any individual force simply broke to pieces. So what was the good?

"I agree," said Lupin in a friendly voice, as though answering Ganimard's unspoken thought, "you would do better to let things be as they are. Besides, friend of my youth, think of all that this incident had brought you: fame, the certainty of quick promotion and, thanks to that, the prospect of a happy and comfortable old age! Surely, you don't want the discovery of the sapphire and the head of poor Arsène Lupin in addition! It wouldn't be fair. To say nothing of the fact that poor Arsène Lupin saved your life. . . . Yes, sir! Who warned you, at this very spot, the Prévailles was left-handed? . . . And is this the way you thank me? It's not pretty of you, Ganimard. Upon my word, you make be blush for you!"

While chattering, Lupin had gone through the same performance as Ganimard and was now near the door. Ganimard saw that his foe was about to escape him. Forgetting all prudence, he tried to block his way and received a tremendous butt in the stomach, which sent him rolling to the opposite wall.

Lupin dexterously touched a spring, turned the handle, opened the door and slipped away, roaring with laughter as he went.

Twenty minutes later, when Ganimard at last succeeded in joining his men, one of them said to him:

"A house painter left the house, as his mates were coming back from breakfast, and put a letter in my hand. 'Give that to your governor,' he said. 'Which governor?' I asked; but he was gone. I suppose it's meant for you."

"Let's have it."

Ganimard opened the letter. It was hurriedly scribbled in pencil and contained these words:—

> This is to warn you, friend of my youth, against excessive credulity. When a fellow tells you that the cartridges in your revolver are damp, however great your confidence in that fellow may be, even though his name be Arsène Lupin, never allow yourself to be taken in. Fire first; and, if the fellow hops the twig, you will have acquired the proof (1) that the cartridges are not damp; and (2) that old Catherine is the most honest and respectable of housekeepers.
>
> One of these days, I hope to have the pleasure of making her acquaintance.
>
> Meanwhile, friend of my youth, believe me always affectionately and sincerely yours,
>
> ARSÈNE LUPIN

Crime in the Rue Sainte-Catherine

Georges Simenon

Georges Simenon was one of the most successful mystery writers of the twentieth century. Introduced in 1930, Inspector Maigret is unlike any other detective. Through his observations of his fellow characters, Maigret's journey toward the understanding of the individual often plays a more central role than the crime and its consequences. Simenon lived to be nearly ninety years of age and left a legacy of books, from which more than fifty films and hundreds of television episodes have been made. Rupert Davies and Michael Gambon remain the most striking British incarnations of Maigret, while in France he has been embodied by Jean Gabin and many others.

A fine, cold drizzle was falling, and it was dark. The only light was toward the end of the street, near the barracks, where at half-past five the trumpets had sounded, and now you could hear the noise of horses being taken to be watered. There the dimly lit rectangle of a window could be seen: someone getting up early or perhaps a sick person who had been awake all night.

The rest of the street was asleep. A wide quiet street, newish with houses all much the same, one- or at the most two-storied, such as is found in the suburbs of most big provincial towns.

The whole district was new, devoid of mystery; its inhabitants were quiet and unassuming—employees, traveling salesmen, people of limited means, peaceable widows.

Inspector Maigret, coat collar turned up, stood pressed into the corner of the entrance to the boys' school; he was waiting, watch in hand and smoking his pipe.

At a quarter to six precisely, the bells of the parish church rang out behind him, and he knew it was, as the boy had said, the "first stroke" of the six-o'clock Mass.

The chimes were still reverberating in the damp air when he heard, or rather sensed, the jarring outburst of an alarm clock in the house opposite. It lasted only a few seconds. In the dark the child's hand must already have stretched out from the warmth of his bed and gropingly turned off the alarm. A few seconds later the attic window on the second floor lit up.

It was happening exactly as the boy had said. He was the first to get up, noiselessly, in the still-sleeping house. Now he must be throwing on his clothes, his socks, splashing water on his face and hands, running a comb through his hair. As for his shoes, he had stated, "I carry them downstairs and put them on on the bottom step in order not to wake my parents."

It had been the same every day, winter and summer, for almost two years, since Justin had started as altar boy at the six-o'clock Mass at the hospital.

He had also told them: "The hospital clock is always three or four minutes behind the parish church."

And the chief Inspector had proof of this. The day before, at the flying squad to which he had been assigned for some months, his Inspectors had shrugged at these detailed stories of bells and first strokes and second strokes. But Maigret, perhaps because he too had served as altar boy for a long time, had not found them laughable.

The parish bells first, at a quarter to six. Then Justin's alarm clock in the attic where he slept. Then, after a few minutes' interval, the higher-pitched, more silvery chimes of the hospital chapel, which made one think of convent bells.

Maigret was still holding his watch in his hand. The child took just a little more than four minutes to dress. His light went out. He must have been groping his way downstairs, still trying not to wake his parents. Sitting down on the bottom step and putting on his shoes, taking his coat and cap from the bamboo hat stand that stood on the right in the hallway.

The door opened. The youngster closed it without a sound, looked anxiously up and down the street, then saw the bulky silhouette of the Inspector approaching.

"I was afraid you wouldn't be there," the boy said. And he started off, walking fast. He was a little fellow of twelve, fair, thin, already self-willed.

"You want me to do just the same as the other days, don't you? I always walk quickly. At first it was to see how many minutes it would take me, and then in winter, when it's dark, I'm afraid. In a month from now, at this time, it'll begin to get light."

He took the first street on the right, another quiet street, rather shorter, which opened out on a square planted round with elm trees and crossed diagonally by streetcar tracks.

Maigret noticed minute details that brought back his own childhood. First, the youngster kept away from the houses as he walked, no doubt because he was afraid someone might step out of the shadow of a doorway. Then, to cross the square, he kept clear of the trees in the same way, for a man could have been hiding behind them.

In fact, he was a pretty brave little chap, as, for two winters, in all weathers, sometimes in thick fog or moonless dark, he had been going along the same route every morning all alone.

"When we get to the middle of the Rue Sainte-Catherine," the boy said, "you'll hear the second stroke of the Mass from the parish church."

"What time does the first streetcar go past?"

"Six o'clock. I've only seen it two or three times when I was late. Once my alarm didn't go off. Another time I went back to sleep. That's why I always jump out of bed when it goes off."

A wan little face in the rainy darkness, eyes that still retained some of the stupor of sleep, a thoughtful expression with only the slighted hint of fear.

"I shan't go on serving at Mass. It's only because you insisted that I came today."

They turned left onto the Rue Sainte-Catherine, where, as in all the other streets in the district, there was a lamp every fifty yards or so, each throwing a pool of light. Between these the child unconsciously walked more quickly than when he was crossing each reassuring circle of lamplight.

The distant noises of the barracks could still be heard. Lights were coming on in some of the windows. Someone was walking somewhere in a cross street.

"When you got to the corner of the street, you didn't see anything?"

That was the critical point, for the Rue Sainte-Catherine was quite straight and deserted. With the pavements straight as a die, and streetlamps at regular intervals, there was not enough shadow between them for one to miss seeing, even at a hundred yards, two men having a row.

"Perhaps I wasn't looking where I was going. I was talking to myself, I remember. I often do in the morning when I'm going this way, talk away to myself under my breath. . . . I wanted to ask my mother something when I got home, and I was repeating to myself what I was going to say to her."

"What did you want to say to her?"

"For a long time I've wanted a bike. I've already saved up one hundred francs out of what I get for the Masses."

It may have been just an impression, but it seemed to Maigret that the child was keeping farther out from the houses. He even stepped off the pavement, then got onto it a little farther on.

"Here it is. Listen—that's the second stroke chiming at the parish church."

Meanwhile Maigret was trying, quite unconscious of the absurdity, to penetrate into that world that was the boy's world each morning.

"I must have raised my head. You know, like when one is running without looking and one finds oneself up against the wall. . . . It was right at this spot." He pointed to the line on the pavement that separated the shadow from the light of a streetlamp, in which the fine rain was dancing like luminous dust.

"First I noticed there was a man stretched out, and he seemed so big that I'd have sworn he took up the whole width of the pavement."

That was impossible, for the pavement was about eight feet wide.

"I don't know what I did exactly. I must have swerved out of the way. I didn't run off right away because I saw the knife in his chest, with a thick brown horn handle—I noticed it because my uncle Henri has a knife almost the same, and he told me it was stag's horn. I'm sure the man was dead."

"Why?"

"I don't know. He looked dead."

"His eyes were closed?"

"I didn't notice his eyes. I don't know any more. But I had a feeling he was dead. It all happened very quickly, as I told you yesterday in your office. But I had to repeat the same things so many times all day yesterday that I'm mixed up. Especially when I feel no one believes me."

"And the other man?"

"When I looked up, I saw there was someone a little farther on perhaps fifteen feet or so away. Someone with very bright eyes. He looked at me for a second, and started to run. It was the murderer."

"How d'you know?"

"Because he ran off as fast as he could."

"Which direction?"

"Straight down there."

"Towards the barracks, in fact?"

"Yes."

It was true that Justin had been questioned at least ten times the previous day. Before Maigret's arrival at the office, the other Inspectors had even made a sort of game of it. But not once had the boy changed the smallest detail.

"What did you do?"

"I started to run, too. It's difficult to explain. I think it was when I saw the man running away that I felt frightened. And then I ran as fast as I could."

"In the opposite direction?"

"Yes."

"You didn't think of calling for help?"

"No. I was too scared. Most of all I was afraid my legs would suddenly give out, for I couldn't feel them any longer. I ran back as far as the Place du Congrès. I took the other street. It also leads to the hospital, but the long way round."

"Let's go on."

Bells again, high-pitched bells, the chapel ones. After another fifty yards or so there was a crossroads and on the left were the loop-holed walls of the barracks, on the right a vast dimly lit doorway surmounted by the greenish dial of a clock.

It was three minutes to six.

"I'm a minute late. Yesterday, in spite of everything, I got here on time because I ran."

In the middle of the oak door there was a heavy knocker, which the boy raised. The din echoed through the porch. A slippered porter came to open up, let Justin through, and placed himself in Maigret's path, looking at him with suspicion. "What is it?"

"Police."

"You've got your identification?"

You crossed a porch, where the first hospital odors greeted you; then, through a second door, you found yourself in a vast courtyard full of outbuildings. Far away in the shadows you could make out the white headdresses of the nuns on their way to the chapel.

"Why didn't you say anything to the porter yesterday?"

"I don't know. I was hurrying to get there."

Maigret could understand that. For the boy it wasn't the lodge with its distrustful, grumpy porter that was a haven, or this cold courtyard where stretchers were borne silently past. It was the warm sacristy, near the chapel, where one of the sisters was lighting the altar candles.

There were two poles, in fact, for the boy each morning, and he went from one to the other in a dizzy rush—his room under the roof, from which the ringing of the alarm clock dragged him, and, at the other end of a sort of void filled only with the chimes of the bells, the sacristy of the chapel.

"You're coming in with me?"

"Yes."

Justin seemed put out, or rather shocked, no doubt at the idea of this Inspector, who was perhaps an unbeliever, penetrating into his sacred world. Maigret could understand now why the child had the courage to get up so early every morning and overcome his fears.

The chapel was warm and cozy. Already the patients in their gray-blue uniforms, some with their heads bandaged, some with their arms in slings, some on crutches, were lined up on the seats in the nave. In the gallery the sisters formed up like a uniform troupe, and all the white coifs dipped at the same time in mystic reverence.

"Follow me."

They had to go up a few steps, pass near the altar, where the candles were already burning. On the right there was a dark-paneled sacristy, a tall bony priest who was finishing putting on his vestments, a lace-trimmed surplice that was ready for the boy, and a nun busy filling the altar vessels.

It was only at this point, the day before, that Justin, panting, his throat dry and his legs shaky, had come to a halt. It was here he had cried out, "A man has just been killed in the Rue Sainte-Catherine."

A small clock set into the paneling showed six o'clock exactly. Bells were ringing again; they were less distinct inside than out. Justin said to the nun who was helping him with his surplice, "It's the police Inspector."

Maigret stood there while the child, preceding the chaplain, shook out the folds of his red cassock and hurried toward the altar steps.

The vestry nun had said, "Justin is a good little boy. Very devout. He has never told us a lie. Sometimes he hasn't turned up to serve the Mass. He could have pretended he was sick. But no, he admitted quite openly that he couldn't bear to get up because it was too cold, or because he had had nightmares during the night and was feeling tired."

And the chaplain, Mass over, had looked at the Inspector with eyes as bright as those of a stained-glass saint, and said, "Why should you think this child would make up such a story?"

Maigret knew now what had happened in the hospital chapel. How Justin's teeth had chattered, and how, at the end of his tether, he had a fit of hysterics. Mass mustn't be held up, so the sacristy nun warned the Sister Superior, and took the place of the child, who meanwhile was being fussed over in the vestry.

It was ten minutes before the Sister Superior thought of informing the police. She had to go through the chapel. Everybody felt something was afoot. At the local headquarters the desk sergeant could not understand.

"What? Sister Superior? Superior to what?"

So she repeated gently in her convent voice that a crime had been committed in the Rue Sainte-Catherine. And the police had found nothing, neither victim nor, of course, murderer. . . .

As he did every day, Justin had gone to school at half-past eight as if nothing had happened, and he was in class when Inspector Besson, a chunky little man who looked like a boxer and played the tough guy, had come for him at half-past nine, when the report had reached the flying squad.

Poor boy, for two hours in a gloomy office that reeked of pipe smoke and the stove that didn't draw, he had been questioned, not as a witness but like a suspect. One after the other, three Inspectors—Besson, Thiberge, and Vallin—had tried to make him waver in his story.

And then, for good measure, his mother had followed the child. She waited in the anteroom, crying and sniffing by turn and telling everyone, "We're honest people. We've never had any trouble with the police."

Maigret, who had been working late the night before on a narcotics case, hadn't arrived in his office until around eleven.

"What's this?" he had asked on seeing the boy, dry-eyed, and looking with his skinny legs for all the world like an indignant little cock.

"A brat who's trying to make fools of us. He says he saw a corpse in the street—he even saw the murderer, who ran away at his approach. But a streetcar passed along the same street four minutes later, and the driver saw nothing. The street is a quiet one, and nobody heard anything. Furthermore, when the police were called, a quarter of an hour later, by some nun or other, there was absolutely nothing on the pavement, not the least speck of blood."

"Come into my office, son."

Maigret was the first person who had spoken civilly to Justin that morning, the first to treat him like a grown-up and not like some brat with a vivid imagination.

Maigret had made him repeat his story, simply and quietly, without interrupting and without taking notes.

"You're going to go on serving Mass at the hospital?"

"No. I never want to go there again. I'm too scared."

But it was a heavy sacrifice. The child was certainly devout, he certainly responded to the poetry of early Mass in the warm, rather mysterious atmosphere of the chapel. And, besides, he was paid for these Masses, not much, but enough to let him put aside a little nest egg. And he did so long to have the bicycle his parents couldn't afford to give him.

"I'm going to ask you to go there once again. Only once. Tomorrow morning."

"I wouldn't dare to walk that way."

"I'll come with you. I'll wait for you in front of your house. And you'll do exactly the same as all the other times."

And that was how Maigret had found himself all alone at seven in the morning at the hospital entrance, in a district that the day before he knew only from having passed through by streetcar or automobile.

An icy drizzle was still falling from the sky, which was now a watery green. Eventually it soaked into the Inspector's coat, and he sneezed twice. There were several people passing by, coat collars turned up and hands in pockets; at the butchers' and grocers' the shutters were being opened.

It was the most ordinary, peaceful district you could possibly imagine. Only with the greatest difficulty could you conceive of two men, even two drunks, having a row at five or six in the morning on the pavement of the Rue Sainte-Catherine.

But then there was the sequel. According to the boy's statement, at his approach the murderer had run off, and it had then been five to six. Now, at six, the first streetcar went by, and the driver insisted he had seen nothing. Of course, he could have had his attention distracted, could have been looking in the opposite direction.

But at five past six, two police constables who were coming off their beat had walked along that very same pavement. And they had seen nothing.

At seven or eight minutes past six, a cavalry officer who lived three houses away from the spot Justin had pointed out had left home as he did every morning to go to the barracks. He hadn't seen anything, either.

Finally, at six-twenty, the constables had cycled from the district police station, and they had found no trace of the victim.

Had someone come meanwhile and removed the body in a car or truck? Soberly and without any fuss, Maigret had set out to envisage all the possibilities, and this one had turned out to be as false as the others. There was a sick woman at Number 42 in the street, and her husband had been up with her all night. He was quite positive.

"We can hear all the noises from outside. I was paying special attention, as my wife, who is in great pain, is upset by the slightest noise. Wait a moment. . . . It was the streetcar that woke her, just as she had dropped off. I can tell you that no car went past before seven that morning. The first thing to go by was the dustcart."

"And you heard nothing else?"

"There was a sound of running at one point."

"Before the streetcar?"

"Yes, for my wife was sleeping. I was getting myself a cup of coffee."

"One person running?"

"More like two."

"You don't know in which direction?"

"The blind was down. As it makes a noise when you pull it up, I didn't look out."

That was the only evidence in support of Justin's story.

There was a bridge about two hundred yards away, and the constable on duty had not seen any car passing. One would have to suppose that only a few minutes after running away, the murderer had come back, heaved his victim onto his shoulders, and carried him off heaven knows where—and all without attracting any attention.

There was worse to come. There was evidence that made people shrug off the child's story. The place he had pointed out was situated just across from 61. Inspector Thiberge had called there the day before, and Maigret, who left nothing to chance, was now ringing there in his turn.

It was a newish house of red brick, with three steps up to the varnished pitch-pine door on which a polished brass letterbox shone. It was only a quarter past seven, but from what he had heard, the Inspector knew he could safely present himself at that hour.

A withered old woman, with a hairy upper lip, first opened a spyhole in the door and parleyed with him before letting him into a hall fragrant with the aroma of freshly made coffee. "I'll find out if the Judge will see you."

The house was occupied by a retired member of the judiciary, who was said to have a private income; he lived there along with his servant.

There was a sound of whispering in the front room, which would normally have been the drawing room. Then the old woman came out and said spitefully, "Come in, but wipe your feet, please. This isn't a stable."

It wasn't a drawing room—it wasn't like anything one normally imagines. The room, which was fairly large, was something of a bedroom, study, library, and even attic, for it was heaped with the most unexpected objects.

"You're coming to look for the corpse?" a voice sneered, and made the Inspector start.

As there was a bed in the room, he had quite naturally looked in that direction, but it was empty. The voice came from the corner of the fireplace, where a thin old man was sunk in the depths of an armchair, a rug around his legs.

"Take your coat off. I love heat, and you won't be able to stand it for long in here."

That was so. The old man, who had a pair of tongs within reach, was doing his best to produce the biggest blaze possible from a log fire.

"I thought that, since my day, the police had made some progress and had learned to distrust the evidence of children. Children and young girls, they're the most dangerous witnesses, and when I was a Judge . . ."

He was wearing a thick dressing gown, and, despite the temperature in the room, around his neck there was a scarf as wide as a shawl.

"So it was right opposite my house that the crime is supposed to have been committed, eh? And you, if I'm not mistaken, are the famous Chief Inspector Maigret, whom they've been good enough to send to our town to reorganize the flying squad?" His voice grated. He was a nasty old man, aggressive and full of savage irony.

"Well, my dear Inspector, unless you accuse me of being in league with the murderer, I regret to inform you, as I already told your colleague yesterday, you're on the wrong track.

"As you've no doubt been told, old men need very little sleep. And there are some people who manage with very little sleep all their lives. That was the case with Erasmus, for instance, and also with a gentleman known by the name of Voltaire." His glance moved complacently to the library shelves stacked up to the ceiling with books.

"I could quote you many other cases you would know equally little about. But, to be brief, it is so in my own case. I pride myself on not having slept more than three hours a night in the last fifteen years. As, for the last ten, my legs have refused to support me and, in any case, I spend my days and my nights in this room, which, as you can see, looks straight out onto the street.

"From four in the morning I sit in this chair, wide-awake, believe me. I could show you the book in which I was immersed this morning, but as it's a Greek philosopher, I suppose that wouldn't interest you. However, if any event of the kind described by your over-imaginative boy had taken place beneath my window, I can assure you I would have noticed it. My legs may have failed, as I told you, but my hearing is as good as ever.

"Besides, I am still curious enough by nature to take an interest in all that happens in the street, and if it amuses you, I can tell at what time every housewife in the neighborhood passes my window on her way to the shops."

He looked at Maigret with a triumphant smile.

"So you're accustomed to hear young Justin going past?" the Inspector asked with saintly sweetness.

"Naturally."

"Hear and see him?"

"I don't understand."

"For more than half the year—for almost two-thirds—it's light at six in the morning. And the child served at Mass in summer as well as winter."

"I used to see him pass."

"Seeing that it was such a regular daily occurrence, like the first streetcar, you must have been expecting it."

"What do you mean?"

"For example, when a factory whistle in the neighborhood goes off every day at the same time, or when a person passes by your window as regular as clockwork, you naturally say to yourself, 'There, it's such-and-such a time.' If one day the whistle doesn't sound, you say to yourself, 'It must be Sunday.' If the person doesn't go past, you wonder, 'What can have happened to him? Is he ill?' "

The Judge's eyes were watching Maigret narrowly. He gave the impression of resenting Maigret's lecture.

"I know all that," he muttered, cracking his fingerjoints. "I was a Judge before you joined the force."

"When the altar boy went past."

"I heard him, if that's what you want to make me admit!"

"And if he didn't go past?"

"I could happen to notice it. But I could also happen not to notice it. As in the case of the whistle you were speaking of just now: one is not struck by the absence of the whistle every Sunday."

"And yesterday?" Maigret might have been mistaken, but he had the impression that the old Judge scowled; there was in his look something sulky, something fiercely shut in. But then old people often sulk just like children, and sometimes show the same childish stubbornness.

"Yesterday?"

"Yes, yesterday." There was no reason for the Judge to repeat the question, except to give himself more time.

"I didn't notice anything."

"You didn't notice if he passed?"

"No."

"Or if he didn't pass?"

"No." Still the same frank and seemingly triumphant "No."

"No tramping of feet, no thud of a falling body, no gasping?"

"Nothing at all."

"Thank you."

"Pray don't mention it."

"Seeing that you were a magistrate, I obviously need not ask if you are ready to repeat your evidence under oath?"

"Whenever you want me to." And the old man said that with a sort of gleeful impatience.

"I must apologize for having disturbed you, sir."

The old servant must have been standing outside the door, for she was right on the threshold to show the Inspector out and close the door behind him.

Maigret had a strange feeling as he stepped out again into the everyday life of that calm suburban street, where the housewives were beginning to make their way to the shops and children could be seen going to school. It seemed to him that he had just been hoaxed, and yet the Judge had not been lying—except for one omission. He had the impression, too, that at one point he had been on the verge of discovering something very odd, very subtle, and very unexpected; at that moment it would have taken only a little effort to bring it off, but he had been incapable of doing it.

In his mind's eye he saw the boy again; he saw the old man again. He tried to see some connection between the two.

He stood on the edge of the pavement, slowly filling his pipe. Then, as he had not yet had breakfast, not even a cup of coffee on getting up, and his drenched overcoat was clinging to his shoulders, he went to the corner of the Place du Congrès and waited for a streetcar to take him back.

The mass of sheets and blankets, heaved like a sea swell, an arm emerged, a red face appeared, shining with sweat; then a surly voice grumbled out, "Pass me the thermometer."

Madame Maigret was sewing by the window, where she had drawn back the lace curtain to be able to see despite the twilight; she rose with a sigh and switched on the light. "I thought you were asleep. It's not half an hour since you took your temperature."

Resigned, knowing from experience that it was useless to thwart her great bear of a husband, she shook the thermometer, then slid it between his lips. He found time to ask, "Nobody's come?"

"You should know, as you haven't been asleep."

He must have dropped off, however, even if it was only for a few minutes. It was that wretched carillon that kept dragging him out of his torpor and bringing him to the surface again.

It wasn't their own home. As his assignment in this provincial town was to last about six months, and as Madame Maigret could not bear the thought of her husband eating in restaurants for such a long period, she had gone with him, and they had rented a furnished apartment in the center of the town.

It was too bright for their liking, with its floral wallpapers and bargain-basement furniture, and the bed that groaned under the Inspector's weight. But at least they had chosen a quiet street, where, as the landlady, Madame Danse, said, not even a cat went by.

What the landlady hadn't said was that, the ground floor being occupied by a dairy, a stale smell of cheese hung about the whole house. Nor had she mentioned—and Maigret had just found out, for it was the first time he had spent the day in bed there—that the door of the dairy below was fitted not with a bell of the usual kind but with a strange apparatus of metal tubes that slowly jangled out a carillon each time a customer entered.

"How much?"

"101."

"A little while ago it was 101."

"It'll be 102 later."

He was furious. He was always bad-tempered when he was ill, and he glowered at Madame Maigret with deep resentment, for she insisted on not going out just when he would have loved to have a smoke.

It was still raining, still the same fine rain that streaked the windows, falling silently, drearily down, and giving one the feeling of being in an aquarium. The electric lightbulb, hanging unshaded at the end of its cord, gave out a harsh light. You could picture street upon street, equally empty, where the windows lit up one after the other, and people went to and fro in their cages like fish in a bowl.

"You're going to have another cup of herb tea."

That would be about the tenth since midday, and he would have to sweat out all that tepid water into his sheets, turning them in the long run into a damp compress.

He must have caught this chill or cold while he was waiting for the boy in the cold morning rain on the school doorstep, or perhaps later while he was roaming round the street. He had hardly got back at ten o'clock to his office at the flying-squad headquarters and embarked on his normal ritual of poking the stove when he started to shiver. Then he felt too hot. His eyelids began to sting, and when he looked into the scrap of mirror in the cloakroom, he saw his eyes were swollen and moist.

Besides, his pipe didn't taste the same, always a sure sign.

"Look here, Besson, if by chance I don't come in this afternoon, you'll go on with the inquiries on this affair of the altar boy."

And Besson, who always thought he knew better than anyone else, said, "You really think, Chief, that there is anything there that a good hiding wouldn't put a stop to?"

"All the same, you'll have the Rue Sainte-Catherine watched by one of your colleagues—by Vallin, for instance."

"In case the corpse comes back to lie down in front of the Judge's house?"

The start of his chill left Maigret too much under the weather to rise to that. He continued heavily, giving instructions. "Give me a list of all the people living in the street. As it isn't a very long one, that won't be too much work."

"Shall I question the boy again?"

"No."

From then on he had been feverish; he could feel the drops of sweat break out on his skin one after the other; he had a stale taste in his mouth, and he kept longing to sink into sleep; but when he did it was only to hear immediately the ridiculous carillon of the brass tubes in the dairy.

He hated being ill, because it humiliated him, and also because Madame Maigret kept a fierce watch on him to prevent him smoking his pipe. If only there had been something she should go and buy at the pharmacist's! But she had taken care to bring the contents of a full medicine cabinet with her from home.

He hated being ill, and yet there were moments when it was almost voluptuous, moments when, on closing his eyes, his years dropped away and he relived his childhood. Then there would come before him the face of young Justin, pale and strong for his years. All that morning's images returned to his memory, no longer with the precision of everyday reality, no longer in the dry light of things that one sees, but with the peculiar intensity of things that one feels.

For instance, he could have described in almost every detail that attic room he had not been in—the iron bed, the alarm clock on the bedside table, the child stretching out his hand, dressing noiselessly, with every gesture the same as always.

The same as always—that was it. That seemed to him important as evidence, as truth. When for two years at a fixed time one serves at Mass, one's actions become absolutely automatic.

The first chimes at a quarter to six . . . the alarm . . . the higher-pitched chapel bells . . . the shoes at the bottom of the stairs . . . the door opening on the cold breath of the morning town.

"You know, Madame Maigret, he's never read a detective story." Ever since they had once done so as a joke, they had called each other Maigret and Madame Maigret, and now they had almost forgotten that they had first names like everyone else.

"He doesn't read the papers, either."

"You should try to get to sleep."

With a last look at his pipe, lying on the black marble of the mantelpiece, he closed his eyes.

"I questioned his mother for a long time. She's a good woman, but far too easily upset by the police."

"Go to sleep."

He was silent for a little while. His breathing became louder, as if he was about to drop off. "She said he'd never seen a corpse. That's something one avoids showing children."

"What's that to do with it?"

"He told me the corpse was so big it seemed to span the pavement. That's exactly the impression you do get from a dead body on the ground. A dead body always looks bigger than a living man. You understand?"

"I don't see why you are worrying about it. Besson's taking care of all that."

"Besson doesn't believe in it."

"In what?"

"In the dead man."

"Would you like me to turn off the light?"

Despite his protests, she got up on a chair and put some oiled paper round the bulb in order to lessen the glare.

"Try to sleep for an hour, and then I'll give you a fresh cup of herb tea. You're not sweating enough."

"D'you think if I just took a puff or two at my pipe—?"

"Are you mad?"

She went into the kitchen to look at the vegetable broth; he could hear her padding about. All the time in front of his eyes he saw the same stretch of the Rue Sainte-Catherine, with streetlamps every fifty yards.

"The Judge claims he didn't hear anything."

"What are you saying?"

"I bet you they loathed each other."

"Who are you talking about?" Her voice came from the other end of the kitchen. "Can't you see I'm busy."

"The Judge and the altar boy. . . . They've never spoken to each other, but I bet you anything they loathe each other. You know, very old people, especially those who live alone, come to be just like children. Justin went by every morning, and every morning the old Judge was there by the window. He looks like a screech owl."

"I don't know what you mean."

She stood there framed in the doorway, a steaming ladle in her hand.

"Try to follow. The Judge claims he didn't hear anything, and it's too serious for me to suspect him of lying."

"I should hope so."

"Only he doesn't dare to say that he did or didn't hear Justin go by yesterday morning."

"Perhaps he fell asleep again."

"No. He doesn't dare to lie, so he is deliberately vague about it. But the husband in Number 42, who was sitting up with his sick wife, heard running in the street."

He kept coming back to that. Sharpened by the fever, his thoughts went round in circles.

"But what could have happened to the corpse?" Madame Maigret's objection showed all the sound sense of a middle-aged woman. "Anyway, don't think about it any more. Besson knows his job—you've often said so yourself."

Discouraged, he sank under the blankets, and tried hard to fall asleep, but it wasn't long before he was thinking again of the altar boy, his legs white against the black socks.

"There's something wrong—" he worried.

"What're you saying? Something wrong? You feel worse? You want me to call the doctor?"

Madame Maigret put down her ladle.

No. He was starting from zero all over again, obstinately. He was setting out again from the entry of the boy's school, crossing the Place du Congrès. "There! It's here something goes wrong—"

First because the Judge hadn't heard anything. Unless one were to accuse him of giving false testimony, it was difficult to accept that there could have been a fight under his window, a few feet away, that a man could have started running in the direction of the barracks while the altar boy rushed off in the other direction without the Judge hearing any of it at all.

"I say, Madame Maigret—"

"What is it now?"

"Suppose they both ran off in the same direction?"

Madame Maigret sighed, picked up her sewing, and settled down dutifully to listen to this monologue interspersed with the hoarse breathing of her husband.

"For one thing, it's more logical—"

"What's more logical?"

"That they should both run off in the same direction. But, in this case, it was not in the direction of the barracks."

"You mean the boy chased the murderer?"

"No. It's the murderer who chased the boy."

"What for, as he didn't kill him?"

"To make him keep quiet, for instance."

"But he didn't manage, as the child has told his story."

"Or to prevent him saying something, giving away some detail. Listen, Madame Maigret—"

"What do you want?"

"I know you'll start by refusing, but it's absolutely essential. Pass me my pipe and my tobacco. Just a few puffs. I have the impression that I'm on the point of understanding—that in a few minutes, if I don't lose the thread—"

She went over for the pipe on the mantelpiece; with a sigh of resignation she held it out to him. "I knew you'd find a good excuse. Anyway, this evening, whether you like it or not, I'm going to make you a mustard plaster."

As luck would have it, there was no telephone in the apartment. You had to go down to the dairy, where the instrument was behind the counter.

"You are going to go downstairs, Madame Maigret, and you will call Besson. It's seven o'clock; maybe he's still at the office. If not, call the Café du Centre; he'll be playing billiards there with Thiberge."

"I'm to ask him to come round?"

"To bring me over as quickly as possible, not the list of everybody who lives in the street, but a list of the tenants of the houses on the left-hand side, and only between the Place du Congrès and the Judge's house."

"Try at least not to get uncovered."

She had hardly started going downstairs when he got himself out of bed, hurried barefoot to his tobacco pouch to fill the pipe, then lay down again, all innocence, in the bed.

Through the thin floorboards he could hear a voice murmuring, the voice of Madame Maigret at the telephone. He smoked with relish, in little greedy puffs, although his throat was very sore. In front of him, raindrops slid slowly down the black windowpanes, and that reminded him afresh of his young days and the childhood illnesses when his mother brought him caramel custard in bed.

Madame Maigret came up again, puffing a little, glanced round the room to see if anything was wrong, but didn't think of the pipe.

"He'll be here in about an hour."

"I must ask you to do something else, Madame Maigret. You must get dressed—" She gave him a suspicious look. "You will go to young Justin's house and you will ask his parents' permission to bring him to me. Be nice to him. If I sent one of the Inspectors, he would be sure to frighten him, and the boy's already too inclined to stiffen up. You will simply tell him that I would like to chat with him for a few minutes."

"And if his mother wants to come with him?"

"Get out of it as best you can. I don't want the mother."

He was all alone, hot, sweaty, deep down in the bed, with his pipe sticking out from the bedclothes and emitting a light cloud of smoke. When he closed his eyes he kept seeing the corner of the Rue Sainte-Catherine; he was no longer Maigret the Chief Inspector—he was the altar boy, hurrying along, going the same way every morning at the same time, speaking to himself under his breath to keep up his courage.

He turned the corner of the Rue Sainte-Catherine.

"Mother, I would like you to buy me a bike—" The boy was practicing the speech he would make to his mother when he got home from the hospital. But it must have been more complex than that. The child would surely think up some more subtle approaches.

"You know, Mother, if I had a bike, I could—"

Or perhaps: "I've already saved up one hundred francs. If you would lend me the rest—I promise to pay it back out of the money I get for the Masses—I could—"

The corner of the Rue Sainte-Catherine . . . a few moments before the parish church bells sound the second stroke . . . and there were only another hundred and fifty meters of black, empty street to go in order to touch the reassuring door of the hospital. . . . A few strides between the pools of light from the streetlamps.

And later the boy would say, "I looked up, and I saw—"

The whole problem was there. The Judge lived almost exactly halfway up the street, equidistant from the Place du Congrès and the barracks corner, and he had neither seen nor heard anything.

The sick woman's husband, the man at Number 42, lived nearer the Place du Congrès, on the right side of the street, and he had heard the hurrying footsteps of a man running.

Yet, five minutes later, there was neither a corpse nor wounded man on the pavement. And neither car nor truck had passed. The constable on duty at the bridge, the other policemen in the district who were on their beats at different places, none of them had seen anything unusual—like, for example, a man carrying another on his back.

His temperature must have been rising, but Maigret no longer thought of consulting the thermometer. It was just like his childhood: when he was ill, it seemed to him that his mother, leaning over him, seemed so big that she filled the house.

There was this body lying across the pavement—so big because it was dead, with a brown-handled knife in its chest.

And behind it a man standing a few yards away, a man with very bright eyes, who had started to run—

To run in the direction of the barracks, while Justin took to his heels and fled in the opposite direction.

"There!"

There what? Maigret had said the word aloud as if it contained the solution to the problem—as if it were the solution to the problem. He was smiling with satisfaction as he drew on his pipe in voluptuous little puffs.

Drunks are like that. Truths suddenly become evident to them which they are incapable of explaining and which fade away as soon as they sober up.

It was there that something was false! And, in his fever, it was exactly at the point that Maigret located the jarring detail.

"Justin didn't make it up—"

His fear, his panic, when he had arrived at the hospital, weren't put on. Nor had he made up the body that looked too long lying on the pavement. And there was at least one person in the street who had heard running.

What was it, then, that the sneering Judge had said? "Are you still pinning your faith on the evidence of children?"

At all events, something of the sort. Yet it was the Judge who was wrong. Children are incapable of creating a story out of nothing, because truths are not built out of nothing—there must be some basis. Children distort the facts, perhaps, but they do not invent them.

There! Again that satisfied "there" that Maigret repeated at each stage, as if congratulating himself.

There had been a corpse on the pavement.

And doubtless, there had been a man nearby. He might even have had bright eyes.

And someone had run away.

And the old Judge, Maigret would have sworn, was not the man to lie in so many words.

Maigret was hot. He was drenched; nevertheless, he emerged from the sheets to go and fill the last pipe before Madame Maigret returned. While he was up he took the opportunity of opening the cupboard and taking a large gulp from a bottle of rum. Too bad if his temperature did rise a little that night, but everything would be tied up.

And it would be a very pretty piece of work—an anything but orthodox inquiry conducted while tucked up in his bed. That was something Madame Maigret would be quite incapable of appreciating.

The Judge hadn't lied, and yet he must have done his utmost to dig at the boy he hated, as two children of the same age can hate one another.

The customers were getting fewer downstairs, for the preposterous door chimes were ringing less often. No doubt the dairyman, his wife, and their daughter, pink as a ham, were at dinner in the rear of the shop.

Footsteps on the pavement. Coming up the stairs. Stumbling footsteps, like a child's. Madame Maigret opened the door and pushed young Justin in in front of her, his thick navy-blue woolen jacket sparkling with little pearls of rain. He smelled like a wet dog.

"Wait a minute, sonny, I'll take off your jacket."

"I can do it myself."

Another suspicious look from Madame Maigret. Oblivious she could not believe that this was still the same pipeful. She may even have suspected the rum.

"Sit down, Justin," said the Inspector, pointing to a chair.

"Thanks. I'm not tired."

"I've had you brought here to have a friendly little chat. What were you busy at?"

"My arithmetic homework."

"So in spite of what you've been through, you've been to school?"

"Why shouldn't I have gone?"

He was a proud little fellow.

He had drawn himself up again to his full height. Perhaps the Inspector too, lying there in bed, seemed to him to be bigger and longer?

"Madame Maigret, be so kind as to go and take a look at the broth in the kitchen and close the door."

This done, he winked at the boy.

"Pass me my tobacco pouch. It's on the mantelpiece. And the pipe that should be in my overcoat pocket. Yes, the one hanging behind the door. Thank you, son. Were you frightened when my wife came to fetch you?"

"No." He said it with pride.

"Have things been difficult for you?"

"Only because everyone keeps saying I'm making it up."

"And you aren't making it up, are you?"

"There was a dead man on the pavement and another who—"

"Hush!"

"What?"

"Not so fast. Sit down."

"I'm not tired."

"You've already said so, but it makes me tired to watch you."

He sat down on the chair, right on the edge, and his feet didn't touch the ground. His legs swung and his knees stuck out bare between his short trousers and his socks.

"What prank have you played on the Judge?"

A rapid instinctive reaction. "I've never done anything to him."

"You know which Judge I'm talking about?"

"The one who's always at his window. He looks like an owl."

"I should have said a screech owl. What's been going on between you?"

"I've never spoken to him."

"What's been going on between you?"

"In winter I never saw him, because his curtains were drawn when I passed."

"But in summer?"

"I stuck out my tongue at him."

"Why?"

"Because he looked at me as if he was laughing at me; he would start snickering to himself while he watched me."

"You've often stuck out your tongue at him?"

"Every time I saw him."

"And he?"

"He'd give a nasty laugh. I thought it was because I served at Mass and because he was an unbeliever."

"So it was he who was lying."

"What did he say?"

"That nothing happened outside his house yesterday morning, as he would have noticed."

The lad stared intently at Maigret, then lowered his head.

"He was lying, wasn't he?"

"There was a corpse with a knife in its chest on the pavement."

"I know."

"How do you know?"

"I know, because it's true," said Maigret softly. "Pass me the matches. I've let my pipe go out."

"Are you too hot?"

"It's nothing. A chill."

"You caught it this morning?"

"That's possible. Sit down."

He came suddenly alert and called, "Madame Maigret! Would you go downstairs? I think that's Besson who's just arrived, and I don't want him to come up till I've finished. You keep him company downstairs. My friend Justin will call you."

He said once more to his young companion, "Sit down. It's true, too, that you both ran away."

"I told you it was true."

"And I'm sure of it. Go and see that there's nobody at the door and it's closed tightly."

The boy went, not understanding, but imbued with the importance of his acts and movements.

"You know, Justin, you're a good little fellow."

"Why'd you say that?"

"The corpse is true, the man who ran is true."

The boy raised his head once again, and Maigret saw that his lip was trembling.

"And the Judge, who didn't lie, because a Judge wouldn't dare to lie, didn't tell the whole truth."

The room was redolent of Maigret's cold, rum, and tobacco. The smell of the vegetable broth wafted in under the door from the kitchen, and it was still raining silver drops on the black windowpanes. Outside, the street was deserted. Was it still a man and a child who found themselves face to face? Or two men? Or two children?

Maigret's head felt heavy, his eyes were watering. His pipe had a strange sickly taste that he did not find unpleasant, and he remembered the odors of the hospital, the chapel, and the sacristy.

"The Judge didn't tell the whole truth, because he wanted to torment you. And you, you didn't tell the whole truth, either. Now, I won't have you crying—it's not worth letting the whole world know what's going on between the two of us at this moment. You understand, Justin?"

The boy nodded. "If what you told us hadn't happened at all, the husband at Number 42 would not have heard running."

"I didn't make it up."

"Exactly. But if it happened as you said, the Judge could not have said that he didn't hear anything. And if the murderer had run in the direction of the barracks, the old man could not have sworn that nobody ran past his house."

The child didn't move; he was staring fixedly at his toes.

"Basically, the Judge was honest when he dared not say that you had gone past his house yesterday morning. But he could perhaps have said that you didn't pass. That is the truth—because you ran away in the opposite direction. No doubt he was also being truthful when he claimed that no man had run past on the pavement outside his window. For the man didn't go off in that direction."

"What do you know about it?" He had stiffened and was staring wide-eyed at Maigret, just as he must have stared the day before at the murderer or the victim.

"Because, inevitably, the man rushed off in the same direction as you, which explains how the husband at 42 heard him pass. Knowing that you had seen him, that you had seen the corpse, that you could get him caught, he ran after you."

"If you tell my mother—"

"Shush. I've no wish to say anything at all to your mother or anyone else. You see, Justin, my boy, I'm going to talk to you like a man. A murderer with enough intelligence and coolness to make a corpse disappear in a few minutes without leaving the slightest trace would not have been so stupid as to let you run away after what you had seen."

"I don't know."

"But I do. It's my business to know. The most difficult thing is not killing a man: it's getting rid of him afterward—and this fellow contrived a magnificent disappearance. He disappeared, even though you saw him and you saw the murderer. In other words, the latter was a very strong man. And a very strong man risking his neck would not have let you get away like that."

"I didn't know—"

"What didn't you know?"

"I didn't know it was so serious."

"It isn't at all serious, as the whole thing has now been put right."

"You've arrested him?" There was tremendous hope in the way he spoke.

"He will no doubt be arrested very shortly. Sit still."

"I won't move."

"First of all, if the scene had taken place in front of the Judge's—that's to say, halfway up the street—you'd have noticed it from farther away, and you'd have had time to run away. That's the only mistake the murderer made, cunning as he was."

"How did you guess?"

"I didn't guess—I too was an altar boy, and I served at the six o'clock Mass. You wouldn't have gone almost a hundred yards down the street without looking in front of you. Therefore, the corpse was nearer, much nearer, almost at the corner of the street."

"Five houses farther on."

"You were thinking of something else—your bicycle—and you probably walked twenty yards without seeing anything."

"You can't possibly know."

"And when you saw it, you ran towards the Place du Congrès to reach the hospital by the other way. The man ran behind you."

"I thought I was going to die of fright."

"He put his hand on your shoulder?"

"He grabbed my shoulders with both his hands. I thought he was going to throttle me."

"He told you to say—"

The child was crying, but not sobbing. He was ashen pale, and the tears were rolling slowly down his cheeks. "If you tell my mother, she'll be at me about it all my life. She's always at me."

"He told you to say that it had all happened farther along?"

"Yes."

"In front of the Judge's?"

"It was I who thought of the Judge's house—because of sticking out my tongue at him. He only said towards the other end of the street. And to say that he ran away in the direction of the barracks."

"And it just missed being the perfect crime, for nobody believed you, seeing that there was no murderer or corpse or trace of any kind, and the whole thing seemed impossible."

"But you?"

"Me? I don't count. It's pure chance that I have been an altar boy and then that I've had a fever today. What did he promise you?"

"He told me that if I didn't say what he wanted he would surely find me wherever I went, in spite of the police, and he'd cut my throat like a chicken."

"And then?"

"He asked me what I'd like to have."

"And you replied, 'A bike.' "

"How did you know that?"

"I keep telling you, I was an altar boy myself."

"And you wanted a bike?"

"That and a lot of things that I'd never had. Why did you say he had bright eyes?"

"I don't know. I didn't see his eyes. He wore thick glasses. But I didn't want them to find him."

"Because of the bike."

"Perhaps. You're going to tell my mother, aren't you?"

"Neither your mother nor anyone else. We're pals, aren't we, you and I? Now, pass me my tobacco again, and don't tell Madame Maigret I've smoked three pipefuls while we've been here. You see, grown-ups don't always tell the whole truth, either. What door was it in front of, Justin?"

"The yellow house next to the pork butcher's."

"Go and find my wife."

"Where is she?"

"Downstairs with Inspector Besson, who was so unkind to you."

"And is he going to arrest me?"

"Open the closet. There's a pair of trousers hanging there."

"What am I to do?"

"In the left-hand pocket you'll find a wallet."

"I've got it."

"In the wallet there are some visiting cards."

"You want them?"

"Give me one. And the pen on the table as well."

And Maigret took and wrote on the card beside his name: Credit for one bicycle.

"Come in, Besson."

Madame Maigret threw a glance at the opaque cloud of smoke that encircled the light veiled with oiled paper, and rushed toward the kitchen, from which there came a smell of burning.

As for Besson, taking the chair the boy had just got out of, he said, "I have the list you wanted me to draw up. I had better tell you straight away—"

"That it's no use. Who lives at Number 40?"

"One moment." He consulted his notes. "Wait . . . 40. The house had only one tenant."

"I thought as much."

"Oh?" A brief uneasy glance toward the child. "A foreigner, a dealer in precious stones. Name of Fross."

And from the depths of the pillows, on which he now reclined, Maigret's voice rose in a nonchalant murmur. "A receiver."

"What did you say, Chief?"

"A receiver. And also, perhaps, head of a gang."

"I don't understand."

"Doesn't matter. Be so kind, Besson, as to pass me the bottle of rum that's in the wall cupboard. Quickly, before Madame Maigret arrives. I bet my temperature's up to 102—the sheets will have to be changed twice tonight. Fross . . . Get a search warrant from the Examining Magistrate—no, at this hour of night that'll take time, for he's sure to be out playing bridge somewhere. Have you had dinner? I'm waiting for my broth. There are some blank warrants in my desk. Fill one out. Search the place. You're bound to find the corpse, even if it means knocking down a cellar wall."

Poor Besson was looking anxiously at his Chief and then at the child, who was waiting good as gold in the corner.

"Do it quickly, old chap. If he knows the lad came here this evening, you'll find the bird has flown. He's a smart one, you'll see."

And indeed he was. While the flying squad were ringing his bell, he was trying to make his getaway over the courtyard walls. It took all night to lay hands on him—he was finally caught on the rooftops—while other detectives were searching the house for hours before they found the corpse buried in the cellar.

Obviously a case of settling an old score. Some fellow, dissatisfied with the boss and feeling cheated, he'd gone and badgered him at his house in the early hours of the morning; Fross had felled him on the doorstep, never thinking an altar boy would be coming round the corner at that moment.

"How much?" Maigret had no longer the courage to look at the thermometer himself.

"102."

"You're not cheating?" He knew that she was cheating and that he had a higher temperature but he didn't care. It was blissfully good to sink into unconsciousness like this, to let himself slip quickly, dizzily away into a world that was hazy but terribly real—a world where an altar boy who looked like the young Maigret of other days was running desperately down the street, thinking he was going to be strangled or that he was going to get a nickel-plated bicycle.

"What are you saying?" asked Madame Maigret, who stood waiting with a hot mustard plaster for his neck in her plump hands.

Meanwhile he was mumbling vaguely like a feverish child, speaking of the "first stroke" and the "second stroke."

"I'm going to be late—"

"Late for what?"

"For Mass. The sister . . ."

He couldn't manage the word "sacristine." "The . . . sister—"

Finally, with a large compress round his neck, he fell asleep and dreamed of the Mass in his village church, of Marie Titin whose inn he used to run past because he was afraid.

"Afraid of what?"

"All the same, I got him—"

"Who?"

"The Judge."

It was so complicated to explain. . . . The Judge looked like someone in his village, someone he had stuck out his tongue at. . . . The blacksmith? No . . . it was the father-in-law of the woman at the bakery. It didn't matter. Someone he didn't like. . . .

It was the Judge who had cheated in order to get his own back on the altar boy. He had said he had not heard footsteps running past his house. He hadn't said that he had heard the sound of a chase in the other direction. Old men have a second childhood. They squabble with children—just like children . . .

Maigret was content, despite everything. He had cheated over the three pipefuls—no, four. There was a fine strong taste of tobacco in his mouth, and he could sink into sleep. . . .

And tomorrow, because he had a chill, Madame Maigret would make his caramel custard.

Trouble Is My Business

Raymond Chandler

"The big foreign car drove itself, but I held the wheel for the sake of appearances" (*Farewell, My Lovely*). This classic one-liner could only have come from the lips of a character that would define the quintessential private eye, Philip Marlowe. Raymond Chandler's masterful creation appeared in his first novel, *The Big Sleep*, in 1939. Chandler was the first writer to establish a code of ethics for private detective stories and felt that the private detective must himself be above all the things he encounters. These classic Marlowe stories unveil betrayal, mistrust and double-dealing on the seamy side of Los Angeles. Marlowe has been immortalized through his adaptation in films, television and radio. Actors ranging from Dick Powell in 1945 (*Murder, My Sweet*) and James Garner in 1969 (*Marlowe*) to Robert Mitchum in 1976 (*Farewell, My Lovely*) and again in 1978 (*The Big Sleep*) have all brought Philip Marlowe to life. However, the actor who best portrays Marlowe as the archetypal private eye is Humphrey Bogart, who in 1946 starred with Lauren Bacall in Howard Hawks's version of *The Big Sleep*.

Anna Halsey was about two hundred and forty pounds of middle-aged putty-faced woman in a black tailor-made suit. Her eyes were shiny black shoe buttons, her cheeks were as soft as suet and about the same color. She was sitting behind a black glass desk that looked like Napoleon's tomb and she was smoking a cigarette in a black holder that was not quite as long as a rolled umbrella. She said: "I need a man."

I watched her shake ash from the cigarette to the shiny top of the desk where flakes of it curled and crawled in the draft from an open window.

"I need a man good-looking enough to pick up a dame who has a sense of class, but he's got to be tough enough to swap punches with a power shovel. I need a guy who can act like a bar lizard and backchat like Fred Allen, only better, and get hit on the head with a beer truck and think some cutie in the leg-line topped him with a breadstick."

"It's a cinch," I said. "You need the New York Yankees, Robert Donat, and the Yacht Club Boys."

"You might do," Anna said, "cleaned up a little. Twenty bucks a day and ex's. I haven't brokered a job in years, but this one is out of my line. I'm in the smooth angles of the detecting business and I make money without getting my can knocked off. Let's see how Gladys likes you."

She reversed the cigarette holder and tipped a key on a large black-and-chromium annunciator box. "Come in and empty Anna's ashtray, honey."

We waited.

The door opened and a tall blonde dressed better than the Duchess of Windsor strolled in.

She swayed elegantly across the room, emptied Anna's ashtray, patted her fat cheek, gave me a smooth rippling glance and went out again.

"I think she blushed," Anna said when the door closed. "I guess you still have it."

"She blushed—and I have a dinner date with Darryl Zanuck," I said. "Quit horsing around. What's the story?"

"It's to smear a girl. A red-headed number with bedroom eyes. She's shill for a gambler and she's got her hooks into a rich man's pup."

"What do I do to her?"

Anna sighed. "It's kind of a mean job, Philip, I guess. If she's got a record of a sort, you dig it up and toss it in her face. If she hasn't, which is more likely as she comes from good people, it's kind of up to you. You get an idea once in a while, don't you?"

"I can't remember the last one I had. What gambler and what rich man?"

"Marty Estel."

I started to get up from my chair, then remembered that business had been bad for a month and that I needed the money.

I sat down again.

"You might get into trouble, of course," Anna said. "I never heard of Marty bumping anybody off in the public square at high noon, but he don't play with cigar coupons."

"Trouble is my business," I said. "Twenty-five a day and a guarantee of two-fifty, if I pull the job."

"I gotta make a little something for myself," Anna whined.

"Okay. There's plenty of coolie labor around town. Nice to have seen you looking so well. So long, Anna."

I stood up this time. My life wasn't worth much, but it was worth that much. Marty Estel was supposed to be pretty tough people, with the right helpers and the right protection behind him. His place was out in West Hollywood, on the Strip. He wouldn't pull anything crude, but if he pulled at all, something would pop.

"Sit down, it's a deal," Anna sneered. "I'm a poor old broken-down woman trying to run a high-class detective agency on nothing but fat and bad health, so take my last nickel and laugh at me."

"Who's the girl?" I had sat down again.

"Her name is Harriet Huntress—a swell name for the part too. She lives in the El Milano, nineteen-hundred block on North Sycamore, very high-class. Father went broke back in thirty-one and jumped out of his office window. Mother dead. Kid sister in boarding school back in Connecticut. That might make an angle."

"Who dug up all this?"

"The client got a bunch of photostats of notes the pup had given to Marty. Fifty grand worth. The pup—he's an adopted son to the old man—denied the notes, as kids will. So the client had the photostats experted by a guy named Arbogast, who pretends to be good at that sort of thing. He said okay and dug around a bit, but he's too fat to do legwork, like me, and he's off the case now."

"But I could talk to him?"

"I don't know why not." Anna nodded several of her chins.

"This client—does he have a name?"

"Son, you have a treat coming. You can meet him in person—right now."

She tipped the key of her call box again. "Have Mr. Jeeter come in, honey."

"That Gladys," I said, "does she have a steady?"

"You lay off Gladys!" Anna almost screamed at me. "She's worth eighteen grand a year in divorce business to me. Any guy that lays a finger on her, Philip Marlowe, is practically cremated."

"She's got to fall some day," I said. "Why couldn't I catch her?"

The opening door stopped that.

I hadn't seen him in the paneled reception room, so he must have been waiting in a private office. He hadn't enjoyed it. He came in quickly, shut the door quickly, and yanked a thin octagonal platinum watch from his vest and glared at it. He was a tall white-blond type in pin-stripe flannel of youthful cut. There was a small pink rosebud in his lapel. He had a keen frozen face, a little pouchy under the eyes, a little thick in the lips. He carried an ebony cane with a silver knob, wore spats and looked a smart sixty, but I gave him close to ten years more. I didn't like him.

"Twenty-six minutes, Miss Halsey," he said icily. "My time happens to be valuable. By regarding it as valuable I have managed to make a great deal of money."

"Well, we're trying to save you some of the money," Anna drawled. She didn't like him either. "Sorry to keep you waiting, Mr. Jeeter, but you wanted to see the operative I selected and I had to send for him."

"He doesn't look the type to me," Mr. Jeeter said, giving me a nasty glance. "I think more of a gentleman—"

"You're not the Jeeter of *Tobacco Road,* are you?" I asked him.

He came slowly toward me and half lifted the stick. His icy eyes tore at me like claws. "So you insult me," he said. "Me—a man in my position."

"Now wait a minute," Anna began.

"Wait a minute nothing," I said. "This party said I was not a gentleman. Maybe that's okay for a man in his position, whatever it is—but a man in my position doesn't take a dirty crack from anybody. He can't afford to. Unless, of course, it wasn't intended."

Mr. Jeeter stiffened and glared at me. He took his watch out again and looked at it. "Twenty-eight minutes," he said. "I apologize, young man. I had no desire to be rude."

"That's swell," I said. "I knew you weren't the Jeeter in *Tobacco Road* all along."

That almost started him again, but he let it go. He wasn't sure how I meant it.

"A question or two while we are together," I said. "Are you willing to give this Huntress girl a little money—for expenses?"

"Not one cent," he barked. "Why should I?"

"It's got to be a sort of custom. Suppose she married him. What would he have?"

"At the moment a thousand dollars a month from a trust fund established by his mother, my late wife." He dipped his head. "When he is twenty-eight years old, far too much money."

"You can't blame the girl for trying," I said. "Not these days. How about Marty Estel? Any settlements there?"

He crumpled his gray gloves with a purple-veined hand. "The debt is uncollectible. It is a gambling debt."

Anna sighed wearily and flicked ash around on her desk.

"Sure," I said. "But gamblers can't afford to let people welsh on them. After all, if your son had won, Marty would have paid him."

"I'm not interested in that," the tall thin man said coldly.

"Yeah, but think of Marty sitting there with fifty grand in notes. Not worth a nickel. How will he sleep nights?"

Mr. Jeeter looked thoughtful. "You mean there is danger of violence?" he suggested, almost suavely.

"That's hard to say. He runs an exclusive place, gets a good movie crowd. He had his own reputation to think of. But he's in a racket and he knows people. Things can happen—a long way off from where Marty is. And Marty is no bathmat. He gets up and walks."

Mr. Jeeter looked at his watch again and it annoyed him. He slammed it back into his vest. "All that is your affair," he snapped. "The district attorney is a personal friend of mine. If this matter seems to be beyond your powers—"

"Yeah," I told him. "But you came slumming down our street just the same. Even if the D.A. is in your vest pocket—along with that watch."

He put his hat on, drew on one glove, tapped the edge of his shoe with his stick, walked to the door and opened it.

"I ask results and I pay for them," he said coldly. "I pay promptly. I even pay generously sometimes, although I am not considered a generous man. I think we all understand one another."

He almost winked then and went on out. The door closed softly against the cushion of air in the door-closer. I looked at Anna and grinned.

"Sweet, isn't he?" she said. "I'd like eight of him for my cocktail set."

I gouged twenty dollars out of her—for expenses.

The Arbogast I wanted was John D. Arbogast and he had an office on Sunset near Ivar. I called him up from a phone booth. The voice that answered was fat. I wheezed softly, like the voice of a man who had just won a pie-eating contest.

"Mr. John D. Arbogast?"

"Yeah."

"This is Philip Marlowe, a private detective working on a case you did some experting on. Party named Jeeter."

"Yeah."

"Can I come up and talk to you about it—after I eat lunch?"

"Yeah." He hung up. I decided he was not a talkative man.

I had lunch and drove out there. It was east of Ivar, an old two-story building faced with brick which had been painted recently. The street floor was stores and a restaurant. The building entrance was the foot of a wide straight stairway to the second floor. On the directory at the bottom I read: John D. Arbogast, Suite 212. I went up the stairs and found myself in a wide straight hall that ran parallel with the street. A man in a smock was standing in an open doorway down to my right. He wore a round mirror strapped to his forehead and pushed back, and his face had a puzzled expression. He went back to his office and shut the door.

I went the other way, about half the distance along the hall. A door on the side away from Sunset was lettered:

John D. Arbogast
EXAMINER OF QUESTIONED DOCUMENTS
PRIVATE INVESTIGATOR
ENTER

The door opened without resistance onto a small windowless anteroom with a couple of easy chairs, some magazines, two chromium smoking stands. There were two floor lamps and a ceiling fixture, all lighted. A door on the other side of the cheap but thick and new rug was lettered:

John D. Arbogast
EXAMINER OF QUESTIONED DOCUMENTS
PRIVATE

A buzzer had rung when I opened the outer door and gone on ringing until it closed. Nothing happened. Nobody was in the waiting room. The inner door didn't open. I went over and listened at the panel—no sound of conversation inside. I knocked. That didn't buy me anything either. I tried the knob. It turned, so I opened the door and went in.

This room had two north windows, both curtained at the sides and both shut tight. There was dust on the sills. There was a desk, two filing cases, a carpet which was just a carpet, and walls which were just walls. To the left another door with a glass panel was lettered:

John D. Arbogast
LABORATORY
PRIVATE

I had an idea I might be able to remember the name.

The room in which I stood was small. It seemed almost too small even for the pudgy hand that rested on the edge of the desk, motionless, holding a fat pencil like a carpenter's pencil. The hand had a wrist, hairless as a plate. A buttoned shirt cuff, not too clean, came down out of a coat sleeve. The rest of the sleeve dropped over the far edge of the desk out of sight. The desk was less than six feet long, so he couldn't have been a very tall man. The hand and the ends of the sleeves were all I saw of him from where I stood. I went quietly back through the anteroom and fixed its door so that it couldn't be opened from the outside and put out the three lights and went back to the private office. I went around an end of the desk.

He was fat all right, enormously fat, fatter by far than Anna Halsey. His face, what I could see of it, looked about the size of a basketball. It had a pleasant pinkness, even now. He was kneeling on the floor. He had his large head against the sharp inner corner of the kneehole of the desk, and his left hand was flat on the floor with a piece of yellow paper under it. The fingers were outspread as much as such fat fingers could be, and the yellow paper showed between. He looked as if he were pushing hard on the floor, but he wasn't really. What was holding him up was his own fat. His body was folded down against his enormous thighs, and the thickness and fatness of them held him that way, kneeling, poised solid. It would have taken a couple of good blocking backs to knock him over. That wasn't a very nice idea at the moment, but I had it just the same. I took time out and wiped the back of my neck, although it was not a warm day.

His hair was gray and clipped short and his neck had as many folds as a concertina. His feet were small, as the feet of fat men often are, and they were in black shiny shoes which were sideways on the carpet and close together and neat and nasty. He wore a dark suit that needed cleaning. I leaned down and buried my fingers in the bottomless fat of his neck. He had an artery in there somewhere, probably, but I couldn't find it and he didn't need it anymore anyway. Between his bloated knees on the carpet a dark stain had spread and spread—

I knelt in another place and lifted the pudgy fingers that were holding down the piece of yellow paper. They were cool, but not cold, and soft and a little sticky. The paper was from a scratch pad. It would have been very nice if it had had a message on it, but it hadn't. There were vague meaningless marks, not words, not even letters. He had tried to write something after he was shot—perhaps even thought he was writing something—but all he managed was some hen scratches.

He had slumped down then, still holding the paper, pinned it to the floor with his fat hand, held on to the fat pencil with his other hand, wedged his torso against his huge thighs, and so died. John D. Arbogast, Examiner of Questioned Documents. Private. Very dammed private. He had said "yeah" to me three times over the phone.

And here he was.

I wiped doorknobs with my handkerchief, put off the lights in the anteroom, left the outer door so that it was locked from the outside, left the hallway, left the building and left the neighborhood. So far as I could tell nobody saw me go. So far as I could tell.

❦ ❦ ❦ ❦

The El Milano was, as Anna had told me, in the 1900 block on North Sycamore. It was most of the block. I parked fairly near the ornamental forecourt and went along to the pale blue neon sign over the entrance to the basement garage. I walked down a railed ramp into a bright space of glistening cars and cold air. A trim light-colored Negro in a spotless coverall suit with blue cuffs came out of a glass office. His black hair was as smooth as a bandleader's.

"Busy?" I asked him.

"Yes and no, sir."

"I've got a car outside that needs a dusting. About five bucks worth of dusting."

It didn't work. He wasn't the type. His chestnut eyes became thoughtful and remote. "That is a good deal of dusting, sir. May I ask if anything else would be included?"

"A little. Is Miss Harriet Huntress's car in?"

He looked. I saw him look along the glistening row at a canary-yellow convertible which was about as inconspicuous as a privy on the front lawn.

"Yes, sir. It is in."

"I'd like her apartment number and a way to get up there without going through the lobby. I'm a private detective." I showed him a buzzer. He looked at the buzzer. It failed to amuse him.

He smiled the faintest smile I ever saw. "Five dollars is nice money, sir, to a working man. It falls a little short of being nice enough to make me risk my position. About from here to Chicago short, sir. I suggest that you save your five dollars, sir, and try the customary mode of entry."

"You're quite a guy," I said. "What are you going to be when you grow up—a five-foot shelf?"

"I am already grown up, sir. I am thirty-four years old, married happily, and have two children. Good afternoon, sir."

He turned on his heel. "Well, good-bye," I said. "And pardon my whiskey breath. I just got in from Butte."

I went back up along the ramp and wandered along the street to where I should have gone in the first place. I might have known that five bucks and a buzzer wouldn't buy me anything in a place like the El Milano.

The Negro was probably telephoning the office right now.

The building was a huge white stucco affair, Moorish in style, with great fretted lanterns in the forecourt and huge date palms. The entrance was at the inside corner of an L, up marble steps, through an arch framed in California or dishpan mosaic.

A doorman opened the door for me and I went in. The lobby was not quite as big as the Yankee Stadium. It was floored with a pale blue carpet with sponge rubber underneath. It was so soft it made me want to lie down and roll. I waded over to the desk and put an elbow on it and was stared at by a pale thin clerk with one of those mustaches that get stuck under your fingernail. He toyed with it and looked past my shoulder at an Ali Baba oil jar big enough to keep a tiger in.

"Miss Huntress in?"

"Who shall I announce?"

"Mr. Marty Estel."

That didn't take any better than my play in the garage. He leaned on something with his left foot. A blue-and-gilt door opened at the end of the desk and a large sandy-haired man with cigar ash on his vest came out and leaned absently on the end of the desk and stared at the Ali Baba oil jar, as if trying to make up his mind whether it was a spittoon.

The clerk raised his voice. "You are Mr. Marty Estel?"

"From him."

"Isn't that a little different? And what is your name, sir, if one may ask?"

"One may ask," I said. "One may not be told. Such are my orders. Sorry to be stubborn and all that rot."

He didn't like my manner. He didn't like anything about me. "I'm afraid I can't announce you," he said coldly. "Mr. Hawkins, might I have your advice on a matter?"

The sandy-haired man took his eyes off the oil jar and slid along the desk until he was within blackjack range of me.

"Yes, Mr. Gregory?" He yawned.

"Nuts to both of you," I said. "And that includes your lady friends."

Hawkins grinned. "Come into my office, bo. We'll kind of see if we can get you straightened out."

I followed him into the doghole he had come out of. It was large enough for a pint-size desk, two chairs, a knee-high cuspidor, and an open box of cigars. He placed his rear end against the desk and grinned at me sociably.

"Didn't play it very smooth, did you, bo? I'm the house man here. Spill it."

"Some days I feel like playing smooth," I said, "and some days I feel like playing it like a waffle iron." I got my wallet out and showed him the buzzer and a small photostat of my license behind a celluloid window.

"One of the boys, huh?" He nodded. "You ought to of asked for me in the first place."

"Sure. Only I never heard of you. I want to see this Huntress frail. She doesn't know me, but I have business with her, and it's not noisy business."

He made a yard and a half sideways and cocked his cigar in the other corner of his mouth. He looked at my right eyebrow. "What's the gag? Why try to apple polish the dinghe downstairs? You gettin' any expense money?"

"Could be."

"I'm nice people," he said. "But I gotta protect the guests."

"You're almost out of cigars," I said, looking at the ninety or so in the box. I lifted a couple, smelled them, tucked a folded ten-dollar bill below them and put them back.

"That's cute," he said. "You and me could get along. What you want done?"

"Tell her I'm from Marty Estel. She'll see me."

"It's the job if I get a kickback."

"You won't. I've got important people behind me."

I started to reach for my ten, but he pushed my hand away. "I'll take a chance," he said. He reached for his phone and asked for suite 814 and began to hum. His humming sounded like a cow being sick. He leaned forward suddenly and his face became a honeyed smile. His voice dripped.

"Miss Huntress? This is Hawkins, the house man. Hawkins. Yeah . . . Hawkins. Sure, you meet a lot of people, Miss Huntress. Say, there's a gentleman in my office wanting to see you with a message from Mr. Estel. We can't let him up without your say so, because he don't want to give us no name. . . . Yeah, Hawkins, the house detective, Miss Huntress. Yeah, he says you don't know him personal, but he looks okay to me. . . . Okay. Thanks a lot, Miss Huntress. Serve him right up."

He put the phone down and patted it gently.

"All you needed was some background music," I said.

"You can ride up," he said dreamily. He reached absently into his cigar box and removed the folded bill. "A darb," he said softly. "Every time I think of that dame I have to go out and walk around the block. Let's go."

We went out to the lobby again and Hawkins took me to the elevator and highsigned me in.

The elevator had a carpeted floor and mirrors and indirect lighting. It rose as softly as the mercury in a thermometer. The doors whispered open, I wandered over the moss they used for a hall carpet and came to a door marked 814. I pushed a little button beside it, chimes rang inside and the door opened.

She wore a street dress of pale green wool and a small cockeyed hat that hung on her ear like a butterfly. Her eyes were wide-set and there was thinking room between them. Their color was lapis-lazuli blue and the color of her hair was dusky red, like a fire under control but still dangerous. She was too tall to be cute. She wore plenty of make-up in the right places and the cigarette she was poking at me had a built-on mouthpiece about three inches long. She didn't look hard, but she looked as if she had heard all the answers and remembered the ones she thought she might be able to use sometime.

She looked me over coolly. "Well what's the message, brown eyes?"

"I'd have to come in," I said. "I never could talk on my feet."

She laughed disinterestedly and I slid past the end of her cigarette into a long rather narrow room with plenty of nice furniture, plenty of windows, plenty of drapes, plenty of everything. A fire blazed behind a screen, a big log on top of a gas teaser. There was a silk Oriental rug in front of a nice rose davenport in front of the nice fire, and beside that there was Scotch and swish on a tabouret, ice in a bucket, everything to make a man feel at home.

"You'd better have a drink," she said. "You probably can't talk without a glass in your hand."

I sat down and reached for the Scotch. The girl sat in a deep chair and crossed her knees. I thought of Hawkins walking around the block. I could see a little something in his point of view.

"So you're from Marty Estel," she said, refusing a drink.

"Never met him."

"I had an idea to that effect. What's the racket, bum? Marty will love to hear how you used his name."

"I'm shaking in my shoes. What made you let me up?"

"Curiosity. I've been expecting lads like you any day. I never dodge trouble. Some kind of a dick, aren't you?"

I lit a cigarette and nodded. "Private. I have a little deal to propose."

"Propose it." She yawned.

"How much will you take to lay off young Jeeter?"

She yawned again. "You interest me—so little I could hardly tell you."

"Don't scare me to death. Honest, how much are you asking? Or is that an insult?"

She smiled. She had a nice smile. She had lovely teeth. "I'm a big girl now," she said. "I don't have to ask. They bring it to me, tied up with ribbon."

"The old man's a little tough. They say he draws a lot of water."

"Water doesn't cost much."

I nodded and drank some more of my drink. It was good Scotch. In fact it was perfect. "His idea is you get nothing. You get smeared. You get put in the middle. I can't see it that way."

"But you're working for him."

"Sounds funny, doesn't it? There's probably a smart way to play this, but I just can't think of it at the moment. How much would you take—or would you?"

"How about fifty grand?"

"Fifty grand for you and another fifty for Marty?"

She laughed. "Now, you ought to know Marty wouldn't like me to mix in his business. I was just thinking of my end."

She crossed her legs the other way. I put another lump of ice in my drink.

"I was thinking of five hundred," I said.

"Five hundred what?" She looked puzzled.

"Dollars—not Rolls-Royces."

She laughed heartily. "You amuse me. I ought to tell you to go to hell, but I like brown eyes. Warm brown eyes with flecks of gold in them."

"You're throwing it away. I don't have a nickel."

She smiled and fitted a fresh cigarette between her lips. I went over to light it for her. Her eyes came up and looked into mine. Hers had sparks in them.

"Maybe I have a nickel already," she said softly.

"Maybe that's why he hired the fat boy—so you couldn't make him dance." I sat down again.

"Who hired what fat boy?"

"Old Jeeter hired a fat boy named Arbogast. He was on the case before me. Didn't you know? He got bumped off this afternoon."

I said it quite casually for the shock effect, but she didn't move. The provocative smile didn't leave the corners of her lips. Her eyes didn't change. She made a dim sound with her breath.

"Does it have to have something to do with me?" she asked quietly.

"I don't know. I don't know who murdered him. It was done in his office, around noon or a little later. It may not have anything to do with the Jeeter case. But it happened pretty pat—just after I had been put on the job and before I got a chance to talk to him."

She nodded. "I see. And you think Marty does things like that. And of course you told the police?"

"Of course I did not."

"You're giving away a little weight there, brother."

"Yeah. But let's get together on a price and it had better be low. Because whatever the cops do to me they'll do plenty to Marty Estel and you when they get the story—if they get it."

"A little spot of blackmail," the girl said coolly. "I think I might call it that. Don't go too far with me, brown eyes. By the way, do I know your name?"

"Philip Marlowe."

"Then listen, Philip, I was in the Social Register once. My family were nice people. Old man Jeeter ruined my father—all proper and legitimate, the way that kind of heel ruins people—but he ruined him, and my father committed suicide, and my mother died and I've got a kid sister back east in school and perhaps I'm not too damn particular how I get the money to take care of her. And maybe I'm going to take care of old Jeeter one of these days, too—even if I have to marry his son to do it."

"Stepson, adopted son," I said. "No relation at all."

"It'll hurt him just as hard, brother. And the boy will have plenty of the long green in a couple of years. I could do worse—even if he does drink too much."

"You wouldn't say that in front of him, lady."

"No? Take a look behind you, gumshoes. You ought to have the wax taken out of your ears."

I stood up and turned fast. He stood about four feet from me. He had come out of some door and sneaked across the carpet and I had been too busy being clever with nothing on the ball to hear him. He was big, blond, dressed in a rough sporty suit, with a scarf and open-neck shirt. He was red-faced and his eyes glittered and they were not focusing any too well. He was a bit drunk for that early in the day.

"Beat it while you can still walk," he sneered at me. "I heard it. Harry can say anything she likes about me. I like it. Dangle, before I knock your teeth down your throat!"

The girl laughed behind me. I didn't like that. I took a step toward the big blond boy. His eyes blinked. Big as he was, he was a pushover.

"Ruin him, baby," the girl said coldly behind my back. "I love to see these hard numbers bend at the knees."

I looked back at her with a leer. That was a mistake. He was wild, probably, but he could still hit a wall that didn't jump. He hit me while I was looking back over my shoulder. It hurts to be hit that way. He hit me plenty hard, on the back end of the jawbone.

I went over sideways, tried to spread my legs, and slid on the silk rug. I did a nose dive somewhere or other and my head was not as hard as the piece of furniture it smashed into.

For a brief moment I saw his red face sneering down at me in triumph. I think I was a little sorry for him—even then.

Darkness folded down and I went out.

❦ ❦ ❦ ❦

When I came to, the light from the window across the room was hitting me square in the eyes. The back of my head ached. I felt it and it was sticky. I moved around slowly, like a cat in a strange house, got up on my knees and reached for the bottle of Scotch on the tabouret at the end of the davenport. By some miracle I hadn't knocked it over. Falling I had hit my head on the clawlike leg of a chair. That had hurt me a lot more than young Jeeter's haymaker. I could feel the sore place on my jaw all right, but it wasn't important enough to write in my diary.

I got up on my feet, took a swig of the Scotch and looked around. There wasn't anything to see. The room was empty. It was full of silence and the memory of a nice perfume. One of those perfumes you don't notice until they are almost gone, like the last leaf on a tree. I felt my head again, touched the sticky place with my handkerchief, decided it wasn't worth yelling about, and took another drink.

I sat down with the bottle on my knees, listening to traffic noise somewhere, far off. It was a nice room. Miss Huntress was a nice girl. She knew a few wrong numbers, but who didn't? I should criticize a little thing like that. I took another drink. The level in the bottle was a lot lower now. It was smooth and you hardly noticed it going down. It didn't take half your tonsils with it, like some of the stuff I had to drink. I took some more. My head felt all right now. I felt fine. I felt like singing the Prologue to Pagliacci. Yes, she was a nice girl. If she was paying her own rent, she was doing right well. I was for her. She was swell. I used some more of her Scotch.

The bottle was still half full. I shook it gently, stuffed it in my overcoat pocket, put my hat somewhere on my head and left. I made the elevator without hitting the walls on either side of the corridor, floated downstairs, strolled out into the lobby.

Hawkins, the house dick, was leaning on the end of the desk again, staring at the Ali Baba oil jar. The same clerk was nuzzling at the same itsy-bitsy mustache. I smiled at him. He smiled back. Hawkins smiled at me. I smiled back. Everybody was swell.

I made the front door the first time and gave the doorman two bits and floated down the steps along the walk to the street and my car. The swift California twilight was falling. It was a lovely night. Venus in the west was as bright as a streetlamp, as bright as life, as bright as Miss Huntress's eyes, as bright as a bottle of Scotch. That reminded me. I got the square bottle out and tapped it with discretion, corked it, and tucked it away again. There was still enough to get home on.

I crashed five red lights on the way back but my luck was in and nobody pinched me. I parked more or less in front of my apartment house and more or less near the curb. I rode to my floor in the elevator, had a little trouble opening the doors and helped myself out with my bottle. I got the key into my door and unlocked it and stepped inside and found the light switch. I took a little more of my medicine before exhausting myself any further. Then I started for the kitchen to get some ice and ginger ale for a real drink.

I thought there was a funny smell in the apartment—nothing I could put a name to offhand—a sort of medicinal smell. I hadn't put it there and it hadn't been there when I went out. But I felt too well to argue about it. I started for the kitchen, got about halfway there.

They came out at me, almost side by side, from the dressing room beside the wall bed—two of them—with guns. The tall one was grinning. He had his hat low on his forehead and he had a wedge-shaped face that ended in a point, like the bottom half of the ace of diamonds. He had dark moist eyes and a nose so bloodless that it might have been made of white wax. His gun was a Colt Woodsman with a long barrel and the front sight filed off. That meant he thought he was good.

The other was a little terrier-like punk with bristly reddish hair and no hat and watery blank eyes and bat ears and small feet in dirty white sneakers. He had an automatic that looked too heavy for him to hold up, but he seemed to like holding it. He breathed open-mouthed and noisily and the smell I had noticed came from him in waves—menthol.

"Reach, you bastard," he said.

I put my hands up. There was nothing else to do.

This little one circled around to the side and came at me from the side. "Tell us we can't get away with it," he sneered.

"You can't get away with it," I said.

The tall one kept on grinning loosely and his nose kept on looking as if it was made of white wax. The little one spat on my carpet. "Yah!" He came close to me, leering, and made a pass at my chin with the big gun.

I dodged. Ordinarily that would have been just something which, in the circumstances, I had to take and like. But I was feeling better than ordinary. I was a world-beater. I took them in sets, guns and all. I took the little man around the throat and jerked him hard against my stomach, put a hand over his little gun hand and knocked the gun to the floor. It was easy. Nothing was bad about it but his breath. Blobs of saliva came out on his lips. He spit curses.

The tall man stood and leered and didn't shoot. He didn't move. His eyes looked a little anxious, I thought, but I was too busy to make sure. I went down behind the little punk, still holding him, and got hold of his gun. That was wrong. I ought to have pulled my own.

I threw him away from me and he reeled against a chair and fell down and began to kick the chair savagely. The tall man laughed.

"It ain't got any firing pin in it," he said.

"Listen," I told him earnestly, "I'm half full of good Scotch and ready to go places and get things done. Don't waste much of my time. What do you boys want?"

"It still ain't got any firing pin in it," Waxnose said. "Try and see. I don't never let Frisky carry a loaded rod. He's too impulsive. You got a nice arm action there, pal. I will say that for you."

Frisky sat up on the floor and spat on the carpet again and laughed. I pointed the muzzle of the big automatic at the floor and squeezed the trigger. It clicked dryly, but from the balance it felt as if it had cartridges in it.

"We don't mean no harm," Waxnose said. "Not this trip. Maybe next trip? Who knows? Maybe you're a guy that will take a hint. Lay off the Jeeter kid is the word. See?"

"No."

"You won't do it?"

"No. I don't see. Who's the Jeeter kid?"

Waxnose was not amused. He waved his long .22 gently. "You oughta get your memory fixed, pal, about the same time you get your door fixed. A pushover that was. Frisky just blew it in with his breath."

"I can understand that," I said.

"Gimme my gat," Frisky yelped. He was up off the floor again, but this time he rushed his partner instead of me.

"Lay off, dummy," the tall one said. "We just got a message for a guy. We don't blast him. Not today."

"Says you!" Frisky snarled and tried to grab the .22 out of Waxnose's hand. Waxnose threw him to one side without trouble but the interlude allowed me to switch the big automatic to my left hand and jerk out my Luger. I showed it to Waxnose. He nodded, but did not seem impressed.

"He ain't got no parents," he said sadly. "I just let him run around with me. Don't pay him no attention unless he bites you. We'll be on our way now. You get the idea. Lay off the Jeeter kid."

"You're looking at a Luger," I said. "Who is the Jeeter kid? And maybe we'll have some cops before you leave."

He smiled wearily. "Mister, I pack this small-bore because I can shoot. If you think you can take me, go to it."

"Okay," I said. "Do you know anybody named Arbogast?"

"I meet such a lot of people," he said with another weary smile. "Maybe yes, maybe no. So long, pal. Be pure."

He strolled over to the door, moving a little sideways, so that he had me covered all the time, and I had him covered, and it was just a case of who shot first and straightest, or whether it was worthwhile to shoot at all, or whether I could hit anything with so much nice warm Scotch in me. I let him go. He didn't look like a killer to me, but I could have been wrong.

The little man rushed me again while I wasn't thinking about him. He clawed his big automatic out of my left hand, skipped over to the door, spat on the carpet again, and slipped out. Waxnose backed after him—long sharp face, white nose, pointed chin, weary expression. I wouldn't forget him.

He closed the door softly and I stood there, foolish, holding my gun. I heard the elevator come up and go down again and stop. I still stood there. Marty Estel wouldn't be very likely to hire a couple of comics like that to throw a scare into anybody. I thought about that, but thinking got me nowhere. I remembered the half-bottle of Scotch I had left and went into executive session with it.

An hour and a half later I felt fine, but I still didn't have any ideas. I just felt sleepy.

The jarring of the telephone bell woke me. I had dozed off in the chair, which was a bad mistake, because I woke up with two flannel blankets in my mouth, a splitting headache, a bruise on the back of my head and another on my jaw, neither of them larger that a Yakima apple, but sore for all that. I felt terrible. I felt like an amputated leg.

I crawled over to the telephone and humped myself in a chair beside it and answered it. The voice dripped icicles.

"Mr. Marlowe? This is Mr. Jeeter. I believe we met this morning. I'm afraid I was a little stiff with you."

"I'm a little stiff myself. Your son poked me in the jaw. I mean your stepson, or your adopted son—or whatever he is."

"He is both my stepson and my adopted son. Indeed?" He sounded interested. "And where did you meet him?"

"In Miss Huntress's apartment."

"Oh I see." There had been a sudden thaw. The icicles had melted. "Very interesting. What did Miss Huntress have to say?"

"She liked it. She liked him poking me in the jaw."

"I see. And why did he do that?"

"She had him hid out. He overheard some of our talk. He didn't like it."

"I see. I have been thinking that perhaps some consideration—not large, of course—should be granted to her for her cooperation. That is, if we can secure it."

"Fifty grand is the price."

"I'm afraid I don't—"

"Don't kid me," I snarled. "Fifty thousand dollars. Fifty grand. I offered her five hundred—just for a gag."

"You seem to treat this whole business in a spirit of considerable levity," he snarled back. "I am not accustomed to that sort of thing and I don't like it."

I yawned. I didn't give a damn if school kept in or not. "Listen, Mr. Jeeter, I'm a great guy to horse around, but I have my mind on the job just the same. And there are some very unusual angles to this case. For instance a couple of gunmen just stuck me up in my apartment here and told me to lay off the Jeeter case. I don't see why it should get so tough."

"Good heavens!" He sounded shocked. "I'll send my car for you. Can you come right away?"

"Yeah. But I can drive myself. I—"

"No. I'm sending my car and chauffeur. His name is George; you may rely upon him absolutely. He should be there in about twenty minutes."

"Okay," I said. "That just give me time to drink my dinner. Have him park around the corner of Kenmore, facing towards Franklin." I hung up.

When I'd had a hot-and-cold shower and put on some clean clothes I felt more respectable. I had a couple of drinks, small ones for a change, and put a light overcoat on and went down to the street.

The car was there already. I could see it half a block down the side street. It looked like a new market opening. It had a couple of head lamps like the one on the front end of a streamliner, two amber fog lights hooked to the front fender, and a couple of sidelights as big as ordinary headlights. I came up beside it and stopped and a man stepped out of the shadows, tossing a cigarette over his shoulder with a neat flip of the wrist. He was tall, broad, dark, wore a peaked cap, a Russian tunic with a Sam Browne belt, shiny leggings and breeches that flared like an English staff major's whipcords.

"Mr. Marlowe?" He touched the peak of his cap with a gloved forefinger.

"Yeah," I said. "At ease. Don't tell me that's Old Man Jeeter's car."

"One of them." It was a cool voice that could get fresh.

He opened the rear door and I got in and sank down into the cushions and George slid under the wheel and started the big car. It moved away from the curb and around the corner with as much noise as a bill makes in a wallet. We went west. We seemed to be drifting with the current, but we passed everything. We slid through the heart of Hollywood, the west end of it, down to the Strip and along the glitter of that to the cool quiet of Beverly Hills where the bridle path divides the boulevard.

We gave Beverly Hills the swift and climbed along the foothills, saw the distant light of the university buildings and swung north into Bel-Air. We began to slide up long narrow streets with high walls and no sidewalks and big gates. Lights on mansions glowed politely through the early night. Nothing stirred. There was no sound but the soft purr of the tires on concrete. We swung left again and I caught a sign which read CALVELLO DRIVE. Halfway up this George started to swing the car wide to make a left turn in at a pair of twelve-foot wrought-iron gates. Then something happened.

A pair of lights flared suddenly just beyond the gates and a horn screeched and a motor raced. A car charged at us fast. George straightened out with a flick of the wrist, braked the car and slipped off his right glove, all in one motion.

The car came on, the lights swaying. "Damn drunk," George swore over his shoulder.

It could be. Drunks in cars go all kinds of places to drink. It could be. I slid down onto the floor of the car and yanked the Luger from under my arm and reached up to open the catch. I opened the door a little and held it that way, looking over the sill. The headlights hit me in the face and I ducked, then came up again as the beam passed.

The other car jammed to a stop. Its door slammed open and a figure jumped out of it, waving a gun and shouting. I heard the voice and knew.

"Reach, you bastards!" Frisky screamed at us.

George put his left hand on the wheel and I opened my door a little more. The little man in the street was bouncing up and down and yelling. Out of the small dark car from which he had jumped came no sound except the noise of its motor.

"This is a heist!" Frisky yelled. "Out of there and line up, you sons of bitches!"

I kicked my door open and started to get out, the Luger down at my side.

"You asked for it!" the little man yelled.

I dropped—fast. The gun in his hand belched flame. Somebody must have put a firing pin in it. Glass smashed behind my head. Out of the corner of my eye, which oughtn't to have had any corners at that particular moment, I saw George make a movement as smooth as a ripple of water. I brought the Luger up and started to squeeze the trigger, but a shot crashed beside me—George.

I held my fire. It wasn't needed now.

The dark car lurched forward and started down the hill furiously. It roared into the distance while the little man out in the middle of the pavement was still reeling grotesquely in the light reflected from the walls.

There was something dark on his face that spread. His gun bounded along the concrete. His little legs buckled and he plunged sideways and rolled and then, very suddenly, became still.

George said, "Yah!" and sniffed at the muzzle of his revolver.

"Nice shooting." I got out of the car, stood there looking at the little man—a crumpled nothing. The dirty white of his sneakers gleamed a little in the side glare of the car's lights.

George got out beside me. "Why me, brother?"

"I didn't fire. I was watching that pretty hip draw of yours. It was sweeter than honey."

"Thanks, pal. They were after Mister Gerald, of course. I usually ferry him home from the club about this time, full of liquor and bridge losses."

We went over to the little man and looked down at him. He wasn't anything to see. He was just a little man who was dead, with a big slug in his face and blood on him.

"Turn some of those damn lights off," I growled. "And let's get away from here fast."

"The house is just across the street." George sounded as casual as if he had just shot a nickel in a slot machine instead of a man.

"The Jeeters are out of this, if you like your job. You ought to know that. We'll go back to my place and start all over."

"I get it," he snapped, and jumped back into the big car. He cut the foglights and the sidelights and I got in beside him in the front seat.

We straightened out and started up the hill, over the brow. I looked back at the broken window. It was the small one at the extreme back of the car and it wasn't shatterproof. A large piece was gone from it. They could fit that, if they got around to it, and make some evidence. I didn't think it would matter, but it might.

At the crest of the hill a large limousine passed us going down. Its dome light was on and in the interior, as in a lighted showcase, an elderly couple sat stiffly, taking the royal salute. The man was in evening clothes, with a white scarf and a crush hat. The woman was in furs and diamonds.

George passed them casually, gunned the car and we made a fast right turn into a dark street. "There's a couple of good dinners all shot to hell," he drawled. "And I bet they don't even report it."

"Yeah. Let's get back home and have a drink," I said. "I never really got to like killing people."

❦ ❦ ❦ ❦

We sat with some of Miss Harriet Huntress's Scotch in our glasses and looked at each other across the rims. George looked nice with his cap off. His head was clustered over with wavy dark brown hair and his teeth were very white and clean. He sipped his drink and nibbled a cigarette at the same time. His snappy black eyes had a cool glitter in them.

"Yale?" I asked.

"Dartmouth, if it's any of your business."

"Everything's my business. What's a college education worth these days?"

"Three squares and a uniform," he drawled.

"What kind of guy is young Jeeter?"

"He'd probably give you a dime—if he didn't have a nickel with him."

"Tsk, tsk, you're talking about your boss."

George grinned. "He's so tight his head squeaks when he takes his hat off. I always took chances. Maybe that's why I'm just somebody's driver. This is good Scotch."

I made another drink, which finished the bottle. I sat down again.

"You think those two gunnies were stashed out for Mister Gerald?"

"Why not? I usually drive him home about that time. Didn't today. He had a bad hangover and didn't go out until late. You're a dick, you know what it's all about, don't you?"

"Who told you I was a dick?"

"Nobody but a dick ever asked so many questions."

I shook my head. "Uh-uh, I've asked you just six questions. Your boss has a lot of confidence in you. He must have told you."

The dark man nodded, grinned faintly and sipped. "The whole set-up is pretty obvious," he said. "When the car started to swing for the turn into the driveway these boys went to work. I don't figure they meant to kill anybody, somehow. It was just a scare. Only that little guy was nuts."

I looked at George's eyebrows. They were nice black eyebrows, with a gloss on them like horsehair.

"It doesn't sound like Marty Estel to pick that sort of helpers."

"Sure. Maybe that's why he picked that sort of helpers."

"You're smart. You and I can get along. But shooting that little punk makes it tougher. What will you do about that?"

"Nothing."

"Okay. If they get to you and tie it to your gun, if you still have the gun, which you probably won't, I suppose it will be passed off as an attempted stickup. There's just one thing."

"What?" George finished his second drink, laid the glass aside, lit a fresh cigarette and smiled.

"It's pretty hard to tell a car from in front—at night. Even with all those lights. It might have been a visitor."

He shrugged and nodded. "But if it's a scare, that would do just as well. Because the family would hear about it and the old man would guess whose boys they were—and why."

"Hell, you really are smart," I said admiringly, and the phone rang.

It was an English-butler voice, very clipped and precise, and it said that if I was Mr. Philip Marlowe, Mr. Jeeter would like to speak to me. He came on at once, with plenty of frost.

"I must say that you take your time about obeying orders," he barked. "Or hasn't that chauffeur of mine—"

"Yeah, he got here, Mr. Jeeter," I said. "But we ran into a little trouble. George will tell you."

"Young man, when I want something done—"

"Listen, Mr. Jeeter, I've had a hard day. Your son punched me on the jaw and I fell and cut my head open. When I staggered back to my apartment, more dead than alive, I was stuck up by a couple of hard guys with guns who told me to lay off the Jeeter case. I'm doing my best but I'm feeling a little frail, so don't scare me."

"Young man—"

"Listen," I told him earnestly. "If you want to call all the plays in this game, you can carry the ball yourself. Or you can save yourself a lot of money and hire an order taker. I have to do things my way. Any cops visit you tonight?"

"Cops?" he echoed in a sour voice. "You mean policemen?"

"By all means—I mean policemen."

"And why should I see any policemen?" he almost snarled.

"There was a stiff in front of your gates half an hour ago. Stiff meaning dead man. He's quite small. You could sweep him up in a dustpan, if he bothers you."

"My God! Are you serious?"

"Yes. What's more he took a shot at George and me. He recognized the car. He must have been all set for your son, Mr. Jeeter."

A silence with barbs on it. "I thought you said a dead man," Mr. Jeeter's voice said very coldly. "Now you say he shot at you."

"That was while he wasn't dead," I said. "George will tell you. George—"

"You come out here at once!" he yelled at me over the phone. "At once, do you hear? At once!"

"George will tell you," I said softly, and hung up.

George looked at me coldly. He stood up and put his cap on. "Okay, pal," he said. "Maybe some day I can put you on to a soft thing." He started for the door.

"It had to be that way. It's up to him. He'll have to decide."

"Nuts," George said, looking back over his shoulder. "Save your breath, shamus. Anything you say to me is just so much noise in the wrong place."

He opened the door, went out, shut it, and I sat there still holding the telephone, with my mouth open and nothing in it but my tongue and a bad taste on that.

I went out to the kitchen and shook the Scotch bottle, but it was still empty. I opened some rye and swallowed a drink and it tasted sour. Something was bothering me. I had a feeling it was going to bother me a lot more before I was through.

They must have missed George by a whisker. I heard the elevator come up again almost as soon as it had stopped going down. Solid steps grew louder along the hallway. A fist hit the door. I went over and opened it.

One was in brown, one in blue, both large, hefty and bored.

The one in brown pushed his hat back on his head with a freckled hand and said: "You Philip Marlowe?"

"Me," I said.

They rode me back into the room without seeming to. The one in blue shut the door. The one in brown palmed a shield and let me catch a glint of the gold and enamel.

"Finlayson, Detective Lieutenant working out of Central Homicide," he said. "This is Sebold, my partner. We're a couple of swell guys not to get funny with. We hear you're kind of sharp with a gun."

Sebold took his hat off and dusted his salt-and-pepper hair back with the flat of his hand. He drifted noiselessly out to the kitchen.

Finlayson sat down on the edge of a chair and flicked his chin with a thumbnail as square as an ice cube and yellow as a mustard plaster. He was older than Sebold, but not so good-looking. He had the frowsy expression of a veteran cop who hadn't got very far.

I sat down. I said: "How do you mean, sharp with a gun?"

"Shooting people is how I mean."

I lit a cigarette. Sebold came out of the kitchen and went into the dressing room behind the wall bed.

"We understand you're a private-license guy," Finlayson said heavily.

"That's right."

"Give." He held his hand out. I gave him my wallet. He chewed it over and handed it back. "Carry a gun?"

I nodded. He held out his hand for it. Sebold came out of the dressing room. Finlayson sniffed at the Luger, snapped the magazine out, cleared the breech and held the gun so that a little light shone up through the magazine opening into the breech end of the barrel. He looked down the muzzle, squinting. He handed the gun to Sebold. Sebold did the same thing.

"Don't think so," Sebold said. "Clean, but not that clean. Couldn't have been cleaned within the hour. A little dust."

"Right."

Finlayson picked the ejected shell off the carpet, pressed it into the magazine and snapped the magazine back in place. He handed me the gun. I put it back under my arm.

"Been out anywhere tonight?" he asked tersely.

"Don't tell me the plot," I said. "I'm just a bit-player."

"Smart guy," Sebold said dispassionately. He dusted his hair again and opened a desk drawer. "Funny stuff. Good for a column. I like 'em that way—with my blackjack."

Finlayson sighed. "Been out tonight, Shamus?"

"Sure. In and out all the time. Why?"

He ignored the question. "Where you been?"

"Out to dinner. Business call or two."

"Where at?"

"I'm sorry, boys. Every business has its private files."

"Had company, too," Sebold said, picking up George's glass and sniffing it. "Recent—within the hour."

"You're not that good," I told him sourly.

"Had a ride in a big Caddy?" Finlayson bored on, taking a deep breath. "Over West L. A. direction?"

"Had a ride in a Chrysler—over Vine Street direction."

"Maybe we better just take him down," Sebold said, looking at his fingernails.

"Maybe you better skip the gang-buster stuff and tell me what's in your nose. I get along with cops—except when they act as if the law is only for citizens."

Finlayson studied me. Nothing I had said made an impression on him. Nothing Sebold said made any impression on him. He had an idea and he was holding it like a sick baby.

"You know a little rat named Frisky Lavon?" he sighed. "Used to be a dummy-chucker, then found out he could bug his way outa raps. Been doing that for say twelve years. Totes a gun and acts simple. But he quit acting tonight at seven-thirty about. Quit cold—with a slug in his head."

"Never heard of him," I said.

"You bumped anybody off tonight?"

"I'd have to look at my notebook."

Sebold leaned forward politely. "Would you care for a smack in the kisser?" he inquired.

Finlayson held his hand out sharply. "Cut it, Ben. Cut it. Listen, Marlowe. Maybe we're going at this wrong. We're not talking about murder. Could have been legitimate. This Frisky Lavon got froze off tonight on Calvello Drive in Bel-Air. Out in the middle of the street. Nobody seen or heard anything. So we kind of want to know."

"All right," I growled. "What makes it my business? And keep that piano tuner out of my hair. He has a nice suit and his nails are clean, but he bears down on his shield too hard."

"Nuts to you," Sebold said.

"We got a funny phone call," Finlayson said. "Which is where you come in. We ain't just throwing our weight around. And we want a forty-five. They ain't sure what kind yet."

"He's smart. He threw it under the bar at Levy's," Sebold sneered.

"I never had a forty-five," I said. "A guy who needs that much gun ought to use a pick."

Finlayson scowled at me and counted his thumbs. Then he took a deep breath and suddenly went human on me. "Sure, I'm just a dumb flatheel," he said. "Anybody could pull my ears off and I wouldn't even notice it. Let's all quit horsing around and talk sense."

"This Frisky was found dead after a no-name phone call to West L. A. police. Found dead outside a big house belonging to a man named Jeeter who owns a string of investment companies. He wouldn't use a guy like Frisky for a penwiper, so there's nothing in that. The servants didn't hear nothing, nor the servants at any of the four houses on the block. Frisky is lying in the street and somebody run over his foot, but what killed him was a forty-five slug smack in his face. West L. A. ain't hardly started the routine when some guy calls up Central and says to tell Homicide if they want to know who got Frisky Lavon, ask a private eye named Philip Marlowe, complete with address and everything, then a quick hang-up.

"Okay. The guy on the board give me the dope and I don't know Frisky from a hole in my sock, but I ask Identification and sure enough they have him and just about the time I'm looking it over the flash comes from West L. A. and the description seems to check pretty close. So we get together and it's the same guy all right and the chief of detectives has us drop around here. So we drop around."

"So here you are," I said. "Will you have a drink?"

"Can we search the joint, if we do?"

"Sure. It's a good lead—that phone call, I mean—if you put in about six months on it."

"We already got that idea," Finlayson growled. "A hundred guys could have chilled this little wart, and two-three of them maybe could have thought it was a smart rib to pin it on you. Them two-three is what interests us."

I shook my head.

"No ideas at all, huh?"

"Just for wisecracks," Sebold said.

Finlayson lumbered to his feet. "Well, we gotta look around."

"Maybe we had ought to have brought a search warrant," Sebold said, tickling his upper lip with the end of his tongue.

"I don't have to fight this guy, do I?" I asked Finlayson. "I mean, is it all right if I leave him his gag lines and just keep my temper?"

Finlayson looked at the ceiling and said dryly: "His wife left him day before yesterday. He's just trying to compensate, as the fellow says."

Sebold turned white and twisted his knuckles savagely. Then he laughed shortly and got to his feet.

They went at it. Ten minutes of opening and shutting drawers and looking at the backs of shelves and under seat cushions and letting the bed down and peering into the electric refrigerator and the garbage pail fed them up.

They came back and sat down again. "Just a nut," Finlayson said wearily. "Some guy that picked your name outa the directory maybe. Could be anything."

"Now I'll get that drink."

"I don't drink," Sebold snarled.

Finlayson crossed his hands on his stomach. "That don't mean any liquor gets poured in the flowerpot, son."

I got three drinks and put two of them beside Finlayson. He drank half of one of them and looked at the ceiling. "I got another killing, too," he said thoughtfully. "A guy in your racket, Marlowe. A fat guy on Sunset. Name of Arbogast. Ever hear of him?"

"I thought he was a handwriting expert," I said.

"You're talking about police business," Sebold told his partner coldly.

"Sure. Police business that's already in the morning paper. This Arbogast was shot three times with a twenty-two. Target gun. You know any crook that packs that kind of heat?"

I held my glass tightly and took a long swallow. I hadn't thought Waxnose looked dangerous enough, but you never knew.

"I did," I said slowly. "A killer named Al Tessilore. But he's in Folsom. He used a Colt Woodsman."

Finlayson finished the first drink, used the second in about the same time, and stood up. Sebold stood up, still mad.

Finlayson opened the door. "Come on, Ben." They went out.

I heard their steps along the hall, the clang of the elevator once more. A car started just below in the street and growled off into the night.

"Clowns like that don't kill," I said out loud. But it looked as if they did.

I waited fifteen minutes before I went out again. The phone rang while I was waiting, but I didn't answer it.

I drove toward the El Milano and circled around enough to make sure I wasn't followed.

The lobby hadn't changed any. The blue carpet still tickled my ankles while I ambled over to the desk, the same pale clerk was handing a key to a couple of horse-faced females in tweeds, and when he saw me he put his weight on his left foot again and the floor at the end of the desk popped open and out popped the fat and erotic Hawkins, with what looked like the same cigar stub in his face.

He hustled over and gave me a big warm smile this time, took hold of my arm. "Just the guy I was hoping to see," he chuckled. "Let's us go upstairs a minute."

"What's the matter?"

"Matter?" His smile became broad as the door to a two-car garage. "Nothing ain't the matter. This way."

He pushed me into the elevator and said, "Eight" in a fat cheerful voice and up we sailed and out we got and slid along the corridor. Hawkins had a hard hand and knew where to hold an arm. I was interested enough to let him get away with it. He pushed the buzzer beside Miss Huntress's door and Big Ben chimed inside and the door opened and I was looking at a deadpan in a derby hat and a dinner coat. He had his right hand in the side pocket of the coat, and under the derby a pair of scarred eyebrows and under the eyebrows a pair of eyes that had as much expression as the cap on a gas tank.

The mouth moved enough to say: "Yeah?"

"Company for the boss," Hawkins said expansively.

"What company?"

"Let me play too," I said. "Limited Liability Company. Gimme the apple."

"Huh?" The eyebrows went this way and that and the jaw came out. "Nobody ain't kiddin' nobody, I hope."

"Now, now, gents—" Hawkins began.

A voice behind the derby-hatted man interrupted him. "What's the matter, Beef?"

"He's in a stew," I said.

"Listen, mugg—"

"Now, now gents—" as before.

"Ain't nothing the matter," Beef said, throwing his voice over his shoulder as if it were a coil of rope. "The hotel dick got a guy up here and he says he's company."

"Show the company in, Beef." I liked this voice. It was smooth quiet, and you could have cut your name in it with a thirty-pound sledge and a cold chisel.

"Lift the dogs," Beef said, and stood to one side.

We went in. I went first, then Hawkins, then Beef wheeled neatly behind us like a door. We went in so close together that we must have looked like a three-decker sandwich.

Miss Huntress was not in the room. The log in the fireplace had almost stopped smoldering. There was still that smell of sandalwood on the air. With it cigarette smoke blended.

A man stood at the end of the davenport, both hands in the pockets of a blue camel's-hair coat with the collar high to a black snap-brim hat. A loose scarf hung outside his coat. He stood motionless, the cigarette in his mouth lisping smoke. He was tall, black-haired, suave, dangerous. He said nothing.

Hawkins ambled over to him. "This is the guy I was telling you about, Mr. Estel," the fat man burbled. "Come in earlier today and said he was from you. Kinda fooled me."

"Give him a ten, Beef."

The derby hat took its left hand from somewhere and there was a bill in it. It pushed the bill at Hawkins. Hawkins took the bill blushing.

"This ain't necessary, Mr. Estel. Thanks a lot just the same."

"Scram."

"Huh?" Hawkins looked shocked.

"You heard him," Beef said truculently. "Want your fanny out the door first, huh?"

Hawkins drew himself up. "I gotta protect the tenants. You gentlemen know how it is. A man in a job like this."

"Yeah. Scram," Estel said without moving his lips.

Hawkins turned and went out quickly, softly. The door clicked gently shut behind him. Beef looked back at it, then moved behind me.

"See if he's rodded, Beef."

The derby hat saw if I was rodded. He took the Luger and went away from me. Estel looked casually at the Luger, back at me. His eyes held an expression of indifferent dislike.

"Name's Philip Marlowe, eh? A private dick."

"So what?" I said.

"Somebody's goin' to get somebody's face pushed into somebody's floor," Beef said coldly.

"Aw, keep that crap for the boiler room," I told him. "I'm sick of hard guys for this evening. I said 'so what,' and 'so what' is what I said."

Marty Estel looked mildly amused. "Hell, keep your shirt in. I've got to look after my friends, don't I? You know who I am. Okay, I know what you talked to Miss Huntress about. And I know something about you that you don't know I know."

"All right," I said. "This fat slob Hawkins collected ten from me for letting me up here this afternoon—knowing perfectly well who I was—and he has just collected ten from your iron man for slipping me the nasty. Give me back my gun and tell me what makes my business your business."

"Plenty. First off, Harriet's not home. We're waiting for her on account of a thing that happened. I can't wait any longer. Got to go to work at the club. So what did you come after this time?"

"Looking for the Jeeter boy. Somebody shot at his car tonight. From now on he needs somebody to walk behind him."

"You think I play games like that?" Estel asked me coldly.

I walked over to a cabinet and opened it and found a bottle of Scotch. I twisted the cap off, lifted a glass from the tabouret and poured some out. I tasted it. It tasted all right.

I looked around for ice, but there wasn't any. It had all melted long since in the bucket.

"I asked you a question," Estel said gravely.

"I heard it. I'm making my mind up. The answer is, I wouldn't have thought it—no. But it happened. I was there. I was in the car—instead of young Jeeter. His father had sent for me to come to the house to talk things over."

"What things?"

I didn't bother to look surprised. "You hold fifty grand of the boy's paper. That looks bad for you, if anything happens to him."

"I don't figure it that way. Because that way I would lose my dough. The old man won't pay—granted. But I wait a couple of years and I collect from the kid. He gets his estate out of trust when he's twenty-eight. Right now he gets a grand a month and he can't even will anything, because it's still in trust. Savvy?"

"So you wouldn't knock him off," I said, using my Scotch. "But you might throw a scare into him."

Estel frowned. He discarded his cigarette into a tray and watched it smoke a moment before he picked it up again and snubbed it out. He shook his head.

"If you're going to bodyguard him, it would almost pay me to stand part of your salary, wouldn't it? Almost. A man in my racket can't take care of everything. He's of age and it's his business who he runs around with. For instance, women. Any reason why a nice girl shouldn't cut herself a piece of five million bucks?"

I said: "I think it's a swell idea. What was it you knew about me that I didn't know you knew?"

He smiled faintly. "What was it you were waiting to tell Miss Huntress—the thing that happened?"

He smiled faintly again.

"Listen, Marlowe, there are lots of ways to play any game. I play mine on the house percentage, because that's all I need to win. What makes me get tough?"

I rolled a fresh cigarette around in my fingers and tried to roll it around my glass with two fingers. "Who said you were tough? I always heard the nicest things about you."

Marty Estel nodded and looked faintly amused. "I have sources of information," he said quietly. "When I have fifty grand invested in a guy, I'm apt to find out a little about him. Jeeter hired a man named Arbogast to do a little work. Arbogast was killed in his office today—with a twenty-two. That could have nothing to do with Jeeter's business. But there was a tail on you when you went there and you didn't give it to the law. Does that make you and me friends?"

I licked the edge of my glass, nodded. "It seems it does."

"From now on just forget about bothering Harriet, see?"

"Okay."

"So we understand each other real good, now."

"Yeah."

"Well, I'll be going. Give the guy back his Luger, Beef."

The derby hat came over and smacked my gun into my hand hard enough to break a bone.

"Staying?" Estel asked, moving toward the door.

"I guess I'll wait a little while. Until Hawkins comes up to touch me for another ten."

Estel grinned. Beef walked in front of him wooden-faced to the door and opened it. Estel went out. The door closed. The room was silent. I sniffed at the dying perfume of sandalwood and stood motionless, looking around.

Somebody was nuts. I was nuts. Everybody was nuts. None of it fitted together worth a nickel. Marty Estel, as he said, had no good motive for murdering anybody, because that would be the surest way to kill his chances to collect his money. Even if he had a motive for murdering anybody, Waxnose and Frisky didn't seem like the team he would select for the job. I was in bad with the police, I had spent ten dollars of my twenty expense money, and I didn't have enough leverage anywhere to lift a dime off a cigar counter.

I finished my drink, put the glass down, walked up and down the room, smoked a third cigarette, looked at my watch, shrugged and felt disgusted. The inner doors of the suite were closed. I went across to the one out of which young Jeeter must have sneaked that afternoon. Opening it I looked into a bedroom done in ivory and ashes of roses. There was a big double bed with no footboard, covered with figured brocade. Toilet articles glistened on a built-in dressing table with a panel light. The light was lit. A small lamp on a table beside the door was lit also. A door near the dressing table showed the cool green of bathroom tiles.

I went over and looked in there. Chromium, a glass stall shower, monogrammed towels on a rack, a glass shelf for perfume and bath salts at the foot of the tub, everything nice and refined. Miss Huntress did herself well. I hoped she was paying her own rent. It didn't make any difference to me—I just liked it that way.

I went back toward the living room, stopped in the doorway to take another pleasant look around, and noticed something I ought to have noticed the instant I stepped into the room. I noticed the sharp tang of cordite on the air, almost, but not quite gone. And then I noticed something else.

The bed had been moved over until its head overlapped the edge of a closet door which was not quite closed. The weight of the bed was holding it from opening. I went over there to find out why it wanted to open. I went slowly and about halfway there I noticed that I was holding a gun in my hand.

I leaned against the closed door. It didn't move. I threw more weight against it. It still didn't move. Braced against it I pushed the bed away with my foot, gave ground slowly.

A weight pushed against me hard. I had gone back a foot or so before anything else happened. Then it happened suddenly. He came out—sideways, in a sort of roll. I put some more weight back on the door and held him like that a moment, looking at him.

He was still big, still blond, still dressed in rough sporty material, with scarf and open-necked shirt. But his face wasn't red anymore.

I gave ground again and he rolled down the back of the door, turning a little like a swimmer in the surf, thumped the floor and lay there, almost on his back, still looking at me. Light from the bedside lamp glittered on his head. There was a scorched and soggy stain on the rough coat—about where his heart would be. So he wouldn't get that five million after all. And nobody would get anything and Marty Estel wouldn't get his fifty grand. Because young Mister Gerald was dead.

I looked back into the closet where he had been. Its door hung wide open now. There were clothes on racks, feminine clothes, nice clothes. He had been backed in among them, probably with his hands in the air and a gun against his chest. And then he had been shot dead, and whoever did it hadn't been quite quick enough or strong enough to get the door shut. Or had been scared and had just yanked the bed over against the door and left it that way.

Something glittered down on the floor. I picked it up. A small automatic, 25 caliber, a woman's purse gun with a beautifully engraved butt inlaid with silver and ivory. I put the gun in my pocket. That seemed a funny thing to do, too.

I didn't touch him. He was as dead as John D. Arbogast and looked a whole lot deader. I left the door open and listened, walked quickly back across the room and into the living room and shut the bedroom door, smearing the knob as I did it.

A lock was being tinkled at with a key. Hawkins was back again, to see what delayed me. He was letting himself in with his passkey.

I was pouring a drink when he came in.

He came well into the room, stopped with his feet planted and surveyed me coldly.

"I seen Estel and his boy leave," he said. "I didn't see you leave. So I come up. I gotta—"

"You gotta protect the guests," I said.

"Yeah. I gotta protect the guests. You can't stay up here, pal. Not without the lady of the house is home."

"But Marty Estel and his hard boy can."

He came a little closer to me. He had a mean look in his eye. He had always had it, probably, but I noticed it more now.

"You don't want to make nothing of that, do you?" he asked me.

"No. Every man to his own chisel. Have a drink."

"That ain't your liquor."

"Miss Huntress gave me a bottle. We're pals. Marty Estel and I are pals. Everybody is pals, don't you want to be pals?"

"You ain't trying to kid me, are you?"

"Have a drink and forget it."

I found a glass and poured him one. He took it.

"It's the job if anybody smells it on me," he said.

"Uh-huh."

He drank slowly, rolling it around on his tongue. "Good Scotch."

"Won't be the first time you tasted it, will it?"

He started to get hard again, then relaxed. "Hell, I guess you're just a kidder." He finished the drink, put the glass down, patted his lips with a large and very crumpled handkerchief and sighed.

"Okay," he said. "But we'll have to leave now."

"All set. I guess she won't be home for a while. You see them go out?"

"Her and the boy friend. Yeah, long time ago."

I nodded. We went toward the door and Hawkins saw me out. He saw me downstairs and off the premises. But he didn't see what was in Miss Huntress's bedroom. I wondered if he would go back up. If he did, the Scotch bottle would probably stop him.

I got into my car and drove off home—to talk to Anna Halsey on the phone. There wasn't any case anymore—for us. I parked close to the curb this time. I wasn't feeling gay anymore. I rode up in the elevator and unlocked the door and clicked the light on.

Waxnose sat in my best chair, an unlit hand-rolled brown cigarette between his fingers, his bony knees crossed, and his long Woodman resting solidly on his leg. He was smiling. It wasn't the nicest smile I ever saw.

"Hi, pal," he drawled. "You still ain't had that door fixed. Kind of shut it, huh?" His voice, for all the drawl, was deadly.

I shut the door, stood looking across the room at him.

"So you killed my pal," he said.

He stood up slowly, came across the room slowly and leaned the .22 against my throat. His smiling thin-lipped mouth seemed as expressionless, for all its smile, as his wax-white nose. He reached quietly under my coat and took the Luger. I might as well leave it home from now on. Everybody in town seemed to be able to take it away from me.

He stepped back across the room and sat down again in the chair.

"Steady does it," he said almost gently. "Park the body, friend. No false moves. No moves at all. You and me are at the jumping-off place. The clock's tickin' and we're waiting to go."

I sat down and stared at him. A curious bird. I moistened my dry lips. "You told me his gun had no firing pin," I said.

"Yeah. He fooled me on that, the little so-and-so. And I told you to lay off the Jeeter kid. That's cold now. It's Frisky I'm thinking about. Crazy, ain't it? Me bothering about a dimwit like that, packin' him around with me, and letting him get hisself bumped off." He sighed and added simply, "He was my kid brother."

"I didn't kill him," I said.

He smiled a little more. He had never stopped smiling. The corners of his mouth just tucked in a little deeper.

"Yeah?"

He slid the safety catch off the Luger, laid it carefully on the arm of the chair at his right, and reached into his pocket. What he brought out made me as cold as an ice bucket.

It was a metal tube, dark and rough-looking, about four inches long and drilled with a lot of small holes. He held his woodsman in his left hand and began to screw the tube casually on the end of it.

"Silencer," he said. "They're the bunk, I guess you smart guys think. This one ain't the bunk—not for three shots. I oughta know, I made it myself."

I moistened my lips again. "It'll work for one shot," I said. "Then it jams the action. That one looks like cast-iron. It will probably blow your hand off."

He smiled his waxy smile, screwed it on, slowly, lovingly, gave it a last hard turn and sat back relaxed. "Not this baby. She's packed with steel wool and that's good for three shots, like I said. Then you got to repack it. And there ain't enough back pressure to jam the action of this gun. You feel good? I'd like you to feel good."

"I feel swell, you sadistic son of a bitch," I said.

"I'm having you lie down on the bed after a while. You won't feel nothing. I'm kind of fussy about my killings. Frisky didn't feel nothing, I guess. You got him neat."

"You don't see good," I sneered. "The chauffeur got him with a Smith and Wesson forty-four. I didn't even fire."

"Uh-huh."

"Okay, you don't believe me," I said. "What did you kill Arbogast for? There was nothing fussy about that killing. He was just shot at his desk, three times with a twenty-two and he fell down on the floor. What did he ever do to your filthy little brother?"

He jerked the gun up, but his smile held. "You got guts," he said. "Who is this here Arbogast?"

I told him. I told him slowly and carefully, in detail. I told him a lot of things. And he began in some vague way to look worried. His eyes flickered at me, away, back again, restlessly, like a hummingbird.

"I don't know any party named Arbogast, pal," he said slowly. "Never heard of him. And I ain't shot any fat guys today."

"You killed him," I said. "And you killed young Jeeter—in the girl's apartment at the El Milano. He's lying there dead right now. You're working for Marty Estel. He's going to be awfully damn sorry about that kill. Go ahead and make it three in a row."

His face froze. The smile went away at last. His whole face looked waxy now. He opened his mouth and breathed through it, and his breath made a restless worrying sound. I could see the faint glitter of sweat on his forehead, and I could feel the cold from the evaporation of sweat on mine.

Waxnose said very gently: "I ain't killed anybody at all, friend. Not anybody. I wasn't hired to kill people. Until Frisky stopped that slug I didn't have no such ideas. That's straight."

I tried not to stare at the metal tube on the end of the Woodsman.

A flame flickered at the back of his eyes, a small, weak, smoky flame. It seemed to grow larger and clearer. He looked down at the floor between his feet. I looked around at the light switch, but it was too far away. He looked up again. Very slowly he began to unscrew the silencer. He had it loose in his hand. He dropped it back into his pocket, stood up, holding the two guns, one in each hand. Then he had another idea. He sat down again, took all the shells out of the Luger quickly and threw it on the floor after them.

He came toward me softly across the room. "I guess this is your lucky day," he said. "I got to go a place and see a guy."

"I knew all along it was my lucky day. I've been feeling so good."

He moved delicately around me to the door and opened it a foot and started through the narrow opening, smiling again.

"I gotta see a guy," he said very gently, and his tongue moved along his lips.

"Not yet," I said, and jumped.

His gun hand was at the edge of the door, almost beyond the edge. I hit the door hard and he couldn't bring it in quickly enough. He couldn't get out of the way. I pinned him in the doorway and used all the strength I had. It was a crazy thing. He had given me a break and all I had to do was stand still and let him go. But I had a guy to see too—and I wanted to see him first.

Waxnose leered at me. He grunted. He fought with his hand beyond the door edge. I shifted and hit his jaw with all I had. It was enough. He went limp. I hit him again. His head bounced against the wood. I heard a light thud beyond the door edge. I hit him a third time. I never hit anything harder.

I took my weight back from the door then and he slid toward me, blank-eyed, rubber-kneed, and I caught him and twisted his empty hands behind him and let him fall. I stood over him panting. I went to the door. His Woodsman lay almost on the sill. I picked it up, dropped it into my pocket—not the pocket that held Miss Huntress's gun. He hadn't even found that.

There he lay on the floor. He was thin, he had no weight, but I panted just the same. In a little while his eyes flickered open and looked up at me.

"Greedy guy," he whispered wearily. "Why did I ever leave Saint Looey?"

I snapped handcuffs on his wrists and pulled him by the shoulders into the dressing room and tied his ankles with a piece of rope. I left him lying on his back, a little sideways, his nose as white as ever, his eyes empty now, his lips moving a little as if he were talking to himself. A funny lad, not all bad, but not so pure I had to weep over him either.

I put my Luger together and left with my three guns. There was nobody outside the apartment house.

The Jeeter mansion was on a nine- or ten-acre knoll, a big colonial pile with fat white columns and dormer windows and magnolias and a four-car garage. There was a circular parking space at the top of the driveway with two cars parked in it—one was the big dreadnought in which I'd ridden and the other a canary-yellow sports convertible I had seen before.

I rang a bell the size of a silver dollar. The door opened and a tall narrow cold-eyed bird in dark clothes looked out at me.

"Mr. Jeeter home? Mr. Jeeter, senior?"

"May I arsk who is calling?" The accent was a little too thick, like cut Scotch.

"Philip Marlowe. I'm working for him. Maybe I ought to of gone to the servant's entrance."

He hitched a finger at a wing collar and looked at me without pleasure. "Aw, possibly. You may step in. I shall inform Mr. Jeeter. I believe he is engaged at the moment. Kindly wait 'ere in the 'all."

"The act stinks," I said. "English butlers aren't dropping their h's this year."

"Smart guy, huh?" he snarled, in a voice from not any farther across the Atlantic than Hoboken. "Wait here." He slid away.

I sat down in a carved chair and felt thirsty. After a while the butler came cat-footing back along the hall and jerked his chin at me unpleasantly.

We went along a mile of hallway. At the end it broadened without any doors into a huge sunroom. On the far side of the sunroom the butler opened a wide door and

I stepped past him into an oval room with a black-and-silver oval rug, a black marble table in the middle of the rug, stiff high-backed carved chairs against the walls, a huge oval mirror with a rounded surface that made me look like a pygmy with water on the brain, and in the room three people.

By the door opposite where I came in, George the chauffeur stood stiffly in his neat dark uniform, with his peaked cap in his hand. In the least uncomfortable of the chairs sat Miss Harriet Huntress holding a glass in which there was half a drink. And around the silver margin of the oval rug, Mr. Jeeter, senior, was trying his legs out in a brisk canter, still under wraps, but mad inside. His face was red and the veins on his nose were distended. His hands were in the pockets of a velvet smoking jacket. He wore a pleated shirt with a black pearl in the bosom, a batwing black tie and one of his patent-leather oxfords was unlaced.

He whirled and yelled at the butler behind me: "Get out and keep those doors shut! And I'm not at home to anybody, understand? Nobody!"

The butler closed the doors. Presumably, he went away. I didn't hear him go.

George gave me a cool one-sided smile and Miss Huntress gave me a bland stare over her glass. "You made a nice comeback," she said demurely.

"You took a chance leaving me alone in your apartment," I told her. "I might have sneaked some of your perfume."

"Well, what do you want?" Jeeter yelled at me. "A nice sort of detective you turned out to be. I put you on a confidential job and you walk right in on Miss Huntress and explain the whole thing to her."

"It worked, didn't it?"

He stared. They all stared. "How do you know that?" he barked.

"I know a nice girl when I see one. She's here telling you she had an idea she got not to like, and for you to quit worrying about it. Where's Mister Gerald?"

Old man Jeeter stopped and gave me a hard level stare. "I still regard you as incompetent," he said. "My son is missing."

"I'm not working for you. I'm working for Anna Halsey. Any complaints you have to make should be addressed to her. Do I pour my own drink or do you have a flunky in a purple suit to do it? And what do you mean, your son is missing?"

"Should I give him the heave, sir?" George asked quietly.

Jeeter waved his hand at a decanter and siphon and glasses on the black marble table and started around the rug again. "Don't be silly," he snapped at George.

George flushed a little, high on his cheekbones. His mouth looked tough.

I mixed myself a drink and sat down with it and tasted it and asked again: "What do you mean your son is missing, Mr. Jeeter?"

"I'm paying you good money," he started to yell at me, still mad.

"When?"

He stopped dead in his canter and looked at me again. Miss Huntress laughed lightly. George scowled.

"What do you suppose I mean—my son is missing?" he snapped. "I should have thought that would be clear enough even to you. Nobody knows where he is. Miss Huntress doesn't know. I don't know. No one at any of the places where he might be knows."

"But I'm smarter than they are," I said. "I know."

Nobody moved for a long minute. Jeeter stared at me fish-eyed. George stared at me. The girl stared at me. She looked puzzled. The other two just stared.

I looked at her. "Where did you go when you went out, if you're telling?"

Her dark blue eyes were water-clear. "There's no secret about it. We went out together—in a taxi. Gerald had had his driving license suspended for a month. Too many tickets. We went down towards the beach and I had a change of heart as you guessed. I decided I was just being a chiseler after all. I didn't want Gerald's money really. What I wanted was revenge. On Mr. Jeeter here for ruining my father. Done all legally of course, but done just the same. But I got myself in a spot where I couldn't have my revenge and not look like a cheap chiseler. So I told Gerald to find some other girl to play with. He was sore and we quarreled. I stopped the taxi and got out in Beverly Hills. He went on. I don't know where. Later I went back to the El Milano and got my car out of the garage and came here. To tell Mr. Jeeter to forget the whole thing and not bother to stick sleuths on to me."

"You say you went with him in a taxi," I said. "Why wasn't George driving him, if he couldn't drive himself?"

I stared at her, but I wasn't talking to her. Jeeter answered me frostily: "George drove me home from the office, of course. At that time Gerald had already gone out. Is there anything important about that?"

I turned to him. "Yeah. There's going to be. Mister Gerald is at the El Milano. Hawkins the house dick told me. He went back there to wait for Miss Huntress and Hawkins let him into her apartment. Hawkins will do you those little favors—for ten bucks. He may be there still and he may not."

I kept on watching them. It was hard to watch all three of them. But they didn't move. They just looked at me."

"Well—I'm glad to hear it," Old Man Jeeter said. "I was afraid he was off somewhere getting drunk."

"No. He's not off anywhere getting drunk," I said. "By the way, among these places you called to see if he was there, you didn't call the El Milano?"

George nodded. "Yes, I did. They said he wasn't there. Looks like the house peeper tipped the phone girl off not to say anything."

"He wouldn't have to do that. She'd just ring the apartment and he wouldn't answer—naturally." I watched Old Man Jeeter hard then, with a lot of interest. It was going to be hard for him to take that up, but he was going to have to do it.

He did. He licked his lips first. "Why—naturally, if I may ask?"

I put my glass down on the marble table and stood against the wall, with my hands hanging free. I still tried to watch them—all three of them.

"Let's go back over this thing a little," I said. "We're all wise to the situation. I know George is, although he shouldn't be, being just a servant. I know Miss Huntress is.

And of course, you are, Mr. Jeeter. So let's see what we have got. We have a lot of things that don't add up, but I'm smart. I'm going to add them up anyhow. First-off a handful of photostats of notes from Marty Estel. Gerald denies having given these and Mr. Jeeter won't pay them, but he had a handwriting man named Arbogast check the signatures, to see if they look genuine. They do. They are. This Arbogast may have done other things, I don't know. I couldn't ask him. When I went to see him, he was dead—shot three times—as I've since heard—with a twenty-two. No, I didn't tell the police, Mr. Jeeter."

The tall silver-haired man looked horribly shocked. His lean body shook like a bulrush. "Dead?" he whispered. "Murdered?"

I looked at George. George didn't move a muscle. I looked at the girl. She sat quietly, waiting, tight-lipped.

I said: "There's only one reason to suppose his killing had anything to do with Mr. Jeeter's affairs. He was shot with a twenty-two—and there is a man in this case who wears a twenty-two."

I still had their attention. And their silence.

"Why he was shot I haven't the faintest idea. He was not a dangerous man to Miss Huntress or Marty Estel. He was too fat to get around much. My guess is he was a little too smart. He got a simple case of signature identification and he went on from there to find out more than he should. And after he had found out more than he should—he guessed more than he ought—and maybe he even tried a little blackmail. And somebody rubbed him out this afternoon with a twenty-two. Okay, I can stand it. I never knew him.

"So I went over to see Miss Huntress and after a lot of finagling around this itchy-handed house dick I got to see her and we had a chat, and then Mister Gerald stepped neatly out of hiding and bopped me a nice one on the chin and over I went and hit my head on a chair leg. And when I came out of that the joint was empty. So I went home.

"And home I found the man with the twenty-two and with him a dimwit called Frisky Lavon, with a bad breath and a very large gun; neither of which matters now as he was shot dead in front of your house tonight, Mr. Jeeter—shot trying to stick up your car. The cops know about that one—they came to see me about it—because the other guy, the one that packs the twenty-two, is the little dimwit's brother and he thought I shot Dimwit and tried to put the bee on me. But it didn't work. That's two killings.

"We now come to the third and most important. I went back to the El Milano because it no longer seemed a good idea for Mister Gerald to be running around casually. He seemed to have a few enemies. It even seemed that he was supposed to be in the car this evening when Frisky Lavon shot at it—but of course that was just a plant."

Old Jeeter drew his white eyebrows together in an expression of puzzlement. George didn't look puzzled. He didn't look anything. He was as wooden-faced as a cigar-store Indian. The girl looked a little white now, a little tense. I plowed on.

"Back at the El Milano I found that Hawkins had let Marty Estel and his bodyguard into Miss Huntress's apartment to wait for her. Marty had something to tell her—that Arbogast had been killed. That made it a good idea for her to lay off young Jeeter for a while—until the cops quieted down anyhow. A thoughtful guy, Marty. A much more thoughtful guy than you would suppose. For instance, he knew about Arbogast and he knew Mr. Jeeter went to Anna Halsey's office this morning and he knew somehow—Anna might have told him herself, I wouldn't put it past her—that I was working on the case now. So he had me tailed to Arbogast's place and away, and he found out later from his cop friends that Arbogast had been murdered, and he knew I hadn't given it out. So he had me there and alone in Miss Huntress's apartment. But this time for no reason at all I poked around. And I found young Mister Gerald, in the bedroom, in a closet."

I stepped quickly over to the girl and reached into my pocket and took out the small fancy .25 automatic and laid it down on her knee.

"Ever see this before?"

Her voiced had a curious tight sound, but her dark blue eyes looked at me levelly.

"Yes. It's mine."

"You kept it where?"

"In the drawer of a small table beside the bed."

"Sure about that?"

She thought. Neither of the two men stirred.

George began to twitch the corner of his mouth. She shook her head suddenly, sideways.

"No. I have an idea now I took it out to show somebody—because I don't know much about guns—and left it lying on the mantel in the living room. In fact, I'm almost sure I did. It was Gerald I showed it to."

"So he might have reached for it there, if anybody tried to make a wrong play at him?"

She nodded, troubled. "What do you mean—he's in the closet?" she asked in a small quick voice.

"You know. Everybody in this room knows what I mean. They know that I showed you that gun for a purpose." I stepped away from her and faced George and his boss. "He's dead, of course. Shot through the heart—probably with this gun. It was left there with him. That's why it would be left."

The old man took a step and stopped and braced himself against the table. I wasn't sure whether he had turned white or whether he had been white already. He stared stonily at the girl. He said very slowly, between his teeth: "You damned murderess!"

"Couldn't it have been suicide?" I sneered.

He turned his head enough to look at me. I could see that the idea interested him. He half nodded.

"No," I said. "It couldn't have been suicide."

He didn't like that so well. His face congested with blood and the veins on his nose thickened. The girl touched the gun lying on her knee, then put her hand loosely around the butt. I saw her thumb slide very gently toward the safety catch. She didn't know much about guns, but she knew that much.

"It couldn't be suicide," I said again, very slowly. "As an isolated event—maybe. But not with all the other stuff that's been happening. Arbogast, the stick-up down on Calvello Drive outside this house, the thugs planted in my apartment, the job with the twenty-two.

I reached into my pocket again and pulled out Waxnose's Woodsman. I held it carelessly on the flat of my left hand. "And curiously enough, I don't think it was *this* twenty-two—although this happens to be the gunman's twenty-two. Yeah, I have the gunman too. He's tied up in my apartment. He came back to knock me off, but I talked him out of it. I'm a swell talker."

"Except that you overdo it," the girl said coolly, and lifted the gun a little.

"It's obvious who killed him, Miss Huntress," I said. "It's simply a matter of motive and opportunity. Marty Estel didn't, and didn't have it done. That would spoil his chances to get his fifty grand. Frisky Lavon's pal didn't, regardless of who he was working for, and I don't think he was working for Marty Estel. He couldn't have got into the El Milano to do the job, and certainly not into Miss Huntress's apartment. Whoever did it had something to gain by it and an opportunity to get to the place where it was done. Well, who had something to gain? Gerald had five million coming to him in two years out of a trust fund. He couldn't wait until he got it. So if he died, his natural heir got it. Who's his natural heir? You'd be surprised. Did you know that in the state of California and some others, but not in all, a man can by his own act become a natural heir? Just by adopting somebody who has money and no heirs!"

George moved then. His movement was once more as smooth as a ripple of water. The Smith & Wesson gleamed dully in his hand, but he didn't fire it. The small automatic in the girl's hand cracked. Blood spurted from George's brown hard hand. The Smith & Wesson dropped to the floor. He cursed. She didn't know much about guns—not very much.

"Of course!" she said grimly. "George could get into the apartment without any trouble, if Gerald was there. He would go in through the garage, a chauffeur in uniform, ride up in the elevator and knock at the door. And when Gerald opened it, George would back him in with the Smith and Wesson. But how did he know Gerald was there?"

I said: "He must have followed your taxi. We don't know where he had been all evening since he left me. He had a car with him. The cops will find out. How much was in it for you, George?"

George held his right wrist with his left hand, held it tightly, and his face was twisted, savage. He said nothing.

"George would back him in with the Smith and Wesson," the girl said wearily. "Then he would see my gun on the mantelpiece. That would be better. He would use that. He would back Gerald into the bedroom, away from the corridor, into the closet, and there, quietly, calmly, he would kill him and drop the gun on the floor."

"George killed Arbogast, too. He killed him with a twenty-two because he knew that Frisky Lavon's brother had a twenty-two, and he knew that because he had hired Frisky and his brother to put over a big scare on Gerald—so that when he was murdered it would look as if Marty Estel had had it done. That was why I was brought out here tonight in the Jeeter car—so that the two thugs who had been warned and planted could pull their act and maybe knock me off, if I got too tough. Only George likes to kill people. He made a neat shot at Frisky. He hit him in the face. It was so good a shot I think he meant it to be a miss. How about it, George?"

Silence.

I looked at old Jeeter at last. I had been expecting him to pull a gun himself, but he hadn't. He just stood there, open-mouthed, appalled, leaning against the black marble table, shaking.

"My God!" he whispered. "My God!"

"You don't have one—except money."

A door squeaked behind me. I whirled, but I needn't have bothered. A hard voice, about as English as Amos and Andy, said: "Put 'em up, bud."

The butler, the very English butler, stood there in the doorway, a gun in his hand, tight-lipped. The girl turned her wrist and shot him just kind of casually, in the shoulder or something. He squealed like a stuck pig.

"Go away, you're intruding," she said coldly.

He ran. We heard his steps running.

"He's going to fall," she said.

I was wearing my Luger in my right hand now, a little late in the season, as usual. I came around with it. Old Man Jeeter was holding on to the table, his face gray as a paving block. His knees were giving. George stood cynically, holding a handkerchief around his bleeding wrist, watching him.

"Let him fall," I said. "Down is where he belongs."

He fell. His head twisted. His mouth went slack. He hit the carpet on his side and rolled a little and his knees came up. His mouth drooled a little. His skin turned violet.

"Go call the law, angel," I said. "I'll watch them now."

"All right," she said, standing up. "But you certainly need a lot of help in your private-detecting business, Mr. Marlowe."

I had been in there for a solid hour, alone. There was the scarred desk in the middle, another against the wall, a brass spittoon on a mat, a police loudspeaker box on the wall, three squashed flies, a smell of cold cigars and old clothes. There were two hard armchairs with felt pads and two hard straight chairs without pads. The electric-light fixture had been dusted about Coolidge's first term.

The door opened with a jerk and Finlayson and Sebold came in. Sebold looked as spruce and nasty as ever, but Finlayson looked older, more worn, mousier. He held a sheaf of papers in his hand. He sat down across the desk from me and gave me a hard bleak stare.

"Guys like you get in a lot of trouble," Finlayson said sourly. Sebold sat down against the wall and tilted his hat over his eyes and yawned and looked at his new stainless-steel wristwatch.

"Trouble is my business," I said. "How else would I make a nickel?"

"We oughta throw you in the can for all this cover-up stuff. How much you making on this one?"

"I was working for Anna Halsey who was working for Old Man Jeeter. I guess I make a bad debt."

Sebold smiled his blackjack smile at me. Finlayson lit a cigar and licked at a tear on the side of it and pasted it down, but it leaked smoke just the same when he drew on it. He pushed papers across the desk at me.

"Sign three copies."

I signed three copies.

He took them back, yawned and rumpled his old gray head. "The old man's had a stroke," he said. "No dice there. Probably won't know what time it is when he comes out. This George Hasterman, this chauffeur guy, he just laughs at us. Too bad he got pinked. I'd like to wrastle him a bit."

"He's tough," I said.

"Yeah. Okay, you can beat it for now."

I got up and nodded to them and went to the door. "Well, good night, boys."

Neither of them spoke to me.

I went out, along the corridor and down in the night elevator to the City Hall lobby. I went out the Spring Street side and down the long flight of empty steps and the wind blew cold. I lit a cigarette at the bottom. My car was still out at the Jeeter place. I lifted a foot to start walking to a taxi half a block down across the street. A voice spoke sharply from a parked car.

"Come here a minute."

It was a man's voice, tight, hard. It was Marty Estel's voice. It came from a big sedan with two men in the front seat. I went over there. The rear window was down and Marty Estel leaned a gloved hand on it.

"Get in." He pushed the door open. I got in. I was too tired to argue. "Take it away, Skin."

The car drove west through dark, almost quiet streets, almost clean streets. The night air was not pure but it was cool. We went up over a hill and began to pick up speed.

"What they get?" Estel asked coolly.

"They didn't tell me. They didn't break the chauffeur yet."

"You can't convict a couple of million bucks of murder in this man's town." The driver called Skin laughed without turning his head. "Maybe I don't even touch my fifty grand now . . . she likes you."

"Uh-huh. So what?"

"Lay off her."

"What will it get me?"

"It's what it'll get you if you don't."

"Yeah, sure," I said. "Go to hell, will you please. I'm tired." I shut my eyes and leaned in the corner of the car and just like that went to sleep. I can do that sometimes, after a strain.

A hand shaking my shoulder woke me. The car had stopped. I looked out at the front of my apartment house.

"Home," Marty Estel said. "And remember. Lay off her."

"Why the ride home? Just to tell me that?"

"She asked me to look out for you. That's why you're loose. She likes you. I like her. See? You don't want any more trouble."

"Trouble—" I started to say, and stopped. I was tired of that gag for that night. "Thanks for the ride, and apart from that, nuts to you." I turned away and went into the apartment house and up.

The door lock was still loose but nobody waited for me this time. They had taken Waxnose away long since. I left the door open and threw the windows up and I was still sniffing at policemen's cigar butts when the phone rang. It was her voice, cool, a little hard, not touched by anything, almost amused. Well, she'd been through enough to make her that way, probably.

"Hello, brown eyes. Make it home all right?"

"Your pal Marty brought me home. He told me to lay off you. Thanks with all my heart, if I have any, but don't call me up anymore."

"A little scared, Mr. Marlowe?"

"No. Wait for me to call you," I said. "Good night, angel."

"Good night, brown eyes."

The phone clicked. I put it away and shut the door and pulled the bed down. I undressed and lay on it for a while in the cold air.

Then I got up and had a drink and a shower and went to sleep.

They broke George at last, but not enough. He said there had been a fight over the girl and young Jeeter had grabbed the gun off the mantel and George had fought with him and it had gone off. All of which, of course, looked possible—in the papers. They never pinned the Arbogast killing on him or on anybody. They never found the gun that did it, but it was not Waxnose's gun. Waxnose disappeared—I never heard where. They didn't touch Old Man Jeeter, because he never came out of his stroke, except to lie on his back and have nurses and tell people how he hadn't lost a nickel in the Depression.

Marty Estel called me up four times to tell me to lay off Harriet Huntress. I felt kind of sorry for the poor guy. He had it bad. I went out with her twice and sat with her twice more at home, drinking her Scotch. It was nice, but I didn't have the money, the clothes, the time or the manners. Then she stopped being at the El Milano and I heard she had gone to New York.

I was glad when she left—even though she didn't bother to tell me good-bye.

Sanctuary

Agatha Christie

In the sixteen novels and collections of short stories featuring Miss Marple, Agatha Christie created one of the most famous female detectives in fiction. On film, Margaret Rutherford created an enduring image of this unlikely amateur detective as an eccentric, bustling with energy, in a series of four pictures made between 1962 and 1964. Miss Marple made her TV debut in America in 1956 when the weekly show *Goodyear Playhouse* adapted *A Murder Is Announced,* with the Lancashire-born singer Gracie Fields cast rather surprisingly in the lead role. Two American actresses have subsequently appeared as the spinster sleuth on TV—Angela Lansbury and Helen Hayes— before Britain's veteran actress Joan Hickson began what is now regarded as the definitive portrayal in 1984 with the mini-series of *The Body in the Library.* Other adaptations have followed, reaffirming the magic of the original stories, including recent versions starring Geraldine McEwan.

The vicar's wife came round the corner of the vicarage with her arms full of chrysanthemums. A good deal of rich garden soil was attached to her strong brogue shoes and a few fragments of earth were adhering to her nose, but of that fact she was perfectly unconscious.

She had a slight struggle in opening the vicarage gate which hung, rustily, half off its hinges. A puff of wind caught at her battered felt hat, causing it to sit even more rakishly than it had done before. "Bother!" said Bunch.

Christened by her optimistic parents Diana, Mrs. Harmon had become Bunch at an early age for somewhat obvious reasons and the name had stuck to her ever since. Clutching the chrysanthemums, she made her way through the gate to the churchyard, and so to the church door.

The November air was mild and damp. Clouds scudded across the sky with patches of blue here and there. Inside, the church was dark and cold; it was unheated except at service times.

"Brrrrrh!" said Bunch expressively. "I'd better get on with this quickly. I don't want to die of cold."

With the quickness born of practice she collected the necessary paraphernalia: vases, water, flower-holders. "I wish we had lilies," thought Bunch to herself. "I get so tired of these scraggy chrysanthemums." Her nimble fingers arranged the blooms in their holders.

There was nothing particularly original or artistic about the decorations, for Bunch Harmon herself was neither original nor artistic, but it was a homely and pleasant arrangement. Carrying the vases carefully, Bunch stepped up the aisle and made her way toward the altar. As she did so the sun came out.

It shone through the east window of somewhat crude colored glass, mostly blue and red—the gift of a wealthy Victorian churchgoer. The effect was almost startling in its sudden opulence. "Like jewels," thought Bunch. Suddenly she stopped, staring ahead of her. On the chancel steps was a huddled dark form.

Putting down the flowers carefully, Bunch went up to it and bent over it. It was a man lying there, huddled over on himself. Bunch knelt down by him and slowly, carefully, she turned him over. Her fingers went to his pulse—a pulse so feeble and fluttering that it told its own story, as did the almost greenish pallor of his face. There was no doubt, Bunch thought that the man was dying.

He was a man of about forty-five, dressed in a dark, shabby suit. She laid down the limp hand she had picked up and looked at his other hand. This seemed clenched like a fist on his breast. Looking more closely she saw that the fingers were closed over what seemed to be a large wad or handkerchief which he was holding tightly to his chest. All round the clenched hand there were splashes of a dry brown fluid which, Bunch guessed, was dry blood. Bunch sat back on her heels, frowning.

Up till now the man's eyes had been closed but at this point they suddenly opened and fixed themselves on Bunch's face. They were neither dazed nor wandering. They seemed fully alive and intelligent. His lips moved, and Bunch bent forward to catch the words, or rather the word. It was only one word that he said:

"Sanctuary."

There was, she thought, just a very faint smile as he breathed out this word. There was no mistaking it, for after a moment he said it again, "Sanctuary . . ."

Then with a faint, long-drawn-out sigh, his eyes closed again. Once more Bunch's fingers went to his pulse. It was still there, but fainter now and more intermittent. She got up with decision.

"Don't move," she said, "or try to move. I'm going for help."

The man's eyes opened again but he seemed now to be fixing his attention on the colored light that came through the east window. He murmured something that Bunch could not quite catch. She thought, startled, that it might have been her husband's name.

"Julian?" she said. "Did you come here to find Julian?"

But there was no answer. The man lay with eyes closed, his breathing coming in slow, shallow fashion.

Bunch turned and left the church rapidly. She glanced at her watch and nodded with some satisfaction. Dr. Griffiths would still be in his surgery. It was only a couple of minute's walk from the church. She went in, without waiting to knock or ring, passing through the waiting room and into the doctor's surgery.

"You must come at once," said Bunch. "There's a man dying in the church."

Some minutes later Dr. Griffiths rose from his knees after a brief examination.

"Can we move him from here into the vicarage? I can attend to him better there—not that it's any use."

"Of course," said Bunch. "I'll go along and get things ready. I'll get Harper and Jones shall I? To help you carry him."

"Thanks. I can telephone from the vicarage for an ambulance, but I'm afraid—by the time it comes . . ." He left the remark unfinished.

Bunch said, "Internal bleeding?"

Dr. Griffiths nodded. He said, "How on earth did he come here?"

"I think he must have been here all night," said Bunch, considering. "Harper unlocks the church in the morning, as he goes to work, but he doesn't usually come in."

It was about five minutes later when Dr. Griffiths put down the telephone receiver and came back into the morning-room where the injured man was lying on quickly arranged blankets on the sofa. Bunch was moving a basin of water and clearing up after the doctor's examination.

"Well, that's that," said Griffiths. "I've sent for an ambulance and I've notified the police." He stood, frowning, looking down on the patient who lay with closed eyes. His left hand was plucking in a nervous, spasmodic way at his side.

"He was shot," said Griffiths. "Shot at fairly close quarters. He rolled his handkerchief up into a ball and plugged the wound with it so as to stop the bleeding."

"Could he have gone far after that happened?" Bunch asked.

"Oh, yes, it's quite possible. A mortally wounded man has been known to pick himself up and walk along a street as though nothing has happened, and then suddenly collapse five or ten minutes later. So he needn't have been shot in the church. Oh no. He may have been shot some distance away. Of course, he may have shot himself and then dropped the revolver and staggered blindly towards the church. I don't quite know why he made for the church and not for the vicarage."

"Oh, I know *that,*" said Bunch. "He said it: 'Sanctuary.' "

The doctor stared at her. "Sanctuary?"

"Here's Julian," said Bunch, turning her head as she heard her husband's steps in the hall. "Julian! Come here."

The Reverend Julian Harmon entered the room. His vague, scholarly manner always made him appear much older than he really was. "Dear me!" said Julian Harmon, staring in a mild, puzzled manner at the surgical appliances and the prone figure on the sofa.

Bunch explained with her usual economy of words. "He was in the church, dying. He'd been shot. Do you know him, Julian? I thought he said your name."

The vicar came up to the sofa and looked down at the dying man. "Poor fellow," he said, and shook his head. "No, I don't know him. I'm almost sure I've never seen him before."

At that moment the dying man's eyes opened once more. They went from the doctor to Julian Harmon and from him to his wife. The eyes stayed there, staring into Bunch's face. Griffiths stepped forward.

"If you could tell us," he said urgently.

But with eyes fixed on Bunch, the man said in a weak voice, "Please—*please*—" And then, with a slight tremor, he died . . .

Sergeant Hayes licked his pencil and turned the page of his notebook.

"So that's all you can tell me, Mrs. Harmon?"

"That's all," said Bunch. "These are the things out of his coat pockets."

On a table at Sergeant Hayes's elbow was a wallet, a rather battered old watch with the initials W.S. and the return half of a ticket to London. Nothing more.

"You've found out who he is?" asked Bunch.

"A Mr. and Mrs. Eccles phoned up the station. He's her brother, it seems. Name of Sandbourne. Been in a low state of health and nerves for some time. He's been getting worse lately. The day before yesterday he walked out and didn't come back. He took a revolver with him."

"And he came out here and shot himself with it?" said Bunch. "Why?"

"Well you see, he's been depressed . . ."

Bunch interrupted him. "I don't mean *that.* I mean, why here?"

Since Sergeant Hayes obviously did not know the answer to that one, he replied in an oblique fashion, "Come out here, he did, on the five-ten bus."

"Yes," said Bunch again. "But *why?*"

"I don't know, Mrs. Harmon," said Sergeant Hayes. "There's no accounting. If the balance of the mind is disturbed—"

Bunch finished for him. "They may do it anywhere. But it still seems to me unnecessary to take the bus out to a small country place like this. He didn't know anyone here, did he?"

"Not so far as can be ascertained," said Sergeant Hayes.

He coughed in an apologetic manner and said, as he rose to his feet, "It may be as Mr. and Mrs. Eccles will come out and see you, ma'am—if you don't mind, that is."

"Of course I don't mind," said Bunch. "It's very natural. I only wish I had something to tell them."

"I'll be getting along," said Sergeant Hayes.

"I'm only so thankful," said Bunch, going with him to the front door, "that it wasn't murder."

A car had driven up at the vicarage gate. Sergeant Hayes, glancing at it, remarked: "Looks as though that's Mr. and Mrs. Eccles come here now, ma'am, to talk with you."

Bunch braced herself to endure what, she felt, might be rather a difficult ordeal. "However," she thought, "I can always call Julian to help me. A clergyman's a great help when people are bereaved."

Exactly what she had expected Mr. and Mrs. Eccles to be like, Bunch could not have said, but she was conscious, as she greeted them, of a feeling of surprise. Mr. Eccles was a stout florid man whose natural manner would have been cheerful and facetious. Mrs. Eccles had a vaguely flashy look about her. She had a small, mean, pursed-up mouth. Her voice was thin and reedy.

"It's been a terrible shock, Mrs. Harmon, as you can imagine," she said.

"Oh, I know," said Bunch. "It must have been. Do sit down. Can I offer you—well, perhaps it's a little early for tea—"

Mr. Eccles waved a pudgy hand. "No, no, nothing for us," he said. "It's very kind of you, I'm sure. Just wanted to . . . well . . . what poor William said and all that, you know?"

"He's been abroad a long time," said Mrs. Eccles, "and I think he must have had some very nasty experiences. Very quiet and depressed he's been, ever since he came home. Said the world wasn't fit to live in and there was nothing to look forward to. Poor Bill, he was always moody."

Bunch stared at them both for a moment or two without speaking.

"Pinched my husband's revolver, he did," went on Mrs. Eccles. "Without our knowing. Then it seems he come here by bus. I suppose that was nice feeling on his part. He wouldn't have liked to do it in our house."

"Poor fellow, poor fellow," said Mr. Eccles, with a sigh. "It doesn't do to judge."

There was another short pause, and Mr. Eccles said, "Did he leave a message? Any last words, nothing like that?"

His bright, rather pig-like eyes watched Bunch closely. Mrs. Eccles, too, leaned forwards as though anxious for the reply.

"No," said Bunch quietly. "He came in the church when he was dying, for sanctuary."

Mrs. Eccles said in a puzzled voice. "Sanctuary? I don't think I quite . . ."

Mr. Eccles interrupted. "Holy place, my dear," he said impatiently. "That's what the vicar's wife means. It's a sin—suicide, you know. I expect he wanted to make amends."

"He tried to say something just before he died," said Bunch. "He began, 'Please,' but that's as far as he got."

Mrs. Eccles put her handkerchief to her eyes and sniffed. "Oh, dear," she said. "It's terribly upsetting, isn't it?"

"There, there, Pam," said her husband. "Don't take on. These things can't be helped. Poor Willie. Still, he's at peace now. Well, thank you very much, Mrs. Harmon. I hope we haven't interrupted you. A vicar's wife is a busy lady, we know that."

They shook hands with her. Then Eccles turned back suddenly to say, "Oh yes, there's just one other thing. I think you've got his coat here, haven't you?"

"His coat?" Bunch frowned.

Mrs. Eccles said, "We'd like all his things, you know. Sentimental-like."

"He had a watch and a wallet and a railway ticket in the pockets," said Bunch. "I gave them to Sergeant Hayes."

"That's all right, then," said Mr. Eccles. "He'll hand them over to us, I expect. His private papers would be in the wallet."

"There was a pound note in the wallet," said Bunch. "Nothing else."

"No letters? Nothing like that?"

Bunch shook her head.

"Well, thank you again, Mrs. Harmon. The coat he was wearing—perhaps the sergeant's got that too, has he?"

Bunch frowned in an effort of remembrance.

"No," she said. "I don't think . . . let me see. The doctor and I took his coat off to examine his wound." She looked round the room vaguely. "I must have taken it upstairs with the towels and basin."

"I wonder now, Mrs. Harmon, if you wouldn't mind. . . . We'd like his coat, you know, the last thing he wore. Well. The wife feels rather sentimental about it."

"Of course," said Bunch. "Would you like me to have it cleaned first? I'm afraid it's rather—well—stained."

"Oh, no, no, no, that doesn't matter."

Bunch frowned. "Now I wonder where . . . excuse me a moment." She went upstairs and it was some few minutes before she returned.

"I'm so sorry," she said breathlessly, "my daily woman must have put it aside with other clothes that were going to the cleaners. It's taken me quite a long time to find it. Here it is. I'll do it up for you in brown paper."

Disclaiming their protests she did so; then once more effusively bidding her farewell the Eccleses departed.

Bunch went slowly back across the hall and entered the study. The Reverend Julian Harmon looked up and his brow cleared. He was composing a sermon and was fearing that he had been led astray by the interest of the political relations between Judaea and Persia, in the reign of Cyrus.

"Yes, dear?" he said hopefully.

"Julian," said Bunch. "What's *Sanctuary* exactly?"

Julian Harmon gratefully put aside his sermon paper.

"Well," he said. "Sanctuary in Roman and Greek temples applied to the *cella* in which stood the statue of a god. The Latin word for altar *'ara'* also means protection."

He continued learnedly: "In A.D. three hundred and ninety-nine the right of sanctuary in Christian churches was finally and definitely recognized. The earliest mention of the right of sanctuary in England is in the Code of Laws issued by Ethelbert in A.D. six hundred . . ."

He continued for some time with his exposition but was, as often, disconcerted by his wife's reception of his erudite pronouncement.

"Darling," she said. "You are sweet."

Bending over, she kissed him on the tip of his nose. Julian felt rather like a dog who has been congratulated on performing a clever trick.

"The Eccleses have been here," said Bunch.

The vicar frowned. "The Eccleses? I don't seem to remember . . ."

"You don't know them. They're the sister and her husband of the man in the church."

"My dear, you ought to have called me."

"There wasn't any need," said Bunch. "They were not in need of consolation. I wonder now . . ." She frowned. "If I put a casserole in the oven tomorrow, can you manage, Julian? I think I shall go up to London for the sales."

"The sails?" Her husband looked at her blankly. "Do you mean a yacht or a boat or something?"

Bunch laughed. "No, darling. There's a special white sale at Burrows and Portman's. You know, sheets, table cloths and towels and glass-cloths. I don't know what we do with our glass-cloths, the way they wear through. Besides," she added thoughtfully, "I think I ought to go and see Aunt Jane."

That sweet old lady, Miss Jane Marple, was enjoying the delights of the metropolis for a fortnight, comfortably installed in her nephew's studio flat.

"So kind of dear Raymond," she murmured. "He and Joan have gone to America for a fortnight and they insisted I should come up here and enjoy myself. And now, dear Bunch, do tell me what it is that's worrying you."

Bunch was Miss Marple's favorite godchild, and the old lady looked at her with great affection as Bunch, thrusting her best felt hat farther on the back of her head, started her story.

Bunch's recital was concise and clear. Miss Marple nodded her head as Bunch finished. "I see," she said. "Yes, I see."

"That's why I felt I had to see you," said Bunch. "You see, not being so clever—"

"But you are clever, my dear."

"No, I'm not. Not clever like Julian."

"Julian, of course, has a very solid intellect," said Miss Marple.

"That's it," said Bunch. "Julian's got the intellect, but on the other hand, I've got the sense."

"You have a lot of common sense, Bunch, and you're very intelligent."

"You see, I don't really know what I ought to do. I can't ask Julian because—well, I mean, Julian's so full of rectitude . . ."

This statement appeared to be perfectly understood by Miss Marple, who said, "I know what you mean, dear. We women—well, it's different." She went on. "You told me what happened, Bunch, but I'd like to know first exactly what you think."

"It's all wrong," said Bunch. "The man who was there in the church, dying, knew all about Sanctuary. He said it just the way Julian would have said it. I mean, he was a well-read, educated man. And if he'd shot himself, he wouldn't drag himself to a church afterwards and say 'sanctuary'. Sanctuary means that you're pursued, and when you get into a church you're safe. Your pursuers can't touch you. At one time, even the law couldn't get at you."

She nodded questioningly at Miss Marple. The latter nodded. Bunch went on, "Those people, the Eccleses, were quite different. Ignorant and coarse. And there's another thing. That watch—the dead man's watch—I opened it—in very small lettering there was 'To Walter from his father' and a date. *Walter*. But the Eccleses kept talking of him as William or Bill."

Miss Marple seemed about to speak but Bunch rushed on. "Oh, I know you're not always called the name you're baptized by. I mean, I can understand that you might be christened William and called 'Porgy' or 'Carrots' or something. But your sister wouldn't call you William or Bill if your name was Walter."

"You mean that she wasn't his sister?"

"I'm quite sure she wasn't his sister. They were horrid—both of them. They came to the vicarage to get his things and to find out if he'd said anything before he died. When I said he hadn't I saw it in their faces—relief. I think myself," finished Bunch, "it was Eccles who shot him."

"Murder?" said Miss Marple.

"Yes," said Bunch. "Murder. That's why I came to you, darling."

Bunch's remarks might have seemed incongruous to an ignorant listener, but in certain spheres Miss Marple had a reputation for dealing with murder.

"He said 'please' to me before he died," said Bunch. "He wanted me to do something for him. The awful thing is I've no idea what."

Miss Marple considered for a moment or two, and then pounced on the point that had already occurred to Bunch. "But why was he there at all?" she asked.

"You mean," said Bunch, "if you wanted sanctuary you might pop into a church anywhere. There's no need to take a bus that only goes four-times a day and come out to a lonely spot like ours for it."

"He must have come there for a purpose," Miss Marple thought. "He must have come to see someone. Chipping Cleghorn's not a big place, Bunch. Surely you must have some idea of who it was he came to see?"

Bunch reviewed the inhabitants of her village in her mind before rather doubtfully shaking her head. "In a way," she said, "it could be anybody."

"He never mentioned a name?"

"He said Julian, or I thought he said Julian. It might have been Julia, I suppose. As far as I know, there isn't any Julia living in Chipping Cleghorn."

She screwed up her eyes as she thought back to the scene. The man lying there on the chancel steps, the light coming through the window with its jewels of red and blue light.

"Jewels," said Miss Marple thoughtfully.

"I'm coming now," said Bunch, "to the most important thing of all. The reason why I've really come here today. You see, the Eccleses made a great fuss about having his coat. We took it off when the doctor was seeing him. It was an old, shabby sort of coat—there was no reason they should have wanted it. They pretended it was sentimental, but that was nonsense.

"Anyway, I went up to find it, and as I was just going up the stairs I remembered how he'd made a kind of picking gesture with his hand, as though he was fumbling with the coat. So when I got hold of the coat I looked at it very carefully and I saw that in one place the lining had been sewn up again with a different thread. So I unpicked it and I found a little piece of paper inside. I took it out and I sewed it up again properly with thread that matched. I was careful and I don't really think that the Eccleses would know I've done it. I don't *think* so, but I can't be sure. And I took the coat down to them and made some excuse for the delay."

"The piece of paper?" asked Miss Marple.

Bunch opened her handbag. "I didn't show it to Julian," she said, "because he would have said that I ought to have given it to the Eccleses. But I thought I'd rather bring it to you instead."

"A cloakroom ticket," said Miss Marple, looking at it. "Paddington Station."

"He had a return ticket to Paddington in his pocket," said Bunch.

The eyes of the two women met.

"This calls for action," said Miss Marple briskly. "But it would be advisable, I think, to be careful. Would you have noticed at all, Bunch dear, whether you were followed when you came to London today?"

"Followed!" exclaimed Bunch. "You don't think—"

"Well, I think it's *possible,*" said Miss Marple. "When anything is possible, I think we ought to take precautions." She rose with a brisk movement. "You came up here ostensibly, my dear, to go to the sales. I think the right thing to do, therefore, would be for us to go to the sales. But before we set out, we might put one or two little arrangements in hand. I don't suppose," Miss Marple added obscurely, "that I shall need the old speckled tweed with the beaver collar just at present."

It was about an hour and a half later that the two ladies, rather the worse for wear and battered in appearance, and both clasping parcels of hardly-worn household linen, sat down at a small sequestered hostelry called the Apple Bough to restore their forces with steak and kidney pudding followed by apple tart and custard.

"Really a pre-war quality face towel," gasped Miss Marple, slightly out of breath. "With a 'J' on it, too. So fortunate that Raymond's wife's name is Joan. I shall put them aside until I really need them and then they will do for her if I pass on sooner than I expect."

"I really did need the glass-cloths," said Bunch. "And they were very cheap, though not as cheap as the ones that woman with the ginger hair managed to snatch from me."

A smart young woman with a lavish application of rouge and lipstick entered the Apple Bough at that moment. After looking around vaguely for a moment or two, she hurried to their table. She laid down an envelope by Miss Marple's elbow.

"There you are, miss," she said briskly.

"Oh, thank you, Gladys," said Miss Marple. "Thank you very much. So kind of you."

"Always pleased to oblige, I'm sure," said Gladys. "Ernie always says to me, 'Everything what's good you learned from that Miss Marple of yours that you were in service with,' and I'm sure I'm always glad to oblige you, miss."

"Such a dear girl," said Miss Marple as Gladys departed again. "Always so willing and so kind."

She looked inside the envelope and then passed it on to Bunch. "Now be very careful, dear," she said. "By the way, is there still that nice young inspector at Melchester that I remember?"

"I don't know," said Bunch. "I expect so."

"Well, if not," said Miss Marple thoughtfully. "I can always ring up the Chief Constable. I *think* he would remember me."

"Of course he'd remember you," said Bunch. "Everybody would remember *you.* You're quite unique." She rose.

❦ ❦ ❦ ❦

Arrived at Paddington, Bunch went to the luggage office and produced the cloakroom ticket. A moment or two later a rather shabby old suitcase was passed across to her, and carrying this she made her way to the platform.

The journey home was uneventful. Bunch rose as the train approached Chipping Cleghorn and picked up the old suitcase. She had just left her carriage when a man, sprinting along the platform, suddenly seized the suitcase from her hand and rushed off with it.

"Stop!" Bunch yelled. "Stop him, stop him. He's taken my suitcase."

The ticket collector, who, at this rural station, was a man of somewhat slow processes, had just begun to say, "Now look here, you can't do that—" when a smart blow in the chest pushed him aside, and the man with the suitcase rushed out from the station. He made his way toward a waiting car. Tossing the suitcase in, he was about to climb after it, but before he could move a hand fell on his shoulder, and the voice of Police Constable Abel said, "Now then, what's all this?"

Bunch arrived, panting from the station. "He snatched my suitcase. I just got out of the train with it."

"Nonsense," said the man. "I don't know what this lady means. It's my suitcase. I just got out of the train with it."

He looked at Bunch with a bovine and impartial stare. Nobody would have guessed that Police Constable Abel and Mrs. Harmon spent long half-hours in Police Constable Abel's off-time discussing the respective merits of manure and bone-meal for rose bushes.

"You say, madam, that this is your suitcase?" said Police Constable Abel.

"Yes," said Bunch. "Definitely."

"And you, sir?"

"I say this suitcase is mine."

The man was tall, dark and well dressed, with a drawling voice and a superior manner. A feminine voice from inside the car said, "Of course it's your suitcase, Edwin. I don't know what this woman means."

"We'll have to get this clear," said Police Constable Abel. "If it's your suitcase, madam, what do you say is inside it?"

"Clothes," said Bunch. "A long speckled coat with a beaver collar, two wool jumpers and a pair of shoes."

"Well, that's clear enough," said Police Constable Abel. He turned to the other.

"I'm a theatrical costumer," said the dark man importantly. "This suitcase contains theatrical properties which I brought down here for an amateur performance."

"Right, sir," said Police Constable Abel. "Well, we'll just look inside, shall we, and see? We can go along to the police station, or if you are in a hurry we'll take the suitcase back to the station and open it there."

"It'll suit me," said the dark man. "My name is Moss, by the way, Edwin Moss."

The police constable, holding the suitcase, went back into the station. "Just taking this into the parcels office, George," he said to the ticket collector.

Police Constable Abel laid the suitcase on the counter of the parcels office and pushed back the clasp. The case was not locked. Bunch and Mr. Edwin Moss stood on either side of him, their eyes regarding each other vengefully.

"Ah!" said Police Constable Abel, as he pushed up the lid.

Inside, neatly folded, was a long rather shabby tweed coat with a beaver fur collar. There were also two wool jumpers and a pair of country shoes.

"Exactly as you say, madam," said Police Constable Abel, turning to Bunch.

Nobody could have said that Mr. Edwin Moss under-did things. His dismay and compunction were magnificent.

"I do apologize," he said. "I really *do* apologize. Please believe me, dear lady, when I tell you how very, very sorry I am. Unpardonable—quite unpardonable—my behavior has been." He looked at his watch. "I must rush now. Probably my suitcase has gone on the train." Raising his hat once more, he said meltingly to Bunch, "Do, *do* forgive me," and rushed hurriedly out of the parcels office.

"Are you going to let him get away?" asked Bunch in a conspiratorial whisper to Police Constable Abel.

The latter slowly closed a bovine eye in a wink.

"He won't get too far, ma'am," he said. "That's to say he won't get far unobserved, if you take my meaning."

"Oh," said Bunch, relieved.

"That old lady's been on the phone," said Police Constable Abel, "the one as was down here a few years ago. Bright she is, isn't she? But there's been a lot cooking up all today. Shouldn't wonder if the inspector or sergeant was out to see you about it tomorrow morning."

It was the inspector who came, the Inspector Craddock whom Miss Marple remembered. He greeted Bunch with a smile as an old friend.

"Crime in Chipping Cleghorn again," he said cheerfully. "You don't lack for sensation here, do you, Mrs. Harmon?"

"I could do with rather less," said Bunch. "Have you come to ask me questions or are you going to tell me things for a change?"

"I'll tell you some things first," said the inspector. "To begin with, Mr. and Mrs. Eccles have been having an eye kept on them for some time. There's reason to believe they've been connected with several armed robberies in this part of the world. For another thing, although Mrs. Eccles *has* a brother called Sandbourne who has recently come back from abroad, the man you found dying in the church yesterday was definitely not Sandbourne."

"I knew he wasn't," said Bunch. "His name was Walter, to begin with, not William."

The inspector nodded. "His name was Walter St. John, and he escaped forty-eight hours ago from Charrington Prison."

"Of course," said Bunch softly to herself, "he was being hunted down by the law, and he took sanctuary." Then she asked, "What had he done?"

"I'll have to go back rather a long way. It's a complicated story. Several years ago there was a certain dancer doing turns at the music halls. I don't expect you'll have ever heard of her, but she specialized in an Arabian Night turn, 'Aladdin in the Cave of Jewels' it was called. She wore bits of rhinestone and not much else.

"She wasn't much of a dancer, I believe, but she was—well—attractive. Anyway, a certain Asiatic royalty fell for her in a big way. Amongst other things he gave her a very magnificent emerald necklace."

"The historic jewels of a Rajah?" murmured Bunch ecstatically.

Inspector Craddock coughed. "Well, a rather more modern version, Mrs. Harmon. The affair didn't last very long, broke up when our potentate's attention was captured by a certain film star whose demands were not quite so modest.

"Zobeida, to give the dancer her stage name, hung on to the necklace, and in due course, it was stolen. It disappeared from her dressing-room at the theater, and there was a lingering suspicion in the minds of the authorities that she herself might have engineered its disappearance. Such things have been known as a publicity stunt, or indeed from more dishonest motives.

"The necklace was never recovered, but during the course of the investigation the attention of the police was drawn to this man, Walter St. John. He was a man of education and breeding who had come down in the world, and who was employed as a working jeweler with a rather obscure firm which was suspected of acting as a fence for jewel robberies.

"There was evidence that this necklace had passed through his hands. It was however, in connection with the theft of some other jewelry that he was finally brought to trial and convicted and sent to prison. He had not very much longer to serve, so his escape was rather a surprise."

"But why did he come here?" asked Bunch.

"We'd like to know that very much, Mrs. Harmon. Following up his trial, it seems that he went first to London. He didn't visit any of his old associates but he visited an elderly woman, a Mrs. Jacobs, who had formerly been a theatrical dresser. She won't say a word of what he came for, but according to other lodgers in the house he left carrying a suitcase."

"I see," said Bunch. "He left it in the cloakroom at Paddington and then he came down here."

"By that time," said Inspector Craddock, "Eccles and the man who calls himself

Edwin Moss were on his trail. They wanted that suitcase. They saw him get on the bus. They must have driven out in a car ahead of him and been waiting for him when he left the bus."

"And he was murdered?" said Bunch.

"Yes," said Craddock. "He was shot. It was Eccles's revolver, but I rather fancy it was Moss who did the shooting. Now, Mrs. Harmon, what we want to know is, where is the suitcase that Walter St. John actually deposited at Paddington Station?"

Bunch grinned. "I expect Aunt Jane's got it by now," she said. "Miss Marple, I mean. That was her plan. She sent a former maid of hers with a suitcase packed with her things to the cloakroom at Paddington and we exchanged tickets. I collected her suitcase and brought it down by train. She seemed to expect an attempt would be made to get it from me."

It was Inspector Craddock's turn to grin. "So she said when she rang up. I'm driving up to London to see her. Do you want to come, too, Mrs. Harmon?"

"Wel-l," said Bunch, considering, "Wel-l, as a matter of fact, it's very fortunate. I had a toothache last night so I really ought to go to London to see the dentist, oughtn't I?"

"Definitely," said Inspector Craddock.

Miss Marple looked from Inspector Craddock's face to the eager face of Bunch Harmon. The suitcase lay on the table. "Of course, I haven't opened it," the old lady said. "I wouldn't dream of doing such a thing till somebody official arrived. Besides," she added, with a demurely mischievous Victorian smile, "it's locked."

"Like to make a guess at what's inside, Miss Marple?" asked the inspector.

"I should imagine you know," said Miss Marple, "that it would be Zobeida's theatrical costumes. Would you like a chisel, Inspector?"

The chisel soon did its work. Both women gave a slight gasp as the lid flew up. The sunlight coming through the window lit up what seemed like an inexhaustible treasure of sparkling jewels, red, blue, green, orange.

"Aladdin's Cave," said Miss Marple. "The flashing jewels the girl wore to dance."

"Ah," said Inspector Craddock. "Now, what's so precious about it, do you think, that a man was murdered to get hold of it?"

"She was a shrewd girl, I expect," said Miss Marple thoughtfully. "She's dead, isn't she, Inspector?"

"Yes, died three years ago."

"She had this valuable emerald necklace," said Miss Marple musingly. "Had the stones taken out of their setting and fastened here and there on her theatrical costume, where everyone would take them for merely colored rhinestones. Then she had a replica made of the real necklace, and that, of course, was what was stolen. No wonder it never came on the market. The thief soon discovered that the stones were false."

"Here is an envelope," said Bunch, pulling aside some of the glittering stones.

Inspector Craddock took it from her and extracted two official-looking papers from it. He read aloud, " 'Marriage Certificate between Walter Edmund St. John and Mary Moss.' That was Zobeida's real name."

"So they were married," said Miss Marple. "I see."

"What's the other?" asked Bunch.

"A birth certificate of a daughter, Jewel."

"Jewel?" cried Bunch. "Why, of course. Jewel! *Jill!* That's it. I see now why he came to Chipping Cleghorn. *That's* what he was trying to say to me. Jewel. The Mundys, you know. Laburnum Cottage. They look after a little girl for someone. They're devoted to her. She's been like their own granddaughter. Yes, I remember now, her name *was* Jewel, only of course, they call her Jill.

"Mrs. Mundy had a stroke about a week ago, and the old man's been very ill with pneumonia. They were both going to the infirmary. I've been trying hard to find a good home for Jill somewhere. I didn't want her taken away to an institution.

"I suppose her father heard about it in prison and he managed to break away and get hold of this suitcase from the old dresser he or his wife left it with. I suppose if the jewels really belonged to her mother, they can be used for the child now."

"I should imagine so, Mrs. Harmon. *If* they're here."

"Oh, they'll be here all right," said Miss Marple cheerfully.

"Thank goodness you're back, dear," said the Reverend Julian Harmon, greeting his wife with affection and a sigh of content. "Mrs. Burt always tries to do her best when you're away, but she really gave me some very peculiar fish-cakes for lunch. I didn't want to hurt her feelings so I gave them to Tiglath Pileser, but even *he* wouldn't eat them so I had to throw them out of the window."

"Tiglath Pileser," said Bunch, stroking the vicarage cat, who was purring against her knee, "is *very* particular about what fish he eats. I often tell him he's got a proud stomach!"

"And your tooth; dear? Did you have it seen to?"

"Yes," said Bunch. "It didn't hurt much, and I went to see Aunt Jane again, too."

"Dear old thing," said Julian. "I hope she's not failing at all."

"Not in the least," said Bunch with a grin.

The following morning Bunch took a fresh supply of chrysanthemums to the church. The sun was once more pouring through the east window, and Bunch stood in the jeweled light on the chancel steps. She said very softly under her breath, "Your little girl will be all right. *I'll* see that she is. I promise."

Then she tidied up the church, slipped into a pew and knelt for a few moments to say her prayers before returning to the vicarage to attack the piled-up chores of two neglected days.

The Case of the Irate Witness

Erle Stanley Gardner

Although he was an environmentalist, fluent in Chinese and a professional attorney for twenty-two years, Erle Stanley Gardner will always be remembered as the creator of legendary protagonist attorney Perry Mason. In fact, it has been reported that when Albert Einstein died, a Perry Mason book was at his bedside. Media contributions for Perry Mason include six films, 3,221 radio episodes, 271 television episodes and more than twenty made-for-television movies, thus making Gardner one of history's all time best-selling mystery writers. "The Case of the Irate Witness" is the first—and only—Perry Mason short story. Raymond Burr is best known for portraying Perry Mason on TV.

The early-morning shadows cast by the mountains still lay heavily on the town's main street as the big siren on the roof of the Jebson Commercial Company began to scream shrilly.

The danger of fire was always present, and at the sound, men at breakfast rose and pushed their chairs back from the table. Men who were shaving barely paused to wipe lather from their faces; men who had been sleeping grabbed the first available garments. All of them ran to places where they could look for the first telltale wisps of smoke.

There was no smoke.

The big siren was screaming urgently as the men formed into streaming lines, like ants whose hill has been attacked. The lines all moved toward the Jebson Commercial Company.

There the men were told that the doors of the big vault had been found wide open. A jagged hole had been cut into one door with an acetylene torch.

The men looked at one another silently. This was the fifteenth of the month. The big, twice-a-month payroll, which had been brought up from the Ivanhoe National Bank the day before, had been the prize.

Frank Bernal, manager of the company's mine, the man who ruled Jebson City with an iron hand, arrived and took charge. The responsibility was his, and what he found was alarming.

Tom Munson, the night watchman, was lying on the floor in a back room, snoring in drunken slumber. The burglar alarm, which has been installed within the last six months, had been bypassed by means of an electrical device. This device was so ingenious that it was apparent that, if the work were that of a gang, at least one of the burglars was an expert electrician.

Ralph Nesbitt, the company accountant, was significantly silent. When Frank Bernal had been appointed manager a year earlier, Nesbitt had pointed out that the big vault was obsolete.

Bernal, determined to prove himself in his new job, had avoided the expense of tearing out the old vault and installing a new one by investing in an up-to-date burglar alarm and putting a special night watchman on duty.

Now the safe had been looted of $100,000 and Frank Bernal had to make a report to the main office in Chicago, with the disquieting knowledge that Ralph Nesbitt's memo stating that the antiquated vault was a pushover was at this moment reposing in the company files.

Some distance out of Jebson City, Perry Mason, the famous trial lawyer, was driving fast along a mountain road. He had planned a weekend fishing trip for a long time, but a jury which had waited until midnight before reaching its verdict had delayed Mason's departure and it was now 8:30 in the morning.

His fishing clothes, rod, wading boots, and reel were all in the truck. He was wearing the suit in which he had stepped from the courtroom, and having driven all night he was eager for the cool, piny mountains.

A blazing red light, shining directly at him as he rounded a turn in the canyon road, dazzled his road-weary eyes. A sign, STOP–POLICE, had been placed in the middle of the road. Two men, a grim-faced man with a .30-30 rifle in his hands and a silver badge on his shirt and a uniformed motorcycle officer, stood beside the sign.

Mason stopped his car.

The man with the badge, deputy sheriff, said, "We'd better take a look at your driving license. There's been a big robbery at Jebson City."

"That so?" Mason said. "I went through Jebson City an hour ago and everything seemed quiet."

"Where you been since then?"

"I stopped at a little service station and restaurant for breakfast."

"Let's take a look at your driving license."

Mason handed it to him.

The man started to return it, then looked at it again. "Say," he said, "you're Perry Mason, the big criminal lawyer!"

"Not a criminal lawyer," Mason said patiently, "a trial lawyer. I sometimes defend men who are accused of crime."

"What are you doing up in this country?"

"Going fishing."

The deputy looked at him suspiciously. "Why aren't you wearing your fishing clothes?"

"Because," Mason said, and smiled, "I'm not fishing."

"You said you were going fishing."

"I also intend," Mason said, "to go to bed tonight. According to you, I should be wearing my pajamas."

The deputy frowned. The traffic officer laughed and waved Mason on.

The deputy nodded at the departing car. "Looks like a live clue to me," he said, "but I can't find it in that conversation."

"There isn't any," the traffic officer said.

The deputy remained dubious, and later on, when a news-hungry reporter from the local paper asked the deputy if he knew of anything that would make a good story, the deputy said that he did.

And that was why Della Street, Perry Mason's confidential secretary, was surprised to read stories in the metropolitan papers stating that Perry Mason, the noted trial lawyer, was rumored to have been retained to represent the person or persons who had looted the vault of the Jebson Commercial Company. All this had been arranged, it would seem, before Mason's "client" had even been apprehended.

When Perry Mason called his office by long-distance the next afternoon, Della said, "I thought you were going to the mountains for a vacation."

"That's right. Why?"

"The papers claim you're representing whoever robbed the Jebson Commercial Company."

"First I've heard of it," Mason said. "I went through Jebson City before they discovered the robbery, stopped for breakfast a little farther on, and then got caught in a road-block. In the eyes of some officious deputy, that seems to have made me an accessory after the fact."

"Well," Della Street said, "they've caught a man by the name of Harvey L. Corbin, and apparently have quite a case against him. They're hinting at mysterious evidence which won't be disclosed until the time of trial."

"Was he the one who committed the crime?" Mason asked.

"The police think so. He has a criminal record. When his employers at Jebson City found out about it, they told him to leave town. That was the evening before the robbery."

"Just like that, eh?" Mason asked.

"Well, you see, Jebson City is a one-industry town, and the company owns all the houses. They're leased to the employees. I understand Corbin's wife and daughter were told they could stay on until Corbin got located in a new place, but Corbin was told to leave town at once. You aren't interested, are you?"

"Not in the least," Mason said. "Except that when I drive back I'll be going through Jebson City, and I'll probably stop to pick up the local gossip."

"Don't do it," she warned. "This man Corbin has all the earmarks of being an underdog, and you know how you feel about underdogs."

A quality in her voice made Perry suspicious. "You haven't been approached, have you, Della?"

"Well," she said, "in a way. Mrs. Corbin read in the papers that you were going to represent her husband, and she was overjoyed. It seems that she thinks her husband's implication in this is a raw deal. She hadn't known anything about his criminal record, but she loves him and is going to stand by him."

"You've talked with her?" Mason asked.

"Several times. I tried to break it to her gently. I told her it was probably nothing but a newspaper story. You see, Chief, they have Corbin dead to rights. They took some money from the wife as evidence. It was part of the loot."

"And she had nothing?"

"Nothing. Corbin left her forty dollars, and they took it all as evidence."

"I'll drive all night," he said. "Tell her I'll be back tomorrow."

"I was afraid of that," Della Street said. "Why did you have to call up? Why couldn't you have stayed up there fishing? Why did you have to get your name in the papers?"

Mason laughed and hung up.

Paul Drake, of the Drake Detective Agency, came in and sat in the big chair in Mason's office and said, "You have a bear by the tail, Perry?"

"What's the matter, Paul? Didn't your detective work in Jebson City pan out?"

"It panned out all right, but the stuff in the pan isn't what you want, Perry," Drake explained.

"How come?"

"Your client's guilty."

"Go on," Mason said.

"The money he gave his wife was some of what was stolen from the vaults."

"How do they know it was the stolen money?" Mason asked.

Drake pulled a notebook from his pocket. "Here's the whole picture. The plant manager runs Jebson City. There isn't any private property. The Jebson Company controls everything."

"Not a single small business?"

Drake shook his head. "Not unless you want to consider garbage collecting as small business. An old coot by the name of George Addey lives five miles down the canyon; he has a hog ranch and collects the garbage. He's supposed to have the first nickel he ever earned. Buries his money in cans. There's no bank nearer than Ivanhoe City."

"What about the burglary? The men who did it must have moved in acetylene tanks and—"

"They took them right out of the company store," Drake said. And then he went on: "Munson, the watchman, likes to take a pull out of a flask of whiskey along about midnight. He says it keeps him awake. Of course, he's not supposed to do it, and no one was supposed to know about the whiskey, but someone did know about it. They doped the whiskey with a barbiturate. The watchman took his usual swig, went to sleep, and stayed asleep."

"What's the evidence against Corbin?" Mason asked.

"Corbin had a previous burglary record. It's a policy of the company not to hire anyone with a criminal record. Corbin lied about his past and got a job. Frank Bernal, the manager, found out about it, sent for Corbin about eight o'clock the night the burglary took place, and ordered him out of town. Bernal agreed to let Corbin's wife and child stay on in the house until Corbin could get located in another city. Corbin pulled out in the morning, and gave his wife this money. It was part of the money from the burglary."

"How do they know?" Mason asked.

"Now there's something I don't know," Drake said. "This fellow Bernal is pretty smart, and the story is that he can prove Corbin's money was from the vault."

Drake paused, then continued: "The nearest bank is at Ivanhoe City, and the mine pays off in cash twice a month. Ralph Nesbitt, the cashier, wanted to install a new vault. Bernal refused to okay the expense. So the company has ordered both Bernal and Nesbitt back to its main office at Chicago to report. The rumor is that they may fire Bernal as manager and give Nesbitt the job. A couple of the directors don't like Bernal, and this thing has given them their chance. They dug out a report Nesbitt had made showing the vault was a pushover. Bernal didn't act on that report." He sighed and then asked, "When's the trial, Perry?"

"The preliminary hearing is set for Friday morning. I'll see then what they've got against Corbin."

"They're laying for you up there," Paul Drake warned. "Better watch out, Perry. That district attorney has something up his sleeve, some sort of surprise that's going to knock you for a loop."

In spite of his long experience as a prosecutor, Vernon Flasher, the district attorney of Ivanhoe County, showed a certain nervousness at being called upon to oppose Perry Mason. There was, however, a secretive assurance underneath that nervousness.

Judge Haswell, realizing that the eyes of the community were upon him, adhered to legal technicalities to the point of being pompous both in rulings and mannerisms.

But what irritated Perry Mason was in the attitude of the spectators. He sensed that they did not regard him as an attorney trying to safeguard the interests of a client, but as a legal magician with a cloven hoof. The looting of the vault had shocked the community, and there was a tight-lipped determination that no legal tricks were going to do Mason any good this time.

Vernon Flasher didn't try to save his surprise evidence for a whirlwind finish. He used it right at the start of the case.

Frank Bernal, called as a witness, described the location of the vault, identified photographs, and then leaned back as the district attorney said abruptly, "You had reason to believe this vault was obsolete?"

"Yes, sir."

"It had been pointed out to you by one of your fellow employees, Mr. Ralph Nesbitt?"

"Yes, sir."

"And what did you do about it?"

"Are you," Mason asked in some surprise, "trying to cross-examine your own witness?"

"Just let him answer the question, and you'll see," Flasher replied grimly.

"Go right ahead and answer," Mason said to the witness.

Bernal assumed a more comfortable position. "I did three things," he said, "to safeguard the payrolls and to avoid the expense of tearing out the old vault and installing a new vault in its place."

"What were those three things?"

"I employed a special night watchman; I installed the best burglar alarm money could buy; and I made arrangements with the Ivanhoe National Bank, where we have our payrolls made up, to list the number of each twenty-dollar bill which was a part of each payroll."

Mason suddenly sat up straight.

Flasher gave him a glance of gloating triumph. "Do you wish the court to understand, Mr. Bernal," he said smugly, "that you have the numbers of the bills in the payroll which was made up for delivery on the fifteenth?"

"Yes, sir. Not all the bills, you understand. That would have taken too much time, but I have the numbers of all the twenty-dollar bills."

"And who recorded those numbers?" the prosecutor asked.

"The bank."

"And do you have that list of numbers with you?"

"I do. Yes, sir." Bernal produced a list. "I felt," he said, glancing coldly at Nesbitt, "that these precautions would be cheaper than a new vault."

"I move the list be introduced in evidence," Flasher said.

"Just a moment," Mason objected. "I have a couple of questions. You say this list is not in your handwriting, Mr. Bernal?"

"Yes, sir."

"Whose handwriting is it, do you know?" Mason asked.

"The assistant cashier of the Ivanhoe National Bank."

"Oh, all right," Flasher said. "We'll go it the hard way, if we have to. Stand down, Mr. Bernal, and I'll call the assistant cashier."

Harry Reedy, assistant cashier of the Ivanhoe Bank, had the mechanical assurance of an adding machine. He identified the list of numbers as being in his handwriting. He stated that he had listed the numbers of the twenty-dollar bills and put that list in an envelope which had been sealed and sent up with the money for the payroll.

"Cross-examine," Flasher said.

Mason studied the list. "These numbers are all in your handwriting?" he asked Reedy.

"Yes, sir."

"Did you yourself compare the numbers you wrote down with the numbers on the twenty-dollar bills?"

"No, sir. I didn't personally do that. Two assistants did that. One checked the numbers as they were read off, one as I wrote them down."

"The payrolls are for approximately a hundred thousand dollars, twice each month?"

"That's right. And ever since Mr. Bernal took charge, we have taken this means to identify payrolls. No attempt is made to list the bills in numerical order. The serial numbers are simply read off and written down. Unless a robbery occurs, there is no need to do anything further. In the event of robbery, we can reclassify the numbers and list the bills in numerical order."

"These numbers are in your handwriting—every number?"

"Yes, sir. More than that, you will notice that at the bottom of each page I have signed my initials."

"That's all," Mason said.

"I now offer once more to introduce this list in evidence," Flasher said.

"So ordered," Judge Haswell ruled.

"My next witness is Charles J. Oswald, the sheriff," the district attorney announced.

The sheriff, a long, lanky man with a quiet manner, took the stand. "You're acquainted with Harvey L. Corbin, the defendant in this case?" the district attorney asked.

"I am."

"Are you acquainted with his wife?"

"Yes, sir."

"Now, on the morning of the fifteenth of this month, the morning of the robbery at the Jebson Commercial Company, did you have any conversation with Mrs. Corbin?"

"I did. Yes, sir."

"Did you ask her about her husband's activities the night before?"

"Just a moment," Mason said. "I object to this on the ground that any conversation the sheriff had with Mrs. Corbin is not admissible against the defendant, Corbin; furthermore, that in this state a wife cannot testify against her husband. Therefore, any statement she might make would be an indirect violation of that rule. Furthermore, I object on the ground that the question calls for hearsay."

Judge Haswell looked ponderously thoughtful, then said, "It seems to me Mr. Mason is correct."

"I'll put it this way, Mr. Sheriff," the district attorney said. "Did you, on the morning of the fifteenth, take any money from Mrs. Corbin?"

"Objected to as incompetent, irrelevant, and immaterial," Mason said.

"Your Honor," Flasher said irritably, "that's the very gist of our case. We propose to show that two of the stolen twenty-dollar bills were in the possession of Mrs. Corbin."

Mason said, "Unless the prosecution can prove the bills were given Mrs. Corbin by her husband, the evidence is inadmissible."

"That's just the point," Flasher said. "Those bills *were* given to her by the defendant."

"How do you know?" Mason asked.

"She told the sheriff so."

"That's hearsay," Mason snapped.

Judge Haswell fidgeted on the bench. "It seems to me we're getting into a peculiar situation here. You can't call the wife as a witness, and I don't think her statement to the sheriff is admissible."

"Well," Flasher said desperately, "in this state, Your Honor, we have a community-property law. Mrs. Corbin had this money. Since she is the wife of the defendant, it was community property. Therefore, it's partially his property."

"Well now, there," Judge Haswell said, "I think I can agree with you. You introduce the twenty-dollar bills. I'll overrule the objection made by the defense."

"Produce the twenty-dollar bills, Sheriff," Flasher said triumphantly.

The bills were produced and received in evidence.

"Cross-examine," Flasher said curtly.

"No questions of this witness," Mason said, "but I have a few questions to ask Mr. Bernal on cross-examination. You took him off the stand to lay the foundation of introducing the bank list, and I didn't have an opportunity to cross-examine him."

"I beg your pardon," Flasher said. "Resume the stand, Mr. Bernal."

His tone, now that he had the twenty-dollar bills safely introduced in evidence, had a gloating note to it.

Mason said, "This list which has been introduced in evidence is on the stationery of the Ivanhoe National Bank?"

"That's right. Yes, sir."

"It consists of several pages, and at the end there is the signature of the assistant cashier?"

"Yes, sir."

"This was the scheme which you thought of in order to safeguard the company against a payroll robbery?"

"Not to safeguard the company against a payroll robbery, Mr. Mason, but to assist us in recovering the money in the event there was a hold-up."

"This was your plan to answer Mr. Nesbitt's objections that the vault was an outmoded model?"

"A part of my plan, yes. I may say that Mr. Nesbitt's objections had never been voiced until I took office. I felt he was trying to embarrass me by making my administration show less net returns than expected." Bernal tightened his lips and added, "Mr. Nesbitt had, I believe, been expecting to be appointed. I believe he still expects to be manager."

In the spectators' section of the courtroom, Ralph Nesbitt glared at Bernal.

"You had a conversation with the defendant on the night of the fourteenth?" Mason asked Bernal.

"I did. Yes, sir."

"You told him that for reasons which you deemed sufficient you were discharging him immediately and wanted him to leave the premises at once?"

"Yes, sir. I did."

"And you paid him his wages in cash?"

"Mr. Nesbitt paid him in my presence, with money he took from the petty-cash drawer of the vault."

"Now, as part of the wages due him, wasn't Corbin given these two twenty-dollar bills which have been introduced in evidence?"

Bernal shook his head. "I had thought of that," he said, "but it would have been impossible. Those bills weren't available to us at that time. The payroll is received from the bank in a sealed package. Those two twenty-dollar bills were in that package."

"And the list of the numbers of the twenty-dollar bills?"

"That's in a sealed envelope. The money is placed in the vault. I lock the list of numbers in my desk."

"Are you prepared to swear that neither you nor Mr. Nesbitt had access to these two twenty-dollar bills on the night of the fourteenth?"

"That is correct."

"That's all," Mason said. "No further cross-examination."

"I now call Ralph Nesbitt to the stand," District Attorney Flasher said. "I want to fix the time of these events definitely, Your Honor."

"Very well," Judge Haswell said. "Mr. Nesbitt, come forward."

Ralph Nesbitt, after answering the usual preliminary questions, sat down in the witness chair.

"Were you present at a conversation which took place between the defendant, Harvey L. Corbin, and Frank Bernal on the fourteenth of this month?" the district attorney asked.

"I was. Yes, sir."

"What time did that conversation take place?"

"About eight o'clock in the evening."

"And, without going into the details of that conversation, I will ask you if the general effect of it was that the defendant was discharged and ordered to leave the company's property?"

"Yes, sir."

"And he was paid the money that was due him?"

"In cash. Yes, sir. I took the cash from the safe myself."

"Where was the payroll then?"

"In a sealed package in a compartment in the safe. As cashier, I had the only key to that compartment. Earlier in the afternoon I had gone to Ivanhoe City and received the sealed package of money and the envelope containing the list of numbers. I personally locked the package of money in the vault."

"And the list of numbers."

"Mr. Bernal locked that in his desk."

"Cross-examine," Flasher said.

"No questions," Mason said.

"That's our case, Your Honor," Flasher observed.

"May we have a few minutes' indulgence?" Mason asked Judge Haswell.

"Very well. Make it brief," the judge agreed.

Mason turned to Paul Drake and Della Street. "Well, there you are," Drake said. "You're confronted with the proof, Perry."

"Are you going to put the defendant on the stand?" Della Street asked.

Mason shook his head. "It would be suicidal. He had a record of a prior criminal conviction. Also, it's a rule of law that if one asks about any part of a conversation on direct examination, the other side can bring out all the conversation. That conversation, when Corbin was discharged, was to the effect that he had lied about his past record. And I guess there's no question that he did."

"And he's lying now," Drake said. "This is one case where you're licked. I think you'd better cop a plea, and see what kind of a deal you can make with Flasher."

"Probably not any," Mason said. "Flasher wants to have the reputation of having given me a licking—wait a minute, Paul. I have an idea."

Mason turned abruptly, walked away to where he could stand by himself, his back to the crowded courtroom.

"Are you ready?" the judge asked.

Mason turned. "I am quite ready, Your Honor. I have one witness whom I wish to put on the stand. I wish a subpoena *duces tecum* issued for that witness. I want him to bring certain documents which are in his possession."

"Who is the witness, and what are the documents?" the judge asked.

Mason walked quickly over to Paul Drake. "What's the name of that character who had the garbage-collecting business," he said softly, "the one who has the first nickel he'd ever made?"

"George Addey."

The lawyer turned to the judge. "The witness that I want is George Addey, and the documents that I want him to bring to court with him are all the twenty-dollar bills that he had received during the past sixty days."

"Your Honor," Flasher protested, "this is an outrage. This is making a travesty out of justice. It is exposing the court to ridicule."

Mason said, "I give Your Honor my assurance that I think this witness is material, and that the documents are material. I will make an affidavit to that effect if necessary. As attorney for the defendant, may I point out that if the court refuses to grant this subpoena, it will be denying the defendant due process of law."

"I'm going to issue the subpoena," Judge Haswell said, testily, "and for your own good, Mr. Mason, the testimony had better be relevant."

George Addey, unshaven and bristling with indignation, held up his right hand to be sworn. He glared at Perry Mason.

"Mr. Addey," Mason said, "you have the contract to collect garbage from Jebson City?"

"I do."

"How long have you been collecting garbage there?"

"For over five years, and I want to tell you—"

Judge Haswell banged his gavel. "The witness will answer questions and not interpolate any comments."

"I'll interpolate anything I dang please," Addey said.

"That'll do," the judge said. "Do you wish to be jailed for contempt of court, Mr. Addey."

"I don't want to go to jail, but I—"

"Then you'll remember the respect that is due the court," the judge said. "Now you sit there and answer questions. This is a court of law. You're in this court as a citizen, and I'm here as a judge, and I propose to see that the respect due to the court is enforced." There was a moment's silence while the judge glared angrily at the witness. "All right, go ahead, Mr. Mason," Judge Haswell said.

Mason said, "During the thirty days prior to the fifteenth of this month, did you deposit any money in any banking institution?"

"I did not."

"Do you have with you all the twenty-dollar bills that you received during the last sixty days?"

"I have, and I think making me bring them here is just like inviting some crook to come and rob me and—"

Judge Haswell banged with his gavel. "Any more comments of that sort from the witness and there will be a sentence imposed for contempt of court. Now you get out those twenty-dollar bills, Mr. Addey, and put them right up here on the clerk's desk."

Addey, mumbling under his breath, slammed a roll of twenty-dollar bills down on the desk in front of the clerk.

"Now," Mason said, "I'm going to need a little clerical assistance. I would like to have my secretary, Miss Street, and the clerk help me check through the numbers on these bills. I will select a few at random."

Mason picked up three of the twenty-dollar bills and said, "I am going to ask my assistants to check the list of numbers introduced in evidence. In my hand is a twenty-dollar bill that has the number L 07083274 A. Is that bill on the list? The next bill that I pick up is number L 07579190 A. Are any of those bills on the list?"

The courtroom was silent. Suddenly Della Street said, "Yes, here's one that's on the list—bill number L 07579190 A. It's on the list, on page eight."

"What?" the prosecutor shouted.

"Exactly," Mason said, smiling. "So, if a case is to be made against a person merely because he had possession of the money that was stolen on the fifteenth of this month, then your office should prefer charges against this witness, George Addey, Mr. District Attorney."

Addey jumped from the witness stand and shook his fist in Mason's face. "You're a cockeyed liar!" he screamed. "There ain't a one of those bills but what I didn't have it before the fifteenth. The company cashier changes my money into twenties, because I like big bills. I bury 'em in cans, and I put the date on the side of the cans."

"Here's the list," Mason said. "Check it for yourself."

A tense silence gripped the courtroom as the judge and the spectators waited.

"I'm afraid I don't understand this, Mr. Mason," Judge Haswell said after a moment.

"I think it's quite simple," Mason said. "And I now suggest the court take a recess for an hour and check these other bills against this list. I think the district attorney may be surprised."

And Mason sat down and proceeded to put papers in his briefcase.

Della Street, Paul Drake, and Perry Mason were sitting in the lobby of the Ivanhoe Hotel.

"When are you going to tell us?" Della Street asked fiercely. "Or do we tear you limb from limb? How could the garbage man have—?"

"Wait a minute," Mason said. "I think we're about to get results. Here comes the esteemed district attorney, Vernon Flasher, and he's accompanied by Judge Haswell."

The two strode over to Mason's group and bowed with cold formality.

Mason got up.

Judge Haswell began in his best courtroom voice. "A most deplorable situation has occurred. It seems that Mr. Frank Bernal has—well—"

"Been detained somewhere," Vernon Flasher said.

"Disappeared," Judge Haswell said. "He's gone."

"I expected as much," Mason said calmly.

"Now will you kindly tell me just what sort of pressure you brought to bear on Mr. Bernal to—?"

"Just a moment, Judge," Mason said. "The only pressure I brought to bear on him was to cross-examine him."

"Did you know that there had been a mistake made in the dates on those lists?"

"There was no mistake. When you find Bernal, I'm sure you will discover there was a deliberate falsification. He was short in his accounts, and he knew he was about to be demoted. He had a desperate need for a hundred thousand dollars in ready cash. He had evidently been planning this burglary, or, rather, this embezzlement, for some time. He learned that Corbin had a criminal record. He arranged to have these lists furnished by the bank. He installed a burglar alarm, and, naturally, knew how to circumvent it. He employed a watchman he knew was addicted to drink. He only needed to stage his coup at the right time. He fired Corbin and paid him off with bills that had been recorded by the bank on page eight of the list of bills in the *payroll on the first of the month.*

"Then he removed page eight from the list of bills contained in the payroll *of the fifteenth,* before he showed it to the police, and substituted page eight of the list for the *first of the month payroll.* It was just that simple.

"Then he drugged the watchman's whiskey, took an acetylene torch, burnt through the vault doors, and took all the money."

"May I ask how you knew all this?" Judge Haswell demanded.

"Certainly," Mason said. "My client told me he received those bills from Nesbitt, who took them from the petty-cash drawer in the safe. He also told the sheriff that. I happened to be the only one who believed him. It sometimes pays, Your Honor, to have faith in a man, even if he has a previous mistake. Assuming my client was innocent, I knew either Bernal or Nesbitt must be guilty. I then realized that only Bernal had custody of the *previous* lists of numbers.

"As an employee, Bernal had been paid on the first of the month. He looked at the numbers on the twenty-dollar bills in his pay envelope and found that they had been listed on page eight of the payroll for the first.

"Bernal only needed to abstract all twenty-dollar bills from the petty-cash drawer, substitute twenty-dollar bills from his own pay envelope, call in Corbin, and fire him.

"His trap was set."

"I let him know I knew what had been done by bringing Addey into court and proving my point. Then I asked for a recess. That was so Bernal would have a chance to skip out. You see, flight may be received as evidence of guilt. It was a professional courtesy to the district attorney. It will help him when Bernal is arrested."

The Inside Story

Colin Dexter

Colin Dexter graduated from Cambridge University in 1953 and has lived in Oxford since 1966. His first novel, *Last Bus to Woodstock*, which features Inspector Morse, was published in 1975. Since then, Morse has appeared in a further twelve novels in this enduringly popular Oxford-set series, ending with *The Remorseful Day*. Among many other accolades and awards, Colin Dexter has received the CWA Diamond Dagger for outstanding services to crime literature and in 2000 was awarded the OBE in the Queen's Birthday Honors List. Inspector Morse is one of the world's most popular detectives, famed not only for his brilliant deductive powers but also the entertaining interplay with Sergeant Lewis. The Inspector Morse novels have been adapted for the small screen with enormous international success by Carlton/Central Television, starring the late John Thaw as Morse and Kevin Whately as Lewis.

PART ONE

Dido attempted to raise her heavy eyes again,
but failed; and the deep wound gurgled in her breast.
(Virgil, *Aeneid* IV, 688–9)

"Get a *move* on!"

"I'll get there as fast as I can, sir—I always do."

"And what's *that* supposed to mean?"

Lewis turned left at Carfax, down into the High, and then over Magdalen Bridge, car siren wailing, before driving past the Asian grocers shops and the Indian restaurants in the Cowley Road.

"I mean," replied Lewis finally, "that here we are with another murder, and *you*'ll get there, won't you? You always do."

"Nearly always," conceded Morse.

"And *I* won't. I've got a second-class mind—"

"Don't underrate yourself, Lewis! Let others do it for you."

Lewis grunted humorlessly. "I'm like a second-class stamp, and well you know it."

"But second-class stamps usually get there in the end."

"Exactly. Just take a dickens of a lot longer—"

"Slow down!"

Morse had been consulting an Oxford street plan, and now jabbed a finger to his right.

"That's it, Lewis: Jowett Place. What number did you say?"

"Probably where those two police cars are parked, sir."

Morse grinned weakly. "Maintain that level of deductive brilliance, Lewis, and we'll be through this case before the pubs are open."

It was 8:50 on the dull, intermittently drizzly morning of Monday, 15 February, 1993.

The Oxford City Police had contacted Kidlington C. I. D. an hour or so earlier after receiving a 999 call from one Paul Bayley, first-floor tenant of the narrow, two-storey property that stood at 14 Jowett Place. Bayley, an erstwhile history graduate from Magdalen College, Oxford, had found himself out of milk that morning—had walked downstairs—knocked on the door of the woman tenant directly below him, Ms. Sheila Poster—had found the door unlocked—and there . . .

Or so he said.

Morse looked down at the fully dressed woman lying just inside the ground-floor living room, the left arm extended, the pleasingly manicured fingernails straining, it appeared, to reach the door. Beneath and in front of the body was a distressingly copious pool of dully matted blood; and although the weapon had been removed it was possible even for such a non-medical man as Morse to unjumble the simple truth that the woman had most probably been stabbed through the heart. Longish dark curls framed the pale face—from which the large brown eyes now stared, forever fixedly, at a threadbare square of the lime-green carpet.

"Lovely-looking girl," said Lewis quietly.

Morse averted his eyes from the terrible sight, glanced across to the curtained window, then stepped outside the room into the narrow hallway, where Dr. Laura Hobson, the police pathologist, stood in subdued conference with a scene-of-crime officer.

"She's all yours," said Morse, in a tone suggesting that the abdication of responsibility for the body was something of a relief. As indeed it was, for Morse had always recoiled from the sight of violent death.

"Funny name—'Poster'!" volunteered Lewis as the two detectives stepped up the narrow stairs of number 14.

"Is it?" asked Morse, his voice betraying no real interest in the matter.

Bayley was sitting beside a police constable in his untidy living room—a large-buttocked, lank-haired, yet handsome sort of fellow, in his late twenties perhaps; unshaven, pony-tailed, with a small earring in his left ear. To whom, predictably, Morse took an instant and intense dislike.

He had been out drinking (Bayley claimed) throughout most of the previous evening, not leaving the King's Arms in Broad Street until closing time. After which he'd gone back to a friend's flat to continue the celebrations, and in fact had slept there—before returning to Jowett Place at about a quarter past seven that morning. The rest he'd already told the police, OK?

As he gave his evidence, Bayley's hands were nervously opening and closing the Penguin translation of Virgil's *Aeneid* and Morse noted (again with distaste) the line of ingrained dirt beneath the fingernails.

"You slept with a woman last night?"

Bayley nodded, eyes downcast.

"We shall have to know her name—my sergeant here will have to check with her. You understand that?"

Again, Bayley nodded. "I suppose so, yes."

"You didn't leave her at all?"

"Went to the loo coupla times."

"You in the habit of sleeping around?"

"I wouldn't put it like that, no."

"Ever sleep with—with the woman downstairs?"

"Sheila? No, never."

"Ever ask her?"

"Once."

"And?"

"She said if we were going to have a relationship it would have to be cerebral—not conjugal."

"Quite a way with words she had, then?"

"You could say that."

"When did you last speak to her?"

"Week or so ago? We were talking—*she* was talking—about epic poetry. She . . . lent me this . . . this book. I was going to give it back to her . . . today."

Lewis looked away in some embarrassment as a curtain of tears now covered Bayley's eyes; but for a while longer Morse himself continued to stare cynically at the young man seated opposite him.

Downstairs, in the second of the two rooms which (along with the kitchen) were offered for rent at 14 Jowett Place, Morse contemplated the double bed in which, presumably, the murdered tenant had usually slumbered overnight. Two fluffy pillows concealed a full-length, bottle-green nightdress, which Morse now fingered lightly before turning back the William-Morris-patterned duvet and examining the undersheet.

"No sign of any recent nocturnal emissions, sir."

"You have a genteel way of putting things," said Morse.

The room was sparsely furnished, sparely ornamented—with a large mahogany wardrobe taking up most of the space left by the bed. On the bedside table stood a lamp; an alarm clock; a box containing half a dozen items of cheap jewelry; and a single book: *Reflections on Inspiration and Creativity,* by Diogenes Small (Macmillan, £14.99).

Picking up the latter, Morse opened its pages at the point where a blue leather bookmarker ('Greetings from Erzincan') had been placed—and then with no obvious enthusiasm read aloud the few sentences which had been highlighted in the text with a yellow felt-tipped pen:

> Obviously our writer will draw upon character and incident taken from personal experience. Inevitably so. Laudibly so. Yet always it is those fictional addenda which will effect the true alchemy; which will elevate our earth-bound artist, and send him forth high-floating on the wings of freedom and creativity.

"Bloody 'ell!"

"Pardon, sir?"

"Can't even spell," muttered Morse, as Lewis picked up the bookmarker.

"Where's Erzincan?"

"Dunno. When I was at school we had to do one of the three G's: Greek, German or Geography."

"And you didn't do Geography . . ."

But a silent Morse was standing now at the window (curtains drawn back) which looked out on to a patch of leaf-carpeted lawn at the rear of the house. Strangely, something had stirred deep down in his mind, like the opening chords of *Das Rheingold;* chords that for the moment, though, remained below his audial range.

Lewis opened the wardrobe doors, exposing a modest collection of dresses and coats hanging from the rail; and half a dozen pairs of cheap shoes stowed neatly along the bottom.

Overhead they heard the creaking of the floorboards as someone—must be Bayley?—paced continuously to and fro. And Morse's eyes rose slowly to the ceiling. But he said nothing.

Neither the bedroom nor the kitchen had yielded anything of significant interest; and Morse was anxious to hear Dr. Hobson's verdict, however tentative, when half an hour later she emerged from the murder-room.

"Sharp knife by the look of things—second attempt—probably entering from above. Bled an awful lot—as you saw . . . still, most of us would—with the knife-blade through the heart. Shouldn't be too difficult to be fairly precise about the time—I'll be having a closer look, of course—but I'd guess, say, eight to ten hours ago? No longer, I don't think. Eleven o'clock, twelve o'clock last night?"

"After the pubs had closed."

"She hadn't been drinking, Inspector."

"Oh!"

Morse placed his hand lightly on the young pathologist's shoulder and thanked her. Her eyes looked interesting—and interested. Sometimes Morse thought he could fall in love with Laura Hobson; and sometimes he thought he couldn't.

It was almost midday before Morse gave the order for the body to be removed. The scene-of-crime personnel had finished their work, and a thick, transparent sheeting had now been laid across the carpet. Lewis, with two DCs, had long since been dispatched to cover the preliminary tasks: to check Bayley's alibi, to question the neighbors, and to discover whatever they could of Sheila Poster's past. And Morse himself now stood alone, and gazed around the room in which Sheila Poster had been murdered.

Almost immediately, however, it was apparent that little was likely to be found. The eight drawers of the modern desk which stood against the inside wall were completely empty; with the almost inevitable conclusion to be drawn that the murderer had systematically emptied the contents of each, as well as whatever had stood on the desk-top, into . . . well, into something—black plastic bag, say? And then disappeared into the night; in gloves, like as not, for Morse had learned that no extraneous prints had been discovered—only those left almost everywhere by the murdered tenant. The surfaces of the desk, the shelving, the furniture, the window—all had been dutifully daubed and dusted with fingerprint powder; but it seemed highly improbable that such a methodical murderer had left behind any easily legible signature.

No handbag, either; no documents of any sort; nothing.

Or was there?

Above the desk, hanging by a cord from the picture-rail, was a plywood board, some thirty inches square, on which ten items were fixed by multicolored drawing-pins: five Medici reproductions of well-known paintings (including two Pre-Raphaelites); a manuscript facsimile of Keats' "Ode to a Nightingale"; a postcard showing the death-mask of Tutankhamen; a photograph of a kingfisher, a large fish balanced in its mouth, perched on a NO FISHING sign; a printed invitation to a St. Hilda's Old Girls' evening in March 1993; and a leaflet announcing a crime short-story competition organized by Oxfordshire County Libraries: "First prize £1,000—Judges Julian Symons and H. R. F. Keating—Final date 10 April 1993."

Huh! Still seven weeks to go. But there'd be no entry from Sheila Poster, would there, Morse?

He methodically unpinned each of the cards and turned them over. Four were blank—obviously purchased for decorative purposes. But two had brief messages written on them. On the Egyptian card, in what Morse took to be a masculine hand, were the words: "Cairo's bloody hot but wish you were here—B." And on the back of Collins's "Convent Thoughts," in what Morse took to be a feminine hand: "On a weekend retreat! I knew I wouldn't miss men. But I do! Susan."

On each side of the boarded-up fireplace were five bookshelves, their contents systematically stacked in order: Austen novels, top left, Wordsworth poems, bottom right. Housman's Collected Poems suddenly caught Morse's eye, and he extracted his old hero, the book falling open immediately at "Last Poems" XXVI, where a postcard (another one) had been inserted: the front showing a photograph of streets in San Jose (so it said) and, on the back, a couplet written out in black Biro:

> And wide apart lie we, my love,
> And seas between the twain.
>
> (7.v.92)

Morse smiled to himself, for the poem from which the lines were taken had been part of his own mental furniture for many moons.

Yet so very soon the smile had become a frown. He'd seen that same handwriting only a few seconds since, surely? He unpinned the postcard from Cairo again; and, yes, the handwriting was more than a reasonable match.

So what?

So what, Morse? Yet for many seconds his eyes were as still as the eyes that stared from the mask of Tutankhamen.

Lewis came briskly into the room twenty minutes later, promptly reading from his notebook:

"Sheila Emily Poster; second-class honors degree in English from St. Hilda's 1990; aged twenty-five—comes from Bristol; Dad died in eighty-four—Hodgkin's disease; Mum in a special home there—Alzheimer's; only child; worked for a while with the University Geology Department in the reference section; here in this property almost ten months—£490 a month, £207 in the Building Society; £69.40 in her current account at Lloyds."

"You can get interest on current accounts these days, did you know that, Lewis?"

"Useful thing for you to know, sir."

"You've been quick."

"Easy! Bursar of St. Hilda's D. S. S., Lloyds Bank—no problems. Murder does help sometimes, doesn't it?"

A sudden splash of rain hatched the front window and Morse stared out at the melancholy day:

"I know not if it rains, my love,

In the land where you do lie . . ."

"Pardon, sir?"

But Morse seemed not to hear. "There's all this stuff here, Lewis . . ." Morse pointed vaguely to the piles of magazines lying around. "You'd better have a look through."

"Can't we get somebody else—"

"No!" thundered Morse. I need help—*your* help, Lewis. Get on with it!"

Far from any annoyance, Lewis felt a secret contentment. In only one respect was he unequivocally in a class of his own as a police officer, he knew that: for there was only one person with whom the curmudgeonly Morse could ever work with any kind of equanimity—and that was himself, Lewis.

He now settled therefore with his accustomed measure of commitment to the fourth-grade clerical chore of sorting through the piles of women's magazines, fashion journals, brochures, circulars, and the like, that were stacked on the floor-space in the two alcoves of the living room.

He was still working when just over an hour later Morse returned from his lunchtime ration of calories, taken entirely in liquid form.

"Found anything?"

Lewis shook his head. "One or two amusing bits, though."

"Well. Let's share the joke. Life's grim enough."

Lewis looked back into one of the piles, found a copy of the *Oxford Gazette* (May 1992), and read from the back page:

CLEANER REQUIRED
Three mornings per week Hourly rate negotiable Graduate preferred

Morse was unimpressed. "We're all of us overqualified in Oxford."

"Not *all* of us."

"How long will you be?"

"Another half-hour or so."

"I'll leave you then."

"What'll you be doing, sir?"

"I'll still be thinking. See you back at H. Q."

Morse walked out again, down Cowley Road to the Plain; over Magdalen Bridge, along the High, and then up Catte Street to the Broad; and was standing, undecided for a few seconds, in front of Blackwell's book shop and the narrow frontage of the adjoining White Horse ("Open All Day")—when the idea suddenly struck him.

He caught a taxi from St. Gile's out to Kidlington. Not to Police H. Q. though, but to 45 Blenheim Close, the address given on the leaflet advertising the Oxfordshire short-story competition.

"You're a bit premature, really," suggested Rex De Lincto, the short, fat, balding, slightly deaf Chairman of the Oxford Book Association. "There's still about a couple of months to go and we'll only receive most of the entries in the last week or so."

"You've had some already, though?"

"Nine."

De Lincto walked over to a cabinet, took out a handwritten list of names, and passed it across.

1. Ian Bradley
2. Emma Skipper
3. Valerie Ward
4. Jim Morwood
5. Christina Collins
6. Una Broshola

7. Elissa Thorpe
8. Richard Elves
9. Mary Ann Cotton

Morse scanned the list, his attention soon focusing on the last name.

"Odd," he mumbled.

"Pardon?"

"Mary Ann Cotton. Same name as that of a woman hanged in Durham jail in the 1880s."

"So?"

"And look at *her!*" Morse's finger pointed to number five, Christina Collins. "She got herself murdered up on the canal in Staffordshire somewhere. Surely!"

"I'm not quite with you, Inspector."

"Do you get phoney names sometimes?"

"Well, you can't really tell, can you? I mean, if you say you're Donald Duck—"

Morse nodded. "You *are* Donald Duck."

"You'd perhaps use a *nom de plume* if you were an established author . . ."

"But this competition's only for first-timers, isn't it?"

"You've been reading the small print, Inspector."

"But how do you know who they are if they've won?"

"We don't sometimes. Not for a start. But every entrant sends an address."

"I see."

Morse looked again at the list, and suddenly the blood was running cold in his veins. The clues, or some of them, were beginning to lock together in his mind: the short-story leaflet; the advice of Diogenes Small, that guru of creative writing; the book that young Bayley had borrowed . . . the translation of Virgil's *Aeneid*, in which Dido, the queen of Carthage, had fallen in love with Aeneas and then stabbed herself in her despair . . . Dido . . . known also by an alternative name—Elissa!

Morse took out a pencil and lightly made twelve oblique strokes through each letter of ELISSA THORPE, in what seemed to De Lincto a wholly random order; but an order which in Morse's mind spelled out in sequence the letters of the name SHEILA POSTER.

Morse rose to his feet and looked across at the cabinet. "You'd better let me have story number seven, if you will, sir."

"Of course. And if I may say so, you've made a very good choice, Inspector."

Only one message was awaiting Morse when he returned to his office at HQ: Dr. Hobson had called to say that Sheila Poster was about twelve weeks' pregnant. But Morse paid scant attention to this new information, for there was something he had to do immediately.

He therefore sat back comfortably in the old black-leather armchair.

And read a story.

PART TWO

Yet always it is those *fictional* addenda which
will effect the true alchemy.
(Diogenes Small, Reflections on *Inspiration and Creativity*)

The story (printed verbatim here) which Morse now began to read was cleanly typed and carefully presented.

I'd seen the advert in the Gazette.

She was going to be a woman who walked silent and unsmiling through any door held open for her, a woman who would speak in a loud voice over the counter at a bank; a woman conscious of her congenital superiority over her fellow beings.

In short she was going to be a North Oxford lady.

And she was—a double-barrelled one.

I was gratified though surprised that my carefully worded application had been considered and I caught the bus in good time.

At 10:30 a.m. to the minute I walked along the flagged path that bisected the weedless front lawn and knocked at the door of The Grange in Squitchey Lane.

A quarter of an hour later, after a last mouthful of some bitter-tasting coffee, I'd landed the job.

How?

I wasn't sure, not then. But when she asked me if I'd enjoyed the coffee, I said I preferred a cup of instant, and she'd smiled thinly.

"That's what my husband says."

I hoped my voice showed an appropriate interest.

"Your husband?"

"He's abroad. The Americans are picking his brains."

She stood up.

"Do you know why I've offered you the job?"

It was a bit risky but I said it: "No one else applied?"

"I'm not surprised you have a degree. You're quite bright really."

"Thank you."

"You need the money, I suppose?"

I lowered my eyes to the deep Wilton and nodded.

"Good-bye," she said.

I left her standing momentarily there at the front door—

slim, elegantly dressed, and young—well, comparatively young.

And, yes, I ought to admit it, uncommonly attractive.

The tasks allotted to me could only just be squeezed into the nine hours a week I spent at The Grange.

But £36 was £36.

And that was a bonus.

Can you guess what I'm saying? Not yet?

You will.

Two parts of the house I was forbidden to enter: the master bedroom (remember that bedroom!) and the master's study—the latter by the look of it a large converted bedroom on the upstairs floor whose door was firmly closed.

Firmly locked, as I soon discovered.

There was no such embargo on the mistress's study—a fairly recent addition at the rear of the house in the form of a semi-conservatory, its shelves, surfaces and floor all crammed with books and littered with loose papers and typescripts. And dozens of houseplants fighting for a little Lebensraum.

I was invariably fascinated with the place as I carefully (too carefully) watered the plants, replaced the books in alphabetical order, shuffled untidy piles into tidy piles, and carefully (too carefully) hoovered the carpeted floor and dusted around.

I love charging around with a duster. It's one of the only jobs I do where I can actually see a result.

And I like seeing a result . . .

There was only one thing wrong with that room.

The cat.

I hate all cats but especially this cat, which occasionally looked at me in a mysterious knowing aristocratic potentially ferocious manner.

Like his mistress.

A small two-way cat-flap had been cut into the door leading from the conservatory to the rear garden through which the frequently filthy-pawed "Boswell" (huh!) would make his exits and his entrances.

Ah, but bless you, Boswell!

I felt confident that Mrs. Spencer-Gilbey could not have taken up my single reference since from the beginning she called me "Virginia" without the slightest hint of suspicion.

For my part, I called her 'ma'am', to rhyme with 'jam'. It

was five syllables shorter than any more formal address, and I think the royal connotation was somewhat pleasing to her.

Early on the Wednesday morning of my third week the amateurish tack-tack-tack of the typewriter in the conservatory stopped and my employer came through into the downstairs lounge to inform me she had to go out for two hours.

It was at that point that I made my first bold move.

I look a leather-bound volume from the bookshelf beside me and blew a miniature dust-storm along the gold channel at the top of its pages.

"Would you like me to give the books a wipe with the duster?"

For a few seconds I thought I saw in those cold gray eyes of hers something very close to hatred.

"If you can put them all back exactly as you found them."

"I'll try, ma'am."

"Don't try. Do it!"

It was going to be a big job.

Bookshelves lined three whole sides of the room, and at mid-morning I had a coffee-break in the kitchen.

Outside by the garden shed I saw the steatopygous odd-job man who appeared intermittently—usually when I was leaving—to fix a few things as I supposed.

I held my coffee-cup up to the window and my eyes asked him if he'd care to join me.

His eyes replied yes and I saw he was younger than I had thought.

More handsome too.

I asked him how well he knew her ladyship but he merely shrugged.

"She's writing a book, did you know?" I asked.

"Really?"

He took a swallow of his coffee and I saw that his hands though grubby enough were not those of a manual laborer.

"On Sir Thomas Wyatt," I continued. "I had a look when I was hoovering."

"Really?"

If his vocabulary seemed rather limited, his eyes ranged over me more widely, and smiled in a curiously fascinating way.

"I don't suppose you know much about Sir Thomas Wyatt?"

He shrugged again. "Not much. But if you're going to tell me he died in 1542, you'll be wasting your time, won't you?"

Wow!

He smiled again, this time at my discomfiture; then leaned forward and kissed me fully on the lips.

"Are you on the pill?"

"It's all right. You see, I'm pregnant," I replied.

❦ ❦ ❦ ❦

Afterwards we dared to have a cigarette together. It was the first I'd smoked for six months and it tasted foul.

Stupid!

His lighter was out of fuel and I used one of the extra-long Bryant & May matches kept in the kitchen for various purposes.

For various purposes...

I'd almost finished the second wall of bookshelves when milady came back.

Just after I had turned round to acknowledge her presence a single sheet of paper fluttered to the floor.

Quickly I bent down to pick it up but she was immediately beside me, snatching it from my hand.

It was only a brief note and its contents could be read almost at a glance:

> Darling J
> Please do try to keep these few lines
> somewhere as a memento of my love

The message had been typed on cheap thin paper with the signatory's name written in light-blue Biro—"Marie," the "i" completed in girlish fashion with a largish ring instead of the usual dot.

But Mrs. S-G said nothing, and half an hour later I was on my way home—unobtrusively as ever.

I had advertised to no one the fact that I was working as a part-time charwoman and I took care to be seen by as few people as possible.

There were reasons for this. You will see.

❦ ❦ ❦ ❦

The following Monday I asked Mrs. S-G if I could vary my time slightly and start half an hour earlier.

"Do you have to?" Her voice was contemptuous of the request.

"It's just that if I caught the earlier bus—"

"Oh, don't explain, for heaven's sake! Do you have to?—that's all I asked."

I said I did, and it was agreed that I should henceforth begin at 8:30 a.m.

On Friday of that same week the postman called at 8:50 a.m., and three letters seemed to slither through the front door: a communication from British Telecom; a letter addressed to Mrs. S-G marked "Strictly Private"; and a letter for Mr. S-G, the name and address written in light-blue Biro, the "i" of "Squitchey" completed in girlish fashion with a largish ring instead of the usual dot.

Even as I picked up the letters I knew that my employer was just behind me.

"Thank you. I'll take them."

Her manner was offensively brusque. But I made no demur and continued wiping the skirting boards around the entrance hall.

"I'm sorry," I said (it was the following Wednesday), "but I shan't be able to come on Friday."

"Oh?"

"You see I've got to go to the ante-natal clinic..."

"Don't explain, for heaven's sake. I thought I told you that before."

"You did, yes."

She said no more.

Nor did I.

The phone was seldom used at The Grange but that morning I heard her ring up someone from the conservatory.

I stood close to the door and tried hard to listen but the only part of the proceedings I caught was "Saturday night ..."

My appointment at the hospital was for 10:30 a.m. but an emergency put the morning's program back by about an hour.

During the wait I read a few articles from various magazines, including an interview with an old gardener now aged one hundred who claimed that for getting rid of dandelions there was nothing quite so effective as arsenic, a small quantity of which he always kept in his garden shed.

Was it at this point I began to think of getting rid of Mrs. S-G? Along with the dandelions?

I suppose I'd already pondered the problems likely to face unmarried mums. Problems so often caused by married dads.

What really irks me more than anything, though, is all that sickening spiel they come up with. You know, about not wanting anyone to get hurt. Above all not wanting the little wife to get hurt.

Hypocrites!

It was my turn for receiving letters on the Thursday of the following week. Two of them.

The first was from the hospital. I was fine. The baby was fine. I felt almost happy.

The second was from the father of my child, with the postmark "Los Angeles."

Here's the bit I want you to read:

Haven't you heard of women's equal rights and responsibilities, you stupid girl? Yes, of course there's such a thing as a condom. OK! And there's also such a thing as the pill! What did you think you were playing at? But that's all water under the bridge. Abortion's the only answer. I'll foot the bill on condition there's a complete break between us. Things can't go on like this. I land at Heathrow at lunchtime on Saturday 13th, so we can meet next Sunday. Let's say the usual—twelve noon in the back room of the Bird and Baby. Please be there—for both our sakes.

How nice and cosy that would be!

And I would be there, perhaps.

Yes, there was a chance I would be there.

The following day, Friday, was to be my last in employment as a cleaning lady, and that morning I put the finishing touches to my plan.

Originally I had intended to kill only Mrs. S-G. But my terms of reference had now widened.

That same afternoon I acted in an uncharacteristically careless way. I wrote a letter to my former employer:

> Dear Mrs. S-G
> I was grateful to you for employing me but
> I shall not be coming to work for you again.
> My circumstances have changed significantly
> in the past few days. I am sure you will
> not have any difficulty in finding a replacement.
> Yours
> Virginia

It would have been tit-for-tat in the resignation-dismissal stakes. But I didn't post the letter that day.

Nor the next.

Mrs. S-G however had clearly been better stocked with first-class stamps and her letter lay on the hall mat the following morning, Saturday 13th, with mine still propped up against the Kellogg's packet on the kitchen table.

> Dear Marie Lawson,
> Oh yes I do know your real name and I made no attempt to take up your bogus reference. At first I

> thought you were quite bright and I told you so. But in truth you must be as stupid as you obviously consider <u>me</u> to be. I was curious about why you'd applied and it amused me to offer you the job. So I watched you. And all the time you thought you were watching <u>me</u>! You see my husband told me all about your affair although I didn't know you were pregnant. Nor, as it happens, do I believe you <u>are</u>. The charades with the note and the letter were prettily performed yet really quite unnecessary. I steamed open the letter as no doubt you wished me to in what (I have to assume) was your futile plan for bringing matters out into the open. I made a photocopy of the letter and forwarded your pathetic plea to America. I think the real reason for my writing—apart from giving you the sack—is to thank you for those two pieces of evidence you provided. I am informed by my lawyer that they will significantly expedite the divorce proceedings I shall be bringing against my husband. After that I expect my own life to turn into happier paths, and I trust that if I remarry I shall be more fortunate with my second husband than I was with the man who amused himself with a whole host of harlots besides yourself.
>
> V. Spencer-Gilbey (Mrs.)

Stupid.

Both of them had called me stupid.

On that same Saturday night—or rather in the early hours of the Sunday morning—I waited with great patience for the light to be switched off in the master bedroom. (You remember it?)

If they were not in the same bed at least they were in the same bedroom, since I had seen the two figures silhouetted several times behind the curtains.

I further waited one whole hour, to the minute, before moving soundlessly along the side of the house and then into the rear garden where I stooped down beside the conservatory door.

Good old Boswell! (Remember him?) I almost hoped he'd decided to sleep out in the open that night.

I struck one of the extra-large Bryant & May matches. (Remember them?) And shielding the flame I pushed my hand slowly through the cat-flap.

Behind the glass-panelled door I could see the loose sheets of paper (so carefully stacked) catching light almost immediately.

No more than ten seconds later I felt rather than heard the sudden "whoosh" of some powerful updraught as a tongue of flame licked viciously at the items (so carefully stacked) beside the conservatory door.

The color of the blaze reminded me so very much of Boswell's eyes.

I departed swiftly via the front path before turning round fifty or so yards down the road.

The window of the master bedroom was still in darkness. But at the rear of the house I had the impression that although it was still only 2:15 a.m. the rosy-fingered dawn was beginning to break already.

It was big news.

Headlined in Monday's edition of The Oxford Mail, for example, I read:

> TWO DIE IN NORTH OXFORD INFERNO
> It seems unlikely that the burned-out shell of the listed thatch-and-timber property in Squitchey Lane (picture p.2) will provide too many clues to the cause of the fire. The blaze spread with such rapid intensity that ...

My eyes skipped on to the next paragraph:

> The remains of two bodies, charred beyond all chance of recognition, have been recovered from a first-floor bedroom and it is feared that these are the bodies of Mr. J. Spencer-Gilbey and of his wife Valerie. Mr. Spencer-Gilbey had just returned from America where ...

But I wasn't really interested about where.

So I turned to look at the picture on page two.

It hadn't after all seemed worthwhile to turn up at the Bird and Baby the previous day. So I hadn't gone. You can see why. The fire was still big (bigger) news in Tuesday evening's edition of The Oxford Mail.

> BLAZE MYSTERY DEEPENS
> The Oxford City Police were amazed to receive a call late yesterday evening from Heathrow. The caller was Mr. John Spencer-Gilbey who, it had been assumed, had perished with his wife in the fire which completely destroyed their home in Squitchey

Lane, Oxford, in the early hours of Sunday morning. Mr. Spencer-Gilbey had been expected back in England on Saturday from a lecture tour in America. However it now appears that industrial action by air-traffic controllers on the western seaboard of America had effected the cancellation of the original flight, and Mr. Spencer-Gilbey told the police that he had earlier rung his wife to inform her of the rescheduling of his return to England. A police spokesman told our reporter that several aspects of the situation were quite extraordinarily puzzling and that further enquiries were being pursued. The police appeal to anyone who might have been in or near Squitchey Lane in the late evening of Saturday 13th or the early morning of Sunday 14th to come forward to try to assist in these enquiries. Please ring (0865) 266000.

'...he had earlier rung his wife...'

Yes.

<u>And he had also rung me</u>.

For a start I was tempted to "come forward" myself—over the phone and anonymously—with a tentative (hah!) suggestion about the identity of that second fire-victim.

God rot his lecherous soul!

But I shan't make that call.

One call I shall quite certainly make though. Once the dust, once the ashes have started to settle.

You see, I think that a meeting between the two of us could possibly be of some value after all. Don't you?

And even as I write I almost hear the words that I shall use:

"John? Sunday? The usual? Twelve noon in the back room of the Bird and Baby? Please be there!"

Yes, John, please be there—for both our sakes . . ."

PART THREE

They flee from me, that sometime did me seek
With naked foot, stalking in my chamber.
(Sir Thomas Wyatt, *Remembrance*)

Lewis came into Morse's office just before four o'clock that afternoon.

"Not much to report, sir. There's a card on the notice board there—looks as if it might be from a boyfriend."

"I saw it."

"And there's this—I reckon it's probably in the same handwriting."

Lewis handed over a postcard showing a caparisoned camel standing in front of a Tashkent mosque. On the back Morse read the brief message: "Traveling C 250 K E."

"What's that all about, do you think, sir?"

Morse shook his head: "Dunno. Probably the number of the airplane or the flight number . . . or something. Where did you find it, anyway?"

"There was an atlas there and I was looking up that place—you know, Erzincan. The postcard was stuck in there. You know, like a sort of marker."

"Oh."

"Don't you want to know where Erzincan is?"

"No. I looked it up when I got back here."

"Oh."

With a glint of triumph in his eyes, Morse now picked up the pink folder containing the Sheila Poster story and quickly explained its provenance.

"I want you to read this."

"What, now, sir?"

"Did you think I meant on your summer holidays?"

"I'm a slow reader, you know that."

"So am I."

"You want me to read it *here?*"

"No. I've got things to be getting on with here. Go and have a sandwich. And take your time. Enough clues there to fill a crossword puzzle."

After Lewis had gone, Morse looked at his watch and started on *The Times* crossword.

When eleven minutes later, he filled in the four blanks left, in – E – S – I – , he knew he should have been quicker in solving the final clue: "Gerry-built semi is beginning to collapse in such an upheaval" (7).

Not bad though.

A further hour passed before Lewis returned from the canteen and sat down opposite his chief.

"Lot's o' clues, you're right, sir. Probably made everything up, though, didn't she?"

"Not *everything,* not by a long chalk—not according to Diogenes Small."

"According to who, sir?"

"To *whom*, Lewis—please!"

"Sorry sir. I'm getting better about spelling, though. She made one mistake herself, didn't she?"

"Don't *you* start making things up!" Morse passed a handwritten list across the desk. "You just rope in Dixon and Palmer—and, well, we can get through this little lot in no time at all."

Lewis nodded: "Have the case sewn up before the pubs close."

For the first time that day there appeared a genuine smile on Morse's face. "And these are only the obvious clues. You'll probably yourself have noticed a good many clues that've escaped *my* notice."

"*Temporarily* escaped," muttered Lewis, as he looked down at Morse's notes:

- Names (road, house, people): all phoney, like as not?
- Gazette: same ad you found? check
- Mr. X (potential father): and academic surely? Lecture tour of USA?
- Boswell: owners of this strange orange-eyed breed? Check with the Cat Society.
- Publishers (OUP etc): any recent work known/commissioned on Sir T W?
- Ante-natal clinics: check—esp. JR2
- Bird and Baby: check, with photograph

"We should come up with *something*, I agree, sir. But it's going to take quite a while."

"You think so?"

"Well, I mean, for a start, *is* there such a thing as the Cat Society?"

"That's what you're going to check *up* on, Lewis!"

"Seven lots of things to check up on, though."

"Six!" Morse rose from his armchair, smiling happily once again. "I'll check up on that last bit myself."

"But where are you going to get a photo from?"

"Good point," conceded Morse, allowing, in his mind, that occasionally it was perfectly acceptable to end a sentence with a preposition.

At 10:15 p.m. Lewis rang Morse's home number, but received no reply. Was the great man still immersed in his self-imposed assignment—with or without a photograph?

In fact Morse was at that moment still sitting in the murder-room at 14 Jowett Place.

His mind had earlier informed him that he had *missed* something there; and at 8.15 p.m. he had re-entered the property, assuring the P. C. guarding the front door that he wouldn't be all that long.

But nothing had clicked in that sad room. And the over-beered Morse had sat in the sole armchair there and fallen asleep—finally awakening half an hour after midnight, and feeling as rough (as they say) as a bear's backside.

The following morning Lewis reported on his failures, Dixon's failures, Palmer's failures; and Morse reported on his own failures.

"You know this *house* business?" volunteered a rather subdued Lewis. "She's very specific about it, isn't she? Listed building, thatched, timbered, conservatory at the back—couldn't we try the Council, some of the up-market estate agents . . ."

"Waste o' time, I reckon."

"So? What do we do next?"

"Perhaps we ought to look at things from the, er, the motivation angle."

"Doesn't sound much like you, sir."

No, it wasn't much like him—Morse knew that. He loved to have some juicy facts in front of him; and he'd never cared to peer too deeply down into the abyss of human consciousness. Yet there now seemed no alternative but to erect some sort of psychological scaffolding around Sheila Porter's hopes and fears, her motives and mistakes . . . and only then to look in turn once more through each of the windows; once more to ask what the murdered woman was trying to tell everyone—trying to tell *herself*—in the story she had written.

Morse sought to put his inchoate thoughts into words whilst Sergeant Lewis sat opposite and listened. Dubiously.

"Let's assume she's had a fairly permanent job in the past—well, we know she has—but she's been made redundant—she's got hardly any money—everything she owns is just that bit cheap—she meets some fellow—falls for him—he's married—but he promises to take her where the lemon trees bloom—she believes him—she carelessly gets herself pregnant—by chance she finds an advert his wife has put in the local rag—she goes to work there—she's curious about the wife—jealous about her—she wants the whole situation out in the open—things turn sour though—lover-boy has second thoughts—he jilts her—the wife gives her the sack into the bargain—and our girl is soon nourishing a hatred for both of them—she wants to *destroy* both of them—but she can't really bring herself to destroy the father of her child—so in her story she changes things a bit—and sticks the wife in bed with a lover of her own—because then her *own* lover, Sheila's lover, will still be around, still alive—so there'll always be the chance of her winning him back—but he's bored with her—there's some academic preferment in the offing perhaps—he wants to get rid of her for good—he's prepared to play the faithful husband again—but Sheila won't play ball—she threatens to expose him—and when he goes to see her she becomes hysterical—he sees red—he sees all the colors of the rainbow—including orange, Lewis—because he knows she *can* ruin everything—*will* ruin everything—and then he knifes her . . ."

"*Who* knifes her?" asked Lewis quietly.

Morse shook his head. "I haven't the faintest idea. I know what, though. I know I'm *missing* something!"

For a few moments the look on Morse's face was potentially belligerent—like that of Boswell in the story; and Lewis felt diffident about asking the favor.

Yet his wife had insisted that he did.

"I hope you won't mind, sir, but if I could take a couple of hours off this lunchtime? The wife—"

Morse's eyebrows rose. "Doesn't she know you're in the middle of a murder enquiry? What's she want you to do? Take her a bag of spuds home?"

Lewis hesitated: "It's just that, well, there's this great big crack that's appeared overnight in the kitchen wall and the wife's worried stiff that if we don't—"

"Bit of subsidence, you reckon?" (The pedantic Morse gave the stress to the first of the three syllables.)

"More like an earthquake, sir."

For several seconds Morse sat utterly immobile in his chair, as if petrified before the sight of the Gorgon. And for the same several seconds, Lewis wondered if his chief had suffered some facial paralysis.

Then Morse's lips slowly parted in a beatific smile. "Lewis, my old friend, you've done it again! You've-gone-and-done-it-once-again! I think I see it. Yes, I think I see *all* of it!"

The happily bewildered Lewis sat back to learn the nature of his latest involuntary feat; but any enlightenment would have to wait awhile—that much was clear.

"Don't you let that missus of yours down!" beamed Morse. "She's one in a million, remember that! Get off and sort things out with the surveyor or something—"

"Or the demolition squad."

"—and get back here" (Morse looked at his watch) "two o'clock, say?"

"You're sure—?"

"Absolutely. I've got a few important things to do here. And, er, just ask Dixon to come in, will you? And Palmer, if he's there?"

Lewis's euphoria was dissipating rapidly; but he had no opportunity to remonstrate, for Morse had already dialled a number and was asking if he was through to the Atlas Department at Oxford University Press.

Sergeant Lewis returned to Kidlington HQ just before 2 p.m., almost three hours later, having finally received some reasonable reassurance that the Lewis residence was in minimal danger of imminent collapse. And at least Mrs. Lewis was now somewhat happier in her mind.

It soon became apparent to Lewis that during his absence someone—the doughnut-addicted Dixon? The pea-brained Palmer?—had been back out to Jowett Place; and Morse himself (what *else* had he been up to?) now sat purring like some cream-crammed orange-eyed long-hair as he surveyed the evidence before him on his desk—ready, it appeared, to lead the way along the path of true enlightenment.

"Clue Number One." Morse opened the magnum opus of Diogenes Small and lovingly contemplated the bookmark: "Greetings from Erzincan." "All right, Lewis?"

"Clue Number Two." He held up the postcard from Tashkent, turned it over, and read out its brief message once more: " 'Travelling C 250 K E.' " Not too bright, were we? It means exactly what it says: Travelling about two hundred and fifty kilometers east, east of Tashkent, where we find, Lewis—the Susamyr Valley in Kyrgyzstan.

"Clue Number Three. Dear old Toot-and-come-in—another postcard, another message, pretty certainly in the same handwriting: 'Cairo's bloody hot but wish you were here.' Remember? Signed 'B.' "

"Clue Number Four." Morse picked up the couplet from "Last Poems." Lines from a love poem, Lewis—with the seas between the pair of them—written from Los Angeles—the place to which the letter was re-addressed by Mrs. S-G in the story. Remember? And we know *why* he went to all these places, don't we?"

Lewis didn't. But he nodded.

Why not?

"Then there was Clue Number Five—that walloping great clue *you* found straightaway: the fact that Sheila Poster had worked in the *Geology* Department here. Huh! I was blind.

"Then there was Clue Number Six . . . from *The Times* crossword yesterday . . . Well, no, perhaps that was just a coincidence.

"And to cap it all you tell me about those almighty cracks in your bedroom wall . . ."

"*Crack*—only *one* crack, sir—in the *kitchen,* actually."

Morse waved his right hand as if dismissing such trivial inaccuracies as of minor moment.

"*And,* Lewis, the dates all match—*all* of 'em. In each case they fall about ten days or a fortnight after the events—I've checked 'em with a lovely girl called Eunice Gill in the OUP cartographical section."

(What *hadn't* Morse done? Lewis was beginning to wonder.)

"And she faxed me this," continued Morse.

Lewis took the sheet and read a newspaper paragraph dated 28.xi.92:

EARTHQUAKE SUMMIT

> Following the major earth tremors which recently shook central Los Angeles, seismologists from all over the world, including the UK, will be assembling in Sacramento early in the new year to discuss improvements in the forecasting of potential disasters. No conference of similar scale has previously been held, and its anticipated 6-week duration reflects the urgency which is attached to this cosmic problem.

It had all taken Lewis far too long, of course, but now he let the information sink in. And finally he spoke:

"So what we need is a list of the delegates at the conference. Shouldn't take—"

But he got no further, for Morse handed him a sheet on which the members of the UK delegation were listed.

"Good man—Sergeant Dixon—you know," said Morse.

Lewis ignored the tribute. "None of 'em with the initial 'B,' though."

"Why not try 'R'?" asked Morse quietly.

So an embarrassed Lewis tried "R," and looked again at the middle name of the five: Robert Grainger, D. Phil., M. A.

"So all we need is to find out his address—"

"Cumnor Hill, Lewis. Not far off, is it? Palmer traced him. Good man—Palmer—you know."

PART FOUR

White on a throne or guarded in a cave
There lives a prophet who can understand
Why men were born . . .
(James Elory Flecker, "The Golden Journey to Samarkand")

"Why do you think he did it?" asked Lewis as they drove along the Botley Road.

"Grainger's possible motives, you mean? Well, he was hot favorite for the chair in Geology—you've just discovered that for yourself. Great honor, you know, having a professorial chair at Oxford. Biggest prize of the lot. For some people."

Lewis nodded, for he half understood now, and himself took up the thread: "And Sheila Poster was going to ruin it all. Just as he's going to claim his birthright, he's suddenly faced with the prospect of scandal and failure and divorce . . . and the nightmare of some squawking infant into the bargain."

Morse was unusually slow in his reply as they started to climb Cumnor Hill. "I wouldn't know about those last two things, Lewis."

They walked along the flagged path that bisected the well-tended lawn, weedless even in winter, and knocked on a front door which was immediately opened by a prematurely gray-haired man, slimly built, in his late forties or so, his eyes looking at them over half-lensed spectacles.

"You're the police, I suppose?"

Morse showed his warranty. "Dr. Grainger?"

For a few seconds the man hesitated. Then stood back and ushered his visitors into a well-appointed lounge, three of its walls completely lined with books.

"Yes, I suppose we'd better get it over with."

He spoke quite slowly, and without emotion—at least to begin with. Yes, he knew that Sheila Poster had been murdered. He'd read it in the *Oxford Mail.* Yes, he'd had an affair with her; she'd been putting pressure on him to leave his wife and go to live with her; she'd told him she was pregnant—though he'd doubted the claim. His wife now knew most of the truth, but had only become directly involved because Sheila had contrived somehow to get a job as a cleaning-woman in the house there, and then had sought to poison the marital relationship—what little there was left of it. . . .

It was at this point that the belittled Lewis (seemingly to Morse's mild amusement?) decided to assert himself.

"It'll be up to Mrs. Grainger to give us details about her side of things, sir. You yourself weren't here, were you, when Miss Poster was working for your wife?"

Grainger, who hitherto had been speaking directly to Morse, now turned his eyes upon Lewis.

"You mean you're not prepared to take my word about what my wife has told me?"

"We're not here to answer questions, Dr. Grainger—we're here to ask them," snapped Lewis.

Irritatedly, Grainger turned back to Morse. "Is it necessary for us to have this man with us, Inspector? I am not used to being spoken to in this way and I find it wholly and unnecessarily offensive!"

"This is a murder enquiry, sir," began Morse rather lamely. "You must understand—"

"But I do understand. And I'm telling you you're wasting your time if you think you'll find any murderer in this house."

"Where were you on Sunday night?" asked Morse quietly.

"Huh! I'll tell you. I was in America—that's where I was."

"And you can prove that?"

Grainger stood up, and followed by Lewis walked over to a bureau, on which, beside a framed wedding-photograph, lay an envelope (as it proved) of travel documents. He handed it to Morse.

"As you'll see, I arrived back only yesterday afternoon—Monday. The plane, believe it or not, landed punctually at 4:15 p.m. I caught the Heathrow bus just after five o'clock, and I got to Oxford about quarter-to-seven."

"It'll certainly be pretty easy to check up, then," said Lewis, smiling serenely; and it was Morse who now looked round at his sergeant, more in admiration than in anger. Yet he himself sat silent and listened only, as Grainger snarled at Lewis once more, the antagonism between the two men now almost physically tangible.

"Oh yes. It'll hardly require a man of your caliber to check up on that. And it'll be pretty easy to check up on my wife as well. But let me tell you something, Sergeant! It won't be you who sees her. Is that clear? She's extremely upset—and you can understand why, can't you? Sheila was here working for her until a fortnight or so ago. All right? Now you might get a bit blasé about murders, Sergeant—but other people don't. My wife is under sedation and she's not going to see anyone—not today she isn't. And she won't see you, in any case! Your inspector here sounds a reasonably humane and civilized sort of fellow—and perhaps there are still a few others like him in the Force. So any of them can see my wife. All right? But it won't be you, Sergeant. Why? Because I say so!"

Phew!

Morse now intervened between the warring parties: "That'll be fine, sir. Have no fears! I'll be interviewing your wife myself. But . . . but it would help us, sir, if you do happen to know where Mrs. Grainger was on Saturday night?"

"She went to some gala do in London with one of her friends—lady-friends. As I understand it, the pair of them missed the 11:20 from Paddington and had to catch the 12:20—the 'milk float,' I think they call it—landing up here at about 2 a.m. They got a taxi home from the station. That's all I know."

"Have you got this friend's telephone number?"

"You won't need it. She lives next door."

Grainger pointed vaguely to the right; and Morse nodded his unspoken instruction to Lewis.

And Lewis left.

Morse was already seated in the Jaguar when Lewis rejoined him ten minutes later.

"He's right, sir. They got back here to Cumnor about half-past two in the early hours of Monday morning."

Morse showed no emotion, for he'd fully expected confirmation of Mrs. Grainger's alibi.

And he began to explain.

"You see, Lewis, it's not the who-dunnit aspect of this particular case that's really important—but the why-dunnit. Why was Sheila Poster murdered? She must surely have posed a threat to someone, either a man or a woman. And more likely a man, I'm thinking. She must have stood in the way of some man's hopes and calculated advancement. So much of a threat that when she refused to compromise, at some show-down between them, she was murdered precisely for that refusal of hers. So we'd no option but to work backwards—agreed? And we knew her side of things, to some extent, from the story she wrote. Now some things in that story reflected actuality fairly closely, didn't they? The Graingers' house—'The Grange,' huh!—her job there—her affair with the husband—her overwhelming wish to force the issue with the wife—"

"Don't forget the baby, sir!"

"No, I won't forget the baby. But Grainger didn't seem to think she was telling the truth about that, did he?"

"She was pregnant, though."

"Yes, she was telling the truth about being pregnant. In fact, she was telling a whole lot more of the truth perhaps than she was prepared to admit—even to herself. Let's make a hypothetical case. What, say, if she really wanted to murder not the married couple she was telling herself she hated? What if—in her story—she wanted to murder the very people she did in fact murder: the lady-of-the-house and that lady's lover? What if the pair of them had fallen deeply in love? What if—again as in the story—the lady-of-the-house had been only too glad to learn of her husband's infidelity? Because then she could divorce him, and marry her new lover . . . the man who stood by the flower-beds and tended the lawns there . . ."

"The man who came in for a cup of coffee, sir?"

"Perhaps so. But don't forget she wasn't just telling us a string of facts in the story—she was making a whole lot of it up as she went along."

"Really, sir?"

Lewis, as Morse could just about make out in the gloaming, was smiling quietly to himself.

"What the hell's got into you, Lewis? You antagonize one of our leading witnesses; you go off and find an unshakeable alibi for his missus; and now you sit there grinning like a Cheshire—"

"By the way, sir, they do have a cat—I asked next door. 'Johnson,' its name is."

"You've nothing else to tell me, have you?" asked Morse, looking curiously at his sergeant.

"Actually, there is, sir—yes."

"Out with it man!"

"Yesterday, sir, when we interviewed Paul Bayley, he said he'd been with his girlfriend all night."

"You told me that. You told me you'd checked."

"I did check. Bayley told me she was in the middle of moving flats that very day—seemed she's been a little bit too generous with her favors for the landlord's liking; and—just temporarily, mind—she was registered as of no fixed address. But Bayley said she'd almost certainly be in the City Centre Westgate Library—where she went most mornings—in the Local History Section—"

"Where she was!"

Lewis nodded. "Doing some research on Nuneham Courtenay and the Deserted Village. So she told me."

"Well?"

"Well . . . that's about it."

"Is it?"

"She's a very beautiful woman, sir."

"More beautiful than Sheila Poster?"

"I'd say so. More to my taste, anyway."

"And most men would fancy her?"

"If they had the chance."

"And Bayley did have the chance."

"I'm pretty sure he did. He's been in Jowett Place for about four months or so now. Unemployed for a start; but then in work—so his landlord says."

"His landlord? When did you see him?"

"He called in yesterday lunchtime, when you were in the pub. And from what he said—"

"You didn't mention this before."

"Thought I'd just do a bit of investigation off my own bat, sir. You didn't mind?"

"See if you could solve the case, you mean?"

"Try to, yes. And the landlord said it was Sheila Poster who'd told Bayley about the vacancy in the flat upstairs and who'd put in a good word for him, you know—gave him a good-behavior reference. Not only that, though. I reckon she was the one who told Bayley about the odd-job vacancy going up at the Graingers' place."

"Phew!" Morse whistled quietly. "You're saying Bayley was the odd-job man?"

"I'm saying exactly that, sir!"

"You're sure of this?"

"Not yet," replied Lewis, beaming happily.

"Let me get this clear. You're suggesting that Bayley goes to work for Mrs. Sylvia Grainger—she falls for him—he falls for her—she knows her husband's having an affair with the charwoman—she's proof of it. Then"—Morse paused slightly for dramatic effect—"just when things are looking hunky-dory, this charwoman claims she's pregnant. Not by Grainger, though . . ."

". . . but by Bayley. Yes, sir."

"And Bayley goes down on Sunday night—has it out with her—she refuses to play ball—and she gets herself murdered. Is that the idea?"

"Exactly!"

"But Bayley's got an alibi! This local history woman of yours—she says she was with him all night."

"From about 9 p.m. to 7 a.m. the following morning. Correct. Slept on the floor together in a friend's house in Cowley somewhere—she refuses to say exactly where."

"She's probably trying to protect her friends or something."

"Or something," repeated Lewis.

"Just you bear in mind all the adverse publicity we're getting about 'confessions under duress,' OK? We've got to tread carefully, you know that."

It was still only four o'clock, yet already the afternoon had darkened into early dusk.

"Can you guess, sir, why Dr. Grainger was so worried about me interviewing his wife?"

"He probably thought you were a bit crude, Lewis—preferred a sensitive soul like me. And by the way, don't forget that there are few in the Force more competent at that sort of thing than me."

"You can't think of any other reason?"

"You obviously can."

Lewis savored his moment of triumph. "Did you see the wedding-photo just now—the one Dr. Grainger had on the bureau?"

"Well, yes—at a distance."

"Beautiful woman, Mrs. Grainger—very beautiful."

"Taken quite a few years ago, that photo—she's probably changed since then."

"No! You're wrong about that, sir."

"How do you know?"

"Because I met her very recently. Met her yesterday morning, in fact. In the Westgate Library. She told me her name was Wendy Allsworth. But it isn't, sir. It's Sylvia Grainger."

"Extraordinary!" said Morse, his voice strangely flat.

"You don't sound at all surprised."

"Just tell me one thing. When you took the statement from—from Mrs. Grainger, do you think she knew about the murder?"

"No, I don't."

"You didn't tell her."

"No. So unless they planned things—"

"Very doubtful!" interposed Morse.

"Bayley must have rung her up early that morning."

"Do you think he told her?"

"I don't think so. If she'd known it was a murder enquiry . . . No, I don't think he told her."

"I agree. She was prepared to go a long way—did go a long way. Not that far, though."

Lewis hesitated. "You'll excuse me for saying so, but as I said you don't sound very surprised about all this."

"What? Of course I am. From where I sat I couldn't have recognized the queen if she'd been in that photo. The old eyes are not as sharp as they were."

"You knew, though, didn't you?" asked Lewis quietly.

"Not all of it, no," lied Morse.

Yet Lewis's silence was saddeningly eloquent, and Morse finally nodded. Then sighed deeply.

"I've always told you, Lewis, haven't I? The person who finds the body is going to be your prime suspect. That's always been my philosophy. It's compulsive with these murderers—they want their victim found. It'd send 'em crackers if the body lay undiscovered somewhere for any length of time."

"So?" asked Lewis dejectedly.

"So! So I had Bayley brought in this morning—this lunchtime."

"While I was with the builder."

"Yes. And Bayley continues to be detained at Her Majesty's Pleasure."

"You interviewed him yourself?"

"Yes. As I just told you, there's no one in the Force so firmly and fairly competent as me—not in that line of business."

Lewis was smiling wryly now—first nodding, then shaking his head. He might well have known. . . .

He nodded toward the Grainger's home: "Shall we go and take her in as well?"

"Actually she's, er, she's already helping with our enquiries."

Lewis almost exploded. "But you can't—you can't mean . . ."

"I do, yes. I had Bayley tailed and he went out to meet Sylvia Grainger—in the bar at The Randolph—about a quarter to twelve, that was. She'd told her husband she was going to her sister's for a few hours. That's what she said. So! So there's really not much point in us sitting here freezing any longer, is there?"

Lewis turned the key in the ignition, the Jaguar spurted into life, and the two detectives now sat silently side by side for several minutes as they drove back down into Oxford.

It was Lewis who spoke first: "You know, it really is nonsense what you say, sir—about the first person finding the body. I just don't know where the evidence is for that. And then you say it's 'compulsive'—didn't you say that?—for murderers to want the body found. But some of 'em take enormous time and trouble for the body never to be found."

"You're right, I agree. I was exaggerating a bit."

"So what did make you think it was Bayley? There must have been something."

"It's all these wretched crosswords I do. You meet some odd words, you know. The first time I saw Bayley in his room I thought what a great big fat-arsed sod he was.

And then, this morning, I read Sheila Poster's story again—and well, things went sort of 'click.' You remember that long word Sheila Poster used—about the odd-job man? Mind you, she was an English graduate."

Lewis did remember, but only vaguely; he'd look it up once they got back to H. Q.

"It was always going to be a straightforward case," continued Morse. "We'd have been sure to find out where Bayley had been working, sooner or later."

"Sooner or later," repeated Lewis. "And for once I thought it was me who was sooner. It's just like I said: I've got a second-class mind—I'm just like a second-class—"

"Ah! That reminds me. Just pull in here a minute, will you?"

Lewis turned into a slip-road alongside a row of brightly lit shops just before the Thames Valley Police HQ buildings.

"Where exactly—?"

"Here! Here's fine."

Morse jabbed a finger to the left, and Lewis braked outside a sub post-office.

"Just nip in and get me a book of stamps, please."

"First- or second-class?" For some reason Lewis was feeling reasonably happy again.

"No need to go wild, is there? I'll have one book of second-class, all right? These days they get there almost as quickly as first, you know that."

Morse had been pushing his hands one after the other into the pockets of overcoat, jacket, trousers—seemingly without success.

"You'll never believe it, Lewis, but . . ."

"I think I will, sir. Remember what that fellow Diogenes Small wrote about people's flights of imagination?"

"You've been soaring up there yourself, you mean?"

"Not quite, no. All I'm saying is it wouldn't take a detective to see what you're trying to tell me."

"Which is?"

"You haven't got any money."

"Ah!"

Morse looked down silently at the car-mat; and Lewis, now smiling happily, opened the driving-seat door of the Jaguar, and was soon to be seen walking toward the premises of the sub post-office in Kidlington, Oxon.

The Strawberry Teardrop

Max Allan Collins

The plaudits for Max Allan Collins continue to grow. He has earned an unprecedented ten Private Eye Writers of America Shamus nominations and won twice for his Nathan Heller novels, *True Detective* and *Stolen Away*. His film novelizations include *The Fugitive, Dick Tracy* and *The Mummy*. Collins has also penned several original novels based on the characters from television's *NYPD Blue, CSI: Crime Scene Investigation* and *Dark Angel*. He scripted the internationally syndicated comic strip *Dick Tracy* and has written the Batman comic book and newspaper strip. His graphic novel, *Road to Perdition*, was brought to the screen in 2002 and starred Tom Hanks and Paul Newman. *The Strawberry Teardrop* has also been expanded into the Eliot Ness novel *Butcher's Dozen* (1988), and has a sequel in the Nathan Heller novel *Angel in Black* (2001). The character Eliot Ness was brilliantly portrayed on television by Robert Stack as well as being brought to the screen by Kevin Costner in Brian De Palma's gangster classic *The Untouchables* (1987).

In a garbage dump on East Ninth Street near Shore Drive, in Cleveland, Ohio, on August 17, 1938, a woman's body was discovered by a cop walking his morning beat.

I got there before anything much had been moved. Not that I was a plainclothes dick—I used to be, but not in Cleveland; I was just along for the ride. I'd been sitting in the office of Cleveland's Public Safety Director, having coffee, when the call came through. The Safety Director was in charge of both the police and fire department, and one would think that a routine murder wouldn't rate a call to such a high muckey-muck.

One would be wrong.

Because this was the latest in a series of anything-but-routine, brutal murders—the unlucky thirteenth, to be exact, not that the thirteenth victim would seem any more unlucky than the preceding twelve.

The so-called "Mad Butcher of Kingsbury Run" had been exercising his ghastly art sporadically since the fall of '35, in Cleveland—or so I understood. I was an out-of-towner myself.

So was the woman.

Or she used to be, before she became so many dismembered parts flung across this rock-and-garbage-strewn dump. Her nude torso was slashed and the blood, splashed here, streaked there, was turning dark, almost black, though the sun caught scarlet glints and tossed them at us. Her head was gone, but maybe it would turn up. The Butcher wasn't known for that, though. The twelve preceding victims had been found headless, and had stayed that way. Somewhere in Cleveland, perhaps, a guy had a collection in his attic. In this weather it wouldn't smell too nice.

It's not a good sign when the Medical Examiner gets sick; and the half dozen cops, and the police photographer, were looking green around the gills themselves. Only my friend, the Safety Director, seemed in no danger of losing his breakfast. He was a ruddy-cheeked six-footer in a coat and tie and vest, despite the heat; hatless, his hair brushed back and pomaded, he still seemed—years after I'd met him—boyish. And he was only in his mid-thirties, just a few years older than me.

I'd met him in Chicago, seven or eight years ago, when I wasn't yet president (and everything else) of the A-1 Detective Agency, but still a cop; and he was still a Prohibition Agent. Hell, *the* Prohibition Agent.

He'd considered me one of the more or less honest cops in Chicago—emphasis on the less, I guess—and I made a good contact for him, as a lot of the cops didn't like him much. Honesty doesn't go over real big in Chicago, you know.

Eliot Ness said, "Despite the slashing, there's a certain skill displayed, here."

"Yeah, right," I said. "A regular ballet dancer did this."

"No, really," he said, and bent over the headless torso, pointing. He seemed to be pointing at the gathering flies, but he wasn't. "There's an unmistakable precision about this. Maybe even indicating surgical training."

"Maybe," I said. "But I think the doctor lost this patient."

He stood and glanced at me and smiled, just a little; he understood me: he knew my wise-guy remarks were just my way of holding on to my own breakfast.

"You ought to come to Cleveland more often," he said.

"You know how to show a guy a good time, I'll give you that, Eliot."

He walked over and glanced at a forearm, which seemed to reach for an empty soap box, fingers stretched toward the Gold Dust twins. He knelt and studied it.

I wasn't here on a vacation, by any means. Cleveland didn't strike me as a vacation city, even before I heard about the Butcher of Kingsbury Run (so called because a number of the bodies, including the first several, were found on that Cleveland street). This was strictly business. I was here trying to trace the missing daughter of a guy in Evanston who owned a dozen diners around Chicago. He was one of those self-made men, who started out in the greasy kitchen of his own first diner, fifteen or so years ago; and now he had a fancy brick house in Evanston and plenty of money, considering the times. But not much else. His wife had died four or five years ago, of consumption; and his daughter—who he claimed to be a good girl and by all other accounts was pretty wild—had wandered off a few months ago, with a taxi dancer from the North Side named Tony.

Well, I'd found Tony in Toledo—he was doing a floor show in a roadhouse with a dark-haired girl named FiFi; he'd grown a little pencil mustache and they did an apache routine—he was calling himself Antoine now. And Tony/Antoine said Ginger (which was the Evanston restauranteur's daughter's nickname) had taken up with somebody named Ray, who owned (get this) a diner in Cleveland.

I'd gotten here yesterday, and had talked to Ray, and without tipping I was looking for her, asked where was the pretty waitress, the one called Ginger, I think her name is. Ray, a skinny balding guy of about thirty with a silver front tooth, leered and winked and made it obvious that not only was Ginger working as a waitress here, she was also a side dish, where Ray was concerned. Further casual conversation revealed that it was Ginger's night off—she was at the movies with some girlfriends—and she'd be in tomorrow, around five.

I didn't push it further, figuring to catch up with her at the diner the next evening, after wasting a day seeing Cleveland and bothering my old friend Eliot. And now I was in a city dump with him, watching him study the severed forearm of a woman.

"Look at this," Eliot said, pointing at the outstretched fingers of the hand.

I went over to him and it—not quickly, but I went over.

"What, Eliot? Do you want to challenge my powers of deduction, or just make me sick?"

"Just a lucky break," he said. "Most of the victims have gone unidentified; too mutilated. And a lot of 'em have been prostitutes or vagrants. But we've got a break, here. Two breaks, actually."

He pointed to the hand's little finger. To the small, gold filigree band with a green stone.

"A nice specific piece of jewelry to try to trace," he said with a dry smile. "And even better . . ."

He pointed to a strawberry birthmark, the shape of a teardrop, just below the wrist.

I took a close look; then stood. Put a hand on my stomach.

Walked away and dropped to my knees and lost my breakfast.

I felt Eliot's hand patting my back.

"Nate," he said. "What's the matter? You've seen homicides before—even grisly ones like this. Brace up, boy."

He eased me to my feet.

My tongue felt thick in my mouth, thick and restless.

"What is it?" he said.

"I think I just found my client's daughter," I said.

Both the strawberry birthmark and the filigree ring with the green stone had been part of my basic description of the girl; the photographs I had showed her to be a pretty but average-looking young woman—slim, brunette—who resembled every third girl you saw on the street. So I was counting on those two specifics to help me identify her. I hadn't counted on those specifics helping me in just this fashion.

I sat in Eliot's inner office in the Cleveland city hall; the mayor's office was next door. We were having coffee with some rum in it—Eliot kept a bottle in a bottom drawer of his rolltop desk. I promised him not to tell Capone.

"I think we should call the father," Eliot said. "Ask him to come and make the identification."

I thought about it. "I'd like to argue with you, but I don't see how I can. Maybe if we waited till . . . till the head turns up."

Eliot shrugged. "It isn't likely to. The ring and the birthmark are enough to warrant notifying the father."

"I can make the call."

"No. I'll let you talk to him when I'm done, but that's something I should do."

And he did. With quiet tact. After a few minutes he handed me the phone; if I'd thought him cold at the scene of the crime, I erased that thought when I saw the dampness in the gray eyes.

"Is it my little girl?" the deep voice said, sounding tinny out of the phone.

"I think so, Mr. Jensen. I'm afraid so."

I could hear him weeping.

Then he said: "Mr. Ness said her body was . . . dismembered. How can you say it's her? How . . . how can you know it's her?"

And I told him of the ring and the strawberry teardrop.

"I should come there," he said.

"Maybe that won't be necessary." I covered the phone. "Eliot, will my identification be enough?"

He nodded. "We'll stretch it."

I had to argue with Jensen, but finally he agreed for his daughter's remains to be shipped back via train; I said I'd contact a funeral home this afternoon, and accompany her home.

I handed the phone to Eliot to hang up.

We looked at each other and Eliot, not given to swearing, said, "I'd give ten years of my life to nail that butchering bastard."

"How long will your people need the body?"

"I'll speak to the coroner's office. I'm sure we can send her home with you in a day or two. Where are you staying?"

"The Stadium Hotel."

"Not anymore. I've got an extra room for you. I'm a bachelor again, you know."

We hadn't gotten into that yet; I'd always considered Eliot's marriage an ideal one, and was shocked a few months back to hear it had broken up.

"I'm sorry, Eliot."

"Me too. But I am seeing somebody. Someone you may remember; another Chicagoan."

"Who?"

"Evie MacMillan."

"The fashion illustrator? Nice-looking woman."

Eliot smiled slyly. "You'll see her tonight, at the Country Club, but I'll arrange some female companionship for you. I don't want you cutting my time."

"How can you say such a thing? Don't you trust me?"

"I learned a long time ago," he said, turning to his desk full of paperwork, "not to trust Chicago cops—even ex-ones."

❦ ❦ ❦ ❦

Out on the Country Club terrace, the ten-piece band was playing Cole Porter and a balmy breeze from Lake Erie was playing with the women's hair.

There were plenty of good-looking women here—low-cut dresses, bare shoulders—and lots of men in evening clothes for them to dance with. But this was no party, and since some of the golfers were still here from late afternoon rounds, there were sports clothes and a few business suits (like mine) in the mix. Even some of the women were dressed casually, like the tall, slender blonde in the pink shirt and pale green pleated skirt who sat down next to me at the little white metal table and asked me if I'd have a Bacardi with her. The air smelled like a flower garden, and some of it was flowers, and some of it was her.

"I'd be glad to buy you a Bacardi," I said clumsily.

"No," she said, touching my arm. She had eyes the color of jade.

"You're a guest. I'll buy."

Eliot was dancing with his girl Evie, an attractive brunette in her mid-thirties; she'd always struck me as intelligent but sad, somehow. They smiled over at me.

The blonde in pink and pale green brought two Bacardis over, set one of them in front of me and smiled. "Yes," she said wickedly. "You've been set up. I'm the girl Eliot promised you. But if you were hoping for somebody in an evening gown, I'm not it. I just had to get an extra nine holes in."

"If you were looking for a guy in a tux," I said, "I'm not it. And I've never been on a golf course in my life. What else do we have in common?"

She had a nicely wry smile, which continued as she sipped the Bacardi.

"Eliot, I suppose. If I have a few more of these, I may tell you a secret."

And after a few more, she did.

And it was a whopper.

"You're an undercover agent?" I said. A few sheets to the wind myself.

"Shhhh," she said, finger poised uncertainly before pretty lips.

"It's a secret. But I haven't been doing it much lately."

"Haven't been doing what?"

"Well, undercover work. And there's a double-entendre there that I'd rather you didn't go looking for."

"I wouldn't think of looking under the covers for it."

The band began playing a tango.

I asked her how she got involved, working for Eliot. Which I didn't believe for a second, even in my cups.

But it turned out to be true (as Eliot admitted to me when he came over to see how Vivian and I were getting along, when Vivian—which was her name, incidentally—went to the powder room with Evie).

Vivian Chalmers was the daughter of a banker (a solvent one), a divorcee of thirty with no children and a lot of social pull. An expert trapshooter, golfer, tennis player and "all-round sportswoman," with a sense of adventure. When Eliot called on her to case various of the gambling joints he planned to raid—as a socialite she could take a fling in any joint she chose, without raising any suspicion—she immediately said yes. And she'd been an active agent in the first few years of Eliot's ongoing battle against the so-called Mayfield Road Mob—who controlled prostitution, gambling and the policy racket in the Cleveland environs.

"But things have slowed down," she said nostalgically. "Eliot has pretty much cleaned up the place, and, besides, he doesn't want to use me anymore."

"An undercover agent can only be effective so long," I said. "Pretty soon the other side gets suspicious."

She shrugged, with resigned frustration, and let me buy the next round.

We took a walk in the dark, around the golf course, and ended up sitting on a green. The breeze felt nice. The flag on the hole—13—flapped.

"Thirteen," I said.

"Huh?"

"Victim thirteen."

"Oh. Eliot told me about that. Your 'luck' today, finding your client's missing daughter. Damn shame."

"Damn shame."

"A shame, too, they haven't found the son-of-a-bitch."

She was a little drunk, and so was I, but I was still shocked—well, amused—to hear a woman, particularly a "society" woman, speak that way.

"It must grate on Eliot, too," I said.

"Sure as hell does. It's the only mote in his eye. He's a hero around these parts, and he's kicked the Mayfield Mob in the seat of the pants, and done everything else from clean up a corrupt police department to throw labor racketeers in jail, to cut traffic deaths in half, to founding Boy's Town, to . . ."

"You're not in love with the guy, are you?"

She seemed taken aback for a minute, then her face wrinkled into a got-caught-with-my-pants-down grin. "Maybe a little. But he's got a girl."

"I don't."

"You might."

She leaned forward.

We kissed for a while, and she felt good in my arms; she was firm, almost muscular. But she smelled like flowers. And the sky was blue and scattered with stars above us, as we lay back on the golf-green to look up.

It seemed like a nice world, at the moment.

Hard to imagine it had a Butcher in it.

I sat up talking with Eliot that night; he lived in a little reconverted boathouse on the lake. The furnishings were sparse, spartan—it was obvious his wife had taken most of the furniture with her and he'd had to all but start over.

I told him I thought Vivian was a terrific girl.

Leaning back in a comfy chair, feet on an ottoman, Eliot, tie loose around his neck, smiled in a melancholy way. "I thought you'd hit it off."

"Did you have an affair with her?"

He looked at me sharply; that was about as personal as I'd ever got with him.

He shook his head no, but I didn't quite buy it.

"You knew Evie MacMillan in Chicago," I said.

"Meaning what?"

"Meaning nothing."

"Meaning I knew her when I was still married."

"Meaning nothing."

"Nate, I'm sorry I'm not the Boy Scout you think I am."

"Hey, so you've slept with girls before. I'll learn to live with it."

There was a stone fireplace, in which some logs were trying to decide whether to burn any more or not; we watched them trying.

"I love Evie, Nate. I'm going to marry her."

"Congratulations."

We could hear the lake out there; could smell it some, too.

"I'd like that bastard's neck in my hands," Eliot said.

"What?"

"That Butcher. That damn Butcher."

"What made you think of him?"

"I don't know."

"Eliot, it's been over three years since he first struck, and you still don't have anything?"

"Nothing. A few months ago, last time he hit, we found some of the . . . body parts, bones and such . . . in a cardboard box in the Central Market area. There's a Hooverville over there, or what used to be a Hooverville . . . it's a shantytown, is more like it, genuine hobos as opposed to just good folks down on their luck. Most of the victims—before today—were either prostitutes or bums . . . and the bums from that shantytown were the Butcher's meat. So to speak."

The fire crackled.

Eliot continued: "I decided to make a clean sweep. I took twenty-five cops through there at one in the morning, and rousted out all the 'bos and took 'em down and fingerprinted and questioned all of 'em."

"And it amounted to . . . ?"

"It amounted to nothing. Except ridding Cleveland of that shantytown. I burned the place down that afternoon."

"Comes in handy, having all those firemen working for you. But what about those poor bastards whose 'city' you burned down?"

Sensing my disapproval, he glanced at me and gave me what tried to be a warm smile, but was just a weary one. "Nate, I turned them over to the Relief department, for relocation and, I hope, rehabilitation. But most of them were bums who just hopped a freight out. And I did 'em a favor by taking them off the potential victims list."

"And made room for Ginger Jensen."

Eliot looked away.

"That wasn't fair," I said. "I'm sorry I said that, Eliot."

"I know, Nate. I know."

But I could tell he'd been thinking the same thing.

❦ ❦ ❦ ❦

I had lunch the next day with Vivian in a little outdoor restaurant in the shadow of Terminal Tower. We were served lemonade and little ham and cheese and lettuce and tomato sandwiches with the crusts trimmed off the toasted bread. The detective in me wondered what became of the crusts.

"Thanks for having lunch with me," Vivian said. She had on a pale orange dress; she sat crossing her brown pretty legs.

"My pleasure," I said.

"Speaking of which . . . about last night . . . "

"We were both a little drunk. Forget it. Just don't ask me to."

She smiled as she nibbled her sandwich.

"I called and told Eliot something this morning," she said, "and he just ignored me."

"What was that?"

"That I have a possible lead on the Butcher murders."

"I can't imagine Eliot ignoring that . . . and it's not like it's just anybody approaching him—you did work for him."

"Not lately. And he thinks I'm just . . . "

"Looking for an excuse to be around him?"

She nibbled at a little sandwich. Nodded.

"Did you resent him asking you to be with me as a blind date last night?"

"No," she said.

"Did . . . last night have anything to do with wanting to 'show' Eliot?"

If she weren't so sophisticated—or trying to be—she would've looked hurt; but her expression managed to get something else across: disappointment in me.

"Last night had to do with showing you," she said. "And . . . it had a little to do with Bacardi rum."

"That it did. Tell me about your lead."

"Eliot has been harping on the 'professional' way the bodies have been dismembered—he's said again and again he sees a 'surgical' look to it."

I nodded.

"So it occurred to me that a doctor—anyway, somebody who'd at least been in medical school for a time—would be a likely candidate for the Butcher."

"Yes."

"And medical school's expensive, so, it stands to reason, the Butcher just might run in the same social circles as yours truly."

"Say, you did work for Eliot."

She liked that.

She continued: "I checked around with my society friends, and heard about a guy whose family has money—plenty of it. Name of Watterson."

"Last name or first?"

"That's the family name. Big in these parts."

"Means nothing to me."

"Well, Lloyd Watterson used to be a medical student. He's a big man, very strong—the kind of strength it might take to do some of the things the Butcher has done. And he has a history of mental disturbances."

"What kind of mental disturbances?"

"He's been going to a psychiatrist since he was a school boy."

"Do you know this guy?"

"Just barely. But I've heard things about him."

"Such as?"

"I hear he likes boys."

Lloyd Watterson lived in a two-story white house at the end of a dead-end street, a Victorian-looking miniature mansion among other such houses, where expansive lawns and towering hedges separated the world from the wealthy who lived within.

This wasn't the parental home, Vivian explained; Watterson lived here alone, apparently without servants. The grounds seemed well-tended, though, and there was nothing about this house that said anyone capable of mass murder might live here. No blood spattered on the white porch; no body parts scattered about the lawn.

It was mid-afternoon, and I was having second thoughts.

"I don't even have a damn gun," I said.

"I do," she said, and showed me a little .25 automatic from her purse.

"Great. If he has a dog, maybe we can use that to scare it."

"This'll do the trick. Besides, a gun won't even be necessary. You're just here to talk."

The game plan was for me to approach Watterson as a cop, flashing my private detective's badge quickly enough to fool him (and that almost always worked), and question him, simply get a feel for whether or not he was a legitimate suspect, worthy of lobbying Eliot for action against. My say-so, Vivian felt, would be enough to get Eliot off the dime.

And helping Eliot bring the Butcher in would be a nice wedding present for my old friend; with his unstated but obvious political ambitions, the capture of the Kingsbury Run maniac would offset the damage his divorce had done him, in conservative, mostly Catholic Cleveland. He'd been the subject of near hero worship in the press here (Eliot was always good at getting press—Frank Nitti used to refer to him as "Eliot Press"); but the ongoing if sporadic slaughter of the Butcher was a major embarrassment for Cleveland's fabled Safety Director.

So, leaving Vivian behind in the roadster (Watterson might recognize her), I walked up the curved sidewalk and went up on the porch and rang the bell. In the dark hardwood door there was opaque glass behind which I could barely make out movement, coming toward me.

The door opened, and a blond man about six-three with a baby-face and ice-blue eyes and shoulders that nearly filled the doorway looked out at me and grinned. A kid's grin, on one side of his face. He wore a polo shirt and short white pants; he seemed about to say, "Tennis anyone?"

But he said nothing, as a matter of fact; he just appraised me with those ice-blue, somewhat vacant eyes. I now knew how it felt for a woman to be ogled—which is to say, not necessarily good.

I said, "I'm an officer of the court," which in Illinois wasn't exactly a lie, and I flashed him my badge, but before I could say anything else, his hand reached out and grabbed the front of my shirt, yanked me inside and slammed the door.

He tossed me like a horseshoe, and I smacked into something—the stairway to the second floor, I guess; I don't know exactly—because I blacked out. The only thing I remember is the musty smell of the place.

I woke up minutes later and found myself tied in a chair in a dank, dark room. Support beams loomed out of a packed dirt floor. The basement.

I strained at the ropes, but they were snug; not so snug as to cut off my circulation, but snug enough. I glanced around the room. I was alone.

I couldn't see much—just a shovel against one cement wall. The only light came from a window off to my right, and there were hedges in front of the window, so the light was filtered.

Feet came tromping down the open wooden stairs. I saw his legs, first; white as pastry dough.

He was grinning. In his right hand was a cleaver. It shone, caught a glint of what little light there was.

"I'm no butcher," he said. His voice was soft, almost gentle. "Don't believe what you've heard."

"Do you want to die?" I said.

"Of course not."

"Well then cut me loose. There's cops all over the place, and if you kill me, they'll shoot you down. You know what happens to cop killers, don't you?"

He thought that over, nodded.

Standing just to one side of me, displaying the cold polished steel of the cleaver, in which my face's frantic reflection looked back at me, he said, "I'm no butcher. This is a surgical tool. This is used for amputation, not butchery."

"Yeah. I can see that."

"I wondered when you people would come around."

"Do you want to be caught, Lloyd?"

"Of course not. I'm no different than you. I'm a public servant."

"How . . . How do you figure that, Lloyd." My feet weren't tied to the chair; if he'd just step around in front of me . . .

"I only dispose of the flotsam. Not to mention jetsam."

"Not to mention that."

"Tramps. Whores. Weeding out the stock. Survival of the fittest. You know."

"That makes a lot of sense, Lloyd. But I'm not flotsam or jetsam.

I'm a cop. You don't want to kill a cop. You don't want to kill a fellow public servant."

He thought about that.

"I think I have to, this time," he said.

He moved around the chair, stood in front of me, stroking his chin, the cleaver gripped tight in his right hand, held about breastbone level.

"I do like you," Lloyd said thoughtfully.

"And I like you, Lloyd," I said, and kicked him in the balls.

Harder than any man tied to a chair should be able to kick; but you'd be surprised what you can do, under extreme circumstances. And things rarely get more extreme than being tied to a chair with a guy with a cleaver coming at you.

Only he wasn't coming at me, now: now, he was doubled over, and I stood, the chair strapped to my back; managed, even so, to kick him in the face.

He tumbled back, gripping his groin, his head leaning back, stretching, tears streaming down his cheeks, cords in his neck taut; my shoe had caught him on the side of the face and broke the skin. Flecks of blood, like little red tears, spattered his cheeks, mingling with the real tears.

That's when the window shattered, and Vivian squeezed down and through; pretty legs first.

And she gave me the little gun to hold on him while she untied me.

He was still on the dirt floor, moaning, when we went up the stairs and out into the sunny day, into a world that wasn't dank, onto earth that was grass-covered and didn't have God-knows-what buried under it.

We asked Eliot to meet us at his boathouse; we told him what had happened. He was livid; I never saw him angrier. But he held Vivian for a moment, and looked at her and said, "If anything had happened to you, I'd've killed you."

He poured all of us a drink; rum as usual. He handed me my mine and said, "How could you get involved in something so harebrained?"

"I wanted to give my client something for his money," I said.

"You mean his daughter's killer."

"Why not?"

"I've been looking for the bastard three years, and you come to town and expect to find him in three days?"

"Well, I did."

He smirked, shook his head. "I believe you did. But Watterson's family would bring in the highest-paid lawyers in the country and we'd be thrown out of court on our cans."

"What? The son-of-a-bitch tried to cut me up with a cleaver!"

"Did he? Did he swing on you? Or did you enter his house under a false pretense, misrepresenting yourself as a law officer? And as far as that goes, you assaulted him. We have very little."

Vivian said, "You have the name of the Butcher."

Eliot nodded. "Probably. I'm going to make a phone call."

Eliot went into his den and came out fifteen minutes later.

"I spoke with Franklin Watterson, the father. He's agreed to submit his son for a lie detector test."

"To what end?"

"One step at a time," Eliot said.

Lloyd Watterson took the lie-detector test twice—and on both instances denied committing the various Butcher slayings; his denials were, according to the machine, lies. The Watterson family attorney reminded Eliot that lie detector tests were not admissible as evidence. Eliot had a private discussion with Franklin Watterson.

Lloyd Watterson was committed, by his family, to an asylum for the insane. The Mad Butcher of Kingsbury Run—which to this day is marked "unsolved" in the Cleveland police records—did not strike again.

At least not directly.

Eliot married Evie MacMillan a few months after my Cleveland visit, and their marriage was from the start disrupted by crank letters, postmarked from the same town as the asylum where Watterson had been committed. "Retribution will catch up with you one day," said one postcard, on the front of which was a drawing of an effeminate man grinning from behind prison bars. Mrs. Ness was especially unnerved by these continuing letters and cards.

Eliot's political fortunes waned, in the wake of the "unsolved" Butcher slayings. Known for his tough stance on traffic violators, he got mired in a scandal when one pre-dawn morning in March of 1942, his car skidded into an oncoming car on the West Shoreway. Eliot and his wife, and two friends, had been drinking. The police report didn't identify Eliot by name, but his license number—EN-1, well-known to Cleveland citizens—was listed. And Eliot had left the scene of the accident.

HIT-AND-RUN, the headlines said. Eliot's version was that his wife had been injured, and he'd raced her to a hospital—but not before stopping to check on the other driver, who confirmed this. The storm blew over, but the damage was done—Eliot's image in the Cleveland press was finally tarnished.

Two months later he resigned as Safety Director.

About that time, asylum inmate Lloyd Watterson managed to hang himself with a bed sheet, and the threatening mail stopped.

How much pressure those cards and letters put on the marriage I couldn't say; but in 1945 Eliot and Evie divorced, and Eliot married a third time a few months later. At the time he was serving as federal director of the program against venereal disease in the military. His attempt to run for Cleveland mayor in 1947 was a near disaster: Cleveland's one-time fair-haired boy was a has-been with a hit-and-run scandal and two divorces and three marriages going against him.

He would not have another public success until the publication of his autobiographical book, *The Untouchables*—but that success was posthumous; he died shortly before it was published, never knowing that television and Robert Stack would give him lasting fame.

I saw Eliot, now and then, over the years; but I never saw Vivian again. I asked him about her, once, when I was visiting him in Pennsylvania, in the early '50s. He told me she'd been killed in a boating accident in 1943.

"She's been dead for years, then," I said, the shock of it hitting me like a blow.

"That's right. But shed a tear for her now, if you like. Tears and prayers can never come too late, Nate."

Amen, Eliot.

Sadie When She Died

Ed McBain

Ed McBain, the nom de plume of Evan Hunter, is one of the most prolific writers of the mystery genre. He has penned more than eighty novels and introduced the 87th Precinct and its memorable cast to the world. The first of the fifty 87th Precinct novels, *Cop Hater,* was published in 1956 and later popularized the combination of the police procedural and the private eye novel. His masterpiece, *The Blackboard Jungle,* remains a classic both as a film and a novel. Under his given name, Evan Hunter, McBain has created some of television's most notable programs, including *The Chisholms* and the *Ed McBain's 87th Precinct* series, starring Randy Quaid. Among McBain's highest achievements are his collaborations with Alfred Hitchcock on *Alfred Hitchcock Presents* as well as scripting one of Hitchcock's most memorable films, *The Birds* (1963), starring Rod Taylor and Tippi Hedren.

"I'm very glad she's dead," the man said.

He wore a homburg, muffler, overcoat and gloves. He stood near the night table, a tall man with a narrow face, and a well-groomed gray mustache that matched the graying hair at his temples. His eyes were clear and blue and distinctly free of pain or grief.

Detective Steve Carella wasn't sure he had heard the man correctly. "Sir," Carella said, "I'm sure I don't have to tell you—"

"That's right," the man said, "you don't have to tell me. It happens I'm a criminal lawyer and am well aware of my rights. My wife was no good, and I'm delighted someone killed her."

Carella opened his pad. This was not what a bereaved husband was supposed to say when his wife lay disemboweled on the bedroom floor in a pool of her own blood.

"Your name is Gerald Fletcher."

"That's correct."

"Your wife's name, Mr. Fletcher?"

"Sarah. Sarah Fletcher."

"Want to tell me what happened?"

"I got home about fifteen minutes ago. I called to my wife from the front door, and got no answer. I came into the bedroom and found her dead on the floor. I immediately called the police."

"Was the room in this condition when you came in?"

"It was."

"Touch anything?"

"Nothing. I haven't moved from this spot since I placed the call."

"Anybody in here when you came in?"

"Not a soul. Except my wife, of course."

"Is that your suitcase in the entrance hallway?"

"It is. I was on the Coast for three days. An associate of mine needed advice on a brief he was preparing. What's your name?"

"Carella. Detective Steve Carella."

"I'll remember that."

While the police photographer was doing his macabre little jig around the body to make sure the lady looked good in the rushes, or as good as any lady can look in her condition, a laboratory assistant named Marshall Davies was in the kitchen of the apartment, waiting for the medical examiner to pronounce the lady dead, at which time Davies would go into the bedroom and with delicate care remove the knife protruding from the blood and slime of the lady, in an attempt to salvage some good latent prints from the handle of the murder weapon.

Davies was a new technician, but an observant one, and he noticed that the kitchen window was wide open, not exactly usual on a December night when the temperature outside hovered at twelve degrees. Leaning over the sink, he further noticed that the window opened onto a fire escape on the rear of the building. He could not resist speculating that perhaps someone had climbed up the fire escape and then into the kitchen.

Since there was a big muddy footprint in the kitchen sink, another one on the floor near the sink, and several others fading as they traveled across the waxed kitchen floor to the living room, Davies surmised that he was onto something hot. Wasn't it possible that an intruder had climbed over the windowsill, into the sink and walked across the room, bearing the switchblade knife that had later been pulled viciously across the lady's abdomen from left to right? If the M.E. ever got through with the damn body, the boys of the 87th would be halfway home, thanks to Marshall Davies. He felt pretty good.

The three points of the triangle were Detective-Lieutenant Byrnes, and Detectives Meyer Meyer and Steve Carella. Fletcher sat in a chair, still wearing homburg, muffler, overcoat and gloves as if he expected to be called outdoors at any moment. The interrogation was being conducted in a windowless cubicle labeled INTERROGATION ROOM.

The cops standing in their loose triangle around Gerald Fletcher were amazed but not too terribly amused by his brutal frankness.

"I hated her guts," he said.

"Mr. Fletcher," Lieutenant Byrnes said, "I *still* feel I must warn you that a woman has been murdered—"

"Yes. My dear, wonderful wife," Fletcher said sarcastically.

". . . which is a serious crime. . . ." Byrnes felt tongue-tied in Fletcher's presence. Bullet-headed, hair turning from iron-gray to ice-white, blue-eyed, built like a compact linebacker, Byrnes looked to his colleagues for support. Both Meyer and Carella were watching their shoelaces.

"You have warned me repeatedly," Fletcher said, "I can't imagine why. My wife is dead—someone killed her—but it was not I."

"Well, it's nice to have your assurance of that, Mr. Fletcher, but this alone doesn't necessarily still our doubts," Carella said, hearing the orders and wondering where the hell they were coming from. He was, he realized, trying to impress Fletcher. He continued, "How do we know it *wasn't* you who stabbed her?"

"To begin with," Fletcher said, "there were signs of forcible entry in the kitchen and hasty departure in the bedroom, witness the wide-open window in the aforementioned room and the shattered window in the latter. The drawers in the dining room sideboard were open—"

"You're very observant," Meyer said suddenly. "Did you notice all this in the four minutes it took you to enter the apartment and call the police?"

"It is my *job* to be observant," Fletcher said. "But to answer your question, no. I noticed all this *after* I had spoken to Detective Carella here."

Wearily, Byrnes dismissed Fletcher, who then left the room.

"What do you think?" Byrnes said.

"I think he did it," Carella said.

"Even with all those signs of a burglary?"

"*Especially* with those signs. He could have come home, found his wife stabbed—but not fatally—and finished her off by yanking the knife across her belly. Fletcher had four minutes, when all he needed was maybe four seconds."

"It's possible," Meyer said.

"Or maybe I just don't like the guy," Carella said.

"Let's see what the lab comes up with," Byrnes said.

The laboratory came up with good fingerprints on the kitchen window sash and on the silver drawer of the dining-room sideboard. There were good prints on some of the pieces of silver scattered on the floor near the smashed bedroom window. Most important, there were good prints on the handle of the switchblade knife. The prints matched; they had all been left by the same person.

Gerald Fletcher graciously allowed the police to take his fingerprints, which were then compared with those Marshall Davies had sent over from the police laboratory. The fingerprints on the window sash, the drawer, the silverware and the knife did not match Gerald Fletcher's.

Which didn't mean a damn thing if he had been wearing his gloves when he'd finished her off.

On Monday morning, in the second-floor rear apartment of 721 Silvermine Oval, a chalked outline on the bedroom floor was the only evidence that a woman had lain there in death the night before. Carella sidestepped the outline and looked out the shattered window at the narrow alleyway below. There was a distance of perhaps twelve feet between this building and the one across from it.

Conceivably, the intruder could have leaped across the shaftway, but this would have required premeditation and calculation. The more probable likelihood was that the intruder had fallen to the pavement below.

"That's quite a long drop," Detective Bert Kling said, peering over Carella's shoulder.

"How far do you figure?" Carella asked.

"Thirty feet. At least."

"Got to break a leg taking a fall like that. You think he went through the window head first?"

"How else?"

"He might have broken the glass out first, then gone through," Carella suggested.

"If he was about to go to all that trouble, why didn't he just open the damn thing?"

"Well, let's take a look," Carella said.

They examined the latch and the sash. Kling grabbed both handles on the window frame and pulled up on them. "Stuck."

"Probably painted shut," Carella said.

"Maybe he *did* try to open it. Maybe he smashed it only when he realized it was stuck."

"Yeah," Carella said. "And in a big hurry, too. Fletcher was opening the front door, maybe already in the apartment by then."

"The guy probably had a bag or something with him, to put the loot in. He must have taken a wild swing with the bag when he realized the window was stuck, and maybe some of the stuff fell out, which would explain the silverware on the floor. Then he probably climbed through the hole and dropped down feet first. In fact, what he could've done, Steve, was drop the bag down first, and then he climbed out and hung from the sill before he jumped, to make it a shorter distance."

"I don't know if he had all that much time, Bert. He must have heard that front door opening, and Fletcher coming in and calling to his wife. Otherwise, he'd have taken his good, sweet time and gone out the kitchen window and down the fire escape, the way he'd come in."

Kling nodded reflectively.

"Let's take a look at that alley," Carella said.

In the alleyway outside, Carella and Kling studied the concrete pavement, then looked up at the shattered second-floor window of the Fletcher apartment.

"Where do you suppose he'd have landed?" Kling said.

"Right about where we're standing." Carella looked at the ground. "I don't know, Bert. A guy drops twenty feet to a concrete pavement, doesn't break anything, gets up, dusts himself off, and runs the fifty-yard dash, right?" Carella shook his head. "My guess is he stayed right where he was to catch his breath, giving Fletcher time to look out the window, which would be the natural thing to do, but which Fletcher didn't."

"He was anxious to call the police."

"I still think he did it."

"Steve, be reasonable. If a guy's fingerprints are on the handle of a knife, and the knife is still in the victim—"

"And if the victim's husband realizes what a sweet setup he's stumbled into, wife lying on the floor with a knife in her, place broken into and burglarized, why not finish the job and hope the burglar will be blamed?"

"Sure," Kling said. "Prove it."

"I can't," Carella said. "Not until we catch the burglar."

While Carella and Kling went through the tedious routine of retracing the burglar's footsteps, Marshall Davies called the 87th Precinct and got Detective Meyer.

"I think I've got some fairly interesting information about the suspect," Davies said. "He left latent fingerprints all over the apartment and footprints in the kitchen. A very good one in the sink, when he climbed through the window, and some middling-fair ones tracking across the kitchen floor to the dining room. I got some excellent pictures and some good blowups of the heel."

"Good," Meyer said.

"But more important," Davies went on, "I got a good walking picture from the footprints on the floor. If a man is walking slowly, the distance between his footprints is usually about twenty-seven inches. Forty for running, thirty-five for fast walking. These were thirty-two inches. So we have a man's usual gait, moving quickly, but not in a desperate hurry, with the walking line normal and not broken."

"What does that mean?"

"Well, a walking line should normally run along the inner edge of a man's heelprints. Incidentally, the size and type of shoe and angle of the foot clearly indicate that this was a man."

"OK, fine," Meyer said. He did not thus far consider Davies's information valuable nor even terribly important.

"Anyway, none of this is valuable nor even terribly important," Davies said, "until we consider the rest of the data. The bedroom window was smashed, and the Homicide men were speculating that the suspect had jumped through the window into the alley below. I went down to get some meaningful pictures, and got some picture of where he must have landed—on both feet, incidentally—and I got another walking picture and direction line. He moved toward the basement door and into the basement. But the important thing is that our man is injured, and I think badly."

"How do you know?" Meyer asked.

"The walking picture downstairs is entirely different from the one in the kitchen. When he got downstairs he was leaning heavily on the left leg and dragging the right. I would suggest that whoever's handling the case put out a physician's bulletin. If this guy hasn't got a broken leg, I'll eat the pictures I took."

A girl in a green coat was waiting in the apartment lobby when Carella and Kling came back in, still retracing footsteps, or trying to. The girl said, "Excuse me, are you the detectives?"

"Yes," Carella said.

"The super told me you were in the building," the girl said. "You're investigating the Fletcher murder, aren't you?" She was quite soft spoken.

"How can we help you, miss?" Carella asked.

"I saw somebody in the basement last night, with blood on his clothes."

Carella glanced at Kling and immediately said, "What time was this?"

"About a quarter to eleven," the girl said.

"What were you doing in the basement?"

The girl sounded surprised. "That's where the washing machines are. I'm sorry, my name is Selma Bernstein. I live here in the building."

"Tell us what happened, will you?" Carella said.

"I was sitting by the machine, watching the clothes tumble, which is simply *fascinating*, you know, when the door leading to the backyard opened—the door to the alley. This man came down the stairs, and I don't even think he saw me. He went straight for the stairs at the other end, the ones that go up into the street. I never saw him before last night."

"Can you describe him?" Carella asked.

"Sure. He was about twenty-one or twenty-two, your height and weight, well, maybe a little shorter, five ten or eleven, brown hair."

Kling was already writing. The man was white, wore dark trousers, high-topped sneakers, and a poplin jacket with blood on the right sleeve and on the front. He carried a small red bag, "like one of those bags the airlines give you."

Selma didn't know if he had any scars. "He went by in pretty much of a hurry, considering he was dragging his right leg. I think he was hurt pretty badly."

What they had in mind, of course, was identification from a mug shot, but the I.S. reported that none of the fingerprints in their file matched the ones found in the apartment. So the detectives figured it was going to be a tough one, and they sent out a bulletin to all of the city's doctors just to prove it.

Just to prove that cops can be as wrong as anyone else, it turned out to be a nice easy one after all.

The call came from a physician in Riverhead at 4:37 that afternoon, just as Carella was ready to go home.

"This is Dr. Mendelsohn," he said. "I have your bulletin here, and I want to report treating a man early this morning who fits your description—a Ralph Corwin of 894 Woodside in Riverhead. He had a bad ankle sprain."

"Thank you, Dr. Mendelsohn," Carella said.

Carella pulled the Riverhead directory from the top drawer of his desk and quickly flipped to the C's. He did not expect to find a listing for Ralph Corwin. A man would have to be a rank amateur to burglarize an apartment without wearing gloves, then stab a woman to death, and give his name when seeking treatment for an injury sustained in escaping from the murder apartment.

Ralph Corwin was apparently a rank amateur. His name was in the phonebook, and he'd given the doctor his correct address.

Carella and Kling kicked in the door without warning, fanning into the room, guns drawn. The man on the bed was wearing only undershorts. His right ankle was taped.

"Are you Ralph Corwin?" Carella asked.

"Yes," the man said. His face was drawn, the eyes in pain.

"Get dressed, Corwin. We want to ask you some questions."

"There's nothing to ask," he said, and turned his head into the pillow. "I killed her."

Ralph Corwin made his confession in the presence of two detectives of the 87th, a police stenographer, an assistant district attorney, and a lawyer appointed by the Legal Aid Society.

Corwin was the burglar. He'd entered 721 Silvermine Oval on Sunday night, December 12, down the steps from the street where the garbage cans were. He went through the basement, up the steps at the other end, into the backyard, and climbed the fire escape, all at about ten o'clock in the evening. Corwin entered the Fletcher apartment because it was the first one he saw without lights. He figured there was nobody home. The kitchen window was open a tiny crack; Corwin squeezed his fingers under the bottom and opened it all the way. He was pretty desperate at the time because he was a junkie in need of cash. He swore that he'd never done anything like this before.

The man from the D.A.'s office was conducting the Q and A and asked Corwin if he hadn't been afraid of fingerprints, not wearing gloves. Corwin figured that was done only in the movies, and anyway, he said, he didn't own gloves.

Corwin used a tiny flashlight to guide him as he stepped into the sink and down to the door. He made his way to the dining room, emptied the drawer of silverware into his airline bag. Then he looked for the bedroom, scouting for watches and rings, whatever he could take in the way of jewelry. "I'm not a pro," he said. "I was just hung up real bad and needed some bread to tide me over."

Now came the important part. The D.A.'s assistant asked Corwin what happened in the bedroom.

A. There was a lady in bed. This was only like close to ten thirty, you don't expect nobody to be asleep so early.

Q. But there was a woman in bed.

A. Yeah. She turned on the light the minute I stepped in the room.

Q. What did you do?

A. I had a knife in my pocket. I pulled it out to scare her. It was almost comical. She looks at me and says, 'What are you doing here?'

Q. Did you say anything to her?

A. I told her to keep quiet, that I wasn't going to hurt her. But she got out of bed and I saw she was reaching for the phone. That's got to be crazy, right? A guy is standing there in your bedroom with a knife in his hand, so she reaches for the phone.

Q. What did you do?

A. I grabbed her hand before she could get it. I pulled her off the bed, away from the phone, you know? And I told her again that nobody was going to hurt her, that I was getting out of there right away, to just please calm down.

Q. What happened next?

A. She started to scream. I told her to stop. I was beginning to panic. I mean she was really yelling.

Q. Did she stop?

A. No.

Q. What did you do?

A. I stabbed her.

Q. Where did you stab her?

A. I don't know. It was a reflex. She was yelling, I was afraid the whole building would come down. I just . . . I just stuck the knife in her. I was very scared. I stabbed her in the belly. Someplace in the belly.

Q. How many times did you stab her?

A. Once. She . . . she backed away from me. I'll never forget the look on her face. And she . . . fell on the floor.

Q. Would you look at this photograph, please?

A. Oh, no.

Q. Is that the woman you stabbed?

A. Oh, no . . . I didn't think . . . Oh, no!

A moment after he stabbed Sarah Fletcher, Corwin heard the door opening and someone coming in. The man yelled, "Sarah, it's me, I'm home." Corwin ran past Sarah's body on the floor, and tried to open the window, but it was stuck. He smashed it with his airline bag, threw the bag out first to save the swag because, no matter what, he knew he'd need another fix, and he climbed through the broken window, cutting his hand on a piece of glass. He hung from the sill, and finally let go, dropping to the ground. He tried to get up, and fell down again. His ankle was killing him, his hand bleeding. He stayed in the alley nearly fifteen minutes, then finally escaped via the route Selma Bernstein had described to Carella and Kling.

He took the subway to Riverhead and got to Dr. Mendelsohn at about nine in the morning. He read of Sarah Fletcher's murder in the newspaper on the way back from the doctor.

On Tuesday, December 14, which was the first of Carella's two days off that week, he received a call at home from Gerald Fletcher. Fletcher told the puzzled Carella that he'd gotten his number from a friend in the D.A.'s office, complimented Carella and the boys of the 87th on their snappy detective work, and invited Carella to lunch at the Golden Lion at one o'clock. Carella wasn't happy about interrupting his Christmas shopping, but this was an unusual opportunity, and he accepted.

Most policemen in the city for which Carella worked did not eat very often in restaurants like the Golden Lion. Carella had never been inside. A look at the menu posted on the window outside would have frightened him out of six months' pay. The place was a faithful replica of the dining room of an English coach house, circa 1627: huge oaken beams, immaculate white cloths, heavy silver.

Gerald Fletcher's table was in a secluded corner of the restaurant. He rose as Carella approached, extending his hand, and said, "Glad you could make it. Sit down, won't you?"

Carella shook Fletcher's hand, and then sat. He felt extremely uncomfortable, but he couldn't tell whether his discomfort was caused by the room or by the man with whom he was dining.

"Would you care for a drink?" Fletcher asked.

"Well, are you having one?" Carella asked.

"Yes, I am."

"I'll have a Scotch and soda," Carella said. He was not used to drinking at lunch.

Fletcher signaled for the waiter and ordered the drinks, making his another whiskey sour. When the drinks came, Fletcher raised his glass. "Here's to a conviction," he said.

Carella lifted his own glass. "I don't expect there'll be any trouble," he said. "It looks airtight to me."

Both men drank. Fletcher dabbed his lips with a napkin and said, "You never can tell these days. I hope you're right, though." He sipped at the drink. "I must admit I feel a certain amount of sympathy for him."

"Do you?"

"Yes. If he's an addict, he's automatically entitled to pity. And when one considers that the woman he murdered was nothing but a—"

"Mr. Fletcher . . ."

"Gerry, please. And I know: it isn't very kind of me to malign the dead. I'm afraid you didn't know my wife though, Mr. Carella. May I call you Steve?"

"Sure."

"My enmity might be a bit more understandable if you had. Still, I shall take your advice. She's dead, and no longer capable of hurting me, so why be bitter? Shall we order, Steve?"

Fletcher suggested that Carella try either the trout au meunière or the beef and kidney pie, both of which were excellent. Carella ordered prime ribs, medium rare, and a mug of beer.

As the men ate and talked, something began happening, or at least Carella *thought* something was happening; he might never be quite sure. The conversation with Fletcher seemed on the surface to be routine chatter, but rushing through this inane, polite discussion was an undercurrent that caused excitement, fear, and apprehension. As they spoke, Carella knew with renewed certainty that Gerald Fletcher had killed his wife. Without ever being told so, he knew it. *This* was why Fletcher had called this morning; *this* was why Fletcher had invited him to lunch; *this* was why he prattled on endlessly while every contradictory move of his body signaled on an almost extrasensory level that he *knew* Carella suspected him of murder, and was here to *tell* Carella (*without* telling him) that, "Yes, you stupid cop, I killed my wife. However much the evidence may point to another man, however many confessions you get, I killed her and I'm glad I killed her. And there isn't a damn thing you can do about it."

Ralph Corwin was being held before trial in the city's oldest prison, known to law enforcers and lawbreakers alike as Calcutta. Neither Corwin's lawyer nor the district attorney's office felt that allowing Carella to talk to the prisoner would be harmful to the case.

Corwin was expecting him. "What did you want to see me about?"

"I wanted to ask you some questions."

"My lawyer says I'm not supposed to add anything to what I already said. I don't even *like* that guy."

"Why didn't you ask for another lawyer? Ask one of the officers here to call the Legal Aid Society. Or simply tell him. I'm sure he'd have no objection to dropping out."

Corwin shrugged. "I don't want to hurt his feelings. He's a little cockroach, but what the hell."

"You've got a lot at stake here, Corwin."

"But I killed her, so what does it matter who the lawyer is? You got it all in black and white."

"You feel like answering some questions?" Carella said.

"I feel like dropping dead, is what I feel like. Cold turkey's never good, and it's worse when you can't yell."

"If you'd rather I came back another time . . ."

"No, no, go ahead. What do you want to know?"

"I want to know exactly how you stabbed Sarah Fletcher."

"How do you think you stab somebody? You stick a knife in her, that's how."

"Where?"

"In the belly."

"Left-hand side of the body?"

"Yeah. I guess so."

"Where was the knife when she fell?"

"I don't know what you mean."

"Was the knife on the *right*-hand side of her body or the *left?*"

"I don't know. That was when I heard the front door opening and all I could think of was getting out of there."

"When you stabbed her, did she *twist* away from you?"

"No, she backed away, straight back, as if she couldn't believe what I done, and . . . and just wanted to get away from me."

"And then she fell?"

"Yes. She . . . her knees sort of gave way and she grabbed for her belly, and her hands sort of—it was terrible—they just . . . they were grabbing *air,* you know? And she fell."

"In what position?"

"On her side."

"*Which* side?"

"I could still see the knife, so it must've been the opposite side. The side opposite from where I stabbed her."

"One last question, Ralph. Was she dead when you went through that window?"

"I don't know. She was bleeding and . . . she was very quiet. I . . . guess she was dead. I don't know. I guess so."

Among Sarah Fletcher's personal effects that were considered of interest to the police before they arrested Ralph Corwin was an address book found in the dead woman's handbag on the bedroom dresser. In the Thursday afternoon stillness of the squad room, Carella examined the book.

There was nothing terribly fascinating about the alphabetical listings. Sarah Fletcher had possessed a good handwriting, and most of the listings were obviously married couples (Chuck and Nancy Benton, Harold and Marie Spander, and so on), some were girlfriends, local merchants, hairdresser, dentist, doctors, restaurants in town or across the river. A thoroughly uninspiring address book—until Carella came to a page at the end of the book, with the printed word MEMORANDA at its top.

Under the word, there were five names, addresses and telephone numbers written in Sarah's meticulous hand. They were all men's names, obviously entered at different times because some were in pencil and others in ink. The parenthetical initials following each entry were all noted in felt marking pens of various colors:

Andrew Hart, 1120 Hall Avenue, 622-8400 (PB&G) (TG)
Michael Thornton, 371 South Linder, 881-9371 (TS)
Lou Kantor, 434 North 16 Street, FR 7-2346 (TPC) (TG)
Sal Decotto, 831 Grover Avenue, FR 5-3287 (F) (TG)
Richard Fenner, 110 Henderson, 593-6648 (QR) (TG)

If there was one thing Carella loved, it was a code. He loved a code almost as much as he loved German measles. He flipped through the phone book and the address for Andrew Hart matched the one in Sarah's handwriting. He found an address for Michael Thornton. It, too, was identical to the one in her book. He kept turning pages in the directory, checking names and addresses. He verified all five.

At a little past eight the next morning, Carella got going on them. He called

Andrew Hart at the number listed in Sarah's address book. Hart answered, and was not happy. "I'm in the middle of shaving," he said. "I've got to leave for the office in a little while. What's this about?"

"We're investigating a homicide, Mr. Hart."

"A *what?* A homicide? Who's been killed?"

"A woman named Sarah Fletcher."

"I don't know anyone named Sarah Fletcher," he said.

"She seems to have known you, Mr. Hart."

"Sarah *who?* Fletcher, did you say?" Hart's annoyance increased.

"That's right."

"I don't know anybody by that name. Who says she knew me? I never heard of her in my life."

"Your name's in her address book."

"My name? That's impossible."

Nevertheless, Hart agreed to see Carella and Meyer Meyer at the offices of Hart and Widderman, 480 Reed Street, sixth floor, at ten o'clock that morning.

At ten, Meyer and Carella parked the car and went into the building at 480 Reed, and up the elevator to the sixth floor. Hart and Widderman manufactured watchbands. A huge advertising display near the receptionist's desk in the lobby proudly proclaimed "H&W Beat the Band!" and then backed the slogan with more discreet copy that explained how Hart and Widderman had solved the difficult engineering problems of the expansion watch bracelet.

"Mr. Hart, please," Carella said.

"Who's calling?" the receptionist asked. She sounded as if she were chewing gum, even though she was not.

"Detectives Carella and Meyer."

"Just a minute, please," she said, and lifted her phone, pushing a button in the base. "Mr. Hart," she said, "there are some cops here to see you." She listened for a moment and then said, "Yes, sir." She replaced the receiver on its cradle, gestured toward the inside corridor with a nod of her golden tresses, said, "Go right in, please. Door at the end of the hall," and then went back to her magazine.

The gray skies had apparently infected Andrew Hart. "You didn't have to broadcast to the world that the police department was here," he said immediately.

"We merely announced ourselves," Carella said.

"Well, okay, now you're here," Hart said, "let's get it over with." He was a big man in his middle fifties, with iron-gray hair and black-trimmed eyeglasses. "I told you I don't know Sarah Fletcher and I don't."

"Here's her book, Mr. Hart," Carella said. "That's your name, isn't it?"

"Yeah," Hart said, and shook his head. "But how it got there is beyond me."

"Is it possible she's someone you met at a party, someone you exchanged numbers with?"

"No."

"Are you married, Mr. Hart?"

"No."

"We've got a picture of Mrs. Fletcher. I wonder—"

"Don't go showing me any pictures of a corpse," Hart said.

"This was taken when she was still very much alive, Mr. Hart."

Meyer handed Carella a manila envelope. He opened the flap and removed from the envelope a framed picture of Sarah Fletcher which he handed to Hart. Hart looked at the photograph, and then immediately looked up at Carella.

"What is this?" he said. He looked at the photograph again, shook his head, and said, "Somebody killed her, huh?"

"Yes, somebody did," Carella answered. "Did you know her?"

"I knew her."

"I thought you said you didn't."

"I didn't know Sarah Fletcher, if that's who you think she was. But I knew this broad, all right."

"Who'd *you* think she was?" Meyer asked.

"Just who she told me she was. Sadie Collins. She introduced herself as Sadie Collins, and that's who I knew her as. Sadie Collins."

"Where was this, Mr. Hart? Where'd you meet her?"

"A singles bar. The city's full of them."

"Would you remember when?"

"At least a year ago."

"Ever go out with her?"

"I used to see her once or twice a week."

"When did you stop seeing her?"

"Last summer."

"Did you know she was married?"

"Who, Sadie? You're kidding."

"She never told you she was married?"

"Never."

Meyer asked, "When you were going out, where'd you pick her up? At her apartment?"

"No. She used to come to my place."

"Where'd you call her when you wanted to reach her?"

"I didn't. She used to call me."

"Where'd you go, Mr. Hart? When you went out?"

"We didn't go out too much."

"What *did* you do?"

"She used to come to my place. The truth is, we never went out. She didn't want to go out much."

"Didn't you think that was strange?"

"No," Hart shrugged. "I figured she liked to stay home."

"Why'd you stop seeing her, Mr. Hart?"

"I met somebody else. A nice girl. I'm very serious about her."

"Was there something wrong with Sadie?"

"No, no. She was a beautiful woman, beautiful."

"Then why would you be ashamed—"

"Ashamed? Who said anything about being ashamed?"

"I gathered you wouldn't want your girlfriend—"

"Listen, what is this? I stopped seeing Sadie six months ago. I wouldn't even talk to her on the phone after that. If the crazy babe got herself killed—"

"Crazy?"

Hart suddenly wiped his hand over his face, wet his lips, and walked behind his desk. "I don't think I have anything more to say to you, gentlemen."

"What did you mean by crazy?" Carella asked.

"Good day, gentlemen," Hart said.

Carella went to see Lieutenant Byrnes. In the lieutenant's corner office, Byrnes and Carella sat down over coffee. Byrnes frowned at Carella's request.

"Oh, come on, Pete!" Carella said. "If Fletcher *did* it—"

"That's only your allegation. Suppose he *didn't* do it, and suppose you do something to screw up the D.A.'s case?"

"Like what?"

"I don't know like what. The way things are going these days, if you spit on the sidewalk, that's enough to get a case thrown out of court."

"Fletcher hated his wife," Carella said calmly.

"Lot of men hate their wives. Half the men in this city hate their wives."

"But her little fling gives Fletcher good reason for . . . Look, Pete, he had a motive; he had the opportunity, a golden one, in fact; and he had the means—another man's knife sticking in Sarah's belly. What more do you want?"

"Proof. There's a funny little system we've got here—it requires proof before we can arrest a man and charge him with murder."

"Right. And all I'm asking is the opportunity to *try* for it."

"Sure, by putting a tail on Fletcher. Suppose he sues the city?"

"Yes or no, Pete? I want permission to conduct a round-the-clock surveillance of Gerald Fletcher, starting Sunday morning. Yes or no?"

"I must be out of my mind," Byrnes said, and sighed.

Michael Thornton lived in an apartment building several blocks from the Quarter, close enough to absorb some of its artistic flavor, distant enough to escape its high rents. A blond man in his apartment, Paul Wendling, told Kling and Meyer that Mike was in his jewelry shop.

In the shop, Thornton was wearing a blue work smock, but the contours of the garment did nothing to hide his powerful build. His eyes were blue, his hair black. A small scar showed white in the thick eyebrow over his left eye.

"We understand you're working," Meyer said. "Sorry to break in on you this way."
"That's okay," Thornton said. "What's up?"
"You know a woman named Sarah Fletcher?"
"No," Thornton said.
"You know a woman named Sadie Collins?"
Thornton hesitated. "Yes," he said.
"What was your relationship with her?" Kling asked.
Thornton shrugged. "Why? Is she in trouble?"
"When's the last time you saw her?"
"You didn't answer my question," Thornton said.
"Well, you didn't answer ours either," Meyer said, and smiled. "What was your relationship with her, and when did you see her last?"
"I met her in July, in a joint called *The Saloon*, right around the corner. It's a bar, but they also serve sandwiches and soup. It gets a big crowd on weekends, singles, a couple of odd ones for spice—but not a gay bar. I saw her last August, a brief, hot thing, and then good-bye."
"Did you realize she was married?" Kling said.
"No. Is she?"
"Yes," Meyer said. Neither of the detectives had yet informed Thornton that the lady in question was now unfortunately deceased. They were saving that for last, like dessert.
"Gee, I didn't know she was married." Thornton seemed truly surprised. "Otherwise, nothing would've happened."
"What *did* happen?"
"I bought her a few drinks and then I took her home with me. Later, I put her in a cab."
"When did you see her next?"
"The following day. It was goofy. She called me in the morning, she said she was on her way downtown. I was still in bed. I said, 'So come on down, baby.' And she did. *Believe* me, she did."
"Did you see her again after that?" Kling asked.
"Two or three times a week."
"Where'd you go?"
"To my pad on South Lindner."
"Never went anyplace but there?"
"Never."
"Why'd you quit seeing her?"
"I went out of town for a while. When I got back, I just didn't hear from her again. She never gave me her number, and she wasn't in the directory, so I couldn't reach her."
"What do you make of this?" Kling asked, handing Thornton the address book. Thornton studied it and said, "Yeah, what about it? She wrote this down the night we met—we were in bed, and she asked my address."
"Did she write those initials at the same time, the ones in parentheses under your phone number?"

"I didn't actually see the page itself. I only saw her writing in the book."

"Got any idea what the initials mean?"

"None at all." Suddenly he looked thoughtful. "She *was* kind of special, I have to admit it." He grinned. "She'll call again, I'm sure of it."

"I wouldn't count on it." Meyer said. "She's dead."

His face did not crumble or express grief or shock. The only thing it expressed was sudden anger. "The stupid . . ." Thornton said. "That's all she ever was, a stupid, crazy . . ."

On Sunday morning, Carella was ready to become a surveillant, but Gerald Fletcher was nowhere in sight. A call to his apartment from a nearby phone booth revealed that he was not in his digs. He parked in front of Fletcher's apartment building until 5:00 p.m. when he was relieved by Detective Arthur Brown. Carella went home to read his son's latest note to Santa Claus, had dinner with his family, and was settling down in the living room with a novel he had bought a week ago and not yet cracked when the telephone rang.

"Hello?" Carella said into the mouthpiece.

"Hello, Steve? This is Gerry. Gerry Fletcher."

Carella almost dropped the receiver. "How are you?"

"Fine, thanks. I was away for the weekend, just got back a little while ago, in fact. Frankly I find this apartment depressing as hell. I was wondering if you'd like to join me for a drink."

"Well," Carella said. "It's Sunday night, and it's late."

"Nonsense, it's only eight o'clock. We'll do a little old-fashioned pub crawling."

It suddenly occurred to Carella that Gerald Fletcher had already had a few drinks before placing his call. It further occurred to him that if played this *too* cozily, Fletcher might rescind his generous offer.

"Okay. I'll see you at eight thirty, provided I can square it with my wife."

"Good," Fletcher said. "See you."

Paddy's Bar & Grill was on the Stem, adjacent to the city's theater district. Carella and Fletcher got there at about nine o'clock while the place was still relatively quiet. The action began a little later, Fletcher explained.

Fletcher lifted his glass in a silent toast. "What kind of person would you say comes to a place like this?"

"I would say we've got a nice lower-middle-class clientele bent on making contact with members of the opposite sex."

"What would you say if I told you the blonde in the clinging jersey is a working prostitute?"

Carella looked at the woman. "I don't think I'd believe you. She's a bit old for the young competition, and she's not selling anything. She's waiting for one of those two or three older guys to make their move. Hookers don't wait, Gerry. Is she a working prostitute?"

"I haven't the faintest idea," Fletcher said. "I was merely trying to indicate that appearances can sometimes be misleading. Drink up, there are a few more places I'd like to show you."

He knew Fletcher well enough by now to realize that the man was trying to tell him something. At lunch last Tuesday, Fletcher had transmitted a message and a challenge: *I killed my wife, what can you do about it?* Tonight, in a similar manner, he was attempting to indicate something else, but Carella could not fathom exactly what.

Fanny's was only twenty blocks away from Paddy's Bar & Grill, but as far removed from it as the moon. Whereas the first bar seemed to cater to a quiet crowd peacefully pursuing its romantic inclinations, Fanny's was noisy and raucous, jammed to the rafters with men and women of all ages, wearing plastic hippie gear purchased in head shops up and down Jackson Avenue.

Fletcher lifted his glass. "I hope you don't mind if I drink myself into a stupor," he said. "Merely pour me into the car at the end of the night." Fletcher drank. "I don't usually consume this much alcohol, but I'm very troubled about that boy."

"What boy?" Carella asked.

"Ralph Corwin," Fletcher said. "I understand he's having some difficulty with his lawyer and, well, I'd like to help him somehow."

"*Help* him?"

"Yes. Do you think the D.A.'s office would consider it strange if I suggested a good defense lawyer for the boy?"

"I think they might consider it passing strange, yes."

"Do I detect a note of sarcasm in your voice?"

"Not at all."

Fletcher squired Carella from Fanny's to, in geographical order, The Purple Chairs and Quigley's Rest. Each place was rougher, in its way, than the last. The Purple Chairs catered to a brazenly gay crowd, and Quigley's Rest was a dive, where Fletcher's liquor caught up with him, and the evening ended suddenly in a brawl. Carella was shaken by the experience, and still couldn't piece out Fletcher's reasons.

Carella received a further shock when he continued to pursue Sarah Fletcher's address book. Lou Kantor was simply the third name in a now wearying list of Sarah's bedmates, until she turned out to be a tough and striking woman. She confirmed Carella's suspicions immediately.

"I only knew her a short while," she said. "I met her in September, I believe. Saw her three or four times after that."

"Where'd you meet her?"

"In a bar called The Purple Chairs. That's right," she added quickly. "That's what I am."

"Nobody asked," Carella said. "What about Sadie Collins?"

"Spell it out, Officer, I'm not going to help you. I don't like being hassled."

"Nobody's hassling you, Miss Kantor. You practice your religion and I'll practice mine. We're here to talk about a dead woman."

"Then talk about her, spit it out. What do you want to know? Was she straight? Everybody's straight until they're *not* straight anymore, isn't that right? She was willing to learn. I taught her."

"Did you know she was married?"

"She told me. So what? Broke down in tears one night, and spent the rest of the night crying. I knew she was married."

"What'd she say about her husband?"

"Nothing that surprised me. She said he had another woman. Said he ran off to see her every weekend, told little Sadie he had out-of-town business. Every weekend, can you imagine that?"

"What do you make of this?" Carella said, and handed her Sarah's address book opened to the MEMORANDA page.

"I don't know any of these people," Lou said.

"The initials under your name," Carella said. "TPC and then TG. Got any ideas?"

"Well, the TPC is obvious, isn't it? I met her at The Purple Chairs. What else could it mean?"

Carella suddenly felt very stupid. "Of course. What else could it mean?" He took back the book. "I'm finished," he said. "Thank you very much."

"I miss her," Lou said suddenly. "She was a wild one."

Cracking a code is like learning to roller-skate; once you know how to do it, it's easy. With a little help from Gerald Fletcher, who had provided a guided tour the night before, and a lot of help from Lou Kantor, who had generously provided the key, Carella was able to crack the code wide open—well, almost. Last night, he'd gone with Fletcher to Paddy's Bar & Grill, or PB&G under Andrew Hart's name; Fanny's, F under Sal Decotto; The Purple Chairs, Lou Kantor's TPC; and Quigley's Rest, QR for Richard Fenner on the list. Probably because of the fight, he hadn't taken Carella to The Saloon, TS under Michael Thornton's name—the place where Thornton had admitted first meeting Sarah.

Except, what the hell did TG mean, under all the names but Thornton's?

By Carella's own modest estimate, he had been in more bars in the past twenty-four hours than he had in the past twenty-four years. He decided, nevertheless, to hit The Saloon that night.

The Saloon was just that. A cigarette-scarred bar behind which ran a mottled, flaking mirror; wooden booths with patched, fake leather seat cushions; bowls of pretzels and potato chips; jukebox gurgling; steamy bodies.

"They come in here," the bartender said, "at all hours of the night. Take yourself. You're here to meet a girl, am I right?"

"There *was* someone I was hoping to see. A girl named Sadie Collins. Do you know her?"

"Yeah. She used to come in a lot, but I ain't seen her in months. What do you want to fool around with her for?"

"Why? What's the matter with her?"

"You want to know something?" the bartender said. "I thought she was a hooker at first. Aggressive. You know what that word means? Aggressive? She used to come dressed down to here and up to there, ready for action, selling everything she had, you understand? She'd come in here, pick out a guy she wanted, and go after him like the world was gonna end at midnight. And always the same type. Big guys. You wouldn't stand a chance with her, not that you ain't big, don't misunderstand me. But Sadie liked them gigantic, and mean. You know something?"

"What?"

"I'm glad she don't come in here anymore. There was something about her—like she was compulsive. You know what that word means, compulsive?"

Tuesday afternoon, Arthur Brown handed in his surveillance report on Gerald Fletcher. Much of it was not at all illuminating. From 4:55 p.m. to 8:45 p.m. Fletcher had driven home, and then to 812 North Crane and parked. The report *did* become somewhat illuminating when, at 8:46 p.m., Fletcher emerged from the building with a redheaded woman wearing a black fur coat over a green dress. They went to Rudolph's restaurant, ate, and drove back to 812 Crane, arrived at 10:35 p.m. and went inside. Arthur Brown had checked the lobby mailboxes, which showed eight apartments on the eleventh floor, which was where the elevator indicator had stopped. Brown went outside to wait again, and Fletcher emerged alone at 11:40 p.m., and drove home. Detective O'Brien relieved Detective Brown at 12:15 a.m.

Byrnes said, "This woman could be important."

"That's just what I think," Brown answered.

Carella had not yet spoken to either Sal Decotto or Richard Fenner, the two remaining people listed in Sarah's book, but saw no reason to pursue that trial any further. If the place listings in her book had been chronological, she'd gone from bad to worse in her search for partners.

Why? To give it back to her husband in spades? Carella tossed Sarah's little black book into the manila folder bearing the various reports on the case, and turned his attention to the information Artie Brown had brought in last night. The redheaded woman's presence might be important, but Carella was still puzzling over Fletcher's behavior. Sarah's blatant infidelity provided Fletcher with a strong motive, so why take Carella to his wife's unhappy haunts, why *show* Carella that he had good and sufficient reason to kill her? Furthermore, why the offer to get a good defense attorney for the boy who had already been indicted for the slaying?

Sometimes Carella wondered who was doing what to whom.

At five o'clock that evening, Carella relieved Detective Hal Willis outside Fletcher's office building downtown, and then followed Fletcher to a department store in midtown Isola. Carella was wearing a false mustache stuck to his upper lip, a wig with longer hair than his own and of a different color, and a pair of sunglasses.

In the department store, he tracked Fletcher to the Intimate Apparel department. Carella walked into the next aisle, pausing to look at women's robes and kimonos, keeping one eye on Fletcher, who was in conversation with the lingerie salesgirl.

"May I help you, sir?" a voice said, and Carella turned to find a stocky woman at his elbow, with gray hair, black-rimmed spectacles, wearing army shoes and a black dress. Her suspicious smile accused him of being a junkie shoplifter or worse.

"Thank you, no," Carella said. "I'm just looking."

Fletcher made his selections from the gossamer undergarments which the salesgirl had spread out on the counter, pointing first to one garment, then to another. The salesgirl wrote up the order and Fletcher reached into his wallet to give her either cash or a credit card; it was difficult to tell from an aisle away. He chatted with the girl a moment longer, and then walked off toward the elevator bank.

"Are you *sure* I can't assist you?" the woman in the army shoes said, and Carella answered, "I'm positive," and moved swiftly toward the lingerie counter. Fletcher had left the counter without a package in his arms, which meant he was *sending* his purchases. The salesgirl was gathering up Fletcher's selections and looked up when Carella reached the counter.

"Yes, *sir,*" she said. "May I help you?"

Carella opened his wallet and produced his shield. "Police officer," he said. "I'm interested in the order you just wrote up."

The girl was perhaps nineteen years old, a college girl working in the store during the Christmas rush. Speechlessly, she studied the shield, eyes bugging.

"Are these items being sent?" Carella asked.

"Yes, *sir,*" the girl said. Here eyes were still wide. She wet her lips and stood up a little straighter, prepared to be a perfect witness.

"Can you tell me where?" Carella asked.

"Yes, sir," she said, and turned the sales slip toward him. "He wanted them wrapped separately, but they're all going to the same address. Miss Arlene Orton, 812 North Crane Street, right here in the city, and I'd guess it's a swell—"

"Thank you very much," Carella said.

It felt like Christmas already.

The man who picked the lock on Arlene Orton's front door, ten minutes after she left her apartment on Wednesday morning, was better at it than any burglar in the city, and he happened to work for the Police Department. It took the technician longer to set up his equipment, but the telephone was the easiest of his jobs. The tap would become operative when the telephone company supplied the police with a list of so-called bridging points that located the pairs and cables for Arlene Orton's phone. The monitoring equipment would be hooked into these and whenever a call went out of or came into the apartment, a recorder would automatically tape both ends of the conversation. In addition, whenever a call was made from the apartment, a dial indicator would ink out a series of dots that signified the number being called.

The technician placed his bug in the bookcase on the opposite side of the room. The bug was a small FM transmitter with a battery-powered mike that needed to be changed every twenty-four hours. The technician would have preferred running his own wires, but he dared not ask the building superintendent for an empty closet or workroom in which to hide his listener. A blabbermouth superintendent can kill an investigation more quickly than a squad of gangland goons.

In the rear of a panel truck parked at the curb some twelve feet south of the entrance to 812 Crane, Steve Carella sat behind the recording equipment that was locked into the frequency of the bug. He sat hopefully, with a tuna sandwich and a bottle of beer, prepared to hear and record any sounds that emanated from Arlene's apartment.

At the bridging point seven blocks away and thirty minutes later, Arthur Brown sat behind equipment that was hooked into the telephone mike, and waited for Arlene Orton's phone to ring. He was in radio contact with Carella.

The first call came at 12:17 p.m. The equipment tripped in automatically and the spools of tape began recording the conversation, while Brown simultaneously monitored it through his headphone.

"Hello?"

"Hello, Arlene?

"Yes, who's this?"

"Nan."

"Nan? You sound so different. Do you have a cold or something?"

"Every year at this time. Just before the *holidays*. Arlene, I'm terribly rushed, I'll make this short. Do you know Beth's dress size?"

The conversation went on in that vein, and Arlene Orton spoke to three more girlfriends in succession. She then called the local supermarket to order the week's groceries. She had a fine voice, deep and forceful, punctuated every so often (when she was talking to her girlfriends) with a delightful giggle.

At 4:00 p.m., the telephone in Arlene's apartment rang again.

"Hello?"

"Arlene, this is Gerry."

"Hello, darling."

"I'm leaving here a little early. I thought I'd come right over."

"Good."

"I'll be there in, oh, half an hour, forty minutes."

"Hurry."

Brown radioed Carella at once. Carella thanked him, and sat back to wait.

On Thursday morning, two days before Christmas, Carella sat at his desk in the squad room and looked over the transcripts of the five reels from the night before. The conversation on that reel had at one point changed abruptly in tone and content. Carella thought he knew why, but he wanted to confirm his suspicion:

FLETCHER: I meant after the holidays, not the trial.
MISS ORTON: I may be able to get away, I'm not sure. I'll have to check with my shrink.
FLETCHER: What's he got to do with it?
MISS ORTON: Well, I have to pay whether I'm there or not, you know.
FLETCHER: Is he taking a vacation?
MISS ORTON: I'll ask him.
FLETCHER: Yes, ask him. Because I'd really like to get away.
MISS ORTON: Ummm. When do you think the case (inaudible).
FLETCHER: In March sometime. No sooner than that. He's got a new lawyer, you know.
MISS ORTON: What does that mean, a new lawyer?
FLETCHER: Nothing. He'll be convicted anyway.
MISS ORTON: (Inaudible).
FLETCHER: Because the trial's going to take a lot out of me.
MISS ORTON: How soon after the trial . . .
FLETCHER: I don't know.
MISS ORTON: She's dead, Gerry, I don't see . . .
FLETCHER: Yes, but . . .
MISS ORTON: I don't see why we have to wait, do you?
FLETCHER: Have you read this?
MISS ORTON: No, not yet. Gerry, I think we ought to set a date now. A provisional date, depending on when the trial is. Gerry?
FLETCHER: Mmmm?
MISS ORTON: Do you think it'll be a terribly long, drawn-out trial?
FLETCHER: What?
MISS ORTON: Gerry?
FLETCHER: Yes?
MISS ORTON: Where are you?
FLETCHER: I was just looking over some of these books.
MISS ORTON: Do you think you can tear yourself away?
FLETCHER: Forgive me, darling.
MISS ORTON: If the trial starts in March, and we planned on April for it . . .
FLETCHER: Unless they come up with something unexpected, of course.
MISS ORTON: Like what?
FLETCHER: Oh, I don't know. They've got some pretty sharp people investigating this case.
MISS ORTON: What's there to investigate?
FLETCHER: There's always the possibility he didn't do it.
MISS ORTON: (inaudible) a signed confession?
FLETCHER: One of the cops thinks I killed her.
MISS ORTON: You're not serious. Who?
FLETCHER: A detective named Carella. He probably knows about us by now. He's

a very thorough cop. I have a great deal of admiration for him. I wonder if he realizes that.

Miss Orton: Where'd he even get such an idea?

Fletcher: Well, I told him I hated her.

Miss Orton: What? Gerry, why the hell did you do that?

Fletcher: He'd have found out anyway. He probably knows by now that Sarah was sleeping around with half the men in this city. And he probably knows I knew it, too.

Miss Orton: Who cares what he found out? Corwin's already confessed.

Fletcher: I can understand his reasoning. I'm just not sure he can understand me.

Miss Orton: Some reasoning. If you were going to kill her, you'd have done it ages ago, when she refused to sign the separation papers. So let him investigate, who cares? Wishing your wife dead isn't the same thing as killing her. Tell that to Detective Copolla.

Fletcher: Carella. (Laughs).

Miss Orton: What's so funny?

Fletcher: I'll tell him, darling.

According to the technician who had wired the Orton apartment, the living-room bug was in the bookcase on the wall opposite the bar. Carella was interested in the tape from the time Fletcher had asked Arlene about a book—"Have you read this?"—and then seemed preoccupied. It was Carella's guess that Fletcher had discovered the bookcase bug. What interested Carella more, however, was what Fletcher had said after he knew the place was wired. Certain of an audience now, Fletcher had:

1. Suggested the possibility that Corwin was not guilty.
2. Flatly stated that a cop named Carella suspected him.
3. Expressed admiration for Carella, while wondering if Carella was aware of it.
4. Speculated that Carella had already doped out the purpose of the bar crawling last Sunday night, was cognizant of Sarah's promiscuity, and knew Fletcher was aware of it.
5. Made a little joke about "telling" Carella.

Carella felt as eerie as he had when lunching with Fletcher and later when drinking with him. Now he'd spoken, through the bug, directly to Carella. But what was he trying to say? And why?

Carella wanted very much to hear what Fletcher would say when he didn't know he was being overheard. He asked Lieutenant Byrnes for permission to request a court order to put a bug in Fletcher's automobile. Byrnes granted permission, and the court issued the order.

Fletcher made a date with Arlene Orton to go to The Chandeliers across the river, and the bug was installed in Fletcher's 1972 car. If Fletcher left the city, the effective range of the transmitter on the open road would be about a quarter of a mile. The listener-pursuer had his work cut out for him.

By ten minutes to ten that night, Carella was drowsy and discouraged. On the way out to The Chandeliers, Fletcher and Arlene had not once mentioned Sarah or the plans for their impending marriage. Carella was anxious to put them both to bed and get home to his family. When they finally came out of the restaurant and began walking toward Fletcher's automobile, Carella actually uttered an audible, "At *last,*" and started his car.

They proceeded east on Route 701, heading for the bridge, and said nothing. Carella thought at first something was wrong with the equipment, then finally Arlene spoke and Carella knew just what had happened. The pair had argued in the restaurant, and Arlene had been smoldering until this moment when she could no longer contain her anger.

"Maybe you don't want to marry me at all," she shouted.

"That's ridiculous," Fletcher said.

"Then why won't you set a date?"

"I have set a date."

"You haven't set a date. All you've done is say after the trial. When, after the trial? Maybe this whole damn thing has been a stall. Maybe you never planned to marry me."

"You know that isn't true, Arlene."

"How do I know there really were separation papers?"

"There were. I told you there were."

"Then why wouldn't she sign them?"

"Because she loved me."

"If she loved you, then why did she do those horrible things?"

"To make me pay, I think."

"Is that why she showed you her little black book?"

"Yes, to make me pay."

"No. Because she was a slut."

"I guess. I guess that's what she became."

"Putting the little TG in her book every time she told you about a new one *Told Gerry,* and marked a little TG in her book."

"Yes, to make me pay."

"A slut. You should have gone after her with detectives. Gotten pictures, threatened her, forced her to sign—"

"No, I couldn't have done that. It would have ruined me, Arl."

"Your precious career."

"Yes, my precious career."

They both fell silent. They were approaching the bridge now. Carella tried to stay close behind them, but on occasion the distance between the two cars lengthened and he lost some words in the conversation.

"She wouldn't sign the papers and I (– –) adultery because (– –) have come out."

"And I thought (– –)."

"I did everything I possibly could."

"Yes, Gerry, but now she's dead. So what's your excuse now?"

"I'm suspected of having *killed* her, damn it!"

Fletcher was making a left turn, off the highway. Carella stepped on the accelerator, not wanting to lose voice contact now.

"What difference does that make?" Arlene asked.

"None at all, I'm sure," Fletcher said. "I'm sure you wouldn't mind at all being married to a convicted murderer."

"What are you talking about?"

"I'm talking about the possibility . . . never mind."

"Let me hear it."

"All right, Arlene. I'm talking about the possibility of someone accusing me of the murder. And of my having to stand trial for it."

"That's the most paranoid—"

"It's not paranoid."

"Then what is it? They've caught the murderer, they—"

"I'm only saying suppose. How could we get married if I killed her, if someone says I killed her?"

"No one has said that, Gerry."

"Well, *if* someone should."

Silence. Carella was dangerously close to Fletcher's car now, and risking discovery. Carella held his breath and stayed glued to the car ahead.

"Gerry, I don't understand this," Arlene said, her voice low.

"Someone could make a good case for it."

"They could say I came into the apartment and . . . They could say she was still alive when I came into the apartment. They could say the knife was still in her and I . . . I came in and found her that way and . . . finished her off."

"Why would you do that?"

"To end it."

"You wouldn't kill anyone, Gerry."

"No."

"Then why are you even suggesting such a terrible thing?"

"If she wanted it . . . If someone accused me . . . If someone said I'd done it . . . that I'd finished the job, pulled the knife across her belly, they could claim she *asked* me to do it."

"What are you saying, Gerry?"

"I'm trying to explain that Sarah might have—"

"Gerry. I don't think I want to know."

"I'm only trying to tell you—"

"No, I don't want to know. Please. Gerry, you're frightening me."

"*Listen* to me, damn it! I'm trying to explain what *might* have happened. Is that so hard to accept? That she might have *asked* me to kill her?"

"Gerry, please, I—"

"I *wanted* to call the hospital, I was *ready* to call the hospital. Don't you think I could *see* she wasn't fatally stabbed?"

"Gerry, please, I—"

"She begged me to kill her, Arlene. She begged me to end it for her, she . . . Damn it, can't *either* of you understand that? I tried to show him, I took him to all the places, I thought he was a man who'd understand. Is it that difficult?"

"Oh, my God, *did* you kill her? *Did* you kill Sarah?"

"No. Not Sarah. Only the woman she'd become, the slut I'd forced her to become. She was Sadie, you see, when I killed her—when she died."

"Oh, my God," Arlene said, and Carella nodded in weary acceptance.

Carella felt neither elated nor triumphant. As he followed Fletcher's car into the curb in front of Arlene's building, he experienced only a familiar nagging sense of repetition and despair. Fletcher was coming out of his car now, walking around to the curb side, opening the door for Arlene, who took his hand and stepped onto the sidewalk, weeping. Carella intercepted them before they reached the front of the building. Quietly, he charged Fletcher with the murder of his wife, and made the arrest without resistance.

Fletcher did not seem at all surprised.

So it was finished, or at least Carella thought it was.

In the silence of his living room, the telephone rang at a quarter past one. He caught the phone on the third ring.

"Hello?"

"Steve," Lieutenant Byrnes said, "I just got a call from Calcutta. Ralph Corwin hanged himself in his cell, just after midnight. Must have done it while we were still taking Fletcher's confession in the squad room."

Carella was silent.

"Steve?" Byrnes said.

"Yeah, Pete."

"Nothing," Byrnes said, and hung up.

Carella stood with the dead phone in his hands for several seconds and then replaced it on the hook. He looked into the living room, where the lights of the tree glowed warmly, and thought of a despairing junkie in a prison cell, who had taken his own life without ever having known he had not taken the life of another.

It was Christmas Day.

Sometimes, none of it made any sense at all.

The Theft of the Royal Ruby

Agatha Christie

In Hercule Poirot, the professional Belgian detective of immaculate dress and manners, Agatha Christie created one of crime fiction's greatest, if most unlikely, heroes. Poirot is best known for his unflinching self-belief, as witnessed in his rather turbulent relationship with Inspector Japp of Scotland Yard. Based in London but often portrayed as an outsider in the society of the period, Poirot views the English as a rather puzzling race. Featured in over forty novels and short stories, Hercule Poirot has been played on the big screen by, among others, Tony Randall, Albert Finney, Ian Holm, and perhaps most accurately by Sir Peter Ustinov in the film adaptations of *Murder on the Orient Express* and *Evil Under the Sun.* Poirot was also portrayed by David Suchet in many TV appearances.

"I regret exceedingly . . ." said M. Hercule Poirot.

He was interrupted. Not rudely interrupted. The interruption was suave and dexterous.

"Please don't refuse offhand, Monsieur Poirot. There are grave issues of State. Your cooperation will be appreciated in the highest quarters."

"You are too kind," Hercule Poirot waved his hand, "but I really cannot undertake to do as you ask. At this season of the year . . ."

Again, Mr. Jesmond interrupted. "Christmas time," he said persuasively. "An old-fashioned Christmas in the English countryside."

Hercule Poirot shivered. The English countryside at this season of the year did not attract him.

"A good old-fashioned Christmas!" Mr. Jesmond stressed it.

"Me—I am not an Englishman," said Hercule Poirot. "In my country Christmas, it is for the children. The New Year, that is what we celebrate."

"Ah," said Mr. Jesmond, "but Christmas in England is a great institution and I assure you at Kings Lacey you would see it at its best. It's a wonderful house, you know. Why, one wing of it dates from the fourteenth century."

Again, Poirot shivered. The thought of a fourteenth century English manor house filled him with apprehension. He had suffered too often in the historic country houses of England. He looked round appreciatively at his comfortable modern flat with its radiators and the latest patent devices for excluding any kind of draft.

"In the winter," he said firmly, "I do not leave London."

"I don't think you quite appreciate, Monsieur Poirot, what a very serious matter this is." Mr. Jesmond glanced at his companion and then back at Poirot.

Poirot's second visitor had up to now said nothing but a polite and formal "How do you do." He sat now, gazing down at his well-polished shoes, with an air of the utmost dejection on his coffee-colored face. He was a young man, not more than twenty-three, and he was clearly in a state of complete misery.

"Yes, yes," said Hercule Poirot. "Of course the matter is serious. I do appreciate that. His Highness has my heartfelt sympathy."

"The position is one of utmost delicacy," said Mr. Jesmond.

Poirot transferred his gaze from the young man to his older companion. If one wanted to sum up Mr. Jesmond in a word, the word would have been discretion. Everything about Mr. Jesmond was discreet. His well-cut but inconspicuous clothes, his agreeable, well-bred voice, which rarely soared out of an agreeable monotone, his light brown hair just thinning a little at the temples, his pale serious face. It seemed to Hercule Poirot that he had known not one Mr. Jesmond but a dozen Mr. Jesmonds in his time, all using sooner or later the same phrase—"a position of the utmost delicacy."

"The police," said Hercule Poirot, "can be very discreet, you know."

Mr. Jesmond shook his head firmly.

"Not the police," he said. "To recover the—er—what we want to recover will almost inevitably involve taking proceedings in the law courts and we know so little. We *suspect,* but we do not know."

"You have my sympathy," said Hercule Poirot again.

If he imagined that his sympathy was going to mean anything to his two visitors, he was wrong. They did not want sympathy, they wanted practical help. Mr. Jesmond began once more to talk about the delights of an English Christmas.

"It's dying out, you know," he said, "the real old-fashioned type of Christmas. People spend it at hotels nowadays. But an English Christmas with all the family gathered round, the children and their stockings, the Christmas tree, the turkey and plum pudding, the crackers. The snowman outside the window . . ."

In the interests of exactitude, Hercule Poirot intervened.

"To make a snowman one has to have the snow," he remarked severely. "And one cannot have the snow to order, even for an English Christmas."

"I was talking to a friend of mine in the meteorological office only today," said Mr. Jesmond, "and he tells me that it is highly probable there *will* be snow this Christmas."

It was the wrong thing to have said. Hercule Poirot shuddered more forcefully than ever.

"Snow in the country!" he said. "That would be still more abominable. A large, cold, stone manor house."

"Not at all," said Mr. Jesmond. "Things have changed very much in the last ten years or so. Oil-fired central heating."

"They have oil-fired central heating at Kings Lacey?" asked Poirot. For the first time he seemed to waver.

Mr. Jesmond seized his opportunity. "Yes, indeed," he said, "and a splendid hot water system. Radiators in every bedroom. I assure you, my dear Monsieur Poirot, Kings Lacey is comfort itself in the wintertime. You might even find the house *too* warm."

"That is most unlikely," said Hercule Poirot.

With practiced dexterity Mr. Jesmond shifted his ground a little.

"You can appreciate the terrible dilemma we are in," he said, in a confidential manner.

Hercule Poirot nodded. The problem was, indeed, not a happy one. A young potentate-to-be, the only son of the ruler of a rich and important native State had arrived in London a few weeks ago. His country had been passing through a period of restlessness and discontent. Though loyal to the father whose way of life had remained persistently Eastern, popular opinion was somewhat dubious of the younger generation. His follies had been Western ones and as such looked upon with disapproval.

Recently, however, his betrothal had been announced. He was to marry a cousin of the same blood, a young woman who, though educated at Cambridge, was careful to display no Western influences in her own country. The wedding day was announced and the young prince had made a journey to England, bringing with him some of the famous jewels of his house to be reset in appropriate modern settings by Cartier. These had included a very famous ruby which had been removed from its cumbersome old-fashioned necklace, and had been given a new look by the famous jewelers.

So far so good, but after this came the snag. It was not to be supposed that a young man possessed of much wealth and convivial tastes, should not commit a few follies of the pleasanter type. As to that there would have been no censure. Young princes were supposed to amuse themselves in this fashion. For the prince to take the girlfriend of the moment for a walk down Bond Street and bestow upon her an emerald bracelet or a diamond clip as a reward for the pleasure she had afforded him would have been regarded as quite natural and suitable, corresponding in fact to the Cadillac cars which his father invariably presented to his favorite dancing girl of the moment.

But the prince had been far more indiscreet than that. Flattered by the lady's interest, he had displayed to her the famous ruby in its new setting, and had finally been so unwise as to accede to her request to be allowed to wear it—just for one evening!

The sequel was short and sad. The lady retired from their supper table to powder her nose. Time passed. She did not return. She had left the establishment by another door and since then had disappeared into space. The important and distressing thing was that the ruby in its new setting had disappeared with her.

These were the facts that could not possibly be made public without the most dire consequences. The ruby was something more than a ruby, it was a historical possession of great significance, and the circumstances of its disappearance were such that any undue publicity might result in the most serious political consequences.

Mr. Jesmond was not the man to put these facts into simple language. He wrapped them up, as it were, in a great deal of verbiage. Who exactly Mr. Jesmond was,

Hercule Poirot did not exactly know. He had met other Mr. Jesmonds in his career. Whether he was connected with the Home Office, the Foreign Office, or some more discreet branch of public service was not specified. He was acting in the interests of the Commonwealth. The ruby must be recovered.

Monsieur Poirot, so Mr. Jesmond delicately insisted, was the man to recover it.

"Perhaps—yes," Hercule Poirot admitted, "but you can tell me so little. Suggestion—suspicion—all that is not very much to go upon."

"Come now, Monsieur Poirot, surely it is not beyond your powers. Ah, come now."

"I do not always succeed."

But this was mock modesty. It was clear enough from Poirot's tone that for him to undertake a mission was almost synonymous with succeeding in it.

"His Highness is very young," Mr. Jesmond said. "It will be sad if his whole life is to be blighted for a mere youthful indiscretion."

Poirot looked kindly at the downcast young man. "It is the time for follies, when one is young," he said encouragingly, "and for the ordinary young man it does not matter so much. The good papa, he pays up; the family lawyer, he helps to disentangle the inconvenience; the young man, he learns by experience and all ends for the best. In a position such as yours, it is hard indeed. Your approaching marriage . . ."

"That is it. That is it exactly." For the first time words poured from the young man. "You see she is very, very serious. She takes life very seriously. She has acquired at Cambridge many very serious ideas. There is to be education in my country. There are to be schools. There are to be many things. All in the name of progress, you understand, of democracy. It will not be, she says, as it was in my father's time. Naturally she knows that I will have diversions in London, but not the scandal. No! It is the scandal that matters. You see it is very, very famous, this ruby. There is a long trail behind it, a history. Much bloodshed—many deaths!"

"Deaths," said Hercule Poirot thoughtfully. He looked at Mr. Jesmond. "One hopes," he said, "it will not come to that?"

Mr. Jesmond made a peculiar noise rather like a hen who has decided to lay an egg and then thought better of it.

"No, no, indeed," he said, sounding rather prim. "There is no question, I am sure, of anything of *that* kind."

"You can be sure," said Hercule Poirot. "Whoever has the ruby now, there may be others who want to gain possession of it, and who will not stick at a trifle, my friend."

"I really don't think," said Mr. Jesmond, sounding more prim than ever, "that we need enter into speculations of that kind. Quite unprofitable."

"Me," said Hercule Poirot, suddenly becoming very foreign, "me, I explore all avenues, like the politicians."

Mr. Jesmond looked at him doubtfully. Pulling himself together, he said, "Well, I can take it that it is settled, Monsieur Poirot? You will go to Kings Lacey?"

"And how do I explain myself there?" asked Hercule Poirot.

Mr. Jesmond smiled with confidence.

"That, I think, can be arranged very easily," he said. "I can assure you that it will all seem quite natural. You will find the Laceys most charming. Delightful people."

"And you do not deceive me about the oil-fired central heating?"

"No, no, indeed." Mr. Jesmond sounded quite pained. "I assure you, you will find every comfort."

"*Tout confort moderne,*" murmured Poirot to himself reminiscently. "*Eh bien,*" he said, "I accept."

The temperature in the long drawing room at Kings Lacey was a comfortable 68 as Hercule Poirot sat talking to Mrs. Lacey by one of the big mullioned windows. Mrs. Lacey was engaged in needlework. She was not doing *petit point* or embroidering flowers on silk. Instead, she appeared to be engaged in the prosaic task of hemming dishcloths. As she sewed she talked in a soft reflective voice that Poirot found very charming.

"I hope you will enjoy our Christmas party here, Monsieur Poirot. It's only the family you know. My granddaughter and a grandson and a friend of his and Bridget who's my great-niece, and Diana who's a cousin and David Welwyn who is a very old friend. Just a family party. But Edwina Morecombe said that that's what you really wanted to see. An old-fashioned Christmas. Nothing could be more old-fashioned than we are!

"My husband, you know, absolutely lives in the past. He likes everything to be just as it was when he was a boy of twelve years old, and used to come here for his holidays." She smiled to herself. "All the same old things, the Christmas tree and the stockings hung up and the oyster soup and the turkey—two turkeys, one boiled and one roast—and the plum pudding with the ring and the bachelor's button and all the rest of it in it. We can't have sixpences nowadays because they are not pure silver any more. But all the old desserts, the Elvas plums and Carlsbad plums and almonds and raisins, and crystallized fruit and ginger. Dear me, I sound like a catalogue from Fortnum and Mason!"

"You arouse my gastronomic juices, madame."

"I expect we'll all have frightful indigestion by tomorrow evening," said Mrs. Lacey. "One isn't used to eating so much nowadays, is one?"

She was interrupted by some loud shouts and whoops of laughter outside the window. She glanced out.

"I don't know what they're doing out there. Playing some game or other, I suppose. I've always been so afraid, you know, that these young people would be bored by our Christmas here. But not at all, it's just the opposite. Now my own son and daughter and their friends, they used to be rather sophisticated about Christmas. Say it was all nonsense and too much fuss and it would be far better to go out to a hotel somewhere and dance. But the younger generation seem to find all this terribly attractive. Besides," added Mrs. Lacey practically, "schoolboys and schoolgirls are always hungry, aren't they? I think they must starve them at these schools. After all, one does know children of that age each eat about as much as three strong men."

Poirot laughed and said, "It is most kind of you and your husband, madame, to include me in your family party."

"Oh, we are both delighted, I'm sure," said Mrs. Lacey. "And if you find Horace a little gruff," she continued, "pay no attention. It's just his manner, you know."

What her husband, Colonel Lacey, had actually said was: "Can't think why you want one of these damned foreigners here cluttering up Christmas. Why can't we have him some other time? Can't stick foreigners! All right, all right, so Edwina Morecombe wished him on us. What's it got to do with her, I should like to know? Why doesn't *she* have him for Christmas?"

"Because you know very well," Mrs. Lacey had said, "that Edwina always goes to Claridge's."

Her husband had looked at her piercingly and said, "Not up to something are you, Em?"

"Up to something?" said Em, opening her blue eyes. "Of course not. Why should I be?"

Old Colonel Lacey laughed, a deep rumbling laugh. "I wouldn't put it past you, Em," he said. "When you look your most innocent is when you are up to something."

Revolving these things in her mind, Mrs. Lacey went on, "Edwina said she thought perhaps you might help us. . . . I'm sure I don't know quite how, but she said that friends of yours had once found you very helpful in—in a case something like ours. I—well, perhaps you don't know what I am talking about?"

Poirot looked at her encouragingly. Mrs. Lacey was close to seventy, as upright as a ramrod, with snow-white hair, pink cheeks, blue eyes, a ridiculous nose, and a determined chin.

If there is anything I can do I shall only be too happy to do it," said Poirot. "It is, I understand, a rather unfortunate matter of a young girl's infatuation."

Mrs. Lacey nodded. "Yes. It seems extraordinary that I should—well, want to talk to you about it. After all, you *are* a perfect stranger."

"*And* a foreigner," said Poirot in an understanding manner.

"Yes," said Mrs. Lacey, "but perhaps that makes it easier, in a way. Anyhow, Edwina seemed to think that you might perhaps know something—how shall I put it—something useful about this young Desmond Lee-Wortley."

Poirot paused a moment to admire the ingenuity of Mr. Jesmond and the ease with which he had made use of Lady Morecombe to further his own purposes.

"He has not, I understand, a very good reputation, this young man?" he began delicately.

"No, indeed, he hasn't! A very bad reputation! But that's no help so far as Sarah is concerned. It's never any good, is it, telling young girls that men have a bad reputation? It—it just spurs them on!"

"You are so very right," said Poirot.

"In my young day," went on Mrs. Lacey. "Oh dear, that's a very long time ago! We used to be warned, you know, against certain young men, and of course it *did* heighten one's interest in them, and if one could possibly manage to dance with them, or to be alone with them in a dark conservatory . . ." She laughed. "That's why I wouldn't let Horace do any of the things he wanted to do."

"Tell me," said Poirot, "exactly what it is that troubles you?"

"Our son was killed in the war," said Mrs. Lacey. "My daughter-in-law died when Sarah was born so that Sarah has always been with us, and we've brought her up. Perhaps we've brought her up unwisely—I don't know. But we thought we ought to leave her as free as possible."

"That is desirable, I think," said Poirot. "One cannot go against the spirit of the times."

"No," said Mrs. Lacey, "that's just what I felt about it. And, of course, girls nowadays do this sort of thing."

Poirot looked at her inquiringly.

"I think the way one expresses it," said Mrs. Lacey, "is that Sarah has got in with what they call the coffee-bar set. She won't go to dances or come out properly or be a deb or anything of that kind. Instead she has two rather unpleasant rooms in Chelsea down by the river and wears these funny clothes that they like to wear, and black stockings, or bright green ones, Very thick stockings. So prickly, I always think! And she goes about without washing or combing her hair."

"Ça, c'est tout à fait naturelle," said Poirot. "It is the fashion of the moment. They grow out of it."

"Yes, I know," said Mrs. Lacey. "I wouldn't worry about *that* sort of thing. But you see she's taken up with this Desmond Lee-Wortley and he really has a very unsavory reputation. He lives more or less on well-to-do girls. They seem to go quite mad about him. He very nearly married the Hope girl, but her people got her made a ward of court or something. And of course that's what Horace wants to do. He says he must do it for her protection.

"But I don't think it's really a good idea, Monsieur Poirot. I mean, they'll just run away together and go to Scotland or Ireland or the Argentine or somewhere and either get married or else live together without getting married. And although it may be contempt of court and all that—well, it isn't really an answer, is it, in the end? Especially if a baby's coming. One has to give in then, and let them get married. And then, nearly always, it seems to me, after a year or two there's a divorce. And then the girl comes home and usually after a year or two she marries someone so nice he's almost dull and settles down.

"But it's particularly sad, it seems to me, if there is a child, because it's not the same thing, being brought up by a stepfather, however nice. No, I think it's much better if we did as we did in my young days. I mean the first young man one fell in love with was *always* someone undesirable. I remember I had a horrible passion for a young man called—now what was his name?—how strange it is, I can't remember his Christian name at all! Tibbitt, that was his surname. Young Tibbitt.

"Of course, my father more or less forbade him the house, but he used to get asked to the same dances, and we used to dance together. And sometimes we'd escape and sit out together and occasionally friends would arrange picnics to which we both went. Of course, it was all very exciting and forbidden and one enjoyed it enormously. But one didn't go to the—well, to the lengths that girls go nowadays. And so, after a while, Mr. Tibbitts faded out. And do you know, when I saw him four years later I was surprised what I could ever have seen in him! He seemed to be such a *dull* young man. Flashy, you know. No interesting conversation."

"One always thinks the days of one's own youth are best," said Poirot, somewhat sententiously.

"I know," said Mrs. Lacey. "It's tiresome isn't it? I mustn't be tiresome. But all the same I *don't* want Sarah, who's a dear girl really, to marry Desmond Lee-Wortley. She and David Welwyn, who is staying here, were such friends and so fond of each other, and we did hope, Horace and I, that they would grow up and marry. But of course she just finds him dull now, and she's absolutely infatuated with Desmond."

"I do not quite understand, madame," said Poirot. "You have him here now, staying in the house, this Desmond Lee-Wortley?"

"That's *my* doing," said Mrs. Lacey. "Horace was all for forbidding her to see him and all that. Of course, in Horace's day, the father or guardian would have called round at the young man's lodgings with a horse whip! Horace was all for forbidding the fellow in the house, and forbidding the girl to see him. I told him that was quite the wrong attitude to take.

" 'No,' I said. 'Ask him down here. We'll have him down for Christmas with the family party.' Of course my husband said I was mad! But I said, 'At any rate, dear, let's *try* it. Let her see him in *our* atmosphere and *our* house and we'll be very nice to him and very polite, and perhaps then he'll seem less interesting to her!' "

"I think, as they say, you *have* something there, madame," said Poirot. "I think your point of view is very wise. Wiser than your husband's."

"Well, I hope it is," said Mrs. Lacey doubtfully. "It doesn't seem to be working much yet. But of course he's only been here a couple of days." A sudden dimple showed in her wrinkled cheek. "I'll confess something to you, Monsieur Poirot. I myself can't help liking him. I don't mean I *really* like him, with my *mind,* but I can feel the charm all right. Oh yes, I can see what Sarah sees in him.

"But I'm an old enough woman and have enough experience to know that he's absolutely no good. Even if I *do* enjoy his company. Though I do think," added Mrs. Lacey rather wistfully, "he has *some* good points. He asked if he might bring his sister here, you know. She's had an operation and was in the hospital. He said it was so sad for her being in a nursing home over Christmas and he wondered if it would be too much trouble if he could bring her with him. He said he'd take all her meals up to her and all that. Well now, I do think that was rather nice of him, don't you, Monsieur Poirot?"

"It shows a consideration," said Poirot thoughtfully, "which seems almost out of character."

"Oh, I don't know. You can have family affections at the same time as wishing to prey on a rich young girl. Sarah will be very rich, you know, not only with what we leave her—and of course that won't be much because most of the money goes with the place to Colin, my grandson. But her mother was a very rich woman and Sarah will inherit all her money when she's twenty-one. She's only twenty now.

"No, I do think it was nice of Desmond to mind about his sister. And he didn't pretend that she was anything very wonderful or that. She's a shorthand typist, I gather—does secretarial work in London. And he's been as good as his word and does carry up trays to her. Not all the time, of course, but quite often. So I think he has some nice points. But all the same," said Mrs. Lacey with great decision, "I don't want Sarah to marry him."

"From all I have heard and been told," said Poirot, "that would indeed be a disaster."

"Do you think it would be possible for you to help us in any way?" asked Mrs. Lacey.

"I think it is possible, yes," said Hercule Poirot, "but I do not wish to promise too much. For the Mr. Desmond Lee-Wortleys of this world are clever, madame. But do not despair. One can, perhaps, do a little something. I shall at any rate put forth my best endeavors, if only in gratitude for your kindness in asking me here for this Christmas festivity."

He looked round him. "And it cannot be so easy these days to have Christmas festivities."

"No indeed," Mrs. Lacey sighed. She leaned forward. "Do you know, Monsieur Poirot, what I really dream of—what I would love to have?"

"But tell me, madame."

"I simply long to have a small modern bungalow. No, perhaps not a bungalow exactly, but a small modern easy-to-run house built somewhere in the park here, and live in it with an absolutely up-to-date kitchen and no long passages. Everything easy and simple."

"It is a very practical idea, madame."

"It's not practical for me," said Mrs. Lacey. "My husband *adores* this place. He loves living here. He doesn't mind being slightly uncomfortable, he doesn't mind the inconveniences, and he would hate, simply *hate,* to live in a small modern house in the park!"

"So you sacrifice yourself to his wishes?"

Mrs. Lacey drew herself up. "I do not consider it a sacrifice, Monsieur Poirot," she said. "I married my husband with the wish to make him happy. He has been a good husband to me and made me very happy all these years, and I wish to give happiness to him."

"So you will continue to live here," said Poirot.

"It's not really too uncomfortable," said Mrs. Lacey.

"No, no," said Poirot hastily. "On the contrary, it is most comfortable. Your central heating and your bathwater are perfection."

"We spent a lot of money in making the house comfortable to live in," said Mrs. Lacey. "We were able to sell some land. Ripe for development, I think they call it. Fortunately out of sight of the house on the other side of the park. Really rather an ugly bit of ground with no nice view, but we got a very good price for it. So that we have been able to have as many improvements as possible."

"But the service, madame?"

"Oh, well, that presents less difficulty than you might think. Of course, one cannot expect to be looked after and waited upon as one used to be. Different people come in from the village. Two women in the morning, another two to cook lunch and wash it up, and different ones again in the evening. There are plenty of people who want to come and work for a few hours a day. Of course for Christmas we are very lucky. My dear Mrs. Ross always comes in every Christmas. She is a wonderful cook, really first-class. She retired about ten years ago, but she comes in to help us in any emergency. Then there is dear Peverill."

"Your butler?"

"Yes, he is pensioned off and lives in the little house near the lodge, but he is so devoted, and he insists on coming to wait on us at Christmas. Really, I'm terrified, Monsieur Poirot, because he's so old and so shaky that I feel certain that if he carries anything heavy he will drop it. It's really an agony to watch him. And his heart is not good and I'm afraid of his doing too much. But it would hurt his feelings dreadfully if I did not let him come.

"He hems and hahs and makes disapproving noises when he sees the state our silver is in and within three days of being here, it is all wonderful again. Yes, he is a dear faithful friend." She smiled at Poirot. "So you see, we are all set for a happy Christmas. A white Christmas too," she added as she looked out of the window. "See? It is beginning to snow. Ah, the children are coming in. You must meet them, Monsieur Poirot."

Poirot was introduced with due ceremony. First, to Colin and Michael, the schoolboy grandson and his friend, nice polite lads of fifteen, one dark, one fair. Then to their cousin, Bridget, a black-haired girl of about the same age with enormous vitality.

"And this is my granddaughter, Sarah," said Mrs. Lacey.

Poirot looked with some interest at Sarah, an attractive girl with a mop of red hair; her manner seemed to him nervy and a trifle defiant, but she showed real affection for her grandmother.

"And this is Mr. Lee-Wortley."

Mr. Lee-Wortley wore a fisherman's jersey and tight black jeans; his hair was rather long and it seemed doubtful whether he had shaved that morning. In contrast to him was a young man introduced as David Welwyn, who was solid and quiet, with a pleasant smile, and rather obviously addicted to soap and water. There was one other member of the party, a handsome, rather intense-looking girl who was introduced as Diana Middleton.

Tea was brought in. A hearty meal of scones, crumpets, sandwiches, and three kinds of cake. The younger members of the party appreciated the tea.

Colonel Lacey came in last, remarking in a noncommittal voice, "Hey, tea? Oh, yes, tea."

He received his cup of tea from his wife's hand, helped himself to two scones, cast a look of aversion at Desmond Lee-Wortley and sat down as far away from him as he could. He was a big man with bushy eyebrows and a red, weather-beaten face. He might have been taken for a farmer rather than the lord of the manor.

"Started to snow," he said. "It's going to be a white Christmas all right."

After tea the party dispersed.

"I expect they'll go and play with their tape recorders now," said Mrs. Lacey to Poirot. She looked indulgently after her grandson as he left the room. Her tone was that of one who says, "The children are going to play with their toy soldiers."

"They're frightfully technical, of course," she said, "and very grand about it all."

The boys and Bridget, however, decided to go along to the lake and see if the ice on it was likely to make skating possible.

"I thought we could have skated on it this morning," said Colin. "But old Hodgkins said no. He's always so terribly careful."

"Come for a walk, David," said Diana Middleton softly. David hesitated for half a moment, his eyes on Sarah's red head. She was standing by Desmond Lee-Wortley, her hand on his arm, looking up into his face.

"All right," said David Welwyn, "yes, let's."

Diana slipped a quick hand through his arm and they turned toward the door into the garden.

Sarah said, "Shall we go, too, Desmond? It's fearfully stuffy in the house."

"Who wants to walk?" said Desmond. "I'll get my car out. We'll go along to the Speckled Boar and have a drink."

Sarah hesitated for a moment before saying, "Let's go to Market Ledbury to the White Hart. It's much more fun."

Though for all the world she would not have put it into words, Sarah had an instinctive revulsion to going down to the local pub with Desmond. It was, somehow, not in the tradition of Kings Lacey. The women of Kings Lacey had never frequented the bar of the Speckled Boar. She had an obscure feeling that to go there would be to let Old Colonel Lacey and his wife down.

And why not? Desmond Lee-Wortley would have said. For a moment of exasperation Sarah felt that he ought to know why not! One didn't upset such old darlings as Grandfather and dear old Em unless it was necessary. They'd been very sweet, really, letting her lead her own life, not understanding in the least why she wanted to live in Chelsea the way she did, but accepting it. That was due to Em, of course. Grandfather would have kicked up no end of a row.

Sarah had no illusions about her grandfather's attitude. It was not his doing that Desmond had been asked to stay at Kings Lacey. That was Em, and Em was a darling and always had been.

When Desmond had gone to fetch his car, Sarah popped her head into the drawing room again.

"We're going over to Market Ledbury," she said. "We thought we'd have a drink there at the White Hart."

There was a slight amount of defiance in her voice, but Mrs. Lacey did not seem to notice it.

"Well, dear," she said, "I'm sure that will be very nice. David and Diana have gone for a walk, I see. I'm so glad. I really think it was a brainwave on my part to ask Diana here. So sad being left a widow so young—only twenty-two—I do hope she marries again *soon.*"

Sarah looked up at her sharply. "What are you up to, Em?"

"It's my little plan," said Mrs. Lacey gleefully. "I think she's just right for David. Of course I knew he was terribly in love with *you,* Sarah dear, but you'd no use for him and I realize that he isn't your type. But I don't want him to go on being unhappy, and I think Diana will really suit him."

"What a matchmaker you are, Em," said Sarah.

"I know," said Mrs. Lacey. "Old women always are. Diana's quite keen on him already, I think. Don't you think she's right for him?"

"I shouldn't say so," said Sarah. "I think Diana's far too—well, too intense, too serious. I should think David would find it terribly boring being married to her."

"Well we'll see," said Mrs. Lacey. "Anyway, *you* don't want him, do you, dear?"

"No, indeed," said Sarah very quickly. She added, in a sudden rush, "You *do* like Desmond, don't you, Em?"

"I'm sure he's very nice indeed," said Mrs. Lacey.

"Grandfather doesn't like him," said Sarah.

"Well, you could hardly expect him to, could you?" said Mrs. Lacey reasonably, "but I daresay he'll come round when he gets used to the idea. You mustn't rush him, Sarah dear. Old people are very slow to change their minds and your grandfather is rather obstinate."

"I don't care what Grandfather thinks or says," said Sarah. "I shall get married to Desmond whenever I like!"

"I know, dear, I know. But do try and be realistic about it. Your grandfather could cause a lot of trouble, you know. You're not of age yet. In another year you can do as you please. I expect Horace will have come round long before that."

"You're on my side, aren't you, darling?" said Sarah. She flung her arms round her grandmother's neck and gave her an affectionate kiss.

"I want you to be happy," said Mrs. Lacey. "Ah, there's your young man bringing his car round. You know, I like these very tight trousers these young men wear nowadays. They look so smart—only, of course, it does accentuate knock-knees."

Yes, Sarah thought, Desmond does have knock-knees; she had never noticed it before . . .

"Go on dear, enjoy yourself," said Mrs. Lacey.

She watched her go out to the car, and then, remembering her foreign guest, she went along to the library. Looking in, however, she saw that Hercule Poirot was taking a pleasant little nap, and smiling to herself, she went across the hall and out into the kitchen to have a consultation with Mrs. Ross.

"Come on, beautiful," said Desmond. "Your family cutting up rough because you're coming out to a pub? Years behind the times here, aren't they?"

"Of course they're not making a fuss," said Sarah sharply as she got into the car.

"What's the idea of having that foreign fellow down? He's a detective, isn't he? What needs detecting here?"

"Oh, he's not here professionally," said Sarah. "Edwina Morecombe, my godmother, asked us to have him. I think he retired from professional work long ago."

"Sounds like a broken-down old cab horse," said Desmond.

"He wanted to see an old-fashioned English Christmas, I believe," said Sarah vaguely.

Desmond laughed scornfully. "Such a lot of tripe, that sort of thing," he said. "How you can stand it I don't know."

Sarah's red hair was tossed back and her aggressive chin shot up.

"I enjoy it!" she said defiantly.

"You can't, baby. Let's cut the whole thing tomorrow. Go over to Scarborough or somewhere."

"I couldn't possibly do that."

"Why not?"

"Oh, it would hurt their feelings."

"Oh, bilge! You know you don't enjoy this sentimental bosh."

"Well, not really perhaps, but . . ." Sarah broke off. She realized with a feeling of guilt that she was looking forward a good deal to the Christmas celebration. She enjoyed the whole thing, but she was ashamed to admit it to Desmond. It was not the thing to enjoy Christmas and family life.

Just for a moment she wished that Desmond had not come down here at Christmastime. In fact, she almost wished that Desmond had not come down here at all. It was much more fun seeing Desmond in London than here at home.

In the meantime the boys and Bridget were walking back from the lake, still discussing earnestly the problems of skating. Flecks of snow had been falling, and looking up at the sky it could have been prophesied that before long there was going to be a heavy snowfall.

"It's going to snow all night," said Colin. "Bet you by Christmas morning we'll have a couple of feet of snow."

The prospect was a pleasurable one.

"Let's make a snowman," said Michael.

"Good lord," said Colin, "I haven't made a snowman since—well, since I was about four years old."

"I don't believe it's a bit easy to do," said Bridget. "I mean, you have to know how."

"We might make an effigy of Monsieur Poirot," said Colin. "Give it a big black mustache. There is one in the dressing-up box."

"I don't see, you know," said Michael thoughtfully, "how Monsieur Poirot could ever have been a detective. I don't see how he'd ever be able to disguise himself."

"I know," said Bridget, "and one can't imagine him running about with a microscope and looking for clues or measuring footprints."

"I've got an idea," said Colin. "Let's put on a show for him!"

"What do you mean, a show?" asked Bridget.

"We'll arrange a murder for him."

"What a gorgeous idea," said Bridget. "Do you mean a body in the snow—that sort of thing?"

"Yes. It would make him feel at home, wouldn't it?"

Bridget giggled.

"I don't know that I'd go as far as that."

"If it snows," said Colin, "we'll have the perfect setting. A body and footprints. We'll have to think that out rather carefully and pinch one of Grandfather's daggers and make some blood."

They came to a halt and oblivious of the rapidly falling snow, entered into an excited discussion.

"There's a paint box in the old schoolroom. We could mix up some blood—crimson-lake, I should think."

"Crimson-lake's a bit too pink, *I* think," said Bridget. "It ought to be a bit browner."

"Who's going to be the body?" asked Michael.

"I'll be the body," said Bridget quickly.

"Oh, look here," said Colin, "*I* thought of it."

"Oh, no, no," said Bridget, "it must be me. It's got to be a girl. It's more exciting. Beautiful girl lying lifeless in the snow."

"Beautiful girl! Ah-ha," said Michael in derision.

"I've got black hair, too," said Bridget.

"What's that got to do with it?"

"Well, it'll show up so well on the snow and I shall wear my red pajamas."

"If you wear red pajamas, they won't show the bloodstains," said Michael in a practical manner.

"But they'd look so effective against the snow," said Bridget, "and they've got white facings, you know, so the blood could be on that. Oh, won't it be gorgeous? Do you think he will really be taken in?"

"He will if we do it well enough," said Michael. "We'll have just your footprints in the snow and one other person's going to the body and coming away from it—a man's, of course. He won't want to disturb them, so he won't know that you're not really dead. You don't think –" Michael stopped, struck by a sudden idea. "You don't think he'll be *annoyed* about it?"

"Oh, I shouldn't think so," said Bridget, with facile optimism. "I'm sure he'll understand that we've just done it to entertain him. A sort of Christmas treat."

"I don't think we ought to do it on Christmas Day," said Colin reflectively. "I don't think Grandfather would like that very much."

"The day after, then," said Bridget.

"The day after would be just right," said Michael.

"And it'll give us more time, too," pursued Bridget. "After all, there are a lot of things to arrange. Let's go and have a look at all the props."

They hurried into the house.

* * * *

The evening was a busy one. Holly and mistletoe had been brought in in large quantities and a Christmas tree had been set up at one end of the dining room. Everyone helped to decorate it, to put up the branches of holly behind pictures, and to hang mistletoe in a convenient position in the hall.

"I had no idea anything so archaic still went on," murmured Desmond to Sarah with a sneer.

"We've always done it," said Sarah defensively.

"What a reason!"

"Oh, don't be tiresome, Desmond. *I* think it's fun."

"Sarah, my sweet, you *can't!* "

"Well, not—not really perhaps, but—I do in a way."

"Who's going to brave the snow and go to midnight mass?" asked Mrs. Lacey at twenty minutes to twelve.

"Not me," said Desmond. "Come on, Sarah."

With a hand on her arm he guided her into the library and went over to the record case.

"There are limits, darling," said Desmond. "Midnight mass!"

"Yes," said Sarah. "Oh, yes."

With a good deal of laughter, donning of coats, and stamping of feet, most of the others got off. The two boys, Bridget, David, and Diana set out for the ten minutes' walk to the church through the falling snow. Their laughter died away in the distance.

"Midnight mass!" said Colonel Lacey, snorting. "Never went to midnight mass in my young days. *Mass,* indeed! Popish that is! Oh, I beg your pardon, Monsieur Poirot."

Poirot waved a hand. "It is quite all right. Do not mind me."

"Matins is good enough for anybody, I should say," said the colonel. "Proper Sunday morning service. 'Hark the Herald Angels Sing,' and all the good old Christmas hymns. And then back to Christmas dinner. That's right, isn't it, Em?"

"Yes, dear," said Mrs. Lacey. "That's what *we* do. But the young ones enjoy the midnight service. And it's nice, really, that they *want* to go."

"Sarah and that fellow don't want to go."

"Well, there dear, I think you're wrong," said Mrs. Lacey. "Sarah, you know, did want to go, but she didn't like to say so."

"Beats me why she cares what that fellow's opinion is."

"She's very young, really," said Mrs. Lacey placidly. "Are you going to bed, Monsieur Poirot? Good night. I hope you'll sleep well."

"And you madame? Are you not going to bed yet?"

"Not just yet," said Mrs. Lacey. "I've got the stockings to fill, you see. Oh, I know they're all practically grown up, but they do *like* their stockings. One puts jokes in them! Silly little things. But it all makes for a lot of fun."

"You work very hard to make this a happy house at Christmastime," said Poirot. "I honor you."

He raised her hand to his lips in a courtly fashion.

"Hm," grunted Colonel Lacey, as Poirot departed. "Flowery sort of fellow. Still—he appreciates you."

Mrs. Lacey dimpled up at him. "Have you noticed, Horace, that I'm standing under the mistletoe?" she asked with the demureness of a girl of nineteen.

Hercule Poirot entered his bedroom. It was a large room well provided with radiators. As he went over towards the big four-poster bed he noticed an envelope lying on his pillow. He opened it and drew out a piece of paper. On it was a shakily printed message in capital letters.

DON'T EAT NONE OF THE PLUM PUDDING.

ONE AS WISHES YOU WELL

Hercule Poirot stared at it. His eyebrows rose. "Cryptic," he murmured, "and most unexpected."

Christmas dinner took place at two o'clock and was a feast indeed. Enormous logs crackled merrily in the wide fireplace and above their crackling rose the babel of many tongues talking together. Oyster soup had been consumed, two enormous turkeys had come and gone, mere carcasses of their former selves. Now, the supreme moment, the Christmas pudding was brought in—in state!

Old Peverell, his hands and knees shaking with the weakness of eighty years, permitted no one but himself to bear it in. Mrs. Lacey sat, her hands pressed together in nervous apprehension. One Christmas, she felt sure, Peverell would fall down dead. Having either to take the risk of letting him fall down dead or of hurting his feelings to such an extent that he would probably prefer to be dead than alive, she had so far chosen the former alternative.

On a silver dish the Christmas pudding reposed in its glory—a large football of a pudding with a piece of holly stuck in it like a triumphant flag and with glorious flames of blue and red rising round it. There was a cheer and cries of "Ooh-ah."

One thing Mrs. Lacey had done: she had prevailed on Peverell to set the pudding in front of her so that she could give out helpings rather than hand the whole pudding in turn around the table. She breathed a sigh of relief as it was deposited safely in front of her. Rapidly the plates were passed round, flames still licking the portions.

"Wish, Monsieur Poirot," cried Bridget. "Wish before the flame goes. Quick, Gran darling, quick."

Mrs. Lacey leaned back with a sigh of satisfaction. Operation Pudding had been a success. In front of everyone was a helping with flames still licking it. There was a momentary silence all round the table as everyone made a wish.

There was nobody to notice the rather curious expression on the face of Monsieur Poirot as he surveyed the portion of pudding on his plate. *"Don't eat none of the plum pudding."* What on earth did that sinister warning mean? There could be nothing different about his portion of plum pudding from that of everyone else! Sighing as he admitted himself baffled—and Hercule Poirot never liked to admit himself baffled—he picked up his spoon and fork.

"Hard sauce, Monsieur Poirot?" Poirot helped himself appreciatively to hard sauce.

"Swiped my best brandy again, eh, Em?" said the colonel good-humoredly from the other end of the table. Mrs. Lacey twinkled at him.

"Mrs. Ross insists on having the best brandy, dear," she said. "She says it makes all the difference."

"Well, well," said Colonel Lacey, "Christmas comes but once a year and Mrs. Ross is a great woman. A great woman and a great cook."

"She is indeed," said Colin. "Smashing plum pudding, this. Mmmm." He filled an appreciative mouth.

Gently, almost gingerly, Hercule Poirot attacked his portion of pudding. He ate a mouthful. It was delicious! He ate another. Something tinkled faintly on his plate. He investigated with a fork. Bridget, on his left, came to his aid.

"You've got something, Monsieur Poirot," she said. "I wonder what it is."

Poirot detached a little silver object from the surrounding raisins.

"Oooh," said Bridget, "it's the bachelor's button! Monsieur Poirot's got the bachelor's button!"

Hercule Poirot dipped the small silver button into the finger bowl of water that stood by his plate and washed it clear of pudding crumbs.

"It is very pretty," he observed.

"That means you're going to be a bachelor, Monsieur Poirot," explained Colin helpfully.

"That is to be expected," said Poirot gravely. "I have been a bachelor for many long years and it is unlikely that I shall change that status now."

"Oh, never say die," said Michael. "I saw in the paper that someone of ninety-five married a girl of twenty-two the other day."

"You encourage me," said Hercule Poirot.

Colonel Lacey uttered a sudden exclamation. His face became purple and his hand went to his mouth.

"Confound it, Emmeline," he roared, "why on earth do you let the cook put glass in the pudding?"

"Glass!" cried Mrs. Lacey, astonished.

Colonel Lacey withdrew the offending substance from his mouth. "Might have broken a tooth," he grumbled. "Or swallowed the damn thing and had appendicitis."

He dropped the piece of glass into the finger bowl, rinsed it, and held it up.

"God bless my soul," he exclaimed. "It's a huge red stone out of one of the cracker brooches."

"You permit?"

Very deftly, Monsieur Poirot stretched across his neighbor, took it from Colonel Lacey's fingers, and examined it attentively. As the squire had said, it was an enormous red stone the color of a ruby. The light gleamed from its facets as he turned it about. Somewhere around the table a chair was pushed sharply back and then drawn in again.

"Phew!" cried Michael. "How wizard it would be it was real."

"Perhaps it is real," said Bridget hopefully.

"Oh, don't be an ass, Bridget. Why, a ruby of that size would be worth thousands and thousands and *thousands* of pounds. Wouldn't it, Monsieur Poirot?"

"It would indeed," said Poirot.

"But what I can't understand," said Mrs. Lacey, "is how it got into the pudding."

"Oooh," said Colin, diverted by his last mouthful, "I've got the pig. It isn't fair."

Bridget chanted immediately, "Colin's got the pig! Colin's got the pig! Colin is the greedy guzzling *pig!*"

"I've got the ring," said Diana in a clear, high voice.

"Good for you, Diana. You'll be married first, of us all."

"I've got the thimble," wailed Bridget.

"Bridget's going to be an old maid," chanted the two boys. "Yah, Bridget's going to be an old maid."

"Who's got the money?" demanded David. "There's a real ten shilling piece, gold, in this pudding. I know, Mrs. Ross told me so."

"I think I'm the lucky one," said Desmond Lee-Wortley.

Colonel Lacey's two neighbors heard him mutter, "Yes, you would be."

"*I've* got a ring, too," said David. He looked across at Diana. "Quite a coincidence, isn't it?"

The laughter went on. Nobody noticed that Monsieur Poirot carelessly, as though thinking of something else, had dropped the red stone into his pocket.

Mince pies and Christmas dessert followed the pudding. The older members of the party then retired for a welcome siesta before the tea-time ceremony of the lighting of the Christmas tree. Hercule Poirot, however, did not take a siesta. Instead, he made his way to the large old-fashioned kitchen.

"It is permitted," he asked, looking round and beaming, "that I congratulate the cook on this marvelous meal that I have just eaten?"

There was a moment's pause and then Mrs. Ross came forward in a stately manner to meet him. She was a large woman, nobly built with all the dignity of a stage duchess. Two lean gray-haired women were beyond in the scullery washing up and a tow-haired girl was moving to and fro between the scullery and the kitchen. But these were obviously mere myrmidons. Mrs. Ross was the queen of the kitchen quarters.

"I am glad to hear you enjoyed it, sir," she said graciously.

"Enjoyed it!" cried Hercule Poirot. With an extravagant foreign gesture he raised his hand to his lips, kissed it, and wafted the kiss to the ceiling. "But you are a genius, Mrs. Ross! A genius! *Never* have I tasted such a wonderful meal. The oyster soup . . ." he made an expressive noise with his lips "and the stuffing. The chestnut stuffing in the turkey, that was quite unique in my experience."

"Well, it's funny that you should say that, sir," said Mrs. Ross. "It's a very special recipe, that stuffing. It was given me by an Austrian chef that I worked with many years ago. But all the rest," she added, "is just good, plain English cooking."

"And is there anything better?" demanded Hercule Poirot.

"Well, it's nice of you to say so, sir. Of course, you being a foreign gentleman might have preferred the continental style. Not but what I can't manage continental dishes, too."

"I am sure, Mrs. Ross, you could manage anything! But you must know that English cooking—*good* English cooking, not the cooking one gets in the second-class hotels or the restaurants—is much appreciated by *gourmets* on the continent, and I believe I am correct in saying that a special expedition was made to London in the early eighteen hundreds, and a report sent back to France of the wonders of the English puddings."

" 'We have nothing like that in France,' they wrote. 'It is worth making a journey to London just to taste the varieties and excellencies of the English puddings.' And above all puddings," continued Poirot, well launched now on a kind of rhapsody, "is the Christmas plum pudding, such as we have eaten today. That was a homemade pudding, was it not? Not a bought one?"

"Yes, indeed, sir. Of my own making and my own recipe such as I've made for many, many years. When I came here Mrs. Lacey said that she'd ordered a pudding from a London store to save me the trouble. But no, madame, I said, that may be kind of you but no bought pudding from a store can equal a homemade Christmas one. Mind you," said Mrs. Ross, warming to her subject like the artist she was, "it was made too soon before the day. A good Christmas pudding should be made some weeks before and allowed to wait. The longer they're kept, within reason, the better they are.

"I mind now that when I was a child and we went to church every Sunday, we'd start listening for the collect that begins 'Stir up O Lord we beseech thee' because that collect was the signal, as it were, that the puddings should be made that week. And so they always were. We had the collect on the Sunday, and that week sure enough my mother would make the Christmas puddings. And so it should have been here this year. As it was, that pudding was only made three days ago, the day you arrived, sir. However, I kept to the old custom. Everyone in the house had to come out into the kitchen and have a stir and make a wish. That's an old custom, sir, and I've always held to it."

"*Most* interesting," said Hercule Poirot. "Most interesting. And so everyone came out into the kitchen?"

"Yes, sir. The young gentlemen, Miss Bridget and the London gentleman who's staying here, and his sister and Mr. David and Miss Diana—Mrs. Middleton, I should say. . . . All had a stir, they did."

"How many puddings did you make? Is this the only one?"

"No sir, I made four. Two large ones and two smaller ones. The other large one I planned to serve on New Year's Day and the smaller ones were for Colonel and Mrs. Lacey when they are alone like and not so many in the family."

"I see, I see," said Poirot.

"As a matter of fact, sir," said Mrs. Lacey, "it was the wrong pudding you had for lunch today."

"The wrong pudding?" Poirot frowned. "How is that?"

"Well, sir, we have a big Christmas mold—a china mold with a pattern of holly and mistletoe on top—and we always have the Christmas Day pudding boiled in that. But there was a most unfortunate accident. This morning, when Annie was getting it down from the shelf in the larder, she slipped and dropped it and it broke. Well, sir, naturally I couldn't serve that, could I? There might have been splinters in it.

"So we had to use the other one—the New Year's Day one, which is in a plain bowl. It makes a nice round but it's not so decorative as the Christmas mold. Really, where we'll get another mold like that I don't know. They don't make things in that size nowadays. All tiddly bits of things. Why, you can't even buy a breakfast dish that'll take a proper eight to ten eggs and bacon. Ah, things aren't what they were."

"No, indeed," said Poirot. "But today that is not so. This Christmas Day has been like the Christmas Days of old, is that not true?"

Mrs. Ross sighed. "Well, I'm glad you say so, sir, but of course I haven't the *help* now that I used to have. Not skilled help, that is. The girls nowadays," she lowered her voice slightly, "they mean very well and they're very willing but they've not been *trained,* sir, if you understand what I mean."

"Times change, yes," said Hercule Poirot. "I, too, find it sad sometimes."

"This house, sir," said Mrs. Ross, "it's too large, you know, for the mistress and the colonel. The mistress, she knows that. Living in a corner of it as they do, it's not the same thing at all. It only comes alive, as you might say, at Christmastime when all the family come."

"It is the first time, I think, that Mr. Lee-Wortley and his sister have been here?"

"Yes, sir." A note of slight reserve crept into Mrs. Ross's voice. "A very nice gentleman he is but, well—it seems a funny friend for Miss Sarah to have, according to our ideas. But there—London ways are different! It's sad that his sister's so poorly. Had an operation, she had. She seemed all right the first day she was here, but that very day, after we'd been stirring the puddings, she was took bad again and she's been in bed ever since. Got up too soon after her operation, I expect. Ah, doctors nowadays, they have you out of hospital before you can hardly stand on your feet. Why, my very own nephew's wife . . ."

And Mrs. Ross went into a long and spirited tale of hospital treatment as accorded to her family, comparing it unfavorably with the consideration that had been lavishly on them in older times.

Poirot duly commiserated with her. "It remains," he said, "to thank you for this exquisite and sumptuous meal. You permit a little acknowledgment of my appreciation?"

A crisp five-pound note passed from his hand into that of Mrs. Ross who said perfunctorily, "You really shouldn't do *that,* sir."

"I insist, I insist."

"Well, it's very kind of you indeed, sir." Mrs. Ross accepted the tribute as no more than her due. "And I wish you, sir, a very happy Christmas and a prosperous New Year."

❦ ❦ ❦ ❦

The end of Christmas Day was like the end of most Christmas Days. The tree was lighted, a splendid Christmas cake came in for tea, was greeted with approval but was partaken of only moderately. There was cold supper.

Both Poirot and his host and hostess went to bed early.

"Good night, Monsieur Poirot," said Mrs. Lacey. "I hope you've enjoyed yourself."

"It has been a wonderful day, madame, wonderful."

"You're looking very thoughtful," said Mrs. Lacey.

"It is the English pudding that I consider."

"You found it a little heavy, perhaps?" asked Mrs. Lacey delicately.

"No, no, I do not speak gastronomically. I consider its significance."

"It's traditional, of course," said Mrs. Lacey. "Well, good night, Monsieur Poirot, and don't dream too much of Christmas puddings and mince pies."

"Yes," murmured Poirot to himself as he undressed. "It is a problem certainly, that Christmas plum pudding. There is here something that I do not understand at all." He shook his head in a vexed manner. "Well—we shall see."

After making certain preparations, Poirot went to bed, but not to sleep.

It was some two hours later that his patience was rewarded. The door of his bedroom opened very gently. He smiled to himself. It was as he had thought it would be. His mind went back fleetingly to the cup of coffee so politely handed him by Desmond Lee-Wortley. A little later, when Desmond's back was turned, he had laid the cup down for a few moments on a table. He had then apparently picked it up again and Desmond had had the satisfaction, if satisfaction it was, of seeing him drink the coffee to the last drop.

But a little smile lifted Poirot's mustache as he reflected that it was not he but someone else who was sleeping a good sound sleep tonight. "That pleasant young David," said Poirot to himself, "he is worried, unhappy. It will do him no harm to have a night's really sound sleep. And now, let us see what will happen."

He lay quite still, breathing in an even manner with occasionally a suggestion, but the very faintest suggestion, of a snore.

Someone came up to the bed and bent over him. Then, satisfied, that someone turned away and went to the dressing table. By the light of a tiny torch the visitor was examining Poirot's belongings neatly arranged on top of the dressing table. Fingers explored the wallet, gently pulled open the drawers of the dressing table, then extended the search to the pockets of Poirot's clothes.

Finally the visitor approached the bed and with great caution slid his hand under the pillow. Withdrawing his hand, he stood for a moment or two as though uncertain what to do next. He walked round the room looking inside ornaments, went into the adjoining bathroom from which he presently returned. Then, with a faint exclamation of disgust, he went out of the room.

"Ah," said Poirot, under his breath. "You have a disappointment. Yes, yes, a serious disappointment. Bah! To imagine, even, that Hercule Poirot would hide something where you could find it!" Then, turning over on his other side, he went peacefully to sleep.

He was aroused the next morning by an urgent soft tapping on his door.

"*Qui est là?* Come in, come in."

The door opened. Breathless, red-faced, Colin stood on the threshold. Behind him stood Michael.

"Monsieur Poirot, Monsieur Poirot."

"But yes?" Poirot sat up in bed. "It is the early tea? But no. It is you, Colin. What has occurred?"

Colin was, for a moment, speechless. He seemed to be under the grip of some strong emotion. In actual fact it was the sight of the nightcap that Hercule Poirot wore that affected for the moment his organs of speech. Presently he controlled himself and spoke.

"I think—Monsieur Poirot, could you help us? Something rather awful has happened."

"Something has happened? But what?"

"It's—it's Bridget. She's out there in the snow. I think—she doesn't move or speak and—oh, you'd better come and look for yourself. I'm terribly afraid—she may be *dead.*"

"What?" Poirot cast aside his bed covers. "Mademoiselle Bridget—dead!"

"I think—I think somebody's killed her. There's—there's blood and—oh, do come!"

"But certainly! I come on the instant."

With great practicality Poirot inserted his feet into his overshoes and pulled a fur-lined overcoat over his pajamas.

"I come," he said. "I come on the moment. You have aroused the house?"

"No. No, so far I haven't told anyone but you. I thought it would be better. Grandfather and Gran aren't up yet. They're laying breakfast downstairs, but I didn't say anything to Peverell. She—Bridget—she's round the other side of the house, near the terrace and the library window."

"I see. Lead the way. I will follow."

Turning away to hide his delighted grin, Colin led the way downstairs. They went out through the side door. It was a clear morning with the sun not yet high over the horizon. It was not snowing now, but it had snowed heavily during the night and everywhere around was an unbroken carpet of thick snow. The world looked very pure and white and beautiful.

"There!" said Colin breathlessly, "I—it's—*there!*" He pointed dramatically.

The scene was indeed dramatic enough. A few yards away Bridget lay in the snow. She was wearing scarlet pajamas and a white wool wrap thrown round her shoulders. The white wool wrap was stained with crimson. Her head was turned aside and hidden by the mass of her outspread black hair. One arm was under her body, the other lay flung out, the fingers clenched, and standing up in the center of the crimson stain was the hilt of a large curved Kurdish knife which Colonel Lacey had shown to his guests only the evening before.

"Mon Dieu!" exclaimed Monsieur Poirot. "It is like something on the stage!"

There was a faint choking noise from Michael. Colin thrust himself quickly into the breach.

"I know," he said. "It—it doesn't seem real somehow, does it? Do you see those footprints? I suppose we mustn't disturb them."

"Ah, yes, the footprints. No, we must be careful not to disturb those footprints."

"That's what I thought," said Colin, "That's why I wouldn't let anyone go near her until we got you. I thought you'd know what to do."

"All the same," said Hercule Poirot briskly, "first we must see if she is still alive? Is that not so?"

"Well—yes—of course," said Michael a little doubtfully, "but you see we thought—I mean, we didn't like . . ."

"Ah, you have the prudence! You have read the detective stories. It is most important that nothing should be touched and that the body should be left as it is. But we cannot be sure as yet if it *is* a body, can we? After all, though prudence is admirable, common humanity comes first. We must think of the doctor, must we not, before we think of the police?"

"Oh, yes. Of course," said Colin, still a little taken aback.

"We only thought—I mean—we thought we'd better get you before we did anything," said Michael hastily.

"Then you will both remain here," said Poirot. "I will approach from the other side so as not to disturb these footprints. Such excellent footprints, are they not—so very clear? The footprints of a man and a girl going out together to the place where she lies. And then the man's footsteps come back but the girl's—do not."

"They must be the footprints of the murderer," said Colin.

"Exactly," said Poirot. "The footprints of the murderer. A long narrow foot with a rather peculiar type of shoe. Very interesting. Easy, I think, to recognize. Yes, those footprints will be very important."

At that moment, Desmond Lee-Wortley came out of the house with Sarah and joined them.

"What on earth are you all doing here?" he demanded in a somewhat theatrical manner. "I saw you from my bedroom window. What's up? Good lord, what's this? It—it looks like . . ."

"Exactly," said Hercule Poirot. "It looks like murder, does it not?"

Sarah gave a quick gasp, then shot a quick suspicious glance at the two boys.

"You mean someone killed the girl—what's-her-name—Bridget?" demanded Desmond. "Who on earth would want to kill her? It's unbelievable!"

"There are many things that are unbelievable," said Poirot. "Especially before breakfast, is it not? That is what one of your classics says. Six impossible things before breakfast." He added, "Please wait here, all of you."

Carefully making a circuit, he approached Bridget and bent for a moment over the body. Colin and Michael were now both shaking with suppressed laughter. Sarah joined them, murmuring, "What have you two been up to?"

"Good old Bridget," whispered Colin. "Isn't she wonderful? Not a twitch!"

"I've never seen anything look so dead as Bridget does," whispered Michael.

Hercule Poirot straightened up.

"This is a terrible thing," he said. His voice held an emotion it had not held before.

Overcome by mirth, Michael and Colin both turned away. In a choked voice Michael said, "What—what must we do?"

"There is only one thing to do," said Poirot. "We must send for the police. Will one of you telephone or would you prefer me to do it?"

"I think," said Colin, "I think—what about it, Michael?"

"Yes," said Michael, "I think the jig's up now." He stepped forward. For the first time he seemed a little unsure of himself. "I'm awfully sorry," he said, "I hope you won't mind too much. It—er—it was a sort of joke for Christmas and all that, you know. We thought we'd—well, lay on a murder for you."

"You thought you would lay on a murder for me? Then this—then this . . ."

"It's just a show we put on," explained Colin, "to—to make you feel at home, you know."

"Aha," said Hercule Poirot. "I understand. You make of me the April fool, is that it? But today is not April the first, it is December the twenty-sixth."

"I suppose we oughtn't to have done it really," said Colin, "but—but—you don't mind very much do you, Monsieur Poirot? Come on, Bridget," he called, "get up. You must be half frozen to death already."

The figure in the snow, however, did not stir.

"It is odd," said Hercule Poirot, "she does not seem to hear you." He looked thoughtfully at them. "It is a joke, you say? You are sure this is a joke?"

"Why, yes." Colin spoke uncomfortably. "We—we didn't mean any harm."

"But why then does Mademoiselle Bridget not get up?"

"I can't imagine," said Colin.

"Come on, Bridget," said Sarah impatiently. "Don't go on lying there playing the fool."

"We really are very sorry, Monsieur Poirot," said Colin apprehensively. "We do really apologize."

"You need not apologize," said Poirot in a peculiar tone.

"What do you mean?" Colin stared at him. He turned again. "Bridget! Bridget! What's the matter? Why doesn't she get up? Why does she go on lying there?"

Poirot beckoned to Desmond. "*You,* Mr. Lee-Wortley. Come here."

Desmond joined him.

"Feel her pulse," said Poirot.

Desmond Lee-Wortley bent down. He touched the arm—the wrist.

"There's no pulse." He stared at Poirot. "Her arm's stiff. Good god, she really is dead!"

Poirot nodded. "Yes, she is dead," he said. "Someone has turned the comedy into a tragedy."

"Someone—who?"

"There is a set of footprints going and returning. A set of footprints that bears a strong resemblance to the footprints *you* have just made, Mr. Lee-Wortley."

Desmond Lee-Wortley wheeled round.

"Are you accusing me? *ME?* You're crazy! Why on earth should I want to kill the girl?"

"Ah—why? I wonder . . . Let us see . . ."

He bent down and very gently prised open the stiff fingers of the girl's clenched hand.

Desmond drew a sharp breath. He gazed down unbelievingly. In the palm of the dead girl's hand was what appeared to be a large ruby.

"It's that damn thing out of the pudding!" he cried.

"Is it?" said Poirot. "Are you sure?"

"Of course it is."

With a swift movement Desmond bent down and plucked the red stone out of Bridget's hand.

"You should not have done that," said Poirot reproachfully. "Nothing should have been disturbed."

"I haven't disturbed the body, have I? But this thing might—might get lost and it's evidence. I'll go at once and telephone."

He wheeled round and ran toward the house. Sarah came swiftly to Poirot's side.

"I don't understand," she whispered. Her face was dead-white. "I don't *understand.*" She caught at Poirot's arm. "What did you mean about—about the footprints?"

"Look for yourself, mademoiselle."

The footprints that led to the body and back again were the same as the ones just made accompanying Poirot to the girl's body and back.

"You mean—that it was Desmond? Nonsense!"

Suddenly the noise of a car came through the clear air. They turned and saw the car driving at a furious pace down the drive.

"It's Desmond," Sarah said. "It's Desmond's car. He—he must have gone to fetch the police instead of telephoning."

Diana Middleton came running out of the house to join them.

"What's happened?" she cried in a breathless voice. "Desmond just came rushing into the house. He said something about Bridget being killed and then he rattled the telephone but it was dead. He couldn't get any answer. He said the wires must have been cut. He said the only thing was to take a car and go for the police. Why the police?"

Poirot made a gesture.

"Bridget?" Diana stared at him. "But surely—isn't it a joke of some kind? I heard something—something last night. I thought that they were going to play a joke on you, Monsieur Poirot."

"Yes," said Poirot, "that was the idea—to play a joke on me. But now come into the house, all of you. We shall catch our deaths of cold here and there is nothing to be done until Mr. Lee-Wortley returns with the police."

"But look here," said Colin, "we can't—can't leave Bridget here alone."

"You can do her no good by remaining," said Poirot gently. "Come, it is sad, a very sad tragedy, but there is nothing we can do any more to help Mademoiselle Bridget. So let us come in and get warm and have a cup of tea."

They followed him obediently into the house. Peverell was just about to ring the gong. If he thought it extraordinary for most of the household to be outside and for Poirot to make an appearance in pajamas and an overcoat, he displayed no sign of it. Peverell in his old age was still the perfect butler. He noticed nothing that he was not asked to notice.

They went into the dining room and sat down. When they all had a cup of tea in front of them and were sipping it, Poirot spoke.

"I have to recount to you," he said, "a little history. I cannot tell you all the details, no. But I can give you the main outline. It concerns a young princeling who came to this country. He brought with him a famous jewel which he was to have reset for the lady he was going to marry, but unfortunately before that he made friends with a very pretty young lady. This pretty young lady did not care very much for the man, but she did care for his jewel—so much so that one day she disappeared with this historic possession which had belonged to his house for generations.

"So the poor young man, he is in a quandary, you see. Above all he cannot have a scandal. Impossible to go to the police. Therefore he comes to me, to Hercule Poirot. 'Recover for me,' he says, 'my historic ruby.' *Eh bien,* this young lady, she has a friend and the friend he has put through several very questionable transactions. He has been concerned with blackmail and he has been concerned with the sale of jewelry abroad. Always he has been very clever. He is suspected, yes, but nothing can be proved.

"It comes to my knowledge that this very clever gentleman, he is spending Christmas here in this house. It is important that the pretty young lady, once she has acquired the jewel, should disappear for a while from circulation, so that no pressure can be put upon her, no questions can be asked her. It is arranged, therefore, that she comes here to Kings Lacey, ostensibly as the sister of the clever gentleman."

Sarah drew a sharp breath.

"Oh, no. Oh, no, not *here!* Not with me here!"

"But so it is," said Poirot. "And by a little manipulation, I, too, become a guest here for Christmas. This young lady, she is supposed to have just come out of the hospital. She is much better when she arrives here. But then comes the news that I, too, arrive, a detective—a well-known detective. At once she has what you call the wind up.

"She hides the ruby in the first place she can think of, and then very quickly she has a relapse and takes to her bed again. She does not want that I should see her, for doubtless I have a photograph and I shall recognize her. It is very boring for her, yes, but she has to stay in her room and her 'brother,' he brings her up the trays."

"And the ruby?" demanded Michael.

"I think," said Poirot, "that at the moment it is mentioned I arrive, the young lady was in the kitchen with the rest of you, all laughing and talking and stirring the Christmas puddings. The Christmas puddings are put into bowls and the young lady she hides the ruby, pressing it down into one of the pudding bowls. Not the one that we are going to have on Christmas Day. Oh no, that one she knows is in a special mold.

"She puts it in the other one, the one that is destined to be eaten on New Year's Day. Before then she will be ready to leave, and when she leaves no doubt that Christmas pudding will go with her. But see how fate takes a hand. On the very morning of Christmas Day there is an accident. The Christmas pudding in its fancy mold is dropped on the stone floor and the mold is shattered to pieces. So what can be done? The good Mrs. Ross, she takes the other pudding—the New Year's Day pudding—and sends it in."

"Good lord," said Colin, "do you mean that on Christmas Day when Grandfather was eating his pudding that that was a real ruby he'd got in his mouth?"

"Precisely," said Poirot, "and you can imagine the emotions of Mr. Desmond Lee-Wortley when he saw that. *Eh bien,* what happens next? The royal ruby is passed round. I examine it and I manage unobtrusively to slip it in my pocket. In a careless way as though I were not interested. But one person at least observes what I have done. When I lie in bed that person searches my room. He searches me. He does not find the ruby. Why?"

"Because," said Michael breathlessly, "you had given it to Bridget. That's what you mean. And so that's why—but I don't understand quite—I mean . . . Look here, what *did* happen?"

Poirot smiled at him.

"Come now into the library," he said, "and look out of the window and I will show you something that may explain the mystery."

He led the way.

"Consider once again," said Poirot, "the scene of the crime."

He pointed out of the window. A simultaneous gasp broke from the lips of all of them. There was no body lying on the snow, no trace of the tragedy seemed to remain except a mass of scuffled snow.

"It wasn't all a dream, was it?" said Colin faintly. "I—has someone taken the body away?"

"Ah," said Poirot. "You see? The Mystery of the Disappearing Body." He nodded his head and his eyes twinkled gently.

"Good lord," cried Michael. "Monsieur Poirot, you are—you haven't—oh, look here, he's been having us on all the time!"

Poirot twinkled more than ever.

"It is true, my children, I also have had my little joke. I knew about your little plot, you see, and so I arranged a counterplot of my own. Ah, voilà Mademoiselle Bridget. None the worse, I hope, for your exposure in the snow? Never should I forgive myself if you *attrapped une fluxion de poitrine.*"

Bridget had just come into the room. She was wearing a thick skirt and a woolen sweater, and was laughing.

"I sent a *tisane* to your room," said Poirot severely. "You have drunk it?"

"One sip was enough!" said Bridget. "Did I do it well, Monsieur Poirot? Goodness, my arm hurts still after that tourniquet you made me put on it."

"You were splendid, my child," said Poirot. "Splendid. But see, all the others are still in the fog. Last night I went to Mademoiselle Bridget. I told her that I knew about your little *complot* and I asked her if she would act a part for me. She did it very cleverly. She made the footprints with a pair of Mr. Lee-Wortley's shoes."

Sarah said in a harsh voice, "But what's the point of it all, Monsieur Poirot? What's the point of sending Desmond off to fetch the police? They'll be very angry when they find out it's nothing but a hoax."

Poirot shook his head gently.

"But I do not think for one moment, Mademoiselle, that Mr. Lee-Wortley went to fetch the police," he said. "Murder is a thing in which Mr. Lee-Wortley does not want to be mixed up. He lost his nerve badly. All he could see was his chance to get the ruby. He snatched that, he pretended the telephone was out of order, and he rushed off in a car on the pretense of fetching the police. I think myself it is the last you will see of him for some time. He has, I understand, his own ways of getting out of England. He has his own plane, has he not, Mademoiselle?"

Sarah nodded. "Yes," she said. "We were thinking of . . ." She stopped.

"He wanted you to elope with him that way, did he not? *Eh bien,* that is a very good way of smuggling a jewel out of the country. When you are eloping with a girl, and that fact is publicized, then you will not be suspected of also smuggling a historic jewel out of the country. Oh yes, that would have made a very good *camouflage*."

"I don't believe it," said Sarah. "I don't believe a word of it!"

"Then ask his sister," said Poirot, gently nodding his head over her shoulder. Sarah turned her head sharply.

A platinum blonde stood in the doorway. She wore a fur coat and was scowling. She was clearly in a furious temper.

"Sister my foot!" she said, with a short unpleasant laugh. "That swine's no brother of mine! So he's beaten it, has he, and left me to carry the can? The whole thing was *his* idea! He put me up to it! Said it was money for jam. They'd never prosecute because of the scandal. I could always threaten to say that Ali had *given* me his historic jewel. Des and I were to have shared the swag in Paris—and now the swine runs out on me! I'd like to murder him!" She switched abruptly. "The sooner I get out of here . . . Can someone telephone for a taxi?"

"A car is waiting at the front door to take you to the station, Mademoiselle," said Poirot.

"Think of everything, don't you?"

"Most things," said Poirot complacently.

But Poirot was not to get off so easily. When he returned to the dining room after assisting Miss Lee-Wortley into the waiting car, Colin was waiting for him.

There was a frown on his boyish face.

"But look here, Monsieur Poirot. *What about the ruby?* Do you mean you've let him get away with it?"

Poirot's face fell. He twirled his mustache. He seemed ill at ease.

"I shall recover it yet," he said weakly. "There are other ways. I shall still . . ."

"Well, I do think!" said Michael. "To let that swine get away with the ruby!"

Bridget was sharper.

"He's having us on again," she cried. "You are, aren't you, Monsieur Poirot?"

"Shall we do a final conjuring trick, Mademoiselle? Feel in my left-hand pocket."

Bridget thrust her hand in. She drew it out with a scream of triumph and held aloft a large ruby blinking in crimson splendor.

"You comprehend," explained Poirot, "the one that was clasped in your hand was a paste replica. I brought it from London in case it was possible to make a substitution. You understand? We do not want the scandal. Monsieur Desmond will try and dispose of that ruby in Paris or Belgium or wherever it is that he has his contacts, and then it will be discovered that the stone is not real! What could be more excellent? All finishes happily. The scandal is avoided, my princeling receives his ruby back again, he returns to his country and makes a sober and we hope a happy marriage. All ends well."

"Except for me," murmured Sarah under her breath.

She spoke so low that no one heard her but Poirot. He shook his head gently.

"You are in error, Mademoiselle Sarah, in what you say there. You have gained experience. All experience is valuable. Ahead of you I prophesy there lies happiness."

"That's what you say," said Sarah.

"But look here, Monsieur Poirot," Colin was frowning. "How did you know about the show we were going to put on for you?"

"It is my business to know things," said Hercule Poirot.

"Yes, but I don't see how you could have managed it. Did someone come and tell you?"

"No, no, not that."

"Then how? Tell us how?"

"But no," Poirot protested. "But no. If I tell you how I deduced that, you will think nothing of it. It is like the conjuror who shows how his tricks are done!"

"Now come on, Monsieur Poirot. *How did you know?*"

"Well, you see, I was sitting in the library by the window in a chair after tea the other day and I was reposing myself. I had been asleep and when I awoke you were discussing your plans just outside the window close to me, and the window was open at the top."

"Is that all?" cried Colin, disgusted. "How simple!"

"Is it not?" cried Hercule Poirot, smiling. "You see? You are disappointed!"

"Oh, well," said Michael, "at any rate we know everything now."

"Do we?" murmured Hercule Poirot to himself. "*I* do not. *I* whose business it is to know everything."

He walked out into the hall, shaking his head a little. For perhaps the twentieth time he drew from his pocket a rather dirty piece of paper. "DON'T EAT NONE OF THE PLUM PUDDING. ONE AS WISHES YOU WELL."

Hercule Poirot shook his head reflectively. He who could explain everything could not explain this! Humiliating. Who had written it? Why had it been written? Until he found that out he would never know a moment's peace.

Suddenly he came out of his reverie to be aware of a peculiar gasping noise. He looked sharply down. On the floor, busy with a dustpan and brush was a towheaded creature in a flowered coverall. She was staring at the paper in his hand with large round eyes.

"Oh, sir," said this apparition. "Oh, *sir. Please,* sir."

"And who may you be, *mon enfant?*" inquired Poirot genially.

"Annie Bates, sir. I come here to help Mrs. Ross. I didn't mean to—to do anything what I shouldn't do. I did mean it well, sir. For your good, I mean."

Enlightenment came to Poirot. He held out the piece of paper.

"Did you write that, Annie?"

"I didn't mean any harm, sir."

"Of course you didn't, Annie." He smiled at her. "But tell me about it. Why did you write this?"

"Well it was them two, sir. Mr. Lee-Wortley and his sister. Not that she *was* his sister, I'm sure. None of us thought so! And she wasn't ill a bit. We could all tell *that.* We thought—we all thought—something queer was going on. I'll tell you straight, sir. I was in her bathroom taking in the clean towels, and I listened at the door. *He* was in her room and they were talking together. I heard what they said plain as plain.

" 'This detective,' he was saying. 'This fellow Poirot who's coming here. We've got to do something about it. We've got to get him out of the way as soon as possible.' And then he says to her in a nasty, sinister sort of way, lowering his voice, 'Where did you put it?' And she answered him, *'In the pudding.'*

"Oh sir, my heart gave such a leap I thought it would stop beating. I thought they meant to poison you in the Christmas pudding. I didn't know what to do! Mrs. Ross, she wouldn't listen to the likes of me. Then the idea came to me as I'd write you a warning. And I did and I put it on your pillow where you'd find it when you went to bed." Annie paused breathlessly.

Poirot surveyed her gravely.

"You see too many sensational films, I think, Annie," he said at last, "or perhaps it is the television that affects you? But the important thing is that you have the good heart and a certain amount of ingenuity. When I return to London I will send you a present."

"Oh, thank you, sir. Thank you very much, sir."

"What would you like, Annie, as a present?"

"Anything I like, sir? Could I have anything I like?"

"Within reason," said Hercule Poirot prudently, "yes."

"Oh, sir, could I have a vanity box? A real posh slap-up vanity box like the one Mr. Lee-Wortley's sister wot wasn't his sister, had?"

"Yes," said Poirot, "yes, I think that could be managed. It is interesting," he mused. "I was in a museum the other day observing some antiquities from Babylon or one of those places, thousands of years old—and among them were cosmetics boxes. The heart of woman does not change."

"Beg your pardon, sir?" said Annie.

"It is nothing," said Poirot, "I reflect. You shall have your vanity box, child."

Annie departed ecstatically. Poirot looked after her, nodding his head in satisfaction.

"Ah," he said to himself. "And now—I go. There is nothing more to be done here."

A pair of arms slipped around his shoulders unexpectedly.

"If you *will* stand just under the mistletoe . . ." said Bridget.

Hercule Poirot enjoyed it. He enjoyed it very much. He said to himself that he had had a very good Christmas.

Man Bites Dog

Ellery Queen

Ellery Queen is the creative brainchild of Frederic Dannay and Manfred Lee, who introduced Queen in the story "The Roman Hat Mystery" (1929). Teamed up with his father, Inspector Richard Queen of the New York Police Department, Ellery Queen would collect and analyze clues and ultimately solve the crime. This duo proved so incredibly popular that Dannay and Lee went on to write thirty-three novels, numerous short stories and hundreds of radio scripts featuring the actor Hugh Marlowe as the voice of Ellery Queen. The legacy of Queen continued in film with Ralph Bellamy as the intellectual detective, while on television, Peter Lawford and Jim Hutton both starred in the title role. In 1941, Dannay and Lee launched *Ellery Queen's Mystery Magazine,* which continues today in the tradition of literary excellence in crime and detective writing and has been heralded as the finest periodical of its kind.

Anyone observing the tigerish pacings, the gnawings of lip, the contortions of brow, and the fierce melancholy which characterized the conduct of Mr. Ellery Queen, the noted sleuth, during those early October days in Hollywood, would have said reverently that the great man's intellect was once more locked in titanic struggle with the forces of evil.

"Paula," Mr. Queen said to Paula Paris, "I am going mad."

"I hope," said Miss Paris tenderly, "it's love."

Mr. Queen paced, swathed in yards of thought. Queenly Miss Paris observed him with melting eyes. When he had first encountered her, during his investigation of the double murder of Blythe Stuart and Jack Royle, the famous motion picture stars, Miss Paris had been in the grip of a morbid psychology. She had been in deathly terror of crowds. 'Crowd phobia,' the doctors called it. Mr. Queen had cured her by the curious method of making love to her. And now she was infected by the cure.

"Is it?" asked Miss Paris, her heart in her eyes.

"Eh?" said Mr. Queen. "What? Oh, no. I mean—it's the World Series." He looked savage. "Don't you realize what's happening? The New York Giants and the New York Yankees are waging mortal combat to determine the baseball championship of the world, and I'm three thousand miles away!"

"Oh," said Miss Paris. Then she said cleverly: "You poor darling."

"Never missed a New York series before," wailed Mr. Queen. "Driving me cuckoo. And what a battle! Greatest series ever played. Moore and DiMaggio have done miracles in the outfield. Giants have pulled a triple play. Goofy Gomez struck out fourteen men to win the first game. Hubbell's pitched a one-hit shutout. And today Dickey came up in the ninth inning with the bases loaded, two out, and the Yanks three runs behind, and slammed a homer over the right-field stands!"

"Is that good?" asked Miss Paris.

"Good!" howled Mr. Queen. "It merely sent the series into a seventh game."

"Poor darling," said Miss Paris again, and she picked up her telephone. When she set it down she said: "Weather's threatening in the East. Tomorrow the New York Weather Bureau expects heavy rains."

Mr. Queen stared wildly. "You mean—"

"I mean that you're taking tonight's plane for the East. And you'll see your beloved seventh game day after tomorrow."

"Paula, you're a genius!" Then Mr. Queen's face fell. "But the studio, tickets . . . *Bigre!* I'll tell the studio I'm down with elephantiasis, and I'll wire Dad to snare a box. With his pull at City Hall, he ought to—Paula, I don't know what I'd do."

"You might," suggested Miss Paris, "kiss me good-bye."

Mr. Queen did so, absently. Then he started. "Not at all! You're coming with me!"

"That's what I had in mind," said Miss Paris contentedly.

And so Wednesday found Miss Paris and Mr. Queen at the Polo Grounds, ensconced in a field box behind the Yankees dugout.

Mr. Queen glowed, he revelled, he was radiant. While Inspector Queen, with the suspiciousness of all fathers, engaged Paula in exploratory conversation, Ellery filled his lap and Paula's with peanut hulls, consumed frankfurters and soda pop immoderately, made hypercritical comments on the appearance of the various athletes, derided the Yankees, extolled the Giants, evolved complicated fifty-cent bets with Detective-Sergeant Velie, of the Inspector's staff, and leaped to his feet screaming with fifty thousand other maniacs as the news came that Carl Hubbell, the beloved Meal Ticket of the Giants, would oppose Senor El Goofy Gomez, the ace of the Yankee staff, on the mound.

"Will the Yanks murder that apple today!" predicted the Sergeant, who was an incurable Yankee worshipper. "And will Goofy mow 'em down!"

"Four bits," said Mr. Queen coldly, "say the Yanks don't score three earned runs off Carl."

"It's a pleasure!"

"I'll take a piece of that, Sergeant," chuckled a handsome man to the front of them, in a rail seat. "Hi, Inspector. Swell day for it, eh?"

"Jimmy Connor!" exclaimed Inspector Queen. "The old Song-and-Dance Man in person. Say, Jimmy, you never met my son Ellery, did you? Excuse me. Miss Paris, this is the famous Jimmy Connor, God's gift to Broadway."

"Glad to meet you, Miss Paris," smiled the Song-and-Dance Man, sniffing at his orchidaceous lapel. "Read your Seeing Stars column, every day. Meet Judy Starr."

Miss Paris smiled, and the woman beside Jimmy Connor smiled back, and just then three Yankee players strolled over to the box and began to jeer at Connor for having had to take seats behind the hated Yankee dugout.

Judy Starr was sitting oddly still. She was the famous Judy Starr who had been discovered by Florenz Ziegfeld—a second Marilyn Miller, the critics called her; dainty and pretty, with a perky profile and great honey-colored eyes, who had sung and danced her way into the heart of New York. Her day of fame was almost over now. Perhaps, thought Paula, staring at Judy's profile, that explained that pinch of her little mouth, the fine lines about her tragic eyes, the singing tension of her figure.

Perhaps. But Paula was not sure. There was immediacy, a defence against the palpable and present danger, in Judy Starr's tautness. Paula looked about. And at once her eyes narrowed.

Across the rail of the box, in the box at their left, sat a very tall, leather-skinned, silent and intent man. The man, too, was staring out at the field, in an attitude curiously like that of Judy Starr, whom he could have touched by extending his big, ropy, muscular hand across the rail. And on the man's other side there sat a woman whom Paula recognized instantly. Lotus Verne, the motion-picture star!

Lotus Verne was a gorgeous, full-blown redhead with deep mercury-colored eyes who had come out of Northern Italy Ludovica Vernicchi, changed her name, and flashed across the Hollywood skies in a picture called *Woman of Bali,* a color-film in which loving care had been lavished on the display possibilities of her dark, full, dangerous body. With fame, she had developed a passion for press-agentry, borzois in pairs, and tall brown men with muscles. She was arrayed in sun-yellow, and she stood out among the women in the field boxes like a butterfly in a mass of grubs. By contrast little Judy Starr, in her flame-colored outfit, looked almost old and dowdy.

Paula nudged Ellery, who was critically watching the Yankees at batting practice. "Ellery," she said softly, "who is that big, brown, attractive man in the next box?"

Lotus Verne said something to the brown man, and suddenly Judy Starr said something to the Song-and-Dance Man; and then the two women exchanged the kind of glance women use when there is no knife handy.

Ellery said absently: "Who? Oh! That's Big Bill Tree."

"Tree?" repeated Paula. "Big Bill Tree?"

"Greatest left-handed pitcher major-league baseball ever saw," said Mr. Queen, staring reverently at the brown man. "Six feet three inches of bull-whip and muscle, with a temper as sudden as the hook on his curve ball and a change of pace that fooled the greatest sluggers of baseball for fifteen years. What a man!"

"Yes, isn't he?" smiled Miss Paris.

"Now what does that mean?" demanded Mr. Queen.

"It takes greatness to escort a lady like Lotus Verne to a ball game," said Paula, "to find your wife sitting within spitting distance in the next box, and to carry it off as well as your muscular friend Mr. Tree is doing."

"That's right," said Mr. Queen softly. "Judy Starr is Mrs. Bill Tree."

He groaned as Joe DiMaggio hit a ball to the clubhouse clock.

"Funny," said Miss Paris, her clever eyes inspecting in turn the four people before her: Lotus Verne, the Hollywood siren; Big Bill Tree, the ex-baseball pitcher; Judy Starr, Tree's wife; and Jimmy Connor, the Song-and-Dance Man, Mrs. Tree's escort. Two couples, two boxes . . . and no sign of recognition. "Funny," murmured Miss Paris. "From the way Tree courted Judy you'd have thought the marriage would outlast eternity. He snatched her from under Jimmy Connor's nose one night at the Winter Garden, drove her up to Greenwich at eighty miles an hour, and married her before she could catch her breath."

"Yes," said Mr. Queen politely. "Come on, you Giants!" he yelled, as the Giants trotted out for batting practice.

"And then something happened," continued Miss Paris reflectively. "Tree went to Hollywood to make a baseball picture, met Lotus Verne, and the wench took the overgrown country boy the way the overgrown country boy had taken Judy Starr. What a fall was there, my baseball-minded friend."

"What a wallop!" cried Mr. Queen enthusiastically, as Mel Ott hit one that bounced off the right-field fence.

"And Big Bill yammered for a divorce, and Judy refused to give it to him because she loved him, I suppose," said Paula softly, "and now this. How interesting."

Big Bill Tree twisted in his seat a little; and Judy Starr was still and pale, staring out of her tragic, honey-colored eyes at the Yankee bat-boy and giving him unwarranted delusions of grandeur. Jimmy Connor continued to exchange sarcastic greetings with Yankee players, but his eyes kept shifting back to Judy's face. And beautiful Lotus Verne's arm crept about Tree's shoulders.

"I don't like it," murmured Miss Paris a little later.

"You don't like it?" said Mr. Queen. "Why, the game hasn't even started."

"I don't mean your game, silly. I mean the quadrangular situation in front of us."

"Look darling," said Mr. Queen. "I flew three thousand miles to see a ball game. There's only one angle that interests me—the view from this box of the greatest li'l ol' baseball tussle within the memory of gaffers. I yearn, I strain, I hunger to see it. Play with your quadrangle, but leave me to my baseball."

"I've always been psychic," said Miss Paris, paying no attention. "This is—bad. Something's going to happen."

Mr. Queen grinned. "I know what. The deluge. See what's coming."

Someone in the grandstand had recognized the celebrities, and a sea of people was rushing down on the two boxes. They thronged the aisle behind the boxes, waving pencils and papers, and pleading. Big Bill Tree and Lotus Verne ignored their pleas for autographs; but Judy Starr with a curious eagerness signed paper after paper with the yellow pencils thrust at her by people leaning over the rail. Good-naturedly Jimmy Connor scrawled his signature, too.

"Little Judy," sighed Miss Paris, setting her natural straw straight as an autograph-hunter knocked it over her eyes, "is flustered and unhappy. Moistening the tip of your pencil with your tongue is scarcely a mark of poise. Seated next to her Lotus-bound husband, she hardly knows what she's doing, poor thing."

"Neither do I," growled Mr. Queen, fending off an octopus which turned out to be eight pleading arms offering scorecards.

Big Bill sneezed, groped for a handkerchief, and held it to his nose, which was red and swollen. "Hey, Mac," he called irritably to a red-coated usher. "Do somethin' about this mob, huh?" He sneezed again. "Damn this hay-fever!"

"The touch of earth," said Miss Paris. "But definitely attractive."

"Should'a seen Big Bill the day he pitched that World Series final against the Tigers," chuckled Sergeant Velie. "He was sure attractive that day. Pitched a no-hit shutout!"

Inspector Queen said: "Ever hear the story behind that final game, Miss Paris? The night before, a gambler named Sure Shot McCoy, who represented a betting syndicate, called on Big Bill and laid down fifty grand in spot cash in return for Bill's promise to throw the next day's game. Bill took the money, told his manager the whole story, donated the bribe to a fund for sick ball players, and the next day shut out the Tigers without a hit."

"Byronic, too," murmured Miss Paris.

"So then Sure Shot, badly bent," grinned the Inspector, "called on Bill for the payoff, Bill knocked him down two flights of stairs."

"Wasn"t that dangerous?"

"I guess," smiled the Inspector, "you could say so. That's why you see that plug-ugly with the smashed nose sitting over there right behind Tree's box. He's Mr. Terrible Turk, late of Cicero, and since that night Big Bill's shadow. You don't see Mr. Turk's right hand, because Mr. Turk's right hand is holding on to an automatic under his jacket. You'll notice, too, that Mr. Turk hasn't for a second taken his eyes off that pasty-cheeked customer eight rows up, whose name is Sure Shot McCoy."

Paula stared. "But what a silly thing for Tree to do!"

"Well, yes," drawled Inspector Queen, "seeing that when he popped Mr. McCoy Big Bill snapped two of the carpal bones of his pitching wrist and wrote finis to his baseball career."

Big Bill Tree hauled himself to his feet, whispered something to the Verne woman, who smiled coyly, and left his box. His bodyguard, Turk, jumped up; but the big man shook his head, waved aside a crowd of people, and vaulted up the concrete steps toward the rear of the grandstand.

And then Judy Starr said something bitter and hot and desperate across the rail to the woman her husband had brought to the Polo Grounds. Lotus Verne's mercurial eyes glittered, and she replied in a careless, insulting voice that made Bill Tree's wife sit up stiffly. Jimmy Connor began to tell the one about Walter Winchell and the Seven Dwarfs . . . loudly and fast.

The Verne woman began to paint her rich lips with short, vicious strokes of her orange lipstick; and Judy Starr's flame kid glove tightened on the rail between them.

And after a while Big Bill returned and sat down again. Judy said something to Jimmy Connor, and the Song-and-Dance Man slid over one seat to his right, and Judy slipped into Connor's seat; so that between her and her husband there was now not only the box rail but an empty chair as well.

Lotus Verne put her arm about Tree's shoulders again.

Tree's wife fumbled inside her flame suede bag. She said suddenly: "Jimmy, buy me a frankfurter."

Connor ordered a dozen. Big Bill scowled. He jumped up and ordered some, too. Connor tossed the vendor two one-dollar bills and waved him away.

A new sea deluged the two boxes, and Tree turned round, annoyed. "All right, all right, Mac," he growled at the red-coat struggling with the pressing mob. "We don't want a riot here. I'll take six. Just six. Let's have 'em."

There was a rush that almost upset the attendant. The rail behind the boxes was a solid line of fluttering hands, arms, and scorecards.

"Mr. Tree—said—six!" panted the usher; and he grabbed a pencil and card from one of the outstretched hands and gave them to Tree. The overflow of pleaders spread to the next box. Judy Starr smiled her best professional smile and reached for a pencil and card. A group of players on the field, seeing what was happening, ran over to the field rail and handed her scorecards, too, so that she had to set her half-consumed frankfurter down on the empty seat beside her. Big Bill set his frankfurter down on the same empty seat; he licked the pencil long and absently and began to inscribe his name in the stiff, laborious hand of a man unused to writing.

The attendant howled: "That's six, now! Mr. Tree said just six, so that's all!" as if God Himself had said six; and the crowd groaned, and Big Bill waved his immense paw and reached over to the empty seat in the other box to lay hold of his half-eaten frankfurter. But his wife's hand got there first and fumbled round; and it came up with Tree's frankfurter. The big brown man almost spoke to her then; but he did not, and he picked up the remaining frankfurter, stuffed it into his mouth, and chewed away, but not as if he enjoyed its taste.

Mr. Ellery Queen was looking at the four people before him with a puzzled, worried expression. Then he caught Miss Paula Paris's amused glance and blushed angrily.

The groundskeepers had just left the field and the senior umpire was dusting off the plate to the roar of the crowd when Lotus Verne, who thought a double play was something by Eugene O'Neill, flashed a strange look at Big Bill Tree.

"Bill! Don't you feel well?"

The big ex-pitcher, a sickly blue beneath his tanned skin, put his hand to his eyes and shook his head as if to clear it.

"It's the hot dog," snapped Lotus. "No more for you!"

Tree blinked and began to say something, but just then Carl Hubbell completed his warming-up, Crosetti marched to the plate, Harry Danning tossed the ball to his second-baseman, who flipped it to Hubbell and trotted back to his position yipping like a terrier.

The voice of the crowd exploded in one ear-splitting burst. And then silence.

And Crosetti swung at the first ball Hubbell pitched and smashed it far over Joe Moore's head for a triple.

Jimmy Connor gasped as if someone had thrust a knife into his heart. But Detective-Sergeant Velie was bellowing: "What'd I tell you? It's gonna be a massacre!"

"What is everyone shouting for?" asked Paula.

Mr. Queen nibbled his nails as Danning strolled halfway to the pitcher's box. But Hubbell pulled his long pants up, grinning. Red Rolfe was waving a huge bat at the plate. Danning trotted back. Manager Bill Terry had one foot up on the edge of the Giant dugout, his chin on his fist, looking anxious. The infield came in to cut off the run.

Again fifty thousand people made no single little sound.

And Hubbell struck out Rolfe, DiMaggio, and Gehrig.

Mr. Queen shrieked his joy with the thousands as the Giants came whooping in. Jimmy Connor did an Indian war dance in the box. Sergeant Velie looked aggrieved, Senor Gomez took his warm-up pitches, the umpire used his whiskbroom on the plate again, and Jo-Jo Moore, the Thin Man, ambled up with his war club.

He walked, Bartell fanned. But Jeep Ripple singled off Flash Gordon's shins on the first pitch; and there were Moore on third and Ripple on first, one out, and Little Mel Ott at bat.

Big Bill Tree got half out of his seat, looking surprised then dropped to the concrete floor of the box as if somebody had slammed him behind the ear with a fast ball.

Lotus screamed. Judy, Bill's wife, turned like a shot, shaking. People in the vicinity jumped up. Three red-coated attendants hurried down, preceded by the hard-looking Mr. Turk. The bench-warmers stuck their heads over the edge of the Yankee dugout to stare.

"Fainted," growled Turk, on his knees beside the prostrate athlete.

"Loosen his collar," moaned Lotus Verne. "He's so p-pale!"

"Have to git him outa here."

"Yes. Oh, yes!"

The attendants and Turk lugged the big man off, long arms dangling in the oddest way. Lotus stumbled along beside him, biting her lips nervously.

"I think," began Judy in a quivering voice, rising.

But Jimmy Connor put his hand on her arm, and she sank back.

And in the next box Mr. Ellery Queen, on his feet from the instant Tree collapsed, kept looking after the forlorn procession, puzzled, mad about something: until somebody in the stands squawked: "SIDDOWN!" and he sat down.

"Oh, I knew something would happen," whispered Paula.

"Nonsense!" said Mr. Queen shortly. "Fainted, that's all."

Inspector Queen said: "There's Sure Shot McCoy not far off. I wonder if—"

"Too many hot dogs," snapped his son. "What's the matter with you people? Can't I see my ball game in peace?" And he howled: "Come o-o-on, Mel!"

Ott lifted his right leg into the sky and swung. The ball whistled into right field, a long fly, Selkirk racing madly back after it. He caught it by leaping four feet into the air with his back against the barrier. Moore was off for the plate like a streak and beat the throw to Bill Dickey by inches.

"Yip-ee!" said Mr. Queen.

The Giants trotted out to their position at the end of the first inning leading one to nothing.

Up in the press box the working gentlemen of the press tore into their chores, recalling Carl Hubbell's similar feat in the All-Star game when he struck out the five greatest batters of the American League in succession; praising Twinkletoes Selkirk for his circus catch; and incidentally noting that Big Bill Tree, famous ex-hurler of the National League, had fainted in a field box during the first inning. Joe William of the *World-Telegram* said it was excitement, Hype Igoe opined that it was a touch of sun—Big Bill never wore a hat—and Frank Graham of the *Sun* guessed it was too many frankfurters.

Paula Paris said quietly: "I should think, with your detective instincts, Mr. Queen, you would seriously question the 'fainting' of Mr. Tree."

Mr. Queen squirmed and finally mumbled: "It's coming to a pretty pass when a man's instincts aren't his own. Velie, go see what really happened to him."

"I wanna watch the game," howled Velie. "Why don't you go yourself, maestro?"

"And possibly," said Mr. Queen, "you ought to go too, Dad. I have a hunch it may lie in your jurisdiction."

Inspector Queen regarded his son for some time. Then he rose and signed: "Come along, Thomas."

Sergeant Velie growled something about some people always spoiling other people's fun and why the hell did he ever have to become a cop; but he got up and obediently followed the Inspector.

Mr. Queen nibbled his fingernails and avoided Miss Paris's accusing eyes.

The second inning was uneventful. Neither side scored.

As the Giants took the field again, an usher came running down the concrete steps and whispered into Jim Connor's ear. The Song-and-Dance Man blinked. He rose slowly. "Excuse me, Judy."

Judy grasped the rail. "It's Bill. Jimmy, tell me."

"Now, Judy—"

"Something's happened to Bill!" Her voice shrilled, and then broke. She jumped up. "I'm going with you."

Connor smiled as if he had just lost a bet, and then he took Judy's arm and hurried her away.

Paula Paris stared after them, breathing hard.

Mr. Queen beckoned the redcoat. "What's the trouble?" he demanded.

"Mr. Tree passed out. Some young doc in the crowd tried to pull him out of it up at the office, but he couldn't and he's startin' to look worried—"

"I knew it!" cried Paula as the man darted away. "Ellery Queen, are you going to sit here and do *nothing?*"

But Mr. Queen defiantly set his jaw. Nobody was going to jockey him out of seeing this battle of giants; no, ma'am!

There were two men out when Frank Crosetti stepped up to the plate for his second time at bat and, with the count two all, plastered a wicked single over Ott's head.

And, of course, Sergeant Velie took just that moment to amble down and say, his eyes on the field: "Better come along, Master Mind. The old man wouldst have a word with thou. Ah, I see Frankie's on first. Smack it, Red!"

Mr. Queen watched Rolfe take a ball. "Well?" he said shortly. Paula's lips were parted.

"Big Bill's just kicked the bucket. What happened in the second inning?"

"He's . . . *dead?*" gasped Paula.

Mr. Queen rose involuntarily. Then he sat down again. "Damn it," he roared, "it isn't fair. I won't go!"

"Suit yourself. Attaboy, Rolfe!" bellowed the sergeant as Rolfe singled sharply past Bartell and Crosetti pulled up at second base. "Far's I'm concerned, it's open and shut. The little woman did it with her own little hands."

"Judy *Starr?*" said Miss Paris.

"Bill's wife?" said Mr. Queen. "What are you talking about?"

"That's right, little Judy. She poisoned his hot dog." Velie chucked. "Man bites dog, and—zowie."

"Has she confessed?" snapped Mr. Queen.

"Naw. But you know dames. She gave Bill the business, all right. C'mon, Joe! And I gotta go. What a life."

Mr. Queen did not look at Miss Paris. He bit his lip. "Here, Velie, wait a minute."

DiMaggio hit a long fly that Leiber caught without moving in his tracks, and the Yankees were retired without a score.

"Ah," said Mr. Queen. "Good old Hubbell." And as the Giants trotted in, he took a fat roll of bills from his pocket, climbed onto his seat, and began waving green-backs at the spectators in the reserved seats behind the box. Sergeant Velie and Miss Paris stared at him in amazement.

"I'll give five bucks," yelled Mr. Queen, waving the money, "for every autograph Bill Tree signed before the game! In this box right here! Five bucks, gentlemen! Come and get it!"

"You nuts?" gasped the sergeant.

The mob gaped, and then began to laugh, and after a few moments a pair of sheepish-looking men came down, and then two more, and finally a fifth. An attendant ran over to find out what was the matter.

"Are you the usher who handled the crowd around Bill Tree's box before the game, when he was giving autographs?" demanded Mr. Queen.

"Yes, sir. But look, we can't allow—"

"Take a gander at these five men . . . You, bud? Yes, that's Tree's handwriting. Here's your fin. Next!" and Mr. Queen went down the line, handing out five-dollar bills with abandon in return for five dirty scorecards with Tree's scrawl on them.

"Anybody else?" he called out, waving his roll of bills.

But nobody else appeared, although there was ungentle badinage from the stands. Sergeant Velie stood there shaking his big head. Miss Paris looked intensely curious.

"Who didn't come down?" rapped Mr. Queen.

"Huh?" said the usher, his mouth open.

"There were six autographs. Only five people turned up. Who was the sixth man? Speak up!"

"Oh." The redcoat scratched his ear. "Say, it wasn't a man. It was a kid."

"A *boy?*"

"Yeah, a little squirt in knee-pants."

Mr. Queen looked unhappy. Velie growled: "Sometimes I think society's takin' an awful chance lettin' you run around loose," and the two men left the box. Miss Paris, bright-eyed followed.

"Have to clear this mess up in a hurry," muttered Mr. Queen. "Maybe we'll still be able to catch the late innings."

Sergeant Velie led the way to an office, before which a policeman was lounging. He opened the door, and inside they found the Inspector pacing, Turk, the thug, was standing with a scowl over a long still thing on a couch covered with newspapers. Jimmy Connor sat between the two women; and none of the three so much as stirred a foot. They were all pale and breathing heavily.

"This is Dr. Fielding," said Inspector Queen, indicating an elderly white-haired man standing quietly by a window. "He was Tree's physician. He happened to be in the park watching the game when the rumor reached his ears that Tree had collapsed, so he hurried up here to see what he could do."

Ellery went to the couch and pulled the newspaper off Bill Tree's still head. Paula crossed swiftly to Judy Starr and said: "I'm horribly sorry, Mrs. Tree," but the woman, her eyes closed, did not move. After a while Ellery dropped the newspaper back into place and said irritably: "Well, well, let's have it."

"A young doctor," said the Inspector, "got here before Dr. Fielding did, and treated Tree for fainting. I guess it was his fault—"

"Not at all," said Dr. Fielding sharply. "The early picture was compatible with fainting, from what he told me. He tried the usual restorative methods—even injected caffeine and picrotoxin. But there was no convulsion, and he didn't happen to catch that odor of bitter almonds."

"Prussic!" said Ellery. "Taken orally?"

"Yes. H.C.N.—hydrocyanic acid, or prussic, as you prefer. I suspected it at once because—well," said Dr. Fielding in a grim voice, "because of something that occurred in my office only the other day."

"What was that?"

"I had a two-ounce bottle of hydrocyanic acid on my desk—I sometimes use it in minute quantities as a cardiac stimulant. Mrs. Tree," the doctor's glance flickered over the silent woman, "happened to be in my office, resting in preparation for a metabolism test. I left her alone. By a coincidence, Bill Tree dropped in the same morning for a physical checkup. I saw another patient in another room, returned, gave Mrs. Tree her test, saw her out, and came back with Tree. It was then I noticed the bottle, which had been plainly marked DANGER—POISON, was missing from my desk. I thought I had mislaid it, but now . . ."

"I didn't take it," said Judy Starr in a lifeless voice, still not opening her eyes. "I never even saw it."

The Song-and-Dance Man took her limp hand and gently stroked it.

"No hypo marks on the body," said Dr. Fielding dryly. "And I am told that fifteen to thirty minutes before Tree collapsed he ate a frankfurter under . . . peculiar conditions."

"I didn't" screamed Judy. "I didn't do it!" She pressed her face, sobbing, against Connor's orchid.

Lotus Verne quivered. "She made him pick up her frankfurter. I saw it. They both laid their frankfurters down on that empty seat, and she picked up his. So he had to pick up hers. She poisoned her own frankfurter and then saw to it that he ate it by mistake. Poisoner!" She glared hate at Judy.

"Wench," said Miss Paris *sotto voce,* glaring hate at Lotus.

"In other words," put in Ellery impatiently, Miss Starr is convicted on the usual two counts, motive and opportunity. Motive—her jealousy of Miss Verne and her hatred—an assumption—of Bill Tree, her husband. And opportunity both to lay hands on the poison in your office, Doctor, and to sprinkle some on her frankfurter, contriving to exchange hers for his while they were both autographing scorecards."

"She hated him," snarled Lotus. "And me for having taken him from her!"

"Be quiet, you," said Mr. Queen. He opened the corridor door and said to the policeman outside: "Look, McGillicuddy, or whatever your name is, go tell the announcer to make a speech over the loud-speaker system. By the way, what's the score now?"

"Still one to skunk," said the officer. "Them boys Hubbell an' Gomez are hot, know what I mean."

"The announcer is to ask the little boy who got Bill Tree's autograph just before the game to come to this office. If he does, he'll receive a ball, bat, pitcher's glove, and an autographed picture of Tree in uniform to hang over his itsy-bitsy bed. Scram!"

"Yes, *sir,*" said the officer.

"King Carl pitching his heart out," grumbled Mr. Queen, shutting the door, "and me strangulated by this blamed thing. Well, Dad, do you think, too, that Judy Starr dosed that frankfurter?"

"What else can I think?" said the Inspector absently. His ears were cocked for the faint crowd-shouts from the park.

"Judy Starr," replied his son, "didn't poison her husband any more than I did."

Judy looked up slowly, her mouth muscles twitching. Paula said gladly: "You wonderful man!"

"She didn't?" said the Inspector, looking alert.

"The frankfurter theory," snapped Mr. Queen, "is too screwy for words. For Judy to have poisoned her husband, she had to unscrew the cap of a bottle and douse her hot dog on the spot with the hydrocyanic acid. Yet Jimmy Connor was seated by her side, and in the only period in which she could possibly have poisoned the frankfurter a group of Yankee ball players was standing before her across the field rail getting her autograph. Were they all accomplices? And how could she have known Big Bill would lay his hot dog on that empty seat? The whole thing is absurd."

A roar from the stands made him continue hastily: "There was one plausible theory that fitted the facts. When I heard that Tree had died of poisoning, I recalled that at the time he was autographing the six scorecards, *he had thoroughly licked the end of a pencil* which had been handed to him with one of the cards. It was possible, then, that the pencil he licked had been poisoned. So I offered to buy the six autographs."

Paula regarded him tenderly, and Velie said: "I'll be a so-and-so if he didn't."

"I didn't expect the poisoner to come forward, but I knew the innocent ones would. Five claimed the money. The sixth, the missing one, the usher informed me, had been a small boy."

"A kid poisoned Bill?" growled Turk, speaking for the first time. "You're crazy from the heat."

"In spades," added the Inspector.

"Then why didn't the boy come forward?" put in Paula quickly. "Go on, darling!"

"He didn't come forward, not because he was guilty but because he wouldn't sell Bill Tree's autograph for anything. No, obviously a hero-worshipping boy wouldn't try to poison the great Bill Tree. Then, just as obviously, he didn't realize what he was doing. Consequently, he must have been an innocent tool. The question was—and still is—of whom?"

"Sure Shot," said the Inspector slowly.

Lotus Verne sprang to her feet, her eyes glittering. "Perhaps Judy Starr didn't poison that frankfurter, but if she didn't then she hired that boy to give Bill—"

Mr. Queen said disdainfully: "Miss Starr didn't leave the box once." Someone knocked on the corridor door and he opened it. For the first time he smiled. When he shut the door they saw that his arm was about the shoulder of a boy with brown hair and quick clever eyes. The boy was clutching the scorecard tightly.

"They say over the announcer," mumbled the boy, "that I'll get a autographed pi'ture of Big Bill Tree if . . ." He stopped, abashed at their strangely glinting eyes.

"And you'll certainly get it, too," said Mr. Queen heartily. "What's your name, sonny?"

"Fenimore Feigenspan," replied the boy, edging toward the door. "Gran' Concourse, Bronx. Here's the scorecard. How about the pi'ture?"

"Let's see that, Fenimore," said Mr. Queen. "When did Bill Tree give you this autograph?"

"Before the game. He said he's on'y give six—"

"Where's the pencil you handed him, Fenimore?"

The boy looked suspicious, but he dug into a bulging pocket and brought forth one of the ordinary yellow pencils sold at the park with scorecards. Ellery took it from him gingerly, and Dr. Fielding took it from Ellery, and sniffed its tip. He nodded, and for the first time a look of peace came over Judy Starr's still face and she dropped her head tiredly to Connor's shoulder.

Mr. Queen ruffled Fenimore Feigenspan's hair. "That's swell, Fenimore. Somebody gave you that pencil while the Giants were at batting practice, isn't that so?"

"Yeah." The boy stared at him.

"Who was it?" Asked Mr. Queen lightly.

"I dunno. A big guy with a coat an' a turned-down hat an' a mustache, an' big black sunglasses. I couldn't see his face good. Where's my pi'ture? I wanna see the game!"

"Just where was it that this man gave you the pencil?"

"In the—" Fenimore paused, glancing at the ladies with embarrassment. Then he muttered: "Well, I hadda go, an' this guy says—in there—he's ashamed to ask her for her autograph, so would I do it for him—"

"What? What's that?" exclaimed Mr. Queen. "Did you say 'her'?"

"Sure," said Fenimore. "The dame, he says, wearin' the red hat an' red dress an' red gloves in the field box near the Yanks dugout, he says. He even took me outside an' pointed down to where she was sittin'. Say!" cried Fenimore, goggling. "That's her! That's the dame!" and he levelled a grimy forefinger at Judy Starr.

Judy shivered and felt blindly for the Song-and-Dance Man's hand.

"Let me get this straight, Fenimore," said Mr. Queen softly. "This man with the sunglasses asked you to get this lady's autograph for him, and gave you the pencil and scorecard to get it with?"

"Yeah, an' two bucks too, sayin' he'd meet me after the game to pick up the card, but—"

"But you didn't get the lady's autograph for him, did you? You went down to get it, and hung around waiting for your chance, but then you spied Big Bill Tree, your hero, in the next box and forgot all about the lady, didn't you?"

The boy shrank back. "I didn't mean to, honest, Mister. I'll give the two bucks back!"

"And seeing Big Bill there, your hero, you went right over to get *his* autograph for *yourself,* didn't you?" Fenimore nodded, frightened. "You gave the usher the pencil and scorecard this man with the sunglasses had handed you, and the usher turned the pencil and scorecard over to Bill Tree in the box—wasn't that the way it happened?"

"Y-yes, sir, an' . . ." Fenimore twisted out of Ellery's grasp, "an' so I—I gotta go." And before anyone could stop him he was indeed gone, racing down the corridor like the wind.

The policeman outside shouted, but Ellery said: "Let him go, officer," and shut the door. Then he opened it again and said: "How's she stand now?"

"Dunno exactly, sir. Somethin' happened out there just now. I think the Yanks scored."

"Damn," groaned Mr. Queen, and he shut the door again.

"So it was Mrs. Tree who was on the spot, not Bill," scowled the Inspector. "I'm sorry, Judy Starr . . . Big man with a coat and hat and mustache and sunglasses. Some description!"

"Sounds like a phony to me," said Sergeant Velie.

"If it was a disguise, he dumped it somewhere," said the Inspector thoughtfully. "Thomas, have a look in the Men's Room behind the section where we were sitting. And Thomas," he added in a whisper, "find out what the score is." Velie grinned and hurried out. Inspector Queen frowned. "Quite a job finding a killer in a crowd of fifty thousand people."

"Maybe," said his son suddenly, "maybe it's not such a job after all. . . . What was used to kill? Hydrocynanic acid. Who was intended to be killed? Bill Tree's wife. And connection between anyone in the case and hydrocyanic acid? Yes—Dr. Fielding 'lost' a bottle of it under suspicious circumstances. Which were? That Bill Tree's wife could have taken that bottle . . . *or Bill Tree himself.*"

"Bill Tree!" gasped Paula.

"Bill?" whispered Judy Starr.

"Quite! Dr. Fielding didn't miss the bottle until *after* he had shown you, Miss Starr, out of his office. He then returned to his office with your husband. Bill could have slipped the bottle into his pocket as he stepped into the room."

"Yes, he could have," muttered Dr. Fielding.

"I don't see," said Mr. Queen, "how we can arrive at any other conclusion. We know his wife was intended to be the victim today, so obviously she didn't steal the poison. The only other person who had opportunity to steal it was Bill himself."

The Verne woman sprang up. "I don't believe it! It's a frame-up to protect *her,* now that Bill can't defend himself!"

"Ah, but didn't he have motive to kill Judy?" asked Mr. Queen. "Yes, indeed; she wouldn't give him the divorce he craved so that he could marry *you.* I think, Miss Verne, you would be wiser to keep the peace. . . . Bill had opportunity to steal the bottle of poison in Dr. Fielding's office. He also had opportunity to hire Fenimore today, for he was the *only* one of the whole group who left those two boxes during the period when the poisoner must have searched for someone to offer Judy the poisoned pencil.

"All of which fits for what Bill had to do—get to where he had cached his disguise, probably yesterday; look for a likely tool; find Fenimore, give his instructions and the pencil; get rid of the disguise again; and return to his box. And didn't Bill know better than anyone his wife's habit of moistening a pencil with her tongue—a habit she probably acquired from *him?*"

"Poor Bill," murmured Judy Starr brokenly.

"Women," remarked Miss Paris, "are *fools.*"

"There were other striking ironies," replied Mr. Queen. "For if Bill hadn't been suffering from a hay-fever attack, he would have smelled the odor of bitter almonds when his own poisoned pencil was handed to him and stopped in time to save his worthless life. For that matter, if he hadn't been Fenimore Feigenspan's hero, Fenimore would not have handed him his own poisoned pencil in the first place.

"No," said Mr. Queen gladly, "putting it all together, I'm satisfied that Mr. Big Bill Tree, in trying to murder his wife, very neatly murdered himself instead."

"That's all very well for *you,*" said the Inspector disconsolately. "But I need proof."

"I've told you how it happened," said his son airily, making for the door. "Can any man do more? Coming, Paula?"

But Paula was already at a telephone, speaking guardedly to the New York office of the syndicate for which she worked, and paying no more attention to him than if he had been a worm.

"What's the score? What's been going on?" Ellery demanded of the world at large as he regained his box seat. "Three to three! What the devil's got into Hubbell, anyway? How'd the Yanks score? What inning is it?"

"Last of the ninth, shrieked somebody. "The Yanks got three runs in the eighth on a walk, a double, and DiMag's homer! Damming hammered in the sixth with Ott on base! Shut up!"

Bartell singled over Gordon's head. Mr. Queen cheered.

Sergeant Velie tumbled into the next seat. "Well, we got it," he puffed. "Found the whole outfit in the Men's Room—coat, hat, fake mustache, glasses and all. What's the score?"

"Three-three. Sacrifice, Jeep!" shouted Mr. Queen.

"There was a rain-check in the coat pocket from the sixth game, with Big Bill's box number on it. So there's the old man's proof. Chalk up another win for you."

"Who cares? *Zowie!*"

Jeep Ripple sacrificed Bartell successfully to second.

"Lucky stiff," howled a Yankee fan nearby. "That's the breaks. See the break they get? See?"

"And another thing," said the sergeant, watching Mel Ott stride to the plate. "Seein' as how all Big Bill did was cross himself up, and no harm done except to his own carcass, and seein' as how organized baseball could get along without a murder, and seein' as how thousands of kids like Fenimore Feigenspan worship the ground he walked on—"

"Sew it up, Mel!" bellowed Mr. Queen.

"And seein' as how none of the newspaper guys know what happened, except that Bill passed out of the picture after a faint, and seein' as everybody's only too glad to shut their traps—"

Mr. Queen awoke suddenly to the serious matters of life. "What's that? What did you say?"

"Strike him out, Goofy!" roared the sergeant to Senor Gomez, who did not hear. "As I was saying, it ain't cricket, and the old man would be broke out of the force if the big cheese heard about it . . ."

Someone puffed up behind them, and they turned to see Inspector Queen, red-faced as if after a hard run, scrambling into the box with the assistance of Miss Paula Paris, who looked cool, serene, and star-eyed as ever.

"Dad!" said Mr. Queen, staring. "With a murder on your hands, how can you—"

"Murder?" panted Inspector Queen. "What murder? And he winked at Miss Paris, who winked back.

"But Paula was telephoning the story—"

"Didn't you hear?" said Paula in a coo, setting her straw straight and slipping into the seat beside Ellery's. "I fixed it all up with your dad. Tonight all the world will know is that Mr. Bill Tree died of heart failure."

They all chuckled then—all but Mr. Queen, whose mouth was open.

"So now," said Paula, "your dad can see the finish of your precious game just as well as *you,* you selfish oaf!"

But Mr. Queen was already fiercely rapt in contemplation of Mel Ott's bat as it swung back and Senor Gomez's ball as it left the Senor's hand to streak toward the plate.

The Criminologists' Club

E. W. Hornung

Encouraged by a suggestion from his brother-in-law Arthur Conan Doyle, Ernest Hornung created a unique form of crime story and introduced the gentleman thief Raffles: daring, debonair, devilishly handsome and a first-class cricketer. Raffles established the prototype for The Saint, James Bond and Cary Grant's character in Alfred Hitchcock's classic *To Catch a Thief*. Ronald Colman portrayed the gentleman cracksman in the 1930 film *Raffles;* David Niven starred in the title role in the 1940 remake.

"But who are they, Raffles, and where's their house? There's no such club on the list in Whitaker."

"The Criminologists, my dear Bunny, are too few for a local habitation, and too select to tell their name in Gath. They are merely so many solemn students of contemporary crime, who meet and dine periodically at each other's clubs or houses."

"But why in the world should they ask us to dine with them?"

And I brandished the invitation which had brought me hotfoot to the Albany: it was from the Right Hon. the Earl of Thornaby, K.G.; and it requested the honor of my company at dinner, at Thornaby House, Park Lane, to meet the members of the Criminologists' Club. That in itself was a disturbing compliment: judge then of my dismay on learning that Raffles had been invited too!

"They have got it into their heads," said he, "that the gladiatorial element is the curse of most modern sport. They tremble especially for the professional gladiator. And they want to know whether my experience tallies with their theory."

"So they say!"

"They quote the case of a league player, *sus per coll*, and any number of suicides. It really is rather in my public line."

"In yours, if you like, but not in mine," said I. "No, Raffles, they've got their eye on us both, and mean to put us under the microscope, or they never would have pitched on me."

Raffles smiled on my perturbation.

"I almost wish you were right, Bunny! It would be even better fun than I mean to make it as it is. But it may console you to hear that it was I who gave them your name. I told them you were a far keener criminologist than myself. I am delighted to hear they have taken my hint, and that we are to meet at their gruesome board."

"If I accept," said I with the austerity he deserved.

"If you don't," rejoined Raffles, "you will miss some sport after both our hearts. Think of it, Bunny! These fellows meet to wallow in all the latest crimes; we wallow with them as though we knew no more about it than themselves. Perhaps we don't, for few criminologists have a soul above murder; and I quite expect to have the privilege of lifting the discussion into our own higher walk. They shall give their morbid minds to the fine art of burgling, for a change; and while we're about it, Bunny, we may as well extract their opinion of our noble selves. As authors, as collaborators, we will sit with the flower of our critics, and find our own level in the expert eye. It will be a piquant experience, if not an invaluable one; if we are sailing too near the wind, we are sure to hear about it, and can trim our yards accordingly. Moreover, we shall get a very good dinner into the bargain, or our noble host will belie a European reputation."

"Do you know him?" I asked.

"We have a pavilion acquaintance, when it suits my lord," replied Raffles, chuckling. "But I know all about him. He was president one year of the M. C. C., and we never had a better. He knows the game, though I believe he never played cricket in his life. But then he knows most things, and has never done any of them. He has never even married, and never opened his lips in the House of Lords. Yet they say there is no better brain in the august assembly, and he certainly made us a wonderful speech last time the Australians were over. He has read everything and (to his credit in these days) never written a line. All round he is a whale for theory and a sprat for practice—but he looks quite capable of both at crime!"

I now longed to behold this remarkable peer in the flesh, and with the greater curiosity since another of the things which he evidently never did was to have his photograph published for the benefit of the vulgar. I told Raffles that I would dine with him at Lord Thornaby's, and he nodded as though I had not hesitated for a moment. I see now how deftly he had disposed of my reluctance. No doubt he had thought it all out before: his little speeches look sufficiently premeditated as I set them down at the dictates of an excellent memory. Let it, however, be borne in mind that Raffles did not talk exactly like a Raffles book: he said the things, but he did not say them in so many conservative breaths. They were punctuated by puffs from his eternal cigarette, and the punctuation was often in the nature of a line of asterisks, while he took a silent turn up and down his room. Nor was he ever more deliberate than when he seemed most nonchalant and spontaneous. I came to see it in the end. But these were early days, in which he was more plausible to me than I can hope to render him to another human being.

And I saw a good deal of Raffles just then; it was, in fact, the one period at which I can remember his coming round to see me more frequently than I went round to him. Of course he would come at his own odd hours, often just as one was dressing to go out and dine, and I can even remember finding him there when I returned, for I had long since given him a key of the flat. It was the inhospitable month of February, and I can recall more than one cosy evening when we discussed anything and everything but our own malpractices; indeed, there were none to discuss just then. Raffles, on the contrary, was showing himself with some industry in the most respectable society and by his advice I used the club more than ever.

"There is nothing like it at this time of year," said he. In the summer I have my cricket to provide me with decent employment in the sight of men. Keep yourself before the public from morning to night, and they'll never think of you in the still small hours."

Our behavior, in fine, had so long been irreproachable that I rose without misgiving on the morning of Lord Thornaby's dinner to the other criminologists and guests. My chief anxiety was to arrive under the aegis of my brilliant friend, and I had begged him to pick me up on his way; but at five minutes to the appointed hour there was no sign of Raffles or his cab. We were bidden at a quarter to eight for eight o'clock, so after all I had to hurry off alone.

Fortunately, Thornaby House is almost at the end of my street that was; and it seemed to me another fortunate circumstance that the house stood back, as it did and does, in its own august courtyard; for, as I was about to knock, a hansom came twinkling in behind me, and I drew back, hoping it was Raffles at the last moment. It was not, and I knew it in time to melt from the porch, and wait yet another minute in the shadows, since others were as late as I. And out jumped these others, chattering in stage whispers as they paid their cab.

"Thornaby has a bet about it with Freddy Vereker, who can't come, I hear. Of course, it won't be lost or won, tonight. But the dear man thinks he's been invited as a cricketer!"

"I don't believe he's the other thing," said a voice as brusque as the first was bland. "I believe it's all bunkum. I wish I didn't, but I do!"

"I think you'll find it's more than that," rejoined the other as the doors opened and swallowed the pair.

I flung out limp hands and smote the air. Raffles bidden to what he had well called this "gruesome board," not as a cricketer but as a suspected criminal! Raffles wrong all the time, and I right for once in my original apprehension! And still no Raffles in sight—no Raffles to warn—no Raffles, and the clocks striking eight!

Well may I shirk the psychology of such a moment, for my belief is that the striking clocks struck out all power of thought and feeling, and that I played my poor part the better for that blessed surcease of intellectual sensation. On the other hand, I was never more alive to the purely objective impressions of any hour of my existence, and of them the memory is startling to this day. I hear my mad knock at the double doors; they fly open in the middle, and it is like some sumptuous and solemn rite. A long slice of silken-legged lackey is seen on either hand; a very prelate of a butler bows a benediction from the sanctuary steps. I breathe more freely when I reach a book-lined library where a mere handful of men do not overflow the Persian rug before the fire. One of them is Raffles, who is talking to a large man with the brow of a demigod and the eyes and jowl of a degenerate bulldog. And this is our noble host.

Lord Thornaby stared at me with inscrutable stolidity as we shook hands, and at once handed me over to a tall, ungainly man whom he addressed as Ernest, but whose surname I never learned. Ernest in turn introduced me, with a shy and clumsy courtesy, to the two remaining guests. They were the pair who had driven up in the hansom; one turned out to be Kingsmill, Q. C.; the other I knew at a glance from his photographs as Parrington, the backwoods novelist. They were admirable foils to each other, the barrister being plump and dapper, with a Napoleonic cast of countenance, and the author one of the shaggiest dogs I have ever seen in evening clothes. Neither took much stock of me, but both had an eye on Raffles as I exchanged a few words with each in turn. Dinner, however, was immediately announced, and the six of us had soon taken our places round a brilliant little table stranded in a great dark room.

I had not been prepared for so small a party, and at first I felt relieved. If the worst came to the worst, I was fool enough to say in my heart, they were but two to one. But I was soon sighing for that safety which the adage associates with numbers. We were far too few for the confidential duologue with one's neighbor in which I, at least, would have taken refuge from the perils of a general conversation. And the general conversation soon resolved itself into an attack, so subtly concerted and so artistically delivered that I could not conceive how Raffles should ever know it for an attack, and that against himself, or how to warn him of his peril. But to this day I am not convinced that I also was honored by the suspicions of the club; it may have been so, and they may have ignored me for the bigger game.

It was Lord Thornaby himself who fired the first shot, over the very sherry. He had Raffles on his right hand, and the backwoodsman of letters on his left. Raffles was hemmed in by the law on his right, while I sat between Parrington and Ernest, who took the foot of the table, and seemed a sort of feudatory cadet of the noble house. But it was the motley lot of us that my lord addressed, as he sat back blinking his baggy eyes.

"Mr. Raffles," he said, "has been telling me about that poor fellow who suffered the extreme penalty last March. A great end, gentlemen, great end! It is true that he had been unfortunate enough to strike a jugular vein, but his own end should take its place among the most glorious traditions of the gallows. You tell them, Mr. Raffles: it will be as new to my friends as it is to me."

"I tell the tale as I heard it last time I played at Trent Bridge; it was never in the papers, I believe," said Raffles gravely. "You may remember tremendous excitement over the Test Matches out in Australia at the time: it seems that the result of the crucial game was expected on the condemned man's last day on earth, and he couldn't rest until he knew it. We pulled it off, if you recollect, and he said it would make him swing happy."

"Tell 'em what else he said!" cried Lord Thornaby, rubbing his podgy hands.

"The chaplain remonstrated with him on his excitement over a game at such a time, and the convict is said to have replied: 'Why, it's the first thing they'll ask me at the other end of the drop!'"

The story was new even to me, but I had no time to appreciate its points. My concern was to watch its effect upon the other members of the party. Ernest, on my left, doubled up with laughter, and tittered and shook for several minutes. My other neighbor, more impressionable by temperament, winced first, and then worked himself into a state of enthusiasm which culminated in an assault upon his shirt cuff with a joiner's pencil. Kingsmill, Q. C., beaming tranquilly on Raffles, seemed the one least impressed, until he spoke.

"I am glad to hear that," he remarked in a high bland voice. I thought, that man would die game."

"Did you know anything about him, then?" inquired Lord Thornaby.

"I led for the Crown," replied the barrister with a twinkle. "You might almost say that I measured the poor man's neck."

The point must have been quite unpremeditated; it was not the less effective for that. Lord Thornaby looked askance at the callous silk. It was some moments before Ernest tittered and Parrington felt for his pencil; and in the interim I had made short work of my hock, though it was Johannisberger. As for Raffles, one had but to see his horror to feel how completely he was off his guard.

"In itself, I have heard, it was not a sympathetic case," was the remark with which he broke the general silence.

"Not a bit."

"That must have been a comfort to you," said Raffles dryly.

"It would have been to me," vowed our author, while the barrister merely smiled. "I should have been very sorry to have had a hand in hanging Peckham and Solomons the other day."

"Why Peckham and Solomons?" inquired my lord.

"They never meant to kill that old lady."

"But they strangled her in her bed with her own pillowcase!"

"I don't care," said the uncouth scribe. "They didn't break in for that. They never thought of scragging her. The foolish old person would make a noise, and one of them tied too tight. I call it jolly bad luck on them."

"On quiet, harmless, well-behaved thieves," added Lord Thornaby, "in the unobtrusive exercise of their humble avocation."

And, as he turned to Raffles with his puffy smile, I knew that we had reached that part of the program which had undergone rehearsal: it had been perfectly timed to arrive with the champagne and I was not afraid to signify my appreciation of that small mercy. But Raffles laughed so quickly at his lordship's humor, and yet with such a natural restraint, as to leave no doubt that he had taken kindly to my own old part, and was playing the innocent inimitably in his turn, by reason of his very innocence. It was a poetic. It was poetic judgment on old Raffles, and in my momentary enjoyment of the novel situation I was able to enjoy some of the good things of this rich man's table. The saddle of mutton more than justified its place in the menu; but it had not spoiled me for my wing of pheasant, and I was even looking forward to a sweet, when a further remark from the literary light recalled me from the table to its talk.

"But, I suppose," said he to Kingsmill, "it's many a burglar you've restored to his friends and his relations."

"Let us say many a poor fellow who had been charged with burglary," replied the cheery Q. C. "It's not quite the same thing, you know, nor is 'many' the most accurate word. I never touch criminal work in town."

"It's the only kind I should care about," said the novelist, eating jelly with a spoon.

"I quite agree with you," our host chimed in. "And of all the criminals one might be called upon to defend, give me the enterprising burglar."

"It must be the breeziest branch of the business," remarked Raffles, while I held my breath.

But his touch was as light as gossamer, and his artless manner a triumph of even his incomparable art. Raffles was alive to the danger at last. I saw him refuse more champagne, even as I drained my glass again. But it was not the same danger to us both. Raffles had no reason to feel surprise or alarm at such a turn in a conversation frankly devoted to criminology; it must have seemed as inevitable to him as it was sinister to me, with my fortuitous knowledge of the suspicions that were entertained. And there was little to put him on his guard in the touch of his adversaries, which was only less light than his own.

"I am not very fond of Mr. Sikes," announced the barrister, like a man who had got his cue.

"But he was prehistoric," rejoined my lord. "A lot of blood has flowed under the razor since the days of Sweet William."

"True; we have had Peace," said Parrington, and launched out into such glowing details of that criminal's last moments that I began to hope the diversion might prove permanent. But Lord Thornaby was not to be denied.

"William and Charles are both dead monarchs," said he. "The reigning king in their department is the fellow who gutted poor Danby's place in Bond Street."

There was a guilty silence on the part of the three conspirators for I had long since persuaded myself that Ernest was not in their secret—and then my blood froze.

"I know him well," said Raffles, looking up.

Lord Thornaby stared at him in consternation. The smile on the Napoleonic countenance of the barrister looked forced and frozen for the first time during the evening. Our author, who was nibbling cheese from a knife, left a bead of blood upon his beard. The futile Ernest alone met the occasion with a hearty titter.

"What!" cried my lord. *"You know the thief?"*

"I wish I did," rejoined Raffles chuckling. "No, Lord Thornaby, I only meant the jeweler, Danby. I go to him when I want a wedding present."

I heard three deep breaths drawn as one before I drew my own.

"Rather a coincidence," observed our host dryly, "for I believe you also know the Milchester people, where Lady Melrose had her necklace stolen a few months afterward."

"I was staying there at the time," said Raffles eagerly. No snob was ever quicker to boast of basking in the smile of the great.

"We believe it to be the same man," said Lord Thornaby, speaking apparently for the Criminologists' Club, and with much less severity of voice.

"I only wish I could come across him," continued Raffles heartily. "He's a criminal much more to my mind than your murderers who swear on the drop or talk cricket in the condemned cell!"

"He might be in the house now," said Lord Thornaby, looking Raffles in the face. But his manner was that of an actor in an unconvincing part and a mood to play it gamely to the bitter end; and he seemed embittered, as even a rich man may be in the moment of losing a bet.

"What a joke if he were!" cried the Wild West writer.

"Absit omen!" murmured Raffles, in better taste.

"Still, I think you'll find it's a favorite time," argued Kingsmill, Q. C. "And it would be quite in keeping with the character of this man, so far as it is known, to pay a little visit to the president of the Criminologists' Club, and to choose the evening on which he happens to be entertaining the other members."

There was more conviction in this sally than in that of our noble host; but this I attributed to the trained and skilled dissimulation of the bar. Lord Thornaby, however, was not to be amused by the elaboration of his own idea, and it was with some asperity that he called upon the butler, now solemnly superintending the removal of the cloth.

"Leggett! Just send upstairs to see if all the doors are open and the rooms in proper order. That's an awful idea of yours, Kingsmill, or of mine!" added my lord, recovering the courtesy of his order by an effort that I could follow. "We should look fools. I don't know which of us it was, by the way, who seduced the rest from the main stream of blood into this burglarious backwater. Are you familiar with De Quincey's masterpiece on 'Murder as a Fine Art,' Mr. Raffles?"

"I believe I once read it," replied Raffles doubtfully.

"You must read it again," pursued the earl. "It is the last word on a great subject; all we can hope to add is some baleful illustration or blood-stained footnote, not unworthy of De Quincey's text. Well, Leggett?"

The venerable butler stood wheezing at his elbow. I had not hitherto observed that the man was an asthmatic.

"I beg your lordship's pardon, but I think your lordship must have forgotten."

The voice came in rude gasps, but words of reproach could scarcely have achieved a finer delicacy.

"Forgotten, Leggett! Forgotten what, may I ask?"

"Locking your lordship's dressing room door behind your lordship, my lord," stuttered the unfortunate Leggett, in the short spurts of a winded man, a few, stertorous syllables at a time. "Been up myself, my lord. Outer door—inner door—both locked inside!"

But by this time the noble master was in worse case than the man. His fine forehead was a tangle of livid cords; his baggy jowl filled out like a balloon. In another second he had abandoned his place as our host, and fled the room; and in yet another we had forgotten ours as his guests and rushed headlong at his heels.

Raffles was as excited as any of us now: he outstripped us all. The cherubic little lawyer and I had a fine race for the last place but one, which I secured, while the panting butler and his satellites brought up a respectful rear. It was our unconventional author, however, who was the first to volunteer his assistance and advice.

"No use pushing, Thornaby!" cried he. "If it's been done with a wedge and gimlet, you may smash the door, but you'll never force it. Is there a ladder in the place?"

"There's a rope ladder somewhere, in case of fire, I believe," said my lord vaguely, as he rolled a critical eye over our faces. "Where is it kept, Leggett?"

"William will fetch it, my lord."

And a pair of noble calves went flashing to the upper regions.

"No need for him to bring it down," cried Parrington, who had thrown back to the wilds in his excitement. "Let him hang it out of the window above your own, and let me climb down and do the rest! I'll undertake to have one or other of these doors open in two two's!"

The fastened doors were at right angles on the landing which we filled between us. Lord Thornaby smiled grimly on the rest of us, when he had nodded and dismissed the author like a hound from the leash.

"It's a good thing we know something about our friend Parrington," said my lord. "He takes more kindly to all this than I do, I can tell you."

"It's grist to his mill," said Raffles charitably.

"Exactly! We shall have the whole thing in his next book."

"I hope to have it at the Old Bailey first," remarked Kingsmill, Q. C.

"Refreshing to find a man of letters such a man of action too!"

It was Raffles who said this, and the remark seemed rather trite for him, but in the tone there was a something that just caught my private ear. And for once I understood: the officious attitude of Parrington, without being seriously suspicious in itself, was admirably calculated to put a previously suspected person in a grateful shade. This literary adventurer had elbowed Raffles out of the limelight, and gratitude for the service was what I had detected in Raffles's voice. No need to say how grateful I felt myself. But my gratitude was shot with flashes of unwonted insight. Parrington was one of those who suspected Raffles, or, at all events, one who was in the secret of those suspicions. What if he had traded on the suspect's presence in the house? What if he were a deep villain himself, and the villain of this particular piece? I had made up my mind about him, and that in a tithe of the time I take to make it up as a rule, when we heard my man in the dressing room. He greeted us with an impudent shout; in a few moments the door was open, and there stood Parrington, flushed and dishevelled, with a gimlet in one hand and a wedge in the other.

Within was a scene of eloquent disorder. Drawers had been pulled out, and now stood on end, their contents heaped upon the carpet. Wardrobe doors stood open; empty stud cases strewed the floor; a clock, tied up in a towel, had been tossed into a chair at the last moment. But a long tin lid protruded from an open cupboard in one corner. And one had only to see Lord Thornaby's wry face behind the lid to guess that it was bent over a somewhat empty tin trunk.

"What a rum lot to steal!" said he, with a twitch of humor at the corners of his canine mouth. "My peer's robes, with coronet complete!"

We rallied round him in a seemly silence. I thought our scribe would put in his word. But even he either feigned or felt a proper awe.

"You may say it was a rum place to keep 'em." continued Lord Thornaby. "But where would you gentlemen stable your white elephants? And these were elephants as white as snow; by Jove, I'll job them for the future!"

And he made merrier over his loss than any of us could have imagined the minute before; but the reason dawned on me a little later, when we all trooped downstairs, leaving the police in possession of the theater of crime. Lord Thornaby linked arms with Raffles as he led the way. His step was lighter, his gaiety no longer sardonic; his very looks had improved. And I divined the load that had been lifted from the hospitable heart of our host.

"I only wish," said he, "that this brought us any nearer to the identity of the gentleman we were discussing at dinner, for, of course, we owe it to all our instincts to assume that it was he."

"I wonder!" said old Raffles, with a foolhardy glance at me.

"But I'm sure of it, my dear sir," cried my lord. "The audacity is his and his alone. I look no further than the fact of his honoring me on the one night of the year when I endeavor to entertain my brother criminologists. That's no coincidence, sir, but a deliberate irony, which would have occurred to no other criminal mind in England."

"You may be right," Raffles had the sense to say this time, though I think it was my face that made him.

"What is still more certain," resumed our host, "is that no other criminal in the world would have crowned so delicious a conception with so perfect an achievement. I feel sure the inspector will agree with us."

The policeman in command had knocked and been admitted to the library as Lord Thornaby spoke.

"I didn't hear what you said, my lord."

"Merely that the perpetrator of this amusing outrage can be no other than the swell mobsman who relieved Lady Melrose of her necklace and poor Danby of half his stock a year or two ago."

"I believe your lordship has hit the nail on the head."

"The man who took the Thimblely diamonds and returned them to Lord Thimblely, you know."

"Perhaps he'll treat your lordship the same."

"Not he! I don't mean to cry over my spilt milk. I only wish the fellow joy of all he had time to take. Anything fresh upstairs by the way?"

"Yes, my lord: the robbery took place between a quarter past eight and the half-hour."

"How on earth do you know?"

"The clock that was tied up in the towel had stopped at twenty past."

"Have you interviewed my man?"

"I have, my lord. He was in your lordship's room until close on the quarter, and all was as it should be when he left it."

"Then do you suppose the burglar was in hiding in the house?"

"It's impossible to say, my lord. He's not in the house now, for he could only be in your lordship's bedroom or dressing room, and we have searched every inch of both."

Lord Thornaby turned to us when the inspector had retreated, caressing his peaked cap.

"I told him to clear up these points first," he explained, jerking his head toward the door. "I had reason to think my man had been neglecting his duties up there. I am glad to find myself mistaken."

I ought to have been no less glad that I was mistaken. My suspicions of our officious author were thus proved to have been as wild as himself. I owed the man no grudge, and yet in my human heart I felt vaguely disappointed. My theory had gained color from his behavior ever since he had admitted us to the dressing room; it had changed all at once from the familiar to the morose; and only now was I just enough to remember that Lord Thornaby, having tolerated those familiarities as long as they were connected with useful service, had administered a relentless snub the moment that service had been well and truly performed.

But if Parrington was exonerated in my mind, so also was Raffles reinstated in the regard of those who had entertained a far graver and more dangerous hypothesis. It was a miracle of good luck, a coincidence among coincidences, which had whitewashed him in their sight at the very moment when they were straining the expert eye to sift him through and through. But the miracle had been performed, and its effect was visible in every face and audible in every voice. I except Ernest, who had never been in the secret; moreover, that gay criminologist had been palpably shaken by his first little experience of crime. But the other three vied among themselves to do honor where they had done injustice. I heard Kingsmill, Q. C., telling Raffles the best time to catch him at chambers, and promising a seat in court for any trial he might ever like to hear. Parrington spoke of a presentation set of his books, and in doing homage to Raffles made his peace with our host. As for Lord Thornaby, I did overhear the name of the Athenaeum Club, a reference to his friends on the committee, and a whisper (as I thought) of Rule II. But he and Raffles had their heads too close together for one to swear honestly to the rule.

The police were still in possession when we went our several ways, and it was all that I could do to drag Raffles up to my rooms, though, as I have said, they were just round the corner. He consented at last as a lesser evil than talking of the burglary in the street; and in my rooms I told him of his late danger and my own dilemma, of the few words I had overheard in the beginning, of the thin ice on which he had cut figures without a crack. It was all very well for him. He had never realized his peril.

But let him think of me—listening, watching, yet unable to lift a finger—unable to say one warning word.

Raffles heard me out, but a weary sight followed the last symmetrical whiff, of a Sullivan which he flung into my fire before he spoke.

"No, I won't have another, thank you. I'm going to talk to you, Bunny. Do you really suppose I didn't see through these wiseacres from the first?"

I flatly refused to believe he had done so before that evening. Why had he never mentioned his idea to me? It had been quite the other way, as I indignantly reminded Raffles. Did he mean me to believe he was the man to thrust his head into the lion's mouth for fun? And what point would there be in dragging me there to see the fun?

"I might have wanted you, Bunny. I very nearly did."

"For my face?"

"It has been my fortune before tonight, Bunny. It has also given me more confidence than you are likely to believe at this time of day. You stimulate me more than you think."

"Your gallery and your prompter's box in one?"

"Capital, Bunny! But it was no joking matter with me either, my dear fellow; it was touch-and-go at the time. I might have called on you at any moment, and it was something to know I should not have called in vain."

"But what to do, Raffles?"

"Fight our way out and bolt!" he answered with a mouth that meant it, and a fine gay glitter of the eyes.

I shot out of my chair.

"You don't mean to tell me you had a hand in the job!"

"I had the only hand in it, my dear Bunny."

"Nonsense! You were sitting at table at the time. No, but you may have taken some other fellow into the show. I always thought you would!"

"One's quite enough, Bunny," said Raffles dryly; he leaned back in his chair and took out another cigarette. And I accepted of yet another from his case; for it was no use losing one's temper with Raffles; and his incredible statement was not, after all, to be ignored.

"Of course," I went on, "if you really had brought off this thing on your own, I should be the last to criticize your means of reaching such an end. You have not only scored off a far superior force, which had laid itself out to score off you, but you have put them in the wrong about you, and they'll eat out of your hand for the rest of their days. But don't ask me to believe that you've done all this alone! By George," I cried, in a sudden wave of enthusiasm, "I don't care how you've done it or who has helped you. It's the biggest thing you ever did in your life!"

And certainly I had never seen Raffles look more radiant, or better pleased with the world and himself, or nearer that elation which he usually left to me.

"Then you shall hear all about it, Bunny, if you'll do what I ask you."

"Ask away, old chap, and the thing's done."

"Switch off the electric lights."

"All of them?"

"I think so."

"There, then."

"Now go to the back window and up with the blind."

"I'm coming to you. Splendid! I never had a look so late as this. It's the only window left alight in the house!"

His cheek against the pane, he was pointing slightly downward and very much aslant through a long lane of mews to a little square light like a yellow tile at the end. But I had opened the window and leaned out before I saw it for myself.

"You don't mean to say that's Thornaby House?"

I was not familiar with the view from my back windows.

"Of course I do, you rabbit! Have a look through your own race glass. It has been the most useful thing of all."

But before I had the glass in focus more scales had fallen from my eyes; and now I knew why I had seen so much of Raffles these last few weeks, and why he had always come between seven and eight o'clock in the evening, and waited at this very window, with these very glasses at his eyes. I saw through them sharply now. The one lighted window pointed out by Raffles came tumbling into the dark circle of my vision. I could not see into the actual room, but the shadows of those within were quite distinct on the lowered blind. I even thought a black thread still dangled against the square of light. It was, it must be, the window to which the intrepid Parrington had descended from the one above.

"Exactly!" said Raffles in answer to my exclamation. "And that's the window I have been watching these last few weeks. By daylight you can see the whole lot above the ground floor on this side of the house; and by good luck one of them is the room in which the master of the house arrays himself in all his nightly glory. It was easily spotted by watching at the right time. I saw him shaved one morning before you were up! In the evening his valet stays behind to put things straight; and that has been the very mischief. In the end I had to find out something about the man, and wire to him from his girl to meet her outside at eight o'clock. Of course he pretends he was at his post at the time: that I foresaw, and did the poor fellow's work before my own. I folded and put away every garment before I permitted myself to rag the room."

"I wonder you had time."

"It took me one more minute, and it put the clock on exactly fifteen. By the way, I did that literally, of course, in the case of the clock they found. It's an old dodge, to stop a clock and alter the time; but you must admit that it looked as though one had wrapped it up all ready to cart away. There was thus any amount of *prima facie* evidence of the robbery having taken place when we were all at table. As a matter of fact, Lord Thornaby left his dressing room one minute, his valet followed him the minute after, and I entered the minute after that."

"Through the window?"

"To be sure. I was waiting below in the garden. You have to pay for your garden in town, in more ways than one. You know the wall, of course, and that jolly old postern? The lock was beneath contempt."

"But what about the window? It's on the first floor, isn't it?"

Raffles took up the cane which he had laid down with his overcoat. It was a stout bamboo with a polished ferrule. He unscrewed the ferrule, and shook out of the cane a diminishing series of smaller canes, exactly like a child's fishing rod, which I afterward found to have been their former state. A double hook of steel was now produced and quickly attached to the tip of the top joint; then Raffles undid three buttons of his waistcoat; and lapped round and round his waist I beheld the finest of Manila ropes, with the neatest of foot loops at regular intervals.

"Is it necessary to go any further?" asked Raffles when he had unwound the rope. "This end is made fast to that end of the hook, the other half of the hook fits over anything that comes its way, and you leave your rod dangling while you swarm up your line. Of course, you must know what you've got to hook on to; but a man who has had a porcelain bath fixed in his dressing room is the man for me. The pipes were all outside, and fixed to the wall in just the right place. You see I had made a reconnaissance by day in addition to many by night; it would hardly have been worthwhile constructing my ladder on chance."

"So you made it on purpose!"

"My dear Bunny," said Raffles as he wound the hemp girdle round his waist once more, "I never did care for ladderwork, but I always said that if I ever used a ladder, it should be the best of its kind yet invented. This one may come in useful again."

"But how long did the whole thing take you?"

"From mother earth to mother earth? About five minutes, tonight, and one of those was spent doing another man's work."

"What!" I cried. "You mean to tell me you climbed up and down, in and out, and broke into that cupboard and that big tin box, and wedged up the doors and cleared out with a peer's robes and all the rest of it in five minutes?"

"Of course I don't, and of course I didn't."

"Then what do you mean, and what did you do?"

"Made two bites at the cherry, Bunny! I had a dress rehearsal in the dead of last night, and it was then I took the swag. Our noble friend was snoring next door all the time, but the effort may still stand high among my small exploits, for I not only took all I wanted, but left the whole place exactly as I found it, and shut things after me like a good little boy. All that took a good deal longer; tonight I had simply to rag the room a bit, sweep up some studs and links, and leave ample evidence of having boned those rotten robes *tonight.* That, if you come to think of it, was what a *Chronicle* critic would call the quintessential Q. E. F. I have not only shown these dear criminologists that I couldn't possibly have done this trick, but that there's some other fellow who could and did, and whom they've been perfect asses to confuse with me."

You may figure me as gazing on Raffles all this time in mute and rapt amazement.

But I had long been past that pitch. If he had told me now that he had broken into the Bank of England, or the Tower, I should not have disbelieved him for a moment. I was prepared to go home with him to the Albany and find the regalia in his hatbox. And I took down my overcoat as he put on his. But Raffles would not hear of my accompanying him that night.

"No, my dear Bunny, I am short of sleep and fed up with excitement. You mayn't believe it—you may look upon me as a plaster devil—but those five minutes you wot of were rather too crowded even for my taste. The dinner was nominally at a quarter to eight, and I don't mind telling you now that I counted on twice as long as I had. But no one came until twelve minutes to, and so our host took his time. I didn't want to be the last to arrive, and I was in the drawing room five minutes before the hour. But it was a quicker thing than I care about, when all is said."

And his last word on the matter, as he nodded and went his way, may well be mine; for one need be no criminologist, much less a member of the Criminologists' Club, to remember what Raffles did with the robes and coronet of the Right Hon. the Earl of Thornaby, K. G. He did with them exactly what he might have been expected to do by the gentlemen with whom we had foregathered; and he did it in a manner so characteristic of himself as surely to remove from their minds the last aura of the idea that he and himself were the same person. Carter Paterson was out of the question, and any labelling or addressing to be avoided on obvious grounds. But Raffles stabled the white elephants in the cloakroom at Charing Cross—and sent Lord Thornaby the ticket.

Saint Nicked

Ian Rankin

Born in the Kingdom of Fife, Scotland, in 1960, Ian Rankin graduated from the University of Edinburgh and has since been employed as a grape picker, swineherd, alcohol researcher, hi-fi journalist and punk musician. His first Rebus novel, *Knots and Crosses,* was published in 1987 and the Inspector Rebus series continues to develop our understanding of this complex character, described as having "the most compelling mind in modern crime fiction." Rankin's noirish settings in his home city of Edinburgh are highly atmospheric and offer an ultrarealistic take on the seamier side of life in Scotland's capital. Rankin is the UK's bestselling crime author and in 2000 Rebus made his television debut in the British feature *Black & White,* starring John Hanna. Other Rebus films for TV include: *The Hanging Tree, Dead Souls* and *Mortal Causes.* In 1988 Rankin was elected a Hawthornden Fellow and was awarded two Gold Daggers and the prestigious Chandler-Fulbright Award, plus an OBE in 2002 for services to literature.

The man dressed as Santa Claus took to his heels and ran, arms held out to stop the branches scratching his face. It was night, but the moon had appeared from its hiding place behind the clouds. The man's shadow stretched in front of him, snared by the car's headlights. He dodged left, deeper into the woods, hoping he would soon outrun the bright beams. There was laughter at his back, the laughter of men who were not yet pursuing him, men who knew his flight was doomed.

"Come back, Santa! Where do you think you're going?"

"You're not exactly in camouflage! Got Rudolph tied to a tree, ready for a quick getaway?"

More laughter, then the first voice again: "Here we come, ready or not . . ."

He didn't pause to look back. His red jacket was heavy, its thick lining padding out a frame that was stocky to begin with. Funny thing was, he'd been stick-thin until his thirties. Made up for it since, though. Chips, chocolate and beer. He knew he could ditch the costume, but that would leave a trail for them to follow. They were right: no way he was going to outrun them. He was already down to a light trot, a stitch developing in his side. The baggy red trousers kept snagging on low branches and bracken. When he paused at last, catching his breath, he heard whistling. "Jingle Bells," it sounded like. The light over to his right was wavering: his pursuers had brought torches. He could hear their boots crunching over the ground. They weren't running. Their steps were steady and purposeful. He started moving again. His plan: to get away. There was a road junction somewhere not far off. Maybe a passing car would save him. The sweat was icy on his neck, steam rising from his body, reminding him of the last horse home in the 2.30.

"You're going to get a kick in the fairy lights for this!" one of the voices called out.

"There won't be enough of you left to fill a Christmas stocking!" yelled the other.

They were still 100, maybe 200 yards behind him. He started picking his way over the ground, trying to muffle any sound. Something scratched his face. He wiped a thumb across his cheek, feeling the prickle of blood. The stitch was getting worse. His heart pounding in his ears, so loud he feared they would hear it. As the pain grew worse, he remembered someone telling him once that the secret to beating a stitch was touching your toes. He paused, bent down, but his hands didn't even make it to his knees. He fell into a crouch instead, resting his forehead against cold bark. There was a piney smell in the air, like those air fresheners you could get for the car. His clenched fists were pushing against the frozen ground. There was something jagged there beneath his knuckles: a thin slice of stone. He prised it from the earth, held it as he would a weapon. But it wasn't a weapon, and never would be. Instead, he got an idea, and started working its edge against the tree trunk.

The movement behind him had stopped, torch-light scanning the night. For the moment they had lost him. He couldn't make out what they were saying: either they were too far away, or keeping their voices low. If they stayed where they were, they would hear him scratching. Sure enough, the beam from at least one torch was arcing toward him. He had a sudden, ludicrous image from films he'd devoured as a kid: he was escaping from Colditz; he'd tunneled out, and now the searchlights were tracking him, the Nazis in pursuit. *The Great Escape:* that's the one they'd always shown at Christmas. He wondered if it would be shown this year, and whether he'd be around to see it.

"Is that you, Santa?" The voice was closer. But he'd finished now, and was back on his feet, moving away from the light, sweat stinging his eyes. It was the smoking that had taken its toll. Time was, he wasn't a bad runner. At school, he'd sometimes come runner-up in races. OK, so that had been 40 years ago, but were his pursuers any fitter? Maybe they would be tiring, thinking of giving up. Was he worth all this effort to them, when the snug warmth of the BMW was waiting?

Of course! The BMW! He could circle back, nick the car from beneath their noses. If only he could keep going. But his sides were burning, his legs buckling. And the truth was, he didn't even know which direction he was headed. He'd been doing anything but run in a straight line. The car could be anywhere. Chances were, he was heading farther into the middle of nowhere. Even if he got away, he might end up freezing to death on the hills. There were pockets of habitation out here: he'd spotted the lights during the drive south. But they were within shouting distance of the roadside, and he felt suddenly he was a long way from any road. He was an achingly long way from home.

He knew now that he would give them what they wanted, but only on his terms. It had to be on his terms, not theirs. And he didn't want a kicking. Didn't deserve it. He'd done everything just the way he'd been told . . . well, almost everything.

His head felt light, but his body was a dead weight. It was like wading through waist-deep water, and he was slowing again. Did he want to escape, to end up alone in this wilderness? The sky was darkening again, clouds closing over the land. Sleet might be on its way. How could it be that he was floating and drowning, both at the same time?

And falling to his knees.

Stretching out, as if on crisp sheets. His eyes closing . . .

And then the glare of the searchlights. The guards with their torches. Hands pulling at him, grabbing him by the hair. The silver wig came away. He'd forgotten he'd been wearing it.

"Sleeping on the job, Santa?"

They had him now, both of them. He didn't care. He didn't feel well enough to care.

"Tell us where it is."

"I . . ." His chest felt ablaze, as if he'd fallen asleep too close to the fire. He started pulling at the front of his costume, trying to shed it.

"Just tell us where it is."

"I . . ." He knew that if he told them, they might leave him here. Or punish him. He knew he had to play for time. Blood pounded through his ears, deafening him.

"No more fun and games."

"Scratched it," he blurted out.

"What's that?"

He tried to swallow. "Scratched it on a tree."

"Which tree?"

"I'll . . . show you."

They were trying to pull him to his feet, but he was too heavy, altogether too large for them. Which was how he'd broken away from them in the first place.

"Just tell us!"

He tried shaking his head. "Show you."

They dropped him then, arguing with one another.

"He's having us on," the taller one said.

The stocky one shrugged. "Tells us or shows us, what's the difference?"

"Difference is . . ." But the tall one didn't seem to have an answer. He sniffed instead. "He's caused us enough grief as it is."

"Agreed, which is why I want this over with."

"So why don't I persuade him?" The tall man slapped his torch against the palm of his hand.

"What do you say, Santa?" The stocky one shone his own torch against Santa's face. The eyes were open, but staring. The face seemed to be going slack. The stocky man knelt down.

"Don't tell me . . ." the tall man groaned.

"Looks like." The stocky man made a few checks, and stood up again. "Heart gave out."

"Don't tell me . . ."

"I just did tell you."

"So what do we do now?"

The stocky man waved his torch around. "Said he'd scratched the answer on one of the trees. Can't be too far. Let's start looking . . ."

But after twenty minutes, they'd found nothing, and reconvened at Santa's cooling body. "So what now?"

"We'll come back tomorrow. The tree's not going anywhere. Plenty of daylight tomorrow."

"And him?" The torch picked out the prone figure.

"What about him?"

"We can't just leave him. Think about it . . ."

The stocky man nodded. "You're right. Can't have the kids finding out Santa's not around anymore." He tucked his torch under his arm. "You take the feet . . ."

Detective Inspector John Rebus was in a bad place, doing a bad thing, at his least favorite time of year.

Which is to say that he was Christmas shopping in Glasgow. It had been his girlfriend's idea: everyone, she'd explained, knew that Glasgow boasted better shops than Edinburgh. Which was why he found himself traipsing around busy stores on the last Saturday before Christmas, carrying more and more bags as Jean consulted the neatly typed list she'd brought with her. Each purchase had been selected carefully beforehand, something Rebus was forced to admire. He, after all, shopped from what some would call instinct and others desperation. What he couldn't work out was why the process took so long: even though Jean knew what she was looking for, and where to find it, they still spent half an hour in each shop. Sometimes—when she was buying something for him—he had to stand outside, shuffling his chilled toes and trying not to look like a man with an impatient wait ahead of him.

It was when they stopped for lunch that Jean, noticing his slumped shoulders, patted his cheek.

"A good impersonation of the condemned man," she told him. "You're not exactly entering into the spirit."

"I'm not the festive sort."

"I'm beginning to realize." She smiled. "The words 'retail' and 'therapy' don't coincide in your world, do they? Maybe we should go our separate ways this afternoon."

Rebus nodded slowly. "That would let me buy a few things for you—without you knowing."

She studied him, seeing through the lie. "Consider yourself off the hook," she said. "Do you want to meet up later?"

Rebus nodded again. "Give me a bell when you're finished."

They parted outside the restaurant, Jean pecking his cheek. Rebus watched her go. Fifty yards down Buchanan Street, she disappeared into an arcade of small, expensive-looking shops. Rebus let his nose guide him to the Horseshoe Bar, where he sat at a corner table, nursing a first and then a second whiskey, perusing a newspaper. Thursday's theft from the First Minister's residence in Edinburgh was still causing plenty of amusement. Rebus had already heard two hardened Glaswegian accents joking about it at the bar.

"Looks like Christmas came early, eh?"

"Only Santa was the one on the receiving end. . . ."

It was all grist to the mill, and rightly so. Doubtless Rebus would have laughed had a man dressed as Father Christmas walked into a reception in Glasgow and wandered out again with a priceless necklace tucked beneath his costume. No ordinary piece of jewelry, but once the property of Mary, Queen of Scots, brought into the light just one day each year so it could be shown off at a party. With the First Minister of the recently devolved Scottish Parliament as victim, Rebus's police station had been a hive of activity, which was why he intended enjoying what was left of today. Finishing his drink, he asked at the bar for a Yellow Pages, jotting down the addresses of local record shops. He was going to find a small gift for himself, a rarity or some new album, something he could play on the big day. Something to take his mind off Christmas. The third shop he tried was a secondhand-record specialist, and Rebus was its only customer. The proprietor had frizzy, graying hair tied in a ponytail, and was wearing a Frank Zappa T-shirt that had shrunk in the wash at some point in the 1970s. As Rebus consulted the racks, the man asked if he was looking for anything.

"I'll know it when I see it," Rebus told him. On an overcast day, it was easy enough to start a conversation. Five minutes in, Rebus realized he knew the man from somewhere. He pointed a finger. "You were in a band yourself once."

The man grinned, showing gaps between his teeth. "That's some memory you've got."

"You played bass for the Parachute Game." The man held up his hands in surrender. "Ted Handsome?" Rebus guessed, eyes narrowed in concentration.

The man nodded. "The name's Hanson, actually. Ted Hanson."

"I had a couple of your albums."

"Almost as many as we made."

Rebus nodded slowly. The Parachute Game had appeared on the Scottish scene in the mid-70s, supporting headliners such as Nazareth and Alex Harvey. Then things had gone quiet.

"Your singer did a runner, didn't he?"

Hanson shrugged. "Bad timing."

Rebus remembered: the band had crept into the lower reaches of the top 30 with a single from their second album. Their first headlining tour was looming. And then their singer had walked out. Jack . . . no, Jake, that was it.

"Jake Wheeler," he said out loud.

"Poor Jake," Ted Hanson said. He was thoughtful for a moment, then checked his watch. "You look like a drinking man, am I right?"

"You've got a good eye."

"Then I reckon this could be my early-closing day."

Rebus didn't like to say, but he got the feeling Ted had a few of those each week . . .

They hit a couple of bars, talking music, bands from the "old days." Hanson had a fund of stories. He'd started the shop with stock ransacked from his own collection.

"And my flat still looks like a vinyl museum."

"I'd like to see that," Rebus said with a smile. So they jumped in a taxi, heading for Hillhead. Rebus called Jean on his mobile, said he might be late going back to Edinburgh. She sounded tired and unbothered. Hanson's Victorian tenement flat was as promised. Albums lay slumped against every wall. Boxes of them sat on tables, singles spilling out from homemade shelves that had warped under the weight.

"A little piece of heaven," Rebus said.

"Try telling that to my ex-wife." Hanson handed him a can of beer.

They spent a couple of hours on the sofa, staring into the space between the loudspeakers and listening to a shared musical heritage. Finally, Rebus plucked up the courage to ask about Jake Wheeler.

"You must have been gutted when he walked out."

"He had his reasons."

"What were they?"

Hanson offered a shrug. "Come to think of it, he never said."

"There were rumors about drugs . . . "

"Rock stars and drugs? Surely not."

"A good way to meet some very bad people." Rebus knew of these rumors, too: gangsters, dealers. But Hanson just shrugged again.

"Jake never resurfaced?" Rebus asked.

Hanson shook his head. Then he smiled. "You said you had a couple of our albums, John . . ." He sprang to his feet, rummaged in a box by the door. "Bet this isn't one of them." He held out the album to Rebus.

"I did own it once upon a time," Rebus mused, recognizing the cover. *The Oldest Tree,* recorded by the remaining trio after Wheeler had walked out. "Lost it at a party, week after I'd bought it." Examining the cover—swirly, late-hippy pencil drawings of dells and hills, a broad oak tree at the center—Rebus remembered something. "You drew this?"

Hanson nodded. "I had more than a few pretensions back then."

"It's good." Rebus studied the drawing. "I mean it."

Hanson sat down again. "Back at the shop, you said you were after something special. Could this be it?"

Rebus smiled. "Could be. How much do you want?"

"Compliments of the season."

Rebus raised an eyebrow. "I couldn't . . ."

"Yes, you could. It's not like it's worth anything."

"Well, OK then, thanks. Maybe I can do you a favor some day in return."

"How's that then?"

Rebus had lifted a business card out of his wallet. He handed it over. "I'm in CID, Ted. Never know when you might need a friend . . ."

Studying the record sleeve again, Rebus failed to notice the look of fear and panic that flitted across his new friend's face.

Sunday morning, Neil Bryant woke up and knew something was wrong. He was the stockier of the two men who'd spent much of the previous evening chasing an overweight, unfit Santa to his death. He was also supposed to be the brains of the outfit, which was why he was so annoyed. He was annoyed because he'd asked Malky Bunker—his tall, skinny partner in crime—to wake him up. It was past ten, and still no sign of Malky. So much for his dawn wake-up call. He phoned Malky and gave him a good roasting.

Twenty minutes later, the BMW pulled up at Bryant's door. Malky's hair was tousled, face creased from sleep. He was yawning.

"You got rid of the deceased?" Bryant asked. Milky nodded. Good enough: the fewer details Bryant knew, the better. They drove out of Glasgow, heading east and south. Different route from last night, and a map neither of them knew how to read.

"Be easier if we drove into Edinburgh and out again," Malky suggested.

"We're late as it is," Bryant snapped. The thing was, as you headed toward the Border country, it all started to look the same. Plenty of forests and crossroads. It was early afternoon before they started to recognize a few landmarks. Passing a couple of flatbed trucks, Bryant sensed they were getting warm.

"Working on a Sunday," Malky commented, glancing out at another truck.

"Run-up to Christmas," Bryant explained. Then his heart sank as he saw what the trucks were carrying.

"This has got to be it," Malky was saying.

"Aye," Bryant agreed, voice toneless.

Malky was parking the car, only now realizing the forest they'd run through the previous night was not a forest. It had been denuded by chainsaws, half its trees missing. Not a forest: a plantation. A fresh consignment of Christmas firs, heading north to Edinburgh.

The two men looked at one another, then sprinted from the car. There were still trees left, plenty of them. Maybe, if they were lucky . . . maybe Santa's tree would still be there.

Two hours and countless arguments later, they were back in the car, heater going full blast. The foreman had threatened to call the police. They'd threatened violence if he did.

"They're all the same," he shouted, meaning the trees.

"Just call us particular," Bryant had snarled back.

"What are we going to do?" Malky asked now. "We go back there without the necklace, our goose is well and truly stuffed."

Bryant looked at him, then got out of the car, marching toward the nervous-looking foreman.

"Where are they headed?" he demanded.

"The trees?" The foreman watched Bryant nod. "Edinburgh," he said.

"Where in Edinburgh?"

"All over." The foreman shrugged. "Probably be sold within the day."

"Addresses," Bryant said, his face inches away from the older man's. "I need addresses."

Rebus and Jean ate Sunday lunch at a hotel in Portobello, surrounded by families who were pulling crackers and wearing lopsided paper crowns.

"Basic training for the big day," Rebus commented, excusing himself from the table as his mobile started ringing. It was his boss, Detective Chief Superintendent Gill Templer.

"Enjoying a lazy Sunday?" she enquired.

"Up until now."

"We're looking at fences, John." Meaning people who might be able to shift an item as hot as the necklace. "You know Sash Hooper, don't you? Wondered if you might pay him a visit."

"Today?"

"Sooner the better."

Rebus glanced back in Jean's direction. She was stirring her coffee, no room for dessert. Rebus had promised to go and buy a Christmas tree.

"Fine," he said into the mouthpiece. "So where can I find Sash?"

"Skating on thin ice, as usual," Gill Templer said.

Ever the entrepreneur, Sash—real name Sacha, courtesy of a mother with a thing for French crooners—has opened an outdoor skating rink on Leith Links.

"Just trying to make an honest dollar," he told Rebus as they walked around the rinks perimeter. "Licenses in place and everything." He watched two teenagers as they shuffled across the slushy ice, the rink's only customers. Then he stared accusingly at the sun, cursing its liquefying powers. Music blared from a faulty loudspeaker: Abba, "Dancing Queen."

"No interest in stolen antiquities, then?"

"All in the past, Mr. Rebus." Hooper was a big man with clenched fists. What was left of his hair was jet black, tightly curled. His thick moustache was black too. He wore sunglasses, through which Rebus could just make out his small, greedy eyes.

"And if anyone came to you with an offer . . ."

"The three wise men could knock on my door tonight, Mr. Rebus, and I'd give them the brush-off." Hooper shrugged a show of innocence.

Rebus looked all around. "Not rushed off your feet, are you?"

"The day's young. Besides, Kiddie Wonderland's doing all right." He nodded at the double-decker bus, decorated with fake snow and tinsel. Mums and young children were lining up for entry. Rebus had passed the bus when he'd first arrived. It promised "a visit you'll never forget—one gift per child." Santa's *grotto on wheels* had been Hooper's explanation, rubbing his hands together. The interior looked to have been decorated with white cotton and sheets of colored crepe paper. The queuing parents appeared dubious, but Kiddie Wonderland was the only show in Leith. Still, to Rebus's mind, there was something missing.

"No Santa," he said, nodding toward the bus.

"Soon as you're gone, there will be." Hooper patted his own stomach.

Rebus stared at him. "You realize some of these kids could be traumatized for life?" Hooper didn't reply. "Let me know if Christmas brings you anything nice, Sash."

Hooper was rehearsing his "ho, ho, ho's" as Rebus walked back to the car.

He knew that there was a place on Dalkeith Road that sold Christmas trees. It was a derelict builders' yard, empty all year round except for the run-up to 25 December. When he arrived, two men were doing a good impression of taking the place apart, studying each tree before dismissing it, while the proprietor watched bemused, arms folded. One man shook his head at the other, and the pair stormed out.

"I got a call half an hour back," the proprietor told Rebus. "They did the same thing to a friend of mine."

"Takes all kinds," Rebus said. But he watched the men get into their rusty BMW and drive off. The elder and shorter of the two—his face was familiar. Rebus frowned in concentration, bought the first five-foot fir offered to him, and took it out to his car. It stretched from boot to passenger seat. He still couldn't put a name to the face, and it bothered him all the way to St. Leonard's police station, where he made his report to Gill Templar.

"Could do with clearing this one up, John," she said.

Rebus nodded. She would have the brass on her back, because the First Minister was on theirs.

"We can but try, Gill," he offered, making to leave. He was driving out of the car park when he saw a face he recognized, and this time the name came easily. It was Ted Hanson. Rebus stopped and wound down his window. "This is a surprise, Ted."

"I was in town, thought I'd look you up." Hanson looked cold.

"How did you find me?"

"Asked a policeman," Hanson said with a smile. "Any chance of a cuppa?"

They were only five minutes from Rebus's tenement flat. He made two mugs of instant coffee while Hanson flicked through his record collection.

"A pale imitation of yours, Ted," Rebus apologized.

"A lot of the same albums." Hanson waved a copy of Wishbone Ash's *Argus*. "Great cover."

"It's not the same with CDs, is it?"

Hanson wrinkled his nose. "Nothing like."

Rebus handed over the coffee and sat down. "What are you doing here, Ted?" he asked.

"Just wanted to get out of the shop—out of Glasgow." Hanson blew across the surface of the mug, then took a sip. "Sorry, John. Got any sugar?"

"I'll fetch some." Rebus got to his feet again.

"Mind if I use your loo meantime?"

"Be my guest." Rebus pointed the way, then retreated to the kitchen. Music was playing in the living room: the Incredible String Band. Rebus returned and placed the sugar beside Hanson's mug. Something was going on. He had a few questions for his new friend. After a couple of minutes, he walked back into the hall, knocked on the bathroom door. No answer. He turned the handle. There was no one inside. Ted Hanson had done a runner.

"Curiouser and curiouser," Rebus muttered to himself. He looked down on to the street from his living room window; no sign of anyone. Then he stared at his record collection. It took him a couple of minutes to decide what was missing.

The last Parachute Game album, the one Hanson himself had given him. Rebus sat in his chair, thinking hard. Then he called Jean.

"Not found a tree yet?" she asked.

"It's on its way, Jean. Could you do me a favor?

"What?"

"Something I'd like for Christmas . . ."

Christmas itself was fine. He'd no complaints about Christmas. There was the slow run-up to Hogmanay, Gill Templar growing less festive as the necklace failed to turn up. New Year's Day, Rebus nursed his accessory of choice: a thumping head. He managed to forgo any resolutions, apart from the usual one to stop drinking.

His Christmas present finally arrived on 4 January, having been posted in Austin, Texas, on 24 December. Jean handed it over, having taken the trouble to wrap it in second-hand paper.

"You shouldn't have," he said. Then he kissed her, and took the album home for a listen. The lyrics were on the inside of the gatefold sleeve. The songs tended to the elegiac, each seeming to refer to Jake Wheeler. Ted Hanson had taken over vocal duties, and though he didn't make too bad a fist of it, Rebus could see why the band had folded. Without Wheeler there was something missing, something irreplaceable. Listening to the title track, Rebus studied the drawing on the front of the sleeve—Ted Hanson's drawing. An old oak tree with the initials JW carved on it, enclosed in a heart, pierced by an arrow that wasn't quite an arrow. Holding the sleeve to the light, Rebus saw that it was a syringe.

And there below the oldest tree, Hanson sung, *You took your last farewell of me. . . .* But was it the bassist talking, or something else? Rebus rubbed a hand across his forehead, and concentrated on other songs, the other lyrics. Then he turned back to the sleeve. So detailed, it couldn't just be imagined. It had to be a real place. He picked up his phone, called Jean's number. She worked at the museum. There were things she could find out.

Such as the location of Scotland's oldest tree.

On the morning of the sixth, he let the office know he'd be late.

"That's got to be a record-breaker: the five-day hangover."

Rebus didn't bother arguing. Instead, he drove to Glasgow, parking on the street outside Ted Hanson's shop. Hanson was just opening up; looked tired and in need of a shave.

"Amazing what you can find on the Internet these days," Rebus said. Hanson turned, saw what Rebus was holding: a near-mint copy of *The Oldest Tree*. "Here's what I think," Rebus went on, taking a step forward. "I think Jake's dead. Maybe natural causes, maybe not. Rock stars have a way of hanging around with the wrong people. They get into situations." He tapped the album sleeve. "I know where this is now. Is that where he's buried?"

The ghost of a smile passed across Hanson's face. "That's what you think?"

"It's why you had to get the album back from me, once you knew what I did for a living."

Hanson bowed his head. "You're right." Then he looked up again, eyes gleaming. "That's exactly why I had to get the album back." He paused, seemed to take a deep breath. "But you're wrong. You couldn't be more wrong."

Rebus frowned, thinking he'd misheard.

"I'll show you," Hanson said. "And by the way, happy new year."

The drive took them over an hour, north out of Glasgow, the scenery stretching, rising, becoming wilderness. They passed lochs and mountains, the sky a vast, bruised skein.

"All your detective work," Hanson said, slouched in the passenger seat, "did you notice where the record was recorded?" Rebus shook his head. Hanson just nodded, then told Rebus to pull over. They were on a stretch of road that would fill with camper vans in the summer, but for now seemed desolate. Below them lay a valley, and across the valley a farmhouse. Hanson pointed toward it. "Owned by our producer at the time. We set up all the gear, did the album in under a month. Braepath Farm, it was called back then."

Rebus had spotted something. On the hillside behind the farmhouse, the tree from the album sleeve. The tree Jean had told him was the oldest in Scotland: the Braepath Oak. And behind it, a small stone bothy, little more than a shelter for shepherds, outside which a man was splitting logs, watched by his sheepdog.

"Jake fell apart," Hanson was saying, voice low. "Maybe it was the company he was keeping, or the industry we were supposed to be part of. He just wanted to be left alone. I promised him I'd respect that. The drawing . . . it was just a way of showing he'd always be part of the band, whatever happened." Hanson paused, clearing his throat. Rebus watched the distant figure as it picked up the kindling, taking it indoors. Long-haired, ragged-clothed: too far away to really be sure, but Rebus knew all the same.

"He's been out here ever since?" he asked.

Hanson nodded. His eyes glistened.

"And you've never . . . ?"

"He knows where I am if he wants me." He angled his head. "So now you know, John. Up to you what you do about it."

Rebus nodded, put the car into gear and started a three-point turn.

"Know what I'd like, Ted?" he said. "I'd like you to sign that album for me. Will you do that?"

"With pleasure," Hanson said with a smile.

Back at St. Leonard's, Rebus was passing the front desk when he saw the duty sergeant emerging from the comms room, shaking his head in disbelief. "I'm not that late," Rebus said.

"It's not that, John. It's mother Hubbard."

Now Rebus knew: Edwina Hubbard from down the road. Two or three times a week she would call to report some imagined mischief.

"What is it this time?" Rebus asked. "The peeping postmen or the disappearing dustbins?"

"Christmas trees," the sergeant said. "Being collected and taken away."

"And did you explain to her that it happens every year, courtesy of our caring, sharing council."

The sergeant nodded. "Thing is, she says they're early. And using a double-decker bus."

"A bus?" Rebus laughed. "Firs, please."

The sergeant laughed, too, turning to retreat into the comms room. "It gets better," he said. "The bus is covered in Christmas decorations."

Rebus was still laughing as he climbed the stairs. After the morning he'd had, he needed something to cheer him up. Then he froze. A Christmas bus . . . Kiddie Wonderland. Collecting Christmas trees . . . two men running around Edinburgh, looking for a tree . . . The name flashed from brain to mouth.

"Neil Bryant!" Rebus took the stairs two at a time, sat down at a computer and typed in Bryant's name. Ex-bouncer, convictions for violence. Clever with it. The other man, the taller one, had looked like bouncer material, too. And hadn't Sash Hooper run a nightclub a few years back? Sash . . . ready to take an unlikely turn as Santa on the bus.

"Santa," Rebus hissed. Then he was back downstairs and in the comms room, grabbing the sergeant's arm.

"The bus with the trees," he said. "Where did she see it?"

Rink.

The bus was full of trees, both decks. But finally they'd found one with that single word scratched on its trunk.

Rink.

The way Bryant had explained it to Sash Hooper, they needed the bus so they could collect as many trees as possible, as quickly as possible. Eventually, Hooper had seen the

wisdom of the plan. He had got a buyer for the necklace, but the sale had to be quick.
Rink.

Well, it didn't take a genius, did it? They'd turned the bus round and headed for Leith Links. The costume had been Bryant's idea, too, when he'd heard that the First Minister was throwing a party. Send someone in there dressed as Santa, they could walk out with anything they liked. He'd gone to Sash with the idea, and Sash had suggested Benn Welsh, a pretty good housebreaker in his time, now down on his luck. Benny had been good as gold—until he'd found out how much the necklace was worth. After which he'd tried upping out. Wasn't going to hand it over until they had a deal.

Three of them now—Sash, Malky and Bryant—slipping and sliding across the ice. Looking for the telltale dark patch, finding it. Benny had cut himself a hole, stuffed the necklace in, then poured in some water, letting it freeze over again. Sash had his penknife out. It took a while, the day darkening around them.

"Give me the knife," Malky said, chipping away with it.

"Watch the blade doesn't snap," Sash Hooper warned, as if the knife were somehow more precious than the necklace. Eventually, all three men clambered to their feet. Hooper holding the necklace, examining it. A string of shimmering diamonds, embracing a vast, blood-red ruby. He actually gasped. They came off the ice and back onto solid earth. They were almost in the shadow of the bus before they noticed Rebus. And he wasn't alone.

Two uniforms could be seen through the upper-deck windows. Two more were downstairs. Another was outside, circling the bus.

"Nice little stocking-filler," Rebus said, motioning toward the necklace.

"You got a warrant?" Hooper asked.

"Do I look as if I need one?"

"You can't just go trampling all over my bus. That's private property." Hooper was attempting to slide the necklace into his pocket.

Malky tugged at Bryant's sleeve. His eyes had widened. They were on the policeman who'd been circling the bus, the policeman who was now turning the handle which would open the bus's luggage compartment. Bryant saw his friend's look, and his own mouth dropped in dismay.

"Malky, for the love of God, tell me you didn't."

Hooper was still concentrating on protesting his innocence. He knew this was the most important speech he would ever make. He felt that if he could just get the words right, then maybe . . .

"DI Rebus," the constable was saying. "Something here you should take a look at . . ."

And Hooper turned his eyes, and saw what everyone else was seeing. Benny Welsh, still dressed in the telltale red suit, lying at peace on the floor of the luggage bay.

Rebus turned to face the three men.

"I'm guessing that means you're Saint Nicked," he said.

Now's the Time

John Harvey

Both a poet and author, John Harvey has over ninety published books to his credit. Principally known for his Charlie Resnick novels, Harvey has been praised for being perhaps the first British crime novelist to effectively and successfully transplant the hard-boiled American aesthetic to the milieu of the British police station. The background for the series is set in the industrial, gritty sectors of Nottingham. Resnick, with his Polish background and roots, is characterized as a slightly sad, solitary figure whose pleasures include jazz, sandwiches and beer. Harvey has been short-listed for every major crime-literature prize and was awarded the Bronze Medal at The New York Festivals in 1992 for his screenplay of *Lonely Hearts*. He also received a Sony Radio Drama Award in 1999 for his adaptation of Graham Greene's *The End of the Affair*. Resnick was accurately portrayed by actor Tom Wilkinson in the British TV series of the 1990s.

"They're all dying, Charlie."

They had been in the kitchen, burnished tones of Clifford Brown's trumpet, soft like smoke from down the hall. Dark rye bread sliced and ready, coffee bubbling, Resnick had tilted the omelet pan and let the whisked eggs swirl around before forking the green beans and chopped red pepper into their midst. The smell of garlic and butter permeated the room.

Ed Silver stood watching, trying to ignore the cats that nudged, variously, around his feet. Through wisps of gray hair, a fresh scab showed clearly among the lattice-work of scars. The hand which held his glass was swollen at the knuckles and it shook.

"S'pose you think I owe you one, Charlie? That it?"

Earlier that evening, Resnick had talked Silver out of swinging a butcher's cleaver through his own bare foot. "What I thought, Charlie, start at the bottom and work your way up, eh?" Resnick had bundled him into a cab and brought him home, stuck a beer in his hand and set to making them both something to eat. He hadn't seen Ed Silver in ten years or more, a drinking club in Carlton whose owner liked his jazz; Silver had set out his stall early, two choruses of "I've Got Rhythm" solo, breakneck tempo, bass and drums both dropping out and the pianist grinning, open-mouthed. The speed of thought: those fingers then.

Resnick divided the omelet on to two plates. "You want to bring that bread?" he said. "We'll eat in the other room."

The boldest of the cats, Dizzy, followed them hopefully through. The *Clifford Brown Memorial* album was still playing—"Theme of No Repeat."

"They're all dying, Charlie."
"Who?"
"Every bugger!"

And now it was true.

> SILVER Edward Victor Suddenly at home, on February 16, 1993. Acclaimed jazz musician of the be-bop era. Funeral service and memorial meeting, Friday, February 19 at Golders Green Crematorium at 11:45 am.
>
> Inquiries to Mason Funeral and Monumental Services, High Lanes, Finchley.

Resnick was not a *Guardian* reader; not much of a reader at all, truth to tell. *Police Review,* the local paper, Home Office circulars and misspelt incident reports, *Jazz Journal*—that was about it. But Frank Delaney had called him Tuesday morning; Frank, who had continued booking Ed Silver into his pub long after most others had turned their backs, left Ed's calls unanswered on their answer-phones. "Seen the *Guardian* today, Charlie?" Resnick had taken it for a joke.

Now he was on the train as it approached St. Pancras, that copy of the newspaper folded on the seat beside him, the debris of his journey—plastic cups, assorted wrappings from his egg mayonnaise sandwich, bacon and tomato roll, lemon iced gingerbread—pushed to one side of the table. There was the Regent's canal and as they passed the gas holders at King's Cross, Resnick got to his feet, lifted his coat down from the rack and shrugged his way inside it. He would have to walk the short distance from one terminal to another and catch the underground.

Even at that hour, King's Cross seemed jaded, sour, down at heel, broad corners and black cabs; bare-legged girls whose pallid skin was already beginning to sweat; men who leaned against the walls and railing and glanced up at you as you passed, ready to sell you anything that wasn't theirs. Ageless and sexless, serious alcoholics sat or squatted, clutching brown bottles of cider, cans of Special Brew. High about the entrances, inside the wide concourse, security cameras turned slowly with remote-control eyes.

The automatic doors slid back at Resnick's approach and beyond the lights of the computerized arrivals board, the Leeds train spilled several hundred soccer fans across the shiny floor. Enlivened by the possibility of business, two girls who had been sharing a breakfast of french fries outside Casey Jones, began to move toward the edges of the throng. One of them was tall, with badly hennaed hair that hung low over the fake fur collar of her coat; the other, younger, smudging a splash of ketchup like crazy lipstick across her cheek, called for her to wait. "For God's sake, Brenda." Brenda bent low to pull up the strap of her shoe, lit a cigarette.

"We are the champions!" chanted a dozen or more youths, trailing blue and white scarves from their belts.

In your dreams, Resnick thought.

A couple of hapless West Ham fans, on their way to catch an away special north, found themselves shunted up against the glass front of W. H. Smith. Half a dozen British Rail staff busied themselves looking the other way.

"Come on, love," the tall girl said to one of the men, an ex-squaddie with regimental colors and a death's head tattooed along his arms, "me and my mate here. We've got a place."

"Bugger off!" the man said. "Just bugger off!"

"Bugger you too!" Turning away from the tide of abuse, she saw Resnick watching. "And you. What the hell d'you think you're staring at, eh? Wanker!"

Loud jeers and Resnick moved away between the supporters but now that her attention had been drawn to him, Brenda had him in her sights. Middle-aged man, visitor, not local, not exactly smart but bound to be carrying a pound or two.

"Don't go."

"What?"

The hand that spread itself against him was a young girl's hand. "Don't go."

"How old are you?" Resnick said. The eyes that looked back at him from between badly applied make-up had not so long since been a child's eyes.

"Whatever age you want," Brenda said.

A harassed woman with one kiddie in a pushchair and another clinging to one hand banged her suitcase inadvertently against the back of Brenda's legs and, even as she swore at her, Brenda took the opportunity to lose her balance and stumble forwards. "Oops, sorry," she giggled, pressing herself against Resnick's chest.

"That's all right," Resnick said, taking hold of her arms and moving her, not roughly, away. Beneath the thin wool there was precious little flesh on her bones.

"Don't want the goods," her friend said tartly, "don't mess them about."

"Lorraine," Brenda said, "mind your own business, right?"

Lorraine pouted a B-movie pout and turned away.

"Well?" Brenda asked, head cocked.

Resnick shook his head. "I'm a police officer," he said.

"Right," said Brenda, "and I'm Julia Roberts!" And she wandered off to join her friend.

The undertaker led Resnick into a side room and unlocked a drawer; from the drawer he took a medium-size manila envelope and from this he slid onto the plain table Ed Silver's possessions. A watch with a cracked face that had stopped at seven minutes past eleven; an address book with more than half the names crossed through; a passport four years out of date; dog-eared at the edges: a packet of saxophone reeds; one pound, thirteen pence in change. In a second envelope there were two photographs. One, in color, shows Silver in front of a poster for the North Sea Jazz Festival, his name, partly obscured, behind him in small print. He is wearing dark glasses but, even so, it is clear from the shape of his face he is squinting up his eyes against the sun. His gray hair is cut in a once-fashionable crew cut and the sports coat he is wearing is bright dogtooth check and overlarge. His alto sax is cradled across his arms. If that picture were ten, fifteen years old, the other is far older—black and white faded almost to sepia. Ed Silver on the deck of the *Queen Mary,* the New York skyline rising behind him. Docking or departing, Resnick couldn't tell. Like many a would-be bopper, he had been part of Geraldo's navy, happy to play foxtrots and waltzes in exchange for a fervid forty-eight hours in the clubs on 52nd Street, listening to Monk and Bird. Silver had bumped into Charlie Parker once, almost literally, on a midtown street and been too dumbstruck to speak.

Resnick slid the photographs back from sight. "Is that all?" he asked.

Almost as an afterthought, the undertaker asked him to wait while he fetched the saxophone case, with its scuffed leather coating and tarnished clasps; stuck to the lid was a slogan: *Keep Music Live!* Of course, the case was empty, sax long gone to buy more scotch when Ed Silver had needed it most. Resnick hoped it had tasted good.

In the small chapel there were dried flowers and the wreath that Frank Delaney had sent. The coffin sat, cheap, before gray curtains and Resnick stood in the second row, glancing round through the vicar's perfunctory sermon to see if anyone else was going to come in. Nobody did. "He was a man, who in his life, brought pleasure to many," the vicar said. Amen, thought Resnick, to that. Then the curtains slowly parted and the coffin slid forward, rocking just a little, just enough, toward the flames.

Ashes to ashes, dust to dust,
If the women don't get you, the whiskey must.

While the taped organ music wobbled through "Abide with Me," inside his head Resnick was hearing Ed Silver in that small club off Carlton Hill, stilling the drinking and the chatter with an elegiac "Parker's Mood."

"No family, then?" the vicar said outside, anxious to find time for a cigarette and a pee before the next service.

"Not as far as I know."

The vicar nodded sagely. "If you've nothing else in mind for them, we'll see to it the ashes are scattered here, on the rose garden. Blooms are a picture, let me tell you, later in the year. We have one or two visitors, find time to lend a hand keeping it in order, but of course there's no funding as such. We're dependent upon donations."

Resnick reached into his pocket for his wallet and realized it was gone.

The "meat rack" stretched back either side of the station, roads lined by lock-up garages and hole-in-the-wall businesses offering third-hand office furniture and auto parts. Resnick walked the gauntlet, hands in pockets, head down, the best part of three blocks and neither girl in sight. Finally, he stopped by a woman in a red coat, sitting on an upturned dustbin and using a discarded plastic fork to scrape dog doo from the sole of her shoe. There were bruises on her neck, yellow and violet, fading under the soiled white blouse which was all she was wearing above the waist.

"Ought to be locked up," the woman said, scarcely glancing up, "letting their animals do their business anywhere. Fall and get your hand in this, God knows what kind of disease you could pick up." And then, flicking the contents of the fork out toward the street, "Twenty-five, short time."

"No," Resnick said, "I don't . . ."

She shook her head and swore as the fork snapped in two. "Fifteen, then, standing up."

"I'm looking for someone," Resnick said.

"Oh, are you? Right, well," she stood straight and barely came level with his elbows, "as long as it's not Jesus."

He assured her it was not.

"You'd be amazed, the number we get round here, looking to find Jesus. Mind you, they're not above copping a good feel while they're about it. Took me, one of them, dog collar an'all, round that bit of waste ground there. Mary, he says, get down on your knees and pray. Father, I says, I doubt you'll find the Lord up there, one hand on his rosary beads, the other way up my skirt. Mind you, it's my mother I blame, causing me to be christened Mary. On account of that Mary Magdalene, you know, in the Bible." Resnick had the impression that even if he walked away she would carry on talking just the same. "This person you're looking for," she said, "does she have a name or what?"

The hotel was in a row of similar hotels, cream paint flaking from its walls and a sign that advertised all modern conveniences in every room. And then a few, Resnick thought. The manager was in Cyprus and the youth behind the desk was an archaeology student from King's, working his way, none too laboriously, through college. "Brenda?" he said, slipping an unwrapped condom into the pages of his book to keep his place. "Is that the one from Glasgow or the one from Kirkby-in-Ashfield?"

"Where?"

"Kirkby. It's near . . ."

"I know where it's near."

"Yes? Don't sound as though you're from around there."

"Neither do you."

"Langwith," the student said. "It's the posh side of Mansfield."

Resnick had heard it called some things in his time, but never that. "That Brenda," he said. "Is she here?"

"Look," you're not her father, are you?"

Resnick shook his head.

"Just old enough to be." When Resnick failed to crack a smile, he apologized. "She's busy." He took a quick look at his watch. "Not for so very much longer."

Resnick signed and stepped away. The lobby was airless and smelt of . . . he didn't like to think what it smelt of. Whoever had taped the print of Van Gogh's sunflowers to the wall had managed to get it upside down. Perhaps it was the student, Resnick thought, perhaps it was a statement. A—what was it called?—a metaphor.

If Brenda was as young as she looked and from Kirkby, chances were she'd done a runner from home. As soon as this was over, he'd place a call, have her checked out. He was still thinking that when he heard the door slam and then the scream.

Resnick's shoulder spun the door wide, shredding wood from around its hinges. At first the man's back was all he could see, arm raised high and set to come thrashing down, a woman's heeled shoe reversed in his hand. Hidden behind him, Brenda shrieked in anticipation. Resnick seized the man's arm as he turned and stepped inside his swing. The shoe flew high and landed on top of the plywood wardrobe in the corner of the room. Resnick released his grip and the man hit the doorjamb with a smack and fell to his knees. His round face flushed around startled eyes and a swathe of hair hung sideways from his head. His pale blue shirt was hanging out over dark striped trousers and at one side his suspenders were undone. Resnick didn't need to see the briefcase in the corner to know it was there.

From just beyond the doorway the student stood thinking, there, I was right, he is her father.

"She was asking . . ." the man began.

"Shut it!" said Resnick. "I don't want to hear."

Brenda was crying, short sobs that shook her body. Blood was meandering from a cut below one eye. "Bastard wanted to do it without a condom. Bastard! I wouldn't let him. Not unless he give me another twenty pound."

Resnick leaned over and lifted her carefully to her feet, held her there. "I don't suppose," he said over his shoulder, "you've got anything like first-aid."

The man snatched up his briefcase and ran, careening between the banister and the wall. "I think there's Band-aids or something," the student said.

Resnick had gone to the hospital with her and waited while they put seven stitches in her cheek. His wallet had been in her bag, warrant card, return ticket and, astonishingly, the credit card he almost never used were still there; the cash, of course, was gone. He used the card to withdraw money from the change kiosk in the station. Now they were sitting in the Burger King opposite St. Pancras and Resnick was tucking into a double cheeseburger with bacon, while Brenda picked at chicken pieces and chain-smoked Rothmans King Size.

Without her make-up, she looked absurdly young.

"I'm eighteen," she'd said, when Resnick had informed her he was contacting her family. "I can go wherever I like."

She was eleven weeks past her fifteenth birthday; she hadn't been to school since September, had been in London a little over a month. She had palled up with Lorraine the second or third night she was down. Half of her takings went to Lorraine's pimp boyfriend, who spent it on crack; almost half the rest went on renting out the room.

"You can't make me go back," she said.

Resnick asked if she wanted tea or coffee and she opted for a milk shake instead. The female police officer waiting patiently outside would escort her home on the last train.

"You know you're wasting your time, don't you?" she called at Resnick across the pavement. "I'll only run off again. I'll be back down here inside a week!"

The officer raised an eyebrow toward Resnick, who nodded, and the last he saw was the two of them crossing against the traffic, Brenda keeping one clear step ahead.

The maitre d' at Ronnie Scott's had trouble seating Resnick because he was stubbornly on his own; finally he slipped him in to one of the raised tables at the side, next to a woman who was drinking copious amounts of mineral water and doing her knitting. Spike Robinson was on the stand, stooped and somewhat fragile-looking, Ed Silver's contemporary, more or less. A little bit of Stan Getz, a lot of Lester Young, Robinson had been one of Resnick's favorite tenor players for quite a while. There was an album of Gershwin tunes that found its way onto his record player an awful lot.

Now Resnick ate spaghetti and measured out his beer and listened as Robinson took the tune of "I Should Care" between his teeth and worried at it like a terrier with a favorite ball. At the end of the number, he stepped back to the microphone. "I'd like to dedicate this final tune of the set to the memory of Ed Silver, a very fine jazz musician who this week passed away. Charlie Parker's 'Now's the Time.' "

And when it was over the musicians had departed backstage and Ronnie Scott himself was standing there encouraging the applause—"Spike Robinson, ladies and gentlemen, Spike Robinson." Resnick blew his nose and raised his glass and continued to sit there with the tears drying on his face. Seven minutes past eleven, near as made no difference.

The Burglar Who Dropped In on Elvis

Lawrence Block

Lawrence Block is a Grand Master of the Mystery Writers of America. He has won more awards than almost any other living mystery writer: four Shamus awards, four Edgar Allan Poe awards, the Cartier Diamond Dagger and many more. One of the leading writers of contemporary crime fiction, he is the creator of Matt Scudder and other great characters, including Bernie Rhodenbarr, Evan Tanner and Chip Harrison. Bernie Rhodenbarr, Greenwich Village bookseller by day and burglar by night, features in ten novels and many short stories. Bernie is remarkable for his gentlemanly charm and expert skill as he relieves wealthy Manhattan residents of their treasured possessions. In this surprising story, he takes up his alternative trade in Memphis, with a twist. Among other TV work, a Lawrence Block short story, "Bradford in My Dreams," was featured in the *Spine Chillers* BBC series starring Chris Langham. Block has also recently acted as executive story editor and staff writer on the nine-episode miniseries *Tilt,* set in Las Vegas. Ironically, Bernie was once played by Whoopi Goldberg in the movies.

"I know who you are," she said. "Your name is Bernie Rhodenbarr. You're a burglar."

I glanced around, glad that the store was empty save for the two of us. It often is, but I'm not usually glad about it.

"Was," I said.

"Was?"

"Was. Past tense. I had a criminal past, and while I'd as soon keep it a secret I can't deny it. But I'm an antiquarian bookseller now, Miss Uh—"

"Danahy," she supplied. "Holly Danahy."

"Miss Danahy. A dealer in the wisdom of the ages. The errors of my youth are to be regretted, even deplored, but they're over and done with."

She gazed thoughtfully at me. She was a lovely creature, slender, pert, bright of eye and inquisitive of nose, and she wore a tailored suit and flowing bow tie that made her look at once yieldingly feminine and as coolly competent as a Luger.

"I think you're lying," she said. "I certainly hope so. Because an antiquarian bookseller is no good at all to me. What I need is a burglar."

"I wish I could help you."

"You can." She laid a cool-fingered hand on mine. "It's almost closing time. Why don't you lock up? I'll buy you a drink and tell you how you can qualify for an all-expenses-paid trip to Memphis. And possibly a whole lot more."

"You're not trying to sell me a time-share in a thriving lakeside resort community, are you?"

"Not hardly."

"Then what have I got to lose? The thing is, I usually have a drink after work with—"

"Carolyn Kaiser," she cut in. "Your best friend, she washes dogs two doors down the street at the Poodle Factory. You can call her and cancel."

My turn to gaze thoughtfully. "You seem to know a lot about me," I said.

"Sweetie," she said, "that's my *job*."

"I'm a reporter," she said. "For the *Weekly Galaxy.* If you don't know the paper, you must never get to the supermarket."

"I know it," I said. "But I have to admit I'm not what you'd call one of your regular readers."

"Well, I should hope not, Bernie. Our readers move their lips when they think. Our readers write letters in crayon because they're not allowed to have anything sharp. Our readers make the *Enquirer*'s readers look like Rhodes scholars. Our readers, face it, are D-U-M."

"Then why would they want to know about me?"

"They wouldn't, unless an extraterrestrial made you pregnant. That happen to you?"

"No, but Bigfoot ate my car."

She shook her head. "We already did that story. Last August, I think it was. The car was an AMC Gremlin with a hundred and ninety-two thousand miles on it."

"I suppose its time had come."

"That's what the owner said. He's got a new BMW now, thanks to the *Galaxy*. He can't spell it, but he can drive it like crazy."

I looked at her over the brim of my glass. "If you don't want to write about me," I said, "what do you need me for?"

"Ah, Bernie," she said. "Bernie the burglar. Sweetie pie, you're my ticket to Elvis."

"The best possible picture," I told Carolyn, "would be a shot of Elvis in his coffin. The *Galaxy* loves shots like that but in this case it would be counterproductive in the long run, because it might kill their big story, the one they run month after month."

"Which is that he's still alive."

"Right. Now the second-best possible picture, and better for their purposes overall, would be a shot of him alive, singing 'Love Me Tender' to a visitor from another planet. They get a chance at that picture every couple of days, and it's always some Elvis impersonator. Do you know how many full-time professional Elvis Presley impersonators there are in America today?"

"No."

"Neither do I, but I have a feeling Holly Danahy could probably supply a figure, and that it would be an impressive one. Anyway, the third-best possible picture, and the one she seems to want almost more than life itself, is a shot of the King's bedroom."

"At Graceland?"

"That's the one. Six thousand people visit Graceland every day. Two million of them walked through it last year."

"And none of them brought a camera?"

"Don't ask me how many cameras they brought, or how many rolls of film they shot. Or how many souvenir ashtrays and paintings on black velvet they bought and took home with them. But how many of them got above the first floor?"

"How many?"

"None. Nobody gets to go upstairs at Graceland. The staff isn't allowed up there, and people who've worked there for years have never set foot above the ground floor. And you can't bribe your way up there, either, according to Holly, and she knows because she tried, and she had all the *Galaxy's* resources to play with. Two million people a year go to Graceland, and they'd all love to know what it looks like upstairs, and the *Weekly Galaxy* would just love to show them."

"Enter a burglar."

"That's it. That's Holly's masterstroke, the one designed to win her a bonus and a promotion. Enter an expert at illegal entry, i.e., a burglar. *Le* Burglar, *c'est moi.* Name your price, she told me."

"And what did you tell her?"

"Twenty-five thousand dollars. You know why? All I could think of was that it sounded like a job for Nick Velvet. You remember him, the thief in the Ed Hoch stories who'll only steal worthless objects." I sighed. "When I think of all the worthless objects I've stolen over the years, and never once has anyone offered to pay me a fee of twenty-five grand for my troubles. Anyway, that was the price that popped into my head, so I tried it out on her. And she didn't even try to haggle."

"I think Nick Velvet raised his rates," Carolyn said. "I think his price went up in the last story or two."

I shook my head. "You see what happens? You fall behind on your reading and it costs you money."

Holly and I flew first class from JFK to Memphis. The meal was still airline food, but the seats were so comfortable and the stewardess so attentive that I kept forgetting this.

"At the *Weekly Galaxy,*" Holly said, sipping an after-dinner something-or-other, "everything's first class. Except the paper itself, of course."

We got our luggage, and a hotel courtesy car whisked us to the Howard Johnson's on Elvis Presley Boulevard, where we had adjoining rooms reserved. I was just about unpacked when Holly knocked on the door separating the two rooms. I unlocked it for her and she came in carrying a bottle of Scotch and a full ice bucket.

"I wanted to stay at the Peabody," she said. "That's the great old downtown hotel and it's supposed to be wonderful, but here we're only a couple of blocks from Graceland, and I thought it would be more convenient."

"Makes sense," I agreed.

"But I wanted to see the ducks," she said. She explained that ducks were the symbol of the Peabody, or the mascot, or something. Every day the hotel's guests could watch the hotel's ducks waddle across the red carpet to the fountain in the middle of the lobby.

"Tell me something," she said. "How does a guy like you get into a business like this?"

"Bookselling?"

"Get real, honey. How'd you get to be a burglar? Not for the edification of our readers, because they couldn't care less. But to satisfy my own curiosity."

I sipped a drink while I told her the story of my misspent life, or as much of it as I felt like telling. She heard me out and put away four stiff Scotches in the process, but if they had any effect on her I couldn't see it.

"And how about you?" I asked after a while. "How did a nice girl like you—"

"Oh, Gawd," she said. "We'll save that for another evening, okay?" And then she was in my arms, smelling and feeling better than a body had a right to, and just as quickly she was out of them again and on her way to the door.

"You don't have to go," I said.

"Ah, but I do, Bernie. We've got a big day tomorrow. We're going to see Elvis, remember?"

She took the Scotch with her. I poured out what remained of my own drink, finished unpacking, took a shower. I got into bed, and after fifteen or twenty minutes I got up and tried the door between our two rooms, but she had locked it on her side. I went back to bed.

Our tour guide's name was Stacy. She wore the standard Graceland uniform, a blue-and-white-striped shirt over navy chinos, and she looked like someone who'd been unable to decide whether to become a stewardess or a cheerleader. Cleverly, she'd chosen a job that combined both professions.

"There were generally a dozen guests crowded around this dining table," she told us. "Dinner was served nightly between nine and ten p.m., and Elvis always sat right there at the head of the table. Not because he was head of the family but because it gave him the best view of the big color TV. Now that's one of fourteen TV sets here at Graceland, so you know how much Elvis liked to watch TV."

"Was that the regular china?" someone wanted to know.

"Yes ma'am, and the name of the pattern is Buckingham. Isn't it pretty?"

I could run down the whole tour for you, but what's the point? Either you've been there yourself or you're planning to go or you don't care, and at the rate people are signing up for the tours, I don't think there are many of you in the last group. Elvis was a good pool player, and his favorite game was rotation. Elvis ate his breakfast in the Jungle Room, off a cypress coffee table. Elvis's own favorite singer was Dean Martin. Elvis liked peacocks, and at one time over a dozen of them roamed the grounds of Graceland. Then they started eating the paint off the cars, which Elvis liked even more than he liked peacocks, so he donated them to Memphis Zoo. The peacocks, not the cars.

There was a gold rope across the mirrored staircase, and what looked like an electric eye a couple of stairs up. "We don't allow tourists into the upstairs," our guide chirped. "Remember, Graceland is a private home and Elvis's aunt Miss Delta Biggs still lives here. Now I can tell you what's upstairs. Elvis's bedroom is located directly above the living room and music room. His office is also upstairs, and there's Lisa Marie's bedroom, and dressing rooms and bathrooms as well."

"And does his aunt live up there?" someone asked.

"No sir. She lives downstairs, through the door over to your left. None of us have ever been upstairs. Nobody goes there anymore."

"I bet he's up there now," Holly said. "In a La-Z-Boy with his feet up, eating one of his famous peanut-butter-and-banana sandwiches and watching three television sets at once."

"And listening to Dean Martin," I said. "What do you really think?"

"What do I really think? I think he's down in Paraguay playing three-handed pinochle with James Dean and Adolf Hitler. Did you know that Hitler masterminded Argentina's invasion of the Falkland Islands? We ran that story but it didn't do as well as we hoped."

"Your readers didn't remember Hitler?"

"Hitler was no problem for them. But they didn't know what the Falklands were. Seriously, where do I think Elvis is? I thinks he's in the grave we just looked at, surrounded by his nearest and dearest. Unfortunately, 'Elvis Still Dead' is not a headline that sells papers."

"I guess not."

We were back in my room at the HoJo, eating a lunch Holly had ordered from room service. It reminded me of our in-flight meal the day before, luxurious but not terribly good.

"Well," she said brightly, "have you figured out how we're going to get in?"

"You saw the place," I said. "They've got gates and guards and alarm systems everywhere. I don't know what's upstairs, but it's a more closely guarded secret than Zsa Zsa Gabor's true age."

"That'd be easy to find out," Holly said. "We could just hire somebody to marry her."

"Graceland is impregnable," I went on, hoping we could drop the analogy right there. "It's almost as bad as Fort Knox."

Her face fell. "I was sure you could find a way in."

"Maybe I can."

"But—"

"For one. Not for two. It'd be too risky for you, and you don't have the skills for it. Could you shinny down a gutterspout?"

"If I had to."

"Well, you won't have to, because you won't be going in." I paused for thought. "You'd have a lot of work to do," I said. "On the outside, coordinating things."

"I can handle it."

"And there would be expenses, plenty of them."

"No problem."

"I'd need a camera that can take pictures in full dark. I can't risk a flash."

"That's easy. We can handle that."

"I'll need to rent a helicopter, and I'll have to pay the pilot enough to guarantee his silence."

"A cinch."

"I'll need a diversion. Something fairly dramatic."

"I can create a diversion. With all the resources of the *Galaxy* at my disposal, I could divert a river."

"That shouldn't be necessary. But all of this is going to cost money."

"Money," she said, "is no object."

"So you're a friend of Carolyn's," Lucian Leeds said. "She's wonderful, isn't she? You know, she and I are the next-closest thing to blood kin."

"Oh?"

"A former lover of hers and a former lover of mine were brother and sister. Well, sister and brother actually. So that makes Carolyn my something-in-law, doesn't it?"

"I guess it must."

"Of course," he said, "by the same token, I must be related to half the known world. Still, I'm real fond of our Carolyn. And if I can help you—"

I told him what I needed. Lucian Leeds was an interior decorator and a dealer in art and antiques. "Of course I've been to Graceland," he said. "Probably a dozen times, because whenever a friend or relative visits that's where one has to take them. It's an experience that somehow never palls."

"I don't suppose you've ever been on the second floor."

"No, nor have I been present at court. Of the two, I suppose I'd prefer the second floor at Graceland. One can't help wondering, can one?" He closed his eyes, concentrating. "My imagination is beginning to work," he announced.

"Give it free rein."

"I know just the house, too. It's off Route 51 across the state line, just this side of Hernando, Mississippi. Oh, and I know someone with an Egyptian piece that would be perfect. How soon would everything have to be ready?"

"Tomorrow night?"

"Impossible. The day after tomorrow is barely possible. Just barely. I really ought to have a week to do it right."

"Well, do it as right as you can."

"I'll need trucks and schleppers, of course. I'll have rental charges to pay, of course, and I'll have to give something to the old girl who owns the house. First I'll have to sweet-talk her, but there'll have to be something tangible in it for her as well, I'm afraid. But all of this is going to cost you money."

That had a familiar ring to it. I almost got caught up in the rhythm of it and told him money was no object, but I managed to restrain myself. If money wasn't the object, what was I doing in Memphis?

"Here's the camera," Holly said. "It's all loaded with infrared film. No flash, and you can take pictures with it at the bottom of a coal mine."

"That's good," I said, "because that's probably where I'll wind up if they catch me. We'll do it the day after tomorrow. Today's what, Wednesday? I'll go in Friday."

"I should be able to give you a terrific diversion."

"I hope so," I said. "I'll probably need it."

Thursday morning I found my helicopter pilot. "Yeah, I could do it," he said. "Cost you two hundred dollars, though."

"I'll give you five hundred."

He shook his head. "One thing I never do," he said, "is get to haggling over prices. I said two hundred, and—wait a darn minute."

"Take all the time you need."

"You weren't haggling me down," he said. "You were haggling me up. I never heard tell of such a thing."

"I'm willing to pay extra," I said, "so that you'll tell people the right story afterward. If anybody asks."

"What do you want me to tell 'em?"

"That somebody you never met before in your life paid you to fly over Graceland, hover over the mansion, lower your rope ladder, raise the ladder and fly away."

He thought about this for a full minute. "But that's what you said you wanted me to do," he said.

"I know."

"So you're fixing to pay me an extra three hundred dollars just to tell people the truth."

"If anybody should ask."

"You figure they will?"

"They might," I said. "It would be best if you said it in such a way that they thought you were lying."

"Nothing to it," he said. "Nobody ever believes a word I say. I'm a pretty honest guy, but I guess I don't look it."

"You don't," I said. "That's why I picked you."

That night Holly and I dressed up and took a cab downtown to the Peabody. The restaurant was there named Dux, and they had *canard aux cerises* on the menu, but it seemed curiously sacrilegious to have it there. We both ordered the blackened redfish. She had two dry Rob Roys first, most of the dinner wine, and a Stinger afterward. I had a Bloody Mary for openers, and my after-dinner drink was a cup of coffee. I felt like a cheap date.

Afterward we went back to my room and she worked on the Scotch while we discussed strategy. From time to time she would put her drink down and kiss me, but as soon as things threatened to get interesting she'd draw away and cross her legs and pick up her pencil and notepad and reach for her drink.

"You're a tease," I said.

"I am not," she insisted. "But I want to, you know, save it."

"For the wedding?"

"For the celebration. After we get the pictures, after we carry the day. You'll be the conquering hero and I'll throw roses at your feet."

"Roses?"

"And myself. I figured we could take a suite at the Peabody and never leave the room except to see the ducks. You know, we never did see the ducks do their famous walk. Can't you just picture them waddling across the red carpet and quacking their heads off?"

"Can't you just picture what they go through cleaning that carpet?"

She pretended not to have heard me. "I'm glad we didn't have duckling," she said. "It would have seemed cannibalistic." She fixed her eyes on me. She'd had enough booze to induce coma in a six-hundred-pound gorilla, but her eyes looked as clear as ever. "Actually," she said, "I'm very strongly attracted to you, Bernie. But I want to wait. You can understand that, can't you?"

"I could," I said gravely, "if I knew I was coming back."

"What do you mean?"

"It would be great to be the conquering hero," I said, "and find you and the roses at my feet, but suppose I come home on my shield instead? I could get killed out there."

"Are you serious?"

"Think of me as a kid who enlisted the day after Pearl Harbor, Holly. And you're his girlfriend, asking him to wait until the war's over. Holly, what if that kid doesn't come home? What if he leaves his bones bleaching on some little hellhole in the South Pacific?"

"Oh my God," she said. "I never thought of that." She put down her pencil and notebook. "You're right, dammit, I *am* a tease. I'm worse than that." She uncrossed her legs. "I'm thoughtless and heartless. Oh Bernie!"

"There, there," I said.

Graceland closes every evening at six. At precisely five-thirty Friday afternoon, a girl named Moira Beth Calloway detached herself from her tour group. "I'm coming Elvis!" she cried, and she lowered her head and ran full speed for the staircase. She was over the gold rope and on the sixth step before the first guard laid a hand on her.

Bells rang, sirens squealed, and all hell broke loose. "Elvis is calling me," Moira Beth insisted, her eyes rolling wildly. "He needs me, he wants me, he loves me tender. Get your hands off me. Elvis! I'm coming, Elvis!"

I. D. in Moira Beth's purse supplied her name and indicated that she was seventeen years old, and a student at Mount St. Joseph Academy in Millington, Tennessee. This was not strictly true, in that she was actually twenty-two years old, a member of Actors Equity, and a resident of Brooklyn Heights. Her name was not Moira Beth Calloway, either. It was (and still is) Rona Jellicoe. I think it may have been something else in the dim dark past before it became Rona Jellicoe, but who cares?

While a variety of people, many of them wearing navy chinos and blue-and-white-striped shirts, did what they could to calm down Moira Beth, a middle-aged couple in the Pool Room went into their act. "Air!" the man cried, clutching at his throat. "Air! I can't breathe!" And he fell down, flailing at the wall where Stacy had told us some 750 yards of pleated fabric had been installed.

"Help him," cried his wife. "He can't breathe! He's dying! He needs AIR!" And she ran to the nearest window and heaved it open, setting off whatever alarms hadn't already been shrieking over Moira Beth's assault on the staircase.

Meanwhile, in the TV room, done in the exact shades of yellow and blue used in Cub Scout uniforms, a gray squirrel had raced across the rug and was now perched on top of the jukebox. "Look at that awful squirrel!" a woman was screaming. "Somebody get that squirrel! He's gonna kill us all!"

Her fear would have been harder to credit if people had known that the poor rodent had entered Graceland in her handbag, and that she'd been able to release it without being seen because of the commotion in the other room. Her fear was contagious, though, and the people who caught it weren't putting on an act.

In the Jungle Room, where Elvis's *Moody Blue* album had actually been recorded, a woman fainted. She'd been hired to do just that, but other unpaid fainters were dropping like flies all over the mansion. And, while all of this activity was hitting its absolute peak, a helicopter made its noisy way through the sky over Graceland, hovering for several long minutes over the roof.

The security staff at Graceland couldn't have been better. Almost immediately two men emerged from a shed carrying an extension ladder, and in no time at all they had it propped against the side of the building. One of them held it while the other scrambled up it to the roof.

By the time he got there, the helicopter was going *pocketa-pocketa-pocketa,* and disappearing off to the west. The security man raced around the roof but didn't see anyone. Within the next ten minutes, two others joined him on the roof and searched it thoroughly. They found a tennis sneaker, but that was all they found.

At a quarter to five the next morning I let myself into my room at the Howard Johnson's and knocked on the door to Holly's room. There was no response. I knocked again, louder, then gave up and used the phone. I could hear it ringing in her room, but evidently she couldn't.

So I used the skills God gave me and opened her door. She was sprawled out on the bed, with her clothes scattered where she had flung them. The trail of clothing began at the Scotch bottle on top of the television set. The set was on, and some guy with a sport jacket and an Ipana smile was explaining how you could get cash advances on your credit cards and buy penny stocks, an enterprise that struck me as a lot riskier than burglarizing mansions by helicopter.

Holly didn't want to wake up, but when I got past the veil of sleep she came to as if transistorized. One moment she was comatose and the next she was sitting up, eyes bright, an expectant look on her face. "Well?" she demanded.

"I shot the whole roll."

"You got in."

"Uh-huh."

"And you got out."

"Right again."

"And you got the pictures." She clapped her hands, giddy with glee. "I knew it," she said. "I was a positive genius to think of you. Oh, they ought to give me a bonus, a raise, a promotion. Oh, I bet I get a company Cadillac next year instead of a lousy Chevy. Oh, I'm on a roll, Bernie, I swear I'm on a roll!"

"That's great."

"You're limping," she said. "Why are you limping? Because you've only got one shoe on, that's why. What happened to your other shoe?"

"I lost it on the roof."

"God," she said. She got off the bed and began picking up her clothes from the floor and putting them on, following the trail back to the Scotch bottle, which evidently had one drink left in it. "Ahhhh," she said, putting it down empty. "You know, when I saw them race up the ladder I thought you were finished. How did you get away from them?"

"It wasn't easy."

"I bet. And you managed to get down onto the second floor? And into his bedroom? What's it like?"

"I don't know."

"You don't *know?* Weren't you in there?"

"Not until it was pitch-dark. I hid in a hall closet and locked myself in. They gave the place a pretty thorough search but nobody had a key to the closet. I don't think there is one, I locked it by picking it. I let myself out somewhere around two in the morning and found my way into the bedroom. There was enough light to keep from bumping into things but not enough to tell what it was I wasn't bumping into. I just walked around pointing the camera and shooting."

She wanted more details, but I don't think she paid very much attention to them. I was in the middle of a sentence when she picked up the phone and made a plane reservation to Miami.

"They've got me on a ten-twenty flight," she said. "I'll get these right into the office and we'll get a check out to you as soon as they're developed. What's the matter?"

"I don't think I want a check," I said. "And I don't want to give you the film without getting paid."

"Oh, come on," she said. "You can trust us, for God's sake."

"Why don't you trust me instead?"

"You mean pay you without seeing what we're paying for? Bernie, you're a burglar. How can I trust you?"

"You're the *Weekly Galaxy*," I said. "*Nobody* can trust you."

"You've got a point," she said.

"We'll get the film developed here," I said. "I'm sure there are some good commercial photo labs in Memphis and that they can handle infrared film. First you'll call your office and have them wire cash here or set up an interbank transfer, and as soon as you see what's on the film you can hand over the money. You can even fax them one of the prints first to get approval, if you think that'll make a difference."

"Oh, they'll love that," she said. "My boss loves it when I fax him stuff."

"And that's what happened," I told Carolyn. "The pictures came out really beautifully. I don't know how Lucian Leeds turned up all those Egyptian pieces, but they looked great next to the 1940s Wurlitzer jukebox and the seven-foot statue of Mickey Mouse. I thought Holly was going to die of happiness when she realized the thing next to Mickey was a sarcophagus. She couldn't decide which tack to take—that he's mummified and they're keeping him in it or he's alive and really weird and uses it for a bed."

"Maybe they can have a reader poll. Call a nine hundred number and vote."

"You wouldn't believe how loud helicopters are when you're inside them. I just dropped the ladder and pulled it back in again. And tossed an extra sneaker on the roof."

"And wore its mate when you saw Holly."

"Yeah, I thought a little verisimilitude wouldn't hurt. The chopper pilot dropped me back at the hangar and I caught a ride down to Burrell house in Mississippi, I walked around the room Lucian decorated for the occasion, admired everything, then turned out all the lights and took my pictures. They'll be running the best ones in the *Galaxy*."

"And you got paid."

"Twenty-five grand, and everybody's happy, and I didn't cheat anybody or steal anything. The *Galaxy* got some great pictures that'll sell a lot of copies of their horrible paper. The readers get a peek at a room no one has seen before."

"And the folks at Graceland?"

"They get a good security drill," I said. "Holly created a peach of a diversion to hide my entering the building. What it hid, of course, was my not entering the building, and that fact should stay hidden forever. Most of the Graceland people have never seen Elvis's bedroom, so they'll think the photos are legit. The few who know better will just figure my pictures didn't come out, or that they weren't exciting enough so the *Galaxy* decided to run fake instead. Everybody with any sense figures the whole paper's a fake anyway, so what difference does it make?"

"Was Holly a fake?"

"Not really. I'd say she's an authentic specimen of what she is. Of course her little fantasy about a hot weekend watching the ducks blew away with the morning mist. All she wanted to do was get back to Florida and collect her bonus."

"So it's just as well you got your bonus ahead of time. You'll hear from her again the next time the *Galaxy* needs a burglar."

"Well, I'd do it again," I said. "My mother was always hoping I'd go into journalism. I wouldn't have waited so long if I'd known it would be so much fun."

"Yeah," she said.

"What's the matter?"

"Nothing, Bern."

"Come on. What is it?"

"Oh, I don't know. I just wish, you know, that you'd gone in there and got the real pictures. He could be in there, Bern. I mean, why else would they make such a big thing out of keeping people out of there? Did you ever stop to ask yourself that?"

"Carolyn—"

"I know," she said. "You think I'm nuts. But there are a lot of people like me, Bern."

"It's a good thing," I told her. "Where would the *Galaxy* be without you?"

The Christmas Present

Jeffery Deaver

Jeffery Deaver has created one of the most fascinating and unusual investigators in Lincoln Rhyme. Unlike the traditional heroes in the suspense genre, Rhyme is a paraplegic whose focus is to outwit his opponents, much like Sherlock Holmes before him. The stories are multifaceted, fast-paced psychological thrillers. Deaver is credited with twenty novels and has been nominated for four Edgar Awards from the Mystery Writers of America, an Anthony Award and is a three-time recipient of the Ellery Queen Reader's Award for Best Short Story of the Year. In 2004 he was awarded the Crime Writers Association of Great Britain's Ian Fleming Steel Dagger Award. He has appeared on the bestseller lists around the world, including *The New York Times, The London Times* and the *Los Angeles Times.* His novel *The Bone Collector* has been adapted into a film starring Denzel Washington and Angelina Jolie, while his book *A Maiden's Grave* was the basis for the HBO film *Dead Silence,* starring James Garner and Marlee Matlin.

"How long has she been missing?"

Stout Lon Sellitto—his diet shot because of the holiday season—shrugged. "That's sort of the problem."

"Go on."

"It's sort of—"

"You said that already," Lincoln Rhyme felt obliged to point out to the NYPD detective.

"About four hours. Close to it."

Rhyme didn't even bother to comment. An adult was not even considered missing until at least twenty-four hours had passed.

"But there're circumstances," Sellitto added. "You have to know who we're talking about."

They were in an impromptu crime scene laboratory—the living room of Rhyme's Central Park West town house in Manhattan—but it had been impromptu for years and had more equipment and supplies than most small-town police departments.

A tasteful evergreen garland had been draped around the windows, and tinsel hung from the scanning electron microscope. Benjamin Britten's *Ceremony of Carols* played brightly on the stereo. It was Christmas Eve.

"It's just, she's a sweet kid. Carly is, I mean. And here her mother knows she's coming over but doesn't call her and tell her she's leaving or leave a note or—anything. Which she always does. Her mom—Susan Thompson's her name—is totally buttoned up. Very weird for her just to vanish."

"She's getting the girl a Christmas present," Rhyme said. "Didn't want to give away the surprise."

"But her car's still in the garage." Sellitto nodded out the window at the fat confetti of snow that had been falling for several hours. "She's not going to be walking anywhere in this weather, Linc. And she's not at any of the neighbors'. Carly checked."

Had Rhyme had the use of his body—other than his left ring finger, shoulders and head—he would have given Detective Sellitto an impatient gesture, perhaps a circling of the hand, or two palms skyward. As it was, he relied solely on words. "And how did this not-so-missing-person case all come about, Lon? I detect you've been playing Samaritan. You know what they say about good deeds, don't you? They never go unpunished. . . . Not to mention, it seems to *sort of* be falling on my shoulders, now, doesn't it?"

Sellitto helped himself to another homemade Christmas cookie. It was in the shape of Santa, but the icing face was grotesque. "These're pretty good. You want one?"

"No," Rhyme grumbled. Then his eye strayed to a shelf. "But I'd be more inclined to listen agreeably to your sales pitch with a bit of Christmas cheer."

"Of . . . ? Oh. Sure." He walked across the lab, found the bottle of Macallan and poured a healthy dose into a tumbler. The detective inserted a straw and mounted the cup in the holder on Rhyme's chair.

Rhyme sipped the liquor. Ah, heaven. . . . His aide, Thom, and the criminalist's partner, Amelia Sachs, were out shopping; if they'd been here Rhyme's beverage might have been tasty but, given the hour, would undoubtedly have been nonalcoholic.

"All right. Here's the story. Rachel's a friend of Susan and her daughter."

So it was a friend-of-the-family good deed. Rachel was Sellitto's girlfriend. Rhyme said, "The daughter being Carly. See, I was listening, Lon. Go on."

"Carly—"

"Who's how old?"

"Nineteen. Student at NYU. Business major. She's going with this guy from Garden City—"

"Is any of this relevant, other than her age? Which I'm not even sure is relevant."

"Tell me, Linc: You always in this good a mood during the holidays?"

Another sip of the liquor. "Keep going."

"Susan's divorced, works for a PR firm downtown. Lives in the burbs, Nassau County—"

"Nassau? Nassau? Hmm, would they sort of be the right constabulary to handle the matter? You understand how that works, right? That course on jurisdiction at the Academy?"

Sellitto had worked with Lincoln Rhyme for years and was quite talented at deflecting the criminalist's feistiness. He ignored the comment and continued. "She takes a couple days off to get the house ready for the holidays. Rachel tells me she and her daughter have a teenage thing—you know, going through a rough time, the two of them. But Susan's trying. She wants to make everything nice for the girl, throw a big party on Christmas Day. Anyway, Carly's living in an apartment in the Village near her school. Last night she tells her mom she'll come by this morning, drop off some things and then's going to her boyfriend's. Susan says good, they'll have coffee, yadda yadda. . . . Only when Carly gets there, Susan's gone. And her—"

"Car's still in the garage."

"Exactly. So Carly waits for a while. Susan doesn't come back. She calls the local boys but they're not going to do anything for twenty-four hours, at least. So, Carly thinks of me—I'm the only cop she knows—and calls Rachel."

"We can't do good deeds for everybody. Just because 'tis the season."

"Let's give the kid a Christmas present, Linc. Ask a few questions, look around the house."

Rhyme's expression was scowly but in fact he was intrigued. How he hated boredom. . . . And, yes, he was often in a bad mood during the holidays—because there was invariably a lull in the stimulating cases that the NYPD or the FBI would hire him to consult on as a forensic scientist, or "criminalist" as the jargon termed it.

"So . . . Carly's upset. You understand."

Rhyme shrugged, one of the few gestures allowed to him after the accident at a crime scene some years ago had left him a quadriplegic. Rhyme moved his one working finger on the touch pad and maneuvered the chair to face Sellitto. "Her mother's probably home by now. But, if you really want, let's call the girl. I'll get a few facts, see what I think. What can it hurt?"

"That's great, Linc. Hold on." The large detective walked to the door and opened it.

"What was this?"

In walked a teenage girl, looking around shyly.

"Oh, Mr. Rhyme, hi. I'm Carly Thompson. Thanks so much for seeing me."

"Ah, you've been waiting outside," Rhyme said, and offered the detective an acerbic glance. "If my friend Lon here had shared that fact with me, I'd've invited you in for a cup of tea."

"Oh, that's okay. Nothing for me."

Sellitto lifted a cheerful eyebrow and found a chair for the girl.

She had long, blond hair and an athletic figure and her round face bore little makeup. She was dressed in MTV chic—flared jeans and a black jacket, chunky boots. To Rhyme the most remarkable thing about her, though, was her expression: Carly gave no reaction whatsoever to his disability. Some people grew tongue-tied, some chatted mindlessly, some locked their eyes on to his and grew frantic—as if a glance at his body would be the faux pas of the century. Each of those reactions pissed him off in its own way.

She smiled. "I like the decoration."

"I'm sorry?" Rhyme asked.

"The garland on the back of your chair."

The criminalist swiveled but couldn't see anything.

"There's a garland there?" he asked Sellitto.

"Yeah, you didn't know? And a red ribbon."

"That must have been courtesy of my aide," Rhyme grumbled. "Soon to be ex, if he tries that again."

Carly said, "I wouldn't've bothered Mr. Sellitto or you. . . . I wouldn't have bothered *anyone* but it's just so weird, Mom disappearing like this. She's never done that before."

Rhyme said, "Ninety-nine percent of the time there's just been a mix-up of some kind. No crime at all . . . and only four hours?" Another glance at Sellitto. "That's nothing."

"Except, with Mom, whatever else, she's dependable."

"When did you talk to her last?"

"It was about eight last night, I guess. She's having this party tomorrow and we were making plans for it. I was going to come over this morning and she was going to give me a shopping list and some money and Jake—that's my boyfriend—and I were going to go shopping and hang out."

"Maybe she couldn't get through on your cell," Rhyme suggested. "Where was your friend? Could she have left a message at his place?"

"Jake's? No, I just talked to him on my way here." Carly gave a rueful smile. "She likes Jake okay, you know." She played nervously with her long hair, twining it around her fingers. "But they're not the best of friends. He's . . ." The girl decided not to go into the details of the disapproval. "Anyway, she wouldn't call his house. His dad's . . . difficult."

"And she took today off from work?"

"That's right."

The door opened and Rhyme heard Amelia Sachs and Thom enter, the crinkle of paper from the shopping bags.

The tall woman, dressed in jeans and a bomber jacket, stepped into the doorway. Her red hair and shoulders were dusted with snow. She smiled at Rhyme and Sellitto. "Merry Christmas and all that."

Thom headed down the hall with the bags.

"Ah, Sachs, come on in here. It seems Detective Sellitto has volunteered our services. Amelia Sachs, Carly Thompson."

The women shook hands.

Sellitto asked, "You want a cookie?"

Carly demurred. Sachs too shook her head. "I decorated 'em, Lon—yeah, Santa looks like Boris Karloff, I know. If I never see another cookie again it'll be too soon."

Thom appeared in the door, introduced himself to Carly and then walked toward the kitchen, from which Rhyme knew refreshments were about to appear. Unlike Rhyme, his aide loved the holidays, largely because they gave him the chance to play host nearly every day.

As Sachs pulled off her jacket and hung it up, Rhyme explained the situation and what the girl had told them so far.

The policewoman nodded, taking it in. She reiterated that a person's missing for such a short time was no cause for alarm. But they'd be happy to help a friend of Lon's and Rachel's.

"Indeed we will," Rhyme said with an irony that everyone except Sachs missed.

No good deed goes unpunished. . . .

Carry continued. "I got there about eight-thirty this morning. She wasn't home. The car was in the garage. I checked all the neighbors'. She wasn't there and nobody's seen her."

"Could she have left the night before?" Sellitto asked.

"No. She'd made coffee this morning. The pot was still warm."

Rhyme said, "Maybe something came up at work and she didn't want to drive to the station, so she took a cab."

Carly shrugged. "Could be. I didn't think about that. She's in public relations and's been working real hard lately. For one of those big Internet companies that went bankrupt. It's been totally tense. . . . But I don't know. We didn't talk very much about her job."

Sellitto had a young detective downtown call all the cab companies in and around Glen Hollow; no taxis had been dispatched to the house that morning. They also called Susan's company to see if she'd come in, but no one had seen her and her office was locked.

Just then, as Rhyme had predicted, his slim aide, wearing a white shirt and a Jerry Garcia Christmas tie, carted in a large tray of coffee and tea and a huge plate of pastries and cookies. He poured drinks for everyone.

"No figgy pudding?" Rhyme asked acerbically.

Sachs asked Carly, "Has your mom been sad or moody?"

Thinking for a minute, she said, "Well, my grandfather—her dad—died last February. Grandpa was a great guy and she was totally bummed for a while. But by the summer, she'd come out of it. She bought this really cool house and had a lot of fun fixing it up."

"How about other people in her life, friends, boyfriends?"

"She's got some good friends, sure."

"Names, phone numbers?"

Again the girl fell quiet. "I know some of their names. Not exactly where they live. I don't have any numbers."

"Anybody she was seeing romantically?"

"She broke up with somebody about a month ago."

Sellitto asked, "Was this guy a problem, you think? A stalker? Upset about the breakup?"

The girl replied, "No, I think it was his idea. Anyway, he lived in L.A. or Seattle or some place out west. So it wasn't, you know, real serious. She just started seeing this new guy. About two weeks ago." Carly looked from Sachs to the floor. "The thing is, I love Mom and everything. But we're not real close. My folks were divorced seven, eight years ago, and that kind of changed a lot of things. . . . Sorry I don't know more about her."

Ah, the wonderful family unit, thought Rhyme cynically. It was what made Park Avenue shrinks millionaires and kept police departments around the world busy answering calls at all hours of the day and night.

"You're doing fine," Sachs encouraged. "Where's your father?"

"He lives in the city. Downtown."

"Do he and your mother see each other much?"

"Not anymore. He wanted to get back together but Mom was lukewarm and I think he gave up."

"Do you see him much?"

"I do, yeah. But he travels a lot. His company imports stuff, and he goes overseas to meet his suppliers."

"Is he in town now?"

"Yep. I'm going to see him on Christmas, after Mom's party."

"We should call him. See if he's heard from her," Sachs said.

Rhyme nodded and Carly gave them the man's number. Rhyme said, "I'll get in touch with him. . . . Okay, get going, Sachs. Over to Susan's house. Carly, you go with her. Move fast."

"Sure, Rhyme. But what's the hurry?"

He glanced out the window, as if the answer were hovering there in plain view.

Sachs shook her head, perplexed. Rhyme was often piqued that people didn't tumble to things as quickly as he did. "Because the snow might tell us something about what happened there this morning." And, as he often liked to do, he added a dramatic coda: "But if it keeps coming down like this, there won't be any story left to read."

A half hour later Amelia Sachs pulled up on a quiet, tree-lined street in Glen Hollow, Long Island, parking the bright red Camaro three doors from Susan Thompson's house.

"No, it's up there," Carly pointed out.

"Here's better," Sachs said. Rhyme had drummed into her that access routes to and from the site of the crime could be crime scenes in their own right and could yield valuable information. She was ever-mindful about contaminating scenes.

Carly grimaced when she noticed that the car was still in the garage.

"I'd hoped . . ."

Sachs looked at the girl's face and saw raw concern. The policewoman understood: Mother and daughter had a tough relationship that was obvious. But you never cut parental ties altogether—can't be done—and there's nothing like a missing mother to set off primal alarms.

"We'll find her," Sachs whispered.

Carly gave a faint smile and pulled her jacket tighter around her. It was stylish and obviously expensive but useless against the cold. Sachs had been a fashion model for a time but when not on the runway or at a shoot she'd dressed like a real person, to hell with what was in vogue.

Sachs looked over the house, a new, rambling two-story Colonial on a small but well-groomed lot, and called Rhyme. On a real case she'd be patched through to him on her Motorola. Since this wasn't official business, though, she simply used her hands-free cord and cell phone, which was clipped to her belt a few inches away from her Glock automatic pistol.

"I'm at the house," she told him. "What's that music?"

After a moment "Hark, the Herald Angels Sing" went silent.

"Sorry. Thom insists on being in the *spirit.* What do you see, Sachs?"

She explained where she was and the layout of the place. "The snow's not too bad here but you're right: in another hour it'll cover up any prints."

"Stay off the walks and check out if there's been any surveillance."

"Got it."

Sachs asked Carly what prints were hers. The girl explained that she had parked in front of the garage—Sachs could see the tread marks in the snow—and then had gone through the kitchen door.

Carly behind her, Sachs made a circuit of the property.

"Nothing in the back or side yard, except for Carly's footprints," she told Rhyme.

"There are no visible prints, you mean," he corrected. "That's not necessarily 'nothing.' "

"Okay, Rhyme. That's what I meant. Damn, it's cold."

They circled to the front of the house. Sachs found footsteps in the snow on the path between the street and the house. A car had stopped at the curb. There was one set of prints walking toward the house and two walking back, suggesting the driver had picked Susan up. She told Rhyme this. He asked, "Can you tell anything from the shoes? Size, sale prints, weight distribution?"

"Nothing's clear." She winced as she bent down; her arthritic joints ached in the cold and damp. "But one thing's odd—they're real close together."

"As if one of them had an arm around the other person."

"Right."

"Could be affection. Could be coercion. We'll assume hope—the second set is Susan's, and that, whatever happened, at least she's alive. Or was a few hours ago."

Then Sachs noted a curious indentation in the snow, next to one of the front windows. It was as if somebody had stepped off the sidewalk and knelt on the ground. In this spot you could see clearly into the living room and kitchen beyond. She sent Carly to open the front door and then whispered into the microphone, "May have a problem, Rhyme. . . . It looks like somebody was kneeling down, looking through the window."

"Any other evidence there, Sachs? Discernible prints, cigarette butts, other impressions, trace?"

"Nothing."

"Check the house, Sachs. And, just for the fun of it, pretend it's hot."

"But how could a perp be inside?"

"Humor me."

The policewoman stepped to the front door, unzipping her leather jacket to give her fast access to her weapon. She found the girl in the entryway, looking around the house. It was still, except for the tapping and whirs of household machinery. The lights were on—though Sachs found this more troubling than if it'd been dark; it suggested that Susan had left in a hurry. You don't shut out the lights when you're being abducted.

Sachs told the girl to stay close and she started through the place, praying she wouldn't find a body. But, no; they looked everywhere the woman might be. Nothing. And no signs of a struggle.

"The scene's clear, Rhyme."

"Well, that's something."

"I'm going to do a fast grid here, see if we can find any clue where she went. I'll call you back if I find anything."

On the main floor Sachs paused at the mantel and looked over a number of framed photographs. Susan Thompson was a tall, solidly built woman with short blond hair, feathered back. She had an agreeable smile. Most of the pictures were of her with Carly or with an older couple, probably her parents. Many had been taken out-of-doors, apparently on hiking or camping trips.

They looked for any clue that might indicate where the woman was. Sachs studied the calendar next to the phone in the kitchen. The only note in today's square said *C here.*

The girl gave a sad laugh. Were the single letter and terse notation an emblem of how Carly believed the woman saw her? Sachs wondered what exactly the problems were between daughter and mother. She herself had always had a complex relationship with her own mother. "Challenging" was how she'd described it to Rhyme.

"Day-Timer? Palm Pilot?"

Carly looked around. "Her purse is gone. She keeps them in there. I'll try her cell again." The girl did and the frustrated, troubled look told Sachs that there was no answer. "Goes right to voice mail."

Sachs tried all three phones in the house, hitting redial. Two got her directory assistance. The other was the number for a local branch of North Shore Bank. Sachs asked to speak to the manager and told her they were trying to locate Susan Thompson. The woman said she'd been in about two hours ago.

Sachs told this to Carly, who closed her eyes in relief. "Where did she go after that?"

The policewoman asked the manager the question and the woman responded that she had no idea. Then she asked hesitantly, "Are you calling because she wasn't feeling well?"

"What do you mean?" Sachs asked.

"It's just that she didn't look very good when she was in. That man she was with . . . well, he had his arm around her the whole time. I was thinking maybe she was sick."

Sachs asked if they could come in and speak with her.

"Of course. If I can help."

Sachs told Carly what the woman had said.

"Not feeling well? And some man?" The girl frowned. "Who?"

"Let's go find out."

As they approached the door, though, Sachs stopped. "Do me a favor," she said to the girl.

"Sure. What?"

"Borrow one of your mother's jackets. You're making me cold just looking at you."

The branch manager of the bank explained to Sachs and Carly, "She went into her safety deposit box downstairs and then cashed a check."

"You don't know what she did down there, I assume?" the policewoman asked.

"No, no, employees are never around when customers go into their boxes."

"And that man? Any idea who he was?"

"No."

"What did he look like?" Sachs asked.

"He was big. Six-two, six-three. Balding. Didn't smile much."

The police detective glanced at Carly, who shook her head. "I've never seen her with anybody like that."

They found the teller who'd cashed the check, but Susan hadn't said anything to her either, except how she'd like the money.

"How much was the check for?" Sachs asked.

The manager hesitated—probably some confidentiality issue—but Carly said, "Please. We're worried about her." The woman nodded to the teller, who said, "A thousand."

Sachs stepped aside and called Rhyme on her cell. She explained what had happened at the bank.

"Getting troubling now, Sachs. A thousand doesn't seem like much for a robbery or kidnapping, but wealth's relative. Maybe that's a lot of money to this guy."

"I'm more curious about the safe-deposit box."

Rhyme said, "Good point. Maybe she had something he wanted. But what? She's just a businesswoman and mother. It's not like she's an investigative reporter or cop. And the bad news is, if that's the case, he's got what he was after. He might not need her anymore. I think it's time to get Nassau County involved. Maybe . . . Wait, you're at the bank?"

"Right."

"The video! Get the video."

"Oh, at the teller cage, sure. But—"

"No, no, no," Rhyme snapped. "Of the *parking* lot. All banks have video surveillance of the lots. If they parked there it'll have his car on tape. Maybe the tag number too."

Sachs returned to the manager and she called the security chief, who disappeared into a back office. A moment later he gestured them inside and ran the tape.

"There!" Carly cried. "That's her. And that guy? Look, he's still holding on to her. He's not letting her go."

"Looks pretty fishy, Rhyme."

"Can you see the car?" the criminalist asked.

Sachs had the guard freeze the tape. "What kind of—"

"Chevy Malibu," the guard said. "This year's model."

Sachs told this to Rhyme and, examining the screen, added, "It's burgundy. And the last two numbers on the tag are seventy-eight. The one before it could be three or eight, maybe six. Hard to tell. It's a New York plate."

"Good, Sachs. Okay. It's up to the uniforms now. Lon'll have them put out a locator. Nassau, Suffolk, Westchester and the five boroughs. Jersey too. We'll prioritize it. Oh, hold on a minute . . ." Sachs heard him speaking to someone. Rhyme came back on the line. "Susan's ex is on his way over here. He's worried about his daughter. He'd like to see her."

Sachs told Carly this. Her face brightened. The detective added, "There's nothing more we can do here. Let's go back to the city."

Amelia Sachs and Carly Thompson had just returned to the lab in Rhyme's town house when Anthony Dalton arrived. Thom led him inside and he stopped abruptly, looking at his daughter. "Hello, honey."

"Dad! I'm so glad you came!"

With both affection and concern in his eyes, he stepped toward the girl and hugged her hard.

Dalton was a fit man in his late forties with a boyish flop of salt-and-pepper hair. He wore a complicated ski jacket, straps and flaps going every which way. He reminded Rhyme of the college professors he sometimes shared the podium with when he was lecturing on forensics at criminal justice colleges.

"Do they know anything?" he asked, apparently only now realizing that Rhyme was in a wheelchair—and finding the fact unremarkable. Like his daughter, Anthony Dalton earned serious points with Rhyme for this.

The criminalist explained exactly what had happened and what they knew.

Dalton shook his head. "But it doesn't necessarily mean she's been kidnapped," he said quickly.

"No, no, not at all," Sellitto said. "We're just not taking any chances."

Rhyme asked, "Do you know anyone who'd want to hurt her?"

He shook his head. "I have no idea. I haven't seen Susan in a year. But when we were together? No, everybody liked her. Even when some of her PR clients had done some pretty shady things, nobody had a problem with her personally. And she always seemed to have the particularly nasty clients."

Rhyme was troubled—for reasons beyond the danger to Susan Thompson. The problem was that this wasn't a real case. They'd backed into it, doing a favor for someone; it was a Christmas present, as Sellitto had said. He needed more facts; he needed serious forensics. He'd always felt you run a case 110 percent or you don't run it at all.

Thom brought more coffee in and replenished the plate of ugly cookies. Dalton nodded at the aide and thanked him. Then the businessman poured coffee from the pot for himself. "You want some?" he asked Carly.

"Sure, I guess."

He poured it and asked, "Anyone else?"

No one else wanted anything. But Rhyme's eyes flipped to the Macallan on the shelf and, lo and behold, without a syllable of protest; Thom took the bottle and walked to Rhyme's Storm Arrow. He opened the tumbler, then frowned. He sniffed it. "Odd, I thought I washed this out last night. I guess I forgot," he added wryly.

"We can't all be perfect, now," Rhyme said.

Thom poured a few fingers into the tumbler and replaced it in the holder.

"Thank you, Balthazar. You can keep your job for now—despite the weeds on the back of my chair."

"You don't like them? I told you I was going to decorate for the holidays."

"The house. Not me."

"What do we do now?" Dalton asked.

"We wait," Sellitto said. "DMV's running all the Malibus with that fragment of a tag number. Or, if we're real lucky, some officer on the street'll notice it." He pulled his coat off a chair. "I gotta go down to the Big Building for a while. Call me if anything happens."

Dalton thanked him, then he looked at his watch, took out his mobile phone and called his office to say he'd have to miss his office Christmas party. He explained that the police were looking into his ex-wife's disappearance and he was with his daughter at the moment. He wasn't going to leave the girl alone.

Carly hugged him. "Thanks, Dad." Her eyes lifted to the window, staring at the swirling snow. A long moment passed. Carly glanced at the others in the room and turned toward her father. In a soft voice she said, "I always wondered what would have happened if you and Mom hadn't broken up."

Dalton laughed, ran his hand through his hair, mussing it further. "I've thought about that too."

Sachs glanced at Rhyme and they turned away, letting the father and daughter continue talking in relative privacy.

"The guys Mom's dated? They were okay. But nobody special. None of them lasted very long."

"It's tough to meet the right person," Dalton said.

"I guess . . ."

"What?"

"I guess I've always wished you'd get back together."

Dalton seemed at a loss for words. "I tried. You know that. But your mom was in a different place."

"But you stopped trying a couple of years ago."

"I could read the writing on the wall. People have to move on."

"But she misses you. I know she does."

Dalton laughed, "Oh, I don't know about that."

"No, no, really. When I ask her about you, she tells me what a cool guy you were. You were funny. She said you made her laugh."

"We had some good times."

Carly said, "When I asked Mom what happened between you, she said it wasn't anything totally terrible."

"True," Dalton said, sipping his coffee. "We just didn't know how to be husband and wife back then. We got married too young."

"Well, you're not young anymore. . . ." Carly blushed. "Oh, I didn't mean it like that."

But Dalton said, "No, you're right. I've grown up a lot since then."

"And Mom's really changed. She used to be so quiet, you know. Just no fun. But she's into all kinds of things now. Camping and hiking, rafting, all that out-of-doors stuff."

"Really?" Dalton asked. "I never pictured her going in for that kind of thing."

Carly looked off for a moment. "Remember those business trips you'd take when I was a kid? You'd go to Hong Kong or Japan?"

"Setting up our overseas offices, sure."

"I wanted all of us to go. You, Mom and me . . ." She played with her coffee cup. "But she was always like, 'Oh, there's too much to do at home.' Or, 'Oh, we'll get sick if we drink the water,' or whatever. We never did take a family vacation. Not a real one."

"I always wanted that too." Dalton shook his head sadly. "And I'd get mad when she didn't want to come along and bring you. But she's your mother; it's her job to look out for you. All she wanted was for you to be safe." He smiled. "I remember once when I was in Tokyo and calling home. And—"

His words were interrupted when Rhyme's phone rang. He spoke into the microphone on his chair, "Command, answer phone."

"Detective Rhyme?" the voice clattered through the speaker.

The rank was out of date—a "Ret." belonged with it—but he said, "Go ahead."

"This's Trooper Bronson, New York State Police."

"Go ahead."

"We've had an emergency vehicle locator request regarding a burgundy Malibu and understand you're involved in the case."

"That's right."

"We've found the vehicle, sir."

Rhyme heard Carly gasp. Dalton stepped beside the girl and put his arm around her shoulder. What would they hear? That Sue Thompson was dead?

"Go ahead."
"The car's moving west, looks like it's headed for the George Washington Bridge."
"Occupants?"
"Two. Man and a woman. Can't tell anything more."
"Thank God. She's alive." Dalton sighed.
Heading toward Jersey, Rhyme reflected. The flats were among the most popular places for dumping bodies in the metro area.
"Registered to a Richard Musgrave, Queens. No warrants."
Rhyme glanced at Carly, who shook her head, meaning she had no clue who he was.
Sachs leaned forward toward the speaker and identified herself, "Are you near the car?"
"About two hundred feet behind."
"You in a marked vehicle?"
"That's right."
"How far from the bridge?"
"A mile or two east."
Rhyme glanced at Sachs. "You want to join the party? You can stay right on their tail in the Camaro."
"You bet." She ran for the door.
"Sachs," Rhyme called.
She glanced back.
"You have chains on your Chevy?"
Sachs laughed. "Chains on a muscle car, Rhyme? No."
"Well, try not to skid into the Hudson, okay? It's probably pretty cold."
"I'll do my best."

True, a rear-wheel-drive sports car, with more than four hundred eager horses under the hood, was not the best vehicle to drive on snow. But Amelia Sachs had spent much of her youth skidding cars on hot asphalt in illegal races around Brooklyn (and sometimes just because, why not, it's always a blast to do one-eighties); this little bit of snow meant nothing to her.
She now slipped her Camaro SS onto the expressway and pushed the accelerator down. The wheels spun for only five seconds before they gripped and sped her up to eighty.
"I'm on the bridge, Rhyme," she called into her headset. "Where are they?"
"About a mile west. Are you—"
The car started to swerve. "Hold on, Rhyme, I'm going sideways."
She brought the skid under control. "A V. W. doing fifty in the fast lane. Man, doesn't that just frost you?"
In another mile she'd caught up to the trooper, keeping back, just out of sight of the Malibu. She looked past him and saw the car ease into the right lane and signal for an exit.
"Rhyme, can you get me a patch through to the trooper?" she asked.

"Hold on . . ." A long pause. Rhyme's frustrated voice. "I can never figure out—" He was cut off and she heard two clicks. Then the trooper said, "Detective Sachs?"

"I'm here. Go ahead."

"Is that you behind me, in that fine red set of wheels?"

"Yep."

"How do you want to handle this?"

"Who's driving? The man or the woman?"

"The man."

She thought for a moment. "Make it seem like a routine traffic stop. Taillight him or something. After he's on the shoulder I'll get in front and sandwich him in. You take the passenger side and I'll get the driver out. We don't know that he's armed and we don't know that he's not. But the odds are it's an abduction, so assume he's got a weapon."

"Roger that, Detective."

"Okay, let's do it."

The Malibu exited. Sachs tried to look through the rear window. She couldn't see anything through the snow. The burgundy car rolled down the ramp and braked slowly to a stop at a red light. When it turned green the car eased forward through the slush and snow.

The trooper's voice crackled into her ear. "Detective Sachs, are you ready?"

"Yep. Let's nail him."

The light bar on his Police Interceptor Crown Victoria started flashing and he hit the squeal once. The driver of the Malibu looked up into the rearview mirror and the car swerved momentarily. Then it pulled to a stop on the side of road, bleak town houses on the left and reedy marshes on the right.

Sachs punched the accelerator and skidded to a stop in front of the Malibu, blocking it. She was out the door in an instant, pulling her Glock from her holster and jogging fast toward the car.

Forty minutes later a grim Amelia Sachs walked into Rhyme's town house.

"How bad was it?" Rhyme asked.

"Pretty bad." She poured herself a double scotch and drank down half the liquor fast. Unusual for her; Amelia Sachs was a sipper.

"Pretty bad," she repeated.

Sachs was not, however, referring to any bloody shoot-out in Jersey, but to the embarrassment of what they'd done.

"Tell me."

Sachs had radioed in from the roadside to tell Rhyme, Carly and Anthony Dalton that Susan was fine. Sachs hadn't been able to go into the details then, though. Now she explained, "The guy in the car was that man she's been seeing for the past couple of weeks." A glance at Carly. "Rich Musgrave, the one you mentioned. It's his car. He called this morning and they'd made plans to go shopping at the Jersey outlet malls.

Only what happened was, when she went out to get the newspaper this morning she slipped on the ice."

Dalton nodded. "The front path—it's like a ski slope."

Carly winced. "Mom always said that she was a born klutz."

Sachs continued, "She hurt her knee and didn't want to drive. So she called Rich back and asked him to pick her up. Oh, the spot in the snow where I thought somebody was looking in the window? It was where she fell."

"That's why he was so close to her," Rhyme mused. "He was helping her walk."

Sachs nodded. "And at the bank, there was no mystery—she really did need something out of the safe-deposit box. And the thousand bucks was for Christmas shopping."

Carly frowned. "But she knew I was coming by. Why didn't she call me?"

"Oh, she wrote you a note."

"Note?"

"It said she'd be out for the day but she'd be back home by six."

"No! . . . But I never saw it."

"Because," Sachs explained, "after she fell she was pretty shaken up and forgot to leave it on the entryway table like she'd planned. She found it in her purse when I told her it wasn't there. And she didn't have her cell phone turned on."

Dalton laughed. "All a misunderstanding." He put his arm around his daughter's shoulders.

Carly, blushing again, said, "I'm really, really sorry I panicked. I should've known there was an explanation."

"That's what we're here for," Sachs said.

Which wasn't exactly true, Rhyme reflected sourly. No good deed . . .

As she pulled on her coat, Carly invited Rhyme, Sachs and Thom to the Christmas party tomorrow afternoon at her mother's. "It's the least we can do."

"I'm sure Thom and Amelia would be *delighted* to go," Rhyme said quickly. "Unfortunately, I think I have plans." Cocktail parties bored him.

"No," Thom said. "You don't have any plans."

Sachs added, "Nope, no plans."

A scowl from Rhyme. "I think I know my calendar better than anyone else."

Which wasn't exactly true either.

After the father and daughter had gone, Rhyme said to Thom, "Since you blew the whistle on my unencumbered social schedule tomorrow, you can do penance."

"What?" the aide asked cautiously.

"Take the damn decorations off my chair. I feel like Santa Claus."

"Humbug," Thom said, and did as asked. He turned the radio on. A carol streamed into the room.

Rhyme nodded toward the speaker. "Aren't we lucky there are only twelve days of Christmas? Can you imagine how interminable that song would be if there were twenty?" He sang, "Twenty muggers mugging, nineteen burglars burgling. . . .

Thom sighed and said to Sachs, "All I want for Christmas is a nice, complicated jewelry heist right about now—something to pacify him."

"Eighteen aides complaining," Rhyme continued the song. He added, "See, Thom, I am in the holiday spirit. Despite what you think."

Susan Thompson climbed out of Rich Musgrave's Malibu. The large, handsome man was holding the door for her. She took his hand and he eased her to her feet; her shoulder and knee still ached fiercely from the spill she'd taken on the ice that morning.

"What a day," she said, sighing.

"I don't mind getting pulled over by the cops," Rich said, laughing. "I could've done without the guns, though."

Carrying all her shopping bags in one hand, he helped her to the front door. They walked carefully over the three-inch blanket of fine snow.

"You want to come in? Carly's here—that's her car. You can watch me prostrate myself in front of her and apologize for being such a bozo. I could've sworn I left that note on the table."

"I think I'll let you run the gauntlet on your own." Rich was divorced too and was spending Christmas Eve with his two sons at his place in Armonk. He needed to pick them up soon. She thanked him again for everything and apologized once more for the scare with the police. He'd been a nice guy about the whole thing. But, as she fished her keys out of her purse and watched him walk back to the car, she reflected that there was no doubt the relationship wasn't going anywhere. What was the problem? Susan wondered. Rough edges, she supposed. She wanted a gentleman. She wanted somebody who was kind, who had a sense of humor. Somebody who could make her laugh.

She waved good-bye and stepped into the house, pulled the door shut behind her.

Carly had already started on the decorations, bless her, and Susan smelled something cooking in the kitchen. Had the girl made dinner? This was a first. She looked into the den and blinked in surprise. Carly'd decked out the room beautifully, garlands, ribbons, candles. And on the coffee table was a big plate of cheese and crackers, a bowl of nuts, fruit, two glasses sitting beside a bottle of California sparkling wine. The girl was nineteen, but Susan let her have some wine when they were home alone.

"Honey, how wonderful!"

"Mom," Carly called, walking to the doorway. "I didn't hear you come in."

The girl was carrying a baking dish. Inside were some hot canapes. She set it on the table and hugged her mother.

Susan threw her arms around the girl, ignoring the pain from the fall that morning. She apologized for the mistake about the note and for making her daughter worry so much. The girl, though, just laughed it off.

"Is it true that policeman's in a wheelchair?" Susan asked. "He can't move?"

"He's not a policeman anymore. He's kind of a consultant. But, yeah, he's paralyzed."

Carly went on to explain about Lincoln Rhyme and how they'd found her and Rich Musgrave. Then she wiped her hands on her apron and took it off. "Mom, I want to give you one of your presents tonight."

"Tonight? Are we starting a new tradition?"

"Maybe we are."

"Well, okay . . ." Then Susan took the girl's arm. "In that case let me give you mine first." She got her purse from the table and dug inside. She found the small velvet box. "This is what I got out of the safe-deposit box this morning."

She handed it to the girl, who opened it. Her eyes went wide. "Oh, Mom . . ."

It was an antique diamond and emerald ring.

"This was—"

"Grandma's. Her engagement ring." Susan nodded. "I wanted you to have something special. I know you've had a rough time lately, honey. I've been too busy at work. I haven't been as nice to Jake as I should. And some of the men I've dated . . . well, I know you didn't like them that much." A laughing whisper. "Of course, I didn't like them that much either. I'm resolving not to date losers anymore."

Carly frowned. "Mom, you've never dated losers. More like semi-losers."

"That's even worse! I couldn't even find a red-blooded, full-fledged loser to date!"

Carly hugged her mother again and put the ring on. "It's so beautiful."

"Merry Christmas, honey."

"Now, time for your present."

"I think I like our new tradition."

Her daughter instructed, "Sit down. Close your eyes. I'm going outside to get it."

"All right."

"Sit on the couch right there."

She sat and closed her eyes tight.

"Don't peek."

"I won't." Susan heard the front door open and close. A moment later she frowned, hearing the sound of a car engine starting. Was it Carly's? Was she leaving?

But then she heard footsteps behind her. The girl must have come back in through the kitchen door.

"Well, can I look now?"

"Sure," said a man's voice.

Susan jumped in surprise. She turned and found herself staring at her ex-husband. He carried a large box with a ribbon on it.

"Anthony . . ."she began.

Dalton sat on the chair across from her. "Been a long time, hasn't it?"

"What are you doing here?"

"When Carly thought you were missing, I went over to that cop's place to be with her. We were worried about you. We got to talking and, well, that's her Christmas present to you and me: getting us together tonight and just seeing what happens."

"Where is she?"

"She went to her boyfriend's to spend the night with him." He smiled. "We've got the whole evening ahead of us. All alone. Just like the old days."

Susan started to rise. But Anthony stood up fast and swung his palm into her face with a jarring slap. She fell back on the couch. "You get up when I tell you to," he said cheerfully, smiling down at her. "Merry Christmas, Susan. It's good to see you again."

She looked toward the door.

"Don't even think about it." He opened the sparkling wine and poured two glasses. He offered her one. She shook her head. "Take it."

"Please, Anthony, just—"

"Take the damn glass," he hissed.

Susan did, her hand shaking violently. As they touched flutes, memories from when they were married flooded back to her: his sarcasm, his rage. And, of course, the beatings.

Oh, but he'd been clever. He never hurt her in front of people. He was especially careful around Carly. Like the psychopath that he was, Anthony Dalton was the model father to the girl. And the model husband to the world.

Nobody knew the source of her bruises, cuts, broken fingers . . .

"Mommy's such a klutz," Susan would tell young Carly, fighting back the tears. "I fell down the stairs again."

She'd long ago given up trying to understand what made Anthony tick. A troubled childhood, a glitch in the brain? She didn't know and after a year of marriage she didn't care. Her only goal was to get out. But she'd been too terrified to go to the police. Finally, in desperation, she'd turned to her father for help. The burly man owned several construction companies in New York and he had "connections." She'd confessed to him what had happened and her father took charge of the problem. He had two associates from Brooklyn, armed with baseball bats and a gun, pay Anthony a visit. The threats, and a lot of money, had bought her freedom from the man, who reluctantly agreed to a divorce, to give up custody of Carly and not to hurt Susan again.

But, with terror flooding through her now, she realized why he was here tonight. Her father had passed away last spring.

Her protector was gone.

"I love Christmas, don't you?" Anthony Dalton mused, drinking more wine.

"What do you want?" she asked in a quivering voice.

"I can never get too much of the music." He walked to the stereo and turned it on. "Silent Night" was playing. "Did you know that it was first played on guitar? Because the church organ was broken."

"Please, just leave."

"The music . . . I like the decorations too."

She started to stand but he rose fast, slapping her again. "Sit down," he whispered, the soft sound more frightening than if he'd screamed.

Tears filled her eyes and she held her hand to her stinging cheek.

A boyish laugh. "And presents! We all love presents. . . . Don't you want to see what I got you?"

"We are not getting back together, Anthony. I do not want you in my life again."

"Why would I want someone like *you* in my life? What an ego." He looked her over, smiling faintly, with his placid blue eyes. She remembered this too—how calm he could be. Sometimes even when he was beating her.

"Anthony, there's no harm so far, nobody's been hurt."

"Shhhh."

Without his seeing, her hand slipped to her jacket pocket where she'd put her cell phone. She'd turned it back on after the mix-up with Carly earlier. She didn't, however, think she could hit 911 without looking. But her finger found the send button. By pressing it twice the phone would call the last number dialed. Rich Musgrave's. She hoped his phone was still on and that he'd hear what was happening. He'd call the police. Or possibly even return to the house. Anthony wouldn't dare hurt her in front of a witness—and Rich was a large man and looked very strong. He outweighed her ex by fifty pounds.

She pressed the button now. After a moment she said, "You're scaring me, Anthony. Please leave."

"Scaring you?"

"I'll call the police."

"If you stand up I'll break your arm. Are we clear on that?"

She nodded, terrified but thankful, at least, that if Rich was listening, he would have heard this exchange and probably be calling the police now.

Dalton looked under the tree. "Is *my* present there?" He browsed through the packages, seeming disappointed that there was none with his name on it.

She recalled this too: One minute he'd be fine. The next, completely out of touch with reality. He'd been hospitalized three times when they were married. Susan remembered telling Carly that her father had to go to Asia on monthlong business trips.

"Nothing for poor me," he said, standing back from the tree.

Susan's jaw trembled. "I'm sorry. If I'd known—"

"It's a joke, Susan," he said. "Why would you get me anything? You didn't love me when we were married; you don't love me now. The important thing is that I got you something. After the scare about what'd happened to you this afternoon I went shopping. I wanted to find just the right present."

Dalton drank down more wine and refilled his glass. He eyed her carefully. "Probably better if you stay snuggled in right where you are. I'll open it for you."

Her eyes glanced at the box. It had been carelessly wrapped—by him, of course—and he ripped the paper off roughly. He lifted out something cylindrical, made of metal.

"It's a camping heater. Carly said you'd taken that up. Hiking, out-of-doors . . . Interesting that you never liked to do anything fun when we were married."

"I never liked to do anything with *you,*" she said angrily. "You'd beat me up if I said the wrong thing or didn't do what you'd told me."

Ignoring her words, he handed her the heater. Then he took out something else. A red can. On the side: *Kerosene.* "Of course," Anthony continued, frowning, "that's one bad thing about Christmas . . . lot of accidents this time of year. You read that article in *USA Today?* Fires, particularly. Lot of people die in fires."

He glanced at the warning label and took a cigarette lighter from his pocket.

"Oh, God, no! . . . Please. Anthony. "

It was then that Susan heard a car's brakes squeal outside. The police? Or was it Rich? Or was it her imagination?

Anthony was busying himself taking the lid off the kerosene.

Yes, there were definitely footsteps on the walk. Susan prayed it wasn't Carly.

Then the doorbell rang. Anthony looked toward the front door, startled.

And as he did, Susan flung the champagne glass into his face with all her strength and leapt to her feet, sprinting for the door. She glanced behind her to see Anthony stumbling backward. The glass had broken and cut his chin. "You whore!" he roared, starting for her.

But she had a good head start and flung the door open.

Rich Musgrave stood there, eyes wide in shock. "What?"

"It's my ex!" she gasped. "He's trying to kill me!"

"Jesus," Rich said. He put his arm around her. "Don't worry, Susan."

"We have to get away! Call the police."

She took his hand and started to flee into the front yard. But Rich didn't move. What the hell was he doing? Did he want to *fight?* This was no time for any chivalry crap. "Please, Rich. We have to run!"

Then she felt his hand tighten on hers. The grip became excruciating. His other hand took her by the waist and he turned her around. He shoved her back inside. "Yo, Anthony," Rich called, laughing. "Lose something?"

In despair, Susan sat on the couch and sobbed.

They'd tied her hands and feet with Christmas ribbon, which would burn away, leaving no evidence that she'd been bound after the fire, Rich had explained, sounding like a carpenter imparting a construction tip to a homeowner.

It had all been planned for months; her ex-husband was smugly pleased to tell her. As soon as he'd learned that Susan's father had died, he started making plans to get even with her—for her "disobedience" when they were married and then for divorcing him. So he'd hired Rich Musgrave to work his way into her life and wait for an opportunity to kill her.

Rich had picked her up at a shopping mall a few weeks ago and they'd hit it off at once. They'd had a lot in common, it seemed—though Susan realized now that he'd merely been fed information about her from Anthony to make it seem like they were soul mates. Planning the killing itself was tough; Susan led a very busy life and she was rarely alone. But Rich learned that she was taking today off. He suggested they meet in Jersey and go to the malls. Then he'd suggest driving to an inn for lunch. But they'd never make it that far. He'd kill her and dump her body in the flats.

But she'd called Rich this morning, asking him if he'd drive; she'd fallen and hurt her knee. He'd be happy to. . . . Then he'd called Anthony and they'd decided that they could still go ahead with the plan. This worked out even better, in fact, because it turned out that Susan had left the note and shopping list for her daughter on the entryway table after all. When he picked her up that morning he'd pocketed the note and list and slipped them into her purse—to be buried with her—so there'd be no trace of him. Rich had also made sure her cell phone was off so she couldn't call for help if she saw what he was up to.

Then they'd run a few errands and headed toward Jersey.

But it hadn't worked out as planned. Carly had gone to the police and, to Anthony's shock; they'd tracked down Rich's car. Her ex had called Rich from Lincoln Rhyme's apartment, pretending to be talking to a business associate about missing an office party; in fact, he was alerting Rich that the police were after him. Susan remembered him taking a call in the car and seeming uneasy with whatever news he was receiving. Ten minutes later that red-haired cop, Amelia, and the state trooper had pulled them over.

After that incident Rich had been reluctant to proceed with the murder. But Anthony had coldly insisted they go ahead. Rich finally agreed when Anthony said they'd make the death look like an accident—and when he promised that after Susan died and Carly'd inherited a couple of million dollars, Anthony would make certain Rich got some of that.

"You son of a bitch! You leave her alone!" Anthony ignored his ex-wife. He was amused. "So she just called you now?"

"Yeah," Rich said. "Hit redial, I guess. Pretty smart."

"Damn," Anthony said, shaking his head.

"Good thing I was the last person she called. Not Pizza Hut."

Anthony said to Susan, "Nice thought. But Rich was coming back anyway. He was parked up the street, waiting for Carly to leave."

"Please . . . don't do this."

Anthony poured the kerosene on the couch.

"No, no, no . . ."

He stood back and watched her, enjoying her terror.

But through her tears of panic Susan saw that Rich Musgrave was frowning. He shook his head. "Can't do it, man," he said to Anthony as he stared at Susan's tearful face.

Anthony looked up, frowning. Was his friend having pangs of guilt?

Help me please, she begged Rich silently.

"Whatta you mean?" Anthony asked.

"You can't burn somebody to death. That's way harsh. . . . We have to kill her first."

Susan gasped.

"But the police'll know it's not an accident."

"No, no, I'll just—" He held his hand to his own throat. "You know. After the fire they won't have a clue she was strangled."

Anthony shrugged. "Okay." He nodded to Rich, who stepped up behind her, as Anthony poured the rest of the liquid around Susan.

"Oh, no, Anthony, don't! Please . . . God, no . . ."

Her words were choked off as she felt Rich's huge hands close around her neck, felt them tightening.

As she began to die, a roaring filled her ears, then blackness. Finally huge bursts of light speckled her vision. Brighter and brighter.

What were the flashes? she wondered, growing calm as the air was cut off from her lungs.

Were they from her dying brain cells?

Were they the flames from the kerosene?

Or was this, she thought maniacally, the brilliance of heaven? She'd never really believed in it before. Maybe . . .

But then the lights faded. The roaring too. And suddenly she was breathing again, the air flowing into her lungs. She felt a huge weight on her shoulders and neck. Something dug into her face, stinging.

Gasping, she squinted as her vision returned. A dozen police officers, men and women, in those black outfits you saw on TV shows, gripping heavy guns, were filling the room. The guns had flashlights on them; their beams had been the bright lights she'd seen. They'd kicked the door in and grabbed Rich Musgrave. He'd fallen, trying to escape; it had been his belt buckle that'd cut her cheek. They cuffed him roughly and dragged him out the door.

One of the officers in black and that woman detective, Amelia Sachs, wearing a bulletproof vest, pointed their guns toward Anthony Dalton. "On the floor, now, face down!" she growled.

The shock of the ex-husband's face gave way to righteous indignation. Then the madman gave a faint smile. "Put your guns down." He held out the cigarette lighter near the fuel-soaked couch, a few feet away from Susan. One flick and the couch would burst into a sea of fire.

One officer started for her.

"No!" Dalton raged. "Leave her." He moved the lighter closer to the liquid, put his thumb on the tab.

The cop froze.

"You're going to back out of here. I want everybody out of this room, except . . . you," he said to Sachs. "You're going to give me your gun and we're walking out of here together. Or I'll burn us all to death. I'll do it. I *will* do it!"

The redhead ignored his words. "I want that lighter on the ground now. And you face down right after it. Now! I *will* fire."

"No, you won't. The flash from your gun'll set off the fumes. This whole place'll go up."

The policewoman lowered her black gun, frowning as she considered his words. She looked at the cop beside her and nodded. "He's right."

She glanced around her, picked up a pillow from an old rocking chair and held it over the muzzle of her gun.

Dalton frowned and dropped to the couch, started to click the lighter. But the policewoman's idea was a good one. There was no flash at all when she fired through the pillow, three times, sending Susan's ex-husband sprawling back against the fireplace.

The Rollx van was parked at the curb. The Storm Arrow wheelchair, which was devoid of ribbons and spruce, was on the van's elevator platform, lowered to the ground, resting on the snow. Lincoln Rhyme was in the thick parka that Thom had insisted he wear, despite the criminalist's protests that it wasn't necessary since he was going to remain in the van.

But, when they'd arrived at Susan Thompson's house, Thom had thought it would be good for Rhyme to have a little fresh air.

He grumbled at first but then acquiesced to being lowered to the ground outside. He rarely got out in cold weather—even places that were disabled-accessible were often hard to negotiate on snow and ice—and he was never one for the out-of-doors anyway, even before the accident. But he was now surprised to find how much he enjoyed feeling the crisp chill on his face, watching the ghost of his breath roll from his mouth and vanish in the crystalline air, smelling the smoke from fireplaces.

The incident was mostly concluded. Richard Musgrave was in a holding cell in Garden City. Firemen had rendered the den in Susan's house safe, removing the sofa and cleaning up or neutralizing the kerosene Dalton had tried to kill her with, and she'd been given an okay from the medics. Nassau County had run the crime scene, and Sachs was now huddled with two county detectives. There was no question she'd acted properly in shooting Anthony Dalton but there'd still be a formal shooting-incident inquiry. The officers finished their interview, wished her a merry Christmas and crunched through the snow to the van, where they spent a few minutes speaking to Rhyme with a sliver of awe in their voices; they knew the criminalist's reputation and could hardly believe that he was here in their own backyard.

After the detectives left, Susan Thompson and her daughter walked down to the van, the woman moving stiffly, wincing occasionally.

"You're Mr. Rhyme."

"Lincoln, please."

Susan introduced herself and thanked him effusively. Then she asked, "How on earth did you know what Anthony was going to do?"

"He told me himself." A glance at the walkway to the house.

"The path?" she asked.

"I could have figured it out from the evidence," Rhyme muttered, "if we'd had all our resources available. It would have been more *efficient*." A scientist, Rhyme was fundamentally suspicious of words and witnesses. He nodded to Sachs, who tempered

Rhyme's deification of physical evidence with what he called 'people cop' skills, and she explained, "Lincoln remembered that you'd moved into the house last summer. Carly mentioned it this morning."

The girl nodded.

"And when your ex was at the town house this afternoon he said that he hadn't seen you since last Christmas."

Susan frowned and said, "That's right. He told me last year that he was going away on business for six months so he brought two checks for Carly's tuition to my office. I haven't seen him since. Well, until tonight."

"But he also said that the path from this house to the street was steep."

Rhyme took up the narrative. "He said it was like a ski slope. Which meant he had been here, and since he described the walk that way, it was probably recently, sometime after the first snow. Maybe the discrepancy was nothing—he might've just dropped something off or picked up Carly when you weren't here. But there was also a chance he'd lied and had been stalking you."

"No, he never came here that I knew about. He must have been watching me."

Rhyme said, "I thought it was worth looking into. I checked him out and found out about his times in the mental hospitals, the jail sentences, assaults on two recent girlfriends."

"Hospital?" Carly gasped. "Assaults?"

The girl knew nothing about this? Rhyme lifted an eyebrow at Sachs, who shrugged. The criminalist continued. "And last Christmas, when he told you he was going away on business? Well, that 'business' was a six-month sentence in a Jersey prison for road rage and assault. He nearly killed another man over a fender bender."

Susan frowned. "I didn't know about that one. Or that he'd hurt anybody else."

"So we kept speculating, Sachs and Lon and I. We got a down-and-dirty warrant to check his phone calls and it turned out he'd called Musgrave a dozen times in the last couple of weeks. Lon checked on him and the word on the street is that he's for hire muscle. I figured that Dalton met somebody in jail who hooked him up with Musgrave."

"He wouldn't do anything to me while my father was alive," Susan said, and explained how it had been her dad who'd gotten the abusive man away from her.

The woman's words were spoken to all of them, clustered in the snow around the van, but it was Carly's eyes she gazed at. This was, in effect, a stark confession that her mother had been lying to her about her father for years and years.

"When the plan with Musgrave didn't work out this afternoon, Dalton figured he'd do it himself."

"But . . . no, no, no, not Dad!" Carly whispered. She stepped away from her mother, shivering, tears running down her red cheeks. "He . . . It can't be true! He was so nice! He . . ."

Susan shook her head. "Honey, I'm sorry, but your father was a very sick man. He knew how to put on a perfect facade, he was a real charmer—until he decided he didn't trust you or you did something he didn't like." She put her arm around her daughter. "Those trips he took to Asia? No, those were the times in the hospitals and jails. Remember I always said I was banging into things?"

"You were a klutz," the girl said in a small voice. "You don't mean—"

Susan nodded. "It was your father. He'd knock me down the stairs, he'd hit me with a rolling pin, extension cords, tennis rackets."

Carly turned away and stared at the house. "You kept saying what a good man he was. And all I could think of was, well, if he was so damn good, why didn't you want to get back together?"

"I wanted to protect you from the truth. I wanted you to have a loving father. But I couldn't give you one—he hated me so much."

But the girl was unmoved. Years of lies, even those offered for the best of motives, would take a long time to digest, let alone forgive.

If they could ever be forgiven.

There were voices from the doorway. The Nassau County coroner's men were wheeling Anthony Dalton's body out of the house.

"Honey," Susan began. "I'm sorry. I—"

But the girl held up a hand to silence her mother. They watched as the body was loaded into the coroner's van.

Susan wiped the tears from her face. She said, "Honey, I know this is too much for you. . . . I know you're mad. I don't have any right to ask, but can you just do one thing to help me? I have to tell everybody coming to the party tomorrow that we're canceling. It'll get too late if I have to call them all myself."

The girl stared as the van disappeared down the snowy street.

"Carly," her mother whispered.

"No," she answered her mother.

Her face flooding with resignation and pain, Susan nodded knowingly. "Sure, sweetheart, I understand. I'm sorry. I shouldn't've asked. You go see Jake. You don't have to—"

"That's not what I mean," the girl said bluntly. "I mean, we're not canceling the party."

"We can't, not after—"

"Why not?" the girl asked. There was flint in her voice.

"But—"

"We're going to have our party," Carly said firmly. "We'll find a room in a restaurant or hotel somewhere. It's late but let's start making some calls."

"You think we could?" Susan asked.

"Yes," the girl said, "we can."

Susan too invited the three of them to the party.

"I may have other commitments," Rhyme said quickly. "I'll have to check my schedule."

"We'll see," Sachs told her coyly.

Eyes wet with tears, mouth unsmiling, Carly thanked Rhyme, Sachs and Thom.

The two women returned to the house, daughter helping mother up the steep path. They moved in silence. The girl was angry, Rhyme could see. And numb. But she hadn't walked away from her mother. A lot of people would have.

The door to the house closed with a loud snap, carried through the compact, cold air.

"Hey, anybody want to drive around and look at the decorations on the houses?" Thom asked.

Sachs and Rhyme looked at each other. The criminalist said, "I think we'll pass. How 'bout we get back to the city? Look at the hour. It's late. Forty-five minutes till Christmas. Doesn't the time fly when you're doing good deeds?"

Thom repeated, "Humbug." But he said it cheerfully.

Sachs kissed Rhyme. "I'll see you back home," she said, and walked toward the Camaro as Thom swung the door of the van shut. In tandem, the two vehicles started down the snowy street.

Rumpole and the Scales of Justice

John Mortimer

Perhaps the most famous novelist and television dramatist to have defended a murderer at the Old Bailey, John Mortimer is also a barrister whose career has held him in good stead, not only in supporting his early writings but also in terms of inspiration. Although he wrote many film scripts as well as plays for radio and television, including the adaptation of Evelyn Waugh's *Brideshead Revisited,* Mortimer is best known for his creative masterpiece, the character Rumpole of the Bailey. The legacy of Rumpole began in 1975 on the BBC's *Play for Today.* Rumpole is inextricably linked with the veteran actor Leo McKern, who played the savvy, wise barrister to perfection in the *Rumpole of the Bailey* series, one of the most popular in television history, which first aired on Thames Television in 1978. The program was also popular on the American PBS network as part of the *Mystery!* series.

"The Scales of Justice have tipped in the wrong direction. That's all I'm saying, Jenny. Now it's all in favor of the defense, and that makes our job so terribly hard. I mean, we catch the villains and, ten to one, they walk away from Court laughing."

Bob Durden, resplendent in his Commander's uniform, appeared in the living room of Froxbury Mansions in Gloucester Road. He was in conversation with Jenny Turnbull, the hard-hitting and astute interviewer on the *Up to the Minute* program.

"You've got to admit he's right, Rumpole." She Who Must Be Obeyed could be as hard-hitting and astute as Jenny. "Things have gone too far. It's all in favor of the defense."

"Why don't you—and the Commander, of course—try defending some unfortunate innocent before the Mad Bull down at the Old Bailey? You'd have a Judge, who's longing to pot your client and is prepared to use every trick in the book to get the Jury on his side, a prosecutor who can afford to make all the enquiries and is probably keeping quiet about evidence that's slightly favorable to the defense, and a Jury out for revenge because someone stole their car radios. Then you'd find out how much things are slanted in favor of the defense."

"Oh, do be quiet." She Who Must didn't have time for a legal argument. "I'm trying to listen to the Commander."

Bob Durden ruled the forces of law and order in an area half crowded countryside, half sprawling suburbs, to the north of London. When the old East End died, and its streets and squares became inhabited by upwardly mobile media persons, ethnic restaurants, and the studios of conceptual artists, it was to Commander Durden's patch that the forces of lawlessness moved. He was a large, broad-shouldered, loose-lipped man who spoke as though he were enjoying some secret joke.

"But aren't there cases where the police haven't been exactly on the side of the law?" said Jenny Turnbull.

Well done, Jenny, I thought. It's about time someone asked that question.

Hilda, however, took a different view. "That girl," she said, "should learn to show respect to the people she's interviewing. After all, the man is a Commander. She could at least be polite."

"She's far too polite in my opinion. If I were cross-examining I'd be a good deal less respectful." I addressed the television set directly. "When are your officers going to stop bribing witnesses by putting them up in luxurious all-expenses-paid hotels and improving on confession statements?"

"Do be quiet, Rumpole! You're worse than that Turnbull woman, interrupting that poor man."

"You know who I blame, Jenny? I blame the lawyers. The 'learned friends' in wigs. Are they part of the justice system? Part of the injustice system, if you want my honest opinion." The Commander spoke from the television set in a tone of amused contempt to which I took the greatest exception. "It's all a game to them, isn't it? Get your guilty client off and collect a nice fat-cat fee from the Legal Aid for your trouble."

"Have you got any particular lawyer in mind?" Jenny Turnbull clearly scented a story.

"Well, Jenny, I'm not naming names. But there are regular defenders down at the Old Bailey and they'll know who I mean. There was a case some time ago. Theft in the Underground. The villain, with a string of previous convictions, had the stolen wallet in his backpack. Bang to rights, you might say. This old defender pulled a few defense tricks and the culprit walked free. We get to know them, 'Counsel for the Devious Defense,' and quite frankly there's very little we can do about them."

"Absolute rubbish!" I shouted fruitlessly at the flickering image of the Commander. "Trevor Timson got off because he was entirely innocent. Are you saying that everyone with previous convictions should be found guilty regardless of the facts? Is that what you're saying?"

"It's no good at all you shouting at him, Rumpole." Hilda was painfully patient. "He can't hear a word you're saying." As usual, She Who Must Be Obeyed was maddeningly correct.

A considerable amount of time passed, a great quantity of Château Thames Embankment flowed down parched legal throats in Pommeroy's Wine Bar, a large number of custodial sentences were handed out to customers down the Bailey, and relatively few of those detained went off laughing. Gradually, as small shoots of promise appear when spring follows winter, my practice began to show signs of an eventual re-bloom. I progressed from petty thievery (in the Case of the New Year's Resolutions) to more complicated fraud, from actual to grievous bodily harm, and from an affray outside a bingo hall to a hard-fought manslaughter in a sauna. It was in the months before I managed to play my part in the richly rewarding case—in satisfaction rather than money—that I am about to record. I was sitting in my Chambers room enjoying an illicit small cigar (Soapy Sam Ballard was still in the business of banning minor pleasures) and leafing through the Oxford Book of English Verse in search of a suitable quotation to use in my final speech in a case of alleged gross decency in Snaresbrook, when a brisk knock at the door was followed by the entrance of none other than Dame Phillida Erskine-Brown—once the much-admired Portia of our Chambers, now the appealing occupant of Judicial Benched from the Strand and Ludgate Circus to Manchester and Exeter Crown Court.

"You'll never guess what I've seen, Rumpole! Never in a million years!" Her Ladyship was in what can only be described as a state of outrage, and whatever she had seen had clearly not been a pretty sight. "I just dropped in to tell Claude he'll have to look after the children tonight because I've got a dinner booked with the Lord Chancellor and the babysitter's got evening classes."

"All part of the wear and tear of married life?"

"It's not that. It's what I saw in the clerk's room. In front of Henry and Denise. Claude, flagrantly in the arms of another woman!"

"When you say in the arms of," I merely asked for clarification, "what were they doing, exactly? I take it they weren't kissing each other?"

"Not that. No. They were hugging."

"Well, that's all right then." I breathed a sigh of relief. "If they were only hugging."

"What do you mean, 'That's all right then?' I said, 'Am I disturbing something' and walked straight out of the clerk's room and came to see you, Rumpole. I must say I rather expected you to take this extraordinary conduct of Claude's rather more seriously."

I couldn't help remembering the time when Dame Phillida, once the nervous pupil whom I'd found in my room in tears, now a Judge of the Queen's Bench, had herself tugged a little at the strict bonds of matrimony and conceived an inexplicable passion for a Doctor Tom Gurnley, a savagely punitive right wing Tory M. P. who believed in mandatory prison sentences for the first whiff of cannabis, and whom I had had to defend in the Case of the Camberwell Carrot. I suppose it wasn't an exact parallel—the Learned judge had not been discovered embracing the old hanger and flogger in our clerk's room.

Now that the Erskine-Browns' marriage seemed to have sailed into calmer waters, I was unwilling to rock the boat. I offered an acceptable solution.

"Exactly whom was your husband hugging?"

"I couldn't see much of her. She seemed to have blond hair. Not entirely convincing I thought."

"A black trouser suit? Shiny boots?"

"I think so, now you mention it."

"Then that would be our new Director of Marketing and Administration."

"I believe Claude told me you have one of those. So that makes it perfectly all right does it?" I could see that the Judge was not entirely satisfied. "Is part of her job description snogging my husband?"

"Not snogging. Hugging."

"All right then, hugging. Is that her job—is that what you're saying?"

"Provided it's Thursday."

"Rumpole! Are you feeling quite well?"

"Her name is Luci. She spells it with an i."

"Does she do that to irritate people?"

"That might well be part of it. She had the idea we should *all* hug each other at work on Thursday. She said it would improve our corporate spirit and lead to greater harmony in the workplace."

"You mean you all hug each other?"

"If you look on the noticeboard, you'll see that Soapy Sam Ballard has commended the idea to 'Everyone at Number 4 Equity Court.' He's very pro-Luci because I told him she fancied him."

"Rumpole, has the whole world gone mad?"

"Only on Thursdays. That's when we're meant to hug each other. On Fridays Luci has decided that we dress down."

"What does that mean, exactly?"

"It means that Ballard comes in wearing jeans and a red sweater with diamonds on it. Oh, and white gym shoes, of course."

"You mean trainers?"

"Probably."

"Do you dress down, Rumpole?"

"Certainly not. I can't afford the wardrobe. I stick to my working clothes—black jacket and striped pants."

"I thought I saw Claude sneak out of the house in jeans. He hasn't told me."

"Your Claude has a nervous disposition. I expect he was afraid you'd laugh at him."

"I certainly would. And about the hugging. Do you hug, Rumpole?"

"Embrace our clerk Henry? Snuggle up to Ballard? Certainly not! I told them hugging always brings me out in a rash. I have a special dispensation not to do it for health reasons. It's like taking the vegetarian dish."

"What did Ballard say when you told him you wouldn't hug?"

"He said I could just say 'Good morning' in an extra cheerful manner. Does that set your mind at rest?"

"I suppose so." Phillida seemed reluctant to abandon a genuine cause for complaint against the unfortunate Claude. "Provided he doesn't embrace that woman too enthusiastically. She's far too old for that haircut."

"It was pure coincidence that you came in at that moment," I told her. "If you'd come in ten minutes later you'd have found him wrapped around Hoskins, a balding middle-aged man with numerous daughters."

"You're always counsel for the defense, aren't you, Rumpole?"

"I can only say that in any situation which looks guilty, I can sometimes offer an innocent alternative to the Jury."

"Bob Durden would call that another trick of the defender's trade. Did you see him on television the other night?"

"I certainly did. And I just wish I had the chance to wake the Commander up to the reality of life when you're on trial at the Old Bailey."

At this the learned and beautiful Judge looked at me with some amusement—but my chance came sooner than either of us would have expected.

The earthshaking news was read out by Hilda from her tabloid newspaper one morning in Froxbury Mansions. She looked seriously upset.

"Feet of clay, Rumpole! That sensible policeman we saw on *Up to the Minute* turns out to have feet of clay!"

I had been trying to catch up with some last-minute instructions in a fairly complicated long firm fraud when She Who Must handed me the paper, from which the face of Bob Durden loomed solemn and severe from beneath his cap. The headline, however, suggested that not only were his feet clay but that the rest of him was by no means perfect senior-police-officer material. The Commander had been arrested on no less a charge than taking part in a conspiracy to murder. It took a good half-minute before I was able to suppress an unworthy tendency to gloat.

Of course I read every detail of the extraordinary case. It was suggested that the scourge of defense lawyers had been prepared to pay a contract killer to do away with a local doctor, but I was sure that the last member of the Bar he would call upon to defend him was that devious Rumpole who spent his life helping guilty villains walk free from courtrooms, laughing triumphantly at the police. So the Commander took his place at the back of my mind, but I was on the lookout for developments in the newspapers.

One memorable day Ballard appeared in my room with a look of sublime satisfaction and the air of a born commander about to issue battle orders. I have to say that he had smartened up a good deal since I let him know that our Director of Marketing and Administration nursed tender feelings for him. He had invested in a new suit, his hair was more dashingly trimmed by a unisex stylist, and he arrived in a chemical haze of aftershave which happily evaporated during the course of the day.

"This, Rumpole," he told me, "will probably be the most famous case of my career. The story, you'll have to admit, is quite sensational."

"What's happened, Ballard?" I had no wish to fuel Soapy Sam's glowing self-satisfaction. "What have you landed now? Another seven days waiting before the rating burial?"

"I have been offered, Rumpole," the man was blissfully unaware of any note of sarcasm; he was genuinely proud of his eventful days in court with rateable values, "the leading brief for the defense in *R. v. Durden*. It is of course, tragic that a fine police officer should fall so low."

Of course, I realized that the case called for a Q. C.—(Queer Customer is what I called them) and, as I have said, that the defendant policeman would never turn to Rumpole in a time of trouble. I couldn't help, however, feeling a momentary stab of jealousy at the thought of Ballard's landing such a sensational front-page *cause célèbre*.

"He hasn't fallen low yet." I thought it right to remind our head of chambers of the elementary rules of our trade. "And he won't until the Jury come back to Court and pronounces him guilty. It's your job to make sure they never do that."

"I know, Rumpole." Soapy Sam looked enormously brave. "I realize that I have taken on an almost superhuman task and a tremendous responsibility. But I've been able to do you a good turn."

"What sort of good turn, exactly?" I was doubtful about Ballard's gifts.

Then he told me, "You see the Commander went to a local solicitor, Henry Crozier (we were at university together), and Henry knew that Durden wouldn't want any sort of flashy clever dick defense Q. C.—the sort he's spoken out against so effectively on television."

"You mean he picked you because you're not a clever dick?"

"Dependable, Rumpole. And, I flatter myself, trusted by the Courts. And as I believe your practice has slowed a bit since . . ."

"You mean since I died?"

"Since you came back to us. I persuaded Henry Crozier to give you the Junior brief. Naturally, in a case of this importance, I shall do most of it myself. If the chance arises you might be able to call some formal undisputed evidence. And of course you'll take a note of my cross-examination. You'll be capable of that won't you?"

"My near-death experience has left me more than capable of conducting even the most difficult trial."

"Don't worry, old fellow." Soapy Sam was smiling at me in a way I found quite unendurable. "You won't be called on to do anything like that."

As I have said, Commander Durden's patch was an area not far from London, and certain important villains had moved in when London's East End was no longer the crime capital. They ran chains of taxi-cab firms, clubs and wine bars. They were shadowy figures behind Thai restaurants and garden centers. They dealt in hard drugs and protection rackets in what may have seemed, to a casual observer, to be the heart of Middle England. And no one could have been more Middle English than Doctor Petrus Wakefield, who carried on his practice in Chivering. This had once been a small market town with a broad main street, and had now had its heart ripped out to make way for a pedestrian precinct with a multi-storey car park, identical shops, and strict regulations against public meetings or thuggish behavior.

Doctor Wakefield, as I was to discover, was a pillar of this community, tall, good-looking, in his fifties. He was a leading light in the Amateur Dramatics Society, chairman of various charities, and the doting husband of Judy—pretty, blond, and twenty years his junior. Their two children, Simon and Sarah, were high achievers at a local private school. Nothing could have been more quietly successful, some might say even boring, than the Wakefield's lives up to the moment when, so it was alleged, Commander Bob Durden took out a contract on the doctor's life.

The local police force, as local forces did, relied on a body of informers, many of whom came with long strings of previous convictions attached to them, to keep them abreast of the crimes and misdemeanors which took place in this apparently prosperous and law-abiding community. According to my instructions, the use of police informers hadn't been entirely satisfactory. There was a suspicion that some officers had been using them to form relationships with local villains—warning them of likely searches and arrests and arranging in the worst cases, for a share of the spoils.

Commander Bob Durden was commended in the local paper "for the firm line he was taking on the investigation he was carrying out into the rumors of police corruption." One of the informers involved was a certain Len "the Silencer" Luxford—so called because of his old connection with quietened firearms—who had, it seemed, retired from serious crime and started a window-cleaning business in Chivering. He was still able occasionally to pass on information, heard in pubs and clubs from his old associates, to the police.

According to Detective Inspector Mynot, Bob Durden met with Len the Silencer in connection with his enquiry into police informers. Unusually, he saw Len alone and without any other officer being present. According to Len's statement, the Commander then offered him five thousand pounds to "silence" Doctor Wakefield, half down and half on completion of the task, the choice of weapons being left to the Silencer. Instead of carrying out these fatal instructions, Len—who owed, he said, a debt of gratitude to the doctor for the way he'd treated Len's mother—warned his prospective victim, who reported the whole matter to Detective Inspector Mynot. The case might have been thought slender if Doctor Wakefield had not been able to produce a letter he'd found in his wife's possession, telling Judy how blissfully happy they might be if Petrus Wakefield vanished from the face of the earth.

Such were the facts which led to Bob Durden—who thought all Old Bailey defense hacks nothing but wrenches in the smooth works of justice—employing me, as Ballard made painfully clear, as his *junior* counsel.

"I'm afraid I have to ask you this. Did you write this letter to Doctor Wakefield's wife?"

"I wrote the letter, yes. She must have left it lying about somewhere."

"You said you'd both be happy if Doctor Wakefield vanished from the face of the earth. Why did you want that?"

We were assembled in Ballard's room for a conference. The Commander, on bail and suspended from his duties on full pay, wearing a business suit, was looking smaller than in his full-dress appearance on the television screen. His lawyer, Mr. Crozier, a local man and apparently Ballard's old university friend, had a vaguely religious appearance to go with his name; that is to say he had a warm smile, a crumpled gray suit, and an expression of sadness at the sins of the world. His client's answer to my leader's question did absolutely nothing to cheer him up.

"You see, Mr. Ballard, we were in love. You write silly things when you're in love, don't you?" The bark of authority we had heard on television was gone. The Commander's frown had been smoothed away. He spoke quietly, almost gently.

"And send silly e-mails to people who fancy you," I hoped Soapy Sam might say, but of course he didn't. Instead he said, in his best Lawyers as Christians tone of deep solemnity, "You, a married man, wrote like that to a married woman?"

"I'm afraid things like that do happen, Mr. Ballard. Judy Wakefield's an extremely attractive woman."

There had been a picture of her in the paper—small, smiling mother of two who had, apparently, fallen in love with a policeman.

"And you, a police commander, wrote in that way to a Doctor's wife?"

"I'm not particularly proud of how we behaved. But as I told you, we were crazy about each other. We just wanted to be together, that was all."

Ballard apparently remained deeply shocked, so I ventured to ask a question.

"When you wrote that you'd both be much happier if he vanished from the face of the earth, you weren't suggesting the doctor would die. You simply meant that he'd get out of her life and leave you to each other. Wasn't that it?"

"Yes, of course." The Commander looked grateful. "You're putting it absolutely correctly."

"That's all right. It's just a defense lawyer's way of putting it," I was glad to be able to say.

Soapy Sam, however, still looked displeased. "You can be assured," he told our client, "that I shall be asking you the questions, Mr. Durden. Mr. Rumpole will be with me to take notes of the evidence. I'm quite sure the Jury won't want to hear the sordid details of your matrimonial infidelity. It won't do our case any good at all if we dwell on that aspect of the matter."

Ballard was turning over his papers, preparing to venture on another subject.

"If you don't mind me saying so," I interrupted, I hoped not too rudely, "I think the Commander's affair with the doctor's wife the most important factor in the case, whichever way you look at it. I think we need to know all we can about it."

At this Ballard gave a thin watery smile and once again bleated, "As I said, I shall be asking the questions in Court. Now, we can obviously attack the witness Luxford on the basis of his previous convictions, which include two charges of dishonesty. If you could just take us through your meeting with this man . . ."

"Did you use him much as an informer?" I interpreted, much to Ballard's annoyance.

But the Commander answered me. "Hardly at all. In fact, I think it had been a year or two since he had given us anything. I thought he'd more or less retired. That was why I was surprised he came over to me with all that information about one of my officers."

Durden then went through his conversation with the Silencer, which contained no reference to any proposed assassination. This had been made quite clear in our instructions, so I excused myself. I slipped out of the door counted up to two hundred in my head, then re-entered to tell Soapy Sam that our Director of Marketing and Administration wished to see him without delay on a matter of extreme urgency. Our leader excused himself, straightened his tie, patted down his hair and made for the door.

"Now then," I gave our instructing lawyer some quick instructions as I settled myself in Ballard's chair, "have a look at our client's bank statements, Mr. Crozier. Make sure that an inexplicable two and a half thousand didn't get drawn out in cash.

If the account's clean, tell the prosecution you'll disclose it providing they give us the good Doctor's."

"Very well, Mr. Rumpole, but why . . . ?"

"Never mind about why for the moment. You might help me a bit more about Doctor Wakefield. I suppose he is pretty well known in the town. Has he practiced there for years?"

"A good many years. I think he started off in London—a practice in the East End. Bethnal Green, that's what he told us. Apparently a pretty rough area. Then he came out to Chivering."

"To get away from the East End?"

"I don't know. He always said he enjoyed working there."

"I'm sure he did. One other thing. He is a pillar of the Dramatic Society, isn't he? What sort of parts does he play?"

"Oh, leads." The lawyer seemed to brighten up considerably as he told me about it. "The Chivering Mummers are rather ambitious you know. We did a quite creditable *Othello* when it was the A-level play."

"And the Doctor took the lead? You're not suggesting he blacked up? That's not allowed nowadays."

"Oh, no. The *other* great part."

"Of course." I made a mental note. "That's most interesting."

A minute later a flustered Ballard returned to the room and I moved politely out of his chair. He hadn't been able to find Luci with an i anywhere in the Chambers, a fact which came as no surprise to me at all.

When I got home to Froxbury Mansions, I happened to mention over shepherd's pie and cabbage, that Commander Bob Durden had admitted to an affair with the Doctor's attractive and much younger wife.

"That comes as no surprise to me at all," Hilda told me. "As soon as he appeared on the television I was sure there was something fishy about that man."

I was glad to discover that, when it came to telling lies, Hilda could do it as brazenly as any of my clients.

In the weeks before the trial, I thought a good deal about Doctor Petrus Wakefield. Petrus was, as you will have to admit, a most unusual Christian name, perhaps bestowed by a pedantic Latin master and his classically educated wife on a child they didn't want to call anything as commonplace as Peter. What bothered me, when I first read the papers in the *R. v. Durden,* was where and when I had heard it before. And then I remembered old cases, forgotten crimes, and gang rivalry in a part of London to the east of Ludgate Circus in the days when I was making something of a name for myself as a defender at the Criminal Bar. These thoughts led me to remember Bill "Knuckles" Huckersley, a heavyweight part-time boxer, full-time bouncer, and general factotum of a taxi-cab organisation in Bethnal Green. I had done him some service, such as getting his father off of a charge of attempting to smuggle breaking out instruments into Pentonville while Bill was detained there. This unlooked-for success moved him to send me a Christmas card every year and, as I kept his latest among my trophies, I had his address.

I thought he would be more likely to confide in me than some professional investigator such as the admirable Fig Newton. Accordingly, I forsook Pommeroy's one evening after Court and made instead for the Black Spot Pub in Bethnal Green Road. There I sat staring moodily into a pint of Guinness as a bank of slot machines whirred and flashed and loud music filled the room, encrusted with faded gilt, which had become known, since a famous shooting had occurred there in its historic past, as the Lager and Lime Bar.

Knuckles arrived dead on time—a large broad-shouldered man who seemed to move as lightly as an inflated balloon across the bar to where I sat. He pulled up a stool beside me and said, "Mr. Rumpole! This is an honor, sir. I told Dad you'd rung up for a meeting and he was over the moon about it. Eighty-nine now and still going. He sends his good wishes, of course."

"Send him mine." I bought Knuckles the Diet Coke and packet of curry-flavored potato crisps he'd asked for and as he crunched his way through them, the conversation turned to Doctor Petrus Wakefield. "Petrus," I reminded him, "not a name you'd forget. It seemed to turn up in a number of cases I did in my earlier years."

"He treated a friend of mine." Knuckles lifted a fistful of crisps to his mouth and a sound emerged like an army marching through a field of dead bracken. "They did get a few injuries in their line of business."

"What do you mean by that, exactly?"

"Knife wounds, bullet holes. Some of them I went round with used to attract those sorts of complaints. You needed a doctor who wasn't going to get inquisitive."

"And that was Doctor Petrus Wakefield?"

"He always gave you the first name, didn't he? Like he was proud of it. You got any further questions, Mr. Rumpole? Don't they say that in Court?"

"Sometimes. Yes, I have. About Len Luxford. He used to come in here, didn't he?"

"The old Silencer? He certainly did. He's long gone, though. Got a window-cleaning business somewhere outside London."

"Do you see him occasionally?"

"We keep in touch. Quite regular."

"And he was a patient of Doctor Petrus?"

"We all were."

"Anything else you can tell me about the Doctor?"

"Nothing much. Except that he was always on about acting. He wanted to get the boys in the slammer into acting in plays. I had it when I was in the Scrubs. He'd visit the place and start drama groups. I used to steer clear of them. Lot of dodgy blokes dressing up like females."

"Did he ever try to teach Len Luxford acting?"

My source grinned, coughed, covered his mouth with a huge hand, gulped Diet Coke, and said with a meaningful grin, "not till recently, I reckon."

"You mean since they both lived at Chivering?"

"Something like that, yes. Last time I had a drink with Len he told me all about it."

"What sort of acting are you talking about?" I tried not to show my feeling that my visit to the deafening Lager and Lime Bar was about to become a huge success, but Knuckle's had a sudden attack of shyness.

"I can't tell you that, Mr. Rumpole. I honestly can't remember."

"Might you remember if I called you as a witness down the Old Bailey?"

My source was smiling as he answered, but for the first time since I'd known him his smile was seriously alarming. "You try and get me down the Old Bailey as a witness and you'll never live to see me again. Not in this world you won't."

After that I bought him another Diet Coke and then I left him. I'd gotten something out of Knuckles. Not very much, but something.

"This is one of those unhappy cases, Members of the Jury. One of those very rare cases when a member of the police force, in this case a very senior member of the police force, seems to have lost all his respect for the law and set about to plot and plan an inexcusable and indeed a cruel crime."

This was Marston Dawlish Q. C., a large beefy man much given to false smiles and unconvincing bonhomie, opening the case for the prosecution to an attentive Jury. On the bench we had drawn the short straw in the person of the aptly named Mr. Justice Graves. A pale, unsmiling figure with hollow cheeks and bony fingers, he sat with his eyes closed, as though to shut out the painful vision of a dishonest senior copper.

"As I say, it is, happily, rare indeed to see a high ranking police officer occupying that particular seat in an Old Bailey courtroom." Here Marston Dawlish raised one of his ham-like hands and waved it in the general direction of the dock.

"A rotten apple." The words came in a solemn, doom-laden voice from the Gravestone on the Bench.

"Indeed, your Lordship." Marston Dawlish was only too ready to agree.

"We used to say that of police officers who might be less than honest, Members of the Jury." The Judge started to explain his doom-laden pronouncement. "We used to call them 'rotten apples' who might infect the whole barrel if they weren't rooted out."

"Ballard!" This came out as a stentorian whisper at my leader's back. "Aren't you going to point out that that was an appalling thing for the Judge to say?"

"Quiet, Rumpole!" The Soapy Sam whisper was more controlled. "I want to listen to the evidence."

"We haven't gotten to the evidence yet. We haven't heard a word of evidence, but some sort of judicial decision seems to have come from the Bench. Get up on your hind legs and make a fuss about it!"

"Let me remind you, Rumpole, that I'm leading counsel in this case. I make the decisions—"

"Mr. Ballard!" Proceedings had been suspended while Soapy Sam and I discussed tactics. Now the old Gravestone interrupted us. "Does your Junior wish to say something?"

"No, my Lord." Ballard rose with a somewhat sickly smile. "My Junior doesn't wish to say anything. If an objection needs to be made, your Lordship can rely on me to make it."

"I'm glad of that." Graves let loose a small sigh of relief. "I thought I saw Mr. Rumpole growing restive."

"I am restive, my Lord." As Ballard sat down I rose up like a black cloud after sunshine. "Your Lordship seemed to be inviting the Jury to think of my client as a rotten apple, as your Lordship so delicately phrased it, before we have heard a word of evidence against him."

"Rumpole, sit down." Ballard seemed to be in a state of panic.

"I wasn't referring to your client in particular, Mr. Rumpole. I was merely describing unsatisfactory police officers in general."

It was, I thought, a remarkably lame excuse. "My Lord," I told him, "there is only one police officer in the dock and he is completely innocent until he is proven guilty. He could reasonably object to any reference to rotten apples before this case has even begun."

There was a heavy silence. I had turned to look at my client in the dock and I saw what I took to be a small shadowy smile of gratitude. Ballard sat immobile, as though waiting for sentence of death to be pronounced against me.

"Members of the Jury," Graves turned stiffly in the direction of the twelve honest citizens, "you've heard what Mr. Rumpole had to say and you will no doubt give it what weight you think fit." There was a welcoming turn in the direction of the prosecution. "Yes, Mr. Marston Dawlish. Perhaps you may continue with your opening speech now that Mr. Ballard's Junior has finished addressing the Court."

Marston Dawlish finished his opening speech without, I was pleased to notice, any further support from the learned Judge. Doctor Petrus Wakefield was the first witness and he gave, I had to admit, an impressive performance. He was a tall, still, slender man with graying sideburns, slightly hooded eyes and a chin raised to show his handsome profile to the best possible advantage. When he took the oath he held the Bible up high and projected in a way which must have delighted the elderly and hard of hearing in the audience attending the Chivering Mummers. He smiled at the Jury, took care not to speak faster than the movements of the Judge's pencil, and asked for no special sympathy as a betrayed husband and potential murder victim. If he wasn't a truthful witness, he clearly knew how to play the part.

An Old Bailey conference room had been reserved for us at lunchtime so that we could discuss strategy and eat sandwiches. Ballard, after having done nothing very much all morning, was tucking into a prawn and mayo when he looked up and met an outraged stare from Commander Durden.

"What the hell was the Judge up to?"

"Gerald Graves?" Ballard tried to sound casually unconcerned. "Bit of an off-putting manner, I agree. But he's sound, very sound. Isn't he, Rumpole?"

"Sound?" I said. "It's the sound of a distant foghorn on a damp night." I didn't want to depress the Commander, but he was depressed already, and distinctly angry.

"Whatever he sounds like, it seems he found me guilty in the first ten minutes."

"You mean," I couldn't help reminding the man of his denunciation of defense lawyers, "you found the scales of justice tipped towards the prosecution? I thought you said it was always the other way round."

"I have to admit," and the Commander spoke as though he meant it, "I couldn't help admiring the way you stood up to this Judge, Mr. Rumpole."

"That was standing up to the Judge, was it?" I couldn't let the man get away with it. "Not just another courtroom trick to get the Jury on our side and give the scales of justice a crafty shove?"

"I don't think we should discuss tactics in front of the client, Rumpole." Soapy Sam was clearly feeling left out of the conversation. "Although I have to say I don't think it was wise to attack the Judge at this stage of the case or indeed at all." He'd gotten the last morsel of prawn and mayo sandwich on his chin and wiped it with a large white handkerchief before setting out to reassure the client. "From now on, I shall be personally responsible for what is said in Court. As your leading counsel, I shall do my best to get back on better terms with Graves."

"You mean," Commander looked distinctly cheated, "he's going to get away with calling me a rotten apple?"

"I mean to concentrate our fire on this man Luxford. He's got a string of previous convictions." Ballard did his best to look dangerous, but it wasn't a great performance.

"First of all, someone's got to cross-examine the good Doctor Petrus Wakefield," I reminded him.

"I shall be doing that, Rumpole. And I intend to do it very shortly. We don't want to be seen attacking the man whose wife our client unfortunately—"

"Rogered." I was getting tired of Ballard's circumlocutions. "Misconducted himself with." Ballard lowered his voice, and his nose into a paper cup of coffee. This was clearly a part of the case on which Soapy Sam did not wish to dwell.

"You'll have to go into the whole affair," I told him. "It's provided the motive for the crime."

"The alleged victim is a deceived husband," Ballard shook his head. "The Jury are going to have a good deal of sympathy for the Doctor."

"If you ask him the questions I've suggested, they may not have all that much sympathy. You got my list didn't you?"

I had given my good learned leader ten good points for the cross-examination of Doctor Petrus. I had little faith in his putting them particularly clearly, or with more force or power of attack than he might have used if he'd been asking the Doctor if he'd driven up by way of the M25 or had his holiday yet. All the same, the relevant questions were written down, a recipe for good cross-examination, and Ballard only had to lob them out across the crowded courtroom.

"I have read your list carefully, Rumpole," my leader said, "and quite frankly I don't think there's anything in it that it would be helpful to ask Doctor Wakefield."

"It might be very helpful to the prosecution if you don't ask my questions."

"I shall simply say that 'My client deeply regrets his unfortunate conduct with your wife,' and sit down."

"Sit down exhausted?" I couldn't help asking. "Don't you want to get at the truth of this case?"

"Truth? My dear Rumpole," Ballard was smiling, "I didn't know you were interested in the truth. All these questions," he lifted my carefully prepared list and dropped it on the table, "seem like nothing but a sort of smoke screen—irrelevant matter to confuse the Jury."

"You read about my meeting with Knuckles Huckersley in the Black Spot Pub?"

"I did, and I regretted the fact that a Member of the Bar would go to such lengths, or shall I say depths, to meet a potential witness."

"You're not going to ask the good Doctor about his practice in the East End?"

"I think the Jury would find that quite counterproductive. It could look like an attack on his character."

"So you won't take the risk?"

"Certainly not." Ballard's thoughts had strayed back to his lunch. "Are those sandwiches bacon and lettuce?"

"I rather imagine corned beef and chutney," Mr. Crozier, our instructing lawyer from Chivering, made a rare contribution to the discussion.

There was silence then. Ballard chewed his last sandwich. No doubt I had broken every rule and shown a lamentable lack of faith in my learned leader, but I had to make the situation clear to our client, the copper who had shown complete lack of faith in defending counsel.

"Well, Commander," I said, "you've got a barrister who's going to keep the scales tipped in what you said was the right direction."

"Towards justice?" Bob Durden was trying to stick to his old convictions as a drowning man might to a straw.

"No," I said, "towards a conviction. If it's the conviction of an innocent man, well, I suppose that's just bad luck and part of the system as you'd like it to work."

There was a silence in the lunchtime conference room. Ballard was at ease in his position as the leader. No doubt I was being a nuisance and breaking most of the rules, but he seemed to feel that he was still in charge and could demolish the corned beef and chutney in apparently contented silence. Mr. Crozier looked embarrassed and the Commander was seriously anxious as he burst out, "Are you saying, Mr. Rumpole, that the questions you want asked could get me off?"

"At least leave you with a chance." I was prepared to promise him that.

"And Mr. Ballard doesn't want to ask them?"

"I've told you. They'll only turn the Judge against us," Ballard mumbled past the corned beef.

"And why do you want to ask them, Mr. Rumpole?" The Commander was puzzled.

"Oh, I'm just one of those legal hacks you disapprove of," I told him. "I want you to walk out of Court laughing. I know that makes me a very dubious sort of lawyer, the kind you really hate. Don't you, Commander Durden?"

In the silence that followed our client looked around the room uncertainly. Then he made up his mind and barked out an order. "I want Mr. Rumpole's questions asked."

"I told you," Ballard put down his half-eaten sandwich. "I'm in charge of this case and I don't intend to make any attack on a reputable Doctor whose wife you apparently seduced."

"All right." In spite of Ballard's assertion of his authority it was the Commander who was in charge. "Then Mr. Rumpole is going to have to ask the questions for you."

I was sorry for Soapy Sam then, and I felt, I have to confess, a pang of guilt. He had behaved according to his fairly hopeless principles and could do no more. He rose to his feet, left his half-eaten sandwich to curl up on his plate, and spoke to his friend Mr. Crozier who looked deeply embarrassed.

"Under the circumstances," Ballard said, "I must withdraw. My advice has not been taken and I must go. I can't say I expect a happy result for you, Commander, but I wish you well. I suppose you're not coming with me, Mr. Rumpole?"

As I say, I felt for the man, but I couldn't leave with him. Commander Durden had put his whole life in the hands of the sort of Old Bailey hack he had told the world could never be trusted not to pull a fast one.

"Doctor Wakefield, you're suggesting in this case that my client, Commander Durden, instigated a plan to kill you?"

"He did that, yes."

"It wasn't a very successful plan, was it?"

"What do you mean?"

"Well, you're still here, aren't you? Alive and kicking." This got me a little stir of laughter from the Jury and a doom-laden warning from his Lordship.

"Mr. Rumpole, for reasons which we need not go into here, your learned leader hasn't felt able to continue with the case."

"Your Lordship is saying that he will be greatly missed?"

"I am saying no such thing. What I am saying is I hope this defense will be conducted according to the high standards we have come to expect from Mr. Ballard. Do I make myself clear?"

"Perfectly clear, my Lord. I'll do my best." Here I was looking at the Jury. I didn't exactly wink, but I hoped they were prepared to join me in the anti-Graves society. "Of course I can't promise anything."

"Well do your best, Mr. Rumpole." The old Gravestone half closed his eyes as though expecting to be shocked by my next question. I did not disappoint him.

"Doctor Wakefield, were you bitterly angry when you discovered that your wife had been sleeping with Commander Durden?"

"Mr. Rumpole!" The Grave's eyes opened again, but with no friendly expression.

"I'm sure the Jury will assume that Doctor Wakefield had the normal feelings of a betrayed husband."

"I quite agree, my Lord. But the evidence might be more valuable if it came from the witness and not your Lordship." Before Graves could utter again, I launched another question at the good Doctor. "Did you consider divorce?"

"I thought about it, but Judy and I decided to try to keep the marriage together for the sake of the children."

"An admirable decision, if I may say so." And I decided to say so before the doleful Graves could stir himself to congratulate the witness. "You've produced the letter you found in your wife's handbag. By the way, do you make a practice of searching your wife's bag?"

"Only after I'd become suspicious. I'd heard rumors."

"I see. So you found this letter, in which the Commander said they might be happier if you vanished from the face of the earth. Did you take that as a threat to kill you?"

"When I heard about the plot, yes."

"When you heard about it from Luxford?"

"Yes."

"But not at the time you found the letter?"

"It occurred to me that it might be a threat, but I didn't believe that Bob Durden would actually do anything."

"You didn't believe that?"

"No. But I thought he meant he wanted me dead."

"And it made you angry?"

"Very angry."

"So I suppose you went straight round to the Commander's house and confronted him with it?"

"No, I didn't do that."

"You didn't do that." I was looking at the Jury now in considerable surprise with a slight frown and raised eyebrows, an expression which I saw reflected in some of their faces.

"May I ask you why you didn't confront my client with his outrageous letter?"

"I didn't want to add to the scandal. Judy and I were going to try and make a life together."

"That answer," the sepulchral Graves's voice was now almost silky, "does you great credit, if I may say so, Doctor Wakefield."

"What may not do you quite so much credit, Doctor," I tried to put my case as politely as possible, "is the revenge you decided to take on your wife's lover. This letter," I had it in my hand now and held it up for the Jury to see, "gave you the idea. The ingenious revenge you planned would cause Bob Durden, and not you, to vanish. Isn't that the truth of the matter?"

"Are you suggesting, Mr. Rumpole," the Judge over-acted his astonishment, "that we've all got the case the wrong way round and that it was Doctor Wakefield who was planning to murder your client?"

"Not murder him, my Lord. However angry the Doctor was, however deep his sense of humiliation, he stopped short of murder. No. What he planned for Mr. Durden was a fate almost worse than death for a senior police officer. He planned to put him exactly where he is now, in the Old Bailey dock, faced with a most serious charge and with the prospect of a long term of confinement in prison."

It was one of those rare moments in Court of absolute silence. The clerk below the Judge stopped whispering into his telephone; no one came in or went out, opened a law book, or sorted out their papers. The Jury looked startled at this new and extraordinary idea. Everyone seemed to hold their breath, and I felt as though I had just dumped my money on an outside chance and the roulette wheel had started to spin.

"I really haven't the least idea what you mean." Doctor Petrus Wakefield, in the witness box, looked amused rather than shaken, cheerfully tolerant of a lawyer's desperate efforts to save his client, and perfectly capable of dealing with any questions I might have the wits to ask.

Graves swooped to support the Doctor. "Mr. Rumpole, I presume you're going to explain that extraordinary suggestion."

"Your Lordship's presumption is absolutely correct. I would invite your Lordship to listen carefully while I put my case to the witness. Doctor Wakefield," I went on before Graves could summon his voice back from the depths, "your case is that you learnt of the alleged plot to kill you when Luxford called to warn you. We haven't heard from Mr. Luxford yet but that's your story."

"It's the truth."

"Luxford warned you because he was grateful for the way you treated his mother?"

"That is so."

"But you'd known Len Luxford—the Silencer, as he was affectionately known by the regulars in the Black Spot Bethnal Green—long before that, hadn't you?"

Doctor Wakefield took time to think. He must have thought of what the Silencer might say when he came to give evidence and took a gamble on the truth. "I had come across him, yes."

"Because you practiced as a doctor in that part of London?"

"I did, yes."

"And got to know quite a lot of the characters who lived on the shady side of the law?"

"It was my job to treat them medically. I didn't enquire into the way they lived their lives."

"Of course, Doctor. Didn't some of your customers turn up having been stabbed, or with gunshot wounds?"

"They did, yes." Once again the Doctor took a punt on the truth.

"So you treated them?"

"Yes. Just as you, Mr. Rumpole, no doubt represented some of them in Court."

It was a veritable hit. The Jury smiled, the Gravestone looked as though it was the first day of spring, and I had to beware of any temptation to underestimate the intelligence of Doctor Wakefield.

"Exactly so. And, like me, you got to know some of them quite well. You got to know Luxford very well in those old days, didn't you?"

"He was a patient of mine."

"You treated his wounds and kept quiet about them."

"Probably."

"Probably. So would it be right to say that you and the Silencer Luxford went back a long time, and he owed you a debt of gratitude?"

"Exactly!" The Doctor was pleased to agree. "Which is why he told me about your client's plan to pay him to kill me."

"I'm just coming to that. When you're not practicing medicine or patching up old gangsters, you spend a great deal of time acting, don't you?"

"It's my great passion." And here the Doctor's voice was projected and enriched. "Acting can release us from ourselves, call on us to create a new character."

"Which is why you encouraged acting in prisons."

"Exactly, Mr. Rumpole! I'm glad that you understand that, at least."

There was a moment of rapport between myself and the witness, but I now had to launch an attack which seemed, now that I was standing up in a crowded court room, like taking a jump in the dark off a very high cliff.

"I think you encouraged Len Luxford to act?"

"In the old days, when I did some work with prisoners, yes."

"Oh, no, I mean quite recently. When you suggested he go for a chat with Commander Durden about police informers and come out acting the part of a contract killer."

The Doctor's reaction was perfect—good-natured, half amused, completely unconcerned. "I really have no idea what you're suggesting," he said.

"Neither have I." The learned Gravestone was delighted to join the line of the mystified. "Perhaps you'd be good enough to explain yourself, Mr. Rumpole."

"Certainly, my Lord." I turned to the witness. "It was finding the letter that gave you the idea, wasn't it? It could be used to support the idea that Commander Durden wanted you dead. You were going to get your revenge not by killing him, nothing as brutally simple as that, but by getting him convicted of a conspiracy to murder you—by finishing his career, turning him into a criminal, landing him, the rotten apple in the barrel of decent coppers, in prison for a very long time indeed."

"This is absolute nonsense." The Doctor was as calm as ever, but I ploughed on doing my best to sound more confident than I felt.

"All you needed was an actor for your small-cast play. So you got Len Luxford, who owed you for a number of favors, to act for you. All he had to do was lie about what Commander Durden had said to him when he arranged a meeting, and you thought that and the letter would be enough."

"It's an interesting idea, Mr. Rumpole. But of course it's completely untrue."

"You're an excellent actor, aren't you, Doctor?" I took it slowly now, looking at the Jury. "Didn't you have great success in the Shakespeare play you did with the local Mummers?"

"I think we all did fairly well. What's that got to do with it?"

"Didn't you play Iago? A man who ruins his Commander by producing false evidence?"

"Mr. Rumpole!" Graves's patience, fragile as it already was, had clearly snapped at what he saw as my attempt to call a dead dramatist into the witness box. "Have you no other evidence for the very serious suggestions you are making to this witness except the fact that he played, who was it"— he searched among his notes—"the man Iago?"

"Oh, yes, my Lord." I tried to answer with more confidence than I felt. "I'd like the Jury to have a couple of documents."

Mr. Crozier had done his work well. Having surrendered Bob Durden's bank statements to the young man from the Crown Prosecution Service, he seemed to take it for granted that we should get Doctor Wakefield's in return. Now the Judge and Jury had their copies, and I introduced the subject.

"Let me just remind you, Luxford saw Commander Durden on March the fifteenth. On March the twenty-first you went to Detective Inspector Mynot with your complaint that my client had asked Luxford to kill you for a payment of five thousand pounds—two and a half thousand down and the balance when the deed was done."

"That's the truth. It's what I told the Inspector."

"You're sure it's the truth?"

"I am on my oath."

"So you are." I looked at the Jury. "Perhaps you could look at your bank statement. Did you draw out two and a half thousand pounds in cash on March the twenty-first? Quite a large sum, wasn't it? May I suggest what it was for?"

For the first time the Doctor missed his cue. He looked about the court hoping for a prompt, and, not getting one invented. "I think I had to pay . . . I seem to remember things were done to the house."

"It wasn't anything to do with the house, was it? You were paying Len Luxford off in cash. Not for doing a murder, but for pretending to be a part of conspiracy to murder?"

The Doctor looked to Marston Dawlish for help, but no help came from that quarter. I asked the next question.

"When does he get the rest of the money? On the day that Commander Durden's convicted?"

"Of course not!"

"Is that your answer?" I turned to the Judge. "My Lord, may I just remind you and the Jury that there are no large amounts of cash to be seen coming out of Commander Durden's account during the relevant period."

With that I sat down. Counsel for the prosecution suggested that as I had taken up such an unconscionable time with Doctor Wakefield, perhaps the Court would end for the day, and he would be calling Mr. Luxford in the morning.

But he didn't call the Silencer the next morning or any other morning. I don't know whether it was the news of my cross-examination in the evening paper, or a message of warning from Knuckles, but in a fit of terminal stage fright Len failed to enter the Court. A visit by the police to the house from which he carried out his window-cleaning business only revealed a distraught wife who had no idea where he had gotten to. I suppose he had enough experience of the law to know that a charge of conspiracy to murder against the Commander might change into a charge of attempting to pervert the course of justice against Doctor Wakefield and himself. So he went with his cash, perhaps back to his old friends and accustomed haunts, his one unsuccessful stab at the acting profession over.

When Marston Dawlish announced that without his vital witness the prosecution couldn't continue, Mr. Justice Graves gave a heavy sigh and advised the twelve honest citizens.

"Members of the Jury, you have heard a lot of questions put by Mr. Rumpole about the man Iago. And other suggestions which may or may not have seemed to you to be relevant to this case. The simple fact of the matter is that the vital prosecution witness has gone missing and Mr. Marston Dawlish has asked me to direct you to return a verdict of 'not guilty.' It's an unfortunate situation but there it is. So will your foreman please stand?"

I paid a last visit to the conference room to say good-bye to my client and Mr. Crozier. The place had been cleaned up, ready to receive other sandwiches, other paper cups of coffee and other people in trouble.

"I suppose I should thank you." The Commander was looking as confident again as he had on the telly. Only now he was smiling.

"I suppose you should thank me, the shifty old defense hack, and a couple of hard cases like Knuckles and Len Luxford. We doubtful characters saved your skin, Commander, and managed to tip the scales in favor of the defense."

"I shall go on protesting about that, of course."

"I thought you might."

"Not that I have any criticism of what you did in my case. I'm sure you acted perfectly properly. You believed in my innocence."

"No." I had to say it, but I'm afraid it startled him. He looked shocked. His full lips shrank in disapproval and his forehead furrowed.

"You don't believe in my innocence?"

"My belief is suspended. It's been left hanging up in the robbing room for years. It's not my job to find you innocent or guilty. That's up to the Jury. All I can do is put your case as well as you would if you had," and I said it all in modesty, "anything approaching my ability."

"I don't think I'd ever have thought up your attack on the Doctor," he admitted.

"No, I don't believe you would have."

"So, I'm grateful to you."

It wasn't an overgenerous compliment, but I said thank you.

"But you say you're not convinced of my innocence?" Clearly he could hardly believe it.

"Don't worry," I told him. "You're free now. You can go back to work."

"That's true. I've been suspended for far too long." He looked at his watch as though he expected to start immediately. "It's been an interesting experience." I was, I must say, surprised at the imperturbable Commander who could fall passionately in love, wish an inconvenient husband off the face of the earth, and call his own criminal trial merely "interesting." "We live in different worlds, Mr. Rumpole," he told me, "you and I."

"So we do. You believe everyone who turns up at Court is guilty. I suspect some of them may be innocent."

"You suspect, you say, but you never know, do you?"

And so he left with Mr. Crozier. I fully expect to see him again in his impressive uniform complaining from the television in the corner of our living room about the scales of Justice being constantly tipped in favor of the defense.

"You had a bit of luck in *R. v. Durden.*" Ballard caught me up in Ludgate Circus one afternoon when we were walking back from the Old Bailey. "I gather Luxford went missing."

"That's right. I told him. "Are you calling that luck?"

"Lucky for you, Rumpole. From what I read of your cross-examination, you were clearly irritating the Judge."

"I'm afraid I was. I do have a talent for irritating Judges."

"Pity, that. Otherwise you are, in many ways, quite able."

"Thank you, Ballard."

"No, I should thank you for getting me out of that unpleasant case. Our clerk fixed me up with a rating appeal."

"Good old Henry."

"Yes, he has his uses. So, you see I have a lot to thank you for, Rumpole."

"You're entirely welcome, but will you promise me one thing?"

"What's that?"

"Please don't hug me, Ballard."

"I told you, Rumpole, that I could tell at once that there was something fishy about that client of yours." Hilda's verdict on the Commander was written in stone.

"But he was acquitted."

"You know perfectly well, Rumpole, that that doesn't mean a thing. The next time he turns up on the television I shall switch it over to the other channel."

Forget Graves, I thought, leave out Bullingham; you'd search for a long time down the Old Bailey before you found a judge as remorseless and tough as She Who Must Be Obeyed!

A Candle for the Bag Lady

Lawrence Block

Lawrence Block's urban noir character Matthew Scudder—the down-and-out, alcoholic, unlicensed Manhattan P.I.—has featured in sixteen Matt Scudder novels, the latest being *All the Flowers Are Dying*, as well as numerous short fiction and story anthologies. Tough, gritty and as close to the reality of life on the streets of New York as is possible, Scudder's personal and professional experience collides to make him an intensely readable character. The fifth novel in the series, *Eight Million Ways to Die*, was filmed by Hal Ashby (his last film) with an initial screenplay written by Oliver Stone. In the film version, relocated from Manhattan to Los Angeles, Jeff Bridges gave a fine performance as Matt Scudder, with Rosanna Arquette and Andy Garcia in supporting roles.

He was a thin young man in a blue pinstripe suit. His shirt was white with a button-down collar. His glasses had oval lenses in brown tortoiseshell frames. His hair was a dark brown, short but not severely so, neatly combed, parted on the right. I saw him come in and watched him ask a question at the bar. Billie was working afternoons that week. I watched as he nodded at the young man, then swung his sleepy eyes over in my direction. I lowered my own eyes and looked at a cup of coffee laced with bourbon while the fellow walked over to my table.

"Matthew Scudder?" I looked up at him, nodded. "I'm Aaron Creighton. I looked for you at your hotel. The fellow on the desk told me I might find you here."

Here was Armstrong's, a Ninth Avenue saloon around the corner from my Fifty-seventh Street hotel. The lunch crowd was gone except for a couple of stragglers in front whose voices were starting to thicken with alcohol. The streets outside were full of May sunshine. The winter had been cold and deep and long. I couldn't recall a more welcome spring.

"I called you a couple of times last week, Mr. Scudder. I guess you didn't get my messages."

I'd gotten two of them and ignored them, not knowing who he was or what he wanted and unwilling to spend a dime for the answer. But I went along with the fiction. "It's a cheap hotel," I said. "They're not always too good about messages."

"I can imagine. Uh, is there someplace we can talk?"

"How about right here?"

He looked around. I don't suppose he was used to conducting his business in bars but he evidently decided it would be all right to make an exception. He set his briefcase on the floor and seated himself across the table from me. Angela, the new day-shift waitress, hurried over to get his order. He glanced at my cup and said he'd have coffee, too.

"I'm an attorney," he said. My first thought was that he didn't look like a lawyer, but then I realized he probably dealt with civil cases. My experience as a cop had given me a lot of experience with criminal lawyers. The breed ran to several types, none of them his.

I waited for him to tell me why he wanted to hire me. But he crossed me up.

"I'm handling an estate," he said, and paused, and gave what seemed a calculated if well-intentioned smile. "It's my pleasant duty to tell you you've come into a small legacy, Mr. Scudder."

"Someone's left me money?"

"Twelve hundred dollars."

Who could have died? I'd lost touch long since with any of my relatives. My parents went years ago and we'd never been close with the rest of the family.

I said, "Who—?"

"Mary Alice Redfield."

I repeated the name aloud. It was not entirely unfamiliar but I had no idea who Mary Alice Redfield might be. I looked at Aaron Creighton. I couldn't make out his eyes behind the glasses, but there was a smile's ghost on his thin lips, as if my reaction was not unexpected.

"She's dead?"

"Almost three months ago."

"I didn't know her."

"She knew you. You probably knew her, Mr. Scudder. Perhaps you didn't know her by name." His smile deepened. Angela had brought his coffee. He stirred milk and sugar into it, took a careful sip, nodded his approval. "Miss Redfield was murdered." He said this as if he'd had practice uttering a phrase which did not come naturally to him. "She was killed quite brutally in late February for no apparent reason, another innocent victim of street crime."

"She lived in New York?"

"Oh yes. In this neighborhood."

"And she was killed around here?"

"On West Fifty-fifth Street between Ninth and Tenth avenues. Her body was found in an alleyway. She'd been stabbed repeatedly and strangled with the scarf she had been wearing."

Late February. Mary Alice Redfield. West Fifty-fifth between Ninth and Tenth. Murder most foul. Stabbed and strangled, a dead woman in an alleyway. I usually kept track of murders, perhaps out of a vestige of professionalism, perhaps because I couldn't cease to be fascinated by man's inhumanity to man. Mary Alice Redfield had willed me twelve hundred dollars. And someone had knifed and strangled her, and—

"Oh God," I said. "The shopping bag lady."

Aaron Creighton nodded.

New York is full of them. East side, West side, each neighborhood has its own supply of bag women. Some of them are alcoholic but most of them have gone mad without any help from drink. They walk the streets, huddle on stoops or in doorways. They find sermons in stones and treasures in trash cans. They talk to themselves, to passersby, to God. Sometimes they mumble. Now and then they shriek.

They carry things around with them, the bag women. The shopping bags supply their generic name and their chief common denominator. Most of them seem to be paranoid, and their madness convinces them that their possessions are very valuable, that their enemies covet them. So their shopping bags are never out of their sight.

There used to be a colony of these ladies who lived in Grand Central Station. They would sit up all night in the waiting room, taking turns waddling off to the lavatory from time to time. They rarely talked to each other but some herd instinct made them comfortable with one another. But they were not comfortable enough to trust their precious bags to one another's safekeeping, and each sad crazy lady always toted her shopping bags to and from the ladies' room.

Mary Alice Redfield had been a shopping bag lady. I don't know when she set up shop in the neighborhood. I'd been living in the same hotel ever since I resigned from the NYPD and separated from my wife and sons, and that was getting to be quite a few years now. Had Miss Redfield been on the scene that long ago? I couldn't remember her first appearance. Like so many of the neighborhood fixtures, she had been part of the scenery. Had her death not been violent and abrupt I might never have noticed she was gone.

I'd never known her name. But she had evidently known mine, and had felt something for me that prompted her to leave money to me. How had she come to have money to leave?

She'd had a business of sorts. She would sit on a wooden soft drink case, surrounded by three or four shopping bags, and she would sell newspapers. There's an all-night newsstand at the corner of Fifty-seventh and Eighth, and she would buy a few dozen papers there, carry them a block west to the corner of Ninth and set up shop in a doorway. She sold the papers at retail, though I suppose some people tipped her a few cents. I could remember a few occasions when I'd bought a paper and waved away change from a dollar bill. Bread upon the waters, perhaps, if that was what had moved her to leave me the money.

I closed my eyes, brought her image into focus. A thick-set woman, stocky rather than fat. Five-three or -four. Dressed usually in shapeless clothing, colorless gray and black garments, layers of clothing that varied with the season. I remembered that she would sometimes wear a hat, an old straw affair with paper and plastic flowers poked into it. And I remembered her eyes, large guileless blue eyes that were many years younger than the rest of her.

Mary Alice Redfield.

"Family money," Aaron Creighton was saying. "She wasn't wealthy but she had come from a family that was comfortably fixed. A bank in Baltimore handled her funds. That's where she was from originally, Baltimore, though she'd lived in New York for as long as anyone can remember. The bank sent her a check every month. Not very much, a couple of hundred dollars, but she hardly spent anything. She paid her rent—"

"I thought she lived on the street."

"No, she had a furnished room a few doors down the street from where she was killed. She lived in another rooming house on Tenth Avenue before that but moved when the building was sold. That was six or seven years ago and she lived on Fifty-fifth Street from then until her death. Her room cost her eighty dollars a month. She spent a few dollars on food. I don't know what she did with the rest. The only money in her room was a coffee can full of pennies. I've been checking the banks and there's no record of a savings account. I suppose she may have spent it or lost it or given it away. She wasn't very firmly grounded in reality."

"No, I don't suppose she was."

He sipped at his coffee. "She probably belonged in an institution," he said. "At least that's what people would say, but she got along in the outside world, she functioned well enough. I don't know if she kept herself clean and I don't know anything about how her mind worked, but I think she must have been happier than she would have been in an institution. Don't you think?"

"Probably."

"Of course she wasn't safe, not as it turned out, but anybody can get killed on the streets of New York." He frowned briefly, caught up in a private thought. Then he said, "She came to our office ten years ago. That was before my time." He told me the name of his firm, a string of Anglo-Saxon surnames. "She wanted to draw a will. The original will was a very simple document leaving everything to her sister. Then over the years she would come in from time to time to add codicils leaving specific sums to various persons. She made a total of thirty-two bequests by the time she died. One was for twenty dollars—that was to a man named John Johnson whom we haven't been able to locate. The remainder all ranged from five hundred to two thousand dollars." He smiled. "I've been given the task of running down the heirs."

"When did she put me in her will?"

"Two years ago in April."

I tried to think what I might have done for her then, how I might have brushed her life with mine. Nothing.

"Of course the will could be contested, Mr. Scudder. It would be easy to challenge Miss Redfield's competence and any relative could almost certainly get it set aside. But no one wishes to challenge it. The total amount involved is slightly in excess of a quarter of a million dollars—"

"That much."

"Yes. Miss Redfield received substantially less than the income which her holdings drew over the years, so the principal kept growing during her lifetime. Now the specific bequests she made total thirty-eight thousand dollars, give or take a few hundred, and the residue goes to Miss Redfield's sister. The sister—her name is Mrs. Palmer—is a widow with grown children. She's hospitalized with cancer and heart trouble and I believe diabetic complications and she hasn't long to live. Her children would like to see the estate settled before their mother dies, and they have enough local prominence to hurry the will through probate. So I'm authorized to tender checks for the full amount of the specific bequests on the condition that the legatees sign quit-claims acknowledging that this payment discharges in full the estate's indebtedness to them."

There was more legalese of less importance. Then he gave me papers to sign and the whole procedure ended with a check on the table. It was payable to me and in the amount of twelve hundred dollars and no cents.

I told Creighton I'd pay for his coffee.

I had time to buy myself another drink and still get to my bank before the windows closed. I put a little of Mary Alice Redfield's legacy in my savings account, took some cash, and sent a money order to Anita and my sons. I stopped at my hotel to check for messages. There weren't any. I had a drink at McGovern's and crossed the street to have another at Polly's Cage. It wasn't five o'clock yet but the bar was doing business already.

It turned into a funny night. I had dinner at the Greek place and read the *Post*, spent a little time at Joey Farrell's on Fifty-eighth Street, then wound up getting to Armstrong's around ten thirty or thereabouts. I spent part of the evening alone at my usual table and part of it in conversation at the bar. I made a point of stretching my drinks, mixing my bourbon with coffee, making a cup last a while, taking a glass of plain water from time to time.

But that never really works. If you're going to get drunk you'll manage it somehow. The obstacles I placed in my path just kept me up later. By two thirty I'd done what I had set out to do. I'd made my load and I could go home and sleep it off.

I woke around ten with less of a hangover than I'd earned and no memory of anything after I'd left Armstrong's. I was in my own bed in my own hotel room. And my clothes were hung neatly in the closet, always a good sign on a morning after. So I must have been in fairly good shape. But a certain amount of time was lost to memory, blacked out, gone.

When that first started happening I tended to worry about it. But it's the sort of thing you can get used to.

It was the money, the twelve hundred bucks. I couldn't understand the money. I had done nothing to deserve it. It had been left to me by a poor little rich woman whose name I'd not even known.

It had never occurred to me to refuse the dough. Very early in my career as a cop I'd learned an important precept. When someone put money in your hand you closed your fingers around it and put it in your pocket. I learned that lesson well and never had cause to regret its application. I didn't walk around with my hand out and I never took drug or homicide money, but I certainly grabbed all the clean graft that came my way and a certain amount that wouldn't have stood a white glove inspection. If Mary Alice thought I merited twelve hundred dollars, who was I to argue?

Ah, but it didn't quite work that way. Because somehow the money gnawed at me.

After breakfast I went to St. Paul's but there was a service going on, a priest saying Mass, so I didn't stay. I walked down to St. Benedict the Moor's on Fifty-third Street and sat for a few minutes in a pew at the rear. I go to churches to try to think, and I gave it a shot but my mind didn't know where to go.

I slipped six twenties into the poor box. I tithe. It's a habit I got into after I left the department and I still don't know why I do it. God knows. Or maybe He's as mystified as I am. This time, though, there was a certain balance in the act. Mary Alice Redfield had given me twelve hundred dollars for no reason I could comprehend. I was passing on a ten percent commission to the church for no better reason.

I stopped on the way out and lit a couple of candles for various people who weren't alive anymore. One of them was for the bag lady. I didn't see how it could do her any good, but I couldn't imagine how it could harm her, either.

I had read some press coverage of the killing when it happened. I generally keep up with crime stories. Part of me evidently never stopped being a policeman. Now I went down to the Forty-second Street library to refresh my memory.

The *Times* had run a pair of brief back-page items, the first a report of the killing of an unidentified female derelict, the second a follow-up giving her name and age. She'd been forty-seven, I learned. This surprised me, and then I realized that any specific number would have come as a surprise. Bums and bag ladies are ageless. Mary Alice Redfield could have been thirty or sixty or anywhere in between.

The *News* had run a more extended article than the *Times,* enumerating the stab wounds—twenty-six of them—and described the scarf wound about her throat—blue and white, a designer print, but tattered at its edges and evidently somebody's castoff. It was this article that I remembered having read.

But the *Post* had really played the story. It had appeared shortly after the new owner took over the paper and the editors were going all out for human interest, which always translates out as sex and violence. The brutal killing of a woman touches both of those bases, and this had the added kick that she was a character. If they'd ever learned she was an heiress it would have been page three material, but even without that knowledge they did all right by her.

The first story they ran was straight news reporting, albeit embellished with reports on the blood, the clothes she was wearing, the litter in the alley where she was found and all that sort of thing. The next day a reporter pushed the pathos button and tapped out a story featuring capsule interviews with people in the neighborhood. Only a few of them were identified by name and I came away with the feeling that he'd made up some peachy quotes and attributed them to unnamed nonexistent hangers-on. As a sidebar to that story, another reporter speculated on the possibility of a whole string of bag lady murders, a speculation which happily had turned out to be wide of the mark. The clown had presumably gone around the West Side asking shopping bag ladies if they were afraid of being the killer's next victim. I hope he faked the piece and let the ladies alone.

And that was about it. When the killer failed to strike again the newspapers hung up on the story. Good news is no news.

I walked back from the library. It was fine weather. The winds had blown all the crap out of the sky and there was nothing but blue overhead. The air actually had some air in it for a change. I walked west on Forty-second Street and north on Broadway, and I started noticing the number of street people, the drunks and the crazies and the unclassifiable derelicts. By the time I got within a few blocks of Fifty-seventh Street I was recognizing a large percentage of them. Each mini-neighborhood has its own human flotsam and jetsam and they're a lot more noticeable come springtime. Winter sends some of them south and others to shelter, and there's a certain percentage who die of exposure, but when the sun warms the pavement it brings most of them out again.

When I stopped for a paper at the corner of Eighth Avenue I got the bag lady into the conversation. The newsie clucked his tongue and shook his head. "The damnedest thing. Just the damnedest thing."

"Murder never makes much sense."

"The hell with murder. You know what she did? You know Eddie, works for me midnight to eight? Guy with the one droopy eyelid? Now he wasn't the guy used to sell her the stack of papers. Matter of fact that was usually me. She'd come by during the late morning or early afternoon and she'd take fifteen or twenty papers and pay me for 'em, and then she'd sit on her crate down the next corner and she'd sell as many as she could, and then she'd bring 'em back and I'd give her a refund on what she didn't sell."

"What did she pay for them?"

"Full price. And that's what she sold 'em for. The hell, I can't discount papers. You know the margin we got. I'm not even supposed to take 'em back, but what difference does it make? It gave the poor woman something to do is my theory. She was important, she was a businesswoman. Sits there charging a quarter for something she just paid a quarter for, it's no way to get rich, but you know something? She had money. Lived like a pig but she had money."

"So I understand."

"She left Eddie seven-twenty. You believe that? Seven hundred and twenty dollars, she willed it to him, there was a lawyer come around two, three weeks ago with a check. Eddie Halloran. Pay to the order of. You believe that? She never had dealings with him. I sold her the papers, I bought 'em back from her. Not that I'm complaining, not that I want the woman's money, but I ask you this: Why Eddie? He didn't know her. He can't believe she knows his name, Eddie Halloran. Why'd she leave it to him? He tells this lawyer, he says maybe she's got some other Eddie

Halloran in mind. It's a common Irish name and the neighborhood's full of the Irish. I'm thinking to myself, Eddie, schmuck, take the money and shut up, but it's him all right because it says in the will. Eddie Halloran the newsdealer is what it says. So that's him, right? But why Eddie?"

Why me? "Maybe she liked the way he smiled."

"Yeah, maybe. Or the way he combed his hair. Listen, it's money in his pocket. I worried he'd go on a toot, drink it up, but he says money's no temptation. He says he's always got the price of a drink in his jeans and there's a bar on every block but he can walk right past 'em, so why worry about a few hundred dollars? You know something? That crazy woman, I'll tell you something. I miss her. She'd come, crazy hat on her head, spacy look in her eyes, she'd buy her stack of papers and waddle off all businesslike, then she'd bring the leftovers and cash 'em in, and I'd make a joke about her when she was out of earshot, but I miss her."

"I know what you mean."

"She never hurt nobody," he said. "She never hurt a soul."

"Mary Alice Redfield. Yeah, the multiple stabbing and strangulation." He shifted a cud-sized wad of gum from one side of his mouth to the other, pushed a lock of hair off his forehead and yawned. "What have you got, some new information?"

"Nothing. I wanted to find out what you had."

"Yeah, right."

He worked on the chewing gum. He was a patrolman named Andersen who worked out of the Eighteenth. Another cop, a detective named Guzik, had learned that Andersen had caught the Redfield case and had taken the trouble to introduce the two of us. I hadn't known Andersen when I was on the force. He was younger than I, but then most people are nowadays.

He said, "Thing is, Scudder, we more or less put that one out of the way. It's an open file. You know how it works. If we get new information, fine, but in the meantime I don't sit up nights thinking about it."

"I just wanted to see what you had."

"Well, I'm kind of tight for time, if you know what I mean. My own personal time, I set a certain store by my own time."

"I can understand that."

"You probably got some relative of the deceased for a client. Wants to find out who'd do such a terrible thing to poor old Cousin Mary. Naturally you're interested because it's a chance to make a buck and a man's gotta make a living. Whether a man's a cop or a civilian he's gotta make a buck, right?"

Uh-huh. I seem to remember that we were subtler in my day, but perhaps that's just age talking. I thought of telling him that I didn't have a client but why should he believe me? He didn't know me. If there was nothing in it for him, why should he bother?

So I said, "You know, we're just a couple of weeks away from Memorial Day."

"Yeah, I'll buy a poppy from a Legionnaire. So what else is new?"

"Memorial Day's when women start wearing white shoes and men put straw hats on their heads. You got a new hat for the summer season, Andersen? Because you could use one."

"A man can always use a new hat," he said.

A hat is cop talk for twenty-five dollars. By the time I left the precinct house Andersen had two tens and a five of Mary Alice Redfield's bequest to me and I had all the data that had turned up to date.

I think Andersen won that one. I now know that the murder weapon had been a kitchen knife with a blade approximately seven and a half inches long. That one of the stab wounds had found the heart and had probably caused death instantaneously. That it was impossible to determine whether strangulation had taken place before or after death. That *should* have been possible to determine—maybe the medical examiner hadn't wasted too much time checking her out, or maybe he had been reluctant to commit himself. She'd been dead a few hours when they found her—the estimate was that she'd died around midnight and the body wasn't reported until half-past five. That wouldn't have ripened her all that much, not in winter weather, but most likely her personal hygiene was nothing to boast about, and she was just a shopping bag lady and you couldn't bring her back to life, so why knock yourself out running tests on her malodorous corpse?

I learned a few other things. The landlady's name. The name of the off-duty bartender, heading home after a nightcap at the neighborhood after-hours joint, who'd happened on the body and who had been drunk enough or sober enough to take the trouble to report it. And I learned the sort of negative facts that turn up in a police report when the case is headed for an open file—the handful of nonleads that led nowhere, the witnesses who had nothing to contribute, the routine matters routinely handled. They hadn't knocked themselves out, Andersen and his partner, but would I have handled it any differently? Why knock yourself out chasing a murderer you didn't stand much chance of catching?

In the theater, SRO is good news. It means a sellout performance, standing room only. But once you get out of the theater district it means single room occupancy, and the designation is invariably applied to a hotel or apartment house which has seen better days.

Mary Alice Redfield's home for the last six or seven years of her life had started out as an old Rent Law tenement, built around the turn of the century, six stories tall, faced in red-brown brick, with four apartments to the floor. Now all of those little apartments had been carved into single rooms as if they were election districts gerrymandered by a maniac. There was a communal bathroom on each floor and you didn't need a map to find it.

The manager was a Mrs. Larkin. Her blue eyes had lost most of their color and half her hair had gone from black to gray but she was still pert. If she's reincarnated as a bird she'll be a house wren.

She said, "Oh, poor Mary. We're none of us safe, are we, with the streets full of monsters? I was born in this neighborhood and I'll die in it, but please God that'll be of natural causes. Poor Mary. There's some said she should have been locked up, but she got along. She lived her life. And she had her check coming in every month and paid her rent on time. She had her own money, you know. She wasn't living off the public like some I could name but won't."

"I know."

"Do you want to see her room? I rented it twice since then. The first one was a young man and he didn't stay. He looked all right but when he left me I was just as glad. He said he was a sailor off a ship and when he left he said he'd got on with another ship and was on his way to Hong Kong or some such place, but I've had no end of sailors and he didn't walk like a sailor, so I don't know what he was after doing. Then I could have rented it twelve times but didn't because I won't rent to colored or Spanish. I've nothing against them but I won't have them in the house. The owner says to me, Mrs. Larkin he says, my instructions are to rent to anybody regardless of race or creed or color, but if you was to use your own judgment I wouldn't have to know about it. In other words he don't want them either but he's after covering himself."

"I suppose he has to."

"Oh, with all the laws, but I've had no trouble." She laid a forefinger alongside her nose. It's a gesture you don't see too much these days. "Then I rented poor Mary's room two weeks ago to a very nice woman, a widow. She likes her beer, she does, but why shouldn't she have it? I keep my eye on her and she's making no trouble, and if she wants an old jar now and then whose business is it but her own?" She fixed her blue-gray eyes on me. "You like your drink," she said.

"Is it on my breath?"

"No, but I can see it in your face. Larkin liked his drink and there's some say it killed him but he liked it and a man has a right to live what life he wants. And he was never a hard man when he drank, never cursed or fought or beat a woman as some I could name but won't. Mrs. Shepard's out now. That's the one took poor Mary's room. And I'll show it to you if you want."

So I saw the room. It was kept neat.

"She keeps the room tidier than poor Mary," Mrs. Larkin said. "Now Mary wasn't dirty, you understand, but she had all her belongings. Her shopping bags and other things that she kept in her room. She made a mare's nest of the place, and all the years she lived here, you see, it wasn't tidy. I would keep her bed made but she didn't want me touching her things and so I let it be cluttered as she wanted it. She paid her rent on time and made no trouble otherwise. She had money, you know."

"Yes, I know."

"She left some to a woman on the fourth floor. A much younger woman, she'd only moved here three months before Mary was killed, and if she exchanged a word with Mary I couldn't swear to it, but Mary left her almost a thousand dollars. Now Mrs. Klein across the hall lived here since before Mary ever moved in and the two old things always had a good word for each other, and all Mrs. Klein has is the welfare and she could have made good use of a couple of dollars, but Mary left her money instead to Miss Strom." She raised her eyebrows to show bewilderment. "Now Mrs. Klein said nothing, and I don't even know if she's had the thought that Mary might have mentioned her in her will, but Miss Strom said she didn't know what to make of it. She just couldn't understand it at all, and what I told her was you can't figure out a woman like poor Mary who never had both her feet on the pavement. Troubled as she was, daft as she was, who's to say what she might have had on her mind?"

"Could I see Miss Strom?"

"That would be for her to say, but she's not home from work yet. She works part-time in the afternoons. She's a close one, not that she hasn't the right to be, and she's never said what it is that she does. But I'm sure she's a decent sort. This is a decent house."

"I'm sure it is."

"It's single rooms and they don't cost much so you know you're not at the Ritz Hotel, but there's decent people here and I keep it as clean as a person can. When there's not but one toilet on the floor it's a struggle. But it's decent."

"Yes."

"Poor Mary. Why'd anyone kill her? Was it sex, do you know?" Not that you could imagine anyone wanting her, the old thing, but try to figure out a madman and you'll go mad your own self. Was she molested?"

"No."

"Just killed, then. Oh, God save us all. I gave her a home for almost seven years. Which it was no more than my job to do, not making it out to be charity on my part. But I had her here all that time and of course I never knew her, you couldn't get to know a poor old soul like that, but I got used to her. Do you know what I mean?"

"I think so."

"I got used to having her about. I might say Hello and Good morning and Isn't it a nice day and not get a look in reply, but even on those days she was someone familiar to say something to. And she's gone now and we're all of us older, aren't we?"

"We are."

"The poor old thing. How could anyone do it, will you tell me that? How could anyone murder her?"

I don't think she expected an answer. Just as well. I didn't have one.

After dinner I returned for a few minutes of conversation with Genevieve Strom. She had no idea why Miss Redfield had left her the money. She'd received $880 and she was glad to get it because she could use it, but the whole thing puzzled her. "I hardly knew her," she said more than once. "I keep thinking I ought to do something special with the money, but what?"

I made the bars that night but drinking didn't have the urgency it had possessed the night before. I was able to keep it in proportion and to know that I'd wake up the next morning with my memory intact. In the course of things I dropped over to the newsstand a little past midnight and talked with Eddie Halloran. He was looking good and I said as much. I remembered him when he'd gone to work for Sid three years ago. He'd been drawn then, and shaky, and his eyes always moved off to the side of whatever he was looking at. Now there was confidence in his stance and he looked years younger. It hadn't all come back to him and maybe some of it was lost forever. I guess the booze had him pretty good before he kicked it once and for all.

We talked about the bag lady. He said, "Know what I think it is? Somebody's sweeping the streets."

"I don't follow you."

"A clean-up campaign. Few years back, Matt, there was this gang of kids found a new way to amuse theirselves. Pick up a can of gasoline, find some bum down on the Bowery, pour the gas on him and throw a lit match at him. You remember?"

"Yeah, I remember."

"Those kids thought they were patriots. Thought they deserved a medal. They were cleaning up the neighborhood, getting drunken bums off the street. You know, Matt, people don't like to look at a derelict. That building up the block, the Towers? There's this grating there where the heating system's vented. You remember how the guys would sleep there in the winter. It was warm, it was comfortable, it was free, and two or three guys would be there every night catching some z's and getting warm. Remember?"

"Uh-huh. Then they fenced it."

"Right. Because the tenants complained. It didn't hurt them any, it was just the local bums sleeping it off, but the tenants pay a lot of rent and they don't like to look at bums on their way in or out of their building. The bums were outside and not bothering anybody but it was the sight of them, you know, so the owners went to the expense of putting up cyclone fencing around where they used to sleep. It looks ugly as hell and all it does is keep the bums out but that's all it's supposed to do."

"That's human beings for you."

He nodded, then turned aside to sell somebody a *Daily News* and a *Racing Form*. Then he said, "I don't know what it is exactly. I was a bum, Matt. I got pretty far down. You probably don't know how far. I got as far as the Bowery. I panhandled, I slept in my clothes on a bench or in a doorway. You look at men like that and you think they're just waiting to die, and they are, but some of them come back. And you can't tell for sure who's gonna come back and who's not. Somebody coulda poured gas on me, set me on fire."

"The shopping bag lady—"

"You'll look at a bum and you'll say to yourself, 'Maybe I could get like that and I don't wanta think about it.' Or you'll look at somebody like the shopping bag lady and say, 'I could go nutsy like her so get her out of my sight.' And you get people who think like Nazis. You know, take all the cripples and the lunatics and the retarded kids and all and give 'em an injection and Good-bye, Charlie."

"You think that's what happened to her?"

"What else?"

"But whoever did it stopped at one, Eddie."

He frowned. "Don't make any sense," he said. "Unless he did the one job and the next day he got run down by a Ninth Avenue bus, and it couldn't happen to a nicer guy. Or he got scared. All that blood and it was more than he figured on. Or he left town. Could be anything like that."

"Could be."

"There's no other reason, is there? She musta been killed because she was a bag lady, right?"

"I don't know."

"Well, what other reason would anybody have for killing her?"

The law firm where Aaron Creighton worked had offices on the seventh floor of the Flatiron Building. In addition to the four partners, eleven other lawyers had their names painted on the frosted glass door. Aaron Creighton's came second from the bottom. Well, he was young.

He was also surprised to see me, and when I told him what I wanted he said it was irregular.

"Matter of public record, isn't it?"

"Well yes," he said. "That means you can find the information. It doesn't mean we're obliged to furnish it to you."

For an instant I thought I was back at the Eighteenth Precinct and a cop was trying to hustle me for the price of a new hat. But Creighton's reservations were ethical. I wanted a list of Mary Alice Redfield's beneficiaries, including the amounts they'd received and the dates they'd been added to her will. He wasn't sure where his duty lay.

"I'd like to be really helpful," he said. "Perhaps you could tell me just what your interest is."

"I'm not sure."

"I beg your pardon?"

"I don't know why I'm playing with this one. I used to be a cop, Mr. Creighton. Now I'm a sort of unofficial detective. I don't carry a license but I do things for people and I wind up making enough that way to keep a roof overhead."

His eyes were wary. I guess he was trying to guess how I intended to earn myself a fee out of this.

"I got twelve hundred dollars out of the blue. It was left to me by a woman I didn't really know and who didn't really know me. I can't seem to slough off the feeling that I got the money for a reason. That I've been paid in advance."

"Paid for what?"

"To try and find out who killed her."

"Oh," he said. *"Oh."*

"I don't want to get the heirs together to challenge the will, if that was what was bothering you. And I can't quite make myself suspect that one of her beneficiaries killed her for the money she was leaving him. For one thing, she doesn't seem to have told people they were named in her will. She never said anything to me or to the two people I've spoken with thus far. For another, it wasn't the sort of murder that gets committed for gain. It was deliberately brutal."

"Then why do you want to know who the other beneficiaries are?"

"I don't know. Part of it's cop training. When you've got any specific leads, any hard facts, you run them down before you cast a wider net. That's only part of it. I suppose I want to get more of a sense of the woman. That's probably all I can realistically hope to get, anyway. I don't stand much chance of tracking her killer."

"The police don't seem to have gotten very far."

I nodded. "I don't think they tried too hard. And I don't think they knew she had an estate. I talked to one of the cops on the case and if he had known that he'd have mentioned it to me. There was nothing in her file. My guess is they waited for her killer to run a string of murders so they'd have something more concrete to work with. It's the kind of senseless crime that usually gets repeated." I closed my eyes for a moment, reaching for an errant thought. "But he didn't repeat it," I said. "So they put it on a back burner and then they took it off the stove altogether."

"I don't know much about police work. I'm involved largely with estates and trusts." He tried a smile. "Most of my clients die of natural causes. Murder's an exception."

"It generally is. I'll probably never find him. I certainly don't expect to find him. Just killing her and moving on, hell, and it was all those months ago. He could have been a sailor off a ship, got tanked up and went nuts and he's in Macao or Port-au-Prince by now. No witnesses and no clues and no suspects and the trail's three months cold by now, and it's a fair bet the killer doesn't remember what he did. So many murders take place in blackout, you know."

"Blackout?" He frowned. "You don't mean in the dark?"

"Alcoholic blackout. The prisons are full of men who got drunk and shot their wives or their best friends. Now they're serving twenty-to-life for something they don't remember. No recollection at all."

The idea unsettled him, and he looked especially young now.

"That's frightening," he said. "Really terrifying."

"Yes."

"I originally gave some thought to criminal law. My Uncle Jack talked me out of it. He said you either starve or you spend your time helping professional criminals beat the system. He said that was the only way you made good money out of a criminal practice and what you wound up doing was unpleasant and basically immoral. Of course there are a couple of superstar criminal lawyers, the hotshots everybody knows, but the other ninety-nine percent fit what Uncle Jack said."

"I would think so, yes."

"I guess I made the right decision." He took his glasses off, inspected them, decided they were clean, put them back on again. "Sometimes I'm not so sure," he said. "Sometimes I wonder. I'll get that list for you. I should probably check with someone to make sure it's all right but I'm not going to bother. You know lawyers. If you ask them whether it's all right to do something they'll automatically say no. Because inaction is always safer than action and they can't get in trouble for giving you bad advice if they tell you to sit on your hands and do nothing. I'm going overboard. Most of the time I like what I do and I'm proud of my profession. This'll take me a few minutes. Do you want some coffee in the meantime?"

His girl brought me a cup, black, no sugar. No bourbon, either. By the time I was done with the coffee he had the list ready.

"If there's anything else I can do—"

I told him I'd let him know. He walked out to the elevator with me, waited for the cage to come wheezing up, shook my hand. I watched him turn and head back to his office and I had the feeling he'd have preferred to come along with me. In a day or so he'd change his mind, but right now he didn't seem too crazy about his job.

The next week was a curious one. I worked my way through the list Aaron Creighton had given me, knowing what I was doing was essentially purposeless but compulsive about doing it all the same.

There were thirty-two names on the list. I checked off my own and Eddie Halloran and Genevieve Strom. I put additional check marks next to six people who lived outside of New York. Then I had a go at the remaining twenty-three names. Creighton had done most of the spadework for me, finding addresses to match most of the names. He'd included the date each of the thirty-two codicils had been drawn, and that enabled me to attack the list in reverse chronological order, starting with those persons who'd been made beneficiaries most recently. If this was a method, there was madness to it; it was based on the notion that a person added recently to the will would be more likely to commit homicide for gain, and I'd already decided this wasn't that kind of killing to begin with.

Well it gave me something to do. And it led to some interesting conversations. If the people Mary Alice Redfield had chosen to remember ran to any type, my mind wasn't subtle enough to discern it. They ranged in age, ethnic background, in gender and sexual orientation, in economic status. Most of them were as mystified as Eddie and Genevieve and I about the bag lady's largesse, but once in a while I'd encounter someone who attributed it to some act of kindness he'd performed, and there was a young man named Jerry Forgash who was in no doubt whatsoever. He was some form of Jesus freak and he'd given poor Mary a couple of tracts and a GET SMART—GET SAVED button, presumably a twin to the one he wore on the breast pocket of his chambray shirt. I suppose she put his gifts in one of her shopping bags.

"I told her Jesus loved her," he said, "and I suppose it won her soul for Christ. So of course she was grateful. Cast your bread upon the waters, Mr. Scudder. Brother Matthew. You know there was a disciple of Christ named Matthew."

"I know."

He told me Jesus loved me and that I should get smart and get saved. I managed not to get a button but I had to take a couple of tracts from him. I didn't have a shopping bag so I stuck them in my pocket, and a couple of nights later I read them before I went to bed. They didn't win my soul for Christ, but you never know.

I didn't run to the whole list. People were hard to find and I wasn't in any big rush to find them. It wasn't that kind of a case. It wasn't a case at all, really, merely an obsession, and there was surely no need to race the clock. Or the calendar. If anything, I was probably reluctant to finish up the names on the list. Once I ran out of them I'd have to find some other way to approach the woman's murder, and I was damned if I knew where to start.

While I was doing all this, an odd thing happened. The word got around that I was investigating the woman's death, and the whole neighborhood became very much aware of Mary Alice Redfield. People began to seek me out. Ostensibly they had information to give me or theories to advance, but neither the information nor the theories ever seemed to amount to anything substantial, and I came to see that they were merely there as a prelude to conversation. Someone would start off by saying he'd seen Mary selling the *Post* the afternoon before she was killed, and that would serve as the opening wedge of discussion of the bag woman, or bag women in general, or various qualities of the neighborhood, or violence in American life, or whatever.

A lot of people started off talking about the bag lady and wound up talking about themselves. I guess most conversations work out that way.

A nurse from Roosevelt said she never saw a shopping bag lady without hearing an inner voice say *There but for the grace of God.* And she was not the only woman who confessed she worried about ending up that way. I guess it's a specter that haunts women who live alone, just as a vision of the Bowery derelict clouds the peripheral vision of hard-drinking men.

Genevieve Strom turned up at Armstrong's one night. We talked briefly about the bag lady. Two nights later she came back again and we took turns spending our inheritances on rounds of drinks. The drinks hit her with some force and a little past midnight she decided it was time to go. I said I'd see her home. At the corner of Fifty-seventh Street she stopped in her tracks and said, "No men in the room. That's one of Mrs. Larkin's rules."

"Old-fashioned, isn't she?"

"She runs a daycent establishment." Her mock-Irish accent was heavier than the landlady's. Her eyes, hard to read in the lamplight, raised to meet mine. "Take me someplace."

I took her to my hotel, a less decent establishment than Mrs. Larkin's. We did each other little good but no harm, and it beat being alone.

Another night I ran into Barry Mosedale at Polly's Cage. He told me there was a singer at Kid Gloves who was doing a number about the bag lady. "I can find out how you can reach him," he offered.

"Is he there now?"

He nodded and checked his watch. "He goes on in fifteen minutes. But you don't want to go there, do you?"

"Why not?"

"Hardly your sort of crowd, Matt."

"Cops can go anywhere."

"Indeed they do, and they're welcome wherever they go, aren't they? Just let me drink this and I'll accompany you, if that's all right. You need someone to lend you immoral support."

Kid Gloves is a gay bar on Fifty-sixth west of Ninth. The décor is just a little aggressively gay lib. There's a small raised stage, a scattering of tables, a piano, a loud jukebox. Barry Mosedale and I stood at the bar. I'd been there before and knew better than to order their coffee. I had straight bourbon. Barry had his on ice with a splash of soda.

Halfway through the drink Gordon Lurie was introduced. He wore tight jeans and a flowered shirt, sat onstage on a folding chair, sang ballads he'd written himself with his own guitar for accompaniment. I don't know if he was any good or not. It sounded to me as though all the songs had the same melody, but that may just have been a similarity of style. I don't have much of an ear.

After a song about a summer romance in Amsterdam, Gordon Lurie announced that the next number was dedicated to the memory of Mary Alice Redfield. Then he sang:

"She's a shopping bag lady who lives on
the sidewalks of Broadway
Wearing all of her clothes and her years
on her back
Toting dead dreams in an old paper sack
Searching the trash cans for something she
lost here on Broadway—
Shopping bag lady . . .

"You'd never know but she once was an
actress on Broadway
Speaking the words that they stuffed in
her head
Reciting the lines of the life that she led
Thrilling her fans and her friends and her lovers on Broadway—
Shopping bag lady . . .

"There are demons who lurk in the corners
of minds and of Broadway
And after the omens and portents and
signs

> Came the day she forgot to remember her
> lines
> Put her life on a leash and took it out
> walking on Broadway—
> Shopping bag lady . . ."

There were a couple more verses and the shopping bag lady in the song wound up murdered in a doorway, dying in defense of the "tattered old treasures she mined in the trash cans of Broadway." The song went over well and got a bigger hand than any of the other ones that had preceded it.

I asked Barry who Gordon Lurie was.

"You know very nearly as much as I," he said. "He started here Tuesday. I find him whelming, personally. Neither overwhelming nor underwhelming but somewhere in the middle."

"Mary Alice never spent much time on Broadway. I never saw her more than a block from Ninth Avenue."

"Poetic license, I'm sure. The song would lack a certain something if you substituted Ninth Avenue for Broadway. As it stands it sounds a little like 'Rhinestone Cowboy.' "

"Lurie live around here?"

"I don't know where he lives. I have the feeling he's a Canadian. So many people are nowadays. It used to be that no one was Canadian and now simply everybody is. I'm sure it must be a virus."

We listened to the rest of Gordon Lurie's act. Then Barry leaned forward and chatted with the bartender to find out how I could get backstage. I found my way to what passed for a dressing room at Kid Gloves. It must have been a ladies' lavatory in a prior incarnation.

I went in there thinking I'd made a breakthrough, that Lurie had killed her and now he was dealing with his guilt by singing about her. I don't think I really believed this but it supplied me with direction and momentum.

I told him my name and that I was interested in his act. He wanted to know if I was from a record company. "Am I on the threshold of a great opportunity? Am I about to become an overnight success after years of travail?"

We got out of the tiny room and left the club through a side door. Three doors down the block we sat in a cramped booth at a coffee shop. He ordered a Greek salad and we both had coffee.

I told him I was interested in his song about the bag lady.

He brightened. "Oh, do you like it? Personally I think it's the best thing I've written. I just wrote it a couple of days ago. I opened next door Tuesday night. I got to New York three weeks ago and I had a two-week booking in the West Village. A place called David's Table. Do you know it?"

"I don't think so."

"I was there two weeks, and then I opened at Kid Gloves, and afterward I was sitting and drinking with some people and somebody was talking about the shopping bag lady and I had had enough Amaretto to be maudlin on the subject. I woke up Wednesday morning with a splitting headache and the first verse of the song buzzing in my splitting head, and I sat up immediately and wrote it down, and as I was writing one verse the next would come bubbling to the surface, and before I knew it I had all six verses." He took a cigarette, then paused in the act of lighting it to fix his eyes on me. "You told me your name," he said, "but I don't remember it."

"Matthew Scudder."

"Yes. You're the person investigating her murder."

"I'm not sure that's the right word. I've been talking to people, seeing what I can come up with. Did you know her before she was killed?"

He shook his head. "I was never even in this neighborhood before. *Oh*. I'm not a suspect, am I? Because I haven't been in New York since the fall. I haven't bothered to figure out where I was when she was killed but I was in California at Christmastime and I'd gotten as far east as Chicago in early March, so I do have a fairly solid alibi."

"I never really suspected you. I think I just wanted to hear your song." I sipped some coffee. "Where did you get the facts of her life? Was she an actress?"

"I don't think so. Was she? It wasn't really *about* her, you know. It was inspired by her story but I didn't know her and I never knew anything about her. The past few days I've been paying a lot of attention to bag ladies, though. And other street people."

"I know what you mean."

"Are there more of them in New York or is it just that they're so much more visible here? In California everybody drives, you don't see people on the street. I'm from Canada, rural Ontario, and the first city I ever spent much time in was Toronto, and there are crazy people on the streets there but it's nothing like New York. Does the city drive them crazy or does it just tend to draw crazy people?"

"I don't know."

"Maybe they're not crazy. Maybe they just hear a different drummer. I wonder who killed her."

"We'll probably never know."

"What I really wonder is why she was killed. In my song I made up some reason. That somebody wanted what was in her bags. I think it works as a song that way but I don't think there's much chance that it happened like that. Why would anyone kill the poor thing?"

"I don't know."

"They say she left people money. People she hardly knew. Is that the truth?" I nodded. "And she left me a song. I don't even feel that I wrote it. I woke up with it. I never set eyes on her and she touched my life. That's strange, isn't it?"

Everything was strange. The strangest part of all was the way it ended.

It was a Monday night. The Mets were at Shea and I'd taken my sons to the game. The Dodgers were in for a three-game series which they eventually swept as they'd been sweeping everything lately. The boys and I got to watch them knock Jon Matlock out of the box and go on to shell his several replacements. The final count was something like 13-4. We stayed in our seats until the last out. Then I saw them home and caught a train back to the city.

So it was past midnight when I reached Armstrong's. Trina brought me a large double and a mug of coffee without being asked. I knocked back half of the bourbon and was dumping the rest into my coffee when she told me somebody'd been looking for me earlier. "He was in three times in the past two hours," she said. "A wiry guy, high forehead, bushy eyebrows, sort of a bulldog jaw. I guess the word for it is underslung."

"Perfectly good word."

"I said you'd probably get here sooner or later."

"I always do. Sooner or later."

"Uh-huh. You okay, Matt?"

"The Mets lost a close one."

"I heard it was thirteen to four."

"That's close for them these days. Did he say what it was about?"

He hadn't, but within the half hour he came in again and I was there to be found. I recognized him from Trina's description as soon as he came in through the door. He looked faintly familiar but he was nobody I knew. I suppose I'd seen him around the neighborhood.

Evidently he knew me by sight because he found his way to my table without asking directions and took a chair without being invited to sit. He didn't say anything for a while and neither did I. I had a fresh bourbon and coffee in front of me and I took a sip and looked him over.

He was under thirty. His cheeks were hollow and the flesh of his face was stretched over his skull like leather that had shrunk upon drying. He wore a forest green work shirt and a pair of khaki pants. He needed a shave.

Finally he pointed at my cup and asked me what I was drinking. When I told him he said all he drank was beer.

"They have beer here," I said.

"Maybe I'll have what you're drinking." He turned in his chair and waved for Trina. When she came over he said he'd have bourbon and coffee, the same as I was having. He didn't say anything more until she brought the drink. Then, after he had spent quite some time stirring it, he took a sip. "Well," he said, "that's not so bad. That's okay."

"Glad you like it."

"I don't know if I'd order it again, but at least now I know what it's like."

"That's something."

"I seen you around. Matt Scudder. Used to be a cop, private eye, now, blah blah blah. Right?"

"Close enough."

"My name's Floyd. I never liked it but I'm stuck with it, right? I could change it but who'm I kidding? Right?"

"If you say so."

"If I don't somebody else will. Floyd Karp, that's the full name. I didn't tell you my last name, did I? That's it, Floyd Karp."

"Okay."

"Okay, okay, okay." He pursed his lips, blew out air in a silent whistle. "What do we do now, Matt? Huh? That's what I want to know."

"I'm not sure what you mean, Floyd?"

"Oh, you know what I'm getting at, driving at, getting at. You know, don't you?"

By this time I suppose I did.

"I killed that old lady. Took her life, stabbed her with my knife." He flashed the saddest smile. "Steee-rangled her with her skeeee-arf. Hoist her with her own whatchacallit, petard. What's a petard, Matt?"

"I don't know, Floyd. Why'd you kill her?"

He looked at me, he looked at his coffee, he looked at me again. He said, "Had to."

"Why?"

"Same as the bourbon and coffee. Had to see. Had to taste and find out what it was like." His eyes met mine. His eyes were very large, hollow, empty. I fancied I could see right through them to the blackness at the back of his skull. "I couldn't get my mind away from murder," he said. His voice was more sober now, the mocking playful quality had gone from it. "I tried. I just couldn't do it. It was on my mind all the time and I was afraid of what I might do. I couldn't function, I couldn't think, I just saw blood and death all the time. I was afraid to close my eyes for fear of what I might see. I would just stay up, days it seemed, and then I'd be tired enough to pass out the minute I closed my eyes. I stopped eating. I used to be fairly heavy and the weight just fell off me."

"When did all this happen, Floyd?"

"I don't know. All winter. And I thought if I went and did it once I would know if I was a man or a monster or what. And I got this knife, and I went out a couple nights but lost my nerve, and then one night—I don't want to talk about that part of it now."

"All right."

"I almost couldn't do it, but I couldn't *not* do it, and then I was doing it and it went on forever. It was . . ."

"Why didn't you stop?"

"I don't know. I think I was afraid to stop. That doesn't make any sense, does it? I just don't know. It was all crazy, insane, like being in a movie and being in the audience at the same time. Watching myself."

"No one saw you do it?"

"No. I threw the knife down a sewer. I went home. I put all my clothes in the incinerator, the ones I was wearing. I kept throwing up. All that night I would throw up even when my stomach was empty. Dry heaves, Department of Dry Heaves. And then I guess I fell asleep, I don't know when or how but I did, and the next day I woke up and thought I dreamed it. But of course I didn't."

"No."

"And what I did think was that it was over. I did it and I knew I'd never want to do it again. It was something crazy that happened and I could forget it. And I thought that was what happened."

"That you managed to forget about it?"

A nod. "But I guess I didn't. And now everybody's talking about her. Mary Alice Redfield, I killed her without knowing her name. Nobody knew her name and now everybody knows it and it's all back in my mind. And I heard you were looking for me, and I guess, I guess . . ." He frowned, chasing a thought around in his mind like a dog trying to capture his tail. Then he gave it up and looked at me. "So here I am," he said. "So here I am."

"Yes."

"Now what happens?"

"I think you'd better tell the police about it, Floyd."

"Why?"

"I suppose for the same reason you told me."

He thought about it. After a long time he nodded. "All right," he said. "I can accept that. I'd never kill anybody again. I know that. But—you're right. I have to tell them. I don't know who to see or what to say or, hell, I just—"

"I'll go with you if you want."

"Yeah. I want you to."

"I'll have a drink and then we'll go. You want another?"

"No. I'm not much of a drinker."

I had it without the coffee this time. After Trina brought it I asked him how he'd picked his victim. Why the bag lady?

He started to cry. No sobs, just tears spilling from his deep-set eyes. After a while he wiped them on his sleeve.

"Because she didn't count," he said. "That's what I thought. She was nobody. Who cared if she died? Who'd miss her?" He closed his eyes tight. "Everybody misses her," he said. "Everybody."

So I took him in. I don't know what they'll do with him. It's not my problem.

It wasn't really a case and I didn't really solve it. As far as I can see I didn't do anything. It was the talk that drove Floyd Karp from cover, and no doubt I helped some of the talk get started, but some of it would have gotten around without me. All those legacies of Mary Alice Redfield's had made her a nine-day wonder in the neighborhood. It was one of those legacies that got me involved.

Maybe she caught her own killer. Maybe he caught himself, as everyone does. Maybe no man's an island and maybe everybody is.

All I know is I lit a candle for the woman, and I suspect I'm not the only one who did.

Midnight at the Lost and Found

Mark Timlin

Mark Timlin used to work in the music business as a roadie for T.Rex and The Who before turning to crime writing. Timlin, a South Londoner born and bred, cites Raymond Chandler and Elmore Leonard as among the greatest American crime writers to influence his work. Private eye Nick Sharman, perhaps his best-known character, first appeared in the novel *A Good Year for the Roses*, published in 1988. Sharman, an ex-copper with a love for vintage R&B, soul and jazz, inhabits the underbelly of London's crime community, and Mark Timlin is highly successful in evoking the rich street life of South London; his own "patch." Nick Sharman was played in the 1995 five-part television series by Academy Award nominee Clive Owen. The program was shot on location in many of the areas featured in the books.

It all started at a party at Vincent Garibaldi's restaurant near Loughborough Junction. Vinnie's it's called. It's situated about halfway between the railway station and the turning that runs up to the hospital. It was always full of young nurses, which is one of the reasons I started going there. I was in the job then, and Vinnie spotted me right away. He liked having coppers as customers. They drank a lot, and kept the place tidy, so he started giving me free meals. He still does, even though I'm long off the force and run a one-man private investigation firm in Tulse Hill. But I don't take the piss. In fact, before the party I hadn't set foot in the place for six months.

The thrash was all in aid of Vincent's one and only offspring, Vincent Garibaldi Junior, more usually known, at least at home, as Little Vinnie, on the occasion of his engagement to be married to one Claire McCammon. A model, as Big Vinnie told me on the phone when he invited me.

Now I've known Little Vinnie since he'd needed stabilizers on his bike, so naturally I put in an appearance, and even stumped up for a Chinese vase that caught my eye in Harrods one Saturday afternoon, and had it gift wrapped with a big red ribbon on top. Don't ever say I haven't got class.

And besides I was looking forward to seeing Vinnie again. He's a good man. Kind. A friend. And he knew that I'd do anything for him, any time. No questions asked.

I walked into Vinnie's dead on eight. There was a notice in the window declaring the place closed for the night for a private function.

The walls of the restaurant were white with dark beams set in them every six feet or so, and dotted with framed watercolors of Italian scenery. The tablecloths were red and white checked, and most of the tables had been pushed up against one wall and were covered with platters of food. Elvis was on the stereo system and the place smelt wonderful. I felt like I'd come home after a long and difficult journey.

Inside it was already pretty crowded. An eclectic bunch. Guys in smart suits, from where little Vinnie worked, I surmised. Some beautiful young women, who the guys in suits were ogling. Model friends of Claire's, I imagined. In fact one of them would probably be Claire herself. Then there were some of Vinnie's old gang. The Italians he'd grown up with in the East End, friends and family both. And finally, a few honored customers, like myself, who Vinnie had adopted over the years.

Big Vinnie, Little Vinnie, and the Garibaldi matriarch, Maria—Vinnie's missus and Little Vinnie's momma, as she never stopped reminding the world—were sitting in one of the booths holding court. I'd been right about Claire being one of the beautiful young women, as Big Vinnie called her over on my arrival.

She was beautiful, although maybe a little older than the teenage super models who were always popping up on TV these days. Her hair was long and dark. Her heart-shaped face was perfectly made up, her teeth gleamed like she had a personal dentist and, in the little black dress she wore, she was drop-dead gorgeous. I envied little Vinnie.

Big Vinnie introduced me to her. He described me in such glowing terms and was so profuse in his compliments that I almost blushed. Claire offered me her hand and I shook it. Hers was cool and smooth. Mine, I'm sure, wasn't. I gave her the present, and she put it with some others and thanked me. Little Vinnie nodded. He'd always been cool, had Little Vinnie.

Vincent got up to fetch me a drink. We walked over to the bar together, and he reached for the Jack Daniel's bottle, and I said, "You went a bit over the top there, Vinnie. I thought for a minute you were going to get out my baby pictures."

He swung round toward me so fast that the bourbon he'd poured slopped all over his hand. He was as white as a sheet and I said, "What's the matter? Are you all right?"

"Nick," he said. "I've got to talk to you."

"Talk away."

"Not here. In private."

He poured me another drink and one for himself and, taking the bottle, he took me through the kitchen, up the back stairs to the tiny room he called his office, where we'd shared more than one bottle in the past.

He sat behind his desk, and I took the comfortable old chair next to it.

"What's the matter?" I said.

"I just don't know how to tell you."

"Just tell me," I said. "Fast or slow, long or short. We've got all night. I'm going nowhere till we get this sorted."

"It's Claire. You've seen her. A lovely girl. A model like I told you. She's like a daughter to me and Maria already. The daughter we never had." He hesitated for a long moment. "There are some photographs of her."

I was going to say that if she was a model it was a racing certainty, but it didn't seem to be the time for jokes by the look on Vinnie's boat race.

Vinnie squeezed the glass he was holding until I was afraid it would implode from the force. "Such photos. It was when you mentioned 'holiday snaps.' "

"Go on," I said. I was none the wiser.

"I got them through the post. Filth. If Maria was to see them . . ." He hesitated again. "He wanted money."

"He?" I asked.

"Whoever sent the letter."

It was like pulling teeth but, when I spoke, I spoke gently. "What letter?" I said.

"The letter that came with the photographs."

"Blackmail?" I asked.

He looked into my eyes. "You know?"

"It's pretty obvious. Now tell me exactly what happened from the beginning."

He sighed, drank a mouthful of JD and asked for one of my cigarettes. I'd never seen Vinnie smoke before.

"Little Vinnie and Claire have been together for over a year," he explained. "A month ago he asked her to marry him. She accepted. It was the happiest day of Maria's and my life. Our only son. Our only child. They are to be married next year. I already have your invitation to the reception. It will be here in the restaurant. Just like the party tonight."

"Thanks Vinnie," I said.

"It should be a time of rejoicing. Instead . . ."

"Instead?"

"A week after the engagement was announced I received two photographs and a letter."

"Where?"

He looked puzzled. "What?" he said.

"Here or at home?" I said.

"Here at the restaurant. If Maria was to see them . . ." It was the second time he'd said that, and I knew what he meant. I'd seen her moods before.

"What did the letter say?"

"Here," he said. "I kept it." He took a piece of paper from his inside pocket. He held it as if it were contagious. "You and I are the only ones to have seen it."

"Nobody's going to hear about it from me."

"I knew I could trust you." He handed the paper to me. It was typed by an electric typewriter or a word processor on a sheet of A4 bond. It read:

> Mr Garibaldi
> I am enclosing a few snaps of your daughter-in-law to be.
> Nice aren't they?
> These pictures and negatives are a wedding gift to you.

> But there are others. The rest will cost you £10,000.
> I will ring you at your restaurant next Monday at noon.
> If you don't want them, I know plenty who will.

It was unsigned. Naturally.

"And he rang?" I asked.

"Yes. He wanted the money in used twenties and tenners, to be wrapped in newspaper, put in a plastic bag and left in the unlocked boot of my car in the National Theatre car park on the following Thursday at eight p.m. I was to leave the car for at least an hour. He said I'd be watched. If I didn't do exactly as I was told the photos would be sent to Little Vinnie's boss and Maria."

"Did you recognize the voice?"

He shook his head.

"Is Little Vinnie still working at the same place?"

Little Vinnie worked for a city bank. He was a high flyer. Destined for orbit before he was thirty. I knew that Vinnie had always dreamed that one day his son and heir would take over the business. But things had changed. The old Italian creed of the son following in his father's footsteps had been washed away. It was tough. But that was the way it went in the new Britain.

"Yes," said Vincent. "Photos like that would make him a laughingstock. Ruin his career."

"What? In the city? They do it with donkeys up there, don't they?"

"Have you ever seen the place he works in?" he asked. "They'd do the accounts with quill pens if they could still get them. It's the only merchant bank in the square mile with a notice outside that says, 'We don't do it with donkeys in this establishment.' "

I was glad he hadn't lost all of his sense of humor.

"Take my word for it, Nick. It would screw up his career and wreck his marriage before it even took place. Maria would make sure of that."

"So you did as you were told?"

"I didn't know what else to do."

"Police?"

"Are you joking?"

"Why didn't you call me straight away?"

He shrugged. "I thought I could take care of it myself."

"Did you receive the photos as promised?"

"Yes. Another dozen."

"And the negs?"

He nodded again.

"Did you keep them?"

He looked across the room. "In the safe. No one ever goes in there but me."

"And now?"

"Another letter."

"That makes sense. Where is it?"

"In the safe also."

"Let's take a look."

"At the photographs too?"

"I'm afraid so. I won't be able to do much unless I do."

He shook his head sadly, then took a bunch of keys out of his jacket pocket and opened the door of the ancient safe that stood in one corner under the barred window. He took out two large brown envelopes, and a smaller white one, and handed them to me. The first brown envelope was typed by what looked like the same machine as the letter I'd read. It was a piece of cheap stationery sold at thousands of outlets in the UK. It had been postmarked three weeks earlier in London W1. The second one was exactly the same. Same typeface, same postmark, a week or so later. The white envelope was similarly typed, similarly postmarked, two days ago. I opened the brown envelopes first. Inside were fourteen, glossy, professional looking 10 by 8 color prints, and a stack of negatives in little transparent envelopes of their own. They were all of Claire and a dark-haired man with hair long enough to hide his features. Her face was clear enough. She looked a couple of years younger than the woman I'd met downstairs, but not more innocent. Each of the prints was of explicit sex acts. What those two weren't doing to each other wasn't worth doing. I lined the photographs up on Vinnie's desk, much to his distress. "Sorry, Vinnie," I said. "I'm not enjoying this."

And I wasn't. My old friend's eyes were full of tears, and he was wringing his hands together as if he were going to pull them off at the wrists.

"Have you got a magnifying glass?" I asked.

"Nick," he said, and his voice broke with emotion.

"I want to see if the place these were taken can be identified. If you want to go back downstairs, I'll talk to you later."

"No," he said. "I'll stay."

He found me a magnifying glass in a drawer, and I pulled over the lamp that stood on the corner of the desk and switched it on. I studied the pictures closely. They'd all been taken in the same place. A white painted room with a double bed covered in a white sheet. On the wall behind the bed was a framed poster of a holiday advertisement for Athens. On the table by the bed was a digital clock radio. Using the glass, I could see the display clearly. The photos had been taken between 22.10 and 00.20. I couldn't be sure, but it looked as if they'd all been taken on the same day. Or night. There was an empty glass on the table in the earliest photo, and it was still there in the last. The man was unidentifiable. No tattoos or scars on his body. When his hair hadn't hidden his face for the camera, he'd kept it out of shot. Like I said, Claire hadn't been so coy. She looked like she was half-stoned when the photos had been taken. In one, her face was looking directly at the camera lens. Her mouth was open in an 'O' of what could have been pleasure or pain, and her eyes were as vacant as a closed hotel.

When I'd finished studying the photographs, I gathered them together and put them back in the envelopes. Then I took another piece of A4 bond from the white envelope and unfolded it. It was typed on the same machine again, and read:

> Mr Garibaldi
> Thanks for the cash last time.
> Sorry, but expenses are mounting. I need another £10,000.
> I'll phone you next Thursday at noon.
> You know what will happen if you don't help me out.

Once again there was no signature.

"Tomorrow's Thursday," I said. Sometimes the obvious needs stating, just to try and keep hold of normality.

Vinnie nodded again.

"These are pretty explicit," I said, tapping the envelopes. "How do you think little Vinnie would take it?"

He shrugged.

"And how about you?"

"We all make mistakes," he said. "She's a wonderful girl. A diamond. She makes Vinnie happy. That's all I care about. I don't want him to know anything about this unless he positively has to."

"You're a good man, Vinnie." I said. "But we've got to put a stop to this. You did right telling me."

"What can you do?"

"Lots. But first I need another drink."

Vinnie poured me out another large one and I lit a cigarette. "Well," I said. "Some things are obvious."

He looked surprised. "What?"

"Don't get excited, Vinnie," I said. "Nothing that's going to solve the problem in a flash. Just some elementary facts."

"Like?"

"Like the blackmailer knows that Little Vinnie and Claire have got engaged. He knows about the restaurant. He knows you and your motor. He knows that Little Vinnie has the kind of job that a scandal could ruin. And most of all he knows that you'll pay. And if you pay once, it's a reasonable assumption that you'll keep on paying until you're white. That's why he kept some photographs back."

"And how does knowing all that help?"

"I don't know yet. But I know one other thing."

"What?"

"I'll have to speak to Claire about it."

"No."

"I mean it, Vinnie," I said.

"Why?"

"A load of reasons. She's the only one we know who can identify the geezer in the pictures, and who took them. There was either another person there, or the camera was on a timer."

"Couldn't we just fix up another drop and you pinch whoever comes to collect the money?"

"Sure we could. Nothing simpler. But what happens if it's just a mug punter the blackmailer's paid to do the gig? A nobody. The blackmailer sees what's occurred, and the photos are all over London in a few hours."

He sighed again. "Sure, Nick," he said. "You know best."

"It's the only way, Vinnie. It doesn't give me a good feeling. But at least she should be aware of the mess she's got you in."

"But not Little Vinnie. He mustn't know."

"I promise you, Vin. He won't know from me. If Claire gives me a blank, we'll do it your way. But if she's the kind of woman you say she is, she'll understand. And if she isn't. Well, it's better to know now, rather than later."

"What do you mean?"

"I mean she might be in on the plot."

"God no. Not that on top of everything else."

"I'm not saying that she is, Vinnie. But it's best to know, isn't it?"

"I suppose you're right."

"I know I am. Have you got her number?"

He fetched a little notebook out of one of his pockets, took a restaurant card from another, and copied an address and telephone number onto the back and slid it across the desk to me. "I'll phone her in the morning," I said. "And I'll need those photos and letters."

"What?"

"You heard, Vinnie."

"Why?"

"Lots of reasons. Shock value for one. If she knows we've seen them, and you've paid, she'll be much more likely to talk. I want to see her reaction. If she's as horrified about what's happening as I hope she'll be, fine. I won't need to show them to her. I hope I don't. Otherwise I will, just to jog her memory. Either way, she has to know they exist. She was there for God's sake, even if she did look like she'd been dabbling with some serious medication. I want to know who took them, and who's had access to them since."

"I don't know. What will she think?"

I was going to say that she might think about leaving the lens cap on next time, but I wasn't looking for a slap from one of Vinnie's big hands.

"Quite frankly, Vinnie, I don't give a damn what she thinks," I said. "It's you I'm worried about. And one thing's for sure."

"What?"

"If whoever wrote the letters kept some photos back the first time he put the black on you, he'll do it again this time. He'll keep taking your money till you're skint and sold the house and hocked the restaurant. He'll see you in the poorhouse, and Maria too. This is the kind of person you're dealing with. So if Claire gets her nose put out of joint by what I'm going to say to her—tough." I was angrier than I thought I was, so I didn't say more.

"OK, Nick," Vince said eventually. "But don't be too hard on her."

I continued saying nothing.

"And what shall I do?" he asked after a moment.

"When the blackmailer calls?"

"Yes."

"Go along with whatever he says. He thinks he's got you where he wants you. Let him go on thinking that."

He nodded yet again.

"And can I take the photos?"

Another nod, and he said, "I'm trusting you, Nick."

"I appreciate that, Vinnie," I said. "I won't let you down."

"Do I owe you anything?" he asked.

"For what?"

"For helping me."

"Vinnie. You ever ask me a question like that again and we're not friends. Understand?"

He stuck his hand out, and I shook it. "You sort this out for me," he said. "And you need never buy food again."

"Cheers, Vinnie," I said, and we went back to the party. But it didn't seem much fun after what I'd heard, and I left pretty soon, without saying good-bye to anyone.

I called the number Vinnie had given me for Claire the next morning at ten. She was in. "Claire McCammon," she said when she picked up the phone.

"Hello," I said. "It's Nick Sharman here. I met you last night at the party."

"I remember. Thank you for the vase. It's lovely."

"Good."

She paused for a moment. "So what can I do for you?" she asked.

"I'd like to talk to you."

"Why?"

"Not on the phone."

"It sounds serious."

"It is."

"Is it to do with Vinnie's father?"

"Yes."

"Is he ill?"

"No."

"Does he know you're phoning?"

"Yes. Look, can I come and see you?"

There was another pause. "I suppose so. But I wish you'd tell me why."

"I will when I see you."

"When?"

"Today. Now."

A third, shorter pause. "All right. I'll be home all day. Do you know the address?"

"Yes," Vinnie gave it to me. And Miss McCammon . . ."

"Yes."

"Please don't tell your fiancé about this. Just wait until I've spoken to you."

"It does sound serious. And mysterious."

"I'm sure it will be all right. I'll be over soon. I'll tell you then."

When I put the phone down I wondered if she thought I was going to ask her for a date.

She lived in Fulham. I drove over and took the envelopes with me. I hoped I wouldn't have to use them. Her address was in a thirties block. I went up to her floor in an old-fashioned lift that was as slow as it was noisy. She answered my ring immediately, and led me into a warm, airy room with a view of the Fulham Road. The windows were double glazed, and it was very quiet in the flat. She was wearing an old sweatshirt with *Primal Scream* printed on the front in faded letters, and blue jeans. Her feet were bare. She offered me coffee and I accepted. She told me I could smoke. It was all very civilized. But I was about to drop a bomb that might blow her civilized little life into pieces. When she came back with the coffee I was standing by the window watching the people going about their business in the street below. "Do sit down," she said.

I sat on a pink sofa and watched her pour out the coffee. When we'd got a cup each and she was seated in the armchair opposite me, I told her what I'd come to tell her. As I talked, her face paled to a dirty gray color, and her hands shook so much she had to put her coffee cup on the small table next to her, and when she tried to light a cigarette she dropped it twice. I didn't pull any punches. I wanted to know if it was her and an accomplice who had written the letters and made the telephone demands of Vinnie. When I'd finished she said, "My God, I'd almost forgotten about them."

"Whoever is blackmailing Vinnie hasn't."

"Have you seen them?" she asked.

"Yes."

"My God," she said again, got up, dropped her cigarette into her coffee cup where it died with a hiss, and ran for the door. I could hear the sound of retching, then silence. If she was putting on an act, she should give up modeling and take up a career on the stage. She came back about five minutes later. She'd regained some of her color and was carrying a white towel which she used to dab at her lips. The front of her sweatshirt was spotted with water stains. She sat down, lit another cigarette and pulled a face at the taste. "Poor Vincent," she said.

"That's exactly my sentiment."

"I'm not blackmailing him."

"I believe you."

"How can I help?"

"Tell me about them."

"What?"

"You know," I said.

She took a deep breath. "I hardly know you," she said.

"Perhaps I'm the best person to tell then."

It was that simple. "All right," she said.

I took out a notebook.

"You're not going to write anything down."

"No one will see what I've written. That's a promise. But I need to take notes. Now we can do this my way, or I can leave now and let Vincent Garibaldi pay ten, twenty, thirty, forty thousand quid to some scumbag. Until he has to sell the restaurant and his house, and he and Maria are living in twin cardboard boxes on the Embankment begging twenty pence pieces from strangers. Do you want that?"

She shook her head.

"Right. So tell me."

And she did. "It was six years ago. I'd not been in London all that long. I was just a baby. I met a photographer. His name was Damien. Damien Simmons. He's quite well-known, or he was. It's the old story." Her mouth twisted bitterly. "Young, naïve girl. Experienced man in the business. He swept me off my feet. Told me he'd make me a star. I went and lived with him. He was a bastard." She started to cry gently. I gave her a handkerchief. I always carry one when I'm going to screw someone's life up. "He was on drugs. Everything. Booze, dope, coke. Smack sometimes. Pills all the time."

"How old was he?" I asked.

"When I met him? Thirty-five or so. He'd been around."

"And?"

"And he did what he promised. Broke me into the big time. But there was a price to pay. I became his property. He made me take drugs too." She looked at me. "Oh, I know. It's no excuse. I was stupid. But I was so young. He ruled my life. There was money coming in. Big money. We had everything. A beautiful house with a studio. Cars. Clothes. But it couldn't last."

"How long *did* it last?"

"A year. Eighteen months. But I knew that if I didn't get away I'd be an old woman by the time I was twenty-five. Washed up. Literally."

"So?"

"So I left. Packed a few things and ran home as fast as my BMW would take me. And it was mine. Bought out of my own money."

I didn't argue. It was her story.

"My family comes from Manchester," she continued. "I cleaned up my act and got taken on the books of a Manchester agency. Not as glamorous as London maybe, but not far off. It was all happening up there then. Remember? The Happy Mondays. Factory Records. The Hacienda."

It had hardly been my scene, but I knew, so I nodded.

"All gone now, of course. Like everything goes. Anyway, after a couple of years I heard that Damien had got married and moved to New York. So I came back and did even better down here. Then I met Little Vinnie and the rest you know."

"Is he still in the States?"

She shook her head. "No. He came back a couple of years ago."

"Have you seen him?"

The little color she'd regained in her face disappeared again. "God, no. I make sure I don't."

"Is he still married?"

"Oh yes. Damien knows which side of his bread is buttered."

"How do you mean?"

"He married a lady." She saw my look. "A real Lady. With a capital L. Daughter of a Lord. Very rich. And I mean very. But the old man hates Damien."

"How do you know all this if you haven't seen him?"

"Gossip. Modeling is that kind of business."

"So being married to money, he wouldn't need any extra."

"Knowing Damien, he always needs extra money."

"Do you know where he lives?"

"Several places. A house in the country, a flat in town and a studio. And of course the cottage in Provence. And when I say cottage I mean twelve bedrooms."

I was beginning to like Claire. "Have you got any?" I asked.

"Any what?"

"Any of the photographs."

She wouldn't meet my eye.

"Claire. I need to know. I need to know how many were taken."

"He took thousands of photographs of me. Mostly glamor shots. Nothing bad."

"The ones I saw weren't like that."

She blushed. "I know. I remember that session. It was just before I ran away from him. It was the last straw really. He'd been on at me for ages to do some X-rated shots." She paused. "That night I gave in. I didn't know what I was doing. I was on dope, wine and quaaludes."

"That'll get you every time. Who's in the photos with you?"

"Damien."

"And who took them?"

"He did. On a timed exposure. I couldn't do what I did in front of anyone else, no matter what I'd had."

"I see. So only you and he knew about them."

"As far as I know. Are they something you'd boast about?"

"I wouldn't," I said. "But maybe he would. Do you think he's capable of blackmail?"

"He's capable of anything," she said with such certainty that I believed her.

"Do you know how many photos were taken that night?"

"I don't exactly. It was a long time ago, and I was out of it. Three rolls, I think."

"How many on a roll?"

"Twenty-four or thirty-six."

"And Vincent has only fourteen. This could go on for years. How many do you have?"

"I don't know."

"Are they here?"

"Yes."

"Can I see them?"

"Why?"

"Not for kicks, Claire," I said. "Because I need to."

She sighed heavily. "I'll get them," she said.

Once again she got up and left the room.

She came back carrying a plain white envelope, cardboard backed, A4 size, with PHOTOGRAPHS—PLEASE DO NOT BEND printed in one corner. I opened it. Inside were a sheaf of glossies, twenty in all. Plus a bunch of negatives. They were a mixture as before, except that in two the man had not hidden his face. In one in particular his features came across clear and sharp. He was handsome in a rattish kind of way, and he didn't look a tenth as stoned as Claire. "Thanks," I said.

She shrugged.

"I'll need to take these with me."

"Why?"

"I have my reasons. Trust me. No one, and I mean no one will get a glimpse of them."

She hesitated. "I do trust you, Mr. Sharman. Vinnie's father has a real love for you. But you have my life there. My life with Little Vinnie. Don't let me down."

"I won't," I said.

What I *didn't* say was that if I screwed up she probably wouldn't have a life with Little Vinnie. But I think she knew. That was why she let me have them.

I told her not to worry. I don't think it did much good. I also told her that as soon as I had any news I'd call. Finally I told her not to say a word to Little Vinnie, and act as much like normal as she could. She said that she would, and I left.

I got back to my place around one and called Vincent Garibaldi Senior on the phone. When he answered, I asked, "Has he called?"

"Yes."

"And?"

"The deal as before. Ten thousand in tens and twenties in my car at the National Theatre car park, Saturday night, seven o'clock."

"Good."

"Shall I get the money?"

"No. I've had an idea about that. Let me sort it out."

"Ten grand. Where are you going to get that sort of money in a hurry?"

"Let me worry about that."
"Suit yourself. Have you seen Claire?"
"Yes."
"Is she all right?"
"As well as can be expected."
"Could she help?" he asked.
"Yes."
"Good."
"Are you in the restaurant later?" I asked him.
"All day."
"I'll pass by about six."
"I'll see you later then," he said, and rang off.

Next I looked up Damien Simmons in the phone book. As Claire had said, there were two addresses and numbers for him in London. One appeared to be his home, and the other his studio. I copied them both down in my notebook.

After all that I left the flat, got in the motor and headed for Tooting. I parked on a meter outside a vast gin palace of a boozer on the main street. I pushed open the doors and walked in to where another frenetic lunchtime drinking session was just winding down. The bar was smoky, and the tables were covered with empty glasses and full ashtrays. The big screen TV was tuned into SkySport, and the jukebox was pounding out Whitney Houston. The fruit machines were doing great business, and the two pool tables were in use. At the bar, a line of serious drinkers were gazing at their reflections in the mirror behind the optics. The clientele was a rich mixture of the underclass taking their leisure, and spending the D. S. S.'s money, and anything they could cop on the black economy. They ranged in age from fifteen to seventy-five. The men seemed to be either toothless and bald, or shell-suited and gymnasium obsessed. The women were mostly blond, mostly showing too much chest and thigh, and most of them seemed to have O. D.'d on the sun bed, except for a few ratty old crones who sat together with their milk stouts dissecting the morals of everyone else in the place. I strolled up to the bar, and the barman, a thug in black trousers and waistcoat over a white shirt open almost to the waist, put his cigarette down in an ashtray and walked over.

"What?" he said.
"Is Swanson in?"
"Mr. Swanson to you."
"Is *Mr.* Swanson in?" I asked.
"Dunno. Might be."
"Well, his Roller's outside on a double yellow with a traffic warden making sure nobody nicks the hubcaps. So is he in or not?"
"I'll have to check. Wanna drink?"
"No thanks. I've seen the state of your glasses before."
The ice cream frowned then picked up the phone and tapped out a number.

When it was answered, he said, "That geezer Sharman's here."

Mr. Sharman to you I thought, but said nothing. Discretion being the better part, and all that.

"OK, Guv," said the barman and put down the dog. "Go on up," he said. "You know the way."

I did, and I did as he said. I went upstairs and tapped on the last door in the corridor. "Come in," said a deep cockney voice, and I did that too.

Terry Swanson's office was big and plush, befitting his status in the local underworld. It held a huge desk, two upright chairs, a sofa, a cocktail bar and a huge filing cabinet. It also held Terry Swanson, sitting behind the desk on a leather swivel chair. He was about fifty-five, huge, and ugly. He was wearing an immaculate double-breasted suit over a white shirt with a Kray Brothers tie. The suit was too tight, and well out of fashion, only no one dared tell him. In one hand he held a cigar nearly as long as Nelson's column, and in the other a glass of Scotch. The bottle was on the table in front of him.

"Hello, Nick, m'boy," he said when I walked in. "How are ya?"

"Fine, Mr. Swanson. Never better." Note I called him "Mister" to his face.

"So what can I do for you this afternoon? Have a drink, son. Sit down."

I got a glass from the bar and helped myself to a small one from the bottle.

"So?" said Swanson when I was settled.

"Funny money," I said.

He sat up in his seat. "Do what?"

"Funny money," I repeated. "Counterfeit."

"What about it?"

"I need some."

"And you think I know about that sort of thing?"

"Good chance."

"What makes you say that?"

I was on tricky ground. "Word about."

"About where?"

"The manor."

"Interesting."

"I thought so."

"And why would you want snide dough, Nick? You looking for a career change so late in life?"

"I need some flash, Mr. Swanson," I said. "It's a little situation I've got involved in where I don't want to use real money."

He seemed affronted. "Not real," he said. "What I've got is as good as real. Better. Silver strips and aged by experts. Just ask the mug punters who run offies round here, and the Paki shopkeepers who take it every day. This once great country of ours is run on snide money, Nick. How do you think the government's keeping inflation down? They don't print anymore themselves these days. They leave it to people like me."

"I bet you're sorry Maggie's gone, aren't you?" I said.

"Those were the days, Nick," he said nostalgically. "Free enterprise. That's how I made my dough."

"Literally," I remarked.

He smiled. "That's right. I like that. I'll have to tell my old woman that one."

"So you got some?" I said.

"You could say that. You could say I was holding certain assets. Yes."

"Ten grand's worth?"

Swanson sat back and waved his cigar in the air as if ten thousand pounds was nothing much. It probably wasn't to him. "That how much you want?"

I nodded.

"No problem. Now normally I sell it off at three to one. But as it's you, and it's getting late on a Thursday, I'll give you a special discount. You want ten grand. Give me two and it's yours."

"Well, actually, Mr. Swanson," I said. "I don't want to buy it."

"What *do* you want then? Do you want me to pay you to take it off my hands?" And he smiled evilly.

"I thought I might borrow it for a while," I ventured. "Just till Sunday. Early Sunday. Saturday night really."

He laughed a gravelly laugh. "Borrow? No such thing, son." He thought for a moment. "But you're not a bad lad. You've kept a low 'un for me a couple of times, so I might find my way clear to hire it to you for a couple of days."

"Like Avis?"

"No son, Hertz. Number one. See, I've got overheads. Clerical staff to pay. If I just lent it to you, who'd count it when it came back? Anyway, I'd be setting a precedent. A dangerous precedent." You could see Mr. Swanson watched the Open University. "Before you know it, every little slag round here would be asking for sale or return on the gear. Nothing personal, but you do understand, don't you?"

I nodded. "How much?" I asked.

"Give me a monkey and the snide's yours till Sunday. But if I don't get it back by closing time, then you'd better be here opening time Monday with the other fifteen hundred, or I'll have to send someone out to find you, and we wouldn't want that, would we?"

I shook my head. No, we definitely didn't want that. I'd seen Swanson's collectors before. *Jurassic Park* wasn't in it. I took out the sum of my worldly goods and counted out five hundred in twenties, and put them on the desk.

"You don't mind if I check this, do you?" he asked. "There's some very dodgy stuff around at the moment."

I shook my head.

"Help yourself," said Swanson. "Top drawer of the cabinet. There's tens, twenties and fifties in thousand lumps."

"I'll take half and half, tens and twenties. No one takes fifties in this town anymore."

Swanson smiled. "Criminal, innit?" he said as he examined my notes.

I went to the filing cabinet and pulled open the top drawer. Inside were bundles of cash in plastic bags. I took out five packets of tens and five packets of twenties and put them on the desk.

"Not much security here," I said. "Don't you believe in safes?"

"Who'd rob me?" said Swanson. "The last bloke who knocked me for a pint downstairs ended up on Tooting Common with his hand nailed to a tree."

I watched as he checked the snide I'd taken. "Good job he didn't drink double Scotches, wasn't it?"

"For *him*. No, son. No one robs me round here. My justice is swift and hard. You'd do well to remember that."

"I will. Got a bag for this lot?"

"What d'you think this is? Sainsbury's? Bung it in your sky."

I put the bundles of notes into my jacket pockets. "Thanks, Mr. Swanson," I said. "See you Saturday."

"Thank you, Nick. A pleasure doing business with you. Come in the afternoon. Bring your bird, or some of the family. There's a right nice atmosphere down here on Sunday afternoons. Complimentary roast potatoes and all."

"I heard there was nude mud-wrestling in the snug, and Pit Bull fights in the beer garden." I was feeling bolder now I'd got the cash.

"Always the sense of humor. Now bugger off, and be careful with that dough, or you owe me."

I nodded, and buggered off like he said, went home and had a beer.

Around six I drove back to Vinnie's. He fed me up with spaghetti and meatballs, and then came and sat at my table. It was still early and the place was practically empty. I'd got the counterfeit cash with me in a carrier bag.

I told Vinnie what had gone on at Claire McCammon's place, and when I'd finished he asked, "Do you think she was in on the plot?"

"No," I said. "I wouldn't stake my life on it, but I'm pretty sure."

"Thank God for that at least. What now?"

"Now you do exactly what the blackmailer says. You put the cash in the car and the car in the car park. On the top floor. I'll be watching. If Simmons picks up the dough, I'll follow him. I've got a couple of addresses. I've got a pretty good idea where he'll end up. If it's not him, I'll nab whoever it is, there and then, and scare the truth out of him. This is the money you use." I tapped the carrier. "Don't get it mixed up with yours, or try and spend it. It ain't exactly kosher."

"Where did it come from?"

"Contacts. Don't worry about it."

"If you say so. Aren't you going to see Simmons before Saturday?"

"No. I don't want to frighten him off. I need hard evidence that he's the blackmailer. I want to catch him with the readies. And I want all the photos and negs. If I go and see him now, and he is at it, he won't turn up on Saturday. And you and Claire'll know that the pictures still exist. I don't want him to know that anyone else is involved. Stay cool, Vinnie. It's got to be him."

"How will you know him?"

"I've got a couple of photos." Then I wished I hadn't said it.

"What kind of photos?"

"You know."

His face crumpled.

"Sorry mate," I said. "Claire salvaged some when she left him."

He shook his head. "I wish I'd just paid up and never got you into this."

"You'd've never stopped paying."

"I know, but . . ."

I was getting a bit pissed off after all I'd done. "Listen," I said. "Are you sure you want to go through with this? I can go now if you want, and leave you to deal with it on your own."

He looked up with misery written all over his face. "Sorry Nick. I'm behaving like an ungrateful bastard after you've gone to so much trouble to help. Yes. We go through with it."

"Good. Now I'm off. I'll check with you on Saturday that there's been no change of plan. You won't see me on the night. So don't go looking. We don't want to spook our friend, do we?"

He shook his head.

I spent Friday and Saturday morning on other business. I called Vinnie at three on Saturday afternoon. He'd heard nothing. I told him to keep calm, and I'd talk to him after it was all over.

I drove up to Waterloo about six. I'd borrowed a Cortina estate off a friend of mine in the motor trade, because my Jaguar was too noticeable to be any good in a tailing situation. The evening was dull, with a light rain that didn't seem to want to settle, but rather hung like a fine mist over London. I dressed in a woollen shirt, jeans and D. M.'s, with my old Burberry on top. I put all the photographs and negatives into one of the brown envelopes which I slipped into the pocket of my coat. I parked in the N. T. garage, in a space on the ground floor, near the exit to the stairs. Then I took the lift to the top floor and found a niche next to a concrete pillar with a good panoramic view. The only problem was that I might get nicked for loitering with intent. At seven precisely I saw Vinnie's green Mercedes drive up the ramp and park. He got out of the car and walked to the lift without a backward glance. A fair amount of other cars arrived during the next ten minutes, but no one showed any interest in the Merc. At 7.10 precisely, a blue BMW-7 Series came up the ramp and drove slowly round the parking area. The car drew up behind Vinnie's, and a tall, dark-haired man got out. He was an older version of the man in the photos in my pocket. He opened the boot of the Merc, took out a green carrier bag, threw it in the back of the BMW, slammed the boot of the Mercedes, got back into his car and drove off slowly. I legged it for the stairs, and ran down them as fast as I could, and straight to the Cortina. There was a queue at the exit, and the BMW was two cars in front of me when I joined it. I was lucky. But I find you make your own luck in this game.

I saw the BMW turn right outside the car park and fidgeted whilst the driver of the car in front of me paid up. I tossed the geezer in the box a fiver, didn't wait for change, and the tires of the Ford screeched as I took off in the same direction as the Beemer. I had a pretty good idea which direction he'd take. Both the addresses for Simmons had been in Bayswater, and I caught him at the roundabout on the south side of Westminster Bridge. He was in no rush. He'd had a result. It was the second time, so why should he worry? He'd got away with it once and thought he was golden. I kept the BMW in sight as he weaved through the traffic on Parliament Square and headed for the park. I dropped back and let him show off a bit in Park Lane, but it wasn't difficult keeping his car in sight, even through the rain and the gathering darkness. For my part, I did what I could to avoid him spotting me. I kept as many cars as I could between the Cortina and the BMW, and I kept switching from sidelights to dipped headlights to main beam, but I didn't think he had a clue that I was there. He went straight to the studio address. I'd guessed that he would. Saturday night there'd be no one there, and I imagined he'd kept schtum about his little scheme to the wife. He parked his car outside and took the money in with him.

I gave him a couple of minutes inside, then walked over and rang the doorbell. He answered it.

"Mr. Simmons?" I asked.

"Yes."

"My name's Nick Sharman. I'm a private detective. I wonder if I might have a few minutes of your time?"

"Why?"

"It's a private matter."

"Obviously. You being a private detective and all."

What a wit. I knew we weren't going to get on right away. "It concerns Miss Claire McCammon," I said.

"Claire. How is she?" he asked coolly.

"Not bad. I wonder if we could talk inside. It's rather damp out here."

"Talk about what?"

"I think you know."

"No," he said.

"Then we'll talk here. It's about some photographs."

"Photographs?" As if he'd never heard the word.

"Photographs of you and Claire. Do you really want the neighbors to hear about this?"

He looked up and down the street. "You'd better come in," he said. "Go upstairs."

I did as he said, and climbed a narrow flight into a room furnished in Laura Ashley and dark wood. There was a desk with a phone on top, a couple of armchairs. Several framed prints of good-looking women were on the walls. None of them was Claire.

"So what about these photographs?" said Simmons.

"Don't tell me you don't know," I replied, and held up the envelope I'd taken from my pocket. The photographs in here. Photos of you and Claire McCammon in what used to be called compromising positions. Photos that are being used to blackmail her fiancé's father."

"Her fiancé's father," said Simmons. "So that's it. I heard she'd got engaged."

"Don't fool around, Damien," I said. "If you weren't in on this you'd've never let me through the door."

"All right," he said resignedly. "I suppose you're here for the money?"

"That's right," I said.

"You didn't say you'd come and collect it. I thought you'd phone like last time."

"What are you talking about?" I said.

"The money of course. The future father-in-law's and mine."

"Yours?"

"Ten thousand pounds in exchange for the photos. The same as I paid last time. But I warn you. I'm not going to cough up again. This is it. The finish. If you hold any back this time, you can send them to my wife, or her father or whoever. I just don't have any more money. It's all my wife's."

"You say *you're* being blackmailed too."

"Of course I am. You know damn well. By you."

I shook my head slowly.

"Not by you?" he said.

"No."

"Then what the hell are you doing here?"

"Because you collected the cash that Vincent Garibaldi was paying for the photos of Claire McCammon and you, that he left in the boot of his car in Waterloo tonight."

"That's what I was told to do."

"By?"

"By a voice on the telephone. A Londoner's voice. Like yours. You . . . I mean he sent me a letter, some sample photographs and then called. Once, a few weeks ago, and then again the other day."

"Are you winding me up?"

"Like you said before. If I was, I wouldn't've let you in."

"Yeah, I suppose."

"So what photos have *you* got?" he asked.

"The ones that were sent to Vincent Garibaldi after he paid up last time. And some that Claire took when she left you."

"May I see them?"

I handed him the envelope, and he opened it, took out the glossies and gave them a squint. Then he held the negs up to the light and said, "Some of these are the same as the ones I was sold. They must've been internegged."

"Come again?"

"Copied. The bastard sold me copies. Or maybe these are the copies. I just don't know."

"And you never sussed?"

"I took them ten years ago. And I didn't study them too closely when they were sent to me. I just looked at them quickly, and burnt them right away."

"You're a bit of a mug then, aren't you?"

"There could be dozens of copies in existence."

The phone rang all of a sudden, and Simmons jumped. He picked up the receiver, listened for a moment, then said, "You . . . Hello. Hello. Oh crap. He's hung up."

"Who?"

"The blackmailer."

"What did he say?"

"He told me to leave both lots of money in the same place as last time."

"Which was?"

"The Euston NCP at midnight. In a briefcase in the unlocked boot of my car. Park it there, and vanish for half an hour."

"Show me the money," I said. I still wasn't sure I believed him.

Simmons went to one of the framed prints on the wall. It was mounted on hinges, and he pulled it open to show the front of the safe. He worked the combination, opened it, and took out a leather briefcase and the bag containing the snide dough. He put them on the table and opened the case to show me ten banded stacks of notes. Each one had £1,000 printed on it in red.

"What shall I do?" he asked.

"Exactly as you were told."

"But there might be dozens of copies. This could go on forever, and I don't have any more money."

"Tough."

"This is insane."

"Tell you what," I said. "Why don't you hire me to get your money back? I'm not exactly earning out this job at the moment."

He seemed relieved and said, "Will you? How much will it cost me?"

"Twenty percent. Two grand."

"That's a lot."

"Take it or leave it," I said. "But that seems to be the going rate these days."

He pulled a face. "All right."

I reached into the case, took out eight thousand of Simmons's money and gave it to him. I put the other two into my coat pocket, transferred the bent cash from the plastic bag to the case and slammed it shut. "There you go," I said. "Simple. I'll try and get your other ten grand back too. For the same deal. But I can't promise."

"You're not even going to give it to him?"

"No."

"But . . ."

"No buts. I did what I said I'd do. I got you your money back, less commish. Now all you've got to do is to drive your car to Euston at midnight, leave it for a bit, then collect it again and go home to the missus. Or whatever you normally do on a Saturday night. So just shut up. I'm beginning to get tired of you."

"You're as bad as the blackmailer."

"No, I'm not. Think about it. This way it costs you just two thousand, and I take all the stress." I looked at my watch. "We've got some time to kill, I suppose a drink's out of the question?"

As it happens it wasn't, and he broke open a very acceptable brandy and we sat around his place having a few.

At about eleven thirty we got under way. He took the case and slung it in the boot of the BMW and drove off in the direction of Euston. I followed a few minutes later. When I got to the station I stuck my motor into the NCP and went looking for him. It was parked up empty on the second level, and I found a spot where I could watch it without being seen.

At twelve ten when I'd been waiting for about fifteen minutes, a figure appeared at the door marked EXIT and walked over to the car.

It was Little Vinnie. Just what I'd been dreading. Bastard. I watched him open the boot, take out the case, close the boot again, put the case on the roof of the car, and open it. I walked over toward him, silent in my Doc Martens, and said, "Hello, Vinnie."

He jumped at the sound of my voice, looked round and slammed the briefcase shut.

"Mr. Sharman," he said. "God, but you gave me a fright. What are you doing here?"

"You know me. I get around. Firm's car?"

"Yeah."

"You must be doing well."

"Can't complain."

"Working late?"

"Yeah. I've got to get this stuff sent up north, Red Star." He was quick, I'll give him that.

"I didn't know they were open this late."

"I dunno. I came on the off chance on the way home from the office."

"You *are* working later. And on a Saturday too. Come on. I'll walk you. We can get a cup of tea."

"That's all right."

"No, come on. The pubs are shut, and I'm not doing anything. I'll carry it for you."

"You don't have to bother."

"Yes, I do." I took the case from his hand, and we walked back through the car park exit and up in the lift to the concourse level. The station itself was quiet at that hour, with only a few punters wandering around looking lost, and a geezer mopping the floor and nattering to two coppers. We walked past them to the cafeteria. Vinnie got two cups of tea and we went and sat down. I put the briefcase on the floor next to the seat.

I lit a cigarette and said conversationally, "Is she in it with you?"

"Do what?"

"Don't muck about, son. The blackmail, does Claire know about it?"

"I don't know what you're talking about."

"Bollocks. The money's in the bleedin' briefcase. *Red Star*, my ass. How could you do that to your dad?"

He could see there was no point in arguing. "I had to have the money," he said.

"Is it dope? Or have you been cooking the books at work?"

"Both. I'm in a mess, Mr. Sharman. Even this lot won't bail me out for long."

"You're joking."

"Peanuts."

"Not for your old man. It's his life. Why didn't you just ask for it?"

"And let him know that his precious son who he dotes on can't keep it together? No chance."

"So you put him through all this."

"I had no choice."

"You git. So is the blushing bride in on it too?"

He shook his head. "No. She doesn't know a thing about it. She's mad about the old man. Loves him."

"Good job one of you does. So how did you get the evidence?"

"I found it, would you believe? One day when I was in her flat on my own. I was just looking through her stuff."

"You're a real charmer, aren't you?"

"What does it matter? Anyway, I found the snaps and had the negs copied. Dirty cow. I knew all about this Simmons character from what she'd told me. And that he's married to the daughter of a belted earl or something."

"And you thought it would be nice to put the black on him, and include your dad as well?"

"I had to. I keep telling you I need the cash. Anyway it'll all be mine one day, when Mum and Dad drop off the perch."

"I can't believe you."

"Listen, Mr. Sharman. No one has to know about this, do they? I can cut you in for a few bob—"

"Shut up," I interrupted. "Shut up now, or by God I'll shut you up, you little bastard."

Then, all of a sudden Little Vinnie grabbed the case from off the floor and ran out of the door of the café onto the concourse. I jumped up and ran after him and shouted, "Vinnie, it's not . . ." Then I saw the two Old Bills again, still chatting to the cleaner, and so did Little Vinnie, who tried to slow to a walk, but lost his balance on the wet tile flooring and fell on his back. The briefcase went up in the air, crashed down and burst open, spilling out bundles of money and some loose note, right at the coppers' feet. One of the constables went to help Vinnie up, whilst the other rescued the cash. He held one of the twenties up to the light and frowned, which was my cue to walk off in the opposite direction.

Poetic justice.

On the upside, Little Vinnie was nicked. Obviously Swanson's notes weren't as good as he'd promised. On the downside, the counterfeit money was gone, but at least I had Simmons's two grand to pay for it. And on one side, or another, I figured I'd better find something else to do on the day that Little Vinnie and Claire were due to get married.

The Disappearance of Mrs. Leigh Gordon

Agatha Christie

Tommy and Tuppence Beresford, the crime-solving couple first created in the 1920s by Agatha Christie, set the standard for mixing marriage and mystery and provided a prototype for the many male/female detective teams that have followed. An eccentric upper-class couple, Tommy and Tuppence take over a floundering detective agency and delight in solving any case that comes their way. First featured in Christie's second novel, *The Secret Adversary,* and the short-story collection *Partners in Crime* (both published in 1922), the Beresfords' chemistry was beautifully evoked in the 1980s TV series starring Francesca Annis and James Warwick. Christie authored only three more Beresford mysteries: *N or M?,* a Second World War spy thriller; *By the Pricking of My Thumbs,* published in 1968; and the last book written by Christie, *Postern of Fate,* Tommy and Tuppence's final adventure, which was issued in 1973.

"What on earth are you doing?" demanded Tuppence as she entered the inner sanctum of the International Detective Agency (Slogan—Blunt's Brilliant Detectives) and discovered her lord and master prone on the floor in a sea of books.

Tommy struggled to his feet.

"I was trying to arrange these books on the top shelf of that cupboard," he complained. "And the damned chair gave way."

"What are they, anyway?" asked Tuppence, picking up a volume. "*The Hound of the Baskervilles.* I wouldn't mind reading that again some time."

"You see the idea?" said Tommy, dusting himself with care. "Half hours with the Great Masters—that sort of thing. You see, Tuppence, I can't help feeling that we are more or less amateurs at this business—of course amateurs in one sense we cannot help being, but it would do no harm to acquire the technique, so to speak. These books are detective stories by the leading masters of the art. I intend to try different styles, and compare results."

"Hm," said Tuppence. "I often wonder how those detectives would have got on in real life." She picked up another volume. "You'll find a difficulty in being a Thorndyke. You've no medical experience, and less legal, and I never heard that science was your strong point."

"Perhaps not," said Tommy. "But at any rate I've bought a very good camera, and I shall photograph footprints and enlarge the negatives and all that sort of thing. Now, *mon amie*, use your little gray cells—what does this convey to you?"

He pointed to the bottom shelf of the cupboard. On it lay a somewhat futuristic dressing gown, a turkish slipper, and a violin.

"Obvious, my dear Watson," said Tuppence.

"Exactly," said Tommy. "The Sherlock Holmes touch."

He took up the violin and drew the bow idly across the strings, causing Tuppence to give a wail of agony.

At that moment the buzzer rang on the desk, a sign that a client had arrived in the outer office and was being held in parley by Albert, the office boy.

Tommy hastily replaced the violin in the cupboard and kicked the books behind the desk.

"Not that there's any great hurry," he remarked. "Albert will be handing them out the stuff about my being engaged with Scotland Yard on the phone. Get into your office and start typing, Tuppence. It makes the office sound busy and active. No, on second thoughts, you shall be taking notes in shorthand from my dictation. Let's have a look before we get Albert to send the victim in."

They approached the peephole which had been artistically contrived so as to command a view of the outer office.

"I'll wait," the visitor was saying. "I haven't got a card with me, but my name is Gabriel Stavansson."

The client was a magnificent specimen of manhood, standing over six feet high. His face was bronzed and weather-beaten, and the extraordinary blue of his eyes made an almost startling contrast to the brown skin.

Tommy swiftly changed his mind. He put on his hat, picked up some gloves, and opened the door. He paused on the threshold.

"This gentleman is waiting to see you, Mr. Blunt," said Albert. A quick frown passed over Tommy's face. He took out his watch.

"I am due at the Duke's at a quarter to eleven," he said. Then he looked keenly at the visitor. "I can give you a few minutes if you will come this way."

The latter followed him obediently into the inner office where Tuppence was sitting demurely with pad and pencil.

"My confidential secretary, Miss Robinson," said Tommy. "Now, sir, perhaps you will state your business? Beyond the fact that it is urgent, that you came here in a taxi, and that you have lately been in the Arctic—or possibly the Antarctic, I know nothing."

The visitor stared at him in amazement.

"But this is marvelous," he cried. "I thought detectives only did such things in books! Your office boy did not even give you my name!"

Tommy sighed deprecatingly.

"Tut, tut, all that was very easy," he said. "The rays of the midnight sun within the

Arctic circle have a peculiar action upon the skin—the actinic rays have certain properties. I am writing a little monograph on the subject shortly. But all this is wide of the point. What is it that has brought you to me in such distress of mind?"

"To begin with, Mr. Blunt, my name is Gabriel Stavansson—"

"Ah! of course," said Tommy. "The well-known explorer. You have recently returned from the region of the North Pole, I believe?"

"I landed in England three days ago. A friend who was cruising in Northern waters brought me back on his yacht. Otherwise I should not have got back for another fortnight. Now I must tell you, Mr. Blunt, that before I started on this last expedition two years ago, I had the great good fortune of becoming engaged to Mrs. Maurice Leigh Gordon—"

Tommy interrupted.

"Mrs. Leigh Gordon was, before her marriage—"

"The Honorable Hermione Crane, second daughter of Lord Lanchester," reeled off Tuppence glibly.

Tommy threw her a glance of admiration.

"Her first husband was killed in the War," added Tuppence.

Gabriel Stavansson nodded.

"That is quite correct. As I was saying, Hermione and I became engaged. I offered, of course, to give up this expedition, but she wouldn't hear of such a thing—bless her! She's the right kind of woman for an explorer's wife. Well, my first thought on landing was to see Hermione. I sent a telegram from Southampton, and rushed up to town by the first train. I knew that she was living for the time being with an aunt of hers, Lady Susan Clonray, in Pont Street, and I went straight there. To my great disappointment, I found that Hermy was away visiting some friends in Northumberland. Lady Susan was quite nice about it, after getting over her first surprise at seeing me. As I told you, I wasn't expected for another fortnight. She said Hermy would be returning in a few days' time. Then I asked for her address, but the old woman hummed and hawed—said Hermy was staying at one or two different places, and that she wasn't quite sure what order she was taking them in. I may as well tell you, Mr. Blunt, that Lady Susan and I have never got on very well. She's one of those fat women with double chins. I loathe fat women—always have—fat women and fat dogs are an abomination unto the Lord—and unfortunately they so often go together! It's an idiosyncrasy of mine, I know—but there it is—I never can get on with a fat woman."

"Fashion agrees with you, Mr. Stavansson," said Tommy drily. "And everyone has their own pet aversion—that of the late Lord Roberts was cats."

"Mind you, I'm not saying that Lady Susan isn't a perfectly charming woman—she may be, but I've never taken to her. I've always felt, deep down, that she disapproved of our engagement, and I feel sure that she would influence Hermy against me if that were possible. I'm telling you this for what it's worth. Count it out as prejudice, if you like. Well, to go on with my story, I'm the kind of obstinate brute who likes his own way. I didn't leave Pont Street until I'd got out of her the names and addresses of the people Hermy was likely to be staying with. Then I took the mail train North."

"You are, I perceive, a man of action, Mr. Stavansson," said Tommy, smiling.

"The thing came upon me like a bombshell. Mr. Blunt, none of these people had seen a sign of Hermy—of the three houses, only one had been expecting her—Lady Susan must have made a bloomer over the other two—and she had put off her visit there at the last moment by telegram. I returned post haste to London, of course, and went straight to Lady Susan. I will do her the justice to say that she seemed upset. She admitted that she had no idea where Hermy could be. All the same, she strongly negatived any idea of going to the police. She pointed out that Hermy was not a silly young girl, but an independent woman who had always been in the habit of making her own plans. She was probably carrying out some idea of her own.

"I thought it quite likely that Hermy didn't want to report all her movements to Lady Susan. But I was still worried. I had that queer feeling one gets when something is wrong. I was just leaving when a telegram was brought to Lady Susan. She read it with an expression of relief and handed it to me. It ran as follows. *'Changed my plans Just off to Monte Carlo for a week Hermy.'*"

Tommy held out his hand.

"You have got the telegram with you?"

"No, I haven't. But it was handed in at Maldon, Surrey. I noticed that at the time, because it struck me as odd. What should Hermy be doing at Maldon? She'd no friends there that I had ever heard of."

"You didn't think of rushing off to Monte Carlo in the same way that you had rushed North?"

"I thought of it, of course. But I decided against it. You see, Mr. Blunt, whilst Lady Susan seemed quite satisfied by that telegram, I wasn't. It struck me as odd that she should always telegraph, not write. A line or two in her own handwriting would have set all my fears at rest. But anyone can sign a telegram 'Hermy.' The more I thought it over, the more uneasy I got. In the end I went down to Maldon. That was yesterday afternoon. It's a fair-sized place—good links there and all that—two hotels. I inquired everywhere I could think of, but there wasn't a sign that Hermy had ever been there. Coming back in the train I read your advertisement, and I thought I'd put it up to you. If Hermy has really gone off to Monte Carlo, I don't want to set the police on her track and make a scandal, but I'm not going to be sent off on a wild-goose chase myself. I stay here in London, in case—in case there's been foul play of any kind."

Tommy nodded thoughtfully.

"What do you suspect exactly?"

"I don't know. But I feel there's something wrong."

With a quick movement, Stavansson took a case from his pocket and laid it open before them.

"That is Hermione," he said. "I will leave it with you."

The photograph represented a tall willowy woman, no longer in her first youth, but with a charming frank smile and lovely eyes.

"Now, Mr. Stavansson," said Tommy, "there is nothing you have omitted to tell me?"

"Nothing whatever."

"No detail, however small?"

"I don't think so."

Tommy sighed.

"That makes the task harder," he observed. "You must often have noticed, Mr. Stavansson, in reading of crime, how one small detail is all the great detective needs to set him on the track. I may say that this case presents some unusual features. I have, I think, practically solved it already, but time will show."

He picked up a violin which lay on the table, and drew the bow once or twice across the strings. Tuppence ground her teeth and even the explorer blanched. The performer laid the instrument down again.

"A few chords from Mosgovskensky," he murmured. "Leave me your address, Mr. Stavansson, and I will report progress to you."

As the visitor left the office, Tuppence grabbed the violin and putting it in the cupboard turned the key in the lock.

"If you must be Sherlock Holmes," she observed, "I'll get you a nice little syringe and a bottle labeled *Cocaine,* but for God's sake leave that violin alone. If that nice explorer man hadn't been as simple as a child, he'd have seen through you. Are you going on with the Sherlock Holmes touch?"

"I flatter myself that I have carried it through very well so far," said Tommy with some complacence. "The deductions were good, weren't they? I had to risk the taxi. After all, it's the only sensible way of getting to this place."

"It's lucky I had just read the bit about his engagement in this morning's *Daily Mirror,*" remarked Tuppence.

"Yes, that looked well for the efficiency of Blunt's Brilliant Detectives. This is decidedly a Sherlock Holmes case. Even you cannot have failed to notice the similarity between it and the disappearance of Lady Frances Carfax."

"Do you expect to find Mrs. Leigh Gordon's body in a coffin?"

"Logically, history should repeat itself. Actually—well, what do you think?"

"Well," said Tuppence. "The most obvious explanation seems to be that for some reason or other Hermy, as he calls her, is afraid to meet her fiancé, and that Lady Susan is backing her up. In fact, to put it bluntly, she's come a cropper of some kind, and has got the wind up about it."

"That occurred to me also," said Tommy. "But I thought we'd better make pretty certain before suggesting that explanation to a man like Stavansson. What about a run down to Maldon, old thing? And it would do no harm to take some golf clubs with us."

Tuppence agreeing, the International Detective Agency was left in the charge of Albert.

Maldon, though a well-known residential place, did not cover a large area. Tommy and Tuppence, making every possible inquiry that ingenuity could suggest, nevertheless drew a complete blank. It was as they were returning to London that a brilliant idea occurred to Tuppence.

"Tommy, why did they put Maldon Surrey on the telegram?"

"Because Maldon is in Surrey, idiot."

"Idiot yourself—I don't mean that. If you get a telegram from—Hastings, say, or Torquay, they don't put the county after it. But from Richmond, they do put Richmond Surrey. That's because there are two Richmonds."

Tommy, who was driving, slowed up.

"Tuppence," he said affectionately, "your idea is not so dusty. Let us make inquiries at yonder post office."

They drew up before a small building in the middle of a village street. A very few minutes sufficed to elicit the information that there were two Maldons. Maldon, Surrey, and Maldon, Sussex, the latter a tiny hamlet but possessed of telegraph office.

"That's it," said Tuppence excitedly. "Stavansson knew Maldon was in Surrey, so he hardly looked at the word beginning with S after Maldon."

"Tomorrow," said Tommy, "we'll have a look at Maldon, Sussex."

Maldon, Sussex, was a very different proposition from its Surrey namesake. It was four miles from a railway station, possessed two public houses, two small shops, a post and telegram office combined with a sweet and picture postcard business, and about seven small cottages. Tuppence took on the shops whilst Tommy betook himself to the Cock and Sparrow. They met half an hour later.

"Well?" said Tuppence.

"Quite good beer," said Tommy, "but no information."

"You'd better try the King's Head," said Tuppence. "I'm going back to the post office. There's a sour old woman there, but I heard them yell to her that dinner was ready."

She returned to the place, and began examining postcards. A fresh-faced girl, still munching, came out of the back room.

"I'd like these, please," said Tuppence. "And do you mind waiting whilst I just look over these comic ones?"

She sorted through a packet, talking as she did so.

"I'm ever so disappointed you couldn't tell me my sister's address. She's staying near here and I've lost her letter. Leigh Wood, her name is."

The girl shook her head.

"I don't remember it. And we don't get many letters through here either—so I probably should if I'd seen it on a letter. Apart from the Grange, there aren't many big houses round about."

"What is the Grange?" asked Tuppence. "Who does it belong to?"

"Doctor Horriston has it. It's turned into a Nursing Home now. Nerve cases mostly, I believe. Ladies that come down for rest cures, and all that sort of thing. Well, it's quiet enough down here, Heaven knows." She giggled.

Tuppence hastily selected a few cards and paid for them.

"That's Doctor Horriston's car coming along now," exclaimed the girl.

Tuppence hurried to the shop door. A small two-seater was passing. At the wheel was a tall dark man with a neat black beard and a powerful, unpleasant face. The car went straight on down the street. Tuppence saw Tommy crossing the road toward her.

"Tommy, I believe I've got it. Doctor Horriston's Nursing Home."

"I heard about it at the King's Head, and I thought there might be something in it. But if she's had a nervous breakdown or anything of that sort, her aunt and her friends would know about it surely."

"Ye-es. I didn't mean that. Tommy, did you see that man in the two-seater?"

"Unpleasant-looking brute, yes."

"That was Doctor Horriston."

Tommy whistled.

"Shifty-looking beggar. What do you say about it, Tuppence? Shall we go and have a look at the Grange?"

They found the place at last, a big rambling house, surrounded by deserted grounds, with a swift mill stream running behind the house.

"Dismal sort of abode," said Tommy. "It gives me the creeps, Tuppence. You know, I've a feeling this is going to turn out a far more serious matter than we thought at first."

"Oh! don't. If only we are in time. That woman's in some awful danger, I feel it in my bones."

"Don't let your imagination run away with you."

"I can't help it. I mistrust that man. What shall we do? I think it would be a good plan if I went and rang the bell alone first, and asked boldly for Mrs. Leigh Gordon just to see what answer I get. Because, after all, it may be perfectly fair and above-board."

Tuppence carried out her plan. The door was opened almost immediately by a manservant with an impassive face.

"I want to see Mrs. Leigh Gordon if she is well enough to see me."

She fancied that there was a momentary flicker of the man's eyelashes, but he answered readily enough.

"There is no one of that name here, Madam."

"Oh! surely. This is Doctor Horriston's place, The Grange, is it not?"

"Yes, Madam, but there is nobody of the name of Mrs. Leigh Gordon here."

Baffled, Tuppence was forced to withdraw and hold a further consultation with Tommy outside the gate.

"Perhaps he was speaking the truth. After all, we don't *know*."

"He wasn't. He was lying. I'm sure of it."

"Wait until the doctor comes back," said Tommy. "Then I'll pass myself off as a journalist anxious to discuss his new system of rest cure with him. That will give me a chance of getting inside and studying the geography of the place."

The doctor returned about half an hour later. Tommy gave him about five minutes, then he in turn marched up to the front door. But he too returned baffled.

"The doctor was engaged and couldn't be disturbed. And he never sees journalists. Tuppence, you're right. There's something fishy about this place. It's ideally situated—miles from anywhere. Any mortal thing could go on here, and no one would ever know."

"Come on," said Tuppence, with determination.

"What are you going to do?"

"I'm going to climb over the wall, and see if I can't get up to the house quietly without being seen."

"Right. I'm with you."

The garden was somewhat overgrown, and afforded a multitude of cover. Tommy and Tuppence managed to reach the back of the house unobserved.

Here there was a wide terrace, with some crumbling steps leading down from it. In the middle some French windows opened onto the terrace, but they dared not step out into the open, and the windows where they were crouching were too high for them to be able to look in. It did not seem as though their reconnaissance would be much use when suddenly Tuppence tightened her grasp on Tommy's arm.

Someone was speaking in the room close to them. The window was open and the fragment of conversation came clearly to their ears.

"Come in, come in, and shut the door," said a man's voice irritably. "A lady came about an hour ago, you said, and asked for Mrs. Leigh Gordon?"

Tuppence recognized the answering voice as that of the impassive manservant.

"Yes, sir."

"You said she wasn't here, of course?"

"Of course, sir."

"And now this journalist fellow," fumed the other.

He came suddenly to the window, throwing up the sash, and the two outside, peering through a screen of bushes, recognized Doctor Horriston.

"It's the woman I mind most about," continued the doctor. "What did she look like?"

"Young, good-looking, and very smartly dressed, sir."

Tommy nudged Tuppence in the ribs.

"Exactly," said the doctor between his teeth. "As I feared. Some friend of the Leigh Gordon woman's. It's getting very difficult. I shall have to take steps—"

He left the sentence unfinished. Tommy and Tuppence heard the door close. There was silence.

Gingerly, Tommy led the retreat. When they had reached a little clearing not far away, but out of earshot from the house, he spoke.

"Tuppence, old thing, this is getting serious. They mean mischief. I think we ought to get back to town at once and see Stavansson."

To his surprise Tuppence shook her head.

"We must stay down here. Didn't you hear him say he was going to take steps— That might mean anything."

"The worst of it is we've hardly got a case to go to the police on."

"Listen, Tommy. Why not ring up Stavansson from the village? I'll stay around here."

"Perhaps that is the best plan," agreed her husband. "But, I say—Tuppence—"

"Well?"

"Take care of yourself—won't you?"

"Of course I shall, you silly old thing. Cut along."

It was some two hours later that Tommy returned. He found Tuppence awaiting him near the gate.

"Well?"

"I couldn't get on to Stavansson. Then I tried Lady Susan. She was out too. Then I thought of ringing up old Brady. I asked him to look up Horriston in the Medical Directory or whatever the thing calls itself."

"Well, what did Doctor Brady say?"

"Oh! He knew the name at once. Horriston was once a bona fide doctor, but he came a cropper of some kind. Brady called him a most unscrupulous quack, and said he, personally, wouldn't be surprised at anything. The question is, what are we to do now?"

"We must stay here," said Tuppence instantly. "I've a feeling they mean something to happen tonight. By the way, a gardener has been clipping the ivy round the house. Tommy, *I saw where he put the ladder.*"

"Good for you, Tuppence," said her husband appreciatively. "Then tonight—"

"As soon as it gets dark—"

"We shall see—"

"What we shall see."

Tommy took his turn at watching the house whilst Tuppence went to the village and had some food.

Then she returned and they took up the vigil together. At nine o'clock, they decided that it was dark enough to commence operations. They were now able to circle round the house in perfect freedom. Suddenly Tuppence clutched Tommy by the arm.

"Listen."

The sound she had heard came again, borne faintly on the night air. It was the moan of a woman in pain. Tuppence pointed upward to a window on the first floor.

"It came from that room," she whispered.

Again that low moan rent the stillness of the night.

The two listeners decided to put their original plan into action. Tuppence led the way to where she had seen the gardener put the ladder. Between them they carried it to the side of the house from which they had heard the moaning. All the blinds of the ground-floor rooms were drawn, but this particular window upstairs was unshuttered.

Tommy put the ladder as noiselessly as possible against the side of the house.

"I'll go up," whispered Tuppence. "You stay below. I don't mind climbing ladders and you can steady it better than I could. And in case the doctor should come round the corner you'd be able to deal with him and I shouldn't."

Nimbly Tuppence swarmed up the ladder, and raised her head cautiously to look in at the window. Then she ducked it swiftly, but after a minute or two brought it very slowly up again. She stayed there for about five minutes. Then she descended again.

"It's her," she said breathlessly and ungrammatically, "but oh, Tommy, it's horrible. She's lying there in bed, moaning, and turning to and fro—and just as I got there a woman dressed as a nurse came in. She bent over her and injected something in her arm and then went away again. What shall we do?"

"Is she conscious?"

"I think so. I'm almost sure she is. I fancy she may be strapped to the bed. I'm going up again, and if I can, I'm going to get into that room."

"I say, Tuppence—"

"If I'm in any sort of danger I'll yell for you. So long."

Avoiding further argument Tuppence hurried up the ladder again. Tommy saw her try the window, then noiselessly push up the sash. Another second, and she had disappeared inside.

And now an agonizing time came for Tommy. He could hear nothing at first. Tuppence and Mrs. Leigh Gordon must have been talking in whispers if they were talking at all. Presently he did hear a low murmur of voices and drew a breath of relief. But suddenly the voices stopped. Dead silence.

Tommy strained his ears. Nothing. What could they be doing?

Suddenly a hand fell on his shoulder.

"Come on," said Tuppence's voice out of the darkness.

"Tuppence! How did you get here?"

"Through the front door. Let's get out of this."

"Get out of this?"

"That's what I said."

"But—Mrs. Leigh Gordon?"

In a tone of indescribable bitterness Tuppence replied.

"Getting thin!"

Tommy looked at her, suspecting irony.

"What do you mean?"

"What I say. Getting thin. Slinkiness. Reduction of weight. Didn't you hear Stavansson say he hated fat women? In the two years he's been away, his Hermy has put on weight. Got a panic when she knew he was coming back, and rushed off to do this new treatment of Doctor Horriston's. It's injections of some sort, and he makes a deadly secret of it, and charges through the nose. I dare say he is a quack—but he's a damned successful one! Stavansson comes home a fortnight too soon, when she's only beginning the treatment. Lady Susan had been sworn to secrecy, and plays up. And we come down here and make blithering idiots of ourselves!"

Tommy drew a deep breath.

"I believe, Watson," he said with dignity, "that there is a very good concert at the Queen's Hall tomorrow. We shall be in plenty of time for it. And you will oblige me by not placing this case upon your records. It had absolutely no distinctive features."

Van der Valk and the False Caesar

Nicolas Freeling

Often unorthodox in his approach to solving crimes, Chief Inspector Van der Valk of the Amsterdam police is a unique and complex figure. Inspired to create the character following his own experience of unjust arrest, Nicolas Freeling imbues Van der Valk with a sense of justice that far exceeds the normal process of the law, along with a zealous dislike of official red tape. The author lived in the Netherlands for a number of years, and his stories convey a rich and authentic sense of place. Van der Valk first appeared in *Love in Amsterdam,* published in 1962, and has since appeared on-screen in two major television series—one created by Thames Television in 1972 featuring the actor Barry Foster and filmed on location, the second made by a German TV company in 1983 with the seasoned British actor Frank Finlay portraying the Dutch detective.

"Now look," said Van der Valk quietly across his desk, "a simple unsupported charge of hanky-panky is not enough—if the police listened every time they got that there'd be no end to it. I'm not saying for an instant you might be acting from malice or spite, but you do see my point, huh? An official inquiry, casting doubt on a death, is already very serious. Then publicity, gossip, conjecture—not to mention a charge of false prosecution."

"I know," said the young man helplessly. "But it's too much for me. My father gathered and ate mushrooms for thirty years—and then suddenly he dies from eating mushrooms. It's just too big for me to swallow. I cannot—I will not—believe in a mistake."

Van der Valk stared at him for a long minute, then slowly took a piece of paper, slowly unclipped his pen, and stabbed the air with it. "Make a statement—only the things of which you are reasonably certain. Sign it. If it should later show untruth or distortion you could be in big trouble—you accept that?"

"Yes," the young man said resignedly.

"And if anything does show up, and if I decided to act on it, you realize the very heavy responsibility you would be taking on? You've really weighed all the possible consequences? . . . Very well, I'll take your statement and it will be carefully studied, but that's all I can promise you. Now, you say your father ate these mushroom dishes often. Did anybody ever share them?"

"I did, usually. Only that night I wasn't there. Nobody else ever did—they had a terror of them."

"He cooked the mushrooms himself?"

"As a rule, yes. Sometimes she did, if he were tired or busy. This time she did."

"And which mushrooms were they, exactly."

"One only. A Caesar. A big Caesar—best there is. He was very proud of having found it."

"He told you that?"

"He was in a coma when I arrived. She told me—but I recognized it. Huge orange thing."

"But an amanita?"

"A perfectly safe amanita. I've had them before, though not often."

"He had nausea, you say, and drunkenness. Then he fell asleep?"

"Yes. He behaved as though he were drunk. But I called the doctor—he'd had no more than usual, a small bottle of burgundy. The doctor said yes, it might be muscarine poisoning, and he injected atropine. He said there was a serum but that it was difficult to get—antiphalline. He came back about four hours later—he'd been everywhere for it. But by the time the doctor returned it was too late. I don't blame him; he did his best."

"So your father died, in a drunken heavy sleep passing into coma, about ten to twelve hours after eating. Very well. Now tell me—"

Ordinarily Van der Valk never mentioned his work at home. But Arlette was something of a mushroom expert herself—Frenchwoman, countrywoman. She would be interested.

"Sounds very queer. An expert wouldn't make a mistake like that. There is a false orange, a false Caesar—two in fact, the fly killer and the panther. But anybody with experience can tell the difference."

"What about the phalloids?"

"Entirely different—they're pale, brownish or greenish. There's a safe pale one, but it's difficult to tell—and a good red one too which is very like a panther. But not a Caesar—you'd need to be really stupid to mistake a wicked amanita for a Caesar."

"Is the poisoning always the same?"

"No, not a bit. The phalloids are the horrible ones—destroy your liver. Doesn't show for about twelve hours and then it's too late. You die about three days later. There is a serum."

"Yes, the doctor tried to get the serum. But he couldn't."

"He doesn't know mushrooms. The panther isn't phalline at all, so the serum's irrelevant, no use at all. And you die much quicker—in a few hours and in a coma. Muscarine, I think, and it's easier to treat. If you get the doctor in time you don't die at all."

"You know what the treatment is?"

"Atropine, I believe."

"Yes, that checks. That's what the doctor gave him."

"Wait a moment," said Arlette slowly. "I'm trying to remember something. I think I've heard that if you are poisoned with a panther or a fly killer, then atropine is all wrong—makes it even worse. You better look it up."

"A Dutch doctor might not know that."

"A French one might not know it either—unless he were a countryman."

Van der Valk got all the tomes out and spent an hour studying. "True enough. Here in the natural history book. There's a muscarine syndrome, and for that the treatment is atropine. But there's also a panther syndrome, and for that atropine is bad. But it's confusing, because the panther also contains muscarine. The phalloids are quite different, of course."

"Nobody would mistake a phalloid for a Caesar," insisted Arlette. "I don't even see how anyone could mistake a panther for a Caesar."

"Would getting the wrong treatment kill him?"

"Of course not—but it wouldn't stop him from dying either."

"What about after the mushroom was cooked? You couldn't tell then, could you?"

"I don't know," said Arlette simply. "I've never cooked one."

"I asked about it—thought you'd be interested. Done in oil—with tomatoes, garlic, parsley."

"Then it would be impossible to tell," she said with certainty. "It would go yellowish orange—yes, it would look like a Caesar."

It might have been an accident of treatment—and one couldn't accuse a doctor of not recognizing the false Caesar. It might have been a mistake—when old, Arlette had said, or after rain, the colors were much the same, but an experienced picker would never have taken the risk. And it was possible—possible—that a panther had been substituted for the Caesar.

Only an exhumation order would decide—and Van der Valk could see the magistrate's face if he came up with that rigmarole! And there would always remain the doubt—the victim might have picked the panther himself.

It was better, was it not, that a murderer go free than that innocent people, and a doctor who had done his best, should all have their lives ruined? Wasn't it?

Certainly it was. Once Van der Valk started it would be impossible to stop. Exactly like a bobsled run. Which killed people too, sometimes.

"Oddly enough, I've mushrooms for supper," said Arlette.

"Not tonight. I know I'm being childish—but not tonight."

And she mourned all evening, because of the waste.

The Pietro Andromache

Sara Paretsky

Sara Paretsky left the marketing profession to write full-time, and readers today are blessed with her character V. I. Warshawski, a private investigator. V.I., or Vic, as she's known, is a tough, intelligent investigator who takes no prisoners. Warshawski has been described as the female Sam Spade with her grit, passion and ability to take care of herself. Paretsky, her creator, has been celebrated as the inventor of the female private eye. Using Chicago as a background to her stories, Paretsky creates unique, compelling and unpredictable characters. Vic was played by Kathleen Turner in the only movie so far adapted from Paretsky's series. Praised by well-established publications such as *Time, Newsweek, The Los Angeles Times, The Chicago Tribune* and *The Wall Street Journal,* Paretsky has also been awarded the Cartier Diamond Dagger Award, the Silver Dagger Award and the Marlowe Award.

"You only agreed to hire him because of his art collection. Of that I'm sure." Lotty Herschel bent down to adjust her stockings. "And don't waggle your eyebrows like that—it makes you look like an adolescent Groucho Marx."

Max Loewenthal obediently smoothed his eyebrows, but said, "It's your legs, Lotty; they remind me of my youth. You know, going into the Underground to wait out the air-raids, looking at the ladies as they came down the escalators. The updraft always made their skirts billow."

"You're making this up, Max. I was in those Underground stations, too, and as I remember the ladies were always bundled in coats and children."

Max moved from the doorway to put an arm round Lotty. "That's what keeps us together, *Lottchen:* I am a romantic and you are severely logical. And you know we didn't hire Caudwell because of his collection. Although I admit I am eager to see it. The board wants Beth Israel to develop a transplant program. It's the only way we're going to become competitive."

"Don't deliver your publicity lecture to me," Lotty snapped. Her thick brows contracted to a solid black line across her forehead. "As far as I am concerned he is a cretin with the hands of a Caliban and the personality of Attila."

Lotty's intense commitment to medicine left no room for the mundane consideration of money. But as the hospital's executive director Max was on the spot with the trustees to see that Beth Israel ran at a profit. Or at least at a smaller loss than they'd achieved in recent years. They'd brought Caudwell in in part to attract more paying patients—and to help screen out some of the indigent who made up

12 percent of Beth Israel's patient load. Max wondered how long the hospital could afford to support personalities as divergent as Lotty and Caudwell with their radically differing approaches to medicine.

He dropped his arm and smiled quizzically at her. "Why do you hate him so much, Lotty?"

"*I* am the person who has to justify the patients I admit to this—this troglodyte. Do you realize he tried to keep Mrs. Mendes from the operating room when he learned she had AIDS? He wasn't even being asked to sully his hands with her blood and he didn't want me performing surgery on her."

Lotty drew back from Max and pointed an accusing finger at him. "You may tell the board that if he keeps questioning my judgment they will find themselves looking for a new perinatologist. I am serious about this. You listen this afternoon, Max, you hear whether or not he calls me 'our little baby doctor.' I am fifty-eight years old, I am a Fellow of the Royal College of Surgeons besides having enough credentials in this country to support a whole hospital, and to him I am a 'little baby doctor.' "

Max sat on the daybed and pulled Lotty down next to him. "No, no, *Lottchen:* don't fight. Listen to me. Why haven't you told me any of this before?"

"Don't be an idiot, Max: you are the director of the hospital. I cannot use our special relationship to deal with problems I have with the staff. I said my piece when Caudwell came for his final interview. A number of the other physicians were not happy with his attitude. If you remember we asked the board to bring him in as a cardiac surgeon first and promote him to chief of staff after a year if everyone was satisfied with his performance."

"We talked about doing it that day," Max admitted. "But he wouldn't take the appointment except as chief of staff. That was the only way we could offer him the kind of money he could get at one of the university hospitals or Humana. And Lotty, even if you don't like his personality you must agree that he is a first-class surgeon."

"I agree to nothing." Red lights danced in her black eyes. "If he patronizes me, a fellow physician, how do you imagine he treats his patients? You cannot practice medicine if—"

"Now it's my turn to ask to be spared a lecture," Max interrupted gently. "But if you feel so strongly about him, maybe you shouldn't go to his party this afternoon."

"And admit that he can beat me? Never."

"Very well then." Max got up and placed a heavily-brocaded wool shawl over Lotty's shoulders. "But you must promise me to behave. This is a social function we are going to, remember, not a gladiator contest. Caudwell is trying to repay some hospitality this afternoon, not to belittle you."

"I don't need lessons in conduct from you: Herschels were attending the emperors of Austria while the Loewenthals were operating vegetable stalls on the Ring," Lotty said haughtily.

Max laughed and kissed her hand. "Then remember these regal Herschels and act like them, Eure Hoheit, not like your U.S. namesake Herschel Walker."

Lotty gave a reluctant grin. "I don't know who that is, but he must be a thug of some kind."

"That's why I love you, Lotty. Because you must be the only person in America who's never heard of him. He's a football star."

"Oh, football." Lotty gestured dismissively, but she slipped her hand through Mac's arm and made a neutral comment about an upcoming concert as they walked downstairs to his car.

Caudwell had bought an apartment sight unseen when he moved to Chicago. A divorced man whose children are in college only has to consult his own taste in these matters. He asked the Beth Israel board to recommend a Realtor, sent his requirements to them—twenties construction, near Lake Michigan, good security, modern plumbing—and dropped $750,000 for an eight-room condo facing the lake at Scott Street.

Since Beth Israel paid handsomely for the privilege of retaining Dr. Charlotte Herschel as their perinatologist, nothing required her to live in a five-room walk-up on the fringes of Uptown, so it was a bit unfair of her to mutter "parvenu" to Max when they walked into the lobby.

Max relinquished Lotty gratefully when they got off the elevator. Being her lover was like trying to be companion to a Bengal tiger: you never knew when she'd take a lethal swipe at you. Still, if Caudwell were insulting her—and her judgment—maybe he needed to talk to the surgeon, explain how important Lotty was for the reputation of Beth Israel.

Caudwell's two children were making the obligatory Christmas visit. They were a boy and girl, Deborah and Steve, within a year of the same age, both tall, both blond and poised, with a hearty sophistication born of a childhood spent on expensive ski slopes. Max wasn't very big, and as one took his coat and the other performed brisk introductions he felt himself shrinking, losing in self-assurance. He accepted a glass of special *cuvée* from one of them—was it the boy or the girl, he wondered in confusion—and fled into the *mêlée.*

He landed next to one of Beth Israel's trustees, a woman in her sixties wearing a gray textured mini-dress whose black stripes were constructed of feathers. She commented brightly on Caudwell's art collection, but Max sensed an undercurrent of hostility: wealthy trustees don't like the idea that they can't out-buy the staff.

While he was frowning and nodding at appropriate intervals it dawned on Max that Caudwell did not know how much the hospital needed Lotty. Heart surgeons do not have the world's smallest egos: when you ask them to name the world's three leading practitioners they never can remember the names of the other two. Lotty was at the top of her field, and she, too, was used to having things go her way. Since her confrontational style was reminiscent more of the Battle of the Bulge than the Imperial Court of Vienna, he couldn't blame Caudwell for trying to force her out of the hospital.

Max moved away from Martha Gildersleeve to admire some of the paintings and figurines she'd been discussing. A collector himself of Chinese porcelains Max raised his eyebrows and mouthed a soundless whistle at the pieces on display. A small Watteau and a Charles Demuth watercolor were worth as much as Beth Israel paid Caudwell in a year. No wonder Mrs. Gildersleeve had been so annoyed.

"Impressive, isn't it?"

Max turned to see Arthur Gioia looming over him. Max was shorter than most of the Beth Israel staff, shorter than everyone but Lotty. But Gioia, a tall muscular immunologist, loomed over everyone. He had gone to the University of Arkansas on a football scholarship and had even spent a season playing tackle for Houston before starting medical school. It had been twenty years since he last lifted weights, but his neck still looked like a redwood stump.

Gioia had led the opposition to Caudwell's appointment. Max had suspected at the time that it was due more to a medicine man not wanting a surgeon as his nominal boss than from any other cause, but after Lotty's outburst he wasn't so sure. He was debating whether to ask the doctor how he felt about Caudwell now that he'd worked with him for six months when their host surged over to him and shook his hand.

"Sorry I didn't see you when you came in, Loewenthal. You like the Watteau? It's one of my favorite pieces. Although a collector shouldn't play favorites any more than a father should, eh, sweetheart?" The last remark was addressed to the daughter, Deborah, who had come up behind Caudwell and slipped an arm around him.

Caudwell looked more like a Victorian sea-dog than a surgeon. He had a round red face under a shock of yellow-white hair, a hearty Santa Claus laugh and a bluff, direct manner. Despite Lotty's vituperations he was immensely popular with his patients. In the short time he'd been at the hospital, referrals to cardiac surgery had already increased 15 percent.

His daughter squeezed his shoulder playfully. "I know you don't play favorites with us, Dad, but you're lying to Mr. Loewenthal about your collection; come on, you know you are."

She turned to Max. "He's got a piece he's so proud of he doesn't like to show it to people—he doesn't want them to see he's got vulnerable spots. But it's Christmas, Dad, relax, let people see how you feel for a change."

Max looked curiously at the surgeon, but Caudwell seemed pleased with his daughter's familiarity. The son came up and added his own jocular cajoling.

"This really is Dad's pride and joy. He stole it from Uncle Griffen when Grandfather died and kept Mother from getting her mitts on it when they split up."

Caudwell did bark out a mild reproof at that. "You'll be giving my colleagues the wrong impression of me, Steve. I didn't steal it from Grif. Told him he could have the rest of the estate if he'd leave me the Watteau and the Pietro."

"Of course, he could've bought ten estates with what those two would fetch," Steve muttered to his sister over Max's head.

Deborah relinquished her father's arm to lean over Max and whisper back, "Mom, too."

Max moved away from the alarming pair to say to Caudwell, "A Pietro? You mean Pietro D'Alessandro? You have a model, or an actual sculpture?"

Caudwell gave his staccato admiral's laugh. "The real McCoy, Loewenthal. The real McCoy. An alabaster."

"An alabaster? Max raised his eyebrows. "Surely not. I thought Pietro worked only in bronze and marble."

"Yes, yes," chuckled Caudwell, rubbing his hands together. "Everyone thinks so, but there were a few alabasters in private collections. I've had this one authenticated by experts. Come take a look at it—it'll knock your breath away. You come too, Gioia," he barked at the immunologist. "You're Italian, you'll be interested in what your ancestors were up to."

"A Pietro alabaster?" Lotty's clipped tones made Max start—he hadn't noticed her joining the little group. "I would very much like to see this piece."

"Then come along, Dr. Herschel, come along." Caudwell led them to a small hallway, exchanging genial greetings with his guests as he passed, pointing out a John William Hill miniature they might not have seen, picking up a few other people who for various reasons would love to see his prize.

"By the way, Gioia, I was in New York last week, you know. Met an old friend of yours from Arkansas. Paul Nierman."

"Nierman?" Gioia seemed to be at a loss. "I'm afraid I don't remember him."

"Well he remembered you pretty well. Sent you all kinds of messages—you'll have to stop by my office on Monday and get the full strength."

Caudwell opened a door on the right side of the hall and let them into his study. It was an octagonal room carved out of the corner of the building. Windows on two sides looked out onto Lake Michigan. Caudwell drew salmon drapes as he talked about the room, why he'd chosen it for his study even though the view kept his mind from his work.

Lotty ignored him and walked over to a small pedestal which stood alone against the panelling on one of the four walls. Max followed her and gazed respectfully at the statue. He had seldom seen so fine a piece outside a museum. About a foot high, it depicted a woman in classical draperies hovering in anguish over the dead body of a soldier lying at her feet. The grief in her beautiful face was so poignant that it reminded you of every sorrow you had ever faced.

"Who is it meant to be?" Max asked curiously.

"Andromache," Lotty said in a strangled voice. "Andromache mourning Hector."

Max stared at Lotty, astonished equally by her emotion and her knowledge of the figure—Lotty was totally uninterested in sculpture.

Caudwell couldn't restrain the smug smile of a collector with a true coup. "Beautiful, isn't it? How do you know the subject?"

"I should know it." Lotty's voice was husky with emotion. "My grandmother had such a Pietro. An alabaster given her great-grandfather by the Emperor Joseph the Second himself for his help in consolidating imperial ties with Poland."

She swept the statue from its stand, ignoring a gasp from Max, and turned it over.

"You can see the traces of the imperial stamp here still. And the chip on Hector's foot which made the Habsburg wish to give the statue away to begin with. How come you have this piece? Where did you find it?"

The small group that had joined Caudwell stood silent near the entrance, shocked at Lotty's outburst. Gioia looked more horrified than any of them, but he found Lotty overwhelming at the best of times—an elephant confronted by a hostile mouse.

"I think you're allowing your emotions to carry you away, Doctor." Caudwell kept his tone light, making Lotty seem more gauche by contrast. "I inherited this piece from my father, who bought it—legitimately—in Europe. Perhaps from your—grandmother, was it? But I suspect you are confused about something you may have seen in a museum as a child."

Deborah gave a high-pitched laugh and called loudly to her brother, "Dad may have stolen it from Uncle Grif but it looks like Grandfather snatched it to begin with anyway."

"Be quiet, Deborah," Caudwell barked sternly.

His daughter paid no attention to him. She laughed again and joined her brother to look at the Imperial Seal on the bottom of the statue.

Lotty brushed them aside. "*I* am confused about the seal of Joseph the Second?" she hissed at Caudwell. "Or about this chip on Hector's foot? You can see the line where some Philistine filled in the missing piece. Some person who thought his touch would add value to Pietro's work. Was that you, *Doctor?* Or your father?"

"Lotty." Max was at her side, gently prising the statue from her shaking hands to restore it to its pedestal. "Lotty, this is not the place or the manner to discuss such things."

Angry tears sparkled in her black eyes. "Are you doubting my word?"

Max shook his head. "I'm not doubting you. But I'm also not supporting you. I'm asking you not to talk about this matter in this way at this gathering."

"But Max, either this man or his father is a thief!"

Caudwell strolled up to Lotty and pinched her chin. "You're working too hard, Dr. Herschel. You have too many things on your mind these days. I think the board would like to see you take a leave of absence for a few weeks, go someplace warm, get yourself relaxed. When you're this tense, you're no good to your patients. What do you say, Loewenthal?"

Max didn't say any of the things he wanted to—that Lotty was insufferable and Caudwell intolerable. He believed Lotty, believed that the piece had been her grandmother's. She knew too much about it, for one thing. And for another, a lot of artworks belonging to European Jews were now in museums or private collections around the world. It was only the most god-awful coincidence that the Pietro had ended up with Caudwell's father.

But how dare she raise the matter in the way most likely to alienate everyone present? He couldn't possibly support her in such a situation. And at the same time, Caudwell pinching her chin in that condescending way made him wish he were not chained to a courtesy that would have kept him from knocking the surgeon out—assuming he'd been young enough and tall enough to do it.

"I don't think this is the place or the time to discuss such matters," he reiterated as calmly as he could. "Why don't we all cool down and get back together on Monday, eh?"

Lotty gasped involuntarily, then swept from the room without a backward glance.

Max refused to follow her. He was too angry with her to want to see her again that afternoon. When he got ready to leave the party an hour or so later, after a long conversation with Caudwell that taxed his sophisticated urbanity to the utmost, he heard with relief that Lotty was long gone. The tale of her outburst had of course spread through the gathering at something faster than the speed of sound; he wasn't up to defending her to the buzzing throng, and certainly not to Martha Gildersleeve who demanded an explanation of him in the elevator going down.

He went home for a solitary evening in his house in Evanston. Normally such time brought him pleasure, listening to music in his study, lying on the couch with his shoes off reading history, letting the sounds of the lake wash over him.

Tonight, though, he could get no relief. Fury with Lotty merged into images of horror, the memories of his own disintegrated family, his search through Europe for his mother. He had never found anyone who was quite certain what became of her, although several people told him definitely of his father's suicide. And stamped over these wisps in his brain was the disturbing picture of Caudwell's children, their blond heads leaning backward at identical angles as they gleefully chanted, "Grandpa was a thief, Grandpa was a thief" while Caudwell edged his visitors out of the study.

By morning he would somehow have to reconstruct himself enough to face Lotty, to respond to the inevitable flood of calls from outraged trustees. He'd have to figure out a way of soothing Caudwell's vanity, bruised more by his children's behavior than anything Lotty had said. And find a way to keep both important doctors at Beth Israel.

Max rubbed his gray hair. Every week this job brought him less joy and more pain. Maybe it was time to step down, to let the board bring in a young MBA who would turn Beth Israel's finances around. Lotty would resign then and it would be an end to the tension between her and Caudwell.

Max fell asleep on the couch. When he awoke around five, his joints were stiff with cold, his eyes sticky with tears he'd shed unknowingly in his sleep.

But in the morning everything changed. Max found the hospital buzzing when he arrived, not with news of Lotty's outburst, but of Caudwell's not showing up for an early surgery. Work stopped almost completely at noon when his children phoned to say they'd found the surgeon strangled in his own study and the Pietro Andromache missing. And on Tuesday, the police arrested Dr. Charlotte Herschel for Lewis Caudwell's murder.

Lotty would not speak to anyone. She was out on $250,000 bail, the money raised by Max, but she had gone directly to her apartment on Sheffield after two nights in County Jail without stopping to thank him. She would not talk to reporters, she remained silent during all conversations with the police, and she emphatically refused to speak to the private investigator who had been her close friend for many years.

Max, too, stayed behind an impregnable shield of silence. While Lotty went on indefinite leave, turning her practice over to a series of colleagues, Max continued to go to the hospital every day. But he, too, would not speak to reporters: he wouldn't even say "No comment." He talked to the police only after they threatened to lock him up as a material witness, and then every word had to be pried from him as if his mouth were stone and speech Excalibur. For three days V. I. Warshawski left messages which he refused to return.

On Friday when no word came from the detective, when no reporter popped up from a nearby urinal in the men's room to try to trick him into speaking, when no more calls came from the State's Attorney, Max felt a measure of relaxation as he drove home. As soon as the trial was over he would resign, retire to London. If he could only keep going until then, everything would be—not all right, but bearable.

He used the remote release for the garage door and eased his car into the small space. As he got out he realized bitterly he'd been too optimistic in thinking he'd be left in peace. He hadn't seen the woman sitting on the stoop leading from the garage to the kitchen when he drove in, only as she uncoiled herself at his approach.

"I'm glad you're home—I was starting to freeze in here."

"How did you get into the garage, Victoria?"

The detective grinned in a way he usually found engaging. Now it seemed merely predatory. "Trade secret, Max. I know you don't want to see me, but I need to talk to you."

He unlocked the door into the kitchen. "Why not just let yourself into the house if you were cold? If your scruples permit you into the garage why not into the house?"

She bit her lip in momentary discomfort but said lightly, "I couldn't manage my picklocks with my fingers this cold."

The detective followed him into the house. Another tall monster; five-foot-eight, athletic, light on her feet behind him. Maybe American mothers put growth hormones or steroids in their children's cornflakes. He'd have to ask Lotty. His mind winced at the thought.

"I've talked to the police, of course," the light alto continued behind him steadily, oblivious to his studied rudeness as he poured himself a cognac, took his shoes off, found his waiting slippers and padded down to the hall to the front door for his mail.

"I understand why they arrested Lotty—Caudwell had been doped with a whole bunch of Xanax and then strangled while he was sleeping it off. And of course she was back at the building on Sunday night. She won't say why, but one of the tenants ID'd her as the woman who showed up around ten at the service entrance when he walking his dog. She won't say if she talked to Caudwell, if he let her in, if he was still alive."

Max tried to ignore her clear voice. When that proved impossible he tried to read a journal which had come in the mail.

"And those kids, they're marvelous, aren't they? Like something out of the *Fabulous Furry Freak Brothers.* They won't talk to me but they gave a long interview to Murray Ryerson over at the *Star.*

"After Caudwell's guests left they went to a flick at the Chestnut Street Station, had a pizza afterward, then took themselves dancing on Division Street. So they strolled in around two in the morning—confirmed by the doorman—saw the light on in the old man's study. But they were feeling no pain and he kind of overreacted—their term—if they were buzzed, so they didn't stop in to say good night. It was only when they got up around noon and went in that they found him."

V.I. had followed Max from the front hallway to the door of his study as she spoke. He stood there irresolutely, not wanting his private place desecrated with her insistent air-hammer speech, and finally went on down the hall to a little-used living room. He sat stiffly on one of the brocade armchairs and looked at her remotely when she perched on the edge of its companion.

"The weak piece in the police story is the statue," V.I. continued. She eyed the Persian rug doubtfully and unzipped her boots, sticking them on the bricks in front of the fireplace.

"Everyone who was at the party agrees that Lotty was beside herself. Even people who weren't in Caudwell's study when she looked at the thing know that she said she would kill him and threatened to have him de-scalpeled or whatever you do to surgeons. But if that's the case, what happened to the statue?"

Max gave a slight shrug to indicate total lack of interest in the topic.

V.I. ploughed on doggedly. "Now some people think she might have given it to a friend or a relation to keep for her until her name is cleared at the trial. And these people think it would be either her Uncle Stefan here in Chicago, her brother Hugo in Montreal, or you. So the Mounties searched Hugo's place and are keeping an eye on his mail. The Chicago cops are doing the same for Stefan. And I presume someone got a warrant and went through here, right?"

Max said nothing, but he felt his heart was beating faster. Police in his house, searching his things? But wouldn't they have to get his permission to enter? Or did they. Victoria would know, but he couldn't bring himself to ask. She waited for a few minutes, but when he still wouldn't speak she plunged on. He could see it was becoming an effort for her to talk, but he wouldn't help her.

"But I don't agree with those people. Because I know that Lotty is innocent. And that's why I'm here. Not like a bird of prey, as you think, using your misery for carrion. But to get you to help me. Lotty won't speak to me and if she's that miserable I won't force her to. But surely, Max, you won't sit idly by and let her be railroaded for something she never did."

Max looked away from her. He was surprised to find himself holding the brandy snifter and set it carefully on a table beside him.

"Max!" Her voice was shot with astonishment. "I don't believe this. You actually think she killed Caudwell."

Max flushed a little, but she'd finally stung him into a response. "And you are God who sees all and knows she didn't?"

"I see more than you do," V.I. snapped. "I haven't known Lotty as long as you have but I know when she's telling the truth."

"So you are God." Max bowed in heavy irony. "You see beyond the facts to the innermost souls of men and women."

He expected another outburst from the young woman, but she gazed at him steadily without speaking. It was a look sympathetic enough that Max felt embarrassed by his sarcasm and burst out with what was on his mind.

"What else am I to think? She hasn't said anything, but there's no doubt that she returned to his apartment Sunday night."

It was V.I.'s turn for sarcasm. "With a little vial of Xanax that she somehow induced him to swallow? And then strangled him for good measure? Come on, Max, you know Lotty: honesty follows her around like a cloud. If she'd killed Caudwell she'd say something like, 'Yes, I bashed the little vermin's brains in.' Instead, she's not speaking at all?"

Suddenly the detective's eyes widened with incredulity. "Of course. She thinks you killed Caudwell. You're doing the only thing you can to protect her—standing mute. And she's doing the same thing. What an admirable pair of archaic knights."

"No!" Max said sharply. "It's not possible. How could she think such a thing? She carried on so wildly that it was embarrassing to be near her. I didn't want to see her or talk to her. That's why I've felt so terrible. If only I hadn't been so obstinate, if only I'd called her Sunday night. How could she think I would kill someone on her behalf when I was so angry with her?"

"Why else isn't she saying anything to anyone?" Warshawski demanded.

"Shame, maybe," Max offered. "You didn't see her on Sunday. I did. That is why I think she killed him, not because some man saw her return to Caudwell's building."

His brown eyes screwed shut at the memory. "I have seen Lotty in the grip of anger many times, more than is pleasant to remember, really. But never, never have I seen her in this kind of—uncontrolled rage. You could not talk to her. It was impossible."

The detective didn't respond to that. Instead she said, "Tell me about the statue. I heard a couple of garbled versions from people who were at the party, but I haven't found anyone yet who was in the study when Caudwell showed it to you. Was it really her grandmother's, do you think? And how did Caudwell come to have it if it was?"

Max nodded mournfully. "Oh yes. It was really her family's, I'm convinced of that. She could not have known in advance about the details, the flaw in the foot, the Imperial seal on the bottom. As to how Caudwell got it, I did a little looking into that myself yesterday. His father was with the Army of Occupation in Germany after the war. A surgeon attached to Patton's staff. Men in such positions had endless opportunities to acquire artworks after the war."

V.I. shook her head questioningly.

"You must know something of this, Victoria. Well, maybe not. You know the Nazis helped themselves liberally to artwork belonging to Jews everywhere they occupied Europe. And not just the Jews—they plundered Eastern Europe on a grand scale. The best guess is that they stole sixteen million pieces—statues, paintings, altarpieces, tapestries, rare books. The list is beyond reckoning, really."

The detective gave a little gasp. "Sixteen million! You're joking."

"Not a joke, Victoria. I wish it were so, but it is not. The U.S. Army of Occupation took charge of as many works of art as they found in the occupied territories. In theory they were to find the rightful owners and try to restore them. But in practice few pieces were ever traced and many of them ended up on the black market.

"You only had to say that such-and-such a piece was worth less than $5,000 and you were allowed to buy it. For an officer on Patton's staff the opportunities for fabulous acquisitions would have been endless. Caudwell said he had the statue authenticated, but of course he never bothered to establish its provenance. Anyway, how could he?" Max finished bitterly. "Lotty's family had a deed of gift from the Emperor, but that would have disappeared long since with the dispersal of their possessions."

"And you really think Lotty would have killed a man just to get this statue back? She couldn't have expected to keep it. Not if she'd killed someone to get it, I mean."

"You are so practical, Victoria. You are too analytical, sometimes, to understand why people do what they do. That was not just a statue. True, it is a priceless artwork, but you know Lotty, you know she places no value on such possessions. No, it meant her family to her, her past, her history, everything that the war destroyed forever for her. You must not imagine that because she never discusses such matters that they do not weigh on her."

V.I. flushed at Max's accusation. "You should be glad I'm analytical. It convinces me that Lotty is innocent. And whether you believe it or not I am going to prove it."

Max lifted his shoulders slightly in a manner wholly European. "We each support Lotty according to our lights. I saw that she met her bail and I will see that she gets expert counsel. I am not convinced that she needs you making her innermost secrets public."

V.I.'s gray eyes turned dark with a sudden flash of temper. "You're dead wrong about Lotty. I'm sure the memory of the war is a pain that can never be cured, but Lotty lives in the present, she works in hope for the future. The past does not obssess and consume her as, perhaps, it does you."

Max said nothing. His wide mouth turned in on itself in a narrow line. The detective laid a contrite hand on his arm.

"I'm sorry, Max. That was below the belt."

He forced the ghost of a smile to his mouth. "Perhaps it's true. Perhaps it's why I love these ancient things so much. I wish I could believe you about Lotty. Ask me what you want to know. If you promise to leave as soon as I've answered and not to bother me again I'll answer your questions."

❧ ❧ ❧ ❧

Max put in a dutiful appearance at the Michigan Avenue Presbyterian Church Monday afternoon for Lewis Caudwell's funeral. The surgeon's former wife came, flanked by her children and her husband's brother Griffen. Even after three decades in America Max found himself puzzled sometimes by the native's behavior: since she and Caudwell were divorced, why had his ex-wife draped herself in black? She was even wearing a veiled hat reminiscent of Queen Victoria.

The children behaved in a moderately subdued fashion, but the girl was wearing a white dress shot with black lightning forks which looked as though it belonged at a disco or a resort. Maybe it was her only dress or her only dress with black in it, Max thought, trying hard to look charitably at the blond Amazon—after all, she had been suddenly and horribly orphaned.

Even though she was a stranger both in the city and the church, Deborah had hired one of the church parlors and managed to find someone to cater coffee and light snacks. Max joined the rest of the congregation there after the service.

He felt absurd as he offered condolences to the divorced widow: did she really miss the dead man so much? She accepted his conventional words with graceful melancholy and leaned slightly against her son and daughter. They hovered near her with what struck Max as a stagey solicitude. Seen next to her daughter, Mrs. Caudwell looked so frail and undernourished that she seemed like a ghost. Or maybe it was just that her children had a hearty vitality that even a funeral couldn't quench.

Caudwell's brother Griffen stayed as close to the widow as the children would permit. The man was totally unlike the hearty sea-dog surgeon. Max thought if he'd met the brothers standing side-by-side he would never have guessed their relationship. He was tall, like his niece and nephew, but without their robustness. Caudwell had had a thick mop of yellow-white hair; Griffen's domed head was covered by thin wisps of gray. He seemed weak and nervous, and lacked Caudwell's outgoing *bonhomie;* no wonder the surgeon had found it easy to decide the disposition of their father's estate in his favor. Max wondered what Griffen had gotten in return.

Mrs. Caudwell's vague disoriented conversation indicated that she was heavily sedated. That, too, seemed strange. A man she hadn't lived with for four years and she was so upset at his death that she could only manage the funeral on drugs? Or maybe it was the shame of coming as the divorced woman, not a true widow? But then why come at all?

To his annoyance, Max found himself wishing he could ask Victoria about it. She would have some cynical explanation—Caudwell's death meant the end of the widow's alimony and she knew she wasn't remembered in the will. Or she was having an affair with Griffen and was afraid she would betray herself without tranquilizers. Although it was hard to imagine the uncertain Griffen as the object of a strong passion.

Since he had told Victoria he didn't want to see her again when she left on Friday it was ridiculous of him to wonder what she was doing, whether she was really uncovering evidence that would clear Lotty. Ever since she had gone he had felt a little flicker of hope in the bottom of his stomach. He kept trying to drown it, but it wouldn't quite go away.

Lotty of course, had not come to the funeral, but most of the rest of the Beth Israel staff was there, along with the trustees. Arthur Gioia, his giant body filling the small parlor to the bursting point, tried finding a tactful balance between honesty and courtesy with the bereaved family; he made heavy going of it.

A sable-clad Martha Gildersleeve appeared under Gioia's elbow, rather like a furry football he might have tucked away. She made bright, unseemly remarks to the bereaved family about the disposal of Caudwell's artworks.

"Of course, the famous statue is gone now. What a pity. You could have endowed a chair in his honor with the proceeds from that piece alone." She gave a high, meaningless laugh.

Max sneaked a glance at his watch, wondering how long he had to stay before leaving would be rude. His sixth sense, the perfect courtesy which governed his movements, had deserted him, leaving him subject to the gaucheries of ordinary mortals. He never peeked at his watch at functions, and at any prior funeral he would have deftly pried Martha Gildersleeve from her victim. Instead he stood helplessly by while she tortured Mrs. Caudwell and other bystanders alike.

He glanced at his watch again. Only two minutes had passed since his last look. No wonder people kept their eyes on their watches at dull meetings: they couldn't believe the clock could move so slowly.

He inched stealthily toward the door, exchanging empty remarks with the staff members and trustees he passed. Nothing negative was said about Lotty to his face, but the comments cut off at his approach added to his misery.

He was almost at the exit when two newcomers appeared. Most of the group looked at them with indifferent curiosity, but Max suddenly felt an absurd stir of elation. Victoria, looking sane and modern in a navy suit, stood in the doorway, eyebrows raised, scanning the room. At her elbow was a police sergeant Max had met with her a few times. The man was in charge of Caudwell's murder investigation; it was that unpleasant association that kept the name momentarily from his mind.

V.I. finally spotted Max near the door and gave him a discreet sign. He went to her at once.

"I think we may have the goods," she murmured. "Can you get everyone to go? We just want the family, Mrs. Gildersleeve and Gioia."

"*You* may have the goods," the police sergeant growled. "I'm here unofficially and reluctantly."

"But you're here." Warshawski grinned and Max wondered how he could ever have found the look predatory. His own spirits rose enormously at her smile. "You know in your heart of hearts that arresting Lotty was just plain dumb. And now I'm going to make you look real smart. In public, too."

Max felt his suave sophistication return with the rush of elation that an ailing diva must have when she finds her voice again. A touch here, a word there, and the guests disappeared like the host of Sennacherib. Meanwhile he solicitously escorted first Martha Gildersleeve, then Mrs. Caudwell to adjacent armchairs, got the brother to fetch coffee for Mrs. Gildersleeve, the daughter and son to look after the widow.

With Gioia he could be a bit more ruthless, telling him to wait because the police had something important to ask him. When the last guest had melted away the immunologist stood nervously at the window rattling his change over and over in his pockets. The jingling suddenly was the only sound in the room. Gioia reddened and clasped his hands behind his back.

Victoria came into the room beaming like a governess with a delightful treat in store for her charges. She introduced herself to the Caudwells.

"You know Sergeant McGonnigal, I'm sure, after this last week. I'm a private investigator. Since I don't have any legal standing you're not required to answer any questions I have. So I'm not going to ask you any questions. I'm just going to treat you to a travelogue. I wish I had slides but I'll have to imagine the visuals while the audio track moves along."

"A private investigator!" Steve's mouth formed an exaggerated O; his eyes widened in amazement. "Just like Bogie."

He was speaking, as usual, to his sister. She gave a high-pitched laugh and said, "We'll win first prize in the 'how I spent my winter vacation' contests. Our daddy was murdered. Zowie. Then his most valuable possession was snatched. Powie. But he'd already stolen it from the Jewish doctor who killed him. Yowie! And then a P.I. to wrap it all up. Yowie! Zowie! Powie!"

"Deborah, please," Mrs. Caudwell sighed. "I know you're excited, sweetie, but not right now, okay?"

"Your children keep you young, don't they, ma'am?" Victoria said. "How can you ever feel old when your kids stay seven all their lives?"

"Oo, ow, she bites! Debbie, watch out, she bites!" Steve cried.

McGonnigal made an involuntary movement, as though wishing to smack the younger man. "Ms. Warshawski is right: you are under no obligation to answer any of her questions. But you're bright people, all of you: you know I wouldn't be here if the police didn't take her ideas very seriously. So let's have a little quiet and listen to what she's got on her mind."

Victoria seated herself in an armchair near Mrs. Caudwell's. McGonnigal moved to the door and leaned against the jamb. Deborah and Steve whispered and poked each other until one or both of them shrieked. They then made their faces prim and sat with their hands folded on their laps, looking like bright-eyed choirboys.

Griffen hovered near Mrs. Caudwell. "You know you don't have to say anything, Vivian. In fact, I think you should return to your hotel and lie down. The stress of the funeral—then these strangers—"

Mrs. Caudwell's lips curled bravely below the bottom of her veil. "It's all right, Grif; if I managed to survive everything else one more thing isn't going to do me in."

"Great." Victoria accepted a cup of coffee from Max. "Let me just sketch events for you as I saw them last week. Like everyone else in Chicago I read about Dr. Caudwell's murder and saw it on television. Since I know a number of the people attached to the Beth Israel I may have paid more attention to it than the average viewer, but I didn't get personally involved until Dr. Herschel's arrest on Tuesday."

She swallowed some coffee and set the cup on the table next to her with a small snap. "I have known Dr. Herschel for close to twenty years. It is inconceivable that she would commit such a murder, as those who know her well should have realized at once. I don't fault the police, but others should have known better: she is hot-tempered. I'm not saying killing is beyond her—I don't think it's beyond any of us. She might have taken the statue and smashed Dr. Caudwell's head in the heat of rage. But it beggars belief to think she went home, brooded over her injustices, packed a dose of prescription tranquilizer and headed back to the Gold Coast with murder in mind."

Max felt his cheeks turn hot at her words. He started to interject a protest but bit it back.

"Dr. Herschel refused to make a statement all week, but this afternoon, when I got back from my travels, she finally agreed to talk to me. Sergeant McGonnigal was with me. She doesn't deny that she returned to Dr. Caudwell's apartment at ten that night—she went back to apologize for her outburst and to try to plead with him to return the statue. He didn't answer when the doorman called up and on impulse she went around to the back of the building, got in through the service entrance, and waited for some time outside the apartment door. When he neither answered the doorbell nor returned home himself, she finally went away around eleven o'clock. The children, of course, were having a night on the town."

"*She* says," Gioia interjected.

"Agreed." V.I. smiled. "I make no bones about being partisan: I accept her version. The more so because the only reason she didn't give it a week ago was that she herself was protecting an old friend. She thought perhaps this friend had bestirred himself on her behalf and killed Caudwell to avenge deadly insults against her. It was only when I persuaded her that these suspicions were as unmerited as—well, as accusations against herself—that she agreed to talk."

Max bit his lip and busied himself with getting more coffee for the three women. Victoria waited for him to finish before continuing.

"When I finally got a detailed account of what took place at Caudwell's party, I heard about three people with an axe to grind. One always has to ask, what axe and how big a grindstone? That's what I've spent the weekend finding out. You might as well know that I've been to Little Rock and to Havelock, North Carolina."

Gioia began jingling the coins in his pockets again. Mrs. Caudwell said softly, "Grif, I am feeling a little faint. Perhaps—"

"Home you go, Mom," Steve cried with alacrity.

"In a few minutes, Mrs. Caudwell," the sergeant said from the doorway. "Get her feet up, Warshawski."

For a moment Max was afraid that Steve or Deborah was going to attack Victoria, but McGonnigal moved over to the widow's chair and the children sat down again. Little drops of sweat dotted Griffen's balding head; Gioia's face had a greenish sheen, foliage on top of his redwood neck.

"The thing that leapt out at me," Victoria continued calmly, as though there had been no interruption, "was Caudwell's remark to Dr. Gioia. The doctor was clearly upset, but people were so focused on Lotty and the statue that they didn't pay any attention to that.

"So I went to Little Rock, Arkansas, on Saturday and found the Paul Nierman whose name Caudwell had mentioned to Gioia. Nierman lived in the same fraternity with Gioia when they were undergraduates together twenty-five years ago. And he took Dr. Gioia's anatomy and physiology exams his junior year when Gioia was in danger of academic probation so he could stay on the football team.

"Well, that seemed unpleasant, perhaps disgraceful. But there's no question that Gioia did all his own work in medical school, passed his boards, and so on. So I don't think the Board would demand a resignation for this youthful indiscretion. The question was whether Gioia thought they would, and if he would have killed to prevent Caudwell making it public."

She paused, and the immunologist blurted out, "No. No. But Caudwell—Caudwell knew I'd opposed his appointment. He and I—our approaches to medicine were very opposite. And as soon as he said Nierman's name to me I knew he'd found out and that he'd torment me with it forever. I—I went back to his place Sunday night to have it out with him. I was more determined than Dr. Herschel and got into his unit through the kitchen entrance; he hadn't locked that.

"I went into his study but he was already dead. I couldn't believe it. It absolutely terrified me. I could see he'd been strangled and—well, it's no secret that I'm strong enough to have done it. I wasn't thinking straight. I just got clean away from there—I think I've been running ever since."

"You!" McGonnigal shouted. "How come we haven't heard about this before?"

"Because you insisted on focusing on Dr. Herschel," V.I. said nastily. "I knew he'd been there because the doorman told me. He would have told you if you'd asked."

"This is terrible," Mrs. Gildersleeve interjected. "I am going to talk to the Board tomorrow and demand the resignations of Dr. Gioia and Dr. Herschel."

"Do," Victoria agreed cordially. "Tell them the reason you got to stay for this was because Murray Ryerson at the *Herald-Star* was doing a little checking for me here in Chicago. He found out that part of the reason you were so jealous of Caudwell's collection is because you're living in terrible debt. I won't humiliate you in public by telling people what your money has gone to, but you've had to sell your husband's art collection and you have a third mortgage on your house. A valuable statue with no documented history would have taken care of everything."

Martha Gildersleeve shrank inside her sable. "You don't know anything about this."

"Well, Murray talked to Pablo and Eduardo. . . . Yes, I won't say anything else. So anyway, Murray checked whether either Gioia or Mrs. Gildersleeve had the statue. They didn't, so—"

"You've been in my house?" Mrs. Gildersleeve shrieked.

V.I. shook her head. "Not me. Murray Ryerson." She looked apologetically at the sergeant. "I knew you'd never get a warrant for me, being as how you'd made an arrest. And you'd never have got it in time, anyway."

She looked at her coffee cup, saw it was empty and put it down again. Max took it from the table and filled it for her a third time. His fingertips were itching with nervous irritation; some of the coffee landed on his trouser leg.

"I talked to Murray Saturday night from Little Rock. When he came up empty here, I headed for North Carolina. To Havelock, where Griffen and Lewis Caudwell grew up and where Mrs. Caudwell still lives. And I saw the house where Griffen lives, and talked to the doctor who treats Mrs. Caudwell, and—"

"You really are a pooper snooper aren't you," Steve said.

"Pooper snooper, pooper snooper," Deborah chanted. "Don't get enough thrills of your own so you have to live on other people's—"

"Yeah, the neighbors talked to me about you two." Victoria looked at them with contemptuous indulgence. "You've been a two-person wolf-pack terrifying most of the people around you since you were three. But the folks in Havelock admired how you always stuck up for your mother. You thought your father got her addicted to tranquilizers and then left her high and dry. So you brought her newest version with you and were all set—you just needed to decide when to give it to him. Dr. Herschel's outburst over the statue played right into your hands. You figured your father had stolen it from your uncle to begin with—why not send it back to him and let Dr. Herschel take the rap?"

"It wasn't like that," Steve said, red spots burning in his cheeks.

"What was it like, son?" McGonnigal had moved next to him.

"Don't talk to them—they're tricking you," Deborah shrieked. "The pooper snooper and her gopher gooper."

"She—Mommy used to love us before Daddy made her take all this crap. Then she went away. We just wanted him to see what it was like. We started putting Xanax in his coffee and stuff, we wanted to see if he'd screw up during surgery, let his life get ruined. But then he was sleeping there in the study after his stupid party, and we thought we'd just let him sleep through his morning surgery. Sleep forever, you know, it was so easy, we used his own Harvard necktie. I was so sick of hearing 'Early to bed, early to rise' from him. And we sent the statue to Uncle Grif. I suppose the pooper snooper found it there. He can sell it and Mother can be all right again."

"Grandpa stole it from Jews and Daddy stole it from Grif so we thought it worked out perfectly if we stole it from Daddy," Deborah cried. She leaned her blond head next to her brother's and shrieked with laughter.

Max watched the line of Lotty's legs change as she stood on tiptoe to reach a brandy snifter. Short, muscular from years of racing at top speed from one point to the next, maybe they weren't as svelte as the long legs of modern American girls, but he preferred them. He waited until her feet were securely planted before making his announcement.

"The board is bringing in Justin Hardwick for a final interview for chief of staff."

"Max!" She whirled, the Bengal fire sparkling in her eyes. "I know this Hardwick and he is another like Caudwell, looking for cost-cutting and no poverty patients. I won't have it."

"We've got you and Gioia and a dozen others bringing in so many non-paying patients that we're not going to survive another five years at the present rate. I figure it's a balancing act. We need someone who can see that the hospital survives so that you and Art can practice medicine the way you want to. And when he knows what happened to his predecessor he'll be very careful not to stir up our resident tigress."

"Max!" She was hurt and astonished at the same time. "Oh. You're joking, I see. It's not very funny to me, you know."

"My dear, we've got to learn to laugh about it: it's the only way we'll ever be able to forgive ourselves for our terrible misjudgments." He stepped over to put an arm around her. "Now where is this remarkable surprise you promised to show me."

She shot him a look of pure mischief, Lotty on a dare as he first remembered meeting her at fifteen. His hold on her tightened and he followed her to her bedroom. In a glass case in the corner stood the Pietro Andromache.

Max looked at the beautiful, anguished face. I understand your sorrows, she seemed to say to him. I understand your grief for your mother, your family, your history, but it's all right to let go of them, to live in the present and hope for the future. It's not a betrayal.

Tears pricked his eyelids, but he demanded, "How did you get this? I was told the police had it under lock and key until lawyers decided on the disposition of Caudwell's estate."

"Victoria," Lotty said shortly. "I told her the problem and she got it for me. On the condition that I not ask how she did it. And Max, you know damned well that it was not Caudwell's to dispose of."

It was Lotty's. Of course it was. Max wondered briefly how Joseph II had come by it to begin with. For that matter, what had Lotty's great-great grandfather done to earn it from the emperor? Max looked into Lotty's tiger eyes and kept such reflections to himself. Instead he inspected Hector's foot where the filler had been carefully scraped away to reveal the old chip.

When the Wedding Was Over

Ruth Rendell

Few writers can maintain the interest in series characters that Ruth Rendell has achieved with the Detective Inspector Reginald Wexford novels. Rendell's novels and stories are considered the best in psychological suspense dramas. She describes her character Wexford as shrewd, compassionate, witty and solid. Seventeen of her fifty books are devoted to the Chief Inspector and are immensely popular both in Britain and America. The television series *The Ruth Rendell Mysteries,* which features the veteran actor George Baker as Wexford, has been running since 1988. Rendell has won many awards, including four Gold Dagger awards as well as the Cartier Diamond Dagger Award from the Crime Writers' Association and The Sunday Times Literary Award. In 1996 she was honored with the award of Commander of the British Empire and in 1997 was elected to the House of Lords.

"Matrimony," said Chief Inspector Wexford, "begins with dearly beloved and ends with amazement."

His wife, sitting beside him on the bridegroom's side of the church, whispered, "What did you say?"

He repeated it. She steadied the large floral hat which her husband had called becoming but not exactly conducive to *sotto voce* intimacies. "What on earth makes you say that?"

"Thomas Hardy. He said it first. But look in your Prayer Book."

The bridegroom waited, hang-dog, with his best man. Michael Burden was very much in love, was entering this second marriage with someone admirably suited to him, had agreed with his fiancée that nothing but a religious ceremony would do for them, yet at forty-four was a little superannuated for what Wexford called "all this white wedding gubbins." There were two hundred people in the church. Burden, his best man and his ushers were in morning dress. Madonna lilies and stephanotis and syringa decorated the pews, the pulpit and the chancel steps. It was the kind of thing that is properly designed for someone twenty years younger. Burden had been through it before when he was twenty years younger. Wexford chuckled silently, looking at the anxious face above the high white collar. And then as Dora, leafing through the marriage service, said, "Oh, I see," the organist went from voluntaries into the opening bars of the Lohengrin march and Jenny Ireland appeared at the church door on her father's arm.

A beautiful bride, of course. Seven years younger than Burden, blond, gentle, low-voiced, and given to radiant smiles. Jenny's father gave her hand into Burden's and the Rector of St. Peter's began: "Dearly beloved, we are gathered together . . ."

While bride and groom were being informed that marriage was not for the satisfaction of the carnal lusts, and that they must bring up their children in a Christian manner, Wexford studied the congregation. In front of himself and Dora sat Burden's sister-in-law, Grace, whom everyone had thought he would marry after the death of his first wife. But Burden had found consolation with a redheaded woman, wild and sweet and strange, gone now God knew where, and Grace had married someone else. Two little boys now sat between Grace and that someone else, giving their parents a full-time job keeping them quiet.

Burden's mother and father were both dead. Wexford thought he recognized, from one meeting a dozen years before, an aged aunt. Beside her sat Doctor Crocker and his wife, beyond them and behind were a crowd whose individual members he knew either only by sight or not at all. Sylvia, his elder daughter, was sitting on his other side, his grandsons between her and their father, and at the central aisle end of the pew, Sheila Wexford of the Royal Shakespeare Company. Wexford's actress daughter, who on her entry had commanded nudges, whispers, every gaze, sat looking with unaccustomed wistfulness at Jenny Ireland in her clouds of white and wreath of pearls.

"I, Michael George, take thee, Janina, to my wedded wife, to have and to hold, from this day forward . . ."

Janina. *Janina?* Wexford had supposed her name was Jennifer. What sort of parents called a daughter Janina? Turks? Fans of Dumas? He leaned forward to get a good look at these philonomatous progenitors. They looked ordinary enough, Mr. Ireland apparently exhausted by the effort of giving the bride away, Jenny's mother making use of the lace handkerchief provided for the special purpose of crying into it those tears of joy and loss. What romantic streak had led them to dismiss Elizabeth and Susan and Anne in favor of—Janina?

"For those whom God hath joined together, let no man put asunder. Forasmuch as Michael George and Janina have consented together in holy wedlock . . ."

Had they been as adventurous in the naming of their son? All Wexford could see of him was a broad back, a bit of profile, and now a hand. The hand was passing a large white handkerchief to his mother. Wexford found himself being suddenly yanked to his feet to sing a hymn.

"O, Perfect Love, all human thought transcending,
Lowly we kneel in prayer before Thy throne . . ."

These words had the effect of evoking from Mrs. Ireland audible sobs. Her son—hadn't Burden said he was in publishing?—looked embarrassed, turning his head. A young woman, strangely dressed in black with an orange hat, edged past the publisher to put a consoling arm round his mother.

"O Lord, save Thy servant and Thy handmaid."

"Who put their trust in thee," said Dora and most of the rest of the congregation.

"O Lord, send them help from Thy holy place."

Wexford, to show team spirit, said Amen, and when everyone else said, "And evermore defend them," decided to keep quiet in future.

Mrs. Ireland had stopped crying. Wexford's gaze drifted to his own daughters, Sheila singing lustily, Sylvia, the Women's Liberationist, with less assurance as if she doubted the ethics of lending her support to so archaic and sexist a ceremony. His grandsons were beginning to fidget.

"Almighty God, who at the beginning did create our first parents, Adam and Eve . . ."

Dear Mike, thought Wexford with a flash of sentimentality that came to him perhaps once every ten years, you'll be OK now. No more carnal lusts conflicting with a puritan conscience, no more loneliness, no more worrying about those selfish kids of yours, no more temptation-of-St.-Anthony stuff. For is it not ordained as a remedy against sin, and to avoid fornication, that such persons as have not the gift of continence may marry and keep themselves undefiled?

"For after this manner in the old time the holy women who trusted in God . . ."

He was quite surprised that they were using the ancient form. Still, the bride had promised to obey. He couldn't resist glancing at Sylvia.

". . . being in subjection to their own husbands . . ."

Her face was a study in incredulous dismay as she mouthed at her sister "unbelievable" and "antique."

". . . Even as Sarah obeyed Abraham, calling him Lord, whose daughters ye are as long as ye do well, and are not afraid with any amazement."

At the Olive and Dove hotel there was a reception line to greet guests. Mrs. Ireland smiling, re-rouged and restored, Burden looking like someone who has had an operation and been told the prognosis is excellent, Jenny serene as a bride should be.

Dry sherry and white wine on trays. No champagne. Wexford remembered that there was a younger Ireland daughter, absent, with her husband in some dreadful place—Botswana? Lesotho? No doubt all the champagne funds had been expended on her. It was a buffet lunch, but a good one. Smoked salmon and duck and strawberries. Nobody, he said to himself, has ever really thought of anything better to eat than smoked salmon and duck and strawberries unless it might be caviar and grouse and syllabub. He was weighing the two menus against one another, must without knowing it have been thinking aloud, for a voice said:

"Asparagus, trout, apple pie."

"Well, maybe," said Wexford, "but I do like meat, Trout's a bit insipid. You're Jenny's brother, I'm sorry I don't remember your name. How d'you do?"

"How d'you do? I know who you are. Mike told me. I'm Amyas Ireland."

So that funny old pair hadn't had a one-off indulgence when they had named Janina. Again Wexford's thoughts seemed revealed to this intuitive person.

"Oh, I know," said Ireland, "but how about my other sister? She's called Cunegonde. Her husband calls her Queenie. Look, I'd like to talk to you. Could we get together a minute away from all this crush? Mike was going to help me out, but I can't ask him now, not when he's off on his honeymoon. It's about a book we're publishing."

The girl in black and orange, Burden's nephews, Sheila Wexford, Burden's best man and a gaggle of children, all carrying plates, passed between them at this point. It was at least a minute before Wexford could ask, "Who's we?" and another half-minute before Amyas Ireland understood what he meant.

"Carlyon Brent," he said, his mouth full of duck. "I'm with Carlyon Brent."

One of the largest and most distinguished of publishing houses. Wexford was impressed. "You published the Vandrian, didn't you, and the de Coverley books?"

Ireland nodded. "Mike said that you were a great reader. That's good. Can I get you some more duck? No? I'm going to. I won't be a minute." Enviously Wexford watched him shovel fat-rimmed slices of duck breast onto his plate, take a brioche, have second thoughts and take another. The man was as thin as a rail too, positively emaciated.

"I look after the crime list," he said as he sat down again. "As I said, Mike half-promised. . . . This isn't fiction, it's fact. The Winchurch case?"

"Ah."

"I know it's a bit of a nerve asking, but would you read a manuscript for me?"

Wexford took a cup of coffee from a passing tray. "What for?"

"Well, in the interests of truth, Mike was going to tell me what he thought." Wexford look at him dubiously. He had the highest respect and the deepest affection for Inspector Burden but he was one of the last people he would have considered as a literary critic. "To tell me what he thought," the publisher said once again. "You see, it's worrying me. The author has discovered some new facts and they more or less prove Mrs. Winchurch's innocence." He hesitated. "Have you ever heard of a writer called Kenneth Gandolph?"

Wexford was saved from answering by the pounding of a gavel on the top table and the beginning of the speeches. A great many toasts had been drunk, several dozen telegrams read out, and the bride and groom departed to change their clothes before he had an opportunity to reply to Ireland's question. And he was glad of the respite, for what he knew of Gandolph, though based on hearsay, was not prepossessing.

"Doesn't he write crime novels?" he said when the enquiry was repeated. "And the occasional examination of a real-life crime?"

Nodding, Ireland said, "It's good, this script of his. We want to do it for next spring's list. It's an eighty-year-old murder, sure, but people are still fascinated by it. I think this new version could cause quite a sensation."

"Florence Winchurch was hanged," said Wexford, "yet there was always some margin of doubt about her guilt. Where does Gandolph get his fresh facts from?"

"May I send you a copy of the script? You'll find all that in the introduction."

Wexford shrugged, then smiled. "I suppose so. You do realize I can't do more than maybe spot mistakes in forensics? I did say maybe, mind." But his interest had already been caught. It made him say, "Florence was married at St. Peter's, you know, and she also had her wedding reception here."

"And spent part of her honeymoon in Greece."

"No doubt the parallel ends there," said Wexford as Burden and Jenny came back into the room.

Burden was in a gray lounge suit, she in a pale blue sprigged muslin. Wexford felt an absurd impulse of tenderness toward him. It was partly caused by Jenny's hat which she would never wear again, would never have occasion to wear, would remove the minute they got into the car. But Burden was the sort of man who could never be happy with a woman who didn't have a hat as part of her "going-away" costume. His own clothes were eminently unsuitable for flying to Crete in June. They both looked very happy and embarrassed.

Mrs. Ireland seized her daughter in a crushing embrace.

"It's not for ever, Mother," said Jenny. "It's only for two weeks."

"Well, in a way," said Burden. He shook hands gravely with his own son, down from university for the weekend, and planted a kiss on his daughter's forehead. Must have been reading novels, Wexford thought, grinning to himself.

"Good luck, Mike," he said.

The bride took his hand, put a soft cool kiss on to the corner of his mouth. Say I'm growing old but add, Jenny kissed me. He didn't say that aloud. He nodded and smiled and took his wife's arm and frowned at Sylvia's naughty boys like the patriarch he was. Burden and Jenny went out to the car which had JUST MARRIED written in lipstick on the rear window and a shoe tied on the back bumper.

There was a clicking of handbag clasps, a flurry of hands, and then a tempest of confetti broke over them.

It was an isolated house, standing some twenty yards back from the Myringham road. Plumb in the center of the façade was a plaque bearing the date 1896. Wexford had often thought that there seemed to have been positive intent on the part of late-Victorian builders to design and erect houses that were not only ugly, complex and inconvenient, but also distinctly sinister in appearance. The Limes, though well-maintained and set in a garden as multi-colored, cushiony and floral as a quilt, nevertheless kept this sinister quality. Khaki-colored brick and gray slate had been the principal materials used in its construction. Without being able to define exactly how, Wexford could see that, in relation to the walls, the proportions of the sash windows were wrong. A turret grew out of each of the front corners and each of these turrets was topped by a conical roof, giving the place the look of a cross between Balmoral castle and a hotel in Kitzbuehl. The lime trees which gave it its name had been lopped so many times since their planting at the turn of the century that now they were squat and misshapen.

In the days of the Winchurches it had been called Paraleash House. But this name, of historical significance on account of its connection with the ancient manor of Paraleash, had been changed specifically as a result of the murder of Edward Winchurch. Even so, it had stood empty for ten years. Then it had found a buyer a year or so before the First World War, a man who was killed in that war. Its present owner had occupied it for half a dozen years, and in the time intervening between his purchase of it and 1918 it had been variously a nursing home, the annexe of an agricultural college and a private school. The owner was a retired brigadier. As he emerged from the front door with two Sealyhams on a lead, Wexford retreated to his car and drove home.

It was Monday evening and Burden's marriage was two days old. Monday was the evening of Dora's pottery class, the fruits of which, bruised-looking and not invariably symmetrical, were scattered haphazardly about the room like windfalls. Hunting along the shelves for G. Hallam Saul's *When the Summer Is Shed* and *The Trial of Florence Winchurch* from the Notable British Trials series, he nearly knocked over one of those rotund yet lopsided objects. With a sigh of relief that it was unharmed, he set about refreshing his memory of the Winchurch case with the help of Miss Saul's classic.

Florence May Anstruther had been nineteen at the time of her marriage to Edward Winchurch and he forty-seven. She was a good-looking fair-haired girl, rather tall and Junoesque, the daughter of a Kingsmarkham chemist—that is, a pharmacist, for her father had kept a shop in the High Street. In 1895 this damned her as of no account in the social hierarchy, and few people would have bet much on her chances of marrying well. But she did. Winchurch was a barrister who, at this stage of his life, practiced law from inclination rather than from need. His father, a Sussex landowner, had died some three years before and had left him what for the last decade of the nineteenth century was an enormous fortune, two hundred thousand pounds. Presumably, he had been attracted to Florence for her youth, her looks and her ladylike ways. She had been given the best education, including six months at a finishing school, that the chemist could afford. Winchurch's attraction for Florence was generally supposed to have been solely his money.

They were married in June 1895 at the parish church of St. Peter's, Kingsmarkham, and went on a six-month honeymoon, touring Italy, Greece and the Swiss Alps. When they returned home Winchurch took a lease of Sewingbury Priory while building began on Paraleash House, and it may have been that the conical roofs on those turrets were inspired directly by what Florence had seen on her alpine travels. They moved into the lavishly furnished new house in May 1896 and Florence settled down to the life of a Victorian lady with a wealthy husband and a staff of indoor and outdoor servants. A vapid life at best, even if alleviated by a brood of children. But Florence had no children and was to have none.

Once or twice a week Edward Winchurch went up to London by the train from

Kingsmarkham, as commuters had done before and have been doing ever since. Florence gave orders to her cook, arranged the flowers, paid and received calls, read novels and devoted a good many hours a day to her face, her hair and her dress. Local opinion of the couple at that time seemed to have been that they were as happy as most people, that Florence had done very well for herself and knew it, and Edward not so badly as had been predicted.

In the autumn of 1896 a young doctor of medicine bought a practice in Kingsmarkham and came to live there with his unmarried sister. Their name was Fenton. Frank Fenton was an extremely handsome man, twenty-six years old, six feet tall, with jet black hair, a Byronic eye and an arrogant lift to his chin. The sister was called Ada, and she was neither good-looking nor arrogant, being partly crippled by poliomyelitis which had left her with one leg badly twisted and paralyzed.

It was ostensibly to befriend Ada Fenton that Florence first began calling at the Fentons' house in Queen Street. Florence professed great affection for Ada, took her about in her carriage and offered her the use of it whenever she had to go any distance. From this it was an obvious step to persuade Edward that Frank Fenton should become the Winchurches' doctor. Within another few months young Mrs. Winchurch had become the doctor's mistress.

It was probable that Ada knew nothing, or next to nothing, about it. In the 1890s a young girl could be, and usually was, very innocent. At the trial it was stated by Florence's coachman that he would be sent to the Fentons' house several times a week to take Miss Fenton driving, while Ada's housemaid said that Mrs. Winchurch would arrive on foot soon after Miss Fenton had gone out and be admitted rapidly through a french window by the doctor himself. During the winter of 1898 it seemed likely that Frank Fenton had performed an abortion on Mrs. Winchurch, and for some months afterward they met only at social gatherings and occasionally when Florence was visiting Ada. But their feelings for each other were too strong for them to bear separation and by the following summer they were again meeting at Fenton's house while Ada was out, and now also at Paraleash House on the days when Edward had departed for the law courts.

Divorce was difficult but by no means impossible or unheard-of in 1899. At the trial Frank Fenton said he had wanted Mrs. Winchurch to ask her husband for a divorce. He would have married her in spite of the disastrous effect on his career. It was she, he said, who refused to consider it on the grounds that she did not think she could bear the disgrace.

In January 1900 Florence went to London for the day and, among other purchases, bought at a grocer's two cans of herring fillets marinated in a white wine sauce. It was rare for canned food to appear in the Winchurch household, and when Florence suggested that these herring fillets should be used in the preparation of a dish called *Filets de hareng marinés à la Rosette,* the recipe for which she had been given by Ada Fenton, the cook, Mrs. Eliza Holmes, protested that she could prepare it from fresh fish. Florence, however, insisted, one of the cans was used, and the dish was made and served to Florence and Edward at dinner. It was brought in by the parlormaid, Alice

Evans, as a savory or final course to a four-course meal. Although Florence had shown so much enthusiasm about the dish, she took none of it. Edward ate a moderate amount and the rest was removed to the kitchen where it was shared between Mrs. Holmes, Alice Evans and the housemaid, Violet Stedman. No one suffered any ill-effects. The date was 30 January 1900.

Five weeks later on 5 March Florence asked Mrs. Holmes to make the dish again, using the remaining can, as her husband had liked it so much. This time Florence partook of the marinated herrings, but when the remains of it were about to be removed by Alice to the kitchen, she advised her to tell the others not to eat it as she "thought it had a strange taste and was perhaps not quite fresh." However, although Mrs. Holmes and Alice abstained, Violet ate a larger quantity of the dish than had either Florence or Edward.

Florence, as was her habit, left Edward to drink his port alone. Within a few minutes a strangled shout was heard from the dining room and a sound as of furniture breaking. Florence and Alice Evans and Mrs. Holmes went into the room and found Edward Winchurch lying on the floor, a chair with one leg wrenched from its socket tipped over beside him and an overturned glass of port on the table. Florence approached him and he went into a violent convulsion, arching his back and baring his teeth, his hands grasping the chair in apparent agony.

John Barstow, the coachman, was sent to fetch Doctor Fenton. By this time, Florence was complaining of stomach pains and seemed unable to stand. Fenton arrived, had Florence and Edward removed upstairs and asked Mrs. Holmes what they had eaten. She showed him the empty herring fillet can, and he recognized the brand as that by which a patient of a colleague of his had recently been infected with botulism, a virulent and usually fatal form of food poisoning. Fenton immediately assumed that it was *bacillus botulinus* which had attacked the Winchurches, and such is the power of suggestion that Violet Stedman now said she felt sick and faint.

Botulism causes paralysis, difficulty in breathing and a disturbance of the vision Florence appeared to be partly paralyzed and said she had double vision. Edward's symptoms were different. He continued to have spasms, was totally relaxed between spasms, and although he had difficulty in breathing and other symptoms of botulism, the onset had been exceptionally rapid for any form of food poisoning. Fenton, however, had never seen a case of botulism, which is extremely rare, and he supposed that the symptoms would vary greatly from person to person. He gave jalap and cream of tartar as a purgative and, in the absence of any known relatives of Edward Winchurch, he sent for Florence's father, Thomas Anstruther.

If Fenton was less innocent than was supposed, he had made a mistake in sending for Anstruther, for Florence's father insisted on a second opinion, and at ten o'clock went himself to the home of that very colleague of Fenton's who had recently witnessed a known case of botulism. This was Doctor Maurice Waterfield, twice Fenton's age, a popular man with a large practice in Stowerton. He looked at Edward Winchurch, at the agonized grin which overspread his features, and as Edward went into his last convulsive seizure, pronounced that he had been poisoned not by *bacillus botulinus* but by strychnine.

Edward died a few minutes afterwards. Doctor Waterfield told Fenton that there was nothing physically wrong with either Florence or Violet Stedman. The former was suffering from shock or "neurasthenia," the latter from indigestion brought on by over-eating. The police were informed, an inquest took place, and after it Florence was immediately arrested and charged with murdering her husband by administering to him a noxious substance, to wit *strychnos nux vomica,* in a decanter of port wine.

Her trial took place in London at the Central Criminal Court. She was twenty-four years old, a beautiful woman, and was by then known to have been having a love affair with the young and handsome Doctor Fenton. As such, she and her case attracted national attention. Fenton had by then lost his practice, lost all hope of succeeding with another in the British Isles, and even before the trial his name had become a by-word, scurrilous doggerel being sung about him and Florence in the music halls. But far from increasing his loyalty to Florence, this seemed to make him the more determined to dissociate himself from her. He appeared as the prosecution's principal witness, and it was his evidence which sent Florence to the gallows.

Fenton admitted his relationship with Florence but said that he had told her it must end. The only possible alternative was divorce and ultimately marriage to himself. In early January 1900 Florence had been calling on his sister Ada, and he had come in to find them looking through a book of recipes. One of the recipes called for the use of herring fillets marinated in white wine sauce, the mention of which had caused him to tell them about a case of botulism which a patient of Doctor Waterfield's was believed to have contracted from eating the contents of a can of just such fillets. He had named the brand and advised his sister not to buy any of that kind. When, some seven weeks later, he was called to the dying Edward Winchurch, the cook had shown him an empty can of that very brand. In his opinion, Mrs. Winchurch herself was not ill at all, was not even ill from "nerves," but was shamming. The judge said that he was not there to give his opinion, but the warning came too late. To the jury the point had already been made.

Asked if he was aware that strychnine had therapeutic uses in small quantities, Fenton said he was but that he kept none in his dispensary. In any case, his dispensary was kept locked and the cupboards inside it locked, so it would have been impossible for Florence to have entered it or to have appropriated anything while on a visit to Ada. Ada Fenton was not called as a witness. She was ill, suffering from what her doctor, Doctor Waterfield, called "brain fever."

The prosecution's case was that, in order to inherit his fortune and marry Doctor Fenton, Florence Winchurch had attempted to poison her husband with infected fish, or fish she had good reason to suppose might be infected. When this failed she saw to it that the dish was provided again, and she added strychnine to the port decanter. It was postulated that she obtained the strychnine from her father's shop, without his knowledge, where it was kept in stock for the destruction of rats and moles. After her husband was taken ill, she herself simulated symptoms of botulism in the hope that the convulsions of strychnine poisoning would be confused with the paralysis and impeded breathing caused by the bacillus.

The defense tried to shift the blame to Frank Fenton, at least to suggest a conspiracy with Florence, but it was no use. The jury was out for only forty minutes. They pronounced her guilty, the judge sentenced her to death, and she was hanged just twenty-three days later, this being some twenty years before the institution of a Court of Appeal.

After the execution Frank and Ada Fenton emigrated to the United States and settled in New England. Fenton's reputation had gone before him. He was never again able to practice as a doctor but worked as the traveling representative of a firm of pharmaceutical manufacturers until his death in 1932. He never married. Ada, on the other hand, surprisingly enough, did. Ephraim Hurst fell in love with her in spite of her sickly constitution and withered leg. They were married in the summer of 1902 and by the spring of 1903 Ada Hurst was dead in childbirth.

By then Paraleash House had been re-named The Limes and lime trees planted to conceal its forbidding yet fascinating façade from the curious passer-by.

The parcel from Carlyon Brent arrived in the morning with a very polite covering letter from Amyas Ireland, grateful in anticipation. Wexford had never before seen a book in this embryo stage. The script, a hundred thousand words long, was bound in red, and through a window in its cover appeared the provisional title and the author's name: *Poison at Paraleash, A Reappraisal of the Winchurch Case* by Kenneth Gandolph.

"Remember all that fuss about Gandolph?" Wexford said to Dora across the coffee pot. "About four years ago?"

"Somebody confessed a murder to him, didn't they?"

"Well, maybe. While a prison visitor, he spent some time talking to Paxton, the bank robber, in Wormwood Scrubs. Paxton died of cancer a few months later, and Gandolph then published an article in a newspaper in which he said that during the course of their conversations, Paxton had confessed to him that he was the perpetrator of the Conyngford murder in 1962. Paxton's widow protested, there was a heated correspondence, MPs wanting the libel laws extended to libeling the dead, Gandolph shouting about the power of truth. Finally, the by then retired Detective Superintendent Warren of Scotland Yard put an end to all further controversy by issuing a statement to the press. He said Paxton couldn't have killed James Conyngford because on the day of Conyngford's death in Brighton Warren's sergeant and a constable had had Paxton under constant surveillance in London. In other words, he was never out of their sight."

"Why would Gandolph invent such a thing, Reg?" said Dora.

"Perhaps he didn't. Paxton may have spun him all sorts of tales as a way of passing a boring afternoon. Who knows? On the other hand, Gandolph does rather set himself up as the elucidator of unsolved crimes. Years ago, I believe, he did find a satisfactory and quite reasonable solution to some murder in Scotland, and maybe it went to his head. Marshall, Groves, Folliott used to be his publishers. I wonder if they've refused this one because of the Paxton business, if it was offered to them and they turned it down?"

"But Mr. Ireland's people have taken it," Dora pointed out.

"Mm-hm. But they're not falling over themselves with enthusiasm, are they? They're scared. Ireland hasn't sent me this so that I can check up on the police procedural part. What do I know about police procedure in 1900? He's sent me in the hope that if Gandolph's been up to his old tricks I'll spot what they are."

The working day presented no opportunity for a look at Poison at Paraleash, but at eight o'clock that night Wexford opened it and read Gandolph's long introduction.

Gandolph began by saying that as a criminologist he had always been aware of the Winchurch case and of the doubt which many felt about Florence Winchurch's guilt. Therefore, when he was staying with friends in Boston, Massachusetts, some two years before and they spoke to him of an acquaintance of theirs who was the niece of one of the principals in the case, he had asked to be introduced to her. The niece was Ada Hurst's daughter, Lina, still Miss Hurst, seventy-four years old and suffering from a terminal illness.

Miss Hurst showed no particular interest in the events of March 1900. She had been brought up by her father and his second wife and had hardly known her uncle. All her mother's property had come into her possession, including the diary which Ada Fenton Hurst had kept for three years prior to Edward Winchurch's death. Lina Hurst told Gandolph she had kept the diary for sentimental reasons but that he might borrow it and after her death she would see that it passed to him.

Within weeks Lina Hurst did die and her stepbrother, who was her executor, had the diary sent to Gandolph. Gandolph had read it and had been enormously excited by certain entries because in his view they incriminated Frank Fenton and exonerated Florence Winchurch. Here Wexford turned back a few pages and noted the author's dedication: *In memory of Miss Lina Hurst, of Cambridge, Massachusetts, without whose help this reappraisal would have been impossible.*

More than this Wexford had no time to read that evening, but he returned to it on the following day. The diary, it appeared, was a five-year one. At the top of each page was the date, as it might be 1 April, and beneath that five spaces each headed 18_ _. There was room for the diarist to write perhaps forty or fifty words in each space, no more. On the 1 January page in the third heading down, the number of the year, the eight had been crossed out and a nine substituted, and so it went on for every subsequent entry until March 6, after which no more entries were made until the diarist resumed in December 1900, by which time she and her brother were in Boston.

Wexford proceeded to Gandolph's first chapters. The story he had to tell was substantially the same as Hallam Saul's, and it was not until he came to chapter five and the weeks preceding the crime that he began to concentrate on the character of Frank Fenton. Fenton, he suggested, wanted Mrs. Winchurch for the money and property she would inherit on her husband's death. Far from encouraging Florence to seek a divorce, he urged her never to let her husband suspect her preference for another man. Divorce would have left Florence penniless and homeless and have ruined his career. Fenton had known that it was only by making away with Winchurch and so arranging things that the death appeared natural, that he could have money, his profession and Florence.

There was only his word for it, said Gandolph, that he had spoken to Florence of botulism and had warned her against these particular canned herrings. Of course he had never seriously expected those cans to infect Winchurch, but that the fish should be eaten by him was necessary for his strategy. On the night before Winchurch's death, after dining with his sister at Paraleash House, he had introduced strychnine into the port decanter. He had also, Gandolph suggested, contrived to bring the conversation round to a discussion of food and to fish dishes. From that it would have been a short step to get Winchurch to admit how much he enjoyed *Filets de hareng marinés à la Rosette* and to ask Florence to have them served again on the following day. Edward apparently would have been highly likely to take his doctor's advice, even when in health, even on such a matter as what he should eat for the fourth course of his dinner, while Edward's wife did everything her lover, if not her husband, told her to do.

It was no surprise to Frank Fenton to be called out on the following evening to a man whose spasms only he would recognize as symptomatic of having swallowed strychnine. The arrival of Doctor Waterfield was an unlooked-for circumstance. Once Winchurch's symptoms had been defined as arising from strychnine poisoning there was nothing left for Fenton to do but shift the blame onto his mistress. Gandolph suggested that Fenton attributed the source of the strychnine to Anstruther's chemist's shop out of revenge on Anstruther for calling in Waterfield and thus frustrating his hopes.

And what grounds had Gandolph for believing all this? Certain entries in Ada Hurst's diary. Wexford read them slowly and carefully.

For 27 February 1900, she had written, filling the entire small space:

Very cold. Leg painful again today, FW sent round the carriage and had John drive me to Pomfret. Compton says rats in the cellars and the old stables. Dined at home with F who says rats carry leptosprial jaundice, must be got rid of. 28 February: *Drove in FW's carriage to call on old Mrs. Paget. FW still here, having tea with F when I returned. I hope there is no harm in it. Dare I warn F?* 29 February: *F destroyed twenty rats with strychnine from his dispensary. What a relief!* 1 March: *Poor old Mrs. Paget passed away in the night. A merciful release. Compton complained about the rats again. Warmer this evening and raining.* There was no entry for 2 March. 3 March: *Annie gave notice, she is getting married. Shall be sorry to lose her. Would not go out in carriage for fear of leaving FW too much alone with F. To bed early as leg most painful.* 4 March: *My birthday. 26 today and an old maid now, I think. FW drove over, brought me beautiful Indian shawl. She is always kind. Invited F and me to dinner tomorrow.* There was no entry for 5 March, and the last entry for nine months was the one for 6 March: *Dined last night at Paraleash House, six guests besides ourselves and the Ws. F left cigar case in the dining room, went back after seeing me home. I hope and pray there is no harm.*

Gandolph was evidently basing his case on the entries for 29 February and 6 March. In telling the court he had no strychnine in his dispensary, Fenton had lied. He had had an obvious opportunity for the introduction of strychnine into the decanter when he returned to Paraleash House in pursuit of his mislaid cigar case, and when he no doubt took care that he entered the dining room alone.

The next day Wexford re-read the chapters in which the new information was contained and he studied with concentration the section concerning the diary. But unless Gandolph were simply lying about the existence of the diary or of those two entries—things which he would hardly dare to do—there seemed no reason to differ from his inference. Florence was innocent, Frank Fenton the murderer of Edward Winchurch. But still Wexford wished Burden were there so that they might have one of their often acrimonious but always fruitful discussions. Somehow, with old Mike to argue against him and put up opposition, he felt things might have been better clarified.

And the morning brought news of Burden, if not the inspector himself, in the form of a postcard from Agios Nikolaios. The blue Aegean, a rocky escarpment, green pines. Who but Burden, as Wexford remarked to Dora, would send postcards while on his honeymoon? The post also brought a parcel from Carlyon Brent. It contained books, a selection from the publishing house's current list as a present for Wexford, and on the compliments slip accompanying them, a note from Amyas Ireland. *I shall be in Kingsmarkham with my people at the weekend. Can we meet? AI.* The books were the latest novel about Regency London by Camilla Barnet; *Put Money in Thy Purse,* the biography of Vassili Vandrian, the financier; the memoirs of Sofya Bolkinska, Bolshoi ballerina; an omnibus version of three novels of farming life by Giles de Coverley; the *Cosmos Book of Stars and Calendars,* and Vernon Trevor's short stories, *Raise me up Samuel.* Wexford wondered if he would ever have time to read them, but he enjoyed looking at them, their handsome glossy jackets, and smelling the civilized, aromatic, slightly acrid print smell of them. At ten he phoned Amyas Ireland, thanked him for the present and said he had read *Poison at Paraleash.*

"We can talk about it?"

"Sure. I'll be at home all Saturday and Sunday."

"Let me take you and Mrs. Wexford out to dinner on Saturday night," said Ireland.

But Dora refused. She would be an embarrassment to both of them, she said, they would have their talk much better without her, and she would spend the evening at home having a shot at making a coil pot on her own. So Wexford went alone to meet Ireland in the bar of the Olive and Dove.

"I suppose," he said, accepting a glass of Moselle, "that we can dispense with the fiction that you want me to read this book to check on police methods and court procedure? Not to put too fine a point on it, you were apprehensive Gandolph might have been up to his old tricks again?"

"Oh, well now, come," said Ireland. He seemed thinner than ever. He looked about him; he looked at Wexford, made a face, wrinkling up nose and mouth. "Well, if you must put it like that—yes."

"There may not have been any tricks, though, may there? Paxton couldn't have murdered James Conyngford, but that doesn't mean he didn't tell Gandolph he did murder him. Certainly the people who give Gandolph information seem to die very conveniently soon afterwards. He picks on the dying, first Paxton, then Lina Hurst. I suppose you've seen this diary?"

"Oh yes. We shall be using prints of the two relevant pages among the illustrations."

"No possibility of forgery?"

Ireland looked unhappy. "Ada Hurst wrote a very stylized hand, what's called a *ronde* hand, which she had obviously taught herself. It would be easy to forge. I can't submit it to handwriting experts, can I? I'm not a policeman. I'm just a poor publisher who very much wants to publish this reappraisal of the Winchurch case if it's genuine—and shun it like the plague if it's not."

"I think it's genuine." Wexford smiled at the slight lightening in Ireland's face. "I take it that it was usual for Ada Hurst to leave blanks as she did for March 2nd and March 5th?"

Ireland nodded. "Quite usual. Every month there'd have been half a dozen days on which she made no entries." A waiter came up to them with two large menus. "I'll have the *bouillabaisse* and the lamb *en croûte* and the *médallion potatoes* and French beans."

"*Consommé* and then the Parma ham," said Wexford austerely. When the waiter had gone he grinned at Ireland. "Pity they don't do *Filets de hareng marinés à la Rosette.* It might have provided us with the authentic atmosphere." He was silent for a moment, savoring the delicate tangy wine. "I'm assuming you've checked that 1900 genuinely was a Leap Year?"

"All first years of a century are."

Wexford thought about it. "Yes, of course, all years divisible by four are Leap Years."

"I must say it's a great relief to me you're so happy about it."

"I wouldn't quite say that," said Wexford.

They went into the dining room and were shown, at Ireland's request, to a sheltered corner table. A waiter brought a bottle of Château de Portets 1973. Wexford looked at the basket of rolls, croissants, little plump brioches, miniature wholemeal loaves, Italian sticks, swallowed his desire and refused with an abrupt shake of the head. Ireland took two croissants.

"What exactly do you mean?" he said.

"It strikes me as odd," said the chief inspector, "that in the entry for February 29th Ada Hurst says that her brother destroyed twenty rats with strychnine, yet in the entry for March 1st that Compton, whom I take to be the gardener, is still complaining about the rats. Why wasn't he told how effective the strychnine had been? Hadn't he been taken into Fenton's confidence about the poisoning? Or was twenty only a very small percentage of the hordes of rats which infested the place?"

"Right. It is odd. What else?"

"I don't know why, on March 6th, she mentions Fenton's returning for the cigar case. It wasn't interesting and she was limited for space. She doesn't record the name of a single guest at the dinner party, doesn't say what any of the women wore, but she carefully notes that her brother had left his cigar case in the Paraleash House dining room and had to go back for it. Why does she?"

"Oh, surely because by now she's nervous whenever Frank is alone with Florence."

"But he wouldn't have been alone with Florence, Winchurch would have been there."

They discussed the script throughout the meal, and later pored over it, Ireland with his brandy, Wexford with his coffee. Dora had been wise not to come. But the outcome was that the new facts were really new and sound and that Carylon Brent could safely publish the book in the spring. Wexford got home to find Dora sitting with a wobbly looking half-finished coil pot beside her and deep in the *Cosmos Book of Stars and Calendars.*

"Reg, did you know that for the Greeks the year began on Midsummer Day? And that the Chinese and Jewish calendars have twelve months in some years and thirteen in others?"

"I can't say I did."

"We avoid that, you see, by using the Gregorian calendar and correct the error by making every fourth year a Leap Year. You really must read this book, it's fascinating."

But Wexford's preference was for the Vassili Vandrian and the farming trilogy, though with little time to read he hadn't completed a single one of these works by the time Burden returned on the following Monday week. Burden had a fine even tan but for his nose which had peeled.

"Have a good time?" asked Wexford with automatic politeness.

"What a question," said the inspector, "to ask a man who has just come back from his honeymoon. Of course I had a good time." He cautiously scratched his nose. "What have you been up to?"

"Seeing something of your brother-in-law. He got me to read a manuscript."

"Ha!" said Burden. "I know what that was. He said something about it but he knew Gandolph'd get short shrift from me. A devious liar if ever there was one. It beats me what sort of satisfaction a man can get out of the kind of fame that comes from foisting on the public stories he *knows* aren't true. All that about Paxton was a pack of lies, and I've no doubt he bases this new version of the Winchurch case on another pack of lies. He's not interested in the truth. He's only interested in being known as the great criminologist and the man who shows the police up for fools."

"Come on, Mike, that's a bit sweeping. I told Ireland I thought it would be OK to go ahead and publish."

Burden's face wore an expression that was almost a caricature of sophisticated scathing knowingness. "Well, of course, I haven't seen it, I can't say. I'm basing my objection to Gandolph on the Paxton affair. Paxton never confessed to any murder and Gandolph knows it."

"You can't say that for sure."

Burden sat down. He tapped his fist lightly on the corner of the desk. "I *can* say. I knew Paxton, I knew him well."

"I didn't know that."

"No, it was years back, before I came here. In Eastbourne, it was, when Paxton was with the Garfield gang. In the force down there we knew it was useless ever trying to get Paxton to talk. He *never* talked. I don't mean he just didn't give away any info, I mean he didn't answer when you spoke to him. Various times we tried to interrogate him he just maintained this total silence. A mate of his told me he'd made it a rule not to talk to policemen or social workers or lawyers or any what you might call establishment people, and he never had. He talked to his wife and his kids and his mates all right. But I remember once he was in the dock at Lewes Assizes and the judge addressed him. He just didn't answer—he wouldn't—and the judge, it was old Clydesdale, sent him down for contempt. So don't tell me Paxton made any sort of confession to Kenneth Gandolph, not *Paxton*."

The effect of this was to reawaken all Wexford's former doubts. He trusted Burden, he had a high opinion of his opinion. He began to wish he had advised Ireland to have tests made to determine the age of the ink used in the 29 February and 6 March entries, or to have the writing examined by a handwriting expert. Yet if Ada Hurst had had a stylized hand self-taught in adulthood . . . What good were handwriting experts anyway? Not much, in his experience. And of course Ireland couldn't suggest to Gandolph that the ink should be tested without offending the man to such an extent that he would refuse publication of Poison at Paraleash to Carylon Brent. But Wexford was suddenly certain that those entries were false and that Gandolph had forged them. Very subtly and cunningly he had forged them, having judged that the addition to the diary of just thirty-four words would alter the whole balance of the Winchurch case and shift the culpability from Florence to her lover.

Thirty-four words. Wexford had made a copy of the diary entries and now he looked at them again. 29 February: *F destroyed twenty rats with strychnine from his dispensary. What a relief! 6 March: F left cigar case in the dining room, went back after seeing me home. I hope and pray there is no harm.* There were no anachronisms—men certainly used cigars in 1900—no divergence from Ada's usual style. The word "twenty" was written in letters instead of two figures. The writer, on 6 March, had written not about that day but about the day before. Did that amount to anything? Wexford thought not, though he pondered on it for most of the day.

That evening he was well into the last chapter of *Put Money in Thy Purse* when the phone rang. It was Jenny Burden. Would he and Dora come to dinner on Saturday? Her parents would be there and her brother.

Wexford said Dora was out at her pottery class, but yes, they would love to, and had she had a nice time in Crete?"

"How sweet of you to ask," said the bride. "No one else has. Thank you, we have a lovely time."

He had meant it when he said they would love to, but still he didn't feel very happy about meeting Amyas Ireland again. He had a notion that once the book was published some as yet unimagined Warren or Burden would turn up and denounce it, deride it, laugh at the glaring giveaway he and Ireland couldn't see. When he saw Ireland again he ought to say, don't do it, don't take the risk, publish and be damned can have another meaning than the popular one. But how to give such a warning with no sound reason for giving it, with nothing but one of those vague feelings, this time of foreboding, which had so assisted him yet run him into so much trouble in the past? No, there was nothing he could do. He sighed, finished his chapter and moved on to the farmer's fictionalized memoirs.

Afterwards Wexford was in the habit of saying that he got more reading done during that week than he had in years. Perhaps it had been a way of escape from fretful thought. But certainly he had passed a freakishly slack week, getting home most nights by six. He even read Miss Camilla Barnet's *The Golden Recticule,* and by Friday night there was nothing left but the *Cosmos Book of Stars and Calendars.*

It was a large party, Mr. and Mrs. Ireland and their son, Burden's daughter Pat, Grace and her husband and, of course, the Burdens themselves. Jenny's face glowed with happiness and Aegean sunshine. She welcomed the Wexfords with kisses and brought them drinks served in their own wedding present to her.

The meeting with Amyas Ireland wasn't the embarrassment Wexford had feared it would be—had feared, that is, up till a few minutes before he and Dora left home. And now he knew that he couldn't contain himself till after dinner, till the morning, or perhaps worse than that—a phone call on Monday morning. He asked his hostess if she would think him very rude if he spoke to her brother alone for five minutes.

She laughed. "Not rude at all. I think you must have got the world's most wonderful idea for a crime novel and Amyas is going to publish it. But I don't know where to put you unless it's the kitchen. And you," she said to her brother, "are not to eat anything, mind."

"I couldn't wait," Wexford said as they found themselves stowed away into the kitchen where every surface was necessarily loaded with the constituents of dinner for ten people. "I only found out this evening at the last minute before we were due to come out."

"It's something about the Winchurch book?"

Wexford said eagerly, "It's not too late, is it? I was worried I might be too late."

"Good God, no. We hadn't planned to start printing before the autumn." Ireland, who seemed about to disobey his sister and help himself to a macaroon from a silver dish, suddenly lost his appetite. "This is serious?"

"Wait till you hear. I was waiting for my wife to finish dressing." He grinned. "You should make it a rule to read your own books, you know. That's what I was doing, reading one of those books you sent me and that's where I found it. You won't be able to publish Poison at Paraleash." The smile went and he looked almost fierce. "I've not hesitation in saying Kenneth Gandolph is a forger and a cheat and you'd be advised to have nothing to do with him in future."

Ireland's eyes narrowed. "Better know it now than later. What did he do and how do you know?"

From his jacket pocket Wexford took the copy he had made of the diary entries. "I can't prove that the last entry, the one for March 6th that says, *F left cigar case in the dining room, went back after seeing me home,* I can't prove that's forged, I only think it is. What I know for certain is a forgery is the entry for February 29th."

"Isn't that the one about the strychnine?"

"F destroyed twenty rats with strychnine from his dispensary. What a relief!"

"How do you know it's forged?"

"Because the day itself didn't occur," said Wexford. "In 1900 there was no February 29th, it wasn't a Leap Year."

"Oh, yes, it was. We've been through all that before." Ireland sounded both relieved and impatient. "All years divisible by four are Leap Years. All century years are divisible by four and 1900 was a century year. 1897 was the year she began the diary, following 1896 which was a Leap Year. Needless to say, there was no February 29th in 1897, 1898 or 1899 so there must have been one in 1900."

"It wasn't a Leap Year," said Wexford. "Didn't I tell you I found this out through that book of yours, the *Cosmos Book of Stars and Calendars?* There's a lot of useful information in there, and one of the bits of information is about how Pope Gregory composed a new civil calendar to correct the errors of the Julian calendar. One of his rulings was that every fourth year should be a Leap Year except in certain cases . . ."

Ireland interrupted him. "I don't believe it!" he said in the voice of someone who knows he believes every word.

Wexford shrugged. He went on, "Century years were not to be Leap Years, unless they were divisible not by four but by four hundred. Therefore, 1600 would have been a Leap Year if the Gregorian calendar had by then been adopted, and 2000 will be a Leap Year, but 1800 was not and 1900 was not. So in 1900 there was no February 29th and Ada Hurst left the space on that page blank for the very good reason that the day following February 28th was March 1st. Unluckily for him, Gandolph, like you and me and most people, knew nothing of this as otherwise he would surely have inserted his strychnine entry into the blank space of March 2nd and his forgery might never have been discovered."

Ireland shook his head at man's ingenuity and perhaps his chicanery. "I'm very grateful to you. We should have looked fools, shouldn't we?"

"I'm glad Florence wasn't hanged in error," Wexford said as they went back to join the others. "Her marriage didn't begin with dearly beloved, but if she was afraid at the end it can't have been with any amazement."

Acknowledgments

Ngaio Marsh, © 1946, reprinted by permission of Peters, Fraser & Dunlop, agents for the author's Estate

Margery Allingham, © 1937, reprinted by permission of Chorion PLC

Howard Engel, © 1989, reprinted by permission of the author and Beverley Slopen Literary Agency

Mickey Spillane, © 2005, reprinted by permission of the author

Georges Simenon, © 1962, reprinted by permission of Chorion PLC

Raymond Chandler, © 1950, renewed 1978 by Helga Greene. Reprinted by permission of Ed Victor Ltd, agents for the author's estate

Erle Stanley Gardner, © 1953, C. Crowell-Collier Publishing Co., renewed 1981 by Jean Bethel Gardner and Grace Naso. Reprinted by permission of Lawrence Hughes Literary Agency, agents for the author's Estate

Colin Dexter, © 1993, reprinted by permission of Macmillan Publishers

Ed McBain, © 1972, by Evan Hunter. Reprinted by permission of Curtis Brown Ltd

Agatha Christie, © 1929 (*The Case of the Missing Lady*), © 1953 (*Sanctuary*) and © 1960 (*The Theft of the Royal Ruby*). Reprinted by permission of Chorion PLC

Ellery Queen, © 1940, reprinted by permission of Larry Gannen, on behalf of the Richard Dannay estate

Ian Rankin, © 2002, reprinted by permission of the author and Curtis Brown Ltd

John Harvey, © 1994, reprinted by permission of the author

Lawrence Block, © 1999, reprinted by permission of Baror International

Jeffery Deaver, © 2003 reprinted by permission of Curtis Brown Ltd

John Mortimer, © 2003, Adrian Press Ltd, reprinted by permission of Peters, Fraser & Dunlop Ltd

Mark Timlin, © 1994, reprinted by permission of the author

Max Allan Collins, © 1990, by Max Allan Collins and Tribune Media Services. Reprinted by permission of the author

Nicolas Freeling, © 1963, reprinted by permission of Chorion PLC

Sara Paretsky, © 1988, reprinted by permission of David Grossman Literary Agency

Ruth Rendell, © 1978, Kingsmarkham Enterprises, reprinted by permission of Peters, Fraser & Dunlop Ltd